COBBLESTONES

A New Orleans Tragedy

S. R. Perricone

HISTORIUM PRESS U.S.A.

Visit S.R. Perricone's website at
www.srperricone.com

Library of Congress Cataloging-in-Publication Data on file
TXu 2-457-046
Date of Registration: November 18, 2024

Hardcover ISBN: 978-1-964700-15-1
Paperback ISBN: 978-1-964700-16-8
Ebook ISBN: 978-1-964700-17-5

This work is dedicated to the late Salvadore A. Serio, who curated the Italian-American Resources Center at the Jefferson Parish Library in Metairie, Louisiana for his dedication to absolving the names of the eleven innocent Italians lynched in New Orleans of March 14, 1891. It was Mr. Serio who encouraged the author to undertake the new investigation of the Lenten slaughter, which is the core subject matter of *Cobblestones*.

Finally, the author would offer a dedication to the eleven Italians who suffered from mob violence, and their memory will never be forgotten.

Part I
DARK HORIZONS

Chapter 1

Bisacquino, Sicily
June 1, 1889
6:10 A.M.

From his first breath, he became eligible for death, but nothing impaled his mortal existence more than the murder of his best friend. On this day, the young Sicilian *contandini* began his mournful morning with dreadful thoughts. The misty dawn coiled him in a flint-gray shroud, reminding him of life's fragility—his and others. As the shards of sunlight beamed through the narrow alleys and streets of his mountain village, he knew his innocence and his humble life's tillage in the undulating soil on the green hills of his family's olive groves and grape-laden vineyards were changing with every fleeting step. Even the air he breathed stung his senses with a tomb-like stench.

The clopping hooves of a solitary black horse on the ancient cobblestone streets echoed against the old tan and yellow stucco homes and shops that framed the Piazza Triona. The horse needed no guidance, as it often made this trip. It required no stinging whip to force him to tug the black-lacquered hearse up the hill toward the yawning doors of St. John the Baptist Church, where a French Jesuit, Jacques Fontebuis, waited with his hands clasped around his Missal for the Requiem Mass.

As the undertaker, Vincenzo Trambatore, stomped on the hearse's wooden brakes, Father Fontebuis nodded and doffed his black *biretta*. The undertaker silently removed his black *coppola* and nodded. Across the piazza, a lamplighter extinguished the village's lamps. For a moment, they were the only men near the church, but that was about to change.

As Father Fontebuis and the undertaker approached the rear doors of the hearse, their funereal countenance diverted to the hobnail thumping of young peasants' boots against one of Bisacquino's six-hundred-year-old cobblestone streets, leading down from the outskirts of town to the piazza.

The young peasant, Antonio Carravella, panting from his run, slowly approached the priest and the undertaker. He stopped and looked past the priest and through the oval glass doors of the hearse. He took one step closer, snatched his brown *coppola*, and placed it over his heart.

"Antonio, did you know this boy?" Father Fontebuis asked, in a mixed Sicilian and French dialect.

"Yes, Father. He was my friend—my only friend."

"Do you know what happened to him?"

Trambatore put his fingers to his lips in an effort to silence Carravella.

"Yes, Father. He was beaten to death by the *gambelloti*—Cascioferro's *gambelloti*. They wanted his family's land. They want all the land in Sicily. They want our land, but we will fight them," young Carravella cried.

Trambatore grabbed the boy and muzzled him by slapping his hand over the boy's mouth. But Carravella resisted and pulled away.

"Let him speak, Mr. Trambatore. I know what's going on here. I want to hear him," Father Fontebuis demanded. "So, you knew him, Antonio?"

"Yes, Father. His name was Santo Depaola. He was my best friend. They beat him with clubs until his brains were in the dirt. But I will fight. My father will fight."

"How old was Santo?" Father Fontebuis asked.

"He was sixteen. I am fifteen—I think."

"Do you know who Vito Cascioferro is, Antonio?"

"Yes. He's the leader of the *Stuppagghieri*."

"Do you know what that is?"

Antonio paused for a moment. "The Mafia, Father."

"Yes. That's why they again want all the French priests out of Sicily. It all started with the Sicilian Vespers of 1282," Father Fontebuis lamented.

"What's that, Father?" Antonio asked.

"Never mind, son. Ancient prejudices are the hardest stone pillars to tumble." Father Fontebuis leaned over and whispered in young Carravella's ear, "Do you want to die like Santo?"

Carravella recoiled and glared at the priest. "No, Father. Why ask me that?"

"After Santo's funeral, we will talk. But right now, turn around slowly and look over your right shoulder and down the hill beyond the piazza's fountain. Tell me what you see."

Carravella did what Father Fontebuis said and looked down the hill away from the Cathedral. His young eyes focused on four men standing in the shadows, looking back at him. They were all dressed in black suits, white shirts, and dark-colored ties. Two wore hats. "Do you know who they are, Antonio?"

"Yes. They work for Cascioferro. They watch everything that goes on in Bisacquino."

Father Fontebuis nodded and opened the back doors of the hearse. He and Trambatore pulled on the rope handles of Santo DePaola's rough-hewn wooden coffin. Father Fontebuis beckoned the lamplighter to help bring the coffin into the Cathedral, who reluctantly obliged.

"Where is Santo's family?" Antonio asked. "Why aren't they here?"

"You see those four men down the hill? They are there to keep people away. They use fear to intimidate Santo's family. His family can't come to their son's funeral," Father Fontebuis said, clenching his jaw. "Those men sent me a message to complete the funeral before eight o'clock. So, we must hurry. Let's bring Santo into God's house and give him his final Mass." Then the priest made the sign of the cross and in a loud stentorian voice announced in Latin, "*Hic Domus Dei Est Et Porta Coeli.*"

The priest, the undertaker, the lamplighter, and Antonio Carravella struggled with Santo DePaola's coffin as they pulled it from the hearse and carried it to a black-draped bier before the Cathedral's altar. Four elderly weeping women sat in the front row, clutching Rosaries and Missals. Flickering altar candles and the dawning sun streamed through the Cathedral's stained-glass windows, providing the only light for the Requiem Mass.

As Father Fontebuis began the Mass, the four elderly women, clad in black dresses and scarves, began to moan and pray loudly. Carravella knelt next to the undertaker and tugged on his coat sleeve. "Who are those women?" he asks.

"They come to every funeral and mourn the dead. They're not family," Trambatore said. "They'll follow us to the cemetery, too. Those four *stronzo* across the *piazza* won't intimidate them."

After the Mass, the undertaker, the priest, and Carravella carried Santo DePaola's coffin back to the hearse. The lamplighter disappeared during the Mass. After shoving the coffin into the hearse, Trambatore mounted his seat and tapped the horse lightly with the reins. Without further guidance, the old horse turned the hearse around and pulled it down the hill towards the cemetery. Father Fontebuis, Antonio Carravella, and the four wailing women walked behind the hearse for the half-mile walk to St. Anthony's Cemetery. When they reached the cemetery's front gate, the four men appeared from behind a large cedar tree. They said nothing. They just watched the small procession approach an open, unmarked grave. Two sextons lowered Santo DePaola's coffin with two ropes into the grave, as Father Fontebuis gave the final blessing. Trambatore, his horse, and his hearse left the cemetery, followed quickly by the elderly women. Santo DePaola was laid to rest.

As Father Fontebuis turned away from the grave, he pulled young Carravella behind the Bensetta family Mausoleum, which stood above the ground and blocked the curious stares of the four men.

"Antonio, we need to talk," Father Fontebuis said, as he sat on a stone bench and removed his *biretta*. "Things are changing in Sicily, and not for the good."

Antonio hung his head.

"Where is your father right now?"

"When I left our house, he hitched our mule to his wagon and went to the vineyard. Why?"

"Tonight, I want you to bring your father to the back gate of the Rectory. We need to talk about what's about to happen?"

"Why us, Father? What's going on?"

Father Fontebuis looked around the cemetery to ensure they were alone. "I've known you and your father for a long time, and as a priest, I hear things no one else does. So, tonight, bring your father to my back gate. Make sure it's dark. And I will tell you more."

"Are we in trouble?" Antonio asked.

"We're all in trouble, my son. I have to leave Sicily. They're forcing me out. The *Stuppagghieri* only want Sicilian priests on the island and no Jesuits. I am French and a Jesuit. I have to be gone by July 15th."

"Where are you going, Father?"

"I don't know, yet. I have to meet my Superior next week in Palermo. I will find out then. If I don't leave, they will kill me."

"Who told you this?"

"The Bishop in Monreale. The *Giaridinineri* have confiscated all the Church's land. They're in competition with the *Stuppagghieri* and killing each other to see who will control Sicily."

"Father, what about the *Risorgimento*, and the land reforms Rome promised us?"

"Rome lies."

"The Pope lies, too?"

"I hope not, but Pope Leo lost his power after the *Risorgimento*. All he has is the *Vaticano*, and the Church. Things are different in Rome, too. The promised reforms have not reached Sicily, and I doubt they will."

"Do we have to leave, too?"

Father Fontebuis stood up and began to pace behind the mausoleum. He stopped before Antonio, who was almost as tall as the priest, and brushed back the boy's thick black hair. "Have you heard of phylloxera, my son?"

"It's a bug that eats the grapes. We have some in our vineyard."

"That's correct. Soon, your vineyard will stop producing grapes for wine. If you keep the land, you won't be able to pay the high taxes the *gambelloti* will demand. They will take your land and put you in the military. Your father will be a slave for the rest of his life on land he once owned. You are a smart, strong boy, and your father is a very honest, hard-working man. There might be a future for both of you somewhere else— and for me."

"Where? I'll fight for our land. My family has worked that vineyard and olive grove for almost three hundred years. I will not give up without a fight."

Before Father Fontebuis could respond, the sound of clumps of mud thudding on Santo DePaola's coffin echoed through the cemetery. The priest and boy said nothing for a moment. They just listened to the mournful repetition of the sexton's shovel heaving the dirt.

After the earth claimed Santo DePaola, Father Fontebuis turned toward Antonio, and with a stern glare said, "Remember, come tonight and bring your father to my back gate. We must plan our escape."

"Are we the only ones leaving?"

"No. Others are planning to leave, too. In fact, every night, a few leave for the Palermo docks. There's no future here."

Antonio walked to the other side of the Bensetta Mausoleum and stared at a lonely grave about thirty feet away, near the north wall of the cemetery. It was his mother's grave, which was dug ten years earlier. She died of a virulent plague which ravaged Bisacquino. Father Fontebuis followed behind him, placing his hands around the boy's shoulders. Antonio's eyes welled with bitter tears, and he looked at the somber face of the priest. "Will there ever be peace in Sicily, Father?"

The priest had only one answer, but knew it wouldn't assuage the boy's grief. "Antonio, we must pray and search for peace. Let's pray wherever we are going, we will find peace." Father Fontebuis pulled the boy away from the sight of his mother's grave and said, "Now, go home and pack your things for a long trip. Then, you and your father meet me at the back gate of my Rectory about midnight."

"What if my father refuses?"

"Tell him I said your lives are worth more than the land. Once I talk to him, he will understand."

"Do you think we will ever return?"

"Yes, I do. But now, we must cross other horizons to find peace and let this land heal. And remember this, Antonio: wherever you go, seeds planted in jealous soil will only yield the rancid fruit of hate, which the planter will try to consume, but never swallow."

Chapter 2

The Vineyard
June 1, 1889
9:35 A.M.

Near a dusty, rocky, and hilly road, about two miles from the Cathedral, sat a vineyard, which the Carravella family had cultivated since 1633. It was triangular-shaped, with the point of the land sloping downward in a southeasterly direction for about a mile, where it widened to a distance of four hundred yards. There, the verdant vale became the riparian land of a rippling stream. At the vineyard's apex, several rows of grape vines marched downhill towards the stream. From Via Camerano, the vineyard appeared as lush green legions, ready to yield its fruitful bounty. But appearances deceived the eye. While the leaves were full and green, their harvest shriveled and died. Instead of bunches of deep purple grapes ready for harvest, rancid, decaying fruit dangled from the vine. The phylloxera, or grape lice, sucked the life from the Carravella family. There would be no harvest, no wine, and no money to pay the *macinato*, or land tax, to the *gambelloti*. The dagger of reality pierced Pietro Carravella's heart, as he sat about fifty feet from the road on his homemade wooden bench, among his fallow vines. He hung his head and wept.

As Pietro pondered his future, his attention drew to a carriage stopping on the road. Two men stepped down onto a pathway that ran between the vines. As they walked towards him, Pietro's vision, even occluded by tears, recognized who they were—the *gambelloti*. Both men were well-dressed, and one carried a brown leather pouch over his left shoulder. The other held a heavy, black brass-knobbed walking stick with a brass ferrule. Pietro wiped his eyes with his sleeves, stood, and faced the men.

"*Buongiorno*, Signore Carravella. Beautiful day, isn't it?" the man with the leather pouch called out.

"Who are you, and what do you want?" Carravella asked.

"My name is Angelo Pendenza, and my friend's name is Gaetano

Galanti. We want to discuss buying your vineyard and your olive grove."

"Not for sale. Go away."

"Please, Signore Carravella. Hear us out before you decide," Pendenza implored.

"Not for sale. You leave now. I have work to do."

"Signore Carravella, you have no work to do. Look at your grapes. They're dead. There will be no harvest this year, and you will not be able to pay your taxes."

"Who sent you here?"

"We are not thieves, Signore Carravella," Galanti said. "We were sent here to help you sell this dying land for a fair price."

"My land is not for sale. You go, now."

Pendenza opened his leather pouch and pulled out a printed contract for the sale of the land. "An anonymous buyer is willing to pay five thousand Liras for the vineyard and the olive grove, or about one-tenth of its worth. Signore Carravella, please look at what is being offered. Your taxes will exceed five thousand Liras, and you will lose everything. You and your son will be homeless and beggars in the streets," Pendenza warned.

Pietro Carravella's blood roiled. "Who sent you here? Cascioferro? You work for him? You're the *gambelloti* going around Sicily stealing people's land? Well, let me tell you something. This land has been in my family for over three hundred years. The olive trees are healthy, and I will get the bugs out of my vineyard. I will have a harvest next year. I will never give up my family's land. Never! Now, go."

"It ceased being your land when Garabaldi captured Sicily," Pendenza intoned. "Remember the *Risorgimento*?"

"*Risorgimento*?" Carravella spat on the ground. "That was just an excuse to steal our land."

Galanti leaned towards Carravella and said, "*Li mortacci, tua.*"

Carravella knotted his fist and swung at Galanti's jaw, knocking the well-dressed man to the ground. "You will not insult my family like that," Carravella screamed. "Now, *vaffanculo*! Go!"

Pendenza pushed Carravella back and helped Galanti up. After dusting his friend off, Pendenza picked up Galanti's walking stick and handed it to his friend. Pendenza and Galanti exchanged a feral glance, as Galanti gripped his walking stick near the brass knob. "You have made a terrible mistake, Signore Carravella. The offer is withdrawn."

"Vaffanculo, truffatori," Carravella exclaimed, turned around, and walked away. When he did, Galanti swung his walking stick and struck Pietro Carravella on the head, knocking the peasant vintner to the ground. Blood gushed from a three-inch wound on the crown of Carravella's head. Galanti approached the helpless Carravella and raised his walking stick again. As he did, Antonio Carravella stood at the top of the path, watching Galanti repeatedly strike his defenseless father on the head and body. Seeing this, the younger Carravella ran back to his father's mule-drawn wagon and dug under the seat for the family's *lupara*—a twelve-gauge double-barreled sawed-off shotgun.

Armed, he ran back to the path and yelled, *"Assassini,* stop!" Galanti ignored Antonio's order, but he didn't see what was in the boy's hands. Antonio cocked the hammers of both barrels and ran down the path. Without saying another word, he squeezed one of the triggers. The shot vaporized Galanti's head, sending his headless body into the vines. Pendenza dropped to his knees and begged for his life. Antonio glanced at his bleeding father, who struggled to sit up and gasped for air. Streams of blood flood in his father's eyes as the elder Carravella tried to speak.

Antonio turned back to the begging Pendenza, shouldered the shotgun, and said, "This is for all the *Stuppagghieri.* May you all burn in hell." Antonio rested his cheek on the gun's stock and allowed his right eye to take careful aim at Pendenza's forehead. And with a slight tug on the trigger, Pendenza's head vanished in a cloud of blood and smoke. His body fell over and landed on top of Galanti's.

Antonio ran to his father's side and examined Pietro's wounds, four deep head wounds, which exposed the elder Carravella's skull and brain. A jagged bone pierced his left forearm's skin, and blood soaked his white cotton shirt. Antonio ripped off his blue working shirt and dabbed his father's head wounds, but the loving effort proved useless. Pietro mustered enough strength to look at his son for the last time.

"Antonio," he gasped. "Go. Leave Sicily. This is not a good place for a young man. They will take the land and kill you, too. Go, hide. Leave the *lupara* at my side. Whoever finds us will think I did this. It might save your life. But you must go and go now."

Pietro's head fell back as he exhaled his last breath. Antonio wept over his father, but after a few moments, he gathered his thoughts and realized what he had done. He stood up, and looked at the three dead men, his young face slurried with mud and tears. Honoring one of his father's last wishes, he kicked the *lupara* to his father's side. Slowly, he backed away from the carnage and realized this would be the last time he would see his father. Mournfully, he ran and tripped up the path towards the road. He unhitched the mule and drove the wagon home, but decided to leave it on Via Camerano to perfect his father's dying illusion.

><

The Carravella family built their home in 1750 using materials quarried from the rocky soil around Bisacquino. It had two stories and a cellar where they kept the grape presses and kegs of aging wine. Two stairways ran through the house—one inside and one along its external northern wall. Since Sicilians cooked inside their homes in large hearths, the fear of fire was ever-present, and an external stairway provided an escape if needed. Antonio's bedroom was on the second floor, facing the road that led into the town's center. He could see the bell tower of the Cathedral and hear the bells pealing on the Angelus and on Sundays. His father's room was next to his, as well as his father's small office.

The house was hemmed by a corral, which had some livestock, chickens, a privy, and a well. For the most part, the Carravellas were neither wealthy nor poor, but despite their family holdings, the upper caste system viewed them as the *contandini*, or peasant class. No matter how hard they tried to scrape a living from the land, they would always be peasants and would be treated that way. Their wine was good and their olive oil, always in demand, but at prices set by others. Upward mobility was a foreign term in the Carravella home and among other Sicilians. It was understood that where you were born was where you would die.

The War of Unification of 1861, which created the Nation of Italy and promised a new life for everyone from Milan to Palermo, was a boastful charade propagated by the rich and powerful to preserve their status. The Sicilians knew this because they heard it, not only on the streets but from the pulpits, where Jesuit priests preached social justice of the times. For the ruling class of Sicily, which included the *Stuppagghieri* and the *Giardinieri*, the Jesuits posed a threat to their power and the status quo.

When Antonio arrived home, his eyes darted around the property, looking for anyone or anything unusual. Every sound startled him. His guilt raced through his blood. He ran inside and saw and smelled his father everywhere. But he had no time to think of the past. Panic drove him from room to room. His father's dying words rang in his ears. *He must leave, but how?* He darted up the inside steps and went into his small bedroom. Before a crucifix mounted on his wall, he dropped to his knees and asked God for His forgiveness. Two lives taken at his young age, but he truly felt he had no choice. After praying, he sat on his lumpy bed and planned his next move. He was alone. No father, mother, or siblings to help him. His external family, like other Sicilian families, continued to feud over something that happened fifty years ago, which left him alone with his fear, his guilt, and his thoughts.

When he heard a creaking wooden wagon pass his front gate, he snuck towards his window to see if anyone approached his house. To his relief, they kept going, but as he stepped away from his window, he noticed the bell tower of the Cathedral and remembered Father Fontebuis's admonition. Quickly, Antonio filled a gray cotton sack with clothes—his and his father's. He rummaged through his father's office and found a steel-locked box. Using a keg maul and a steel spike, he broke the lock and opened the box. He found four hundred Liras—the most money he had ever seen. He folded the large notes, stuffed them in his shoes and pockets, then placed fifty Liras in the sweatband of his *coppola*. Swinging the sack over his shoulder, he took one last look around, feeling confident that Father Fontebuis would help him… *But how?*

Antonio left his house and descended the cellar steps, hiding in the corner behind two large kegs of wine. As he sat on the mud-packed floor, the adrenaline seeped from his body, and he shook with chills. Balling himself into a fetal position, he rocked and wept. His chest heaved with grief as the images of what happened in the vineyard flashed through his mind. For a moment, he sat up and leaned against the wall, but the tears continued to flow. He noticed his blue shirt, blood-splattered and tattered, then ripped it off and replaced it with a black one from his sack. Racing up the cellar stairs, he stuffed the blue shirt in the privy and returned to his redoubt. When he leaned against the cellar wall, he realized the cellar had four small windows, which allowed the sun to cast different shadows through them, revealing the passing hours. Forced to bide his time until darkness swallowed the Rectory, he watched the windows, tracing the dying light as though it marked his doom. His heart thudded, loud and ragged, against his chest.

After about two hours, Antonio fell asleep. The evening Angelus startled him awake, and he sprang to his feet. Twilight fell, and since it was not dark enough to walk the streets of Bisacquino without drawing attention, he decided to wait another hour. Hunger seized his stomach. As the cellar darkened, his eyes found a sack of cheese hanging from a rafter.

His father often used goat milk to make cheese while pressing grapes for wine. He cut open the sack and bit into the ball of cheese. The salty treat made him thirsty, and the only thing to drink in the cellar was aging wine. He approached a keg and put a tin cup under the spigot. After eating a large ball of goat cheese and drinking several cups of wine, Antonio lost some of his inhibitions and felt brave enough to venture towards Father Fontebuis's back gate. After ascending the cellar stairs, he opened the door, and a gust of cool mountain air brushed across his face. Images of how his day started crept across his mind, but he had no idea how it was going to end.

From dawn to dusk, his young peasant day coursed through grief, blood, death, fear, and now, flight. As he swung the sack over his right shoulder and walked towards the front gate, his mind exploded with emotions. He stopped and looked back at the only home he had ever known as a frisson of nostromania gripped him like an eagle's claw.

He knew he must flee.

Chapter 3

Bisacquino, Sicily
June 1, 1889
9:45 P.M.

Like a feral cat, Antonio crept from the shadows and under the amber flickering gas lamps lining the streets and alleys of his hometown. With every step, his old boots banged against the cobblestones, betraying his presence. So, he sat on the street, removed his boots, and stuffed them into his sack. His threadbare socks offered little protection from the hardened, uneven stones, but he preferred the pain to being noticed. In a small-town square, three *uoma vecchio* sat on benches discussing the dire news of the past three days in their small mountain town. Four dead. They didn't notice Antonio passing through the shadows as he wound his way to the rectory's back gate.

Antonio smelled the various home-cooked scents wafting through the town's chimneys and across the terracotta-tile roofs, like epicurean specters competing for prominence. His stomach churned with hunger, but he pressed on. When he arrived at Father Fontebuis's back gate, he knocked four times. No answer. He knocked again. No answer. The six-foot wall posed no problem for the wiry-framed boy as he scaled it and peered into the courtyard behind the rectory. He noticed an elderly woman staring at him from her iron balcony next to the rectory, so he slipped back to the street and knocked again. After a few moments, the gate creaked open, and the silhouette of Father Fontebuis stood in front of him. "Hurry. Come in, Antonio. You're early."

The priest led the boy inside and down a long corridor lit by candle-bearing sconces, and into his office. It was sparsely furnished with three straight-back chairs, a desk, and several shelves filled with books. "Sit down, Antonio. We need to talk."

Antonio did as he said, as Father Fontebuis turned the brass knob on the oil lamp to increase the flame. The room brightened, and Antonio noticed several Catholic icons hanging on the wall, compelling him to blurt out, "Father, I need to confess some mortal sins!"

"This is a small town, Antonio. I heard what happened. When they brought your father to the hospital, the doctors called me. I went there and saw his wounds. I gave him Extreme Unction. But tell me what happened in your own words," the priest replied as he handed Antonio a handkerchief. Antonio wiped his eyes and told the entire story from the time he left the cemetery to what happened in the vineyard.

Antonio fell to his knees, begged for absolution of his sins, and began to writhe on the floor. The priest helped Antonio back into his chair and knelt next to him. "My son, your sins are forgiven. As I see it, and I believe God does too, you had no choice. What you did was terrible, and you will live with it for the rest of your life, but God has forgotten it. But we have to worry about those who will never forget. And that's what we need to discuss."

Antonio nodded and wiped his eyes again. "Am I in trouble, Father?"

"Well, the *Stuppagghieri* and the *Carabinieri* are looking for you. They think you are hiding up on the mountain near the Sanctuary of Mount Tritone."

"The *Carabinieri*, too, Father?"

"The police want to question you because the two men they found next to your father were *gambelloti* with ties to Cascioferro. The *Carabinieri* are trying to stop this Mafia, but it's a Sisyphean task."

"A what, Father?"

"Never mind. The police have a tough job, and for the most part, I think they're honest. But we must stay away from them, too."

"Thank you for taking care of my father. He didn't deserve to die like that."

"Antonio, your father was a good man—an honest man. He donated all the wine we use for our Masses. As I anointed him today, I promised him I would take care of you until you are a man. And that's what I intend to do. Do you know how old you are?"

"I think I am fifteen."

"Not yet. I checked your Baptismal records, and you will be fifteen on July thirtieth. That means Italy can still try you for the murders of those men in the vineyard if the *Stuppagghieri* doesn't get to you first. I won't let either happen."

"What are we going to do, Father?"

The priest considered his question, then replied, "Can you read?"

"Yes, Father. I went to the sixth level."

"Good." The priest pulled a green book off his shelf and gave it to Antonio. "This is an Italian-French dictionary. Study it every day. I will test you on your language skills. You must know some French to enter France. I will change your name in our Baptismal records. Our records have some prominence over the civil records."

"We're going to lie, Father?"

"Oh, no. We're only going to adjust the truth for the greater good. Your new name will be… let's see… how about, Pierre Caravelle. Your father was French, and your mother Sicilian. Forget about Antonio Carravella. He died in that vineyard, too. Understand?"

Antonio hung his head and tears streamed down his cheeks. "What about my father? Will he have a funeral?"

"Yes. We will have a Requiem the day after tomorrow, but you can't come. I'm sure the *Stuppagghieri* and the *Carabinieri* will be there. You can hide in the Sacristy and listen to the entire Mass. There is no Sanctuary from the *Stuppagghieri*."

"What about my father's coffin? Where will you bury him?"

"The Bishop has donated church funds for your father's funeral. He just doesn't know it yet. Mr. Trambatore will have your father buried next to your mother. Everything is taken care of, Pierre."

"Then what?"

"You ask too many questions. But that's good. Your mind is working. After your father's funeral, I will go to the telegraph office and send a message to my Superior in Palermo. I will tell him to expect me by the end of June. Telegraph offices are great places to start rumors. We will leave early the next morning and I will borrow the Bishop's new carriage and horse. I don't believe he will mind. He wants me to leave anyway. We will take a route over the mountains and away from the other towns. I expect we will arrive in Palermo in two days. I'll pack some food and water for the trip. By the way, are you hungry?"

"Yes, Father. Thirsty, too."

"Follow me, and I will show you our cellar. There's a cot down there and a stairway to the garden. If you need to go outside, stay in the garden. The privy is there. No one will see you. It's a good place to study and pray."

"I think your neighbor saw me trying to climb the wall."

"That's Isabella. She's blind. She probably heard you banging on the gate."

Father Fontebuis lit a large, thick candle from his oil lamp, and he and Antonio descended the dark stairs to the Rectory's cellar. There, he lit two oil lamps and unfolded a blanket to chase the cellar's chill. "I will bring you some food soon. Tomorrow, when the Bishop makes his rounds to Chiusa Sclafani, I will let you take a bath in his new indoor bathtub. He won't mind."

"For a greater good, Father?" Antonio quipped.

"*Oui*, Pierre. *Pour un plus grand bien.*"

Chapter 4

St. John the Baptist Cathedral
Bisacquino
June 3, 1889
6:50 A.M.

The sacristan unbolted the huge wooden doors of the cathedral, and slowly, defiant townspeople filed in to pay their respects to Pietro Carravella. Four black-clad elderly ladies wobbled to the front row near the main altar and began to wail, as they did for every funeral. Vincenzo Trambatore nudged his horse up the hill towards the Cathedral, as several old friends of Pietro waited to serve as pallbearers. As the hearse stopped, each man removed their *coppolas* and stuffed them in their waistband. Each man grabbed the brass handles on the black-oak coffin and carried it to the black-draped bier near the front altar. Father Fontebuis stood near the altar and waited for the coffin. Once the pallbearers rested the coffin on the bier, the priest swung a silver thurible over the coffin, casting clouds of pungent incense throughout the Cathedral. Pietro Carravella's last Mass had commenced.

It was a rainy morning, so the weather denied the sun from streaming through the stained-glass windows. Iron candelabra, stationed at each corner of the coffin, and on both sides of the altar, provided the only light for the Mass. But despite the funereal gloom, which pervaded the cavernous Cathedral, a pair of darting black eyes, hiding behind the scarlet curtain, separating the Sacristy from the Sanctuary, spotted four *Stuppagghieri* leaning against one of the cathedral's massive pillars. Antonio's heart pounded as his eyes switched from his father's coffin to the men looking for him. As the Mass proceeded, the front doors of the cathedral flung open, and six *Carabinieri* stormed down the side aisle of the church. Their black knee-high boots pounded against the flagstone floor, and their black uniforms, with silver piping and epaulets, pierced the darkness with authority. Each officer wore the distinctive bicorn *Lucerna* hat with the plume of black feathers jetting from the Italian National Cockade.

Antonio's breathing shallowed, and he sweated through his shirt. The *Carabinieri* marched towards the Sanctuary and the Sacristy. *They know I'm here,* Antonio thought. He cast his gaze towards Father Fontebuis, who paid the marching troops no notice. Antonio continued to peek through the scarlet curtain, but when he was about to run, the lead officer stopped, grabbed one of the *Stuppagghieri,* and slammed him against the wall. The other officers grabbed the remaining *Mafiosi* and treated them the same. A vociferous interrogation by the *Carabinieri* commenced. Father Fontebuis continued the Mass.

The lead officer demanded to know why the *Stuppagghieri* were attending the funeral. When he didn't get the desired response, the officer knocked one of them to the floor with a thunderous blow of his rifle. He asked the next one. Silence. He received a similar official response. When the lead officer approached the third *Stuppagghieri,* the mobster uttered some indecipherable words, and the troops grabbed the four and dragged them from the Cathedral. Father Fontebuas continued Pietro Carravella's Mass, while Antonio released a sigh of relief.

><

Antonio slipped down the cellar stairs and lit an oil lamp near his cot. He opened the book Father Fontebuis gave him and began to study. But after a minute, his mind wandered back to the cemetery and his father's burial. Visions of the grave diggers dumping mud on his father's coffin slashed through his young mind, and hot tears stung his eyes. Despite receiving absolution for his sins, the grief of losing his father alloyed his guilt. He couldn't study, so he paced the length of the cellar like a caged animal. As he paced, his grief and guilt morphed into anger. His youthful outlook on life dimmed. The confluence of the past few day's events —the murder of his friend, the murder of his father before his eyes, killing two men, losing his home, being hunted, given a new name, and now forced to leave his homeland—caused him to view his new world in hues of contradictions. Cynicism attacked his faith. Despair attacked his hope. Emptiness attacked his future. The only thing he had left was a glimmer of trust in Father Fontebuis.

About two hours after the Mass, Father Fontebuis descended the cellar stairs and found Antonio sitting on his cot, reading the little green book.

"Great, Antonio—I mean Pierre. Keep studying. Are you packed? We leave right after midnight. I will feed the horse about nine tonight."

Antonio said nothing and cast a vacant stare towards the priest.

"Did you hear me, my son?"

"Yes, Father," Antonio replied. "Will you tell me more about my father's funeral?"

"Of course. Many people came to the cemetery. I guess they wanted to show their respect for your father and defiance to the *Stuppagghieri*. In fact, there were no *Mafiosi* at the cemetery. I guess the *Carabinieri* solved that problem for us. Your father had a great service."

"How did the *Carabinieri* know the *Stuppagghieri* would be at my father's Mass?"

"Well, yesterday, I went to the telegraph office to send my Superior a message about my arriving in Palermo soon. While I was there, I told the telegrapher that the Bishop had heard that *Stuppagghieri* was going to burn down the Cathedral if we had Pietro Carravella's funeral there. The poor man became enraged and sent out a series of telegraphs. He assured me we would be safe."

"Was that true, Father?"

"Not exactly, but we now have the police and the *Mafiosi* at war with one another, instead of looking for you. *Un mensonge pour un plus grand bien, Pierre.*"

"*Une tromperie necessaire, Pere Fontebuis?*"

"*Tres bon, Pierre.* Yes, Antonio, it was a necessary deception. It will give us time to get to Palermo, and then to France. Now, go upstairs and take a bath in the Bishop's new tub. I have laid out some clothes for you to wear—some black pants and a white shirt. I have some new clerics to wear, too. We must look good when we arrive in Palermo. If anyone questions us, you are to be a seminarian. It's another necessary deception."

Antonio hung his head for a moment and then asked, "Father, do you think it's possible we can stop at the cemetery tonight? It will be dark and everyone will be in bed."

"Sure, my son. I will bring a lantern. You won't be scared of going into a cemetery in the dark? I know about the old Sicilian superstitions."

"No. My father always told me the dead can't hurt you—only the living can."

Chapter 5

Bisacquino to Monreale, Sicily
June 4, 1889
1:15 A.M.

Father Fontebuis, dressed in a long black cassock, Roman collar and a saturno hat, and Antonio, dressed in black trousers, white shirt, a black woolen jacket, and black *coppola*, snuck out the rectory's back gate, and walked through the winding alleys of Bisacquino. It took fifteen minutes to get to Gino Scarpuzzo's livery service, where the bishop kept his new black canopied carriage and horse. With the exception of the flickering gas lamps, the moonless night shrouded the town in an eerie darkness and solitude. When the travelers arrived, Scarpuzzo hitched the horse to the carriage. Scarpuzzo took Father Fontebuis's leather suitcase and Antonio's sack, and stored it in the rear of the carriage. When the priest and the boy climb aboard the carriage, the horse began to buck, which required Scarpuzzo the yank on the long leather reins.

"He's young, Father, and eager to go," Scarpuzzo said.

"Good. We have a long trip ahead of us. He'll need his strength. We're going over the mountains to Palermo," Father Fontebuis said. "Signore Scarpuzzo, do you have a lantern I can borrow? I will leave it in the carriage when it's returned in a couple of days."

Scarpuzzo retrieved an old miner's lamp from his livery stable, and put it on the floor of the carriage. "I used to use this in the sulphur mines. It has enough oil for about two hours, Father."

"*Grazie*, Gino. We'll take good care of it. Well, *addio*, Gino."

"*Addio*, Father. Be careful on those mountain roads. The *Banditi* hide up there. Do you want to borrow a *lupara*, too?"

Father Fontebuis glanced at Antonio. "No, *grazie*. We'll be fine. And with a snap of the reins on the horse's back, they were on their way. The priest gripped the reins, as the young horse began to clop quickly through the narrow streets of the ancient town. As promised, Father Fontebuis drove the horse to the front gates of St. Anthony's Cemetery. In the dark, its foreboding countenance gave the bravest man chills and quivers, but the priest and Antonio had to pay one last visit before leaving. After tying the reins to the front gates of the cemetery, they braved the aura of death and entered the cemetery. Father Fontebuis struck a sulphur-tipped match and lit the miner's lamp, casting a bright four-foot radial glow as they walked among the legions of tombs and towards Antonio's father's grave.

Pietro Carravella's grave wasn't hard to find, even in the dim light. The newly tilled soil and humble bouquets were easy to see. Antonio knelt on the ground, folded his hands and prayed for his father. After a few moments, Father Fontebuis tapped the boy on the shoulder. "We must be going, Antonio. You'll come back one day. I promise."

Antonio stood up and backed away from his father's grave, but continued to pray. He promised his father to fight the *Stuppagghieri* anywhere he found them. "They took our land and your life. I promise to fight them for all my days," Antonio said. The priest tugged on Antonio's jacket, and they left the cemetery and mounted the carriage. "Which way are we going, Father?"

"We're going to take a longer route to avoid the *Banditi*. First, we will go past Contessa Entellina and then to Salapartua. Then, we will turn north and go straight to Monreale. Hopefully, we will make it by dusk. I have a fellow Jesuit there, and we'll stay the night with him. Then tomorrow morning, we will go to Palermo. Have you been to Palermo, Antonio?"

"No, Father. I have never left Bisacquino."

"Well, open your eyes and your mind. You are about to embark on a new adventure. We both are. Your life will change every day. Just remember to pray and study your French."

As the carriage left Bisacquino, Antonio turned around and looked one last time at the only place he had known. His heart sank, but he found courage in Father Fontebuis's words. Through the dark, he could see the faint outline of the jagged terracotta-tiled roofs, the flickering gas lamps, and wisps of gray chimney smoke floating over the town. As the carriage crunched the rocky road beneath its wooden-spoked wheels, Antonio crossed his arms and drifted off to sleep.

When they reached the outskirts of Salapartua, Father Fontebuis stopped the carriage and allowed the horse to drink from a flowing stream. The sudden jerk of the carriage stirred Antonio. He reached back to his sack and grabbed some cured meat and a wineskin filled with water, while the priest shared slices of an apple with the horse.

In the distance, they heard the galloping of several horses approaching from the north. As the riders came closer, Antonio noticed that one of them had a lantern on a pole stuffed in his left stirrup. In the faint glow of the light, their faces were recognizable—the *Carabinieri*. As the five riders approached, the lead officer gave the order to stop and dismount. He walked towards Father Fontebuis and said, *"Buongiorno, Padre,"* and bowed. "I am Lieutenant Ferranzzo. May I ask why you and the boy are out here in the middle of the night?"

"We are on our way to Palermo to see my superior. As you know, the Jesuits have been ordered out of Sicily. I am a Jesuit, and the boy is a seminarian."

"Are you Arbereshe—Albanian? Are you coming from Contessa Entellina?"

"No. We are French and we are coming from Bisacquino."

"Bisacquino? Ah, the home of Vito Cascioferro. You know him, *Padre*?"

"No. But I know who he is. He's part of the reason we're leaving Sicily."

"The *Stuppagghieri*?" Lieutenant Ferranzzo asked.

"And the *Carabinieri*. Both seem to have control of Sicily right now."

Ferranzzo shrugged his shoulders and said, "We are hunting them, and the *Banditi*. In fact, the *Banditi* are hiding in the hills around us. I wouldn't be surprised if they're not watching us right now. You must be careful. Trust no one. Understand?"

"I understand."

"Good. Now, I must see your identification papers—just to make sure you are who you say you are."

As Father Fontebuis walked to the rear of the carriage to retrieve their identification papers, the trooper with the lantern approached Antonio, who was seated in the carriage. He held the lantern against the boy's face and stared into his eyes. "You look Sicilian. Are you Sicilian, boy? What is your name?"

"His name is Pierre Caravelle. His father was French, but his mother was from Bisacquino. He's an orphan now—both parents are dead. Here is his Baptismal record from the Church," Father Fontebuis said, handing the identification papers to Lieutenant Ferranzzo. Ferranzzo stepped towards the light and examined the papers. After a few moments, Lieutenant Ferranzzo handed the papers back to the priest.

"I am satisfied. You may go, but you must be careful. Do you know what time it is?"

Father Fontebuis dug into his pocket and produced a small gold pocket watch. "It's 3:10," he said, as he wound the stem.

"You have a long ride ahead of you. Be on your way, but be careful," Lieutenant Ferranzzo enjoined.

"*Grazie*, Lieutenant. God is with us."

"I hope so. Good luck." The *Carabinieri* mounted their horses and rode south towards Salapartua. Father Fontebuis mounted the carriage, slapped the horse with the reins, and proceeded north.

"Well, Antonio, it looks like we passed our first test," the priest said with a sigh of relief.

Antonio smiled and looked at the deep, expansive, star-studded firmament, which seemed to follow them over every hill and hollow. *There must be a God,* he thought to himself.

><

About twenty miles north of Salapartua, and at the junction of two roads near the hillside village of Camporeale, the carriage lurched and stopped as it approached the knoll of a small hill. In the distance, Father Fontebuis could see a glow of a fire against the dark sky and smelled wood burning. "Our horse senses something, Antonio. When we get to the top of the hill, we will stop." The priest slapped the reins against the horse's back again and again. The horse tugged the carriage to the crown of the hill and stopped. Father Fontebuis and Antonio dismounted the carriage and looked down the hill. About one hundred yards ahead of them, a roaring bonfire burned in the middle of the road. Sparks and embers flew into the night sky, like demons from hell. Antonio's eyes searched for anyone who could be attending the fire, but saw no one.

"Who would set a fire in the middle of the road in the middle of the night, Father?"

"The *Carabinieri* were right, Antonio," the priest lamented. And as he was going to explain his answer, two *Banditi* jumped from the bushes lining the side of the road, and pointed their shotguns at Father Fontebuis and Antonio Carravella.

"Stop! Don't move," a bearded *Banditi* demanded. "Give us all your money and valuables.

"As you can see, I am just a priest, and he's a poor seminarian. We have no valuables."

"Bullshit. Rome has more money than all of Europe. Hand it over or I'll blow your brains all over this road."

The other *Banditi,* a younger and taller man, went to the rear of the carriage, slung his shotgun over his shoulder, and rummaged through Antonio's sack and Father Fontebuis's suitcase. He lit a candle to give himself some light and discovered the priest's communion kit, which included a silver chalice and paten.

"You have no valuables?" he asked, showing them to his bearded partner. "A priest who lies deserves to die," he snarled. He ripped the saturno off the priest's head, flung it towards the fire, and jammed the muzzle of his shotgun into Father Fontebuis's ribs, snarling, "Both of you, walk to the fire, and get on your knees and pray."

The bearded *Banditi* stopped Antonio and searched his pockets. There, he found two hundred Liras. "No money?" he yelled and smacked Antonio between the eyes with the butt of the shotgun, knocking him to the ground. He grabbed the boy by the collar of his shirt and told him to kneel next to the priest. Blood trickled down Antonio's face and into his mouth. The taste of his own blood triggered his last vision of his father's face, as the flames seared his skin.

"We're also taking your horse and carriage, because you'll not need them anymore," the elder *Banditi* said. Now both of you face the fire and stare deeply into it, for that's where you are going." The *Banditi* place the muzzles of their shotguns against the backs of Father Fontebuis's and Antonio's heads. "You have ten seconds to pray."

Just as the priest and the boy braced for what they believed would be their final breath, a sudden volley of rifle fire shattered the stillness of the night. Both *banditi* collapsed—toppling over the priest and the boy—then crumpling to the earth. Their skulls had been cleft as though struck by an executioner's axe, and thick, dark blood spilled from their mortal wounds, snaking its way toward the fire. Their shotguns fell uselessly at their sides. From the shadows beyond, Father Fontebuis and Antonio heard distant cheers of triumph. Slowly, they rose and peered into the darkness.

"Please forgive us, Father, for using you and the boy as bait," Lieutenant Ferranzzo said with a big smile as he emerged from the darkness with his troops. "But we have been looking for these two for a long time. I hope you understand. *Carabinieri* is grateful for your service."

Antonio dropped to his knees next to the man who hit him with the shotgun, punching, kicking, and spitting on his corpse. Lieutenant Ferranzzo and the other *Carabinieri* cheered him on until he had exhausted himself. Ferranzzo dismounted his horse and retrieved some rags, bandages, and his canteen from a leather bag slung over his saddle. He bent down over Antonio and cleaned and bandaged his wounds. "Calm down, seminarian," he said with a wink. When you get to Palermo, have a doctor look at that wound. It's small, but deep," Ferranzzo said.

"Lieutenant, may I ask a question?" Father Fontebuis asked.

"Of course."

"You followed us all the way here?"

"Yes."

"You knew these *Banditi* were in the hills?"

"I had a good idea they were there. They've been robbing and killing people going to Palermo for almost a year. We could not find them until tonight. Their fire made them excellent targets."

"But they almost killed us."

"We had them in our sights from the moment they started that fire. You were safe."

Ferranzzo ordered his men to strip the *Banditi* and bury them deep on the hillside. He gave Antonio the two hundred Liras stolen from him, and put the chalice and paten in the priest's suitcase. "Father, you and the seminarian can go now. Again, thank you for your service."

"I can't go, yet. I must say prayers over these men's graves."

"What? *Figlio di puttana! Scusa*, Father, but these men tried to kill you."

"But you said they were in your sights from the moment they started the fire. Right?"

Ferranzzo slapped his hands on the sides of his legs and said, "I suppose there's no arguing with God."

Chapter 6

Monreale, Sicily
Via Piave
June 4, 1889
7:35 P.M.

Tens miles south of Palermo, snuggled against Monte Caputo, lay the ancient town Monreale, which was once occupied by hordes of Muslims, but now the exclusive domain of a Benedictine Archbishop Gaspere di Brolo. The town's twenty-thousand inhabitants, nearly all Roman Catholic, had anticipated the benefits of the 1861 Italian Unification, but twenty-two years later, hardly any of the promises have trickled down the Italian peninsula to Sicily. In fact, much of Sicily's land, once under the control of the Archbishop of Monreale for centuries, now belonged to a corrupt puppet government in Palermo, and factions of the *Stuppagghieri* and the *Giardinieri.* But to most Sicilians, who only wanted to scratch out a life, live in peace, and own the land under their feet, didn't care who wanted power and wealth. Since the days of William II in 1172, the towns occupants had lived and worked as vassals of a higher power, and in 1889, they felt little had changed. The inexorable currents of time flowed through Sicily, and for some of the island's oldest families, they sought change, if not on their soil, somewhere else.

At dusk, Father Fontebuis and Antonio entered Monreale. The cobblestone streets glowed with gas lamps, and a new invention: electricity. Antonio's eyes bulged as his head swiveled, ensnaring all the sights and smells he could absorb. Horse-drawn carriages tangled in small knots, waiting for their drivers to get control of their horses, and rolled through the streets and alleys. Father Fontebuis chuckled as he watched two men yell invectives at each other, questioning their driving skills. Antonio watched two well-dressed ladies stop at a shop window and gaze at a well-dressed mannequin.

"Father, is Palermo like this?" Antonio asked.

"It's much bigger," he said, as he unfolded a hand-drawn map of Monreale.

"Are we lost, Father?"

"No, I'm just looking for a quick way to get to the *Duomo*. My friend, Father Philippe Consere, lives in a small apartment behind it. He is from Paris and probably being asked to leave Sicily, too."

"Why only Jesuits and not the other priests?" Antonio asked.

"Well, that's hard to explain, Antonio. My order has a history of preaching God's Word and mixing it with social issues, much like Jesus did. Some people can't handle the truth. Some people want God and religion contained in a box called a church, and never allowed to walk the streets. They find words threatening, and the Italian government seems to be threatened by this. So, I suppose I am ready to go home and leave all this."

Father Fontebuis edged the carriage down a narrow alley towards the *Duomo,* and when Antonio saw the immensity of Monreale's Cathedral, he gasped. "Is that their cathedral, Father?"

"Yes, it is. And it's been there for over six hundred years." Father Fontebuis turned the horse down Via Palermo and then right on Via Piave. A young stable boy sat on a step waiting for their arrival.

"*Buongiorno*, Father, my name is Giuseppe, and I have been waiting all day for you. I will take care of the horse and carriage for you. Father Consere is inside waiting for you."

"*Grazie,* Guiseppi. I will need the carriage first thing in the morning. Here is something for your time," Father Fontebuis said as he gave the stable boy a few coins.

After unloading their baggage, Father Fontebuis pulled a brass rod near the door, which rang a bell inside Number 12 Via Piave. After a few moments, the door opened, and a short, clerically dressed, balding man appeared. Father Fontebuis and Father Consere embraced and exchanged some words in French. After Antonio was introduced to Father Consere, the weary travelers were led into the small apartment. The apartment had three bedrooms, a sitting room, and a kitchen. Father Consere explained the other Jesuits had already left, and he would like to leave with them in the morning, if possible.

After a roasted chicken, pasta, and red wine dinner, the priest discussed the current situation. Antonio listened, but their conversation would drift into French when the priest sought confidentiality. Father Consere was curious about Antonio and why he was traveling with Father Fontebuis. He also showed concern for the bandage on the boy's head.

Being deferentially silent, Antonio was encouraged to speak about the last few days. As he did, Father Consere blanched and looked at Father Fontebuis for confirmation.

"It's true. He's an orphan," Father Fontebuis lamented. "And if that's not enough, the *Carabinieri* used us as bait to kill two *Banditi* on our way here." Shocked, Consere went to the cabinet and brought back a bottle of Cognac and three glasses.

"After hearing those stories, we all need a drink," Father Consere said, as he poured Antonio a glass. "Go ahead, son. Drink. This is very expensive Cognac. I only bring it out for special occasions and special people. I won't give any to the Archbishop—so feel special." Antonio took a small sip and grimaced as the Cognac slipped down his throat, like a lit fuse. Father Consere laughed.

"Philippe, what do you think will happen tomorrow when we meet with Father Wertz in Palermo?"

"I don't know. He seems to have a stern countenance. Where do you think they will send us?"

"I hope it's back to France," Father Consere said, slugging back his Cognac and pouring another. "I love Sicily, but it's just too corrupt here. I read all the promises Victor Emanuel and Giuseppe Garibaldi made years ago about reform, and none have happened. We're just Rome's stepchild. Whatever the *Mafioso* want, the politicians give them. And our Black Pope seems like he doesn't care. He's trying to stay in the good graces of the Pope. I hear things are in turmoil in the Vatican, too. Do you know the Black Pope?"

"I was in Rome when Father Anton Anderledy was installed as our General Superior. He's Swiss and seems to be a kind man, but he's a politician. You must be to survive in Rome," Father Fontebuis said. "Well, no use worrying about things we have no control over. I hope Father Wertz allows me to continue my care for Antonio. I promised his dying father."

"I'm sure he will." Father Consere paused and sipped his drink. "To be completely honest, I had a conversation with the Archbishop about leaving, and where I would go. He mumbled something about America. I'm sure I heard him correctly."

"America?" Father Fontebuis said. "Isn't there a war there?"

"It's over. While Italy was having its War of Unification, America was having a war among its states. I heard it was a very bloody affair, and di Brolo said they need priests in some of their cities. As you know, many

Sicilians have left for New York and they're sending money home, which hasn't gone unnoticed by the government or the Church. So things must be improving there."

"New York? I've seen pictures of that city. I think it's bigger than Rome."

"I know. And two ships are leaving Palermo for New York every week. How's your English?"

"It's good, but I'm not fluent. How's yours?"

"I just know the bad words," Father Consere said, laughing.

Chapter 7

Palermo, Sicily
June 5, 1889

At dawn, Fathers Fontebuis and Consere, accompanied by Antonio, left number 12 Via Piave, and walked to the livery stable to hitch their horse to their carriage for the trip to Palermo. On the way, Father Consere dropped a farewell letter in Archbishop di Brolo's mail slot, thanking him for allowing Jesuits to serve in Monreale. There was no need for a face-to-face discussion regarding his departure, as it was understood among the parties how political forces sometimes drove ecclesiastical policies. Both priests knew the history of the Jesuits in Europe, and how their Order was exiled from parts of Italy and Sicily in 1769. To them, they were experiencing the swing of history's pendulum and accepted it.

As they left Monreale, they passed the fertile fields of blood oranges, almonds, lemons, olive groves, and some atrophying vineyards. Despite the variety of what the earth had to offer, Antonio's eyes were locked on the vineyards and their shriveling crop. For the two priests and the boy, the trip on the busy road to Palermo seemed uneventful, but each pondered the future.

About noon, Father Consere drove the carriage through the narrow, bustling streets of Palermo. Antonio coughed as the dust kicked up by the horses and mules choked him. The clear mountain air and the quietude of Bisacquino seemed miles away now, but Antonio was pleasantly stunned at the frenetic pace of the big city. He snapped his head in every direction. Everywhere he looked there was someone engaged in some type of activity. As they passed the market, he saw row upon row of various merchants selling everything from strands of garlic to knives, barrels of lemons to casks of olive oil, mounds of vegetables to sacks of almonds, rosaries to shotguns, and Sicilian citrus stacked upon each other like cannon balls. The air hung heavy with a cacophony of scents pouring from the narrow market passages. Freshly butchered animals hung on iron hooks. Men and women yelled at each other, but what Antonio first thought was anger was merely blandishments, seeking the bargain of the day. Freshly slaughtered chickens hung by their feet, while others, stuffed in wooden cages, waited for a similar fate. The marketplace exploded with life, and what sustained it was money, being pushed and pulled. Antonio mused to himself: *nothing remains still, not even the dead chickens.* He watched as the herds of merchants whirled among their tables with the alacrity and celerity wrought by the drive for self-survival. The exciting desperation oozed from everyone's pores under the blazing sun, but peacefully, they all knew they would return home satisfied. This was the quotidian ritual which kept Palermo alive.

Father Consere stopped the carriage as Father Fontebuis consulted another hand-drawn map. They conversed in French, but it was clear to Antonio they were looking for the office of their superior, Father Franz Wertz. After wending their way through the streets of Palermo, Father Consere found Via Vicolo Casa Professa, a wide cobblestoned street which fronted the Jesuit baroque cathedral and cloister of *Chiesa de Gesu*. After asking for directions to Father Wertz's office, Father Fontebuis tethered the horse to an iron ring next to a water trough. The thirsty beast wasted no time driving its parched snout into the cool water.

The priests took turns brushing the dust from each other's cassocks, as they wanted to make a positive impression on their superior. Father Consere dipped his handkerchief into the water trough, wiped dust from Antonio's face, and adjusted his bandage. "Remember, Antonio, remove your *coppola* while in the presence of Father Wertz," Father Fontebuis cautioned. Antonio nodded. And after retrieving their bags, they sloughed their way up a small hill to a baroque cloister, which led to several pairs of massive iron-studded Gothic doors.

As they approached the doors of Father Wertz's residence, a black-habited nun appeared with a large brass key. After unlocking the doors, she allowed them to enter, but not before yanking Antonio's hat. She glared at him and said, "What happened to your head, boy?"

"Some *Banditti* struck him with a gun," Father Fontebuis said.

The nun shook her head and said, "Follow me."

They followed the nun down a dark corridor to a candle-lit anteroom furnished with leather sofas and stuffed chairs. Large oil paintings of the four Evangelists hung on the walls. As the priests sat down, a smaller arched door opened, and a large, balding, rotund priest wearing round metal spectacles stood in the doorway. Immediately, Father Consere and Father Fontebuis shot up and greeted Father Franz Wertz with a bow. After polite introductions and a partial explanation of why a bandaged Antonio was in their company, Father Wertz directed his two subordinates to his private office and instructed Antonio to make himself comfortable in the anteroom.

Father Wertz's office was spacious. A large oil portrait of Saint Ignatius Loyola hung behind his large, black oak desk. The brick floor was covered with a large Turkish rug, and the walls were covered with various icons of Catholic saints. As Fathers Fontebuis and Consere sat down, Father Wertz opened a locked drawer and retrieved a large file with two large envelopes. Both envelopes had red wax seals of the Jesuit order, which indicated their importance and secrecy. Wertz adjusted his spectacles and, after a few moments, broke the tense silence.

"How old are you, Father Fontebuis?" Wertz asked.

"I'm thirty-two, sir."

"Father Consere?"

"I'm thirty-eight, sir."

"How old is the boy?"

"He will be fifteen on July the thirtieth," Father Fontebuis responded.

Wertz took a deep breath and looked at both priests. "We are in very tough times here in Sicily. Not as bad when Popes Clement XIII and XIV were in Rome, but nonetheless, tough. As you both know, the *Risorgimento* has not yet brought the promised reforms to Sicily. The government is corrupt and is rife with the *Stuppagghieri* and their hated rivals, the *Giaridinineri.* The politicians are risible puppets. For the last several years, some of our brethren have been very vocal and critical of the lack of reforms from the pulpit. Some things are better left unsaid, but nothing is better undone. That is why the local government is asking us to leave Sicily. Those in power fear our words will lead to social unrest, particularly among the *Contandini.* Father Anderledy has consulted with Pope Leo, and he thinks it's best we make some reassignments—for our own good."

"Are you leaving, too, Father Wertz?" Father Consere asked.

"Yes, in September. I am being recalled to Rome. But this reassignment should be temporary. The government wants only an Italian priest in Sicily. I am German, and you both are French, and the French have a bitter history on this island."

"Yes, we've heard history many times. Where are we going?" Father Consere braved.

Father Wertz separated the papers before him into two stacks and paged through them. He broke the red seals and emptied the contents of the envelopes onto his desk, and began to read through them. "Your records indicate great acumen in teaching, so both of you are being assigned teaching positions in America. Our records indicate that since the American Civil War, things have improved. Sicilian families who have left here are sending money home to their families, which has raised the government's curiosity, but not in a good way."

"Are we going to New York?" Father Consere asked.

"No. It appears Rome received a Transatlantic cable about ten days ago. We have a young men's college in New Orleans, Louisiana called The College of the Immaculate Conception. The headmaster, Father O'Shanahan, has requested more teachers, particularly in math, science, and the languages. Your resumes seem to satisfy his needs."

"New Orleans?" Father Fontebuis asked. "I know nothing about the place, other than many Sicilians go there for work."

"It appears there remains a critical shortage of agriculture workers and city laborers in and around New Orleans," Father Wertz sighed. He held several sheets of paper between his stubby fingers. Fathers Consere and Fontebuis followed their superior's eyes as he scanned the pages. "I have a report from our Provincial Superior in New Orleans here. I will share some of the salient aspects of New Orleans with you. It looks pretty detailed. Here's the good and the bad."

Father Wertz cleared his throat and began to read the report to his subordinates. After a brief chuckle, he said, "It appears that the Jesuits were expelled in New Orleans in 1763—just about the time we were expelled from here by Popes Clement XIII and XIV. I hope that doesn't presage anything for the moment." All three priests allowed a nervous laugh.

"Well, let's see. The estimated population of New Orleans is 236,000 people. While it is primarily Catholic, Protestants control the city's government. There is tension among the faiths and races. The city is composed of an admixture of nationalities and races. There are Anglos, French Catholics, Huguenots, Germans, Irish, Greeks, Croats, Africans, Italians—mostly Sicilians—and indigenous people they call Indians. There are also Creoles, a mixture of African, French, and Spanish. Complete assimilation of the people has not been realized, nor desired. While their civil war has been over for twenty years, vestiges of the conflict remain. The Anglo city government seems to tolerate the former African slaves. Still, there seems to be a palpable dislike for the Sicilians, who seem to have assimilated with the former slaves or their descendants.

"It appears the secret Sicilian groups have taken advantage of the

Sicilian immigration to New Orleans. While most immigrants are hardworking, the *Stuppagghieri* and the *Giardinieri* have formed secret societies in New Orleans and are preying upon the good Sicilian immigrants. An extortion method known as the *Mano Nero* or Black Hand seems to rule certain parts of the city, which has drawn the ire of the city's civil authorities. Looks like we can't escape it, Fathers.

"The Neapolitan *Camorra* and the Calabrian *'Ndrangheta* are also in New Orleans, and openly compete in the extortion trade. According to Father O'Shanahan, this criminal activity has exacerbated the suspicions and hostilities toward all Sicilians. He writes that 'There is a *Mafia*-related murder nearly every month in an area known as the *Carré de la Ville or Vieux Carré,* which is the original city of New Orleans, and is contiguous with the docks of the Mississippi River. Many Sicilians settled there in small hovels, and the area acquired the appellation of the Italian Colony *or Piccolo Palermo.* The police are corrupt, very aggressive, and sometimes very brutal towards the immigrants. Entreaties by the Archbishop of New Orleans, Francis Jenssens, have gone ignored, because the Protestant-control city doesn't like the Sicilians or the Catholic Church. Sounds familiar, Fathers?"

"Father Wertz, with all due respect, how can we be effective in such a hostile place? We are leaving one Sicily for another?" Father Fontebuis asked.

"As Jesuits, we always go into hostile environments. That's our history and calling. Besides, you will love the irony in this. The Anglos, the very people who dislike us, send their sons to our college in New Orleans. There seems to be no shortage of hypocrisy in that city, and as we know it, it is a driving force behind all political power."

"Protestants in a Jesuit college?" Father Consere asked.

"Oh, yes. I suppose they don't participate in any religious courses, but they want our priests to teach them some secular skills. You'll be safe there," Father Wertz promised. "Just busy yourselves with academics, and stay away from the local politics. Father O'Shanahan writes that the Jesuit community enjoys a respectable peace in New Orleans and doesn't want to disturb the fragile harmony. Understand?"

Both Father Consere and Fontebuis nodded.

For a moment, the room fell silent as Father Wertz thumbed through Father O'Shanahan's report. A florid red shade flowed from Wertz's collar to the top of his bald head. His brow furrowed in anger as he clenched his jaw. His chest heaved under his cassock.

"Is something wrong, sir?" Father Fontebuis asked.

"According to Father O'Shanahan's report, members of the city's government and the business community have their own secret societies, which date back before their civil war, and have been aggressive in their treatment of Negroes and Sicilians. He cautions against staying away from those controversies. It appears we can't escape secret societies," Father Wertz said.

"Father Wertz, is there any way you or Rome will reconsider this assignment?" Father Consere asked.

"I can't. It comes from the Vatican. O'Shanahan sent his request directly to Father Anderledy, and he knows we're being asked to leave Sicily. Both of you have teaching experience. While New Orleans sounds hostile, we're not being asked to leave there. Like I said, they want us to teach their sons. We might not win in the pulpit, but we could win in the classroom, if you understand my thinking. But be careful, deliberate, but subtle. Perhaps, you can cozen your way into their cold, sterile hearts. Let God do the rest."

"When do we leave for New Orleans?" Father Fontebuis asked.

"We have you both booked on the *SS Neustria*. It sails on July the thirtieth."

"What about Antonio? I can't leave him here," Father Fontebuis said. "I promised his father I would take care of him."

"Is that the man killed in the vineyard in Bisacquino?" Father Wertz asked. "Don't worry. I heard the news about some killings in the wine country."

"Yes. I gave him Extreme Unction at the small hospital in the village."

Wertz sat back in his chair and steepled his fingers. "Was the man dead when you made that promise?"

"I don't know. But it was still a promise I must honor. Antonio has no family, and if he stays in Sicily, the *Stuppagghieri* will find him and kill him. He is an orphan."

"Did Antonio kill those two men in the vineyard?" Father Wertz probed. "I heard all about it. Sicily is a small island."

"Father Wertz, you know I can't discuss anything the boy confessed to me."

Wertz put his hand up and said, "Say no more. But I understand the *Carabinieri* are looking for him, too. They are having a hard time believing Antonio's father killed both men in the vineyard, given the fatal wounds he sustained. Don't respond. We will protect the boy and claim him as our own. We've done it before. Does he have any money?"

"He has a few *Lira*. How much is the passage to America?" Father Fontebuis asked.

"They want thirty-five American dollars—about a dollar a day for the voyage, I guess," Father Wertz opined. "I think that translates to about 200 *Liras*. Does he have that? If not, I will front his passage to the *Padrone*. They run the docks."

"I don't know, but can we get him some work around Palermo, until the ship sails? We have nearly two months."

Father Wertz rubbed his chin and smiled. "Sister Consolata, the nun you met when you arrived, has a brother who works on the docks loading ships with citrus, fish, and other cargo. That's how we get our food. I will ask her to get him a job until the ship sails. We have room in the cloister so he can stay here, too. But I have to caution you. Remember, he's Sicilian, has no family, doesn't speak English, is going to a place where he knows no one, and might not be welcomed when he gets there. Do you still want to take him with you?"

"If I leave him here, he might be arrested, killed, or conscripted in the Italian army. I don't know why Italy needs to build a large army and navy. I guess they're looking for another war to express their new national identity," Father Fontebuis lamented. "I am teaching him French now, and I have changed his name to Pierre Caravelle. I will start teaching him English, too. We both can use the lessons."

Father Wertz pushed back from his desk, stood, and went to a cabinet to retrieve a file. "Do you know what this is?" he asked.

His subordinates shook their heads.

"These are my original orders when I was sent here, some fifteen years ago. I will share some things my superior wrote me about this place. Have you ever heard of Gerolamo Nino Bixio?"

His subordinates shook their heads.

"He was a General under Garabaldi who killed several people in Bronte, a small village in Catania. He was brutal, and though he was Italian, he hated Sicilians. He feared them. It was his invasion of Sicily that brought it under the crown of Victor Emmanuel. Sicily has been washed and stained with blood for many centuries. The people on this island have suffered under the sword of many nations for thousands of years, yet they remain tenacious fighters. Let me read you something Bixio wrote to the Sicilian population in 1866, after the War of Unification or *Il Risorgimento*. Remember, he feared them."

Father Wertz adjusted his spectacles. "'Be peaceful, people of Sicily, or we will destroy you as enemies of humanity.' This is what I was told about Sicilians. I don't see anything changing. Take him with you to New Orleans, but be careful. Considering the *Neustria* leaves in about sixty days, and the voyage is about thirty-three days, you three have about ninety days for everyone to learn English. Start tonight."

><

When the three priests left Father Wertz's office, they found Sister Consolata changing Antonio's bandage, while he ate grapes and sliced blood oranges from a silver platter.

"That's fine, Antonio," Father Wertz said, "you need to eat and become strong." Turning his attention to Sister Consolata, Father Wertz said, "Sister, would you be kind enough to have three rooms prepared in the cloister. Our travelers will be staying with us for the next two months. And, do you think your brother can help Antonio get a job on the docks?"

Sister Consolata smiled and nodded. "I will send a message to him tonight, Father. They always need help down there."

"Thank you, Sister," Father Wertz said, turning towards Father Fontebuis and Consere, he asked them to accompany him back to his office. "I have something to tell you. Follow me."

After closing the door, Wertz said, "I know your next assignment is dangerous. A friend of mine is a Redemptorist, and they have priests in New Orleans ministering to the German population. It's a port city filled with vice and corruption, and life is cheaply disposed of on a regular basis. So, I am asking you to go there and do your best for at least two years. When I get to Rome, I will ask Father Anderledy to make the assignment temporary. Our Community has a Novitiate in Louisiana, and they can replace you then. Afterwards, I will see that you return to France. If Father Anderledy agrees, I will send a cable to Father O'Shanahan. That should be sometime in September, after you arrive in New Orleans. Is that acceptable with you?"

Both priests agreed, smiled, and shook their Superior's hand. "Father

Wertz," Father Fontebuis began, "I think we will assimilate well. From what you have told us, we are not actually leaving Sicily."

Chapter 8

The Pickwick Club
New Orleans
June 8, 1889
7:30 P.M.

When Charles Dickens created his character, Samuel Pickwick, in *The Pickwick Papers* in 1837, he could have not imagined that twenty years later a group of *soi desant* elite white male Protestants in New Orleans would have appropriated his character's name, and fictional club as inspiration for the formation of a secret society, which fostered white supremacy. Dickens was an ardent abolitionist. The club's first president, Adley Hogan Gladden, wanted to celebrate his fledgling observance on the city's Mardi Gras while preserving New Orleans' own variety of eugenics. Only the finest families from selected professions were chosen to join. Most of the membership were attorneys, doctors, non-Jewish merchants, businessmen, and owners of the local newspapers. Most claim to be of an Anglo-Saxon pedigree and refuse to tolerate anyone whom they view as having an inferior social standing in a city carved from a cypress swamp by French Catholics, Indians, and African slaves. Every member, during the Civil War, swore allegiance to the Confederacy and was an inveterate Democrat. Indeed, Gladden, who joined the Confederate army, was killed on April 12, 1862, during the battle of Shiloh, Tennessee. But the Pickwick Club endured. It endured the Union occupation of New Orleans and the post-war Reconstruction.

The Pickwick Club had a companion club, which had many of the same social aspirations—the Boston Club. It took its name from a popular card game of the time, but some viewed its membership as a social notch below the Pickwick Club, though both clubs shared and welcomed each other's members. And both enforced and enjoyed the caste system, which controlled New Orleans. Despite some political differences, however, the clubs sometimes found their members supporting different candidates for mayor and other elected and appointed offices, which sometimes caused confused feelings. The Pickwickian self-identified as Bourbonist and more sophisticated than their Bostonian counterparts, who self-identified as The Ring or the Regular Democratic Organization. Every election found candidates in heated campaigns between the Bourbonists and The Ring, and often, the mayor's office and city council would switch sides every election. Since the end of Reconstruction, no republican dared to run for public office in New Orleans. In fact, the last Republican mayor of New Orleans, Benjamin Flanders, was voted out of office in November 1872. The insular city despised republicans and avoided them like yellow fever. Though it had been twenty-three years since the end of the Civil War, many nativists recalled vividly the Union yoke of Reconstruction. Long memories have long knives.

On the night of April 23, 1889, Joseph Ansoetigui Shakspeare, age fifty-two, had just completed his first year of his second term as the twenty-ninth mayor of New Orleans. This was the second time he was elected mayor—the first in 1880. Shakspeare self-identified as a Bourbonist, but was a member of both the Boston and Pickwick clubs, and their associated Mardi Gras clubs, Comus and Rex. In fact, he was the King of Rex in 1882 and enjoyed a high social standing in New Orleans. His family owned a foundry and iron works on Girod Street, and he attended an Episcopal church, though his father was a Quaker. He was politically savvy and street smart, despite the aristocratic countenance he projected. When he was elected the second time, he was determined to pull New Orleans into the Gilded Age and enhance its status among the cities of the world.

In 1884, New Orleans hosted the Cotton Centennial Exposition, which drew crowds from throughout the United States and some foreign countries. Shakspeare's family company helped build the exposition center, and witnessed some out-of-state firms' keen interest in establishing branch offices in New Orleans, given its port along the Mississippi River. But not every New Orleanian shared Shakspeare's dream, because most New Orleanians did not belong to the Boston or Pickwick clubs, or supported the cotton commerce and its ancillary industries. They sweated for them and had to be content with putting hot food on the table every night, next to flickering candles or oil lamps. Others, however, pursued more nefarious means of supporting themselves in the dark back alleys and dank, narrow streets of New Orleans.

But Shakspeare's adamantine determination and ego knew no bounds. He viewed his second term as an opportunity, not only for himself, but for New Orleans. He refused to allow competing political ideas any chance of denying his dream. So, upon assuming his second term as mayor, he selected people he could trust the most to work for him. He demanded fealty to his aspirations and would not tolerate anyone who offered any opposition. And to ensure his plans, he installed a select group of men from his social clubs as executors of his dreams. None of these men were part of his governmental cabinet, as he wanted to keep their names and participation secret, to ensure compliance.

They worked clandestinely, as they commenced through the city and the surrounding environs. This inner circle of like-minded men would report to him regularly and target anyone who stood in the Mayor's way. Shakspeare knew he could not trust every city worker, because many were part of The Ring and a lesser class. But he needed their sweat and their votes. He felt he finally had an opportunity to cast his shadow internationally, and he would use New Orleans to do it.

So, on this night, Shakspeare called a secret meeting in the private dining room on the second floor of the Feibleman Building, located at the corner of Carondelet and Canal Streets in the heart of the commercial district of New Orleans. The Feibleman Building was a four-story, Queen Anne-style structure with large Oriel-arched windows and massive castle-like corner turrets, which ran from the second floor to the roof. Inside the second floor, the Pickwick Club enjoyed many amenities often found in exclusive men's clubs of the Northeast. There were smoking rooms, card rooms, a library, and a dining room, which had a private area near the corner of the building, tucked inside a turret. A large arched window was built into the turret facing Canal Street and towards the Mississippi River. Inside the turret, a large round dining table, covered with a white linen tablecloth, rested on an Oriental rug. A coal gas-lit crystal chandelier hung over the table, which provided a dulcet ambiance.

After parking their barouche coaches on Carondelet Street, Shakspeare's nine selected guests ascended the mahogany stairway, where they were met by tuxedo-dressed black men who escorted them to Shakspeare's inner sanctum. When they arrived, they found their names printed on white cards on china plates. The mayor sat in a chair with his back to the open Oriel window. It was dusk, and a summer afternoon rain had cooled New Orleans, but with the drop in temperature came a waft of steamy stench from Canal Street's cobblestoned surface. Since Shakspeare had the windows opened to catch the evening breeze, he placed expensive Cuban cigars next to each plate to compensate for the invading street vapors, a floor below. Also, a fifty-foot iron tower stood at the corner of Carondelet and Canal Streets, which held a moon-shaped carbon-arc light. When lit, the rudimentary electric utility provided a lunar glow upon the street below, accompanied by the audible crackle and hiss of the arc. The light provided some primitive lighting for the busy intersection, but Shakspeare had more ambitious plans for *his* New Orleans.

Seated clockwise around the table from the mayor were William Sterling Parkerson, a well-respected attorney, Walter Denegre, another attorney, George Denegre, an attorney and Walter's brother, James "J.D." Houston, a merchant, planter and former Chief Deputy for the Orleans Parish Criminal Sheriff's Office, Franklin B. Hayne, a merchant and member of the New Orleans Cotton Exchange, Maurice Hart, a merchant and stockbroker, General Algeron S. Badger, a customs appraiser, Thomas Boylan, Chief of the Boylan Detective Agency, and Theodore D. Wharton, publisher of the *Times-Democrat,* one of New Orleans' most prominent newspapers. Though these nine men represented the type of people the mayor trusted, there were others, but he wanted their input on his secret plans.

After greeting his guests, Shakspeare invited the men to light their cigars, as the white waiters poured expensive bourbon into crystal glasses. Franklin Hayne sat in his chair and covered his nose with his handkerchief. "What's wrong, Frank? Light your cigar and have a drink. We have a long night ahead of us," the mayor said.

"No, thank you. The smell of cigars and mule shit has killed my appetite. I'll just have a glass of bourbon. You have to do something about those streets. Don't you have enough men to clean up after those horses and mules?"

"At least there's enough light to prevent you from stepping in it," Shakspeare said. "Besides, that's one of the things we are going to discuss. A renaissance for New Orleans, but I need your help," Shakspeare responded, as he lit his cigar. "Dinner will be served in about an hour. In the meantime, I have a list of things I want to discuss," he said, unfolding a large piece of paper from the inside pocket of his blue suit jacket.

"Look around the table, gentlemen. Each of you represents an important segment of New Orleans culture, society, breeding, and most importantly, commerce. New Orleans is about to emerge from its dark days of Union occupation and imposed servitude disguised as Reconstruction. The days of other people telling us what to do and how to do it are over. We are about to embark on a new day for this city—our city." Shakspeare stood and approached the open window facing Canal Street. "You see that street out there? That is the heart of our city's commerce. It is one hundred and seventy feet wide—one of America's widest and busiest streets. And at the end of Canal Street is the Mississippi River—our river, ninety-four miles from the Gulf of Mexico, and the rest of the world. For too long, we have been subjugated by forces that only want to exploit our city. That's over."

"Excuse me, Mr. Mayor," Maurice Hart interrupted. "But I must lodge an objection to General Badger sitting at the same table with these gentlemen. As I recall, General Badger, who is from Massachusetts, not only fought for the Union army but was also part of their oppressive occupation of this city. Then, as I clearly recall, he fought for the Republicans right outside that window on September 14, 1874. You speak of oppression, sir, but with all due respect, General Badger participated in that oppression. How can we trust he has the same desires and goals as we do?"

"General Badger, you may have the floor," the mayor responded.

Algeron Badger slowly stood up, rested on his walking stick, drew on his cigar, exhaled a cloud of smoke, and allowed a slight smile through his bushy mustache. "Mr. Hart, I take no offense at how you feel or what you said. For everything you have uttered is correct. But allow me to defend myself." The room fell quiet, and the mayor sat down. "Yes, I am from Massachusetts, and I was an officer in the United States Army. Yes, I admit I was part of the occupying force, which controlled New Orleans during the Civil War. But I committed no atrocities here. I have grown to love this city. If I didn't, I would have gone back to Massachusetts. And yes, I fought in the Battle of Liberty Place in 1874. I did so to preserve the rule of law and to maintain the integrity of the governor's election. And as you remember, Mr. Hart, I was shot four times, and it was a band of *your* supporters who carried me on a door to the hospital. They saved my life. But I must walk with this cane for the rest of my life."

"That was a band of Italians commanded by Joseph P. Macheca, who only wanted to be on the winning side," Hart responded. "They will never be part of us. They used us, and we used them. We needed their votes and unfortunately, still do."

"I understand your sentiment," Badger said, focusing on J.D. Houston. "Mr. Houston, I know you remember Arthur Guerin."

"I do," Houston responded. "Why do you ask, sir?"

"Mr. Guerin shot and killed David Hennessy, Sr., on St. Ann Street in 1869. He was never prosecuted for that killing. Perhaps it was because of Hennessy's position in the Union army during the war. I don't know. Some say it was self-defense, but no jury did. And as you recall, it was I who gave his young son, David, Jr., a job as a police messenger when I was the Superintendent of the Metropolitan Police. If I hadn't done that, Hennessy's widow and son would have starved. He was twelve years old when I gave him that job, and he put his heart into it. And today, our mayor has chosen young David to be *his* Superintendent of Police. Isn't that correct, Mr. Mayor?"

"Yes, I did. David Hennessy will make a good chief. I can control him, and hopefully his rueful temper. Go on, General," the mayor said.

"Mr. Houston, as I recall, you and Mr. Guerin had a problem at one time, which resulted in you shooting and killing him in St. Patrick's Hall, the Criminal Courts building of this city. I think that was in 1871, when you were a Chief with the Sheriff's Office. Is that correct?"

"Yes, it is," Houston said, as he stood and faced Badger. "And as everyone in this room knows, I went to trial and was found not guilty. What is your point, General?"

"I want no fight with you, Mr. Houston. Everyone here knows your prowess with a gun, as some of our cemeteries can attest. All I want is fairness," Badger said, returning his attention to Hart. "Mr. Hart, I recall you witnessing the killing of Detective Thomas Devereaux back in 1881 on Gravier Street. Is that correct?"

"I was there," Hart admitted. "And it was murder. David Hennessy shot Detective Devereaux in the back of the head while defending himself after his cousin, Michael, shot at him first. Devereaux was a fine man and had many friends in New Orleans. The Hennessys made many enemies in this city. It's a shame Michael Hennessy was mysteriously killed in Houston, Texas, two years ago. People in New Orleans have long memories, sir. Remember that."

"I understand, Mr. Hart. And both men stood trial for Detective Devereaux's death and were found not guilty, is that correct?"

"You are, and they went to trial like Mr. Houston but were unfortunately acquitted. They were lucky—they had the best lawyer in New Orleans, Lionel Adams. The jury ruled it self-defense," Hart said. "Chief Hennessy, his cousin, and Detective Devereaux had a long-running feud. I must admit I was a good friend of Detective Devereaux, and I never cared for either Hennessy—and I still don't. I must admit I enjoyed reading Michael Hennessy's obituary. Justice has a way of moving slowly, but it moves. But the mayor has made his choice, and I will live with it."

"So you were friends with Detective Devereaux, Mr. Hart?" Badger pressed.

"Yes, I considered him a close friend, and so were many other respectful people of New Orleans. Look, I am not on trial here. I was invited to join the mayor in his efforts to make this city a better place to live, not to be questioned by you."

"So was I, Mr. Hart. So was I. But it appears that our fraternal paths have crossed over the past years, and I see no reason for you to object to my presence or service to this city."

"You are a damn Republican, and a former member of the Union army —like Hennessy's dead father," Hart yelled.

"Easy, Maurice," the mayor interrupted. "No one here is without a past, but our future is outside that window. As I see it, David Hennessy, like his father, has many enemies. General Badger saved the boy and his mother after the father was killed. Mr. Houston killed the man who killed his father. And Mr. Hart thought then–Detective Hennessy murdered Detective Devereaux. It was ruled self-defense, and I assure you tonight, I have plans for Chief Hennessy, which will make all of us proud. But I need everyone's cooperation. And as you all know, there is too much gunplay in this city, and it must stop if my plans are to succeed. Now, can you men work together and stop living in the past? Each of you will reap the rewards of what I have planned, but you must work together."

Hart, Houston, and Badger slowly relaxed, returned to their seats, and the nine men nodded in agreement. Then the Mayor untied a leather valise and removed a small stack of papers he called "The Shakspeare Plan."

"Gentlemen, I have before me a series of methodical steps that will convert New Orleans from a grid work of bloody and concupiscent streets to a gleaming star in the constellation of the world's commercial capitals. The damn war is over, and Washington doesn't care about us, so we must do this on our own. But with General Badger's connections in Washington, we will not get any resistance from the Union—I mean, Federal government."

The nine men puffed on their cigars and took sips of bourbon as the mayor continued. But as Shakspeare began to read from his list, Hart cast a penetrating and fierce glare at Badger, which did not go unnoticed by Houston, who just smiled.

"The first thing I want to do is complete the electrification of New Orleans and the replacement of gas lamps throughout the city. Gas is dangerous and kills about ten people a year. Electricity is also dangerous, but can be controlled and monitored. I am having two new coal-fired furnaces built with gas retorts to fuel electric generators. Once they are ready, we can start electrifying the city lights and streetcars. Franklin, that should make you happy, since you will have less mule shit to smell."

The comment broke the tension in the room, as all the men laughed and imbibed. But a restive Maurice Hart shifted in his chair and then leaned forward. "Mr. Mayor, may I interrupt your presentation?"

"Sure, Maurice. You have the floor," Shakspeare said.

"I know you have grand ideas for New Orleans, and everyone in this room welcomes them excitedly. But, as you know, I have good friends in the exchanges and other commercial enterprises that depend upon our river for their commerce and the commerce of this entire city. But given the existing conditions of our docks and who controls them, we are impeded in fulfilling our full potential as profitable businessmen."

"What do you mean, Maurice?" the mayor probed.

"Well, sir, your plans call for a complete modernization of New Orleans, and its streets, byways, drainage, bridges, railroads, and international commerce. Such a renaissance will be futile without some significant changes in our population's occupations. As you referenced earlier, the river is ours, and the gateway to international commerce, and the revenue is immeasurable. But all your efforts will be for naught if we do not control the docks and port of New Orleans."

"What do you propose, Maurice?" the mayor asked. "My plan recognizes the river as the *raison d'être* for our existence. The Union army and navy recognized its importance when they seized New Orleans in 1862," the mayor quipped, winking at General Badger.

"I will be as delicate as possible in deference to General Badger and his friends. The Italians, Sicilians, dagoes, whatever you want to call them, control the port of New Orleans. Joseph Macheca, Charles Matranga, and Joseph Provenzano essentially control the docks and all commerce coming into the Port of New Orleans. They control the shipping, the docking spaces, the stevedores, what ships get loaded and unloaded first, and those who must wait in anchorage. They control the cartage carriers from the docks to the railroads and markets. They even control the stalls at the French Market, the Orleans Market, and the Poydras Market. As Mr. Hayne can attest, our exchanges are at their discretion and capricious whims."

Franklin Hayne, of the Cotton Exchange, stood and said, "I must agree with Mr. Hart. The receiving and shipping of tons of cotton bales are in the hands of these miscreants. Okay, I will assert it—the *Mafia*. They are gangsters, and the proof is printed in our daily papers with every killing in the Italian Colony. Am I correct, Mr. Wharton?"

"You are, Mr. Hayne," Theodore D. Wharton, of the *Times-Democrat,* responded. "Just this morning, a body was found floating in the river, near the Picayune Tier. He had been sliced to death. Another was shot to death on Gallatin Street. That's the fifth murder on that street this year. And, of course, nobody saw anything. I have three reporters walking the docks day and night to get the stories. The other newspapers do, too. In fact, there are more reporters near the docks than policemen," Wharton chuckled.

Shakspeare stood and walked to the window behind his chair. In his right hand was a crystal glass of bourbon—his third—and his left hand a stub of a smoldering cigar. His eyes followed the string of gaslights from Carondelet Street to the river. In the dark, the wide aorta of commerce glowed like a flaming strand of pearls. Merchants on both sides of the street began their closing rituals, as their gas lamps flicked off for the night. Men and women scurried home along the cypress board and flagstone banquettes, as mule-drawn wagons clopped towards the local livery for the evening. The mayor sipped his bourbon and began to compose his response to Hart's statement.

"I thought I could avoid this subject tonight by impressing my friends with my plans. But it appears my plans cannot achieve fruition, without addressing the problem of the immigrant population amassing in large numbers in the *Carrer de la Ville, Vieux Carré, Piccolo Palermo,* or the Italian Colony. I know all the names. I have heard them. I have seen them. Every time my wife and I go to the French Opera House on Bourbon Street, I see them. I see them lurking in the shadows, in the doorways, and on the balconies. They are everywhere. Some work very hard at their various trades. Some work on the docks. Some work in the markets. And some don't work at all."

"Why do we have so many dagoes in New Orleans, Mr. Mayor?" Hart asked. "Aren't there other cities that will take them?"

"Mr. Hart, if you recall after the War for Southern Independence— sorry General Badger, that's what we called it—the Louisiana legislature created the Bureau of Immigration to attract immigrants from southern Europe to work the fields abandoned by the liberated negro, and to do the work in the cities and towns no one wanted to do. It appears the climate of New Orleans is similar to that of southern Italy, and with the current civil strife in Sicily, many answered the call and immigrated here. Mr. Houston, your family owns the Ben Hur Plantation near Baton Rouge. Don't you employ them to pick your cotton, and cut your cane?"

"Yes. We rent to the Sicilians, who are a stubborn, hardworking breed of people, but render good harvests. But what is growing here in this city is disturbing me, and the other men around this table. New Orleans is changing, and it's not for the good."

"Explain yourself, Mr. Houston," the mayor demanded.

J.D. Houston stared at General Badger, and without unlocking his eyes from Badger's, he stood up and grabbed his lapels. "Gentlemen, as I stand here today, there are approximately fifty thousand Italian immigrants in this city, and more arrive every month from Naples and Palermo. General Badger, you work at the Custom House. Am I correct?"

"That is correct. Once they arrive, they are registered at the Custom House, and told if they want to become citizens, they must declare their intent after they have been here a year. And many have done so."

Houston began to prance around the room, like a lawyer giving his closing argument to a jury. "We have too many here now and should refuse to accept anymore. They are fundamentally from a criminal class that goes back centuries. A criminal element has invaded this city and controls the docks and our shipping industry. They control the markets, and those who are not criminals have succumbed to this thing called the 'Black Hand.'"

"Aren't there some good people among them, Mr. Houston?" Badger asked.

"No! And I am not finished. This filthy race of people who easily compromise the negro. As I stand before you now, there are meetings almost every night among the negro, the creole, and the dago. Our challenge is not only economic, but also political. I see our voting population changing and changing rapidly. Soon, we will have them in public office, and that, Mr. Mayor, will destroy your ambitious vision for New Orleans."

"What do you propose, Mr. Houston?" the mayor asked.

"You need to contact Governor Nicholls and put an end to these immigrants swarming like rats from the steamers every month."

"You can't do that, Mr. Mayor," Badger said.

"Why not?" Houston asked as he approached Badger.

"Because Washington would be down here again if we started banning people from congregating, immigrating, or voting. As I see it, it's a police problem, not a political one."

"Are you insane, Badger?" Houston yelled as he bent over and placed his face within inches of Badger's.

The smell of bourbon and cigar smoke stung General Badger's nose, and he pushed the brass knob of his walking stick into Houston's chest. Houston stumbled back and reached for a small Smith and Wesson revolver in his vest pocket. Immediately, Hart and Hayne grabbed Houston by his arms and restrained him. Shakspeare jumped from his chair, pounded the table and yelled, "Enough gun play in my city, J.D. Too many people are being shot or stabbed in New Orleans every day. And we don't need a murder in the Pickwick Club. You must control yourself. Now, sit down or leave."

Houston relaxed, and when Hart and Hayne released him, he returned to his seat and gulped his bourbon. "I am sorry, Mr. Mayor, but I love this city as much as you, and I see it being destroyed daily."

"Everybody, calm down and have another drink," the mayor enjoined. "Dinner will be ready soon. Let me say this for everybody's understanding. We need the immigrants in New Orleans to build what needs to be built. I have miles of streets covered in chert and tar, while I have mountains of Belgium ballast sitting on the docks ready to be laid for our road surfaces. Who will handle those two- and three-hundred-pound granite blocks and pave our streets? The negro and the dago, that's who. Who is going to shovel mule shit all day long? The negro and the dago. Who is going to dig our ditches and gutters? The negro and the dago. Who will sink the new telephone and telegraph poles into the ground? The negro and the dago. Who is going to collect our trash and dump it in Jefferson Parish? The negro and the dago. And Mr. Houston, who is going to muck out your privy? We need the immigrant, and if he makes friends with the negro, we will keep them so busy they won't have a chance to vote. And if they do, they will vote for the people who put the food in their bellies."

"What about the *Mafia*?" Parkinson asked.

"I will have General Badger talk to David Hennessy about our police problem," the mayor assured.

"Mr. Mayor," Thomas Boylan interrupted. "As you know, I have several detectives assigned to the Italian Colony, and they report that the *Mafia* problem is getting worse. Right now, most of their victims are other immigrants—Italian and Greek. But they are also robbing the seamen, as they get off the ships and go on Gallatin Street. And I hate to tell you this, but I must. Hennessy is in business with Provenzano. They are both interested in a brothel and casino at the river, on Girod Street, an area known as the Swamp. And who among us doesn't know about the Red

Lights Club on Customhouse Street? It's owned by Provenzano and frequented by your new Superintendent of Police."

"I am aware of that unfortunate arrangement and will be discussing that with David soon. I am also aware that Hennessy has many enemies in this city, and a few of them are sitting at this table. Rest assured, I can control him and the police department."

"He's a stubborn Irishman and a killer," Hayne said.

"He's not the only killer in New Orleans who has been found not guilty," the mayor said, looking at Houston. "But, if we are going to achieve a renaissance for this city, we must put aside our differences and strive for a common good."

"And will the Italian Colony continue to control the docks, markets, and police corruption?" Hart asked.

"I have a plan for that, too. But you must trust me."

For a moment, the room fell into a pensive silence. At the same time, white waiters in tuxedos wheeled in carts of roasted lamb, oyster soup, assorted vegetables, citrus produce, and twelve bottles of imported French wine, all sold to the Pickwick Club by Italians at the Poydras Market, just five blocks away.

><

Thick cigar smoke wrapped and whirled around the chandelier, which hung over the round linen-draped dinner table, while the waiters collected ten empty wine bottles, two empty bourbon bottles, and five ashtrays filled with cigar butts. A breeze tossed the lace curtains, but it had little effect on the heavy gray layers of smoke hovering over the table and the remnants of the mayor's conspiratorial repast. What wasn't consumed, the waiters would sneak home for their families, because everyone in New Orleans occupied a link in the city's food chain.

As the mayor and his political courtesans left the dining room and approached the mahogany stairway, Shakspeare tugged on Badger's arm and motioned for him to allow the other eight to go. "We need to talk," the mayor whispered in Badger's ear.

Badger nodded as he watched the other men descend the stairway and leave the Pickwick Club. It was midnight, and a large grandfather's clock chimed twelve times. When Shakspeare was satisfied his guest had left, he turned to Badger and said, "Allow me to take you home, General."

"I have my horse outside, Mr. Mayor. I'll be safe."

"We need to talk and talk tonight. Tether your horse to the back of my carriage. Do you still live at Number 22 Coliseum Street?"

"Yes, sir, since before the war. But may I ask you a question?" asked Badger, as he limped down the stairs.

"Sure."

"Can you handle a team of horses in your condition?"

Shakspeare laughed. "I'm not drunk, General. I feel good, but I'm not drunk. Why do you ask?"

"I remember when you were the King of Rex, you fell off your horse in front of City Hall—early on Mardi Gras morning, some years ago."

"You have a good memory. That was six years ago. But I'm fine. Now hop up in my carriage. We need to talk."

After tethering the dark horse to the mayor's black lacquered carriage, Badger, with the help of Pickwick Club butler, Creed Baptiste, climbed onto the mayor's coach and sank into the black-leather tufted seat. After slapping the reins on the back of two large draft horses, the carriage tugged away and bobbed along the cobblestones of Carondelet Street, towards Coliseum Street.

"General, I need your help," Shakspeare began. "We're alone now, and I feel I can express myself clearly, but confidentially. Do you understand?"

"Yes, Mr. Mayor. I do."

"I need your help with controlling David Hennessy. Since you have known him since his childhood, and were in the Union army with his father, he will listen to you more than anyone I know. Several men at dinner tonight hate him and would love to see him floating in the river."

"Like Maurice Hart?"

"And J.D. Houston, Thomas Boylan, and Franklin Hayne. While Boylan pretends to be friends with Hennessy, he is very jealous of him and wants me to appoint him as the Superintendent of Police. He wanted his old job back, but I couldn't do that and be viewed as a reform mayor. Hennessy proved himself worthy by doing an excellent job protecting the Cotton Expedition. He made national news, too. I think it was a good political move, but I have my reservations about some of his habits and friends."

"The Provenzanos?"

"Yes. Those people and others who run the brothels and those buckets-of-blood establishments on Gallatin Street. I need you to watch him and counsel him. I can't have a corrupt police department while building an international city."

"Mr. Mayor, David is making new enemies among the ranks of the police department. I had a conversation with a police commissioner, and he is concerned Hennessy is too heavy-handed with disciplining officers."

"I spoke to the entire Board of Police Commissioners and told them Hennessy is doing what I want him to do. I want him to cut asunder the secret, corrupt factions within the ranks of the police department. Most of them belong to the Ring. There is too much graft and payoffs."

"And I am sure you don't want him to suffer the same fate as his cousin?"

Shakspeare didn't respond, but when the mayor's carriage reached the intersection of Carondelet and Poydras, two men on horseback, bearing kerosene torches, blocked the street to allow twenty heavy wagons of goods and produce to pass on their way from the docks to the Poydras Market.

"You see that, General. That's what Hart and Hayne were complaining about earlier. These goods arrive on our docks and are immediately transported to the city's markets. Our exchanges are deprived of making any income from this commerce, while the Italians, Greeks, and Slavs control a significant portion of our city's wealth. They set the prices. Why? Because they control the docks and the markets. Look at those teamsters. They all look Italian or Greek. Only cotton, lumber, and other manufactured goods pass through our exchanges, denying our friends the opportunity to participate fully in this city's commerce. This must be stopped."

"What do you propose Mr. Mayor? It's late at night, and these men are working. The men who operate the exchanges are home in bed."

"I don't know, General, but we must control our river's commerce, if we are going to have prosperity for all and make New Orleans an international city."

Shakspeare's eyes squinted with anger as the string of wagons rumbled by the mayor's carriage. His fists twirled the reins around his wrists. After the last wagon had passed and the men with torches waved them across Poydras Street, the mayor grabbed his whip and lashed his horses' backs. The beasts jumped and lurched the carriage forward, tossing Shakspeare and Badger back into their seats. Badger braced himself with his walking stick, while the mayor maintained a feral glare into the darkened streets.

No words passed between either man until the carriage reached the intersection of Melpomene and Coliseum streets. Badger gingerly dismounted the carriage and untethered his horse from the carriage. As he stopped to bid the mayor good night, Shakspeare said, "General, as Customs Collector of this city, I need you to help me regain control of our docks. I don't know how you can do that, but you must help me. If you need Hennessy to help you, use him. Control him. But get me control of that river."

Badger looped the reins of his horse over his shoulder and stared into the flickering flame of the gas lamp on the corner. "Mr. Mayor, tonight, I believe you ignited a small flame, which will grow into a fire, and that fire will combust into a conflagration beyond your or my control. Look at me," Badger said, holding his walking stick out from his body. "I've been through wars and felt the burning sting of shot piercing my skin. I felt doctors slicing through my body to save my life. I have seen death. I have smelled death. I've been threatened by people you know well. And now I feel my destiny is destroying a man to save this city and the vestiges of your former life. I only pray it is only one man who will be destroyed. I wonder if New Orleans is worth it. I pray you don't make this city's *status quo* its destiny."

"Wait a minute, General," Shakspeare ordered. "Tell me, now. Do you believe in this thing called the *Mafia,* and will you help David?"

"Indeed, I do. It's just like the Ku Klux Klan, and the tattered remnants of the Knights of the White Camelia, some of whom are your friends, and still ride the darkened streets of New Orleans with floursack masks, concealing their pedigree, and terrorizing the negro wards. Perhaps when you control your port, they can dismount and participate in *your* renaissance. And yes, I will do anything to protect David from anyone, including you, Mr. Mayor. You're using him. All politicians use people, until their worth and purpose are exhausted."

"General, New Orleans' wards are carved up like a butchered calf for a reason," Shakspeare said, ignoring the oblique insult.

"Mr. Mayor, you don't want a renaissance. You want to resurrect antebellum ghosts frolicking on Canal Street."

Chapter 9

Palermo, Sicily
June 15, 1889
4:30 A.M.

S ince 734 BCE, when the Phoenicians discovered a scalloped-shaped deep-water port on a mountainous island on the southern edge of the Tyrrhenian Sea, Palermo, Sicily, has been a maritime stepping stone strategically located between Southern Europe and Northern Africa. Throughout the centuries, Sicily has been a coveted commercial and military redoubt for many nations, and many have died trying to conquer it. The last time Sicilians defended their insular sovereignty was in 1861, when Giuseppe Garibaldi claimed it as part of the new Kingdom of Italy, placing the island's four million inhabitants under the control of secular Rome. Despite the *Risorgimento,* or War of Unification, Sicilians remained proud of their heritage, and suspicious of a government enforced by its military policing arm, the *Giardinieri,* which targeted the ancient secret criminal societies, which preyed upon the peasant classes. By the late 1800s, much of Sicily's population found itself in the struggle for subsistence, and immigration to other lands held their only hope for survival.

By 1888, thousands of Sicilians had already immigrated to the United States, particularly to its major cities, like New York, Boston, and Philadelphia. But when a clarion call went abroad from Louisiana seeking agricultural and urban laborers, New Orleans was added to that list of destinations. Many tales buzzed around Palermo's docks about how well Sicilians were treated in their new homeland, and the work was plentiful and rewarding. Some of these stories were true, while others were apocryphal. Rumors feed starving minds.

On this morning, Antonio Carravella followed the regimen established by Father Fontebuis. He would rise at 4:00 A.M. and study his English assignments, seeking some degree of fluency. An hour later, he would eat breakfast, leave the cloister, and run down Via Vittoria Emanuele to an area known as *Il Cala,* or the Cove. There, he waited for dawn to cast its pale glow over the Gulf of Palermo. and the fishing docks, near the *Molo Sud,* or the South Pier. When he arrived at the Cove, Antonio could see the flickering lanterns of the fishing boats bobbing towards the rocky jetties, which protected the inner harbor and cove from the tidal vagaries of the Tyrrhenian Sea. The lanterns dotted the blackened waters like hundreds of fireflies buzzing on the waves. A salty sea breeze brushed against his face, while he smiled at the sight of returning fishermen, who spent the night trolling waters miles offshore. A pre-dawn return meant a fruitful catch. And as the fishing boats passed the breakwater and entered the sanctuary of the placid waters of the inner harbor, their lanterns cast an eerie amber glow against their solitary triangular sails, which reminded Antonio of butterflies hovering in his family's vineyard.

As the boats sailed closer to the piers, the fishermen dropped their sails and maneuvered their boats with heavy oars until they could toss hawse lines to waiting dockhands. In the dark, Antonio could identify some familiar faces of the men he worked with to unload the boats. But this morning, he saw two strangers—a man and a boy—standing on the dock. The boy appeared to be about two years younger than Antonio. Antonio heard the man asking the dock master about a job, and the dock master agreed to hire them to unload the fishing boats on the spot. Fearing the loss of his job, Antonio approached the dock master and asked about his assignment, whereupon he was assigned the first three boats moored at the docks. Antonio jumped on the first boat, stripped off his black wool jacket, and began the laborious work of loading the catch into large barrels for shipment to various Palermo markets. He didn't pause until the sun broke the eastern horizon, revealing the serrated promontory of Mount Pellegrino, two thousand feet above Palermo. Even in the early sunlight, Antonio could see the Sanctuary of St. Rosalie embedded in the mountainside, whereupon he made the cross sign and thanked her for his new life and job.

At about noon, Antonio finished unloading his three boats and then helped an elderly man finish his job on a fourth. All the workers were on the docks to earn their passage to America. The dock master, Vito Battistella, began his daily ritual of cooking fresh fish over a charcoal fire, to express his appreciation for their labor, and since Battistella could only pay ten liras a day per man, he supplemented the pay with a free lunch, to ensure their return the next morning, There was no market for rotting fish.

As Antonio sat on an old crate eating his lunch, the man and the boy he had seen earlier approached him and asked if they could join him. Antonio smiled, stood, removed his hat, and welcomed their company. After a few moments of idle chatter about their work, the man spoke. "My name is Antonio Marchesi, and this is my son, Asperi. We are *Cefalutana*. Are you *Palermitani*?"

"My name is Antonio, too, I am *Bisacquinesi*."

"Are you going to America, too?" the elder Marchesi asked.

"Yes. I leave at the end of next month and work for my passage."

"Us, too. You have family?"

"No. I'm an orphan, but I'm traveling with two Jesuit priests to a place called New Orleans. Have you heard of it?"

Marchesi smiled and clapped his hands. "Yes. We are going there, too, on a ship called the *Neustria*."

"Me, too. We leave at the end of next month. What is this place, New Orleans, like?"

"We have a friend there now. His name is Pietro Monasterio. He is a cobbler. He wrote me a letter, and said the city is like Palermo, but no mountains: lots of work. So we go. No work here, except on the docks, and it's hard to get a job here. We are lucky."

Antonio Caravella smiled, nodded, and continued the conversation for a few minutes, until Vito Battistella attracted his attention and waved him over to where Battistella was cooking. Antonio complied. and Battistella put his arm around him and said, "Do you know those people?"

"No. I just met them. They will be traveling with me to New Orleans next month."

Battistella bent down and whispered in his ear, "Don't tell people too much about yourself. These docks have more ears than fish. Do you know how we survived the Spanish many years ago?"

Antonio shook his head.

"*Omerta*. Do you know what that means?"

"Yes, but they are Sicilian, too."

"So were the men who killed your father," Battistella said, placing his forehead against Antonio's. "Yes, I know who you are, and I am proud of you. Many people on this dock know who you are and why you are here. They are proud of you, too. The *Stuppagghieri* probably know you are somewhere in Palermo. There are no secrets here. I would guess the *Carabinieri* know you are here and will use you as bait to flush out the *Mafioso*."

"They have done that before," Antonio lamented.

"Take this box of fish to the nuns and priests," Battistella said, handing Antonio a large, heavy crate filled with fresh fish. "Be careful going up the hill to the cloister. Don't drop it. And remember, don't talk about yourself to anyone. Understand? In Sicily, silence is life."

Chapter 10

Central Police Station
New Orleans, Louisiana
June 18, 1889

With a 12:12 pitched gray slated roof, and three stories wrapped in red brick, the Romanesque-designed New Orleans Central Police Station cast an ominous aura from every angle, for it was, indeed, intentionally conceived to instill fear, order, and power, especially in men of a fragile nature. The pulse-racing structure even caused the strongest men to question their presence near or around it. Few ventured near it, unless they worked within its dungeon-thick walls. New Orleans' architects spared no expense designing buildings which evoked emotions, for they believed that man should not only walk into a building, but must feel it and wear it, and carry its memory long after they have left. The architects who designed the Central Police Station exceeded those expectations.

Its wide corridors and high ceilings facilitated air flow on humid days, and it had several warrens of spacious offices on all three floors. With a population growing monthly, the New Orleans Police Department needed to create a Bureau of Identification to log the identity of new residents, immigrants, and arrestees. Police personnel were now experimenting with a new technology, photography, and the Bertillon System to capture the physical features of every arrestee through a process known as anthropometric physical measuring, to enhance the accuracy of their record keeping. Police messengers would go to the Custom House on Canal Street every week to collect the identities of immigrants who would arrive by ship, and the police clerks would create handwritten indices on all new arrivals. They would also go to the city's three railroad stations and monitor the new arrivals to New Orleans, especially those lugging heavy portmanteaus or carpet-clad satchel bags, indicating their intent to stay.

The police department's new superintendent was a thirty-year-old tough, lanky Irishman with a dubious history and a mixed reputation for strict law enforcement. His name was David C. Hennessy. With his coveted power, supported by the new mayor, he insisted on building a new police department, evocative of the larger cities in the Northeast, and desired every possible new innovation in policing. On this day, Hennessy believed the population of New Orleans was about 275,000 people, and growing. Mixed demographics presented the city with new challenges. On nearly every street corner where people gathered, one could hear several foreign dialects spoken, which aroused suspicion among the Anglos and descendants of the original French. He could gaze out three tall arched windows from his third-floor corner office to a grassy park created by the intersection of two well-trodden streets and hemmed on the riverside by Orleans Street, where a cluster of Jewish merchants toiled.

Indeed, Basin Street was a hive of commerce, which ran between two navigable canals, the New Basin Canal and the Carondelet Canal, two miles apart. These aortas of commerce stocked the various markets located throughout the city with everything a man could consume or use, which was built, grown, or raised on the farms, factories, and ranches on the north shore of Lake Pontchartrain. From his open windows, Hennessy could hear the rumbling of large wooden wagons carrying freight between the canals and markets, punctuated by the grinding iron wheels of mule-drawn streetcars dragged along their forged rails, which were embedded in large cobblestones of Belgian granite.

Under Hennessy, anyone wanting to work for the police department had to be literate and have no convictions for a serious crime. Though the pay was low, one hundred dollars a month, many black and white men sought a coveted position within the ranks. Hennessy personally reviewed the application of every man, and if he could satisfactorily complete the two-page application on site, that would satisfy the literacy requirement. Then the applicant's name would be sent to the first floor's Bureau of Identification for a record check. With great hesitancy and some regret, Hennessy would not hire men of Italian descent, by order of Mayor Joseph A. Shakspeare and his hand-picked Police Commission. It would be nearly a decade before that policy would be rescinded. Of course, having political connections would accelerate one's appointment to the police department, and many positions were supernumerary. Hennessy wanted to change that.

The Central Police Station occupied half a city square and housed the offices for the First Precinct and a small lockup in the rear of the building. Any arrestee who was going to be in jail longer than a night would be transferred to the police jail, four blocks away on Perrilliat Street, behind the Girod Street Cemetery. If an arrestee were going to be bound over for trial, the police would transfer the person to the custody of Orleans Parish

Sheriff, Gabriel Villere, who would lock them in the large, vermin-infested Orleans Parish Prison, bounded by Basin, Treme, Marais, and St. Ann Streets. The police Fourth Precinct station was incorporated within the prison walls and sat at the corner of Basin and Marais Streets.

At about 10:00 a.m., a horse-drawn cab stopped in front of the Central Police Station, and General Algeron S. Badger carefully dismounted the carriage. He asked the driver if he didn't have a fare, to return in an hour and take him to his first-floor office in the Custom House. The driver doffed his hat and agreed. With the aid of his walking stick, Badger limped up the granite steps to the station's front door, where he met Senior Captain John Journee and Hennessy's secretary, George W. Vandervoort. Both men were in the main lobby showing off their new uniforms, which consisted of a dark blue thigh-length tunic with a double row of descending brass buttons and matching trousers. Each man had the well-recognized badge of the New Orleans Police Department, a silver crescent, symbolizing the city's shape, carved by the Mississippi River, superimposed over a five-pointed star, symbolizing police authority. Both officers immediately recognized Badger and greeted him warmly.

"How can we assist you, General?" Journee asked.

"I would like to see the Chief, if he isn't too busy. I don't have an appointment."

"General, you don't need an appointment. Vandervoort and I will accompany you upstairs. Can you handle three flights of steps, sir?"

"Oh, yes, but not as fast as you can."

Both officers assisted Badger up the stairs to Hennessy's office, where a surprised Hennessy hugged his old benefactor and requested Vandervoort to retrieve some coffee for his guest. After exchanging pleasantries, Badger's visage turned serious, which didn't escape Hennessy's keen eye. Hennessy invited Badger to join him on a brown leather Queen Anne sofa. Badger allowed one last pleasantry before digging into Hennessy.

"How's your mother, David?"

"Fine, Sir. But she is worried about my new position."

"I am, too, son," Badger said. "David, I have always looked after you like you were my real son. I gave you your first job with the Metropolitan Police when you were twelve."

"Excuse me, sir. I was sixteen."

"Sorry. You have a precise mind, and I like that. Anyway, you did a great job. Over the years, you have made a name for yourself. Capturing the notorious Sicilian brigand, Guiseppi Esposito, in Jackson Square, and then spiriting him off to New York, and then back to Italy bestowed international fame upon you, and your late cousin, Michael."

Hennessy listened pensively, waiting to see where Badger was taking the conversation. Vandervoort returned with a tray with two china cups and a white porcelain coffee pot, with steam pouring from its spout. After placing the tray on a small table, Vandervoort excused himself and closed the door behind him. Badger and Hennessy sipped their coffees, and Badger continued. "Dave, your mother has good reason to worry about your new position. You have made many enemies inside the police department and around town. Your capture of Esposito led directly to you killing Detective Devereaux."

"General, I was found not guilty. It was self-defense."

"I understand that, but Devereaux still has many powerful friends in New Orleans—on both sides of Canal Street. You understand what I am saying?"

"Yes, and Devereaux had friends in the Italian Colony, like I do. In fact, he ordered Michael and me *not* to arrest Esposito. Chief Boylan helped us capture him with information from Antonio Labousse, whom Esposito owed money for building him a boat. He crossed the wrong man and paid for it. Now, he is in an Italian prison for life."

"And Michael is dead, too," Badger intoned.

"Do you think his death is related to Devereaux's death? Hennessy asked.

"Like I said, Devereaux had friends in very high places, on both sides of Canal Street. They have long memories."

"Like Maurice Hart and Franklin Hayne?" Hennessy pressed.

"Among others, David. What was once the White League is now New Orleans' society elites. They control almost everything, except the docks, and your boss wants that to change. The Italians control—"

"General, what are you trying to tell me? We captured Esposito in May of 1881, and several months later, Devereaux shot Michael in the face and stomach. It was an act of vengeance wrought by envy. Devereaux was convinced he was about to lose his job as Chief of Detectives because he interfered with the Esposito investigation. Perhaps Devereaux was protecting Esposito. I don't know for sure. But when I saw Michael's blood pouring from his face, I had to do something, and I am damn proud I did. It's a miracle the surgeons at Charity Hospital saved Michael."

"Only to be killed in Houston, Texas," Badger responded.

"General, you didn't come here to walk down memory lane. What's on your mind, sir?"

"I will get to the point. There is talk about your relationships with the Provenzanos, who are at war with the Matrangas. And as you know, Esposito was a close friend of Charles Matranga, who some people believe has *Mafia* ties back to Sicily. When you arrested Esposito, you made more enemies. On the docks, everybody sees everything. People speak languages we don't understand. But the word on the street is you are aligned with the Provenzano and Locascio Stevedores."

"I also have a civil relationship with Mr. Matranga, and your friend, J.P. Macheca. All three run those docks, and they are constantly fighting for a marketplace for their goods and stevedores to unload their ships and steamboats. I understand there is a family feud that goes back several hundred years. I don't feel threatened when I ride through the docks or the markets."

"You are, and let me tell you how. That feud is about money and power. Whoever controls those docks controls New Orleans. If either side perceives any favoritism coming from your police department, there will be hell to pay. And another perilous element is at play here—the Boston and Pickwick Clubs and the people who control the exchanges."

"The White League, again?" Hennessy asked.

"Yes. The Italians control the docks, and what ships get unloaded and when. They set the prices and dictated what product goes to what market and when. By passing the exchanges, they control the pricing of the commodities. Other than cotton and lumber, our uptown friends are losing money, while they perceive their police chief as being controlled by the *Mafia*. David, as I see it, you are caught in the middle of a triangular feud —the Provenzanos on one side, and the Matrangas on the other, with the silky elites of New Orleans on the third side."

Hennessy stood, walked toward his three windows, and peered at the streets below. With the palms of both hands, he matted down his dark brown hair, which was parted down the middle of his head, removed a handkerchief from his coat pocket, and wiped his handlebar mustache. Badger's words echoed in his ears. He felt the pressure of his new position squeeze him like a vise. He turned and stared at a pile of papers on his large oak desk. Badger broke his concentration.

"David, do you have any financial interest with the Provenzanos at the Red Lights Club on Customhouse Street?"

Hennessy shot a startled glare at Badger and dipped his head. "No, but I play poker there with chips I purchase from the bar. I keep my winnings, but I get nothing from the gambling or what goes on upstairs. I swear."

"That's bad enough, son. You go there too much. You have to divest yourself of all the concupiscence of New Orleans and focus only on enforcing the law. You can't have any entanglements with those people if you want to remain objective. The Matrangas know, Pickwickians know, the Ring knows, the Police Commission knows, the newspapers know, and the mayor knows."

"And I remember things from the Cotton Centennial," Hennessy said, as he picked up a letter sent to him by the mayor. Hennessy walked over to Badger and handed him the letter. Badger hooked his reading glasses to his ears and read the letter. As he did, his face reddened in anger. After reading the letter, Badger dropped it on his lap.

"I guess this is part of the 'Shakspeare Plan,'" Badger said. "You do know this is illegal, don't you?"

"Yes, I do. But what can I do? He's the mayor and controls the newspapers, the Police Commission, and now wants control of the docks. I have no choice. If I don't, he will replace me with Journee, or God forbid, Dexter Gaster."

"Does the District Attorney know about this?"

"Ha! He owes his job to Shakspeare. Charles Luzenberg is a cheap wooden marionette. My attorney, Lionel Adams, holds him in low regard."

"How are you going to force these sixty-seven casinos and brothels to pay a tax to the city, when their very existence violates state law?" Badger asked, pointing to the mayor's letter. "That's called common law extortion, which is worse than what's being taxed. Consult with Mr. Adams. Is Shakspeare crazy?"

"He has the power and plans on using it. He wants to use the money to electrify the entire city, pave the streets, dig more drainage canals, expand the police department, and get rid of the *Mafia*. Now, who's in trouble?"

"Not him. You are. Shakspeare will drop you like a hot coal if he feels threatened. That's what politicians do, David. You are now officially Shakspeare's pawn."

"What do I do, sir? Look at me. I am a shanty Irishman who crawled his way up the ladder to be the police chief, and I will never be truly accepted. I feel like my arse is naked and sitting on a straight razor. Anyway, I get cut."

"That's why I am here, unannounced. I want to protect you like the day I hid you and your mother in the Custom House in 1874. I knew your father. He served under me. He was neither accepted nor I accepted because of our Union pedigree. I believe they tolerate me because of contacts in Washington, and I will exploit their beliefs to protect you. But you must cut your losses and your ties."

Badger stood and limped around Hennessy's office in deep thought. After a few moments, he suggested something, which he considered counterintuitive, but given the roiling blood on both sides of Canal Street, he had to take a chance. "What is your relationship with J.P. Macheca?" Badger asked.

"Since he knows we are friends and saved your life fourteen years ago, I believe it's cordial. He has complained to me about all the killings between the Matrangas and the Provenzanos. About two weeks ago, he told me to put men on Rocco Geraci, whom he believes has killed several men on both sides of this feud. But he won't testify."

"Macheca is a smart and practical businessman. He needs both Matranga and Provenzano to unload his ships. I still get along with him. Let's do this. Let you and I message him to come to the Custom House. We will take him to my office and ask him to broker a peace between the Matrangas and the Provenzanos. If we can stop the killing on the docks and streets, it might take the pressure off them and you from the Pickwickians and The Ring."

"Who is more violent?"

"Well, the *Mafia* kills each other with great regularity and efficiency, while our friends uptown are Democrats, which is the political party who started a Civil War, The Battle of Liberty Place, the Knights of the White Camellia, the White League, and are members of the Boston and Pickwick Clubs," Badger said, with a slight giggle. "What do they call that strip of ground that runs down the middle of Canal Street, where the mules pull the streetcars?"

"The neutral ground," Hennessy answered. "It's understood by everyone that there is to be no gun play on Canal Street anymore. People need a place to commerce in peace."

"Well, someone in New Orleans had the rare sense to put a statue of Henry Clay at Canal and Royal Streets in 1860. Ironically, he was called the "Great Compromiser" for his work in the United States Senate to end slavery. It's a miracle the Democrats didn't tear him down when the war started. Did you know Henry Clay and Andrew Jackson opposed each other for the Presidency in 1832? Both had different opinions about slavery, and now both have monuments in the South's largest city. New Orleans will always be a city of contradictions, lacey passions concealed in lavender whispers, knotted with purple bows and splashed with blood," Badger asserted, banging the brass ferrule of his walking stick against the cypress floor.

Chapter 11

Chiesa de Gesu
The Cloister
Palermo
June 20, 1889
5:15 A.M.

Under the pale amber light of his oil lamp, Antonio dragged his quill across his tablet of thick, rough paper and completed his English vocabulary homework for the day. Every night before retiring, the priests would assign fifty Italian words, which Antonio had to find in an extensive English-Italian dictionary, then write a short, simple English sentence using those words. Antonio did that every morning before leaving the cloister and going to work on the fishing docks. Father Fontebuis would correct Antonio's work, punch two holes in the homework, and bind them into a notebook for their long voyage to America.

After placing his homework in a wooden box outside Father Fontebuis's door, Antonio, hearing the rain splashing against the tile roof, sleeved a black, slick coat made of vulcanized Indian rubber, pushed his head in this black *coppola*, and left the cloister. Though very dark, Antonio could see the sheets of rain blowing through the streets and alleys, but despite the weather, he knew the fisherman would be looking for safe harbor from the storm. He sprinted through the rain, praying he would not slip on the slippery cobblestones and tumble in the street. When he reached the Via Vicolo Casa Professa and Via del Ponticello intersection, Antonio took refuge under a small loggia, hoping the heavy rain would abate.

After a few minutes and realizing it was raining harder by the moment, Antonio decided to suffer the lashing sheets and run to the docks. As he stepped into the rain, a large, strong arm grabbed him around the neck and dragged him back under the loggia. His eyes bulged with fear, and his heart pounded. He attempted to free himself from the crushing grip of a large man.

"Relax, Antonio. It's me, Battistella. Calm down."

Antonio relaxed and spun around to see the drenched face of his dock master. "Sir, why did you grab me so hard? Why are you here and not at the dock?"

"You can't go there anymore."

"Why?"

"Late yesterday and again this morning, several *Stuppagghieri* were searching the docks for you."

"Me? Why?"

"Antonio, everyone on the docks knows who you are, and knows you are *Bisacquinesi*. They know what happened down there. Cascioferro is sending out his monsters to find you. He cannot be disgraced by what you did. You can't return to the docks. You must hide until your ship leaves."

"Did those Marchesi people tell them I worked there?"

"Oh, no. They thought Asperi was you and grabbed him. His father had to show them his identity papers before they released him. I saw it. They asked everyone on the docks about you, but no one said anything. But someone did," Battistella said, shaking his head. "When I arrived on the docks this morning, even in this storm, they were waiting for you. I had to come here to stop you."

With what Battistella said, and the wind belting the rain under the loggia, Antonio began to shiver. "You must come with me to the cloister and tell the priests what you know. They have to know I am in danger."

"Let's go," Battistella said.

"What about the fishermen?" Antonio asked when they arrived under the cloister's colonnade.

"They are okay. They came in over an hour ago. They know how to read the skies and the wind. It's in their blood."

Antonio and Vito Battistella stood on the stone floor of the main corridor of the cloister, dripping water wherever they walked. Seeing their wet trail in the glow of her lantern, Sister Consolata yelled, "Stop. Take off those wet coats and hang them on the hooks by the door. What are you doing here? Shouldn't you be on the docks by now?"

"We must talk to Father Fontebuis and Father Wertz. It's important," Antonio pleaded.

"They're having breakfast. Put your coats on the hooks and follow me, "Sister Consolata ordered. "And take off those boots, too."

Antonio and Battistella did what they were told and followed the nun down the corridor to a small dining room adjacent to the kitchen. When they arrived, both priests stopped eating and stood to greet them. "You look like two drowned wharf rats," Father Wertz said. "What's going on?"

"I'm in trouble," Antonio said. "Mr. Battistella will explain."

As the dock master told the story, Sister Consolata put plates of fresh fruit in front of Antonio and Battistella. She also poured four cups of black coffee, with a dash of black Sambuca, "to stiffen the spine," she murmured.

After hearing the threat to Antonio's life, Father Wertz told the boy he had to remain in the cloister until the end of next month. "You can study your English and help with the many chores around here. I don't want you away from the church, the garden, or the cloister. Understand?"

"Yes, Father."

Father Wertz rubbed his chubby chin and began to pace around the room. He stopped, looked at Battistella, and asked, "How many *Stuppagghieri* are looking for Antonio?"

"It's hard to say, Father. I see them every day walking around. You can easily spot them—they are the only ones with clean collars and hands."

"And the *Carabinieri*? What are they doing about this?"

"They prance around on their big black horses, but they can be spotted coming, and the *Stuppagghieri* hide."

"Well, finish your breakfast, Mr. Battistella, and return to the docks. Please keep us informed as to what's happening down there. And if you have time, can you bring us some fish every week?"

"*Si*, Father. Every Friday—as usual."

><

After breakfast, Fathers Fontebuis and Wertz discussed the situation, while Antonio returned to his room, changed his clothes, and studied again. The priests had to find a way to get Antonio from the cloister to the docks on the day of their voyage, which was just over a month away. "Do you have any ideas, Father Wertz?" Father Fontebuis asked.

"Only one. Every Friday, Colonel Salvani, the Commandant of the *Carabinieri* for all of Sicily, comes to me for confession. We meet in the church after morning Mass, and he confesses his sins in German, so no one can understand him. He's from Milano and speaks several languages. I know him well, and if he can't help us, no one can, but God. He hates all the *Mafioso*, from Napoli to Palermo. You heard what Mr. Battistella said? The *Stuppagghieri* knows Antonio is here, and that means we, too, are in jeopardy. So, I am going to ask Colonel Salvani for help. Knowing his past, like I do," Father Wertz said, with a mischievous wink, "he won't let those *jarbroni* near us.

"Do we have any guns in the cloister?" Father Fontebuis asked.

"There is an old *lupara* in my room, but it hasn't been fired in many years. It's a muzzleloader, and I have some powder, a ramrod, and some shot. Should I get it ready?"

"I don't know. Ask Colonel Salvani for his advice," Father Fontebuis said.

"I don't want you or Father Consere to leave the grounds. I won't go until my ship arrives. I will instruct the nuns to travel in fours to the markets. I don't think the *Stuppagghieri* or the *Carabinieri have* the *coraggio* to take on Sister Consolata or her nuns," Father Wertz said with a chuckle.

Chapter 12

Chiesu de Gesu
Palermo,
June 22, 1889
10:00 A.M.

Consecrated in 1636, *Chiesu de Gesu,* was originally built as a baroque cathedral dedicated to the Jesuits for the Nation of Sicily. However, since its construction and serial tumults on the island, the Jesuits were accustomed to being evicted from their motherhouse several times. With the current problems and prejudices, all non-Italian Jesuits were packing again, leaving Sicily for various parts of the world, including New Orleans. But this morning, Father Wertz hurried through the cloister, his cassock flapping, to keep his regularly scheduled appointment with *Carabinieri* Commandant, Silvio Salvani, to hear his confession, and plead for help. Never before has he felt the hot dagger of fear piercing his heart, both for himself and others.

Father Wertz knelt in the massive church's last pew of the west transept. The heavy smell of incense lingered in the air from the morning Mass, as it mixed with the pungent odor of burning votive candles. His eyes traced the many ornate Biblical figures carved in marble in full dimension, reliefs, and friezes. He wondered about the hands of the craftsmen, long stilled by time, who created wreaths, seraphim, cornices, and cherubs, which adorned the columns and walls everywhere he looked. The artwork attacked the senses, like a lion's claws dragging anyone into a state of prayer.

From a distance, he heard the pounding heels of Salvani's knee-high black boots against the multicolored marble inlaid floor of the 237-foot-long nave. When they met, they hugged, and both looked around to ensure their privacy.

In German, Salvani began, "Bless me, Father, for sin is upon me."

"Your sins are forgiven," Father Wertz said, accelerating the Sacrament of Confession in the Roman Rite. "We need to talk. I need your help."

"But Father, you must hear my sin. It is grievous and mortal," Salvani insisted.

"It's fine. Your sins are forgiven. Read Psalm 51 for your penance. Now listen to me. I need your help, Silvio."

"Father, you might not want my help after I tell you what we did last night."

Frustrated, Father Wertz relented. "Fine. Whatever it is, make a good confession, and your sins will be forgiven, but then you must help me."

Salvani looked around the transept's chapel to ensure they were alone. "I killed a man last night, or should I say, I allowed him to be killed."

"What happened, Silvio?"

"You probably know the *Stuppagghieri* are looking for the boy you are giving Sanctuary. We know he is here. Don't worry. The *Mafioso* were sent here by Cascioferro, who we believe is hiding in Monreale with the *Giardinieri*. Imagine that! I want him badly."

"Go on."

"Last night, we caught one outside your cloister, hiding in the shadows. We took him to the docks. My men borrowed a fishing boat and took him out into the sea. We interrogated him about why he was hanging around your cloister. He wouldn't tell us. So we wrapped him in an old fishing net and threw him overboard."

Father Wertz winched and rubbed his face. He glanced at the purple marble crucifix over the altar and offered a silent prayer. After composing himself, he said, "Silvio, you acknowledge before God you killed a man?"

"Yes, Father, but we did it to protect you and the boy. Besides, Palermo is full of *Stuppagghieri* and the *Giardinieri,* and soon the word will get out not to bother the Jesuits or the boy."

"I understand your motives, and they are noble, indeed. But you killed a man and must atone for that sin. And you can't report it to the authorities, because you *are* the authorities—at least on this earth. Are you sorry for your actions?"

"But of course. If I weren't, I wouldn't have told you. But it had to be done. If we had brought him back to the docks and released him, we would have brought more attention to the Jesuits and the boy. It would have given them permission to sit in front of the church and cloister until they got him. It would have made us look weak and vulnerable."

"Let me think about this for a minute, Silvio." With that, Father Wertz stood, approached the altar, and knelt for a few minutes. The Commandant sat motionless in the pew, watching every crease and movement in Father Wertz's black cassock. After a few minutes, Father Wertz returned to the pew, and sat next to Salvani and said, "We are both sinners, Silvio, because today, I needed to ask you for your help in guarding our cloister, and see that our priests, and the boy get to the docks safely next month. It appears you have already taken the first step in doing that. In some way, I feel complicit in your actions, but I feel God will understand the justification of your actions and the good that shall flow from your actions. So, your sins are forgiven."

"Thank you, Father. What is the name of the ship, and when does it sail?"

"It's the *Neustria,* and it leaves on July thirtieth from the *Lanterna Batteria del Molo.*"

"I know that ship. It's French and has a French crew. I know it well. I will tell you another secret—"

"I hope it's not another sin," Father Wertz pleaded.

"Oh, no. I put men on every ship going to America to watch who among the passengers are *Stuppagghieri* or *Giardinieri.* I have them dress like passengers. Then, they let the American police know who they need to watch. I will have men on the *Neustria,* too. Your priests and the boy will have safe passage." Salvani stood, banged his saber against the pew, and asked, "Father, is there a penance for my sin?"

"Yes, for both of us. We will both read Psalm 51."

Salvani bowed his head, crossed himself, and whispered, "Father, what name will the boy be traveling under? He can't use his real name?"

"We will have baptismal documents and give him a French name."

"No. No. No. You can't do that. The *Padrone* will catch him and force him to disclose his real name. I must do something. We must give him a Sicilian name."

"What is this *Padrone* thing?" Father Wertz asked.

"They get paid to send children to America from Sicily. Their families pay them. Once they arrive in America, there are *Padrone* there, too, and decide where the children are to work. My men tell me it's sad to see the children sent from the docks to wherever. They know nobody. I read America fought to free slaves, but they are allowing this. I don't understand."

Father Wertz shook his head in disgust. "I think I do, Silvio. What do we do about Antonio?"

"I will create special documents for him and give him a new Sicilian name. I have that power, and no one will question me. You need to create some baptismal documents, too, which will identify him with his new name. How old is he?"

"I think he is sixteen."

"My official documents will say he was born on July 30, 1873, and your documents will say he was baptized in Palermo shortly after that date. The *Padrone* will not ask any questions. Besides, he will be traveling with two priests, and I will alert my men on the ship to protect them."

"Thank you, Silvio. What name will we give him?" Father Wertz asked.

"Since he is going to a new land and getting a new start, we will call him Antonio Terranova."

Chapter 13

The United States Custom House
Canal Street
New Orleans, Louisiana
Monday, July 16, 1889

When construction started on the new United States Custom House in New Orleans in 1847, it was designed to be the most significant government building in the country, outside of Washington, D.C. With four stories of thick, brick walls, clad in dark gray Massachusetts granite, the colossal edifice announced the United States' dominion over the commerce on the Mississippi River, just four squares away. Architects wasted no effort mastering their authoritative image when they decided to occupy an entire city square of New Orleans, bounded by Canal, Custom House, North Peters, and Decatur Streets. To complete their dominating message, the builders designed the entire building in a mixture of Egyptian and Greek Revival, which was anachronistic in appearance and size at that time. Just one glimpse and one knew the building was the official domain of the United States of America, and any challenge thereto would be quickly suppressed.

Indeed, though unfinished at the time of the Civil War, the Union Army used its bottom floor to imprison about 2,000 Confederate soldiers after New Orleans surrendered in 1862. And when it was finally completed in 1881, the Customhouse was home to the United States District Courts, the United States Attorney, the United States Post Office, and the United States Customs Bureau, for which Algeron S. Badger worked and occupied a first-floor office.

On this morning, Badger told Ellis Overton, a customs clerk who collected tariffs at a bank-like teller's window in the center hall, to accompany Joseph P. Macheca to Badger's office when he arrived. Badger knew Macheca's schedule because two of his vessels had unloaded shipments of bananas and oranges from South America over the weekend, and the tariffs were due. While waiting for Macheca to arrive,

Badger and his guest, Superintendent of Police David C. Hennessy, gazed out Badger's large corner-office window onto Canal Street and watched how the people, dressed in various attire, interacted with one another on the busy street. Since it was hot this morning, ladies deployed their frilly parasols to shade themselves from the sun, while men, dressed in suits and bowler hats, greeted each other with feigned, but obligatory Southern gentility.

As Badger and Hennessy looked upon the streetscape, a carriage, drawn by a single but well-nourished brown horse, stopped in front of the Custom House, and J.P. Macheca stepped down, crossed the banquette, and entered the building. "Are you ready for this?" Badger asked Hennessy.

"Well, he looks like he is in a good mood, but we both know that can change in the blink of an eye," Hennessy responded.

Both men sat and waited for Overton to escort Macheca to Badger's office. It didn't take long before a soft knock sounded on the door. Badger opened it and warmly greeted the man who saved his life fourteen years earlier, just two squares from where they were standing.

"Good morning, J.P., and how are you doing?" Badger asked.

"Fine, Mr. Badger. But Mr. Overton said you need to talk to me. Is anything wrong?" After greeting Badger, Macheca saw Hennessy standing across the room, and his smiling visage dropped from his face. "What's he doing here?" Macheca asked.

"We need you to bestow upon us your favor and time. J.P., please sit down," Badger entreated.

Macheca, clutching a white straw, wide-brimmed hat, sat down but didn't take his eyes off Hennessy. The office air was edgy with suspicion. "What do you need, Mr. Badger?"

"J.P., we need your help, and we believe you are the only one who can do what we need," Badger said.

"What's that, sir?"

"We need you to broker a peace between the Matrangas and the Provenzanos."

Macheca laughed and tossed his hat over his shoulder. "Are you joking? Don't you realize that part of the problem between the Matrangas and the Provenzanos is sitting right there?" Macheca asked, pointing to Hennessy.

"What do you mean?" asked Hennessy.

"Your men harass and pick fights with their men on the docks. The police are always attacking the Italians and the negroes, or should I say the dagoes, so you can understand," Macheca snarled.

"No one has complained to me about that," Hennessy responded.

"I just did. Now, do something about it." Macheca began to shift and bounce in his chair. "Every time a drayman pulls up to the dock to load, your officers stop them and tell the men they can't stop near the dock. Where do you expect them to stop? But if they give him a buck or two or a sack of oranges, the cop goes away. That shit must stop before there's any peace on the docks. Everybody is tired of paying off cops."

"Are you telling us it's the police's fault that there are so many killings on the docks and Gallatin Street? Are you telling us there's no animosity between the Matrangas and the Provenzanos?" Badger asked.

No. Not entirely. Those two families have been at war since they left Sicily. The Matrangas are the *Stuppagghieri,* and the Provenzanos are the *Giardinieri*. They've been hating each other for hundreds of years, and they brought that shit to America. But the cops pour coal oil on the fire. Nobody trusts anybody on the docks."

"What about the Machecas?" Hennessy asked.

"My name is Maltese. We are neither. We are honest businesspeople who have been here before the Matrangas and Provenzanos arrived. Look at me. Where am I? I am in the United States Custom House, paying the government money. If I were a criminal, would I be here?"

"J.P., didn't you form the *Innocenti* in 1868 after the war?" Badger asked.

"Mr. Badger, you know we did that to protect our Italian neighborhoods. We were being raided by the Knights of the White Camelia every night, who were just looking for trouble with us. We had no real police department. So, we had to protect ourselves and our little businesses."

"The *Innocenti* killed many people," Badger asserted. "Do you deny there is no blood on Sicilian hands?"

"Wait a minute, Mr. Badger. You have known me for a long time. I saved your life right down the street in 1874. In 1868, the *Innocenti* was not just Sicilian. We had Irish, German, Creoles, and Frenchmen. In fact, it was a Frenchman who started the *Innocenti*—Pascalis Labarre. Remember him? We needed protection after the war. And remember that poor Irish kid the democrats killed on Dryades Street—Edward Malone? He was

Innoceni, too." Macheca turned towards Hennessy and said, "That's right, Chief, he was shanty Irish, just like you. And a group of negroes chop him up with meat cleavers."

"Aren't you Sicilian, but adopted by the Macheca family?" Hennessy asked.

"Mr. Badger, did you bring me to your office to be insulted by Chief Hennessy? Are we going to sit here and exchange insults all day?"

"I'm sorry, Mr. Macheca. I meant no offense. We are looking for peace on the docks and need your help to make that a reality. I apologize," Hennessy said.

Macheca seemed to have calmed down, but his face was still florid with anger. "What do you need, Mr. Badger?" Macheca asked, ignoring Hennessy.

"We know there is bad blood between the Matrangas and the Provenzanos, and we need the shootings and stabbings to stop. I don't think the police are the real problem, but as you alluded, it has ancient origins. We want you to call a truce—a meeting for all of us to meet and discuss our differences."

"When? Where?"

"How about the Red Lantern Club on Customhouse Street?" Badger asked.

Macheca bowed over in laughter. "Are you kidding me? You don't need me. Chief Hennessy owns part of that joint with the Provenzanos. He drinks and gambles there. Get *him* to call the meeting."

"I don't own any part of the Red Lantern Club, and I don't drink. Yes, I will visit and play cards with my own money, but that's it," Hennessy asserted.

"Have you ever visited the third floor, Chief?" Macheca asked slyly with a wink.

"Never!" Hennessey growled. "I don't need any incurable diseases."

"They have new medicine for that, Chief. Besides, New Orleans is full of various diseases; some can be seen, and others can't. And most of it is in the city hall," Macheca said. "It's called hatred, greed, and prejudice. Chief, your boss and his secret society friends are the real problem in New Orleans, not the Italians. We work."

"Please explain, J.P.," Badger said.

"Everybody knows Shakspeare and his friends want control of the docks, the ships, the screwmen, the stevedores, and the markets. He wants his friends to take our businesses and everything to do with the waterfront. He doesn't care if one dago kills another. He wants the port. Don't you understand?"

"That's not true," Hennessy said.

"No? Why isn't the mayor going after Antonio Monteleone? He buys the old Commercial Hotel, and no one bothers him. The *Stuppagghieri* and the *Giardinieri* stay there. No one cares. Why isn't he going after Joseph Solari? He runs the biggest grocery store in the French Quarter—across Royal Street from Monteleone's hotel. I make deliveries to him every week, and we talk. No one bothers him, and *everybody* shops there."

"Calm down, J.P.," Badger said, patting Macheca on his left shoulder.

Macheca ignored him. "I run a shipping company, and stalls in the markets. I get harassed by your officers. Matranga and Provenzano operated the screwmen, stevedores, drayage, and some markets, and they get harassed, too, by your officers and city inspectors, but Matranga gets it the worst. Why? I will tell you why. Because Shakspeare, and his friends want to control everything on the river, because that's where the money is. They want it all. It's only the Italians on the river who catch hell from this city. Well, you can tell your mayor he will have to kill me to get my business. I worked too long and hard to get what I have, and I'm not giving it to people who never worked hard a day in their lives," Macheca yelled while rubbing his chest.

"Calm down, J.P.," Badger said. "No one wants to take your business away from you. All we want is peace on the docks. It seems every day, someone is shot or stabbed along the river. It must stop and stop now. That's why you are here. If we didn't respect you or your position, we wouldn't be asking you for help."

Macheca removed a large handkerchief from his breast jacket pocket and wiped his brow. He requested a glass of water, which Hennessy poured from a silver pitcher on Badger's desk. Macheca guzzled down the entire glass. "Nice, I can tell this isn't cistern water. Must be nice to have spring water," Macheca said, wiping his mouth and bushy mustache. But, I must be honest with you," Macheca said. "I can't talk to Provenzano. He hates me and Matranga. I can talk to Matranga, but you, Chief Hennessy, need to talk to Provenzano. He's your friend, not mine."

"Will you talk to Matranga?" Badger asked. "He owes you a favor."

"What do you mean?" Macheca asked.

"Who killed Rafaele Agnello on Toulouse Street by your family's fruit store in 1869? And who rose to prominence in the Italian Colony afterwards?"

Macheca cast his eyes to the floor and mumbled, "I don't know."

"Didn't you become great friends with the Matrangas after, and made enough money to open your shipping company?" Badger probed.

"That's a long time ago. I am an honest businessman today. We all did stupid things when we were young. Remember, I saved your life while General Ogden's Democrats were shooting you and killing your horse? And the Democrats, the Ring, the Bourbonists, the Knights of the White Camellia, and the Young Democrats Association have never let me forget that day."

"I remember. I walk with a limp every day. How many times are you going to remind me?" Badger asked. "So, are you going to talk to the Matrangas?"

"Yes, but this is going to be tough. Like I said, Matranga hates Provenzano and Provenzano hates Matranga and me, too. Matranga doesn't like you, Chief Hennessy, because of your relationship with Provenzano." J.P. Macheca stood, picked up his hat, and raked it to the right. "I have to go, but do you want some advice, Chief?"

"Sure, Mr. Macheca."

"If we have this meeting, you better bring a bunch of your cops with you—a bunch of cops who like you. Other than Mr. Badger, they will be the only ones in that room who won't want you dead."

Chapter 14

The Cotton Exchange Building
New Orleans, Louisiana
3:00 P.M.
July 2, 1889

Almighty God blessed the Mississippi River Valley with rich alluvial and loess deposits of fertile soil from St. Louis to Baton Rouge. Man cursed that soil with the irons of slavery, and indentured servitude needed to harvest a woolly substance, which made their masters wealthy and powerful. Indeed, every Southern cotton baron ignored the anguish, moans, sweat, toil, and tears of those men and women who labored under the scorching sun to produce the softest crop the soil could ever yield, for the King was cotton, and the King must be served, and the King's court were the planters, shippers, and brokers who sustained the value of their Crown. They ignored the human toll thrust upon the black, brown, and rufescent calloused hands who nurtured their masters' suzerain bounty, from seed to boll.

After the Civil War, the harvesting of cotton remained the same, with the exception that the burlap sacks slung over the field workers' shoulders were filled by people plied with meager wages for their broiling toil in the charred soil—White: a dollar a day, Negroes: seventy-five cents a day, and Dagoes: fifty cents a day.

Once a sack was filled with cotton bolls, the harvest was dumped into a waiting bin and then wrapped in burlap sheets, creating bales weighing as much as five hundred pounds. From the plantations, teams of mules pulled laden wagons to the docks along the Mississippi Delta. Shirtless men in Vicksburg and Natchez loaded steam-driven paddle wheelers from the docks, to gins, presses, and into the avarice arms of cotton brokers in New Orleans, where the earth's ransom was designed by the brokers, and sold to mills in England and France.

Though the Mississippi River was nearly a mile wide at New Orleans, the cotton commerce was being choked by competing interests along the city's docks. Perishables took precedence over cotton, as cotton would not rot while waiting for the market. Delays in cotton shipping, however, meant time lost, and time lost meant money was delayed. Money delayed meant fortunes delayed, and in New Orleans, fortunes delayed meant status delayed, which was intolerable, for in New Orleans, one's status was his *raison d'être,* for which killing was no obstacle to sustain.

From his second-floor office window, Charles Chaffe, the tall, lean President of the New Orleans Cotton Exchange, watched the hum of commerce below his window, as his private Italian barber, Francisco "Frank" Trapani, shaved the nape of his neck with an ivory-handled straight razor. Chaffe could feel the razor chip away at his errant brown hairs, which grew below his high-collar line. Once that was done, the barber's boar brush soaped Chaffe's face around the borders of his sideburns, the margins of his large, brown, bushy mustache, which most men in New Orleans fashioned proudly. With the precision of a Renaissance painter, Trapani guided his blade carefully and created sharp lines between Chaffe's bare face and his boastful facial hair.

As Trapani was finishing, Franklin Hayne, accompanied by cotton brokers Harry Labousse, Maurice Hart, S.P. Walmsley, Whitney Bank president, James T. Hayden, and Harbor Master, Armand Blackmar, entered Chaffe's office. From their facial expressions, they wanted Trapani to leave, as they had important private business to conduct. The barber folded his razor and towel-dried Chaffe's face. Chaffe paid him twenty-five cents for his services, and Trapani excused himself. Chaffe greeted each man, as he knew them well. All the men were deeply involved in the cotton trade except for Blackmar and Hayden, and their impatient countenance signaled a problem brewing in their world.

"You trust that dago with a razor against your neck?" Hart asked.

"He's a good man with a family, Maurice. But you men didn't come here to talk about Mr. Trapani, did you?"

"No," Hart said, as he and the other men took seats in the luxurious leather chairs, which formed a semi-circle around Chaffe's large mahogany desk. "We need to talk about the upcoming cotton harvest and how we are going to handle it."

Chaffe thumbed through a pile of yellow telegraphs on his desk he received that morning from cotton ports upriver from New Orleans. "The planters report that this harvest is going to be a great one. The press houses are ready. Armand, is the port ready?"

"Yes, the port is ready, but we still have that persistent problem, which cuts deeply into our businesses," Blackmar said. "It's who controls what boats and ships get loaded, unloaded, and when. Firms like the Matrangas and the Provenzanos control New Orleans' cotton commerce. I can only do so much in saying what ships can dock at what wharfs, but I can't make the stevedores load or unload the ships. The other stevedore companies upriver are small and can't compete."

"Don't they want to work the steamboat or steamers?" Chaffe asked.

"The ships with citrus products and other foodstuffs take precedence in loading and unloading," Hart said. "Since cotton can't be eaten, our cargo has to sit and wait. When the steamboats carrying the cotton bales reach New Orleans, they must dock between the steamers and wait. The planters have tried to send down their own stevedores, but that's when the fights break out and people get dumped in the river. The steamboat captains have to burn excess coal to keep their boats pushed against the levees to fight the river's current. They are losing money, everybody is losing money, especially us. We have to do something."

"Is there a shortage of stevedores in New Orleans? Every time I go down to the docks, it's a beehive of activity. People push and pull hand trucks and drive drayage wagons to and from the docks. You have to watch where you stand, or you will get run over. And horse and mule shit is everywhere. You must admit, that's one indication of commerce," Chaffe laughed.

"May I say something?" Walmsley asked.

"Please, go ahead, sir," Chaffe responded.

"When those paddle wheelers come down river this fall, they will be piled with bales from the gunwales to the wheelhouses. Tons of cotton are ready to be pressed and loaded on the ocean-going steamers. None of that can happen if the stevedores are directed away from those vessels. As I sit here, Mobile, Alabama, is poised to compete and thus lower our prices."

"How so?" Chaffe asked.

"The docks at Mobile are a few miles from the Gulf of Mexico. Our docks are ninety-four miles from the Gulf. That means we need to unload the steamboats and load the steamships much faster to be competitive with Mobile. Our docks draw more tonnage from Louisiana, Mississippi, Arkansas, and Missouri than Alabama's. But we need more attention paid to our boats and ships, or we will lose our market position."

"I understand, but what can I do?" Chaffe asked. "I can control our price per pound, which is at seven dollars now. I have no control over the stevedores."

"Yes, you do," Hart said. "You and the mayor are close friends, and he, too, is invested in cotton, as many of our Pickwick Club members are. We need the city government to force those stevedore companies to service our vessels. The cotton exporting business is our largest economic engine, and we are forced to wait for banana boats to be unloaded. How are you going to explain that to the mills in England? Remember, Charles, in 1884, we had the Cotton Centennial in the park upriver. It wasn't called the Banana Centennial."

"I understand. I will talk to the mayor tonight. We're having dinner tonight at the Club. Gentlemen, your timing is impeccable," Chaffe said, turning his attention to Hayden. "James, how's the Whitney Bank doing? Are you concerned, too?"

Hayden, attired in a dark blue suit with gray trousers, looked like a nervous banker as he gripped the arms of his chair. "Yes, Charles, I am. The bank has financed the crops of several plantations up the river and the improvement of several steam presses near our docks. If this year's crop and next aren't sold at the top of market price, we will lose those loans, and the bank does not need to own empty cotton presses or fallow fields. We need Shakspeare to get involved. Perhaps he can get his police chief to encourage the Provenzanos to divert some of his laborers to the steamboats when they come downriver. I understand they are close friends."

"Too damn close," Hart lamented.

"Is there a shortage of laborers on the docks?" Chaffe asked.

"Nearly every month, another steamer docks near the Picayune Tier, and hundreds of grimy and grubby Sicilians waddle down the gangplank into the arms of someone they call the *Padrone*. He is Italian, too, and he decides where the immigrants go from there. Some are put on boats and sent upriver to work the plantations, some are sent across the lake to work the farms and ranches, and some stay in New Orleans to work at whatever job they can get. And some refuse to work and operate their "Black Hand" operations in the Italian Colony. Frankly, Charles, it's a disgusting mess down there, and we must do something about it now," Hart complained.

"Why do we have so many Sicilians in New Orleans?" Hayden asked. "They don't use our banks, and I don't know how Monteleone bought that hotel on Royal Street. As the president of the largest bank in this city, I should know where the money originates, where it is flowing, and to whom it is flowing. However, the Italians have their own secret banking system, which could potentially compromise the city's economy. We don't need an underground economy in New Orleans."

"I understand, James. As you know, the state brought those immigrants here to work after the war. We had a shortage of laborers everywhere, but now it seems we have too many immigrants and not enough workers. However, my cousin, William Chaffe, an attorney, informed me that Congress passed a law forbidding the Padrone system in 1874. It's now a felony to entice immigrants into involuntary servitude, and from what I understand, the paltry wages the Italians receive approach involuntary servitude. If you want to stop Italian immigration, I recommend we consult with the United States Attorney and seek indictments of everyone involved in this practice."

Maurice Hart shot up from his chair and exclaimed, "That's crazy, Charles. First, the United States Attorney, William Grant, is a republican and would be very suspicious of anything a democrat would suggest. Second, who would work the fields, and third, who would unload the steamboats? The Negroes? We must do something, but stopping immigration isn't the answer. The problem is that this race of people controls our commerce and *our* money. It should be stopped before they consume New Orleans brick by brick and stone by stone."

"So, gentlemen, we have a conundrum, don't we? We can't halt the immigration of Italians. It's a state and federal issue. And we can't make enemies with the planters, and we must stabilize the wages for all. If we assert ourselves too much, Washington will view it as another form of racial control or insurrection. The last thing we need are federal troops on Canal Street regulating our labor force," Chaffe calmly advised. "We must be judicious in our approach. We must attack this problem incrementally, devoid of emotion and motive. We must assist the mayor in his plan, which puts New Orleans' economy first. After all, his fortunes are linked to the docks, too."

"What do you suggest, Charles?" Walmsley asked.

"We need to get the newspapers involved and start printing stories about the Italian community—negative stories. We know there's a killing down there nearly every week. The papers must start reporting those stories with the appropriate emphasis. Tonight, I will encourage Shakspeare to get his police department on the problem and detain those who prefer leisure to work. Anyone caught loitering on street corners can do it in the police jail. Every newspaper story will be accompanied by our planted exhortations that the mayor moves quickly to solve the problem. Shakspeare loves to read his name in the papers, and a man who loves notoriety can be controlled. There will be more stevedores loading and unloading vessels. They must work. Shakspeare is a politician, and his image means everything to him, as well as his bank account. He will have no choice. Remember, the Cotton Exchange controls this city, but the mayor doesn't understand that yet."

"Do you think the papers will seriously affect public opinion?" Hart asked.

"Maurice," Hayden began, "our good friend, Colonel John Wickliffe of the *Daily States,* once told me his newspaper could make the archbishop look like a heretic. In New Orleans, ink is more lethal than a bullet."

Chapter 15

The Pickwick Club
New Orleans, Louisiana
July 2, 1889
Evening

As Charles Chaffe sat at his desk writing notes for tonight's meeting with the mayor, a blinding vein of lightning seared down Gravier Street, accompanied by window-rattling thunder, which caused the cotton baron to jump in his chair. With his heart thumping beneath his white, high-collar, starched shirt, Chaffe looked at his banjo clock on the wall and realized it was best to be early and dry, rather than soaked and on time. He looked out his window and saw gusts of wind kicking up the debris and dust along the cobblestoned streets, and decided to dash to his meeting at the Pickwick Club.

When he arrived at the front door of the private club, Charles was greeted by the smiling face of the club's valet, Creed Baptiste, who dutifully opened the door and allowed Chaffe's admittance. After a perfunctory greeting, Chaffe stopped and engaged the valet in an unusual and rare jesting conversation. "Creed, may I ask you a question?"

"Sure, Mr. Chaffe."

"Earlier today, I looked out my window and saw several men working on the large cobblestones under the streetcar tracks. One of them looked like you. Was it?"

"Yes, sir, Mr. Chaffe. I have two jobs. In the daytime, I works for the New Orleans Railway and Light company, and at night, I goes home and shower under the spigot of my cistern and put on this tuxedo and work here. Am I doing something wrong?"

"Of course not, Creed. But today, you were working with some men who looked Italian. Were they?"

"Yes, sir. They work with me every day. They good people and work hard and don't stop until the job is done. If we don't fix them stones and tighten 'em up, the streetcar will roll off those tracks and kill someone."

"I understand. Do you get along with the Italians?" Chaffe probed.

"Yes, sir. They bring me lunch and share their food with me. I can't bring my lunch some days—I have seven children. So, they always share. They talk funny, but they're nice people. And they cook as good as my momma," Baptiste said with a wink.

Chaffe was about to ask another question, but was interrupted when a carriage stopped in front of the club and splashed water onto the banquette. Mayor Shakspeare and J.D. Houston carefully stepped down and jumped across the wide gutter, which was filling quickly with the storm's water. The men greeted each other, but Chaffe and Houston exchanged curious stares. After thanking Baptiste, Chaffe, Houston, and Shakspeare ascended the grand stairway leading to the dining room.

As the men sat at the linen-draped table, Shakspeare asked Chaffe, "I saw you talking to our valet. Any problems, Charles?"

"No. Just some small talk."

Houston shot Chaffe another glance as the three men settled in for dinner, but this one had a feral element. Chaffe ignored the passive provocation and placed his napkin across his lap, while the mayor lit a cigar. "Charles, I sent a messenger to you this morning inviting you to have dinner with us, because of a storm on our horizon, and it's not the one blowing outside the window."

"Well, to be honest with you, Joseph, I was going to send you a messenger and request a meeting alone because there is a confluence of issues we must deal with immediately. But you go first."

"Well, I invited J.D. because of his contacts with many planters upriver and throughout the state. And, as you know, his family owns cotton and sugarcane fields between New Orleans and Baton Rouge. His knowledge in that area will help us with this burgeoning problem."

"What problem?" Chaffe asked.

"We might be facing a serious labor issue, which will impact the port and our cotton exports. I know that one-third of the cotton exports from the United States to Europe pass through New Orleans. It's the engine of our economy."

"I guess coincidences are not coincidental," Chaffe quipped.

"Is that remark meant for me?" Houston snarled.

"No, it means I have the same concerns," Chaffe retorted.

"Calm down, J.D.," Shakspeare enjoined. "Honestly, I don't know who has the worst temper—you or Maurice Hart. Let me tell Charles what I told you earlier." The mayor took a puff on his cigar, placed his gold-frame pince-nez on the bridge of his nose, opened his leather valise, and removed some notes he had scrawled earlier.

"This morning, I was walking down the center hallway in city hall, when I had a fortuitous encounter with our local republican United States Attorney, William Grant, the nephew of the former president. I asked him what brought him to our city hall, since he is well ensconced at the Custom House, or should I say *palace*. He told me he was checking our immigration and occupation records—the same ones the Soards Company uses to publish our official city directory."

"Why does that concern you, Joseph?" Chaffe asked.

Shakspeare glanced at his notes. "Grant told me that fifteen years ago, Congress passed a law forbidding the enticement of immigrants to the United States and introducing them to slavery or involuntary servitude. He was investigating whether our port is practicing this through something called the *Padrone* system. He said if he determines our port is allowing this practice, federal and maritime law require him to seize our docks and vessels that bring immigrants to Louisiana. He told me the government is investigating New York and Boston now. Did you know about this law?"

"Yes, I do. My cousin, William, told me about it and warned me that the immigrants must be paid the same as whites and negroes. Any disparity in wages could constitute involuntary servitude, and if the disparity becomes common knowledge, the Italians could strike the plantations and the docks, paralyzing our cotton industry. In fact, it's one of the things I wanted to discuss with you, since the city has many Italians working for it, at a reduced wage. William says we are inviting the federal government to sue our industry and the city. That would damage our image, Joseph. We don't need federal troops in New Orleans, again."

Shakspeare blanched. "This is utter nonsense," Houston said. "The Italians are paid a fair wage in New Orleans and on the plantations. Some are tenant farmers. Some have saved enough money to buy their own land or return to Sicily, where they belong."

"I've heard that some Italians have been accidentally shot in hunting accidents, *after* they try to buy the land they have worked," Chaffe said. "Is that true, Mr. Houston?"

"Hunting is a dangerous enterprise, Mr. Chaffe. One must always be careful in the fields and woods of Louisiana."

"And the streets of New Orleans?" Chaffe asked.

"There, too, Mr. Chaffe. Besides, it appears more Italians kill people in New Orleans than vice versa. Just this morning, Chief Hennessy's men pulled a dago out the river whose head was nearly severed. The only thing holding his head on his body was the skin on the back of the poor bastard's neck. And this afternoon, Hennessy's men found a wagon driven by two dagoes, which had three boxes of dynamite under a canvas tarpaulin. They told the police it was for extracting cypress stumps near Milneburg. We don't have a labor problem in Louisiana. We have a dago problem. Fortunately, they never kill on the uptown side of Canal Street."

Chaffe drew a deep breath to stanch his emotions and not allow Houston's caustic words to cloud his thinking, but he could not resist, at least, one retort. "You're not a member of this club, are you, Mr. Houston?"

"No, but I am a member of the Boston Club—right down Canal Street."

"Is that the same Boston Club who started the Battle of Liberty Place in 1874, which required our United States Attorney's uncle to send federal troops to patrol New Orleans, not to mention seven navy gunboats? And doesn't your family's plantations profit from the *Padrone* system?"

Houston shot up, reached inside his coat, and stared down at the composed Chaffe. Shakspeare, knowing Houston's history with a gun, stood and grabbed Houston by the shoulder. "Sit down, J.D. Let's hear what Charles has to say, for God's sake."

"Mr. Mayor, I think Mr. Chaffe has too much sympathy for the Italian Colony," Houston said.

"No. That's not true. All I want is to make New Orleans prosperous, without having the United States Army bivouac on Canal Street, or controlling our port," Chaffe responded.

"Tell us what's on your mind, Charles," Shakspeare said.

"Earlier today, I had a meeting with several members of the New Orleans Cotton Exchange, a banker, and a newspaper editor."

"Newspaper?" Shakspeare asked.

"Yes. They came to me and told me about the Italian problem, among other things. I made some notes, from which I will read," Chaffe said, as he removed his notes from his inside coat pocket. Houston craned his neck to read them, but Chaffe's poor penmanship and numerous ink blots prevented Houston's furtive eyes from a pre-emptive understanding of the issues.

After flattening his notes on the table, Chaffe began his presentation. "As I sit here, Mobile, Alabama, and Galveston, Texas are presenting formidable competition to our cotton exports. Both ports are closer to the Gulf of Mexico than we are. I have spoken to several ship masters, and they claim a ship leaving New Orleans can be in the Gulf before a ship from Galveston reaches the mouth of the Mississippi. But given our geographical advantage over Texas, we could lose that advantage if our riverboats are not unloaded and the cotton pressed and reloaded on steamers in a deliberate manner."

"Is that being done?" the Mayor asked.

"No. We are now on the precipice of a labor crisis. Allow me to explain. Three years ago, Charles Matranga and Antonio Locascio formed a huge stevedore company, which has taken business away from the Provenzano brothers. In fact, one of Provenzano's former supervisors, Rocco Geraci, and a shoemaker named Vincent Raffo, and a close friend of the Provenzano brothers, got into a shootout near Gallatin Street. Geraci killed Raffo, but it took several months for the police to arrest him. After the police arrested Geraci, Joseph Macheca and others convinced the District Attorney that both men had shot at each other, and the disposition should be settled as self-defense. It was."

"One less dago to worry about," Houston intoned.

Chaffe ignored Houston and continued his presentation. "Do you know the detective on the case back then?"

"Who?" Shakspeare asked.

"David Hennessy."

"I thought Hennessy and the Provenzano brothers were close friends. I understand they are partners in the Red Lantern on Customhouse Street," Houston asserted. "Besides, when Hennessy captured Esposito in Jackson Square eight years ago, didn't the Matrangas or the Provenzanos swear they would kill him and his cousin?"

"Maybe. But they may have had some type of rapprochement, but I don't know if that's true. Anyway, the Provenzanos appear to be friendly with Hennessy. But the feud continues. Remember January 5th of last year, at the Café De Monde?" Chaffe asked.

"Wasn't there another murder down there?" Shakspeare asked.

"Yes. Another friend of the Provenzanos tried to kill Geraci while he was drinking coffee early that morning. Shots were exchanged, and Geraci killed Anthony Bonura. Again, it was ruled self-defense and probably was, according to the witnesses. Hennessy had no choice but to release Geraci. And last night, there was another slashing on the docks."

"Dago killing dago. What does that have to do with our cotton being exported?" Houston asked.

"Mr. Houston, these families control the stevedores, and what boats and ships get unloaded and loaded. Soon, you will see steamboats laden with bales of cotton docking or trying to dock on our waterfront. If those bales are not loaded on the steamers and exported to Liverpool, and elsewhere in a deliberate manner, Mobile and Galveston will surpass New Orleans as the primary exporter of cotton, and we all lose money. Does that answer your question?"

"Charles, what do you recommend?" the mayor asked.

"We must devise a way for the city to take over the docks, stevedores, and wharves. We cannot allow an ancient Sicilian war to be planted on the Mississippi's banks and collapse the industry that breathes life into New Orleans. Sure, there are other commodities coming through our port, but cotton has made us all who we are today. The issue is beyond debate," Chaffe said, as he pounded the table with his fist, surprising the mayor.

"What do you propose, Charles?" the mayor asked, again.

"As I see it, we must take control of the port. In doing so, we must end the *Padrone* system, to the extent it treats the immigrants like indentured servants. Selecting them for the work they are best suited for is one thing, but paying them a disparate wage will force Grant to sue and seize the port, which is worse than the Sicilians killing each other over a barrel of lemons."

"You want them to be paid as much as the whites? That's insane," Houston said.

"Yes, and as much as the negro. Any disparity of wages or conditions will be evidence against the port and the city, not to mention the plantations up the river. If you recall Mr. Houston, it was the *Louisiana Planters and Sugar Manufacturers*—your relatives and friends—who lobbied for the state legislature to create *The Louisiana Bureau of Immigration,* to replace the negroes who moved North after the war. As I see it, their plantations are at risk, as much as our port."

Houston seethed and slumped into his chair.

"Grant seemed very determined to do something this morning," the mayor said. "But he only has three attorneys working for him. What can he discover with only a couple of attorneys?"

"Wrong, Joseph. William told me he saw Grant dining with the Pinkerton Brothers at Antoine's Restaurant last week."

"The Pinkertons are in New Orleans?" the Mayor asked. "Does Hennessy know this?"

"I think so. William Pinkerton has been seen at the Central Police Station. And given their skill as investigators, I wouldn't be surprised that some of them are already working as stevedores and reporting back to Grant or Hennessy," Chaffe responded.

"Dammit. Hennessy should have told me about the Pinkertons being in New Orleans," the mayor said.

"Joseph, it's okay. Let Hennessy and Pinkerton investigate the *Mafia* or whatever they call themselves. I have some people exhorting the newspapers to report on all the activities in the Italian Colony, especially linking all killings to the *Mafia*. It's a necessary diversion, which will mold public opinion. We need Hennessy to pursue the *Mafia*. Anyway, it appears Hennessy is still friends with the Provenzanos, which could redound in our favor, as we seek control of the docks," Chaffe said.

"I'm confused, Charles. Please explain," the mayor asked.

"My cousin, William, told me the city has contracted with the Joseph A. Aiken & Company to manage the French Market. Are you aware of that?"

"Yes. Aiken is a good businessman."

"Did you know he contracted with the Provenzanos to operate the entire French Market?"

"Hell, no. When did that happen?"

"I don't know," Chaffe said. "But the word on the streets and cafes is that Aiken had no choice. The Black Hand paid him a visit, which has caused more tension between the Matrangas and the Provenzanos. The Matrangas control the docks, and the Provenzanos control the market. Now, factor in the race-based pay schedule on the docks, and Grant has a good case to seize the docks and put them under the control of the Army. If that happens, the Cotton Exchange will be closed. In short, our cotton and sugar industries are caught between a centuries-old Sicilian feud and the United States government. We must thread this needle very carefully."

Shakspeare sat back in his chair and said nothing. His breathing was noticeably heavy. Tuxedoed waiters brought in the dinner, but Shakspeare pushed his plate away and stared out the window. "Y'all eat. I have some thinking to do. Besides, I lost my appetite," the stunned Mayor said.

While Chaffe and Houston dined, Shakspeare wrote some notes and drew lines, connecting his notes, as if he were designing a structure. He sipped his bourbon, puffed on his cigar, and occasionally watched the people and wagons on Canal Street as the indigo twilight descended on the summer day.

After twenty minutes, Shakspeare spoke. "If we lose the docks, we lose New Orleans. If Grant seizes the docks, he seizes New Orleans. If the Matrangas and the Provenzano control the docks, they control New Orleans. Anyone interested in the port, directly or indirectly, will be financially ruined. We can't let that happen. I won't let that happen. I have plans for New Orleans, and no one will stop me. We surrendered this city once in 1862. We won't do it again."

"What are you going to do, Mr. Mayor?" Houston asked.

"I will assemble a committee of everyone involved, in any way, with the cotton industry. They need to know what is at stake. As I see it, New Orleans is under siege. We could have the United States Attorney working with the Pinkerton Detective Agency while we have the *Mafia* controlling the docks and markets in this town. And I have a police chief who might have divided loyalty or has had his integrity unwittingly compromised. I need to speak with Hennessy. This committee will be assembled, and we will devise a plan to take back the docks from the *Mafia* and Washington. Charles, can we use the large meeting room at the Exchange? I don't want my committee seen at City Hall or here."

"Of course. We'll keep it a secret. Most of those men are in the Exchange daily to use our telegraph system and check the prices of stocks and commodities. Their presence will arouse no suspicion."

"I have already assembled a small committee to facilitate the improvements I want for this city, but I want to expand it to be composed of every businessman, lawyer, doctor, ship chandler, cotton presser, shipping agent, shipping company in this city," Shakspeare said.

"You mean the Boston and Pickwick Clubs, Mr. Mayor?" Houston asked.

"Exactly, and the Ring. Things might get perilous for some people, and we must distance ourselves from the pigs in the mud. I want no attribution whatsoever, visiting the doorstep of the Boston or Pickwick Clubs. J.D., you are my campaign manager and have political purchase with the Ring and their sinewed associates. You know what needs to be done."

Houston allowed a wide, sinister smile to cut across his face.

"And I want every man with over twenty-five thousand dollars in the bank to know what could happen if we do nothing. Charles, do you want to be on the committee?"

For a moment, Chaffe was surprised by the invitation. "Thank you, Joseph, but I think as president of the Exchange, I should detach myself from any formal membership in the committee. I have a fiduciary relationship with the cotton industry. But I will facilitate the goals and objectives of the committee. But in the meantime, I must assert we do something about the pay inequity on the docks. With Pinkerton's detectives operating in New Orleans, they might find what those men who are being paid and tell Grant. In my opinion, this is something we must do now. Joseph, you must do something. Perhaps a city council resolution acknowledging past inequities—throughout the city."

"I like that. Will the Matrangas and Provenzanos resist? After all, the increase in wages will cost them, too." Shakspeare asked.

"They'll just pass the cost on to the shippers, who will do the same. They have no choice. We control the newspapers, and we can print stories about how pay equity can save a man's business from government seizure. I will have the *Daily Picayune* write an analysis on how the increase in wages will be offset by an increase in the price per pound for cotton— pennies, actually. In the final analysis, all they have to do is stevedore more boats and ships, in a timely manner. Come to think of it, such publicity might assuage Grant's concerns without admitting guilt. Then, all we must do is devise a plan to take control of the docks and set the price of *everything*."

"Brilliant, Charles," Shakspeare said.

"Well, I still oppose paying the dago the same as a white man," Houston persisted. "They are *not* white. I prefer to call them the other people, who belong back in Sicily. Just yesterday, I heard one was getting married to a creole or mulatto girl. That poses another problem—a political one. We can't have the dagoes and negroes mixing and forming a political voting bloc, which opposes the Ring. Doesn't Louisiana have a miscegenation law?"

Chaffe and Shakspeare erupted in laughter. "Did you hear what you just said, J.D.?" Shakspeare asked.

"What?"

"You don't want to pay the Italians a white man wage, but you want to prosecute them for being white and marrying a woman of negro blood? Which is it, J.D.?"

Chapter 16

City Hall
New Orleans, Louisiana
July 5, 1889
9:00 A.M.

When architect James Gallier designed New Orleans city hall in 1853, his vision was to install on the city's Lafayette Square an edifice, which exuded the city's developing culture, economy, society, and sophistication, worthy of joining similar Greek Revival shrines found in the Valley of the Temples in Agrigento, Sicily. He wanted a structure that would endure the harsh climatic conditions of South Louisiana, so he chose gleaming-white Tuckahoe marble from New York State mounted on a dark-gray Connecticut granite foundation. With double rows of fluted Ionic-capped columns, the building, ninety feet wide and two hundred and fifteen feet deep, evoked the city's sovereign Southern power, after unbidden Reconstruction.

At 9 o'clock on this cloudless Friday morning, Police Superintendent David Hennessy parked his carriage in front of City Hall and ascended the eighteen granite steps to the building's front double doors. He was greeted by several workers who readily identified the chief, dressed in a dark blue cutaway coat, a white high-collar shirt, a black bow tie, and gray trousers. He had an appointment with the mayor and didn't want to be late, so he didn't dawdle in the building's center hallway. He politely acknowledged workers and walked swiftly to his boss's office on the second floor.

When he arrived at Mayor Shakspeare's office, a nervous mayor was in the hallway, waiting for him. "Come in, David, and thank you for being on time. Please sit down. I have several important matters to discuss with you."

Hennessy sat in a leather tufted chair in front of the mayor's massive desk. The morning sun streamed through the office's large windows, suffusing the mayor's domain with natural light. Shakspeare spent a moment rearranging some papers on his desk and asked, "David, do you know what historic event occurred right here in this office?"

"No, sir."

"You were just a child then. This is the very room where Mayor John Monroe surrendered New Orleans to Admiral David Farragut on April 29, 1862, and this city was under the Union boot for nearly four years. Then came Reconstruction. Those were horrible years, and I refuse to surrender this city to anyone, for any reason, anymore. Understand?"

Hennessy furrowed his brow and tried to understand the mayor's point. "I don't think I understand, Mr. Mayor. Is the city in trouble, again?"

"Let me ask you a few questions, David. Were the Pinkerton brothers in New Orleans recently?"

"Yes, sir."

"Why didn't you tell me? Didn't you think I wanted to meet these famous men while visiting my city?"

"I'm sorry, sir. I didn't think of it. They were here to share information they received from Rome regarding the *Mafia*. They know we have a problem and want to help. So, we exchanged notes and ideas."

"Did you know they also met with the United States Attorney?"

"Grant? Why?"

"That's what I want you to find out. As you probably have guessed, we have several problems on the docks, and how much the Italians and Negroes are paid is a major problem."

"What do you mean, Mr. Mayor?"

Shakspeare began a long discussion about how vulnerable the docks were to seizure by the United States, if it were determined Louisiana, through its *Padrone System,* was responsible for wage disparity, which could be interpreted by a court to be involuntary servitude, making the docks sizable.

"Hold on, Mr. Mayor. That problem might be solved."

"What do you mean, David?"

"Do you know Pasquale Corte?"

"That little Italian man who works for the Italian government? He's always pestering me about something to do with the Italian Colony and the water system down there. I can't understand a word he says—he talks too fast."

"That's him. He went to the Matrangas and the Provenzanos, and is trying to get them to pay the same wages they pay the white stevedores and the negroes. I don't know what happened, but I heard the Italian stevedores are excited about it. But the increase in wages will be passed on to the shipping companies and the various exchanges."

"Don't worry about the exchanges. We can't have pay disparity on our docks," Shakspeare demanded. "Unfortunately, the Italians are a necessary inconvenience, which we must deal with."

"What do you mean, Mr. Mayor?"

"If that little pain-in-the-ass Italian is successful in correcting the pay disparity among the stevedores, then he should do something about the war between the Matrangas and the Provenzanos, not to mention Macheca. What are you doing about it? I am being asked by many people, 'What's Hennessy doing about the *Mafia* and the Black Hand?'"

"We are studying the problem closely. That's why the Pinkertons were here. They are monitoring the immigration of brigands from Sicily to New York, Boston, and New Orleans. They gave me a list of people who are here, which the Italian police said we should watch. Sir, remember that the Black Hand only victimizes other Italians, and the victims are scared to cooperate with the police."

"Are your friends on that list?"

"My friends?" Hennessy asked.

"The Provenzanos. Aren't they *Mafia*, too?"

"To be honest, sir, I suspect they were, at one time. But now they have a booming business on the docks and the markets. In fact, they are victims of the Black Hand, but they are big enough to ignore it. The little shop owners and fruit vendors aren't. They pay those bastards, or they will lose their businesses."

"What about the Red Lantern Club? Are you a part owner of that establishment?"

Hennessy shook his head and sighed. "No, sir. I have been accused of that many times. Do I go there? Yes. Do I drink there? No. Do I gamble there? Sometimes, but only table stakes. But, if I win, I win fairly, and if I lose, I lose fairly."

"David, people talk in this town. Gossip is a disease of the weak mind, and there is no cure. It doesn't look good for my police chief to be in a saloon, gambling hall, and whorehouse. You need to stop going there."

"Sir, while playing cards, I collect information and record it in my journal at the Central Police Station. If I don't go there, I will blind myself to their activities. I can't trust anyone else to do that. My cousin, Michael, is dead."

"You have no one who can blend in down there and collect information?" Shakspeare asked.

"No. These men like playing cards with the police chief, and they talk. For example, just the other day, some of Provenzano's men told me about brigands with a wagon-full of dynamite parked in front of the mint. My men seized it. God only knows the damage they could have caused."

Shakspeare leaned on the arm of his chair and seemed frustrated. He cast his eyes over the papers on his desk, and after a few moments spoke again. "David, do you know why I picked you to be my police chief?"

"You told me I did a great job as Security Director at the Cotton Centennial in 1884."

"What kind of Centennial?"

"Cotton."

"Remember that word. Cotton controls this city's commerce and everything else, while important, is secondary. Cotton is the number one business in this city, and our cotton exports support many people. Do you understand that?"

"Yes, sir."

"Then tell me why there are still bales of cotton stacked along the docks from the spring harvest, which have not been loaded onto steamers heading to England? You do understand there are two cotton harvests in the South—Spring and Fall? And the Fall harvest is due in New Orleans at the end of September. If those Spring bales are not loaded and shipped to Europe, where are we going to put the Fall harvest? Other ports, like Galveston and Mobile, are clamoring for our share of the trade."

"Mr. Mayor, I am just the police chief. I don't control the docks or the stevedores."

"Dammit, David! You play cards with the Provenzanos and others. Can't you convince them to load those steamers quicker? Their lethargy is costing people money. And those people are losing their patience with my decision for police chief. Understand?"

"Yes, sir. But what do you want me to do?" The Matrangas and the Provenzanos hate each other and have carved out territories along the docks and the markets. I am trying to get Joseph Macheca to broker a peace, but those families won't meet. They're stubborn people. Their hatred for each other goes back centuries."

"I'm just as stubborn," Shakspeare said, pounding his fist on his desk. "I want you to demand a peace with those families and get them to load those steamships with our cotton—NOW! And they have to stop shooting and stabbing each other. Every killing is printed in the newspapers. Did you see the morning *Times-Democrat*? One of their reporters found a body on the riverbank near Gallatin Street with an anchor chain wrapped around his neck and chest. I guess they didn't bring him far enough into the river before they dumped him."

"I heard about it. We are investigating it."

"David, a reporter found the body, not a policeman. Do you have men patrolling the docks?"

"Yes, but I need to hire more officers."

"Well, that's another thing. I have a list of forty officers you have fired in the last six months. Every city councilman is angry about these firings. You are creating more political enemies, too. Why did you fire so many officers in a short period of time? Now, you need more policemen?"

"I am trying to make the police department more professional. The officers I fired were sleeping on the beat, taking payoffs, demanding payoffs, cavorting with women, when they should have been working. I need officers who will abide by their oath, and can read and write, not just swing a truncheon or pull a trigger. In fact, the Pinkertons gave me some advice on hiring and testing new officers."

"Well, I might assuage the city council, but I will not assuage the cotton industry until their cargo is gone to market. As we sit here now, you are not making many friends. Get the *Mafia* under control. Get the Matrangas and Provenzanos to settle their differences peacefully. Get that cotton moving from steamboat to steamship. Get the *Padrones* off the docks and away from Grant's eyes. Remember, there are a lot of men who want your job."

"J.D. Houston?"

"He wants your job, too?"

"He wants me to give him a badge, and I won't. He likes to remind me he killed the man who killed my father in 1871. I know he's your friend, but I don't trust him. Besides, his family has an interest in the *Padrones*. They work the docks looking for workers for their plantations."

"I didn't know that, or care about his family upriver. As you know, J.D. is my campaign manager and sometimes bodyguard. I had the City Council authorize him to carry a gun. Hell, everybody in New Orleans carries a gun. But do you know about Billy O'Connor? Dexter Gaster? John Journee?"

"My Secretary, George Van Dervort, told me about Gaster and Journee, but O'Connor is my close friend."

"You can't trust anyone. They all want your job. You have a very coveted position, so be careful and don't give too many people your back or your trust. And remember this: when you killed Thomas Devereaux, you made many enemies in this city. And they know you know about their dalliances during the Cotton Centennial.

"I also made enemies with the Sicilians when I arrested Esposito and with the white people when I killed Devereaux," Hennessy lamented.

"New Orleans is a city of ever-changing fidelities. It's a spider web— always waiting in the shadows for an unwitting victim. First, it snares, then it kills. Remember, your father joined the Union army after this city surrendered. Many people remember that, and believe Arthur Guerin did the right thing. Your father fell into that web on St. Ann Street. I caught hell when I appointed you the Superintendent because I want an honest police force. Don't make me regret my decision."

Shakspeare stood and approached two oil portraits hanging on his office wall. One was of Jean-Baptiste Le Moyne de Bienville, the recognized French founder of New Orleans, and Etienne de Bore, the first mayor of New Orleans, after Thomas Jefferson purchased Louisiana.

"You see these two men, David?" Shakspeare asked, pointing to the portraits. "Both tried to tame this wicked termagant of a city, but today, we must live with her distemper, foul ways, and blood-dripping fangs. From the day the French displaced the tribes, New Orleans has been a redoubt for brigands, pirates, thieves, killers, demimondes, slave mongers, grifters, gamblers, the corrupt, and now, the *Mafia*. They all seek power, position, and wealth in our society, and will do anything to acquire it. It's the immutable character of man. And slicing through her is Canal Street, which putatively offers neutrality and peace for her people, but in reality, it's a hate-built rampart, warning all who traverse its cobblestones of the perils that lie beyond, on both sides. And you, David, must cross that rampart daily and minister to the city's insatiable dark desires. I wouldn't want your job."

"Mr. Mayor, I must agree with you, but *every* cobblestone on every street and alley of this city is stained with someone's blood. Those who do nothing bestow silent benediction upon the thrust of the dagger or trigger pull. I understand what you're saying, but I want my benediction to be over my body, only after I try to make New Orleans a better place to live."

"David, when you were at that Jesuit school on Baronne Street, did you study Greek mythology?"

"Yes, along with some Greek and Latin languages, too."

"Do you remember the story of Sisyphus?"

"Yes."

"Well, New Orleans is either your boulder or the venue of your benediction—perhaps, both. Be careful, son."

Chapter 17

The Bridge of the SS Neustria
Palermo, Sicily
July 30, 1889
6:00 A.M.

At 328 feet long and forty feet wide, the French-built *SS Neustria* edged closer to the dock on the west side of the Port of Palermo. Its deckhands scurried around its deck, tossing hawse and mooring lines to eager dock workers below. They wrapped the lines tightly around iron bollards, securing the ship to the wharf. From the bridge, Captain Paul Vermie yelled orders through a metal megaphone to his crew and the dock workers to secure the lines tight, to prevent the 23,000-ton ship from shifting, while loading its cargo of citrus products, olive oil, wine, small machinery, and doleful immigrants.

Captain Vermie could see them from his high perch in the dawning light. A queue of dingy, brown, forlorn immigrants snaking about one hundred yards from a white hut, where waiting Italian immigration authorities sat at a long table, next to Palermo's *Padrones*. Each immigrant carried their most valuable possessions to their new home—America. Some women were carrying babies, swaddled in old scarves. Their sagging eyes swelled with hope even in the dim light as they stared at the black, iron-hulled ship of mercy, spewing acrid coal smoke from its funnel.

Captain Vermie instructed his First Officer, Calais Berot, to establish three gangways from the wharf to the ship—one for cargo, one for food stores, and one for people. As his eyes surveyed the long line of patient immigrants fleeing Sicily for a better life in a land of unknown fortune, his attention was directed to a phalanx of *Carabinieri* escorting a black carriage, pulled by two black horses. Leading the column of officers was a man he was very familiar with—Colonel Silvio Salvani.

With his curiosity ablaze, Captain Vermie quickly descended four ladders to the promenade deck, stepped on the bouncing gangway to the wharf, and greeted his old friend. "*Buongiorno,* Silvio. What brings you out to these smelly wharfs so early?"

"I had to escort a special cargo to your ship. I have two Jesuits and a seminarian who are under threat from the *Stuppagghieri.* I have their passage and papers with me. Their fare is paid, and they will be assigned one of your eighteen staterooms." Then Salvani bent over and whispered in Vermie's ear, "I also have two of my men assigned to a stateroom, too—as usual."

"I understand, my good friend. Let's get them through your immigration. There will be no need to talk to the *Padrone*, as God has already assigned their work," Vermie said, leading Fathers Jacque Fontebuis and Philippe Consere, and Antonio Terranova to the front of the line of immigrants. Each priest wore full black cassocks, while Antonio wore an ill-fitting, clean, black suit, white shirt, and black tie. Both priests carried two brown leather suitcases, while Antonio carried one.

When they reached the immigration hut, Antonio glanced over his shoulder and caught the eye of his friends from the docks, Asperi Marchesi and his father. They were about thirty feet from the immigration hut, and were clothed in ragged clothes, not worthy of prisoners. Antonio smiled and gave a short wave, which was politely returned. Once cleared through immigration and the ticketing process, Captain Vermie escorted Colonel Salvani, the priests, and Antonio to Stateroom Number One, located one deck below the ship's bridge, on the port side. Inside the stateroom, they found four bunks, two dressers, a wardrobe, three kerosene lamps, two desks, and two twelve-inch portholes. Antonio gasped when he realized this would be his home for the next thirty to forty days. He expected much worse conditions, based on stories he had heard about shipboard conditions to America.

"Stow your bags, and I will give you a tour of the bridge," Captain Vermie proudly said. "This ship is equipped with all the newest navigational aids. We even have ship-to-ship telegraphs, in the event of trouble."

Antonio, the priests, and Salvani followed Vermie up one ladder and entered the bridge. They were stunned by the array of nautical equipment fastened to the bulkheads. In the middle of the deck was a large brass binnacle, with a large ship's wheel attached to its brass tackle box. A large desk stood on the starboard side of the binnacle and the ship's wheel, upon which a thick stack of navigational charts sat. A fully uniformed officer sat on a stool at the table. Captain Vermie introduced him to his guest as *Neustria's* navigation officer, Chimel Standite. "This man is responsible for getting us to America," Captain Vermie said. "He knows the Atlantic well and will help us make a safe crossing."

Standite observed Antonio's curiosity as his young eyes scanned the charts and brass instruments on the table. "Parlez vous Francais?" Standite asked.

"Oui, but I have been instructed to only speak English, since I am going to America," Antonio replied. "Do you speak English?"

"Yes, I do," Standite responded. "Do you know what I am doing?"

Antonio shook his head. "I am plotting our course from Palermo to New Orleans, America. The world has invisible numbers around the globe, called longitude and latitude. We use those numbers and a compass to find our way around the world. Look, our course will take us from Palermo to Gibraltar," Standite said, using a two-pointed instrument he flipped through his fingers. "We will sail west, which is two hundred and seventy degrees on the compass. Once we pass through the Strait of Gibraltar, we will change course to two hundred and forty-one degrees, which is southwest, and remain on that course until we reach Florida, America. Then we sail west again through the Strait of Florida, and then northwest at three hundred and twenty-five degrees, until we reach the mouth of the Mississippi River. Once there, we just follow the river for about ninety miles and find New Orleans. Sounds simple, right?"

Antonio beamed a big smile and nodded, with an excited sparkle in his eyes.

"How old are you, Antonio?" Standite asked.

Father Fontebuis interrupted and said, "Today is his birthday. He is sixteen."

"Fabulous," Captain Vermie said. "I will have a cook bake a cake, and we will celebrate in the dining room tonight. Follow me and I will show you our spacious dining room. We are immensely proud of it. It's our library, too."

As Captain Vermie and his guests left the bridge, Mr. Standite invited Antonio to come to the bridge anytime to learn geometry and navigation. Antonio beamed a smile and nodded. On his way to the dining room, however, Antonio's dulcet visage changed when he saw a single file of immigrants shuffling along the main deck and descending a metal ship's ladder into a dark hole. He stopped, as a surge of guilt coursed through his body. He tugged on Captain Vermie's cuff and asked, "Sir, where are those people going?"

"They are going to their berths. It's called steerage. Single men are separated from married men with wives and children. Single women are separated and berthed near the front of the ship. They are allowed to go to the main and promenade decks but are restricted from roaming the ship without permission from a crew member," Vermie said.

"Will they be able to wash their clothes and eat well?" Father Fontebuis asked.

"Yes. Once we sail, everyone will be given new clothes donated by the people of Paris and the nuns in Marseille. The plight of the Sicilians is well known in France. We have wash tubs on the ship's fantail, and they will eat the same food as we do, but on the decks, not in the dining room. Father, will you say Mass for them?"

"Of course. Everyday. Where would be the best place to set up an altar?"

"The aft main deck. It will be less windy there. And I have a surprise for you. Our galley has a small oven, which can bake unleavened bread. The nuns gave us two sacks of flour for our voyage. So, if they want, everyone can receive communion," Vermie said.

"Excuse me, Captain," Antonio said. May I go down to the steerage to visit a friend?"

"Yes. But he cannot go with you to your stateroom. It's the rules."

"I understand."

><

10:00 A.M.

After touring the ship, Captain Vermie escorted the priests and Antonio to their stateroom. There, they bid Colonel Salvani goodbye. Everybody hugged each other, silently knowing they would never see him again. Each expressed their gratitude for the *Carabinieri's* protection. Antonio felt that familiar pang of loneliness, which accompanies a farewell, but drew a deep breath of courage and visualized his horizons.

Once inside the stateroom, Father Fontebuis gave Antonio a copy of Charles Dickens' *Great Expectations* and instructed him to sit at a desk and copy the first chapter, underlining all the English words he didn't understand. "I pulled this book off the shelf in the dining room. It's the best book you could read on our voyage. It was written in 1861 by the great English author, Charles Dickens. I want you to pay attention to its vocabulary and the sentence structure of his work. Don't be intimidated by its size. We have over a month to get through it. And if we are successful, you will have a great appreciation for the English language."

"Thank you, Father. You want me to write every word I don't understand?"

"Yes, then we will look up the word in our English dictionary after dinner each night. I read the book a long time ago. So, it will help both of us—maybe Father Consere, too. We all must master English."

Antonio smiled, nodded, opened his suitcase, and removed a tablet of writing paper, his nibbed pen, and a vial of black ink. Father Fontebuis opened both portholes and the door to the stateroom to capture any cross breeze flowing through the ship. After Antonio sat at one of the desks, Father Fontebuis and Consere left the stateroom and went to the steerage section of the ship to minister to the needs of the other passengers.

><

1:00 P.M.

After Antonio scrawled another unfamiliar word on his tablet, he stood, stretched, and yawned. He gazed upon his work and counted twenty new words he must learn. But for the most part, he understood the first chapter of this classic work about an orphan. Filled with a sense of pride, but very hungry, he walked to the dining room to search for food. Since Fathers Fontebuis and Consere were still in steerage, Antonio began to explore the ship.

When he arrived at the dining room, only two other men were sitting at a table, near the starboard side. They stopped talking when they saw him, but locked their eyes on his every move. Antonio found biscuits, butter, a jar of molasses, and a silver pitcher of cold water on an oak sideboard. As the hungry boy stuffed his face with biscuits, he became aware of the glare of the two men across the room. As Antonio enjoyed his late lunch, one of the men, tall, with a dark reddish complexion, hollow cheeks, and a large bushy mustache, dressed in a gray suit, with a white shirt and an open collar, approached him. In Italian, he asked if Antonio was traveling alone. Antonio shook his head, and the man returned to his table. After gorging himself on four buttered and molasses biscuits, Antonio scampered out of the dining room and went to the bridge to see Mr. Standite.

"Hello, Mr. Standite," Antonio said.

"Good afternoon, Antonio. How are you? Are you hungry?"

"No, sir. I just ate some biscuits in the dining room."

"Oh no. You need more than that. You are a growing young man, and need nourishment," Standite said, gesturing to a steward to bring a tray of fruit water to his navigation table. "I'm hungry, too. Plotting our passage has given me an appetite."

Antonio crawled up on a stool next to Standite and examined the charts. He also noticed the *Neustria* still moored at the Palermo docks, while cargo and people crossed the gangplanks to the ship. "What time do we leave, Mr. Standite?"

"Judging from the line of people still on the dock, I would say in about an hour," Standite said. "If so, we should pass through the Strait of Gibraltar about midnight, under sail and steam."

"This ship has sails, too?" Antonio asked.

"Yes, we can make about ten knots in the Mediterranean, but once we cross into the Atlantic, the seas will slow us down slightly," Standite said, pointing to the charts.

When the steward arrived with a silver tray of fruits and nuts, Antonio reached for a helping, but Standite grabbed his wrist. "Antonio, your fingers are black with ink. Have you been writing something?"

"My studies, Father Fontebuis assigned me."

"Come with me," Standite said, leading Antonio to a tiny lavatory to scrub his hands. When they returned to the navigation table, Standite opened a drawer and handed Antonio a new ten-inch-long red navigational pencil. "Here, use this for your studies. The rubber plug on the end is the eraser. You make a mistake, rub the eraser over the mistake, and it disappears—like magic."

A wide-eyed Antonio thanked Standite in three languages—Italian, French, and English. "Excellent, Antonio. Plug your inkwell and use the pencil if we hit rough seas. We only use ink for the ship's log, and when the seas are calm. Here, write something on the chart and erase it. Come back when the point gets dull, and I will sharpen it."

Before Antonio could write anything, Father Fontebuis and Consere raced onto the bridge. They were breathless and in a state of frenzy. Their eyes darted around the bridge, looking for Captain Vermie. "Where is the captain?" Father Fontebuis panted.

"He's in his office. I will get him for you," Standite said.

Father Fontebuis grabbed Antonio's shoulders and said, "I have been looking for you. You left our state-room door open. I thought something happened to you."

"I'm sorry, Father. I was hungry and went looking for food."

"It's okay, but you must be careful. You are not in a little mountain village anymore. And where we are going may present new challenges for us all. So be careful, and don't talk to strangers on this ship."

"Yes, Father."

Mr. Standite and Captain Vermie returned to the bridge, whereupon Father Fontebuis gestured for them to join him on the starboard side. "Stay here, Antonio, while I speak with the captain."

Antonio nodded and started to doodle on some paper next to the charts. On the bridge, Father Fontebuis told Captain Vermie, "I was just approached by two men standing near the dining room. They asked me to sell Antonio to them. Who are these men? Can we force them to leave the ship? Are they *Padrone*?"

Captain Vermie and Mr. Standite became visibly agitated and started cursing in French. "We can't let Antonio know this. He's been through too much in his short life," Father Fontebuis said. "Are they *Padrone*?"

"Probably, or worse. But don't worry, Fathers. Antonio is safe. Colonel Salvani has two of his men on this ship, lodged down the hall from you. I will alert them. Please write down what they looked like and what they were wearing. It's been my experience that these types never finish the voyage. Sorry, Fathers, but the sea has its own rules, which the land will never understand."

><

3:30 P.M.

Captain Vermie stood on the starboard flying bridge and barked orders through his megaphone to the deckhands below. "Cast off all lines and prepare to sail," he yelled. First Officer Calais Berot reported to Vermie there was sufficient steam pressure in the compound engine to generate enough revolutions on the shaft and turn the single screw to propel the ship. Vermie gazed at the ship's funnel and gave a satisfied nod to the billowing black smoke flowing into the azure sky.

"Telegraph the engine room to give us more revolutions to pull us away from the dock, Mr. Berot."

Berot cranked the ship's telegraph to "slow," and a loud metallic clank reverberated through the ship, accompanied by a sudden lurch forward. Vermie then ordered the helmsman to turn the ship's wheel hard to starboard, and the *Neustria's* bow swung past the jetties and out to the blue waters of the Tyrrhenian Sea.

As the ship left port, Fathers Consere, Fontebuis, and Antonio Terranova descended a ship's ladder from the dining room to the fantail deck of the ship. There, they were joined by a crowd of other immigrants stuffed shoulder-to-shoulder to watch the ship's single screw churn the blue sea waters into an iridescent display of hues, unknown to most of them, including Antonio. As the *Neustria* left the Tyrrhenian and entered the choppy waves of the Mediterranean, the water became a darker blue, which enhanced the western-descending sun's bronze dance upon the ship's roiling wake. Antonio stood on his toes to watch the ship cut through the tossing waves, but his new experiences were stabbed by Sicily's Mount Pellegrino shrinking on the eastern horizon. While his eyes welled with tears, he gulped a breath of fresh salty air and sighed hopefully as Sicily slipped beneath the horizon.

Chapter 18

Central Police Station
New Orleans, Louisiana
August 18, 1899
10:30 A.M.

Algernon Badger slid down his carriage seat and tethered his horse to the ring of a black-iron hitching post a few yards away from the front steps of the Central Police Station. Using his cane, he walked up the front steps and entered the building's vestibule. The center hallway was covered with long strands of black wire, which workers were pulling from a large wooden spool attached to a mule-drawn wagon, parked in the rear of the police station. A man, with a large set of scissor-like cutters, was measuring one-hundred-foot segments and cutting them before tacking them to the oak moldings of the various offices. Badger carefully walked over the wire and up the stairs to David Hennessy's office. Since his visit was unplanned, Badger's presence stunned Hennessy's secretary, George W. Van Dervoort, who was testing his new typewriter.

"Oh, General, I didn't know you were coming. Did I miss recording your appointment?"

"No, George. This is an unannounced visit. Is the Chief available to talk?"

"Of course. Please go in."

Badger knocked on Hennessy's door and admitted himself, whereupon the young chief warmly greeted him. "General, what brings you here on such a hot morning?"

"We need to talk about our friends on the docks. By the way, what's going on with all the wiring and hammering?"

"We are getting a new telephone system installed. Soon, we will have the ability to talk to other police departments, as well as telegraphing them. My new number is going to be three hundred. Do you have a telephone?"

"Yes, but I hardly use it. My number is 847. When you get ready, call me. It might make these hot trips from the Custom House to the police station unnecessary. But I always like to look at a man when I talk to him."

"Same here, General. Now, what's this about our friends on the docks?" Hennessy asked.

Badger was about to tell him when a large map of New Orleans hanging on the wall drew his attention. The city streets and squares were described accurately, but the map was festooned with red dots. "What does that map mean, David?"

"That's the new location for the police call boxes. When ready, people will be able to call a switchboard downstairs, and we can send an officer from the nearest precinct. Each red dot represents a call box location. I mapped them myself. Take a look. Do you agree with my placements?"

After a few moments, Badger examined the map, turned toward Hennessy, and said, "David, you're thinking more like a cop than a politician."

"What do you mean?"

"David, the placements look great. If you were a war general, positioning troops. But you are the police chief in a city where everyone thinks they are important, especially the ones who want you replaced. Who lives at Number 616 Carondelet Street?"

"The mayor."

"There are no call boxes near his residence. Why?"

"Because the people in that neighborhood can afford their own telephones."

"You are missing my point. Put a call box at the corner of Euterpe and Carondelet. And then tell the mayor it's for his protection. He might never use it, but it's a sign of homage to the man who appointed you. Then get the addresses of each city councilman and judge. Put one near their homes. Tell them the same thing. You will accrete great favor among the ruling class of this city, which might inure to your benefit one day."

"I guess I'm not a very good politician."

"No, you're not. But you can learn the art of feigned honor and respect, as much as they have. Politics is the art of human insincerity," Badger asserted. "Learn it well, and it will advance your career. And you have to smile more, especially in public. A smile from the police chief means all is well, even when all is a dung heap. Strategic deception has carried many a man a long way in this world, especially in a city like New Orleans, where deception is valued more than truth. You must learn to absorb the culture of this city to survive. Coming from Massachusetts, I had to learn an entirely new way of navigating people, and this city is filled with reefs and shoals; a man can run aground very easily."

Hennessy studied the map pensively, tapping his red pencil against his bushy mustache. "I have a great deal to learn, General. Thank you for opening my eyes."

"Speaking of opening your eyes, we must get our friends to have a peace settlement before the fall harvest of cotton descends the river. Those silk-ass bastards at the Cotton Exchange want their commodities unloaded and shipped to England with great dispatch. Matranga and Provenzano must be made aware that their feud is costing this city money, which can only result in them losing their businesses. We don't need another 1874."

"Why us, General?" Hennessy asked.

"David, now is a good time to think like a peace-making politician, not a beat cop. You and I are in unique positions to control the actions of that port. I control the commerce, to an extent, and you control the people. We both know the men who are responsible for moving cargo on the docks. They know us. We must exploit those relationships, for if we don't, we will have another war, and it won't start on Canal Street, but on the docks. Now, stuff that handsome head of yours in your bowler, and let's take a ride."

"You want me to talk to Provenzano?" Hennessy asked.

"Yes, while I talk to Macheca. We have a month before those steamboats arrive at the docks. We have to make sure the bales get from those steamboats, pressed, and onto the steamships. I know maritime commerce is not part of your job, but if our negotiations fail, it will be your job to deal with the consequences."

><

Hennessy helped Badger into his carriage and walked around to the front of Badger's horse. He noticed a gooey sheet of saliva dripping from the beast's mouth. Hennessy also noticed a thick froth of sweat under the horse's collar, which streamed from its withers. "General, we need to water your horse soon."

"I'll tie him in front of Jackson Square. There's a water trough there and a shade tree. That's where I usually park my carriage when I visit the docks."

Hennessy climbed into the carriage and removed his jacket, revealing his silver star-and-crescent badge, pinned to his white shirt, and his nickel-plated, breech-break, Smith and Wesson .38 caliber revolver, tucked in a black leather holster. "New pistol, David?" Badger asked.

"Yes. It cost forty-five dollars, and I haven't shot it yet. I need to go out to Milneburg and practice."

"Well, given your prowess with a gun, you won't have to practice much."

Hennessy was slightly stunned by the Badger's response, not knowing if it was a compliment or a reminder that he had killed Thomas Devereaux several years earlier. Hennessy decided to let the comment pass, as Badger directed his horse towards Canal Street. When Badger reached the corner of Canal and St. Charles, he stopped the carriage near a Cuban cigar shop. "I'm a little short on cigars. Do you want me to buy you any?" Badger asked.

"No, thank you. It's too damn hot to smoke, General. Besides, I don't smoke."

"That's right. You don't drink either. How about ladies, David?"

"When the right one comes along. But now, I must take care of my mother."

Badger stepped down from the carriage and hobbled into the cigar shop, leaving Hennessy alone in the carriage with his thoughts. The intersection was very busy with long-dressed ladies carrying open parasols, businessmen, legless Civil War veterans begging near the large granite base of the Henry Clay Monument, and mule-drawn street cars circling the monument. A brown-tinged cloud of dirt, dust, and street matter hovered about two feet above the cobblestoned intersection, layering the city's central meeting spot with a choking, dingy fog. Hennessy cast his eyes upon the face of the bronzed Clay and hoped the "Great Compromiser" would attend his upcoming meetings.

Badger returned to the carriage, settled in his seat, bit the end of a cigar, and spit the plug of tobacco into the street. He scraped a match on the sole of his boot and puffed life into the cigar. Hennessy watched this ritual and noticed streams of sweat rolling down Badger's jawline. Hennessy said nothing but understood the inner toughness of a focused survivor.

Badger snapped the reins against his horse's lathered back and proceeded to an area of the docks known as the Picayune Tier, which ran several squares between Decatur Street and the Mississippi River. The Tier was the aorta of maritime commerce in New Orleans, which facilitated loading and unloading all types of cargo, mostly cotton. The area bustled with all types of movement of men, push carts, and drayage wagons. Everywhere one looked, there was movement choreographed for New Orleans' survival. To encourage the relentless movement of cargo, the city installed a fifty-foot carbon-light tower on the Tier to facilitate stevedoring into the night.

As Badger and Hennessy reached the intersection of Bienville and Decatur Streets, they noticed a circle of men standing around an object on the ground. At first, Hennessy thought it was another murder, but as they approached, they saw a dead mule lying on the packed mud. Badger and Hennessy dismounted the carriage and pushed their way through the crowd. The dead mule, still harnessed to a drayage wagon, laden with large barrels of molasses and lemons, was already attracting flies. Its dead tongue draped from its mouth, while its lifeless eyes stared into the dirt.

"Whose mule is this?" Hennessy yelled. The driver of the wagon said nothing. Hennessy climbed up the wagon and grabbed the driver by his sweaty collar. "Who owns this mule and wagon?"

The driver began to shiver with fear and pointed to a man standing in the crowd.

"The mule and wagon are mine, but the cargo belongs to Joseph Macheca," the man said.

Hennessy jumped down from the wagon and approached the man, who was several inches shorter than the chief. "What's your name?" Hennessy asked.

"Joseph Giacomino. I have a drayage service at 234 Decatur Street, and I live at 624 St. Philip Street. I am an American."

Hennessey began to pace in anger, but composed himself for a moment. "This mule died of exhaustion and thirst, Mr. Giacomino. When a draft animal dies on the docks, it stops commerce on the docks. You must take care of your animals as much as your men."

Giacomino nodded. "Now, someone get another mule and pull this wagon to market. Then someone get another mule and wagon, and drag this poor beast to the swamp for disposal," Hennessy ordered.

The circle of men scampered around the Tier, while others began to unhitch the dead mule from the wagon. Hennessy approached Giacomino and was about to continue his tirade, but he noticed a tear dripping from the little Italian's eye. Hennessy drew a deep breath and said, "Mr. Giacomino, do you have another mule to work the docks?"

"I only have one left, and it's working down the Tier. If it dies, I am out of business."

"Go make sure it's watered. The people who operate these docks must build more water troughs for these animals," Hennessy said, as he walked back to Badger's carriage.

After climbing into the carriage, Badger and Hennessy rolled down Decatur Street to the intersection of St. Peter. There, they found a young black man enjoying a nap under the shade of an oak tree. Badger kicked the man's boot and aroused him from his dreams. "What's your name?" Badger asked.

"They call me John T., sir."

"Well, John T., if you water my horse and feed him while I am gone, I will give you a dollar. And if you do it well, I will give you another dollar when I return."

A wide grin sliced across John T.'s face, and he agreed. "You will find a water bucket and a sack of oats under the carriage seat. We will be back in an hour. Take care of my horse."

"Yes, sir. What's your name, sir?"

"I am General Badger, and this is police chief Hennessy?"

John T. stiffened with fear and respect. He saw Hennessy's badge and gun. "No problem, General. I'll take good care of your horse."

"Thank you, John T.," Badger said, flipping a silver dollar to the young man.

Badger and Hennessy walked to the corner and stopped. Hennessy whispered in Badger's ear, "That's probably the most money John T. has ever held in his hand at one time. You are very generous, General."

"After watching you talk to Mr. Giacomino, I realized life in this city is very tenuous and temporary. That blazing sun burns us all—beast and man. We are all equal, and death is the great equalizer. From man to mule, our shadows upon the ground are as temporary as the breath in our lungs." Badger drew a last puff on his cigar, and tossed the butt into the wide, deep gutter.

"I am looking forward to making John T. richer when we return. His smile and Giacomino's tear, only a few hundred yards apart, tell me no one is expendable. Come to think of it, David, we all live somewhere between a smile and a tear, which are the borders of our existence. Now, with that in mind, we must try and achieve some peace here or prepare ourselves for the flow of blood."

"I'll go see Provenzano?" Hennessy said.

"No. I changed my mind. I want you to come with me to see Macheca. I don't want you to be seen around Provenzano. Let's see if Macheca will be willing to broker a meeting. After all, he needs both Matranga and Provenzano to unload his ships. His blood, cards, and chips are on the table, too."

><

Badger and Hennessy walked down Decatur Street, doffing their hats to ladies who were brave enough to shop during the midday heat. Many merchants, seeing Hennessy with his jacket slung over his shoulder, exposing this badge and silver gun, stopped and gawked. Even children playing under the green-canvased market stalls stopped and whispered to each other. "I can feel their eyes burning through me," Hennessy told Badger, as he slowed his lanky gait to accommodate Badger's limp.

"And I thought they were looking at me," Badger quipped. "Just smile and be pleasant. They will remember every gesture you make and interpret it as friendly or intimidating. You are now in the heart of the Italian Colony of New Orleans, and your presence here will be discussed in many dialects for days. They know who you are. No need to prove it."

Both men maintained a dulcet countenance as they walked to a red brick building at 129 Decatur Street, with a blue and white sign hanging from its upper gallery, which read, *Macheca Brothers & Company.* Near the front door, a small brass sign read, *J.P. Macheca, Bolivian Consulate.* "What does that mean?" Hennessy asked, pointing to the brass sign.

"Since before the battle on Canal Street in '74, J.P. always wanted to be somebody. He has worked hard to burnish his image, and it wasn't until he saved my ass, he enjoyed the society of men, who now hate him and the other Italians. You know who they are. Even his brothers, who have their own problems, try to avoid him, but the shipping business is doing well, and members of the family seem content. Don't try to understand the relationships down here. One day they love each other—the next they're killing each other. Their blood boils close to the surface. Loyalties are conditional and grudges endure centuries."

"And people complain about the Irish," Hennessy said.

"Believe it or not, there are some similarities between the two people, which make them formidable foes, if you cross them, as you know."

Their attention was drawn by a small Italian man dragging a shovel down Decatur Street with his left hand, while pushing a cart carrying a large wooden barrel with his right. The barrel was so heavy that the little man, dressed in old, soiled dungarees and a slouch hat, struggled. Badger and Hennessey stood still and watched the man scrape and scoop the filth from the bottom of the gutter to allow the free flow of rainwater, which usually accompanies hot August afternoons. Repeatedly, the man, oblivious to the police chief's presence, scooped the muck from the gutter and dumped it into the barrel, and dutifully moved down the street.

"You see that little man, David? He is at the bottom of society's social ladder, but toils his way down the street. These gutters were dug by Negroes and Shanty Irish, and now you're the Superintendent of Police. Now, the Italians are at the bottom, and they are working on being accepted by New Orleans' rigid society. They might never get acceptance, but can live comfortably with tolerance."

"Have they accepted me or do they tolerate me?" Hennessy asked.

"Tolerate. Your position, like mine, is temporary, as is everything in life. The problem with the faux royalty of this city is that they think their positions are permanent. When they are finished with you, they will dump you like that dead mule. Sorry to be so blunt, son. But, as I told you before, that's New Orleans."

Hennessy said nothing and followed Badger as he climbed a long, winding wooden staircase. *Clop, thud, click* announced Badger's ascent up the stairs to Macheca's office. The noise echoed throughout the 1834-built building, and aroused Macheca to look over the banister to see who or what was making that noise.

"Well, I be damned. What brings you two to the working side of New Orleans?" Macheca asked.

Badger paused, looked up, and said, "J.P., do you have some water you can spare?"

"Sure. It's cistern water, not the fancy stuff you are accustomed to."

"We'll gratefully accept it," Badger said, reaching the top of the stairs.

Macheca gave Hennessy a hard, flinty look. "I see you brought your friend with you. Am I in trouble?" Macheca asked.

"No. We are here to ask you for a favor," Badger said.

"Me? A favor? I got to hear this. Come into my office and rest a while," Macheca said, pouring two glasses of water. "Now, what kind of favor do you need, General?"

Badger took a long gulp of water and said, "We need you to broker a peace meeting between Matranga and Provenzano."

Macheca sat behind his desk and laughed. "Are you serious? Those guys hate me as much as they hate each other. I give them business, and they leave me alone. But soon I might be causing more problems, because I am unhappy with Provenzano's stevedores. They're lazy and careless. They're costing me money every day."

"Don't do anything, yet," Badger said. "We need peace on the docks, or I fear the city will take over everything down here, regarding shipping and cargo. Then everyone loses."

Macheca stood and went to three very large windows facing the Picayune Tier, hoping to catch any breeze from a darkening sky approaching from the southeast. Dressed in brown trousers, matching vest, and white shirt, Macheca unfastened his starched high collar from his shirt and placed it on a table by the window. "I hope you don't mind me getting comfortable, but I feel this conversation will take a while. What's going on, General?"

"The gentlemen at the Cotton Exchange are not happy with the pace at which the stevedores are moving their cargo. Neither is the Sugar Exchange, whose membership has allied with the Cotton Exchange. If things don't improve down here, I fear a takeover. And the mayor is behind the move."

"Why do you care? The government will get paid regardless of who controls the docks. And why me? I don't operate stevedores. I ship citrus products from South and Central America to New Orleans, and then up the river."

"If there is a takeover of the docks by the city, the state, or a chosen few, everyone down here will suffer. Do you think your citrus cargo will be unloaded for the market? Who will set the prices? Cotton and molasses will come first, J.P., and you ship molasses from the sugar plantations. They will take your business. Your ships coming from South America will sit at anchorage until they make space for you to dock, if you have ships. You need the stevedores to move your cargo, and right now, despite this feud, you can still talk to Matranga and Provenzano. You are the perfect person to broker a peace. Besides, just about half an hour ago, one of your citrus ships lost a drayage mule on the Tier. That dead mule will delay the movement of your cargo as much as lazy stevedores. I'm returning the favor for saving my life."

Macheca nodded and asked, "Giacomino lost another mule? That poor bastard is trying so hard to make it. I'll get him another one. I also spoke to Salvatore Oteri this morning, and he isn't happy with Provenzano either. He thinks his cargo is being pilfered by Provenzano's men."

"Pilfering is a way of life on the docks. Tell Oteri not to do anything now. Wait. Keep the peace. We need Matranga and Provenzano to sit down with us and resolve their differences, or the Cotton Exchange will resolve them, and everybody loses. And to answer your other question, I know the government will get paid, but a dock war will interrupt commerce and probably invite the city or Washington to take over the docks. It will be 1874 again. The same people who started that insurrection control the city and the Cotton Exchange. They want control of the docks, the prices, and the markets. If they are willing to start a war on Canal Street in 1874, they'll start one on Decatur Street in 1890," Badger said.

"Do you really believe they will take over the docks?" Macheca asked.

"J.P., wake up!" Badger yelled. "Don't be so stubborn. We are both old enough to remember 1874. Look at my leg. I feel the same forces are gathering now, as they did then, to take over the governor's office. Most of those bastards are still alive, like us. Fifteen years ago, they felt they were losing their city to the Republicans, and the growing Negro vote. Now, they believe they are losing money, because the Italians and the Negroes are controlling the commerce of this city. And you and Frank Romero are growing a voting block among the negro and the Italians. Shakspeare still blames the Italians and Negroes for losing the mayor's election in 1882."

"It was the Ring who defeated him in 1882, and they still hate him. He beat their candidate last year with sixty-seven percent of the vote."

"And who comprised thirty-three percent of the vote last year?" Badger asked. "It was the Italians and the Negroes. And Houston and Parkinson know this. Shakspeare has successfully created a bond between The Ring and Parkerson's Regulators. They now have a common interest —the docks and the markets."

"Shakspeare is not liked on this side of Canal Street and never will be. He's a pompous ass. Sorry, Chief Hennessy, for speaking badly about your boss, but he's also corrupt and you know it." Macheca said.

"What do you mean, Mr. Macheca?" Hennessy probed.

"You know damn well what I mean. He had your police department and his Parkerson's Regulators raid over sixty casinos owned by the Ring members. He has extorted them out of business, while others, owned by his supporters, are allowed to stay in business. Hell, we know that some of his best friends are customers at those brothels, and you do nothing about it. He calls it the *Shakspeare Plan*."

"That's not true," Hennessy fumed.

"It is true. Have you closed down any of Tom Anderson's joints, yet?"

Hennessy didn't respond.

Macheca seized the moment. "Look at General Badger's leg, Chief. You were a kid hiding in the Customhouse when your boss's friends tried to kill one police chief, and I saved him. Better be careful you're not the next one."

Badger stood and leaned on his cane. "Hold on, J.P., I am here to return that favor and keep you in business. There's no need to alarm David. He's doing a good job, under challenging circumstances. He has to walk a fine line between the mayor's enemies and his own, while trying to reform the police department, which is creating *more* enemies."

"I have my enemies, too," Macheca said, opening his desk drawer. "Look at this," he said, handing a crumpled piece of white paper to Badger.

Badger and Hennessy looked at the paper. On the page were two crude drawings: one of a skull with a dagger plunged through it, and another of a black open hand.

"What is this? I can't read Italian," Badger said.

"It's an extortion note—the Black Hand or *Mano Nera*, as it's called down here. They want me to pay them five hundred dollars, or they will blow up one of my boats. So, you see, Shakspeare has his plan and the *Stuppagghieri or Giardinieri* have theirs. Extortion is extortion. The result is the same," Macheca said.

"Are you going to pay them?" Hennessy asked.

"I will give them fifty dollars, and they will go away for a month or two. So, Mr. Hennessy, ask your boss if I were in the *Mafia*, why would I extort myself? I am trying to make a straight living in a crooked city. Maybe Giacomino's mule didn't die of the heat. Strange things happen on the docks. Every day, I expect to be done up by some brigand who wants to make a name for himself. Fear is the duty we all pay to live and work in New Orleans. I pay it and you pay it."

"J.P., are you willing to broker a meeting, or are we wasting our time?" Badger persisted.

Macheca looked out his office window and gazed at the many boats, luggers, and ships docked along the river. As an ominous thunderstorm clouds gathered over the mighty bend of the Mississippi, the wind blew, and the sky seemed streaked by the black serpentine exhaust of the vessels' coal-fired boilers. Dock workers scurried about the docks, covering vulnerable cargo with canvas tarpaulins. The advancing wind filled Macheca's office with the scent of damp ozone, as sheets of rain began to wash over Decatur Street and the docks. After pulling his large windows down several inches to prevent the rain from blowing into his office, Macheca turned and asked, "Do I have a choice?"

"No," Badger said, "Now, let's sit down and wait out this storm."

Macheca flopped in his chair, mindful of Badger's symbolic words.

Chapter 19

SS Neustria

78° West Longitude, 32° North Latitude

September 5, 1889

5:45 P.M.

After the ship's galley steward cleared their dinner table, Father Fontebuis and Consere began to pepper Antonio with questions about *Great Expectations*, from vocabulary to reading comprehension. Earlier that day, Father Fontebuis gave Antonio a list of one hundred words and asked him to define them in English, while Father Consere asked him to pronounce them, without an Italian accent. Both priests were amazed at how far their student had advanced since sailing from Palermo. Even his conjugation of English subjects and verbs stunned them, as did his knowledge of math, courtesy of Mr. Standite, the ship's navigator.

"Antonio, you are an amazing and dedicated student," Father Fontebuis said, clapping his hands. "Your diction is improving, and soon Americans will understand you well. Keep studying. It appears we have another week before we land in New Orleans. The English language has many expressions that mean the same thing and many words that sound alike but mean different things. Keep your sentences and questions short and to the point. Understand?"

"Yes, Father. May I go outside and walk on the deck while there is still daylight?"

"Excellent question and use of the English language. Very polite, too. Yes, you may go, but the sky looks ominous, and it will likely rain. The sea is getting rough, too. Look at the white caps lacing the top of the waves. Did you understand what I said?"

"Yes."

"What does ominous mean?"

"It means scary?"

"Close enough. Go outside and fill your lungs with some fresh salty air, but return to our cabin, if it gets too rough," Father Fontebuis cautioned.

Antonio nodded, left the dining room through its aft door, and descended the steps to the main deck of the *Neustria*. A large group of steerage passengers hung onto the rail as the wind blew against them. The ship heaved with each swell. To the west, the horizon beamed the golden glow of the setting sun, while dark gray clouds streaked through its radiance, refracting its glow into shafts of sunlight against the ocean's choppy horizon. To the east, the sky was black and yielded a strong wind, blowing stinging seawater drops against the passengers' faces. The passengers braved the conditions, as it was better than the stifling air of steerage.

Since he couldn't find a place at the rail, Antonio walked forward on the port deck, listening to the wind sing through the shroud lines and the ship's two billowing sails. As he passed the ship's modest superstructure, he noticed Asperi Marchesi sitting on the forward hatch cover with two girls. As he approached, the two girls saw him and dashed away.

"Grazie, Antonio. I was just about to get their names," Asperi said.

"Sorry. I see you speak English," Antonio said.

"Yes, your priests are teaching all of us English, while you study in your cabin, during the day."

Antonio smiled and asked, "Why did the girls run away?"

"Because they believe you are a seminarian and belong to God. That's why you study alone. They believe it would be sinful to talk to a boy pledged to God. Are you really a seminarian?" Asperi asked.

Antonio paused and cast his eyes to the east. "I know who you are," Asperi said. "It's okay. I am running from Sicily, too. My real last name is Grimando. My father and I are fugitives, too. The army was going to conscript me. My father told them I was too young, and he got into a fight with an officer and stabbed him. Like you, a parish priest gave us new names and church papers. The only money we had was spent on the passage to America. We know about what happened in Bisacquino. You were right to defend your father."

Antonio began to wonder if Asperi would betray him, but given that he had betrayed himself, he determined he could trust the younger, and seemingly wiser boy. "Where are you from, again?" Antonio asked.

"We are from Cefalu. The army was moving south and taking every teenage boy into the army, and the land. If you had not escaped, the army would have taken you and part of your father's land. Cascioferro's men would have taken the rest. We did the right thing, leaving Sicily. Maybe we can buy back our land when we make enough money in America."

"You think?"

"Sure. My father told me that some people on this ship are going to America for just a few years to make enough money to repurchase their land."

"Won't you still be a fugitive?" Antonio asked.

"Yes, but they will look for Asperi Grimando, not Marchesi. Besides, we will buy land in another part of Sicily or Calabria."

The wind began to howl and moan. Antonio noticed the bow of the ship taking a sharp starboard shift to the west and then the northwest. Two crew members warn the boys to return to their quarters before climbing the mast and retracting the sails.

"What's happening?" Antonio screamed up to the crewman.

The crew member yelled in English. "Hurricane. "We are going to circle it. Go now."

Asperi ran to the ladder leading to the steerage, while Antonio wobbled back to the aft stairway leading to the dining room. Since the blackened sky had overtaken the ship, the main deck was slippery and dark. The waves mercilessly cast the Neustria side-to-side, causing Antonio to slip headlong down the deck towards the fantail. The rain pelted his eyes. He rubbed them to find the ladder to the dining room. The peasant boy was alone on the pitching deck, clutching anything to avoid being hurled overboard.

As he stood and braced himself against a bulkhead, two men grabbed Antonio and dragged him toward the aft rail. Antonio yelled, but the howling wind muffled his screams. He kicked his legs. One of the men punched him in the stomach. Antonio fought hard, torquing and twisting his body, but the two men had overpowered him. He craned his neck and saw the men carrying him towards the top of the aft rail. As they got to the rail, Antonio kicked the rail with all his might and pushed the men backwards. He twisted his body to break their grip. As he fell to the deck, he heard four muffled shots and saw his captors fall to the deck. He looked up and saw two other men tucking pistols inside their coat pockets.

"Don't move," one of the men ordered Antonio. Every muscle in Antonio's body stiffened as he watched the two armed men toss his captors overboard into the stormy waters of the Atlantic Ocean. "Get up and return to your cabin," one man ordered. "And don't tell anyone what you saw. Compliments of Colonel Salvani," the man said. Antonio did precisely what the man said and bounded up the stairs to the dining room. In the dining room, he found an open bottle of wine and took several gulps to calm his nerves. His heart pounded through his chest as he recalled his imminent death and his lethal rescue. The ship's gimbaled lanterns began to sway. Antonio, again, felt death's grip as the ocean waves crashed against the dining room windows. Resigned to his fate, he flipped the bottle of wine up and drained it in one massive gulp. *"Al diavolo al morte!"* he yelled defiantly in Italian.

When he left the dining room and walked down the darkened corridor towards his cabin, since several bulkhead lanterns had failed, his eyes focused on several figures standing outside his cabin door. Father Fontebuis recognized Antonio staggering towards him through the faint light as the *Neustria* rocked and yawed. Antonio said nothing as his eyes darted from Father Fontebuis and Consere to Captain Vermie to Mr. Standite. At their feet was a sobbing young woman hovering over a newborn baby wrapped in a canvas bag.

"What's happening?" Antonio braved in English.

Father Fontebuis cupped his hands around Antonio's face and felt his forehead. "You are freezing," the priest said. "And your clothes are drenched. Go into the cabin and change, before we have another tragedy onboard this ship."

"What happened?" Antonio asked, looking at the young woman and the baby.

"The baby was born dead," Father Fontebuis whispered in Antonio's ear. "I just gave it *Extreme Unction*. Now go inside and change your clothes. Captain Vermie has a job for you. We need you. Now go dry off."

As Antonio turned to go into his cabin, a boatswain's mate appeared with a link to an anchor chain and placed it inside the canvas bag next to the baby. He then took a large wooden fid, some coarse twine, and stitched the bag closed. The mother began to wail louder than the wind. When the boatswain mate handed the bag to Captain Vermie, the mother, her dress still drenched in blood, howled and grabbed the captain's arms. Father Fontebuis and Consere pulled her away and dragged her down the corridor towards the dining room. She pulled and tugged as she watched Captain Vermie and Mr. Standite leave the corridor through the forward door. She knew.

Antonio ran into the cabin and slammed the door. He could still hear the mother's wails and buried his head under his pillow. and began to sob. His body shivered and shook with grief, knowing his life was spared, while an innocent baby was being consigned to the roiling seas and God. In the span of a few minutes, Antonio's turbid thoughts augured through his young mind. His life was threatened, two men were killed, and a baby lost its chance at life, while his mind was sadistically hurled by the flashbacks of his vineyard. He felt ensnared and trapped in his own thoughts. At that moment, he surrendered his future to the next moment, and then the next. If there were to be a next breath, he would take it. If not, he would accept that, too.

Father Fontebuis entered the cabin and found a sobbing Antonio stretched out across his bunk. He sat down next to the boy, patted him on the back, and softly said, "Antonio, let's get you out of these wet clothes. The captain needs your help in the engine room, now. Our ship needs you, now."

"Why me, Father?"

"Because you are brave and strong. He has selected several strong boys to help keep the boiler stoked with coal to maintain enough pressure and steam so that we can sail around the storm. If the ship loses steam, the Captain can't control the ship's direction, and we will sink."

Antonio sat up and wiped his face with his sleeves. He changed his clothes and followed Father Fontebuis to the ship's bridge. When he arrived, Captain Vermie and Mr. Standite sat at the navigation table, sipping cognac, to still their nerves. "Here, Antonio, have a glass. We are all in for a rough night, and I need you," Captain Vermie said. "Go down five decks to the engine room and report to Mr. Ellington. He's English and our engineer. He needs your help to keep our ship sailing and under control. We must maintain pressure in the boiler by feeding all the coal it can take. We also need to keep lubricating all the moving parts of the steam engine. We are going to push everything to its limits, until we sail around this storm. I will pay your passage, like the other boys, if we make it. Our company will honor your service to the survival of the ship and the passengers. Are you willing to do that?"

Antonio took a sip of the cognac and nodded.

Antonio put his empty glass on the navigation table and walked past the telegraph room, where the signal officer received messages from other ships about the storm. He paused and recognized panic on the officer's face.

Antonio braced himself and scampered down the five ladders to the engine room. The deeper he descended the ship's bowels, the hotter it got. As he opened the iron passageway into the engine room, he slammed into a wall of hot dry air and a cacophony of clanging, grunting and hissing of the *Neustria's* heart. Except for a few lanterns hanging by hooks, the hellish rooms' only light came from the two open boiler doors. In the flare of the flames, Antonio saw Asperi Marchesi shoveling coal into the mouth of the burning furnace. His shirtless friend was smeared with coal dust, soot, and sweat. Another Sicilian boy stood next to Asperi, trying to catch his breath.

The *Neustria's* engineer, James Ellington, half-naked and covered in dust, grime, and oil, waved to Antonio to join him at the rear of the boiler. "What is your name?" Ellington yelled.

"Antonio."

"Good. Thanks for helping me. My other boys are hurt and sick, and I need help maintaining the boiler and the engine," Ellington yelled.

"Do you want me to shovel coal?" Antonio screamed.

"No. I need you to grease the shaft and gears. Follow me," Ellington said.

Ellington, a tall gray-haired man with a creased face and blue eyes, led Antonio to the main gear assembly at the rear of the boiler. He pointed to a large bucket of thick black grease using hand signals. and a long-handled brush. He picked up the brush and lathered the main drive shaft, attached to the engine's steam pistons, with grease. He bent over and yelled, "We must keep the gears and shaft greased to reduce friction in this heat. Do you understand?"

Antonio nodded.

"Good. Follow me," Ellington said, unhooking a lantern and handing it to Antonio. He walked towards a cave-like structure and stopped. "This is the shaft alley. It is about a hundred feet long. The shaft has four ball-bearing iron collars every twenty-five feet. They must be kept greased when we shift into full speed. You must go down this alley and grease every collar. At the end of the shaft, where it meets the stern's hull, is the last collar and the most important one. It allows the shaft to turn the propeller on the ship. You must keep it greased. If there is too much friction, we will lose power. If that happens, the ship will founder and sink. Do you understand?"

Antonio nodded again.

"Good. Take this brush and bucket and paint the collars with grease.

Go up and down the alley until I tell you to stop. Soon, the Captain will order full speed, and you will see the shaft spin faster. The faster it spins, the more grease the collars will need. Now go into the alley and good luck," Ellington said, patting Antonio on his shoulder. Before Antonio could enter the shaft alley, Ellington grabbed him by his shirt. "Wait," he yelled. "You might want to do this job naked."

Antonio's visage revealed shock. "Why?" he yelled.

"If any part of your clothes gets caught around that spinning shaft or the bearings, it will wrap you around the shaft and trap you or squeeze you to death. We can't stop the ship to free you. Understand?"

Antonio nodded and removed all his clothes. Ellington gave him a canteen of warm water and said, "You must drink it anyway. If not, you will faint in this heat. Understand?"

Antonio nodded and stepped into the shaft alley with the bucket of grease in his left hand and the coal miner's lantern in his right. He wrapped the canteen around his shoulder and neck. At the first gear collar, he lathered the bearings and shaft with the black, thick grease. As the eighteen-inch shaft spun, it splattered Antonio's body with grease.

Each trip down the shaft alley took about twenty minutes before his third trip down the alley. In the dim light of the engine room, he saw more Sicilian boys shoveling coal into the blazing boilers. Asperi was sitting on a pile of coal, breathing deeply. He looked at Antonio's greasy naked body and began to laugh. Antonio shrugged his shoulders, laughed, and waved.

Mr. Ellington approached Antonio and motioned for him to follow him to a small gear, which ran a generator. Ellington yelled, "Put a blob of grease on its gear. This generator runs our navigation lights and the telegraph on the bridge. We need to keep them running. Then go back into the alley and grease those collars. I'm about to kick the engine into full speed. I hope the boiler doesn't blow, but if it does, we won't know it," Ellington said, with a wink.

Antonio stepped into the abyss of the shaft alley. Even in the bleak glow of his lantern, he could tell the shaft was spinning faster. The faster the shaft spun, the more grease Antonio would splash on the bearings. He took a swig of water from his canteen, which his body immediately converted to perspiration, but the suffocating dry heat evaporated every bead of sweat. He felt the ship list to starboard as the shaft spun faster. A deafening rattling vibration shook the ship. Antonio felt the bulkheads were about to buckle. He ran towards the mouth of the alley, where he met Ellington.

"Don't worry. That noise and vibration means the screw is coming out the water, as the ship is turning east. It's normal. We are still at full speed, and the boiler exceeds its pressure capacity. So, get back down the alley and grease those collars."

Antonio took a deep breath, re-entered the alley, and resumed his routine. As he jabbed grease into the third collar, his mind shifted back to his deadly encounter with the men on the aft deck, about two hours earlier. He began to shiver, despite the laboring dry heat. As he moved to the stern collar, he noticed the shaft spinning more slowly, and the ship stopped rolling from side to side. He thought it was his imagination, so he held his lantern closer against the spinning shaft. Even the roar of the engine room, which blew down the alley like a bent bugle, subsided. The shaft continued to spin, but at lower revolutions. Antonio stepped towards the alley's mouth, but his legs weakened. He could not move. He began to shiver and laugh uncontrollably. His naked, oily body slid down the bulkhead as he crumbled into a ball, laughing and shivering, like a warrior after an exhausting battle.

Ellington peered down the shaft alley and saw Antonio's lantern's faint, flickering wick. Armed with his own lantern and a warm, wet blanket, the ship's engineer followed the glow down the alley until he saw Antonio, convulsing and shaking on the filthy, grimy deck. Ellington wrapped the blanket around Antonio and lifted him on his feet. "Come on, lad. Tonight, you earned your passage and the respect of everyone on this ship. Let me clean you up and take you topside for food and well-deserved rest."

"Are we going to die?" Antonio asked.

"Not tonight, lad."

Chapter 20

The Cotton Exchange
New Orleans, Louisiana
September 11, 1889
1:30 P.M.

Colonel Abner Crandall, President of the Great Southern Telephone and Telegraph Company of New Orleans, skipped up the front steps of the Cotton Exchange building to attend a secret meeting with members of the cotton and sugar cane industries. The meeting was scheduled for 2:00 o'clock on the second floor of the ornate building. In 1874, two years after New York City inaugurated its own cotton exchange, far from the cotton fields of the South, New Orleans, to preserve its dominance over the export of cotton and other commodities, commenced its own exchange, which quickly became the commercial nerve center of New Orleans.

Crandall personally oversaw the elaborate installation of the largest telegraph room in Louisiana and was preparing to upgrade the exchange with the newest technology—the telephone. Over twenty telegraph operators in the first-floor room monitored the incessant beeping and clacking of the telegraph keys twenty-four hours a day. Each operator had a specific assignment, which ranged from tracking the news from around the world, the current market price for commodities, Trans-Atlantic cables, the cost of stocks issued from the New York Stock Exchange, and the status of maritime traffic to and from the United States. Each operator worked eight-hour shifts and had two messengers at their disposal to physically deliver telegraph traffic to the intended parties or post messages on a large board in the first-floor meeting room.

Crandall walked among the legions of operators, peering over their shoulders in an attempt to capture the most current news from around the world. When he came upon the operator monitoring the maritime traffic along the Mississippi River and the Gulf of Mexico, Percival McBride, paused, looked at Crandall, and handed him the transcribed message from Morse Code to English. It read:

"SS Neustria feared lost in the Atlantic Ocean. Hurricane. Last message received from the Neustria was on September 5, 1889, at 7:00 P.M. Two hundred miles north of the Bahamas. All efforts to contact the vessel, to no avail. Over four hundred lives feared lost. Ships in area will continue to send messages and search for vessel. Vessel embarked in Palermo, Italy, on July 30th. Destination: New Orleans, Louisiana."

Crandall asked McBride to make another copy of the message and post it on the maritime traffic board in the exchange's first-floor meeting room. "I will notify the other appropriate parties. Who originated this message?" Crandall asked.

"The vessel's owners, the Fabre Line of Marseilles, France," McBride replied. "I'm somewhat familiar with that vessel. It usually steams between Naples and New York, but was making a special voyage to New Orleans, with less-than-usual passengers, and returning for a full load of our cotton for La Harve. Damn shame," McBride lamented.

><

Crandall approached the steam-operated elevator's large brass-barred door and went to the second floor. When the doors opened, he was greeted by two men whom he knew as William Sterling Parkerson's Regulators, and they were assigned to guard the doors of a large conference room. The men, dressed in business attire, well-groomed, with pistol grips bulging from their waistbands, respectfully requested Crandall's invitation. The Colonel obliged, and the men admitted him to the conference room. Inside, the room had been configured in a theater fashion with four rows of chairs arched around a dais, upon which a long conference table commanded attention. There were about thirty chairs before the dais and five perched on the dais. Crandall's eyes searched the room, thinking he was alone, but he was stunned when he saw Algernon Badger sitting alone in a shadowy corner behind the dais. Badger just smiled, resting his chin on the brass cap of his walking stick.

"Good afternoon, General," Crandall said with a bow.

Badger leaned on his walking stick and stood. "Good afternoon, Colonel. It appears we are early. Who do you think is demanding our and others' presence today?"

"Well, judging by the quality of the stationery and the print, it appears to have come from City Hall."

"That's my guess, too. Shakspeare uses this room as his private redoubt whenever he wants something done without too much notice. Too many eyes and ears at city hall, and he doesn't want to sully the Pickwick Club with plebeian matters," Badger said.

"Hence, the Regulators guarding the second floor?"

"Exactly, Colonel. I guess we will hear more about the *Shakspeare Plan* today," Badger said.

At that moment, Mayor Joseph A. Shakspeare and his retinue of sycophantic followers filed into the room and took seats before the dais. These men all represented the cotton industry of New Orleans: two newspapers, four attorneys, and J.D. Houston. As most men took seats in the audience, Houston, William Sterling Parkerson, Edgar Farrar, and the Denegre brothers took seats on the dais. Except for Houston and Shakspeare, the dais occupants were prominent attorneys, and represented the cotton, sugar, lumber, stock exchange and all ancillary enterprises serving the port. The mayor had no chair, as he intended to prance upon the dais in his usual aristocratic countenance.

As Badger took his seat in the second row, on the end, he noticed the tempestuous Maurice Hart seated in the center of the front row. Badger remembered the last time they were in the same room, and felt his pulse quicken. After the room was filled, the armed Regulators closed and guarded the doors. As the mayor paced the length of the dais, he paged through his notes, and after a few moments, he stood next to Farrar and began his presentation.

"Good afternoon, gentlemen, and thank you for attending this very important meeting on short notice. Did everyone have to dress in a black suit? You look like a conference of undertakers."

The audience laughed.

"I assure you, the agenda is essential to all of you because it will impact your respective businesses, if not the entire economic health of this city.

"As you know, I have great plans for this city, and its growth beyond my political career. We are already installing electric lights on Magazine and Dryades Streets, and soon Canal Street will glow like Paris in the night. Our streets are slowly being paved, and I want to quicken the process with the Belgium granite, so when it rains, our streetlights will reflect our progress. I see Colonel Crandall in the audience and will shortly ask him to update us on our new telephone system. Soon, we can talk to each other from the comfort of our parlors or offices. In short, gentlemen,

New Orleans is progressing like other great American cities, but we have a long way to go to shed the yoke of Reconstruction. It's our destiny to restore New Orleans to its greatness."

The room erupted in applause.

"We have one major problem which is impeding our progress: the lethargic operation of our docks and port. And we must address that now, and develop a plan to place the port, from Poland Avenue to Louisiana Avenue, under the control of our city, the city council, or a local enterprise. So, I have asked our esteemed bar members to address the situation and Mr. Parkerson to address our rights. Mr. Parkerson, you may have the floor."

William Sterling Parkerson was regarded as one of New Orleans' most learned civil attorneys. He graduated from the University of Louisiana's law school in 1880, just four years before the university changed its name to Tulane University of Louisiana. From early in his career, he studied the Napoleonic origins of the Louisiana Civil Code and its survival in Louisiana after statehood in 1812. Early in his career, he was regarded as one of the city's greatest orators. He was second only to Reverend Benjamin Morgan Palmer, Pastor of the First Presbyterian Church on Lafayette Square, where many of the city's elites worshiped.

Parker stood at the dais with a thick stack of notes cradled and began lecturing the audience.

"Gentlemen, Mayor Shakspeare has requested I conduct certain legal research into the dominion and control of the docks and port of New Orleans, and what our rights are appertaining thereto as citizens of this city, state, and nation. I am not speaking as the city attorney, a job I have rejected, but as someone who is a student of the law.

"I have written some notes about our shared origins and the history of New Orleans. I want to share them with you, hoping we can mutually arrive at a plan that will preserve New Orleans as a vibrant port and the economic engine of this city. As an attorney, I travel in various circles of scholars and politicians, some are easily disguisable."

The audience roared with laughter.

"To fully understand *our* rights to *our* port, allow me your indulgence to trace our history, as a city, and where that history has taken us to this moment in time. As you know, New Orleans was founded and declared French soil in 1699; from that moment in history, it has been a port city. If not for the Mississippi River, New Orleans would not exist. It's that simple.

"From 1699, the French used New Orleans as a gateway to the seas and controlled the entire Mississippi River, until it sold it to Spain in 1762, reserving its rights to use the port and river. Spain retained control over the port and river, and gave our new nation, the United States of America, use of the port and river through the *Pinckney Treaty of 1795*. In 1800, Spain sold the Louisiana territory back to France. In 1803, Thomas Jefferson bought the Louisiana territory, which ran from the Gulf of Mexico to Canada and the Mississippi River to the Continental Divide.

"But what did Jefferson really purchase? My research indicated he bought New Orleans and the right to control and use the Mississippi River to its headwaters. The contiguous lands were essential to him, but New Orleans' port and the river were what he really wanted. Remember when New Orleans was founded and transferred to Spain, it wasn't a state. When Spain transferred it back to France, it wasn't a state. And when Jefferson purchased it from Napoleon, it wasn't a state. Louisiana didn't become a state until 1812, after the city and port of New Orleans were established.

"So, I ask you, who owned the city and port from 1803 to 1812? The United States of America? Probably."

"Hold on, Mr. Parkerson," Maurice Hart interrupted. "Behind me sits a representative of the United States government. His interests have always been with the Union. In fact, he was a General in the Union Army. Are you about to tell us that our port belongs to the federal government, again?"

"No, Mr. Hart. But if you allow me to finish, I hope to answer your question," Parkerson responded.

"Sit down, Maurice," the mayor intoned.

Parkerson continued. "Gentleman, after statehood, the city and the many enterprises along the river controlled the commerce of the river. Never once did the state of Louisiana exercise control over our port. It was the city's gem. In fact, when Admiral David Farragut and General Benjamin Butler demanded that Mayor John Monroe surrender the city and port on May 16, 1862, they didn't demand that the governor of Louisiana surrender it. They went to City Hall and demanded that Monroe surrender New Orleans, and he did. The city was then placed under a military governor. In fact, we had no real mayor during the Civil War, but after the Civil War, the city and the port were returned to Mayor Monroe on May 12, 1866."

"What's your point, Mr. Parkerson?" Hart asked.

"My point, gentlemen, is simply this: who controls the port of New Orleans today? Is it the city? Is it the state? Is it the federal government?

It's not France or Spain anymore. So, who controls our port?"

"Who?" Franklin Hayne asked.

"Well, it is my belief that the city controls the port, along with the recognized riparian owners," Parkerson asserted.

"What does that mean?" Hayne asked.

"Well, under the Louisiana Civil Code of 1870, the riparian owners—those who own the land next to a stream of navigable water—have control and use over that portion of the stream which passes through their land or by their land. That includes the Mississippi River. If the city owns the land, and since it owns most of it near the river, it is the riparian owner and controls what goes on its land."

"Does Macheca, Matranga, or Provenzano own any land along the Mississippi River?" J.D. Houston asked.

"As far as I can tell, no. They own structures on the river, which assist in their shipping and stevedoring enterprises, but the riparian owner of the land is the city."

"Can the city evict them from those properties?" Houston asked.

"Let me answer that," Shakspeare said. "They have paid fees to the city to operate their business. They rent market stalls at the various markets throughout the city. But all the mayors before me, including me, have allowed them to operate their businesses for nominal fees."

"That must be stopped and stopped now," Hart yelled.

"Calm down, Maurice," Shakspeare said. "If we must take control of the port and its operations, we must do it carefully. Mr. Parkerson will explain."

"Thank you, Mr. Mayor," Parkerson said. "As you know, I circulate among this state's legal and legislative community. In fact, I had a fortuitous encounter with Governor Nicholls last week. As most of you know, he is part-owner of the Ridgefield sugar cane plantation near Thibodaux and has an interest in our port's activities. During our conversation, I asked him who actually controls the Port of New Orleans. He said, 'It's a local matter.'"

"He hinted there's a movement in Baton Rouge to have a state constitutional convention either in 1896 or 1898, to modernize our post-Reconstruction laws, to meet the commercial demands of the Twentieth Century, and to place our state under firm control of the Democratic party. But our legislature recognizes the many advancements in steam and electric power and wants Louisiana to prosper, like other states. Some legislators see our port as a revenue generator and want to put it under state control."

The room erupted in profane protest. The discordant bellows continued for about five minutes, until the Mayor returned the meeting to order. "Gentlemen, please listen to a plan Mr. Parkerson has developed," Shakspeare yelled.

"Thank you, Mr. Mayor. Gentlemen, don't worry. If the convention is held, it will be held in New Orleans, but we must act very carefully and deliberately in the next few years. This is what I propose, and it's just a proposal for you to consider. Since you represent this city's shipping and export businesses, and the port is essential to your continued success, I propose we start a trust or corporation, which will be designed to purchase the land adjacent to the river, not owned by the city. This trust will become the riparian owners of those lands. According to the Civil Code, if the state tries to appropriate those lands, it would have to indemnify you."

"Who would be in control of this trust?" Franklin Hayne asked.

"The trust will be held at the Whitney Bank and controlled by the cotton, shipping, and sugar industry members. You will elect a board of directors to oversee the trust, and husband the funds for all acquisitions and future construction. If the city owns the land, the trust will pay the city for a long-term lease to build wharfs, warehouses, presses, or any other facility needed to execute your enterprise. In short, the trust will control all operations of the docks, ports, and ancillary businesses associated with importing and exporting all commodities through the Port."

"How are we to fund this trust?" John Moore, a cotton factor, asked.

"Once the trust or corporation is established, and the directors selected, bylaws should be drafted to include financial contributions from all parties concerned. Annual contributions from your various companies should be held at the bank and readily inspected to ensure all funds are received and recorded properly. Then the board of directors should decide what lands and improvements should be made. This will all be designed to prevent the state or anyone from ever controlling the port, except the men in this room or your designees."

"When do we start this?" J.D. Houston asked.

"I suggest you get together as soon as possible and select a group of men to help organize this trust or corporation, and then contact me, or Mr. Farrar, to help in the legal drafting of all necessary papers. Select a name that will not betray the true purpose of the company's mission. Every contributor should be a stockholder in the corporation, and the shares should be apportioned ratably to the company's contribution."

"What about the Matrangas and the Provenzanos?" Maurice Hart asked.

Parkerson giggled. "Are you going to allow them to be stockholders?"

The room erupted in a disdainful gale of laughter. Maurice Hart stood and began to wave his arms to speak. The room fell silent and allowed Hart the floor. "I like your thoughts, Mr. Parkerson, but I would like to know how Mr. Badger feels about this, since he represents the federal government."

Algernon Badger stood and supported himself on his cane. "Well, Mr. Hart and others, let me begin by saying I am not here as a representative of the United States. I am merely the customs officer assigned to the port. Mr. Grant, the U.S. attorney, is the only one who can legally represent the federal government. That said, I don't care what you do with controlling the port, as long as all duties are paid. That's my only concern."

"What about your friends, Macheca, Matranga, and Provenzano?" Hart probed.

"I don't consider them friends, but business acquaintances associated with my job. What you do with their companies is not my concern."

"Didn't Macheca save your life once?" Hart sneered.

"Yes, Mr. Hart, he did, and I have thanked him many times. But he still must pay his duties to the United States government."

"General, I understand you and my police chief are trying to get Matranga and Provenzano from killing each other down there. How is that coming?" Shakspeare asked.

"Mr. Mayor, David Hennessy, and I are speaking to both of them and have elicited the help of J.P. Macheca to broker a peace. As I stand here now, Macheca has secured their agreement to meet, but after the fall crops are loaded and unloaded on the boats and steamers. The only snag is the venue—where to meet. We are working on that now. But it appears it will be around Christmas, before we have the meeting. In the meantime, we are seeing some reduction in the violence down there, except for the cuttings, shootings, and murders on Gallatin Street, which are unrelated to the Matranga and Provenzano operations."

"Dagoes killing dagoes. I don't care," Hart exclaimed. "I just want them all gone—kith and kin."

"Who will do the work, Maurice?" the mayor asked. "We need workers on the docks. We just need them under our control. And that is what Mr. Parkerson is trying to accomplish."

"But do we need so many of them in New Orleans. Not all of them work the docks. How many banana salesmen do we need?" Hart asked.

Abner Crandall stood and asked to be recognized. Shakspeare obliged. "Gentlemen, I fully endorse Mr. Parkerson's idea of a trust or corporation to take over the docks, and my company stands ready to serve any and all your needs in this endeavor. New Orleans' telephone system is growing and soon will be comparable to our telegraph system. I offer my company as a stockholder when the time comes. Communication between the port and the exchanges is vital for the growth of New Orleans.

"As for Mr. Hart's concerns, I have good news. When I arrived here today, I stopped in the telegraph room and spoke to an operator monitoring the maritime key." Crandall dug inside his coat pocket and removed the message, which Percival McBride received. He read it aloud. "So, Mr. Hart, it appears there will be fewer *Italians* arriving in New Orleans. Does that make you happy?"

><

After the meeting, Abner Crandall stepped off the elevator and onto the first floor of the Cotton Exchange. He bumped into an excited Percival McBride, who was waving another telegraph message in his hand. "Colonel Crandall, I just received another message, which seems to have originated in Key West, Florida."

"May I see it?" Crandall asked.

McBride handed it to Crandall, and a gloomy visage etched across his face.

It read:

"SS Neustria survived hurricane. Passing through the Straits of Florida now. Vessel's sails damaged, but steaming under its own power. Should arrive in New Orleans in four to five days."

"Make me another copy of this message and post a really large one on the board. I want everyone to see it," Crandall said. "After that, Mr. McBride, send it to all the newspapers in New Orleans."

Part II
THE OTHER PEOPLE

Chapter 21

SS Neustria
29° North Latitude & 89° West Longitude
September 16, 1889
6:30 A.M.

Antonio twitched in his bunk and rubbed his nose, as a pungent organic aroma filled his cabin. A few feet away, he heard the slumbering breaths of Father Fontebuis and Consere. He blinked his eyes open and noticed the cabin filled with a pinkish-orange hue, revealing a new day at sea. As his senses met the new day, he noticed something different from last night. Eight hours earlier, when he opened the portholes for ventilation, he could smell the salty sea and feel the gentle rolling of the ship. But as he sat up on his bunk, the strange smell stunned his nose, and the ship seemed to sail smoothly.

He quietly jumped from his bunk, approached a porthole, and poked his head through its opening. He immediately noticed the origin of the smell—land and the brown waters of the Mississippi River. His eyes darted from side to side as the morning sky grew brighter. His first sight of America—tall swamp grass, duck weed, and oyster fishermen—filled his senses. Seagulls and pelicans glided over the *Neustria,* hoping the ship's wake would serve breakfast. Some ducks glided in for a soft landing next to the marshy shores of the river. Antonio yelled, "America. America?"

His cries aroused the priests, and Father Consere bolted from his bunk and poked his head out the porthole. "That's America, Antonio! We made it." As Antonio and Father Consere danced around the cabin joyfully, a knock rapped upon the cabin door. Dressed only in his nightshirt, Consere cracked the door open.

"Good morning, Father, and welcome to America," Captain Vermie said. "I hope I'm not disturbing you, but I wanted to be the first to announce your arrival into American waters. We just entered the mouth of the Mississippi River and should be in New Orleans in about nine hours. We are about ninety-four miles from the city, and Mr. Ellington says our boiler has a leak, but it's providing enough steam for us to finish our trip. Of course, we will have to make repairs in New Orleans, and our company has authorized our bursar to pay for the repairs. They also authorized me to pay Antonio one hundred dollars in American currency, which should cover his passage and then some. This ship is grateful to all the boys who helped keep her sailing through the storm." Vermie handed Antonio a thick envelope.

"Thank you, Captain," Antonio said. "Thank you very much."

"Good English, son. Now, when you get to New Orleans, watch your money, and put it in a good bank for safekeeping. I must warn you that New Orleans can be a dangerous place at times, so keep your wits about you."

"Thank you, Captain," Father Consere said. "We'll be careful."

"Our cook is preparing breakfast and lunch for everyone. We will empty our stores and give everyone two great meals before they step on American soil. It's summer, and the river current is mild, so we should arrive sometime this afternoon."

"Where do you go from New Orleans?" Father Fontebuis asked, poking his head around the door.

"Well, we will be in New Orleans for about a week. We're going to take on a cargo of cotton destined for Europe, while our boiler is being repaired."

Thank you, Captain, for everything," Father Fontebuis said.

"No, let me thank Antonio and the other Sicilian boys. Without them, we wouldn't be here. Remember that, Antonio. Remember on your most discouraging days what you have accomplished. Remember the heat, the noise, the sweat, the grease, and the fear. Remember saving this ship and the many people on board. If you do, nothing and no one can stop you."

><

After lunch, Antonio returned to his cabin and began to pack his belongings in an old leather suitcase. Since the weather was very warm, he stuffed his woolen jacket and the other clothes he brought from Bisacquino. Before closing and buckling the lid of his case, he hid most of his money in the jacket's pocket, then placed his tablets and books on top of his clothes. After securing his suitcase under his bunk, he decided to stroll around the ship's deck one more time. Father Consere gave him a black *saturno* hat to perpetuate the illusion of his seminarian status. Its wide brim shielded his eyes from the brilliant sun as he strolled among the throngs of immigrants clutching the rails, waiting for the ship to dock. He found a vacant spot near the bow and noticed how green the American marshland contrasted with the azure sky. Along the banks of the river, people with long poles were casting lines into the water, hoping to catch their dinner. Some waved to him, and Antonio smiled and returned the gesture—his first contact with Americans.

Near a slight bend in the river, Antonio saw a group of children swinging from a rope fastened to the bough of a giant oak tree, rooted in the bank of the river. When the rope swung over the water, the children would drop into the murky river and splash their way back to the bank. He could hear them laughing and yelling. The frolicking punched his gut with wistful feelings of his childhood, splashing in a rocky stream in the Sicilian mountains.

As he looked forward, he saw ships and boats of many designs, dimensions sailing and steaming up and down the Mississippi River. One such boat aroused his curiosity. It was long, wide, and the gunwales were just inches from the brown water. It had a giant red paddle wheel propelling it up the river, while black coal smoke poured from two large stacks, which jetted through its decks. Between the stacks was a small square room encased in windows. From his perch on the *Neustria's* bow, he could see a man in the room, with both hands on a large wooden wheel, steering the vessel through the turbid river currents. The man yanked on a rope hanging from the little house's ceiling and blew several high-pitched, discordant notes from its steam-powered whistle. The *Neustria* returned the signal, with one long baritone blast. Stacked casks and hogshead-sized barrels crowded its decks, from stem to stern, as it steamed upriver toward New Orleans.

Antonio's eyes darted from bank to bank of the river. Everywhere he looked, there was some movement. On the distant banks, farmers worked their fields, harvesting crops from the black fertile soil. The river teemed with commerce, and the vessel traffic got heavier, the closer the *Neustria* approached New Orleans. On the starboard side, Antonio saw the first images of the city's neighborhoods and people. Rows and rows of narrow, long houses, resembling coffins, hemmed by narrow, muddy streets. Some houses were painted white, while others were weather-beaten and clad in brown clapboards. Children of all races played in the streets, while women hung wet clothes on lines between the houses. Among the houses and square neighborhoods, red-brick warehouses, and rickety storehouses lined the roads, while horses and mules trundled large drayage wagons along the rutted ways.

Fathers Consere and Fontebuis found Antonio at the peak of the bow. They were attired in full black cassocks and *saturno* hats crowned their heads. Roman collars ringed their necks, which announced their office. Several immigrants, frissoned by the moment, approached the priests and thanked God for a safe passage to their new homes. The priest obliged every request and blessed each immigrant, and prayed for their new lives on a new horizon.

"Antonio, Captain Vermie said we should be docking soon, and he is going to allow us to disembark the ship first," Father Fontebuis said. "Let's return to our cabins, collect our things, and wait near the ship's bridge."

Antonio and the priests lugged their bags to the deck adjacent to the bridge. In the distance, they saw the ship's bow turn sharply to the port side, as it entered the sweeping bend in the river, which gave the Crescent City its moniker. The ship slowly reduced speed, yawing towards an open pier. The ship's deck crews stood on the decks with hawse lines ready to be tossed to waiting dockworkers. When the ship floated near the dock, the deck crews tossed the lines to the waiting hands of several Blacks, ready to wrap the lines around large iron bollards. Once the lines were wrapped, a gang of Black men tugged the lines and pulled the ship into port and tied the lines fast. Antonio watched in amazement as the sun beat upon the men's dark, leathered skin, which rippled in bulges and sinewed rows across their upper backs and shoulders. "I can't believe they are strong enough to pull this ship," Antonio muttered.

Two wooden gang planks stretched from the dock to the ship. Captain Vermie, Messrs. Standite and Ellington bid a tearful farewell to Antonio and the priests. It was a difficult departure for all, given their shared experiences crossing the Atlantic. As he dried his eyes, Captain Vermie instructed them to leave the ship by the forward gang plank, to avoid congestion and the *Padrone*. They did, but not before waving goodbye as they bounced down the rickety planks to their new land.

In the distance, Father Fontebuis spied a long black carriage with three rows of empty seats hitched to a team of two black horses. Standing next to the carriage was a cassocked priest wearing a *biretta*, waving his arms to attract their attention. Next to the priest was a very tall Black man in a black cut-away suit and a bowler hat. As Antonio and the priest pressed through a gaggle of dock workers and stevedores, a well-attired man carrying a notepad, accompanied by a very tall policeman with a large, red handlebar mustache, grabbed Antonio by his shoulder.

"Hold on, son. Where are you going?" the man asked.

Father Fontebuis asked, "Who are you? And what do you want?"

"My name is James Keller, and I am a labor broker. I believe this boy belongs to my company. He must come with us."

"Labor broker? You mean you are part of the *Padrone,* don't you?" Father Consere asked.

"The name doesn't matter. This boy belongs to our company, because we paid his passage to America."

"Nonsense," Father Fontebuis asserted. "He paid part of his own passage, and the Jesuits paid the balance. Then we sailed through a hurricane, and he helped save the ship. The shipping company reimbursed him for his actions. Now release the boy."

"What is your name, boy?" Keller demanded.

"Antonio…Terranova."

Keller examined his list of passengers from the *Neustria.* "I can't find your name. That tells me you are lying and probably a stowaway. You must come with me," Keller said, tugging on Antonio's jacket.

"He's not going with you. He belongs to the Jesuits and is a seminarian," Father Fontebuis said, breaking Keller's grip on Antonio's jacket.

"Wait a minute," the large policeman said, drawing his truncheon from his wide leather belt, which cinched his dark blue tunic. "You must surrender the boy until we determine his true identity. Do you have any of his identity papers with you?" the policeman demanded.

"Yes, we do," Father Fontebuis said, rummaging through his records. As he was about to produce Antonio's baptism records from Bisacquino and Palermo, Captain Vermie, dressed in his finest nautical uniform and white hat, pushed into the circle of men.

"What's going on here?" Captain Vermie demanded.

"Who are you?" the policeman asked.

"I am the Captain of that ship over there. These people were my passengers. You have no authority to detain them."

"Who paid the boy's fare to America?" the policeman asked.

"Look at my ship's rigging. It's tattered and ripped to shreds. We cannot use our sails until they are repaired here. The storm also ripped one of the lifeboats off the deck. We steamed through a hurricane while in the

Atlantic. You can check my ship's log. This boy, Antonio, and others saved this ship when we were destined to sink. My company paid his passage. If anyone owns him, I do."

Keller looked at the policeman. "What are you going to do?"

"Nothing. The boy is free to go. A ship's captain's word is Gospel on the docks. If the boy is not on your list, you have no claim to him. I must side with the priests and the ship's captain."

"I will call Chief Hennessy about your neglect of duty. What is your name?" Keller fumed.

"Patrolman Gabriel Porteous. Tell the Chief I said hello, Mr. Keller. The priests and the boy are free to go." With that, Porteous tucked his truncheon back into his belt, doffed his gray bell-shaped helmet, and walked away. Keller stomped off and returned to the gangplank near the ship's stern. Captain Vermie hugged the priests and Antonio, and wished them well, stepped away, and disappeared into a crowd of people, horses, mules, and wagons.

><

The Jesuit Provincial Superior, Father John O'Shanahan, waited by his carriage and his attendant, Thomas Charles, as they watched Father Fontebuis and Consere defend Antonio Terranova. A wide smile stretched across the Irish priest's face, knowing the Jesuits were not daunted by the petty processes of a corrupt immigration system. But Father O'Shanahan was very practical and well-trained in the political maneuverings of the Society of Jesus, especially since his Order had been expelled from the Louisiana territory once before. His knowledge of Louisiana's history was etched deep into his mind, and he knew his limits and the tolerance of the protestant-dominated city.

As Father Fontebuis and Consere approached the carriage, Father O'Shanahan spread his arms wide and said, "Welcome to the land of liturgy and lubricity, Fathers. I know you are well-acquainted with the former and have just encountered the latter." The priests embraced each other and exchanged blessings, pleasantries, and thanksgivings, while Antonio looked on. After a few moments, Father O'Shanahan's attention fell upon the forlorn countenance of a young wayfarer, gripping his scuffed leather suitcase with both hands.

"And what is your name, son?" Father O'Shanahan asked, with a light Irish lilt.

"Antonio Terranova, Father. It's an honor to meet you."

Father O'Shanahan's ear discerned Antonio's clear diction and response, braided with an Italian accent. "How old are you, my son?"

"I am sixteen years old."

"You are a fine-looking boy, with strong shoulders and clear eyes. Welcome to America."

"Thank you, Father," Antonio said, with a respectful bow.

Father O'Shanahan's eyes darted to the other two priests and motioned for them to step into the shade of several large bales of cotton, destined to be loaded on the *Neustria*. "Antonio, why don't you get acquainted with Mr. Charles, while I talk to Father Fontebuis and Consere. We'll only be a minute."

Antonio bowed and extended his hand to Thomas Charles, who greeted the young Sicilian with a welcoming smile. As the priests sought refuge from the afternoon sun between the bales of cotton, a worried visage tugged on Father O'Shanahan's face. He removed his *biretta and* wiped his brow with a large white handkerchief. "Fathers, I must be completely honest with you. I received several cables from Father Wertz about the boy, but he didn't go into great detail, making me more curious and suspicious. So, I must ask you, why did you bring the boy with you to America?"

Father Fontebuis began to relate the history of Antonio, his real name, his family, the vineyard, and how and why he decided to shepherd him to America. He left no detail to conjecture, because he knew the baseless presumptions would fill any omissions in the boy's life. The moment demanded the complete truth. Hearing the unexpected details, Father O'Shanahan, weakened by what he heard, leaned against the cotton bales and hung his head.

"So, he isn't a candidate for our seminary?" Father O'Shanahan asked.

"I don't think so," Father Fontebuis said. "But he is a very smart boy, and we have tutored him in Sicily and on the voyage here. He has passed every test we've given him and has a great aptitude for languages and math. He would make a great student at our school."

"I'm sorry, Father, but that can't be," Father O'Shanahan said.

"Why not? We have heard great things about the Jesuit school here. Antonio will make a great student," Father Fontebuis asserted.

"Well, I will be brutally honest with you both," Father O'Shanahan began. "New Orleans is a tough city for Italian immigrants. Though their labor is sought, their presence is discouraged—an incurable social paradox. Despite being part of America, this city is still mired deep in the murky traditions of European aristocracy and class structure, and the Italians are not even recognized as being Negro or Caucasian. They are called the "Other People" because they have no place in New Orleans society.

"After the American Civil War, the Negro was set free, but then came the Italians and Sicilians, and they were welcomed for only one thing—their labor and sweat. Their wages are meager, and less than that of the Negro. Social assimilation is discouraged by the city's Protestant ruling class, if not outright forbidden. And I, being born and bred in Ireland, know how brutal the Anglos can be while enforcing their cherished class system. Our Jesuit order is tolerated because we educate their sons, along with the ascending Irish, German, and French Catholics. Antonio, I am sure, would be ostracized if we admit him to our school, and his enrollment would encourage disruptions among the other students. Besides, we have four hundred boys and nowhere to board them."

"Are there any Negroes in our school?" Father Consere braved.

"No. No Negroes, Italians, Greeks, or Croats. The history of the Jesuit order in Louisiana is a sad one. Like you being expelled from Sicily, we were once expelled from Louisiana. Now, we are back and building our wealth and political strength, which is consubstantial with evolving community tolerances. As the Provincial Superior, I would be remiss if I admitted the boy to our school here, but if he wants to be a seminarian, I can send him to our Novitiate in Grand Coteau, Louisiana. It's the French Catholic part of Louisiana, and Italians are more tolerated there than here. Does he want to be a priest?"

"Given his past, would he be accepted as a priest?" Father Fontebuis asked.

"Ignatius Loyola, I am sure, killed a few men in his time, before his conversion. It's what's in the boy's heart that counts," Father O'Shanahan responded. "Have you asked him?"

"No. I was too occupied to save him from the wolves in his old country," Father Fontebuis lamented. "But give me a minute and I will go ask him."

Father Fontebuis left the shade of the bales and walked back to the carriage. He asked Antonio to step down and walk with him for a minute. As they walked, Antonio spied his friend, Asperi Marchesi, and his father, climbing into an open wagon, with other immigrants. Their eyes met, and both waved, as if it were the last time they would see each other. As the wagon pulled away from the docks, kicking up a cloud of dust and gravel, Father Fontebuis asked Antonio the fateful question. "Antonio, do you want to be a Jesuit priest?"

Antonio's eyes widened, and his shoulders shot back. A slight river breeze tossed his hat onto the cypress planks of the Picayune Tier, but he didn't retrieve it. His mind recalled the gloomy departure of Asperi, his only friend, to parts unknown. "I don't know, Father. I never gave it much thought. I have sinned grievously, as you know, and I don't think I am qualified."

"Where do you see yourself in five years, son?"

"Father, I don't know. I just arrived in a strange place, which looks and smells strange. The people look different. I hear people speaking in languages I've never heard in Sicily. For the last few minutes, I have been sitting in a carriage talking to one of the biggest men I've ever seen, and whose skin looks like boot leather. My only friend has been taken away, and you are asking me where I see myself in five years. I don't know where I will be in five minutes."

Father Fontebuis hugged Antonio and apologized for the questions. He stooped down, picked up the boy's hat, and squared it on his head. "Let God and time direct your steps. You are in a new world with strange customs, but never forget seeking God's guidance in everything. The Lord has brought you this far, and I am sure He won't abandon you now. Go back to the carriage and sit with Mr. Charles. I'll be along soon."

Father Fontebuis returned to the shade of the cotton bales. "I don't think Antonio is ready to make any decisions on his life. He is confused, to say the least. He's in a strange land, and his horizons are dimmed by uncertainty. Unlike us, he has no calling, but survival from moment to moment, Fontebuis said."

"I understand," Father O'Shanahan said. "To be honest with you, I anticipated this and have an alternative plan, which he might accept."

"Alternative plan?" Father Consere probed.

"Yes. I took the liberty to enroll him, at our cost, at another boy's Catholic school, which accepts immigrant orphans and boards them. He will get a good education, and it's only about two miles from ours. It's not far from here, and we have an invitation for dinner with the school's principal. He and I are friends. His name is Brother Stanislaus, and he operates a school named after a young Italian Jesuit priest who died in 1591—Saint Aloysius. I believe Antonio will make an easy transition there."

"So, are we going to orphan Antonio again on this dock?" Father Fontebuis asked.

"Not at all. We are going to expand his new family on these docks. In fact, I am in the process of purchasing land upstream from New Orleans to build a college. I need you two to help me assemble a curriculum for young men. If Antonio does well at St. Aloysius, we will admit him for no cost. The school has a great reputation among the business community, and the curriculum is geared towards commercially minded boys. As I said, his tuition and board are paid for one year, and the school has many contacts in the city where he can work part-time after classes. How much money does he have with him?" Father O'Shanahan asked.

"He has about one hundred and twenty dollars—American," Father Fontebuis said.

"Praise be Jesus!" Father O'Shanahan exclaimed. "Let's keep that among us."

"Should we open a bank account for him?" Father Consere asked.

"No. Most of the Italians don't trust the banks here and keep their money secretly among themselves. There is one bank in the French Quarter or *Piccolo Palermo*, as the Italians call it, but it's still working on gaining the immigrants' trust. It's a slow process. Let's not tell Brother Stanislaus what Antonio has with him. As I see it, he's one of the richest immigrants to set foot in New Orleans."

Chapter 22

St. Aloysius Academy
Chartres and Barracks Streets
New Orleans, Louisiana
September 16, 1889
4:15 P.M.

As Thomas Charles steered the team of horses down Chartres Street, his passenger, Antonio Terranova, swiveled his head from side to side to capture the ambiance and essence of his new home. Fathers Fontebuis and Consere did the same, as they cast their delicate glances upon the neglected side of New Orleans, many refused to travel, unless it was necessary. The streets were either paved with loose granite bricks or tarred with chert. Deep gutters served as the drainage and sewer system for this end of the French Quarter. At the corners of the streets, the residents had covered the wide hand-dug gulches with wooden planks to serve as footbridges. At each intersection, the city had installed solitary carbon-arch lights, protected by large glass globes, suspended from wooden poles over the rutted streets. The pulsating electrical devices provided some illumination, along with flickering gas lamps. With the humid evening drawing long shadows on the brick and stucco buildings, a lamplighter began his rounds, signally the close of another day.

The clopping of the horses' hooves against the cobblestoned and chert streets, combined with the crowing roosters and the smell of garlic, onions roasting with *capra arrosta,* hanging over an open patio fire, made Antonio's first impressions of New Orleans an amalgam of appreciation and apprehension. On either side of the street, the familiar banter of several Italian and Sicilian dialects wafted over the iron railings of the second-floor galleries, which lined Chartres Street. And at the intersection of Chartres and Barracks, a muscular, but rotund woman dressed in a long blue dress, emptied a pan of hot cooking grease into the gutter.

Mr. Charles stopped the carriage and said, "This is Saint Aloysius Academy, Fathers."

Father O'Shanahan patted Antonio on the shoulder and said, "What do you think of New Orleans, so far?"

"It's flat. The streets are bumpy. It looks older than Sicily."

"It's not as old as Sicily, but with some of the same problems, Antonio," Father O'Shanahan said. "It's a big city, but a small town, with growing problems next to a dangerous port. Always remember that, son."

As Antonio and the priest stepped down from the carriage, the lady with the grease pan approached, bowed, and smiled. "You must be Brother Stanislaus' dinner guests. I am Maria Bertucci, his cook and housekeeper. Follow me, and I will get Brother for you."

The Priests and Antonio followed Miss Bertucci across a plank covering the gutter and into a courtyard ringed by a six-foot red brick wall, and secured by a dark green wooden gate. Mr. Charles lingered behind, lit a small kerosene lamp, and hung it on the rear axle of the carriage to warn people that the carriage was parked. He tethered the horses to a conical-shaped bollard on the corner to prevent the team and carriage from wandering off.

Once inside the courtyard, the three-story boys' school towered over the flagstone square. Only the lights on the first floor cast a welcoming amber glow through six large windows. All the windows on the upper floors were dark. The center front door of the building flung open, and two men dressed in black cassocks stepped outside to greet their guests. They both had large crucifixes hanging around their necks, and large smiles beamed across their faces.

"Welcome to Saint Aloysius. I'm Brother Stanislaus, and this is Brother Angelo. We are honored to have you as our guests." The Jesuits returned the greetings and introduced Antonio to the brothers. Mr. Charles slowly approached behind them, carrying Antonio's suitcase. After a brief obligatory chat in the school yard, the brothers welcomed their guests into their parlor. The room was well-appointed in a mixture of Victorian and Queen Anne furniture, and the walls were covered in traditional Catholic iconography. Mr. Charles stealthily slipped Antonio's suitcase behind a winged chair, stepped into the hallway, and sat alone.

The Brothers and the Jesuits exchanged the usual banter about the long, perilous voyage to America, and lavished praise upon their ward, Antonio, for his heroics in the ship's engine room during the hurricane. The Brothers were impressed.

Brother Angelo broached the apparent reasons for the meeting, and Antonio sat straight up in his chair. He knew from this moment on, his future dangled on every word spoken by anyone in that parlor. "Antonio, we are very grateful and honored to have you as one of our students. As you know, your tuition for one year and your room and board have been paid. You will be comfortable here, and we promise to give you a great education. Do you understand?"

"Yes, Brother."

"Don't worry about your accent or nationality. As you can see, I also have a bit of an accent. I am from Rome and speak English, Greek, and Italian. So, I want you to feel at home here. Understand?"

"Yes, Brother."

"The first thing we must do is to evaluate your educational level to place you properly. We have four levels, much like the Jesuit school. But since they have no openings and we have several, we are proud to have you as one of our students. So, I will ask you to step into the next room and take a little test. It will only be about thirty minutes or so. After that, Miss Bertucci will serve us a lavish meal, welcoming you to America. Follow me, please."

Brother Angelo and Antonio stepped out of the parlor and down the hall to a small sitting room with a small desk. On the desk was a four-page entrance exam for Saint Aloysius Academy. "When you are finished the test, bring it back to the parlor," Brother Angelo said. Antonio nodded and began reading the questions.

><

After forty minutes had passed, Antonio appeared in the parlor doorway, clutching his test in his right hand, waiting to be acknowledged. The Brothers and the Jesuits stood, smiled, and beckoned him to enter and sit. Antonio gave the test to Brother Angelo, who began to peruse it. After a few minutes, Miss Bertucci appeared in the doorway and announced that dinner was ready. Brother Stanislaus, the Jesuits, and Antonio followed her into a chandeliered dining room and gathered around an oval table. Brother Angelo remained in the parlor and graded the exam. When Antonio entered the dining room, he noticed Mr. Charles sitting alone at a small table with his empty pblate in the corner.

When Brother Angelo entered the dining room, he boomed, "Magnificent results!" Except for some syntactical irregularities, Antonio's English is excellent. His math is amazing. And his reading comprehension is excellent. I congratulate our Jesuit Fathers for excellently tutoring our new student."

"What level do you recommend, Brother Angelo?" Father O'Shanahan asked.

"I recommend we put him in our third-level math, second-level English, and typing class. One of our benefactors donated three new business machines called typewriters. We have a theology class in our second level, and a history class composed of Louisiana and American history, in our second level."

"Do you think he can do any afternoon and weekend work?" Brother Stanislaus asked.

"Yes. I recommend you message Mr. Jahnke. When I spoke to him last, he needed a boy to help drive the Belgian ballast cobblestones from the docks to the street-paving sites, but he must be good at math, too. Antonio would be a perfect fit for the job, and he will learn the streets of New Orleans—the good and the bad." Everyone laughed and applauded the boy's success.

Antonio seized the moment and motioned for Mr. Charles to bring his plate and sit next to him. Mr. Charles, more familiar with the local customs, looked at Brother Stanislaus, who gave the tall Black man an approving nod.

><

After dinner, Miss Bertucci cleared the table, served an apple pie, and coffee. When Father Fontebuis and Antonio took a sip of the hot coffee, both winced at its strength. Brothers Angelo and Stanislaus laughed. "Coffee too strong?" Brother Angelo asked.

"Yes. What's in it?" Father Fontebuis asked.

"Root Chicory. When the United States Navy blockaded the Mississippi River during the Civil War, it caused a shortage of coffee in New Orleans. Root Chicory was added to extend our supply, and people grew to love its aroma and strength. Now, it's sold like that. You'll get accustomed to it. But Antonio, don't drink the entire cup. You have class early tomorrow morning. You need your sleep," Brother Angelo said.

After dinner, the brothers took the Jesuits and Antonio on a tour of the school and where the boy would live. Antonio's room would be in the third-floor attic, with thick brick walls and dormer windows overlooking

Barracks Street. It was clean, but small. It had a small bed, dresser, a chiffonier, a desk, and two kerosene lamps. A down-the-hall privy was installed because the building was once a hospital for wounded Confederate soldiers after the Civil War. Three other students occupied rooms in the attic, and all were Sicilian orphans. Mr. Charles nodded and smiled when he placed Antonio's suitcase next to his bed.

Brother Angelo raised the dormer window and draped the opening with mosquito netting. Immediately, the discordant sounds of Gallatin Street leapt across the slate rooftops and into Antonio's new home. "There's one problem with our school," Brother Stanislaus began. "It's too close to the most dangerous street in New Orleans. Sorry, Antonio, but you might have to endure the screams and yells of ladies, the breaking of bottles, untuned pianos, and occasional gunfire—a typical night in New Orleans. Gallatin Street is where lost souls lose their bodies. You are to stay away from that street at all times. If you must go to the market for any reason, go early in the morning. By then, those people are deeply immured in a debaucherous repose—at least for a few hours. If you need to study, use the library on the first floor. It's always open. Do you understand?"

"Yes, Brother."

An awkward silence descended on the room. It was time for Antonio to say goodbye to the two men who saved him from the perilous uncertainties of Sicily, only to deposit him in the new uncertainties of New Orleans. Antonio approached Father Fontebuis and wrapped his arms around the priest. Tears flowed from every eye in the room. Father Fontebuis patted Antonio on the back and assured him he would only be a few miles away and would visit him often. Father O'Shanahan quickly sketched a crude map on a piece of paper, revealing the quickest way to get from Saint Aloysius to the Jesuit school on Baronne Street, to assuage any further anxieties.

"Antonio, you have proven in the last three months you're a man smarter and stronger than most. You have the will of a bull and a very keen mind. With that combination and the education these brothers will give you, you will become someone you won't recognize in five years. Don't dwell on your past. The past is to be built on, not dwelt upon. You are in a new land, which will provide many new challenges and opportunities. Be ready every day to meet them," Father Fontebuis said.

"Yes, Father."

"And remember, I am not going anywhere. Reach out to me if you need me. We are both going to experience this new place together. Now, I must leave and go to my new home, and you have to get ready to go to a *real* school. Open your mind to all possibilities. Anyone who can understand *Great Expectations* at your age can handle anything."

"Am I Pip?"

"No. You're Antonio Terranova. Never forget that."

Chapter 23

Jahnke Construction Company
Howard Street
New Orleans, Louisiana
October 5, 1889
8:00 A.M.

After eating a hearty breakfast prepared by Miss Bertucci, Antonio Terranova and his fellow orphaned attic dweller, Vito Vittori, washed their plates in an iron basin under a squeaky hand-cranked pump. As they left the kitchen, Brother Angelo stood in the doorway with two Italian ladies from the neighborhood. They were holding large packages of old clothes, which they were donating to Saint Aloysius students, especially the three in the attic.

"Boys, these ladies have some gifts for you. The clothes might be old, but they are clean and can be worn to class, play, or work," Brother Angelo said. "I want you to take them and hang them in your chiffonier. We have five minutes before we must leave for Mr. Jahnke's construction yard. So, hurry and change your clothes."

Antonio and Vito took the packages, hugged the ladies, and kissed their cheeks as sincere expressions of gratitude. They exchanged some small talk in Italian and were invited to the ladies' homes every Sunday, after Mass, for dinner. "Boys, I would accept the invitations, as I can attest these are two of the best cooks in New Orleans," Brother Angelo intoned. The boys accepted and ran upstairs to their rooms.

Both packages contained old, tattered boots, orphaned like them, but with new soles, cobbler-nailed for more life. Antonio stuffed his feet into them, but they were too big. So, he stuffed old rags into their toes to tighten the fit. Vito did the same, and both thundered down the stairway and into the courtyard, where Brother Angelo was waiting in an old, battered buggy.

"Okay, boys, today you will go to work for one of our benefactors—a German man named Johan Jahnke. He has a contract with the city to pave and repair the streets with large blocks of granite cobblestones. He buys them from the shipping companies. Several of our students work for him on weekends, and he pays them two dollars a day. I want you to keep one dollar, and we will start a bank account with the other. Every time you get paid, you deposit it into your account. I will teach you how to maintain your account, so you will be self-sufficient one day. Understand?"

Both boys nodded as Brother Angelo snapped the reins on the back of the mule. They traveled upriver on Chartres Street, passed an old Italian Catholic church, and a few blocks away, the first Cathedral built on the Mississippi River. The streets were busy with other wagons and buggies, as people commuted. As their buggy bounced on the streets, Brother Angelo directed the boys' attention to the many loosened granite blocks laid without care during and after the Civil War.

"Nearly every stone in this city must be reset and fixed, boys," Brother Angelo said, "or we will have more broken ankles and axles soon. On some streets, only a drunk can walk straight." The boys laughed.

><

Brother Angelo pulled into the Jahnke Construction Company's large yard under a clear sky and with a slightly cool breeze flowing from the northwest. The vast expansive area, adjacent to the New Basin Canal, contained stacks of lumber and large granite blocks, once used as a ship's ballast. Near the gate, an echelon of very large and stout wagons was lined up, with each driver sitting high above their teams of four mules. Each team was hitched to their wagons with heavy brass and leather tack. The wagon beds were empty, and each of them had hand-cranked winches attached to an A-frame boom to facilitate the loading and unloading of the granite stones. A tall, barrel-chested man with red hair and a black leather apron approached Brother Angelo. His sleeves were rolled up to his elbows, revealing forearms thick as tree trunks.

"Good morning, Brother. Have you brought me some new workers?" Johan Jahnke asked with a welcoming smile.

"I did. I want you to meet Antonio Terranova and Vito Vittori. They are two of our best students and have earned the right to work for you."

The boys stepped down from the buggy, and Mr. Jahnke inspected them like they were a pair of mules at an auction. He grabbed their shoulders and shook them. He squeezed their arms and inspected their hands. "They seem strong and sturdy, Brother, but their hands are soft like a baby's butt. That will change after one day of fighting the mules and the stones. Thank you, Brother. We will feed them some lunch, but they will be hungry when they get back to school. I will have them home by dark."

"Thank you, Mr. Jahnke," Brother Angelo said as he drove the buggy out of the yard.

Both Antonio and Vito were quiet and seemed apprehensive about what the day would promise, but were more than willing to make some money in America. Jahnke led the boys to two of the wagons, where he introduced them to two of his weathered-beaten foremen. "This is Mr. John Falcone and Mr. Paolo Borsellino. They are both from Palermo and two of my best men. They speak your language and will teach you what to do. Listen to them. They will take care of you," Jahnke said.

The boys shook the men's hands and immediately knew what it felt like to stick their hands into old leather bags of broken rocks. The men's hands bore the calluses of years of laying bricks and stones. Over the years of chipping, chopping, and cutting large pieces of granite, their bodies had transformed into lean sinew and deep scars. The color and texture of their battered skin made them look as if they were made of hammered bricks wrapped in dungarees. They each wore gray slouch hats to protect their heads from the sun. A bond of trust was formed after exchanging small talk in an ancient Sicilian dialect.

"But remember, when others are around, you speak English and nothing but English," Falcone warned. "The people here don't like foreign languages. Mr. Jahnke speaks German and Italian, but to us, he speaks English. Understand?"

The boys nodded.

"Today, I will take Antonio to the Picayune Tier to get a load of ballast. Vito, you go with Mr. Borsellino. You will get some stones from the Poydras Street docks and deliver the load to the work site on Canal Street. We only load and unload the stones. The city has a crew to lay the stone. If they need cutting, we will help them. But that's all we can do. We don't get paid to pave the streets. Understand?"

The boys nodded.

Antonio and Mr. Falcone climbed onto the wagon. Falcone tossed the wide leather reins to Antonio and said in a low voice, "*Adiamo.*" Having never had such power in his hands, Antonio hesitated but then slapped the reins on the mules' backs. The wagon lurched forward with tremendous power as Mr. Falcone laughed. "These mules are powerful. We just have to keep them happy and fed. Do you know how they get to the Picayune Tier, Antonio?"

"I think so. I think that's where my ship docked a few weeks ago."

"Good. Go down Rampart Street and turn right onto Poydras. Then go towards the river. Then we go left."

Antonio followed Mr. Falcone's instructions, but when he turned onto Poydras near a large market, he saw an old friend, Asperi Marchesi. They waved to each other, and then Asperi yelled, "I knew you weren't a priest." Antonio shrugged and kept moving.

"What was that about?" Mr. Falcone asked. "You a priest?"

"Sir, that's a long story."

"Never mind. Keep your mouth shut. New Orleans is full of long stories, big ears, and wagging tongues. Your mouth is the front door to your mind. Keep it locked, and don't let anybody in unless you know them well. And those you know well, tell them what they already think they know. That way, you keep them stupid."

Antonio laughed but accepted the sage advice from a man he had only known for about an hour. Though his hands were scarred and his skin abraded, Mr. Falcone's words resonated with Antonio, whose orphaned life had already met its share of adversities.

A uniformed policeman stopped their wagon as Antonio and Mr. Falcone approached the Picayune Tire. "I have to stop you right here, men. Looks like we had another Dago killing last night," the policeman said, pointing to a small crowd of uniform policemen and stevedores about a hundred feet away.

"Officer Porteous, do you remember me? I'm John Falcone—the stone mason."

"I recognize you," the officer said. "But it appears someone used your stones to crush a man last night. I can let you take some large stones, but there's a body between the smaller stones and the bales of cotton."

"That will be fine, officer. We need to take them to St. Charles Street to pave near City Hall."

"Go ahead. Back your wagon into the space near the pile of large stones. I'll get some Dagoes and Negroes to help you load your wagon," the policeman said. "But don't get in the way of the investigation."

Mr. Falcone showed Antonio how to back a team of powerful mules into a tight place to load the ballast. With the street skills acquired through time, Mr. Falcone spoke to the left mule team. The mules led the way, while the right team followed. After parking the wagon, Antonio and Mr. Falcone prepared the winch to lift the heavy stones, while a group of Black, Greek, and Italian stevedores, armed with long iron rods, helped.

While the stevedores grunted and manhandled the heavy gray granite, Mr. Falcone tapped Antonio on the shoulder. "Follow me," he whispered. "Don't say a word."

Mr. Falcone crept around the large piles of stone and bales of cotton. They climbed upon the pile of stacked ballast. Falcone wanted to see what the police were investigating. With the morning sun still in the east and their backs to the west, Mr. Falcone and Antonio cast no shadow upon the grisly site.

As they peered down about ten feet, Mr. Falcone and Antonio watched as policemen slowly removed stones from a man flattened by the granite. But as a policeman removed the stones from the man's head, a collective gasp quaked through the crowd. The man's eyes had been carved out of his head. Even the most seasoned cop flinched as they stared into the open skull of the victim. Blood dripped down the victim's face, around his jaw, and down his neck. Then three officers removed a slab of granite from the man's chest and discovered a broken oyster knife plunged through his sternum. The victim's brown shirt was stained and stiffened by the dried blood.

"Son-of-a bitch, someone took an oyster knife to this poor bastard's eyes, and then stabbed him in the heart," a policeman yelled, as he backed away from the body. "I guess they are sending the stevedores some kind of message. Does anyone know who he was?"

"His name was Frank Fiore," Mr. Falcone said. "He worked for either the Provenzanos or the Matrangas. I forget which one. It doesn't matter, does it? This damn war will never end."

"Do you know where he lived?" a policeman asked.

"He lived on Hospital Street, near Dauphine. He had a wife and three children," Mr. Falcone said.

"These Dagoes like to send a message when they kill. Does this mean anything to you?" a Detective asked.

"Open his mouth, and see if he still has a tongue."

A detective bent down and, with his pocketknife, pried open the tightened jaw of the victim. "His tongue is gone. What does that mean?" the detective asked.

"It means he saw something he shouldn't have seen and someone made sure he would never tell anyone what he saw," Mr. Falcone said.

"How do you know these things?" the detective asked.

"I have been moving ballast from the docks to the streets for five years. I keep my mouth shut. I move my stones, and that's all I do. I hear things and say nothing."

Mr. Falcone grabbed Antonio's shirt and said, "Let's get out of here." They descended the pile of stones and returned to their wagon. Laden with several tons of stone, Mr. Falcone gave the mules a savage lash, and they headed to Saint Charles Avenue to meet a paving crew near City Hall. Not a word was exchanged between Mr. Falcone and Antonio until they returned to the yard later that day.

It was near dusk when Falcone drove his mule team into the Jahnke yard. He reached under the seat and handed Antonio several inventory receipts. "Take these to the office, so the ladies can issue the bill to the city."

Antonio jumped down from the wagon and started to walk off. "Wait, Antonio. Come back here," Mr. Falcone said.

Antonio walked to Mr. Falcone's side of the wagon while brushing his hair, face, and clothes covered in gray stone dust. His hands and fingers were streaked with his dried blood. Mr. Falcone bent down and whispered, "*Sai cosa significa Omerta?*"

"*Si,*" Antonio responded. "Say nothing."

"Good. Tell no one what you saw this morning. Forget what you saw this morning. It didn't happen. Have you heard of the *Stuppagghieri ei Giardinieri?*"

Antonio smiled and nodded. "Why do you think I am in New Orleans, Mr. Falcone?"

Mr. Falcone smiled. "We have them here in New Orleans. Be careful. Now go to the office and get paid for your day's work."

Antonio walked back to a brown-brick building near the front of the yard. When he opened the door, his dark, weary eyes locked on the deep blue eyes of a young girl sitting behind a desk. His breath left his lungs, and his heart thudded through his tattered shirt. Her complexion glowed like radiant alabaster, while her golden blonde hair was curled into a bun resembling gold bullion. She smiled at Antonio and stood to greet him. "Hello, I am Ilsa Jahnke. I work for my father." She extended her hand to shake Antonio's.

"Oh no, Miss. My hands are too dirty to shake your hands," Antonio said with a blush. "Here are our receipts for the day."

Ilsa smiled, thanked Antonio, and handed him an envelope with his wages. He opened it and discovered it held three dollars. Antonio paused and said, "Miss, I... I think you made a mistake. My wages are two dollars, and you gave me three dollars."

"Ilsa smiled and said, "Antonio, you need new shoes. Now go before my father comes back. See you next Saturday."

Antonio stumbled out of the office and left the Jahnke yard. He walked two miles back to St. Aloysius Academy, without feeling the cobber's nails stabbing the soles of his feet.

Chapter 24

New Orleans City Hall
November 5,1889
10:30 A.M.

R obert Chaffe pursued his quotidian ritual of having breakfast at the Saint Charles Hotel before going to his office at New Orleans's center of commerce, a block away. His mornings always started in the hotel's reading room, with a glance at the daily broadsheets, and this morning he decided to select his favorite, *The Daily Picayune*. Afterwards, the *Maître d'*, Honore Bourgeois, would seat him at his usual table, near the window, which overlooked St. Charles Avenue. After laying his linen napkin on his lap, he folded and quartered his broadsheet and read the columns about his hometown. Mr. Bourgeois brought him a small bowl of water to dab his fingers in, to liberate the printer's ink from his pallid digits. His breakfast of poached eggs, ham, and slices of oranges arrived precisely fifteen minutes after he sat down. The waiter filled his fine china cup with the blackest of coffee and placed a crystal cruet of cream next to his cup.

As Chaffe read his paper, ate his breakfast, and sipped his coffee, he occasionally glanced out the window and watched a group of Italian and Black men wrestle a large granite block onto the street bed to brace the new streetcar rails. Though it was a cool autumn morning, the workers' perspiration stained their clothes, and beads of sweat dripped down their faces, sparkling in the morning sun. The intense labor mystified Chaffe for some reason, and he mused how lucky he was to make his sybarite living wearing a suit and working indoors. Secretly, he admired the laborer's sinewed strength, given his atrophying muscles caused by a mysterious childhood disorder.

As he flipped over the newspaper folds, Chaffe was disturbed by fellow cotton broker John Moore, who plopped down at the table, uninvited. "Have you seen the morning papers?" Moore panted.

"I am doing that now. What's got you so excited this early?"

"Look," Moore said, as he shoved a copy of the *Chicago Times* inches from Chaffe's nose. Chaffe recoiled and allowed his eyes to focus on the paper's banner.

"John, what are you doing reading a Chicago newspaper. Don't we have enough problems here?"

"Robert, look at the story. It's about us. It's about our port and our cotton."

Chaffe's eyes focused on the text, and as he read the story, his eyes widened as he took deep breaths. His neck became florid as he ground his teeth. "Goddammit," he said, as he stood, dropped three dollars on the table, snatched the Chicago newspaper, and ran out of the hotel. Moore followed him to the front door and watched the wiry Cotton Exchange President run down Saint Charles Avenue towards City Hall.

Breathless, Chaffe climbed the steep front steps of City Hall and walked briskly to the mayor's office. When he arrived, he found Mayor Shakspeare, J.D. Houston, and city councilman and attorney Ferdinand Claiborne poring over the pages of extensive ledger books, listing the names of the men who had registered to vote during the last twelve months. Most were immigrants—Italian immigrants—and the mayor was noticeably agitated. When Shakspeare noticed Chaffe standing near the doorway, he greeted his friend.

"We have problems, Robert," the mayor said.

"I know. Big problems," Chaffe responded. "Read this article in the *Chicago Times.*"

"Robert, I don't have time to read the Chicago newspaper. We have problems right here and right now."

"This article is about us, and we have problems on the docks," Chaffe responded.

Shakspeare took the newspaper from Chaffe and tried to read it. He patted his vest, looking for his spectacles, but they were buried in the voter registration books. "Here, J.D., read the article out loud, so we all can hear it."

Houston took the newspaper and began to read:

"A family named Provosano had enjoyed a monopoly on the stevedore work on the levee for a long time. They became wealthy and arrogant and did as they pleased. Merchants complained of neglected work and the careless handling of goods, but the Provosano brothers were too independent to pay any attention. Taking advantage of the dissatisfaction,

Tony Matringo, who had worked for the Provosanos, organized another gang and set up in opposition to the monopoly, gradually working the Provosanos out of the trade."

"Oh my God," Shakspeare said. "Why would that be in the Chicago papers and not ours. Could it be true?"

"The article quotes William Pinkerton as the source of the information, and except for misspelling Matranga's name, seems accurate. This is why we have war down there, and now the entire country will know our problem on our docks," Houston said. "Merchants and shippers could shift their cargoes to other ports."

"No doubt New York will pick up on that story. How old is it?" the mayor asked.

"Five days ago," Houston said.

"Ferdinand, do you know how many people live in Chicago?" the mayor asked.

"About a million, Mr. Mayor," Claiborne responded. "We get much commerce from Illinois and the Ohio River Valley. Like J.D. said, if the Pinkertons are finding problems with our port and reporting it nationally, we might have trouble exporting goods. No one wants their goods spoiling on our docks."

Shakspeare slumped in his chair and stared at the voter registration books. "We have a fifteen percent increase in Italians— 'The Other People'—registering to vote, along with a ten percent increase in Colored and Creole voters. Now, our dock war is national news. We not only have a serious political problem, but a commercial one, too. Ferdinand, who is our dock administrator?"

"The Joseph A. Aiken Company, which has contracts with the Provenzanos. But there has been tension down there since Rocco Geraci killed Vincent Raffo on Toulouse Street three years ago. It took a couple of years for Geraci to get arrested, and just this year—and this is only a rumor—J.P. Macheca and some members of our Democrat Party friends got the District Attorney to drop the charges. That sent the Provenzanos into a rage, and they threatened all of the Machecas. That's the second killing involving Geraci. Remember Bonura?"

"Yes, I remember that one, too. It was ruled self-defense—by Hennessy," Shakspeare said. Somehow and some way, we must control the docks and this city's commerce. J.D, use that damn new telephone and call Hennessy. Tell him to get his ass over here, now. And then call Badger and tell him I would like to speak with him, too. We've got to get control of the docks."

"You think Hennessy can do the job?" Houston asked.

"J.D., I need you to help me with our political problems," Shakspeare said, tapping the voter registration books with his right index finger. "Besides, you live in a mansion on Saint Charles Avenue. It wouldn't look good if my police chief had your lifestyle. Your talents are needed elsewhere."

><

Noon

Algernon Badger and David Hennessy arrived at the city hall within minutes of each other. Both had quizzical looks on their faces, given the urgency and method employed to summon them for an expected meeting. And being called by J.D. Houston only heightened their curiosity. As both men sat before the mayor, Houston paced behind them, his boot heels thumping against the wooden floor. Shakspeare had the *Chicago Times* article splayed across the voter registration books. He looked up, removed his spectacles, and slumped to one side of his ornate chair.

"Gentlemen, I called you here on short notice to alert you to a problem you are very familiar with, and now the entire country will soon know." The mayor handed the Chicago paper to Badger. "Read that, General."

Badger took the paper and read it, as Hennessy leaned towards him and did the same. Badger stroked his bushy mustache and said, "Mr. Mayor, this is not good, and I'm afraid this will cause New Orleans some problems if we are perceived not to be able to control or operate our port. May I keep this? I want to telegraph Washington to let them know we are aware of the problem and working on it. Any potential loss of revenue to the government should be reported."

"You can keep it. I will get another paper. But if you telegraph Washington, tell them we are aware of the problem and have it under control. I don't want their military down here and taking over control of our port."

"I will so inform them, Mr. Mayor. But this problem is not quite under control, but we are working on it," Badger responded.

"Working on it? David, when are you going to get that meeting with the Matrangas and the Provenzanos? I don't need the Pinkertons telling the world our port is contested territory by Sicilian mobsters. This will close us down, and Mobile and Galveston will take advantage of our loss. And for Christ's sake, watch Rocco Geraci. He has killed twice, and he seems to be immune from prosecution. I want him stopped."

"We have made many entreaties to those firms, and they said they will let us know when it would be a good time to meet," Hennessy said. "As for Geraci, I have some men watching him. In both killings, his actions seemed justified."

"Justified my ass. He's a killer, David, with divided loyalties. One day, he works for the Provenzanos and then walks down Decatur Street to work for the Matrangas. I want him in jail. Now, take that newspaper down to the port today. Let them know if they can't operate in harmony, we all lose. Get them to sit down soon, or else," Shakspeare growled.

"Or else?" Hennessy probed.

"Or else I will have Mr. Houston and his friends handle the matter."

Chapter 25

Provenzano Brothers Stevedores
Front and Bienville Streets
November 5, 1889
2:00 P.M.

David Hennessy hitched his carriage in the *porte cochere,* in the rear of the Custom House, and climbed aboard Algernon Badger's buggy. Hennessy unholstered his pistol to see if it was fully loaded. Badger smiled and patted his gray vest pocket, indicating he was carrying his derringer, to allay any anxieties the young chief might have about their impending visit to the Provenzano Brothers. However, Hennessy was very well acquainted with Joseph Provenzano and considered him a friend; his brother, George, had a volatile temper and could explode under pressure. Both men knew much was at stake with getting the belligerent Sicilians to quell their mutual hatred, which had roots that were several hundred years old.

Badger stopped his buggy on Front Street and tied the reins to an iron ring embedded into a granite block in the gutter. Both men approached a red clapboard, two-story structure with vigilant eyes. Along the Canal Street side of the building, a gaggle of bedraggled black men sat on a bench smoking cigar butts and chatting in murmured tones. They were waiting for work—any kind of work. When they saw Hennessy, they stood, doffed their hats, and smiled. Hennessy, remembering Badger's advice a few weeks earlier, stopped and exchanged polite conversation. The Black men nodded and smiled, revealing their broken teeth, rheumy eyes, and scarred faces.

When Badger and Hennessy entered the front office of the Stevedore company, Joseph Provenzano respectfully stood. At the same time, his brothers George and Peter remained sitting, with deep frowns etched into their faces. There was no pretense. The passing months have worn each man down, and Provenzanos' dwindling revenue created tension. Nevertheless, though obligatory, some proprieties of the moment were thinly observed.

"Well, what brings the police chief to our humble business on a bright afternoon?" Joseph Provenzano asked.

"Joseph, we need to have that meeting very soon, or there will be dire consequences suffered by all," Hennessy said.

"Bullshit," roared George Provenzano, as he jumped to his feet. "We need business, and your friends are choking us. The only reason you want a meeting is to do us up, as a company."

"Calm down, George," Joseph Provenzano said. "Let's hear what they want. Chief, tell us what's on your mind."

Hennessy handed the *Chicago Times* article to Joseph Provenzano. "Read this."

After reading the article, Provenzano threw the paper down on his desk. "The Matrangas have been kissing those Pinkertons' asses for months. They want us off the docks and out of the markets. We'll fight them. We have a right to make a living, just like them."

"Hold on, Joseph," Hennessy said. "Everyone knows your crews can't keep up with the work at the port. Too many vessels are waiting to be unloaded, which costs the shippers money."

"Rocco Geraci has stolen all my good people. He works for Matranga. You saw what's on my bench outside. A bunch of old Negroes whose good days are behind them. That's all I can get. Matranga won't hire them. I will. They want to work. I will give them work. They are waiting for a small banana boat from Honduras to dock."

"Macheca's?" Badger asked.

"No. Salvador Oteri still sends me some work. Don't you understand? Matranga wants me off the docks so that he can get all the work. And I will be stuck with a few stalls at the markets and the Red Lights Club. So, tell me, what do you want us to do?"

"Agree to a meeting with Matranga to solve your differences, so the city doesn't come down here and take over the docks. You both have a lot to lose. Any more killings or delays in shipping will provoke the city hall and the Cotton Exchange."

Joseph Provenzano sat down at his desk and rocked back in his chair. "Do you really think Matranga will meet with me and share the business down here? He wants to control everything from Poland Street to Poydras Street and all the market stalls in between. He hates my family for something that happened years ago in Sicily."

"Have you ever talked to him?" Badger asked.

"It's no use. His head is as hard as those granite cobblestones outside. He is a greedy, stubborn bastard, and his friend, Macheca, is no better."

"Will you meet with them, if they agree?" Badger asked.

Joseph Provenzano looked at his two brothers. George and Peter shrugged their shoulders. "Okay. Set it up. But I want it on my terms, and at the Red Lights Club."

"What are your terms?" Hennessy asked.

"No guns or knives. I want Tom Anderson and you two to mediate and keep order. My brothers and I are on one side, and Matranga and Macheca are on the other. But no Geraci. Everywhere he goes, he causes shit."

"I will have my gun and some men outside to keep order," Hennessy assured.

"No problem," Joseph Provenzano said. "You're a cop. You need a gun in this damn city."

"When?" Badger asked.

Provenzano looked at his nearly empty calendar and pretended to be busy most of November. "Let's meet on December first, at eight o'clock. It's a Sunday night, and the streets should be quiet. We will use the card room on the second floor, and to show good faith, I will provide the food, too. But if they start their shit, the meeting will be over."

"Let me ask a stupid question," Badger said. "Do you want peace down here?"

"Yes. We want peace. We want business, too. I don't need any more Black Hand demands. I don't need any more threats from anybody. We want to make a living," Joseph Provenzano said.

"Okay. Put it on your calendar. Chief Hennessy and I will go to Matranga and Macheca and set it up. Until then, keep the peace down here."

"Are you going to tell the mayor?" George Provenzano asked.

"I have to," Hennessy said. "It will keep his wolves quiet."

Chapter 26

Poydras Market
South Rampart & Poydras Streets
November 23, 1889
9:30 A.M.

Two peg-legged Confederate veterans plunged pickaxes into the brown alluvial dirt, forming the new roadbed for large granite cobblestones on Poydras Street. Both men appeared in their mid-forties by looking at time's tug on their whiskered faces. Their disabilities and scars meant nothing to a society governed by profit, status, and wealth. Regardless of their physical limitations, they had to work wrought by a cause neither really understood.

With every thump of the pick, their hearts pumped faster and harder; at the end of the day, they would collect their weekly wage of seven dollars. Once they had dug a grave-shaped trench, about two feet deep and four feet long, Jahnke Company workers would help them seat a large stone, in a herringbone pattern, to pave the street. Engineers had selected the pattern to prolong a smoother ride for wooden-wheeled wagons and prevent broken axles and splintered wheels. The design succeeded, with less repair business going to New Orleans' wheelwrights.

Near the street crews, Antonio Marchesi and his son, Asperi, began their busy Saturday setting up their fruit stand in a rented stall in the Poydras Market. The elder Marchesi swept his tiny stall with an old broom of cypress limbs wrapped around a long stick. He had purchased two wooden tables to display his produce, which include apples, oranges, tomatoes, green beans, and ropes of garlic hanging from a hook screwed into a post. Two bunches of ripening bananas hung next to the garlic. In a city deeply divided by race and nationalities, marketplaces throughout New Orleans seemed to be neutral respites from the deliberate avoidance of fellow people who dressed, looked, and spoke differently. Next to the Marchesi stall, a group of stout Irish ladies were busy selling linen they wove themselves in the Irish Channel. The din and dust from the various merchants signaled the life and pulse of the city's growing population, with a concomitant need to eat and survive. Throughout New Orleans's Saturdays, the markets and stalls of the various vendors were veritable hives of commerce, where one's color or name was momentarily ignored to effect a sale.

While Asperi Marchesi was stacking tomatoes on the table, like a pyramid, Antonio Scaffidi, a friend of the elder Marchesi, ran into the stall and told him, in Italian, that a group of Croatian luggers had docked at the end of Poydras Street in the river. Each lugger had stacks of freshly caught fish and hampers of oysters scraped from the bogs of St. Bernard Parish. Scaffidi agreed to lend Marchesi an iron tub and a pushcart to go to Poydras Wharf and buy some fish and oysters if he would agree to share in the profits. Since Scafiddi's stall had already been set up with various produce, he had no room for a tub of fish and oysters.

For a moment, they whispered to each other about the potential profit that could be made and decided to contribute ten dollars each to the purchase. With his interest piqued, the elder Marchesi told his son to go to the end of the Poydras Market, two squares away, and collect Scafiddi's pushcart and tub. Before sending the boy off, the elder Marchesi and Scaffidi each slipped ten dollars into the boy's front pocket. Asperi's father gave him a large wooden bucket and instructed him to stop at the icehouse and cover the purchase with a layer of chopped ice. Scaffidi gave the boy an ice pick, fashioned from a large nail, embedded in a piece of an oak branch. With twenty dollars in his pocket, an excited Asperi scampered down Poydras Street to collect the pushcart and tub.

When Asperi approached the intersection of Penn and Poydras Streets, he came upon a Boylan Detective Agency foot patrolman, J. C. Roe, who was assigned as security for the Poydras Market. The Boylan Detective Agency was retained by the city of New Orleans to augment the shrinking numbers of city police officers, due to resignations and terminations, the latter provoked by Superintendent Hennessy's reform policies. Roe, a Confederate Veteran, and dressed in an all-gray uniform with brass buttons, had lost most of his hearing during the war. When Asperi approached him, the boy startled him. Roe reflexively swung his heavy wooden truncheon and struck the boy on the right side of his head. The blow echoed throughout the market stalls, sending Asperi crashing into a pile of wooden chicken cages. Blood gushed from Asperi's head as the women rushed to the unconscious boy. Other merchants chased chickens throughout the market.

An Irish woman, Margaret Brady, approached Roe and cursed him. "He's just a dago. Go away," Roe said and walked away. Other women tied a linen bandage around the boy's head to staunch the blood flow and gave him some cool water. After a few moments, Asperi regained consciousness and said, "I must go to the fish market." He struggled to his feet. The woman urged him to sit for a while or see a doctor. But Asperi refused, thanked the ladies, and staggered towards the end of the market.

With all his might, Asperi put the iron tub inside the pushcart and shoved it over the broken stones and dirt of Poydras Street. With every thrust of his young legs, the wound throbbed, but he couldn't stop. He couldn't disappoint his father or Mr. Scaffidi.

At the intersection of Poydras and Saint Charles, another street crew was swinging pickaxes near a Jahnke wagon laden with stone. Asperi stopped and leaned against the pushcart for a moment. He tapped his bandage, and it was damp with blood. But he had five squares to go and had to return without the ice melting.

From across the street, Asperi heard his name being called. He saw his old friend, Antonio Terranova, sitting high on the Jahnke wagon. Asperi waved, but even through his blurring vision, he saw his friend running towards him.

"What happened to your head? Speak English," Antonio said.

"A policeman hit me with his stick."

Antonio looked at the blood seeping through his bandage, grabbed the younger boy, and escorted him to the Jahnke wagon. Falcone saw the weakened Asperi and reached under the wagon seat for a kit they kept in case a worker got injured. Falcone removed the linen bandage and dabbed the deep oozing wound with a thick salve. It staunched the bleeding, and Falcone re-bandaged the boy's head.

"Where are you going, boy?" Falcone asked.

"To the fish market at the end of the street," Asperi said. "I need to push my cart there before they have no fish."

"Climb up on the wagon. We will take you there," Falcone said.

"But my pushcart and tub—it's not mine to leave," Asperi cried.

Falcone and Antonio went to the wagon's rear and removed stones with the A-frame boom and winch. Falcone loaded the pushcart and tub into the wagon and headed for the fish market on the wharf.

With Falcone's keen eye, Asperi purchased fish and oysters at a fair price.

"Your father will be proud of you," Falcone said, with a wink.

After guiding the mule team away from the fisherman's quay, Falcone headed towards the Consumer Ice Company on Magazine Street, near the corner of Girod Street. Falcone bought a tub of ice for Asperi.

"How much do I owe you, Mr. Falcone?" Asperi asked.

"Don't worry about it, Asperi," Falcone said, patting the boy's leg. "In New Orleans, like in Sicily, blood is money and money is blood. The ice will melt, but blood remains."

Chapter 27

The Red Lights Club
134 Customhouse Street
December 1, 1889
8:00PM

As Nineteenth-Century barrelhouses go, The Red Lights Club enjoyed a particular social prominence in New Orleans, which surpassed many other taverns, casinos, and houses of assignation pocking the municipal streetscape of the grungy port city. While Parisians were completing the Eiffel Tower, New Orleans struggled to sustain enough electrical current to operate its new streetcars and streetlights. The city's inbred parochialism permeated the operations of the Crescent City, especially how it collected taxes on bars, brothels, and casinos, which was the tribute the mayor demanded as a condition to remain open, except on Sundays—maybe.

While ignoring Louisiana state law, which forbade gambling and prostitution, Shakspeare's police department, and its ancillary civilly authorized law enforcement agencies, the Boylan and Farrell Detective agencies, were instructed to allow the loyal establishments to remain open, even if Mass was being celebrated just blocks away. Shuttered front doors and shaded windows increased the narrow back-alley foot traffic between the French Quarter's tightly clustered *briquette entre poteaux* buildings. A cop's blind eye meant needed revenue for the city and the cop.

On this cold Sunday night, the three gas-lit sconces bolted into the façade of the Red Lights Club were ablaze with bold flickering amber flames, and the windows were clear, allowing anyone to view the activity within, at least on the first floor. No pretense of piety or adherence to abstinence was required this night. And while the second and third floors were by invitation only, which was strictly enforced by members of the Boylan Detective Agency, a dim glow of gas and kerosene lamps behind drawn window shades glowed in the darkness.

Built in 1834, the Red Lights Club stood between Bourbon and

Dauphine Streets and towered over the small Creole cottages built along the brick banquettes of Customhouse Street. The first floor had two large windows and an entrance on the riverside of the structure. The top two floors had galleries laced in intricate black wrought iron designed by the Shakspeare iron works and forged in Leeds Foundry on Tchoupitoulas Street. To avoid paying taxes to the "Shakspeare Plan," owner, Joseph Provenzano, converted the shadowy establishment from a public house to a private gentlemen's club, which only required a twenty-dollar annual fee. Anything other than an activity required an additional tribute.

On the first floor, Provenzano built an elaborate mahogany bar on the rear wall of the club, while each of the windowless walls was festooned with stacks of oak barrels of various sizes, filled with various spirits. Large English tun casks filled with whiskeys and bourbons were on the bottom row, one on top of the tuns, where puncheons filled with Caribbean rum. And on top of the puncheons were small firkins of beer, pressurized with carbon dioxide at the local breweries. Racks of bottled wine from France, Italy, and Germany glimmered behind the bar. A club member could stand at the bar or one of the ten tables. Members were encouraged to use the many brass spittoons placed at the bars and tables. Decorum was required, despite women being forbidden on the first floor.

A steep, long staircase, along the riverside of the building, led to the second floor, which housed the casino. It has a large room with six round green-felt card tables, two faro tables, and a baccarat table. Near the head of the stairway, behind a secured door, stood a jail-like cell locked with a large brass key, which was kept in the pocket of the head cashier, who would dispense poker chips for money and vice versa. A trusted relative of Provenzano's sat in the cell-like cage next to the cashier, with a double-barrel sawed-off shotgun, known to the Sicilians as a *Lupara,* cradled in his arms. Every club member knew they could play in a secure environment. Any violation of the house rules would result in a lethal tumble down the stairs.

Down a dimly lit hallway, at the rear of the second floor, a second stairway led to the third floor. It was guarded by another trusted Provenzano relative, armed with a *Lupara,* who required a tip before ascending the stairway, where a small vestibule, beyond a red velvet curtain, waited. Inside the vestibule, a lady who had the countenance of a dyed, painted, and perfumed feral-farrowing sow sat behind a small writing desk. When a member arrived, she would stare at him and slide a menu of services across the desk, which were provided under the dulcet gaslights within a warren of small rooms, called cribs. If the terms were agreeable, the gentleman was instructed to place his tribute in a blue silk bag, sit on a round Victorian sofa, and wait for his demimonde. The "Bill of Fare" ranged from the mulatto *déclassé,* to the tender courtesans for gentlemen from the American section of the city. After the services were rendered, the gentleman was escorted to a rear external stairway to avoid awkward encounters with anyone.

David Hennessy and Algernon Badger arrived at the club a few minutes past eight. They were accompanied by Hennessy's secretary, George Vandervoot, who was assigned to keep the meeting minutes. Because of the dwindling hours and the falling temperature, the streets of the French Quarter were empty, and most of the windows were dark. A large knot of carriages and riderless horses was tied and tethered to the iron support columns in front of the Red Lights Club. Several city policemen and Boylan detectives hovered around an old iron pot filled with burning coal. A northerly wind whistled down the narrow street as the officers stomped their feet and held their hands over the glowing coals. Across the street, newspaper reporters huddled around a pile of glowing coals in the deep gutter.

"How did the papers know about the meeting?" Badger whispered in Hennessy's ear. Hennessy didn't respond but only glanced at Vandervoort.

As the three men entered the club, a Boylan detective saluted the chief and pointed up the stairs. The three men climbed the stairway, ignoring the howling questions from the reporters across the street. At the head of the stairway, Joseph Provenzano greeted the men and ushered them into the casino, which had been converted into a large conference room. Since Badger, Hennessy, and Vandervoort were a few minutes late, all sides of the controversy were already present, but standing at opposite sides of the room, with their arms crossed, glaring at each other.

Hennessy approached the end of the table, and as he slowly scanned the room and its shadowy corners, he asked, "I want the meeting to go peacefully. Now, how many of you are armed?"

Every man in the room raised his hands, including Badger. "You, too, General?" Hennessy asked.

"In this city, I never go anywhere without my derringer," Badger responded, patting his silver silk vest.

Everyone in the room laughed, which broke the tension for a moment. Then Joseph Provenzano reminded everyone in the room that his cage man had a shotgun loaded with buckshot pointed at the table. "If anyone draws a gun, we all get hit. That way, we all have peace," he said.

Again, the room laughed, and each man found a seat and placed their elbows on the green felt and waited. A black waiter placed several bottles of whisky and glasses on the table, followed by a silver wassail bowl filled with a concoction of whisky, bourbon, rum, and absinthe. As the waiter placed a silver ladle into the bowl, Joseph Provenzano enjoined, "I put that on the table to calm everybody down. But drink it slowly, because it can hit you harder than that shotgun over there."

Again, there was more laughter as the men filled their glasses and flared their cigars. To chase the chill, the waiter stoked the coal grates in two small fireplaces at each side of the room, and cracked a door which led to the balcony to allow some ventilation and balance the room's temperature. Hennessy said as everyone got seated and comfortable, "George Vandervoort, my secretary, will keep the meeting minutes. He will write what you say to the best of his ability, but he needs to know your names, so let's go around the tables and identify yourselves. To his left, Algernon Badger announced his name, and Vandervoort wrote it down on a piece of thick writing paper. Then, clockwise around the table, each man said his name.

"Joseph P. Macheca."

"Tom Anderson, State Assemblyman."

"Charles Matranga."

"Anthony Matranga."

"Rocco Geraci."

The group moaned.

"Salvatore Sunzeri."

"Ike Kuhn."

"Luke Scalco."

"Jack Kohl."

"Frank Locascio."

"Salvador Oteri."

At the opposite end of the tables, Joseph Provenzano proudly announced his name, followed by:

"George Provenzano."

"Anthony Provenzano."

"Guiseppi Provenzano."

"Vincent Provenzano."

"Peter Provenzano."

Vandervoort scribbled furiously, pausing only to dab the nib of his pen in a small jar of black ink. Once Hennessy recognized the participants were logged into the meeting, he stood and began to speak. As he did, the waiter returned and slipped a cold glass of milk in front of him, which triggered a round of sneers and snorts from the men at the table.

"What's wrong, Chief, my liquor ain't good enough for you?" Joseph Provenzano asked. The room erupted in laughter.

"Joseph, you know I don't imbibe in spirits of any kind," Hennessy responded. Now that everyone seems in good spirits, let's begin."

The room turned somber as Hennessy removed some notes from his coat pocket, unfolding the papers. Charles Matranga and Joseph Provenzano stared at each other. "First, I want to thank everyone for agreeing to have this meeting," Hennessy began. "It's long past due that we discuss our differences and end the violence on the docks."

"What about a man stealing another man's business?" George Provenzano sneered. "Are we going to discuss that?"

"We will discuss anything you want. But the killings, cuttings, and shootings must stop. The mayor is determined to end the violence down here, anyway he can," Hennessy said.

"Does your mayor know you serve two masters?" Charles Matranga asked.

"What do you mean, Mr. Matranga?" Hennessy asked.

"Did you read the *Mascot* last week? They wrote that you still have an interest in the Boylan Detectives, and the more cops you fire, the more business the Boylans get. Whose detectives are downstairs guarding this whorehouse, now? You're a member here, and your detective agency is making money, as we sit here. So, as I see it, we have a lot to discuss here tonight," Charles Matranga sneered.

"This is not a whorehouse," Joseph Provenzano said. "This is a respectable club where gentlemen from both sides of Canal Street can come to relax. Drink a little. Gamble a little. And enjoy a worldly lady's company."

"And nothing is free here, especially what goes on upstairs," Charles Matranga said.

"Mr. Matranga, I am trying to reform the police department. I have some men who can't read or write but got badges from the city's politicians. Until I get the police department this city needs, we must rely upon the services of private patrols and detectives," Hennessy explained.

"Either way, you make money, Chief, while we are losing business on the docks," Joseph Provenzano said.

"Well, let's see if we can reach a compromise where every shipping firm and stevedore company can make a profit," Hennessy said. "Currently, the people who run this city aren't happy with the operations of the docks, the markets, or the bodies floating in the river. Blood attracts buzzards, not investors."

"That's because their cut isn't big enough. They want more money from us and our businesses," Anthony Matranga said. "I keep the books for our company, and we are just getting by."

"Bullshit. You keep stealing our business from the docks and pushing us out of the stalls in the markets," Joseph Provenzano said. "And you have Rocco Geraci stealing our best workers. All I can get to unload our boats are a few old negroes with back problems, missing fingers, and peg legs."

"I quit you, because you do not treat us well," Rocco Geraci said, pointing his finger at Joseph Provenzano. "The Matrangas treat the workers better and pay better."

"You bastard, you killed for Matranga—two good men—hard workers. You scared our good people away and into the arms of the Matrangas. You won't do that again," Vincent Provenzano yelled.

"*Vaffanculo,*" Geraci screamed, as he jumped from his chair. "I was found not guilty and never charged on the other."

"That's because Macheca and Hennessy spoke for you. Bonura was a good friend. I no forget, "Vincent Provenzano said.

"Hold on, everybody," Badger said. "Sit down, Mr. Geraci, and have a drink. Everybody, calm down. We will not solve any problems for the future if we wander around in the past. What's done has been done. We must discuss how not to repeat the same mistakes, or you will all lose."

"Lose? We are losing our business as we sit here," Joseph Provenzano said. "All we want is a fair chance to make an honest living. But every month we see our business eaten away by the Matrangas."

"You remember what the *Chicago Times* wrote about your company, right?" Badger asked.

"And you remember what I told you about that article? Matranga and the Pinkertons were behind it," Joseph Provenzano responded.

"Bullshit," Charles Matranga said. "Shippers come to me because I can unload their boats and ships better and quicker than you. Your people drop bales of cotton into the river. Fruits spoil waiting to be unloaded. Even Macheca has to hire rat bastards to keep his fruit from being eaten on the wharfs by vermin. Right, J.P.?"

"Whoa. Whoa. What is a rat bastard?" Badger asked.

"I'll explain," Macheca said. "You see, rats don't eat cotton but will devour a boat of bananas in one night. So, I go to the orphanages and hire some of the Sicilian kids, and I pay them fifty cents a night to keep the rats off my boats and docks. If they club a rat, I give them an extra quarter for each rat they smash."

"So, if there is a delay in unloading, you have to hire rat bastards to protect your cargo, right?" Charles Matranga asked.

"Or the ship docks when there are no stevedores available. Look, I want peace down here, too. I will return some of my work to the Provenzanos if they promise to work harder and stop the violence," Macheca said.

Charles Matranga began to seethe in his chair. He tugged on his collar while his neck corded in anger. He leaned over and whispered something in Frank Locascio's ear. After their furtive exchange, Charles Matranga sat up in his chair, took a swill from his glass, and said, "I will give a little. I will give you some spaces in the Orleans, French, and Poydras Markets— two stalls at each market. If J.P. wants to send you work, that's fine with me, but you get no men from me. You have to round up your own crews and gangs. That's the best I will do."

"Why don't you give me back what you stole from me?" Joseph Provenzano pleaded. "Just give me back what you took this year alone, and I will be happy."

"Take my offer or leave it," Matranga said. "But be careful, if you leave it."

"Hold on," Hennessy said. "I want no more violence down here. If you can't solve your problems, everybody loses."

"Well, you can send more of your Boylan detectives down here to watch us," Charles Matranga said. "That way, you will have peace and make money, too."

"Wait a minute, Matranga," Badger interrupted. "There's another little practice which comes to an end tonight. And everyone at this table is guilty of it."

"What?" Macheca asked.

"As I look around this table, I see thousands of dollars in tariffs and taxes not paid to the U.S. government. I am aware of your little practice of unloading cargo from boats and ships on the port side, sailing it downstream to St. Bernard Parish, and getting your favorite drayage firms to haul it back to markets for untaxed profits. So, as I see it, each of you is making money. So, Matranga has an offer on the table. Think about it, Mr. Provenzano. I want an answer in my office at the Custom House by noon in ten days. That's enough time for you to arrive at some accord."

"If there's no agreement?" Joseph Provenzano asked.

"Then, you will suffer the consequences of your actions. If you are wise, you will work together and forget ancient feuds, which started in a country you don't live in anymore," Badger warned.

The men moaned, and sharp stares were exchanged.

A frail Salvador Oteri stood and remained silent by his seat until the room became quiet. Without interrupting anyone and demonstrating old-world respect, he began to speak. "I have been in the fruit import business for many years. Everyone in this room knows me as an honest, reputable man who only wants the best for my adopted home. But I must say this." His voice began to shake, as did his hands, which rested upon the table. "I will soon sign with Matranga and Locascio to unload most of my ships from Central America. The reason is that they charge less for their work. Mr. Provenzano, you cost me too much, and your crews are unreliable. I can't sell rotten fruit. My profits are low, and your stevedores steal too much. It's nothing personal. I consider you a friend, but friendship goes both ways. I will send you my small boats from Cuba, but that's all. I hope you understand. Now, I am tired, and I am going home." No one said a word as Oteri left the casino and descended the stairs. After a few moments, a new voice filled the room.

"May I say something?" Tom Anderson asked.

"Please, sir, go ahead," Badger said.

"Most of you know me as a saloon keeper, among other things."

The room erupted in laughter, given Anderson's entrepreneurial skills in the concupiscent arts along Basin Street.

"Well, as a politician, I enjoy a good laugh, too. But let me get serious for a minute. The state legislature and the governor are keenly aware of the problem on the docks. The very people who were responsible for bringing so many Italian immigrants to New Orleans—the planters—are now complaining that their products, cotton, sugar cane, rice, and everything else grown in Louisiana, are not getting to market on time, and they blame this feud between the Matrangas and Provenzanos. I know you both well. I know your past. But let me warn you both now. If you don't work together, the state will try to take over the docks, and the mayor knows this."

Anderson wiped his right hand over his bushy mustache, grasped the lapels of his dark gray overcoat, and began to pace the room's width.

"Shakspeare won't let the state near those docks. He hates the state government as much as he hates you. This is all about who controls those docks, and he wants his friends to have that control—not you or the state. If you do not reach an agreement soon, and spring is coming in a few months, it won't be the city or state that suffers. It will be you. You *will* lose your business."

"Now, most of you know I am good friends with Dave Hennessy, and he tells me what's happening in this city. You are lucky to have him trying to broker a peace between your families. He doesn't need to be here. I don't need to be here, but enjoy your votes. Dave could be home with his mother on Girod Street, on a cold Sunday night. He could let Shakspeare take over the docks, but he's with you tonight. By the end of next summer, you will be working together or not working at all. Do you understand me?" Anderson asked sternly.

The room went silent as a crypt. And while Anderson began to speak again, he was interrupted by the sharp knocking sounds of hard-sole shoes echoing against the wooden hallway floor outside the casino, followed by the angry voices of several women. Joseph Provenzano went to the locked door and opened it. Immediately, he was pushed aside by three women who worked on the club's third floor. Their leader, Fannie Deckert, dressed in a red calf-length dress, crowned by a black lace collar, pranced into the room carrying an empty porcelain chamber pot. She was followed by two young mulatto prostitutes, who were painted up to appear adults. Their sepia cheeks were rubbed with rouge, and their lips stained with beeswax and extract from red berries. Their raven-black hair flowed down their shoulders and collected above their small lemon-oiled breasts. The illusion failed miserably, for they remained young, soiled doves huddled under the eaves of a house of assignation.

Deckert moved the wassail bowl and planted the chamber pot on the table. "If you gentlemen don't mind, we would appreciate you compensating my ladies for the loss of business you have caused me tonight. Pointing to the open pot, Deckert yelled, "Fill it up with cash, or I will take these ladies back to Number 11 Burgundy Street and lock the door until we are paid. It's your decision. Either your pockets will be empty, or your pants will be full." Deckert looked around the table until her eyes fell upon David Hennessy. "Shit! What is the police chief doing here?"

"Inspecting the premises, Miss Deckert. Is that the faint scent of lemon oil I smell, splashed on those young girls to make them paler under the dim light?" Hennessy asked.

"Very observant, Mr. Hennessy. Why don't you come upstairs with me, while these men fill my pot?"

"No, thank you, Miss Deckert. I don't want to catch the gleet."

"Gleet? You sanctimonious bastard. You cops have never turned me down. You know, most of them hate you, don't you? I hear things you should know."

"Miss Deckert, collect your pot and your girls and leave, before I have you and them arrested."

Deckert snatched the empty pot from the table, but not before Joseph Provenzano stuffed some money in it.

><

As Anderson, Badger, and Hennessy left the Red Lights Club, George Vandervoort approached his boss while tucking his notes in his coat pocket. "Did you get all that down, George?" Hennessy asked.

"Yes, sir. I will use our new typing machine tomorrow and give you my notes. Do you want the Fannie Deckert part in there, too?"

"Why not. It was part of the meeting," Hennessy responded. "Our records should reflect everything that goes on in this city."

"Chief, there's something else I need to ask you?"

"What is it, George?"

"When I was descending the stairs, I heard the Matrangas saying they would no longer negotiate. Do you want that in my notes?"

"Absolutely. If there's a war down here, we can always say we tried," Hennessy lamented. "After you type your notes, we will tell the mayor."

"You think that is the wise thing to do, Chief?" Vandervoort asked.

"George, I think he has already decided what to do, regardless of what the Matrangas and Provenzanos decide. Shakspeare and his friends are going to take the docks. They need a good excuse. They feel the *Mafia* controls the docks, but it appears we have two *Mafias* in this city."

Chapter 28

St. Charles Avenue & Poydras Street
Friday, December 6, 1889
11:30 A.M.

War is man's worst endeavor, because it is forged in hell, burns through the innocent lives, destroys dreams, creates hateful prejudices, and carves deep scars into the bodies and minds of those who have survived. The dead have no memory. It alters man's thinking and excites his imagination by etching conflicts that have occurred, and those marooned in his imagination, and loiter in the darkest recesses of his mind until triggered by some spark of his past. War accomplishes no sustainable peace, only a suspicious pause, crouched in the dark like a bandit, waiting to pounce upon people who bear no responsibility for its cause. War is conceived in feral prejudices created by previous wars that should have never been fought. Man's restive spirit, while praying for peace, is garrisoned behind the political solipsists' aspiration for glory, power, social position, and wealth, while those responsible impiously stamp their boot heels into the soft mud of the graves of boys who died for another man's desires.

Native New Orleanians, as a result of an extorted surrender in 1862, followed by a harsh Union occupation, followed by an imposed Reconstruction, developed a *bête noire* for anything or anyone, which conflicted with their antediluvian and antebellum caste system. Negroes, Octoroons, Mulattos, and Sicilian immigrants, in that descending social order, enjoyed a social tolerance commensurate with their sweaty utility. Strict social boundaries were established and enforced, except behind the scarlet shrouds of Basin Street and the French Quarter, where the enforcers of those boundaries cuddle with indigo taboos, while wrapped in the arms and legs of young girls, paid to say nothing.

This morning, the streets of New Orleans were empty. Though it was a Friday, the only sound which could be heard was the hoof steps of a mule pulling a solitary drayage wagon near the Poydras Market, followed by the lumbering thumping of a Jahnke wagon near the intersection of Saint

Charles Avenue and Poydras Street. John Falcone and Antonio Terranova sat on the wagon looking at the deserted streetscape. In the distance, they could see merchants sitting idly by their wares in the market. There were no customers. When a newsboy passed their wagon, Falcone yelled to him, "Where   is   everybody?"

"For two cents, you can read about it in the *Daily Picayune*," the clever boy responded.

Falcone dug into his pockets, found two pennies, and tossed them to the newsboy, for which he received the broadsheet from the city's largest newspaper. Falcone opened the paper, as Antonio peered over the page. There on the front page, it read in bold print, covering several columns:

"Throughout the South are Lamentations and tears; in every country on the globe where there are lovers of liberty, there is mourning; wherever there are men who love heroic patriotism, dauntless resolution, fortitude, or intellectual power, there is a sincere sorrowing. The beloved of our land, the unfaltering upholder of constitutional liberty, the typical hero and sage, is no more; the fearless heart that beats with sympathy for all mankind is stilled forever, a great light is gone—Jefferson Davis is dead."

"What does it say, Mr. Falcone?" Antonio asked.

"Jefferson Davis died."

"Who is that?"

"Somebody important to these people. That's why the market and streets are empty. Let's drop this load of stones on St. Charles. I don't see anyone from the city to lay them. So, we leave them here."

Before descending from the wagon, Antonio read the broadsheet. He learned the President of the old Confederacy, which he did not understand, had died at the home of Charles Erasmus Fenner, the cousin of Clarence Fenner, a wealthy cotton broker of the city. Davis died just after midnight on December 6, 1889, at Fenner's mansion at First and Camp Streets.

"Mr. Falcone, where are First and Camp Streets?" Antonio asked.

"A neighborhood where we are not allowed to go. Come down here and help me with these stones."

"Is it far from here?"

Falcone laughed. "It's a world away from here, but actually, it's only about a mile from this intersection, and two miles from that big statue of their Confederate General Robert E. Lee, on that circle a few blocks from here. Many people here are still fighting a war that happened over twenty years ago. Now, we are caught in the middle of their lost dreams. Let's drop the stones and get out of here."

As Falcone wound the winch and dropped a large stone, a police officer came up and demanded that they leave and take the stones with them. "Why?" Falcone asked.

"Because we are getting ready for President Davis's funeral at City Hall, and Saint Charles Avenue must be completely cleared."

"Who was President Davis?" Antonio asked, thinking the cop would have more information than the newspaper.

Without a word, the police officer punched Antonio in the face, dropping the boy to his knees, and then face-down on the cobblestoned street. Blood gushed from his nose and an inch-long cut on his nose. Antonio moaned, as his face scraped across the blood and granite. "Why did you hit the boy?" Falcone yelled. The cop laughed, rubbed his right knuckles, and walked down Saint Charles Avenue towards City Hall.

Mr. Falcone grabbed the medical kit under the wagon seat and applied a gauze bandage on Antonio's nose. As he did, Ilsa Jahnke stopped her carriage near the intersection and ran to Antonio's aid.

"What happened?" she asked.

"A policeman hit Antonio," Mr. Falcone said.

"Why?" she asked.

"Because he wanted to know who Jefferson Davis was?"

"Oh. The entire city is in mourning. All the schools are closed, and so is our business. My father sent me to tell you to return to the yard with the stones. The city won't be paving any streets for a week." Ilsa removed the bandage and saw blood oozing from an inch-long jagged cut descending down Antonio's nose. "You go back to the yard. I will take him to Charity Hospital. Tell my father what happened."

Ilsa Jahnke and Mr. Falcone helped a stunned Antonio into her carriage and left for Charity Hospital, about two miles away. Since the streets were empty, except for a few pedestrians, Ilsa made the trip within ten minutes. Doctors in the emergency theater applied some ether on a cloth to place it under Antonio's nose, which caused him to fall asleep. While he slept, a doctor closed the wound with ten black stitches and wrapped a bandage around his nose and head. "When he wakes up, tell him to come back to the hospital in ten days to have those stitches removed. I don't think the nose bone is broken, and the swelling should go down in a few days," a doctor said. No one asked what happened to Antonio.

><

1:30 P.M.

Ilsa left Charity Hospital with Antonio slumping in the carriage's seat. With every bump in the road, he would moan. "Where am I?" he asked.

Ilsa would pat him on his head and answer, "I'm taking you for a ride to get some fresh air in Milneburg. The cool air will make you feel better."

When they arrived at the end of Elysian Fields, near Lake Pontchartrain, Ilsa helped Antonio down from the carriage. Through his blackened and bruised eyes, Antonio gazed into the crystal-blue eyes of the young German girl. They walked on a pier over the lake's shallow waters and found a small weather-beaten café near the Port Pontchartrain lighthouse. There, she bought him lunch and a cup of hot black coffee. A gentle northern breeze flowed over them, as they watched fisherman dock their boats. The smell of fresh coffee, baking bread, and freshly caught fish wafted over them.

"Reminds me of Palermo, without the mountains," Antonio mused. "It's nice out here. Is this part of New Orleans?"

"Yes. People come here to fish and escape the city's smells. Even a small train stops here, which goes back to town."

"I don't understand this place. I ask a question, and a policeman punches me. I did nothing wrong," Antonio said, rubbing his bandage.

"It's New Orleans. My father said the people here are a mixture of love, hate, whiskey, gunpowder, every race and color, dumped in the middle of the swamp and ordained to live together. Everybody nods politely to each other but wishes everybody else were dead or living somewhere else. Your name and address are your legacy and destination. Where you are born is where you will die."

"How do you know so much?" Antonio asked.

"I read books about old Europe and people with titles. Some people here would be happier in old Europe, where they can prance about all day with their titles." Ilsa stood and mockingly affected an exaggerated royal galliard dance along the wooden pier. The calm wind tussled her golden hair.

"Be careful you don't fall into the lake," Antonio warned. The bottom of your dress is getting muddy."

Ilsa twirled and spun into her chair. "That's fine. Our servants will boil the stains out. Can you dance like that?" she asked.

"No. I'm the son of a Sicilian vintner," Antonio responded.

"I like the Sicilian vintners," Ilsa said.

Antonio blushed behind his large bandage. "Tell me. Did Jefferson Davis have a title?" Antonio asked.

Ilsa burst into laughter. "Sorry. I'm not laughing at you, but why do you think you were punched in the nose for asking a simple question like that in New Orleans?"

><

3:30 P.M.

The evanescent late-autumn sun began to slip lower into the southwest horizon, casting a brilliant aureate glow upon the French Quarter's gray-slated roofs and rubescent brick-walled structures bordering Chartres and Barracks Street. The front gate of Saint Aloysius Academy remained open, where passersby could watch Brothers Stanislaus and Angelo pace the school yard with a worried countenance. Since the city demanded that all schools be closed in observance of Jefferson Davis's death, no students were in the schoolyard.

Ilsa Jahnke yanked the reins of her horse and drove into the school yard with Antonio sitting next to her. Immediately, the Brothers noticed the large bandage on Antonio's nose and the gauze band wrapped around his head. By now, both of his eyes were deeply blackened, which only heightened the Brothers' anxiety.

"Antonio, where have you been? What happened to you?" Brother Stanislaus asked.

Before Antonio could answer, Ilsa told the Brothers the entire story about their ride to Milneburg. "Ilsa, your father was here several times looking for you. You'd better get home before it gets too dark. We'll take care of him, and thank you for your care and time," Brother Stanislaus said. But before entering the building, Antonio turned, looked back at Ilsa, and waved. The gesture was politely returned, and she left the yard.

The Brothers helped Antonio to his room on the school's third floor. Brother Angelo put some coal in the fireplace and started a small fire to chase the chill from the room. The housekeeper returned with some ice wrapped in a towel and gently put it on Antonio's cheeks, while another housekeeper brought him dinner of baked fish and vegetable soup. "You can take your meals here until you feel comfortable, Antonio," Brother

Angelo said. "We won't have school until next Thursday. The city is closed down until after Jefferson Davis's funeral.

Antonio tried to eat, but with every bite, he winced in pain. "We understand a policeman punched you. Is that correct?" Brother Stanislaus asked.

Antonio nodded.

"Son, you must understand there are many people in New Orleans who are still fighting a war, which ended many years ago, but in their hearts, they are still struggling with their past. They are trying to keep the important things to them and their fathers alive, while time has marched on like an army of ghosts. Now, the Italians come to this country, and that gives them a new opportunity to impose their will and old values upon a new class of people. Some people can't feel important unless they are hurting others. Does any of this make sense?" Brother Stanislaus asked.

"They want us to go back to Sicily?" Antonio asked.

"Yes and no. They need your labor, but don't want your company. They need your sweat and blood, but don't want to see you toil. They want your results, without witnessing the process. But *we* won't let that happen. Our school is dedicated to educating *all* people. Italians are strong people and work hard. Yes, some are bad, but there were bad people here before the first Italians arrived in New Orleans. That war they fought many years ago was for the freedom of *all* people, including you."

"But I'm not an American."

"You will be." Brother Stanislaus said. "And American laws apply to you, and every other Italian in New Orleans. Now, let's take that bloodied shirt off and put on a clean one. After you are finished eating, rest with the ice on your face. It will keep the swelling down."

"Tomorrow is Saturday. Can I work?" Antonio asked.

"No. The city is shut down until next week. Besides, earlier today, Mr. Jahnke and I had a long conversation. He thinks it would be better if you stayed on this side of Canal Street and worked. He got the contract to lay cobblestones on Basin Street, from the parish prison to Canal Street. You will be safer working there," Brother Stanislaus said.

Antonio slurped his soup and dropped the spoon into his bowl. "He no want me to see Ilsa anymore?"

Brother Stanislaus drew a deep breath. "Remember what I said about old values? The Creoles call it *vieil argent de sang blue*—old money of the blue bloods. Well, Mr. Jahnke needs to get city contracts, and having his daughter see an Italian boy might hurt his opportunities. New Orleans is an American city, but some people here resist American ways. They live in the past while sacrificing their futures. They prefer a city like Europe, with rank, status, and title. Do you understand?"

"Yes, Brother. I understand. They want it like Italy, but without the Italians," Antonio quipped.

"Excellent observation, Antonio. But don't worry. I have a good opportunity for you to succeed in life, once you leave our school."

"What's that, Brother?"

"We have a graduate of Saint Aloysius who is an editor of a small newspaper on Camp Street. The third boy who lives up here with you is an Italian Jew. His name is Abraham Jurrichi—he's Neapolitan. He works there, carving printing blocks, which are used to create images for the newspaper. He's very talented with a carving knife. We hardly ever see him, except for his final science class. He told me the editor needs a copy boy who can write and understand English well. This January, we will teach a course on writing English and using the various newspapers in our lessons. The editor will help teach the class. If you pass the course in May, he might hire you. You can continue to live here through next Summer, and attend your last year, taking classes in the morning and working for the newspaper in the afternoon. And, once you graduate from our school, he might hire you. It's an outstanding job, and you won't have to bust and scrape your knuckles on cobblestones anymore. You like?"

"Yes, Brother. But I can now read and understand English very well. I know I still have an accent, but I speak clearly. Don't I?"

"Yes, you speak very well, but you have to be able to write well, too. You are progressing in all your classes, and I have recommended you for this opportunity. It pays four dollars a week, but it's every afternoon and some nights. And you can wear a white shirt to work."

"A new white shirt and maybe a tie?" Antonio asked excitedly.

"Yes. I will take you shopping on Canal Street *if* you get the job."

Antonio hung his head and softly asked, "Brother, do you think Ilsa's father will respect me then?"

"We'll see, Antonio. As you know, some grapes need to ripen on the vine more than others."

Part III
BLOOD AND JUSTICE

Chapter 29

The Picayune Tier
May 5, 1890
10:15 P.M.

Six armed men sat deep in the shadows under an iron-braced tin awning, which hung low on the façade of a cooperage shop on Decatur Street. Their lethal stares were fixed on seven Matranga stevedores finishing their unloading process of Macheca's citrus ship, *Foxhall*. Several rat bastards lined up like little soldiers in the fog. Waiting for their overnight orders to guard the citrus from the hungry wharf rats. The six angry men thirsted for blood while the vermin waited to eat citrus. After Vincent Caruso hung oil-fueled lanterns on the front and rear of a horse-drawn wagon, he waved his fellow stevedores to get aboard for the thirty-minute ride to Greek Row, a cluster of shotgun houses, about two miles down Esplanade Avenue, from the docks.

As Antonio Matranga, Frank Locascio, Rocco Geraci, James Caruso, Salvatore Sunzeri, and Bastian Incardona climbed aboard the wagon, the six-armed men slinked from the shadows. They scurried to their horses, which were tethered to a lamppost on St. Louis Street. They mounted their horses, secured their guns, and galloped down the streets to their dark lair, hidden in high weeds and shrubs at the intersection of Esplanade and Claiborne Streets. Vincent Caruso climbed into the wagon's driver's seat and tapped the horse with the reins. The beast tugged the wagon along the Decatur Street docks, while its passengers opened a bottle of wine and began to sing songs.

At Dumaine and Decatur Streets, Vincent stopped the wagon and allowed his brother, James, to jump down and walk home, a few blocks away. As the wagon rambled on its way, the stevedores sang and celebrated the possibility of future steady work, as their employer, Matranga and Locascio Stevedores, had won a majority of the dock work, to the detriment of the Provenzano Brothers. Steady work meant survival.

As the wagon rolled under the dark leafy canopy of oak trees along Esplanade Avenue, some of the men dozed off, while others chatted in their native tongue about their good fortune of being paid fifty dollars a month, despite knowing their black and white co-workers were earning more. They knew Geraci protected their jobs because of his fearsome reputation with everyone on the docks. including the police and the *Padrone*.

As Vincent Caruso guided the laboring horse down Esplanade towards Greek Row, the street lost its amber illumination of the gas lamps and entered an inky abyss. The only light about them flowed from the wagon's lanterns. The only sound heard came from the iron bands around the wooden wagon wheels, as they crunched the chert-covered street. Cobblestones were reserved for more gilded vicinages.

In the distance and despite the gloom of night and the faint glow of a gibbous moon, Vincent Caruso saw the silhouettes of several men crossing the street. Though it was approaching midnight, Caruso paid no attention to the foot traffic near the intersection of Esplanade and Claiborne. His eyes begged for sleep.

When he reached the brushy intersection, the black of night erupted in the flares of muzzle blasts from shotguns and pistols, spraying ball and shot from the weeds and shrubs into the wagon. As Vincent Caruso ducked down into the well of the driver's seat, he lashed the horse, but a shadowy figure grabbed its bit, stopping the wagon. The assailants yelled some words in Italian, but the deafening volleys rendered the words meaningless. The blasts continued for about thirty seconds, until the gunmen disappeared into the night and smoke.

Darkened windows began to glow behind drawn shades. Men in long night shirts ventured out of their homes and into the street, hearing the gasping pleas of the wounded stevedores. The smell of burnt sulfur and powder hung heavily in the air for several minutes. A nearby resident sent his shoeless son to Esplanade and Rampart Street, to the new police call box. Other residents held lanterns over the wounded stevedores, while some women tore sheets and made bandages.

In the glow of several lanterns and candles, the residents discovered that Vincent Caruso had been shot twice in the right leg and calf. Salvatore Sunzeri was hit in the right hip by a bullet, and his right calf had also been hit. Antonio Matranga screamed in pain. Buck shot shredded his left leg, and blood gushed from every wound. In a few minutes, a crowd of people gathered and gawked. Those stevedores who escaped the blasts tried to comfort their friends. To exact revenge, Rocco Geraci took off on foot, armed with an old revolver. But the only thing he shot was a stray dog, which jumped out of the shrubs and startled him.

At about half an hour after midnight, the main switchboard at the Central Police station called the telephone number 195, the home phone of Chief David C. Hennessy at 275 Girod Street. A police clerk told Hennessy about the shootings at Esplanade and Claiborne, and Hennessy immediately got dressed, ran three squares to the police station, jumped into a waiting carriage, and raced to the scene. When he arrived, a crowd of people and beat cops waded through the tall weeds, searching for any evidence of the ambush. Their candles and lanterns swarmed the intersection like a cluster of fireflies. Two ambulances from Charity Hospital arrived, kicking up a thick dust cloud and causing onlookers and searchers to choke and cough.

Hennessy took charge of the scene and ordered his officers to search for witnesses and evidence. He confronted Rocco Geraci. "Did you see who did this?" Geraci shook his head and walked off. The chief watched as the wounded were carried on stretchers to the ambulances, as the attendants applied pressure to the gaping wounds. Hennessy felt betrayed after concluding that the Provenzanos pulled the triggers. But old-world hatreds, coupled with new world economics, had dragged a Thirteenth-Century Sicily to the docks of New Orleans. Hennessy stood in the dark and realized how powerless he was to stop the violence, and responded in the only way he could. He gathered his men and ordered the arrest of every member of the *Giardinieri,* including every Provenzano family member.

><

When Hennessy arrived at Charity Hospital, he was met by a group of newspaper reporters. Every one of them wanted to know if the shooting was the start of a *Mafia* war in New Orleans. The chief ignored them and pushed his way into the hospital's lobby. A nun, from the Order of the Sisters of Charity, led him to the surgery theater, where he was informed each victim was near death, but doctors were applying all the new surgical techniques to save their lives. George Vandervoort joined his boss at the hospital and informed him that the arrest of the Provenzano family and associates was underway. Hennessy sat on a long wooden bench, knowing he had just kicked open the unlocked Gates of Hell.

At about two that morning, the unwounded Matranga stevedores walked down the hall and met Hennessy and Vandervoort. At that moment, they would only say they saw six figures shooting at them from shrubs and weeds, but could not identify anyone. Hennessy didn't believe them, but understood their culturally imposed silence, which portended a *vendetta*. He ordered Vandervoort to tell all arresting officers to book the Provenzanos with "Capitol Ambuscade," an English common law crime, carrying the death penalty, because the offense was committed with the intent to kill. Ironically, the word's etymology is from the old Italian word, *imboscata.*

About two hours later, Doctor Jefferson Davis Bloom emerged from the surgical theatre wearing a blood-stained white gown. His young face was drawn and worn by the stress of repairing the victims' ghastly wounds. He told Hennessy, the family members, and friends that the men would survive their wounds, but Antonio Matranga's leg had to be amputated to save his life. As a Catholic priest comforted the friends and family, J.P. Macheca and Charles Matranga stomped into the waiting area. Their angry countenance exacted a fearful stillness in the waiting area.

"I want no more trouble on the docks, Mr. Matranga," Hennessy ordered. Besides, none of your men recognized who shot them. I have ordered the Provenzanos arrested and questioned. Let me handle this."

"After I talk to them, you will have the men who shot my people," Matranga seethed. "No more *Omerta*, now. We'll let you handle this, but we will give them justice if you can't give us justice."

Hennessy, again, exhorted Macheca and Matranga to allow the justice system to work. "The newspapers are ready to announce a *Mafia* war in the city. The mayor and his people will come after you and the Provenzanos. Remember what I told you at the Red Lights Club last December. The mayor's people want to control the docks, and if you start a war, you will have fewer stevedores working on the docks, and the cargo will not move. Everybody loses. You must let me handle this to ensure they get justice, and the docks continue functioning."

"I never started no war. Provenzano did. But I will let you handle this, for now," Matranga said.

As Hennessy and Vandervoort left the hospital, he could hear Matranga speaking to his unwounded stevedores in Italian. That alarmed him. "Come on, George, let's go to the police station. We have work to do," Hennessy said.

Chapter 30

Monday
May 6, 1890
6:00 A.M.
Central Police Station

David Hennessy stood on the backsteps of the central police station, waiting for the police department's Black Maria to enter the backyard, near the jail's entrance. Several police officers on horseback escorted the paddy wagon while brandishing either a shotgun or a Winchester. They were taking no chances with the human cargo chained inside. As Hennessy stepped down and walked to the rear of the wagon, a police officer opened its rear doors and ordered George, Joseph, Peter, and Vincent Provenzano, Nick and Salvatore Giulio, Tony Gianforcarro, Tony Pelligrini, and Gaspare Lombardo—all members of the *Giardinieri*—to step down and enter the cell block attached to the rear of the police station. As the morning sun rose above the building, Hennessy's lanky shadow cast across the forlorn faces of the arrestees. Hennessy stood stone-faced as each man, shackled with wrist and ankle irons, filed past him. The clanking of the chains echoed off the building's brick walls, as each man cast a glance at the Matranga's unhorsed, bullet-ridden wagon parked next to the "Black Maria." Newspaper reporters snuck behind the building, with their notepads and pencils, frantically describing the scene. Typically, the police would not allow such a bold security breach, but Hennessy wanted it. He needed it.

><

Throughout the City
9:15 A.M.
The *Daily Picayune* and other daily broadsheets wasted no time exploiting the event as an Italian issue. Under their front-page banner, the *Picayune* reported:

AMBUSCADED!

A Presumed Vendetta Upon Which
The Wounded Will Cast No Light

"Like all Italian affairs, the whole matter is shrouded in mystery, and not even the wounded will tell all they know. It's supposed, however, to be another case of vendetta."

In daylight, Hennessy ordered a legion of police officers, led by Captain John Journee, to return to Esplanade and Claiborne to find witnesses and search the scene again. While there, officers found two muzzle-loading, sawed-off shotguns and a Remington pistol in the weeds near the intersection of Kerlerec and Claiborne Streets, which was about two hundred feet from the ambush. A young boy, identified only as John, told the police he saw six men scatter after the shooting. Three went down Esplanade towards the river, and three went East on Claiborne. The guns were discovered due to the boy's information, and he was taken to the Fourth Precinct Station at Orleans and Marais Streets for a more thorough interview. The Fourth Precinct was built into the Orleans Parish Prison complex, about a mile away.

New Orleans buzzed with the news of the midnight ambush. Brokers at the Cotton Exchange huddled in small knots to exchange their rumors of the event. Nearly every man on the exchange floor held a creased and folded broadsheet, pointing to the paragraphs supporting their theory of the crime. In Charles Chaffe's second-floor office, a more somber mood pervaded, as he and other members of the various exchanges studied the reports. Phone messages from the docks indicated all work had stopped. No vessels were being loaded or unloaded. In fact, only women could be seen walking the streets, as men huddled in small alleys and patios to discuss the news. With all commerce halted on the docks, the city felt like Sunday morning, without the church bells.

At city hall, the mayor worked his new phones and instructed his staff to call all their contacts on "Newspaper Row," on Camp Street. "I want information, now," Shakspeare bellowed. "Someone find Chief Hennessy, and tell him to get here, now." The mayor stomped into his office, where J.D. Houston and Maurice Hart had slunk in without notice. "What are you two hearing?" the mayor demanded.

"The dagoes are at war with each other, and soon the news will spread through the country. Our docks are shut down. Not even the negroes will go near the river. They are all scared of being shot," Houston said. "Hennessy has to make a quick arrest, or all commerce in the city will stop."

"I understand he has made some arrests—the Provenzano gang. But some reporters are doubting whether they did it or not. Anyway, something has to be done down there and soon. Those dagoes are never going to get along, and the negroes are caught in the middle."

"The city has to take over those docks, or we will lose commerce and credibility throughout this nation. Our port services are in twenty states. If those bastards want to fight each other, send them back to Italy—not here," Hart stated.

As I understand it, this vendetta seems to have no ending. Next, the Matrangas will shoot up the Provenzanos, and it will go on and on," Shakspeare said. "And they won't talk. What is this *Omerta* shit, anyway?"

"It means 'silence.' They won't talk to the police. They handle things their way. That's why we have to take back the docks. Once we control the docks, let the bastards kill each other all day. But we can't let them shut down New Orleans. We need to come up with a plan."

"You have a plan, J.D.?" the mayor asked.

"Several."

"Good. Work on them. If you need Parkerson's people, let me know.

"What about Hennessy?" Hart asked.

"Let me worry about Hennessy. He promised me he could bring peace to those docks. He can't do it, or won't do it. Either way, J.D., come up with a plan. Our main cotton season is coming up in August, September, and October. I want those docks working by then," the mayor ordered.

><

187 Dorgenois Street.

Greek Row

10:30 A.M.

Charles Matranga cried when he saw the stub of his brother's heavily bandaged, amputated left leg. He bellowed revenge throughout the second-floor hospital ward, but a nun shushed him to allow his brother to sleep.

"Come on, Charles, let's go find Rocco and find out who did this," J.P. Macheca said, as he wrapped his arm around Charles Matranga's broad shoulders. Let Tony rest. We have work to do. And we can't rely on the police."

Matranga removed a large handkerchief from his jacket pocket and wiped his eyes. "Do you know where Rocco is? He saw what happened," Matranga said.

"I heard the police rounded up a bunch of Provenzano's men, but we want to get the ones responsible for this, even if it means getting Joseph Provenzano himself. Now let's go to Greek Row. Rocco lives there. I think he's hiding from Provenzano and the police," Macheca said.

Charles Matranga left the ward, but not before glancing over his shoulder at his wounded brother. Outside Charity Hospital, the men boarded Macheca's carriage and rode down newly named Tulane Avenue, towards Dorgenois Street. After about a ten-minute ride, Macheca stopped his carriage in front of a row of gray shotgun double houses. The numbers, 187, were painted over the front door of Geraci's house. Since it was a warm day, several neighbors sat on their stoops outside. They knew who the men were knocking on Geraci's door and why. They pretended to see nothing.

Geraci cracked open the door and let Macheca and Matranga inside his small house. A shaken Antonio Locascio was there, too, wondering what would happen next. The four men gathered in the kitchen and sat around a porcelain pot of coffee and several white mugs. A funereal stillness filled the air for a few moments as Rocco began to pour hot black coffee into each man's mug.

"Tell us what happened, Rocco," Macheca said softly.

"They tried to do us up—all of us," Geraci said.

"Who?" Matranga asked.

"The *Giardinieri*. The Provenzanos."

"Who? Which ones?" Matranga probed.

"Joe Provenzano, Peter Provenzano, Nick Giulio, Tony Pelligrini, Tony, Gianforcarro, and Gaspare Lombardo," Geraci said in a determined whisper.

"Did you tell the police?" Macheca asked.

"No. I no tella the police anything. They're worthless."

"How do you know, Rocco?" Macheca asked.

"The muzzle blasts lit up their faces in the dark, on both sides of the street. Pelligrini held the horse, and we were trapped," Geraci said. "I tried to shoot back, but my aim no good. I only had my pistol."

"You need to tell Hennessy," Macheca said. "He's got the Provenzanos in his jail now. You have to go tell him."

"No. I no trust the police. They let it happen. They hate us."

You must tell the police," Matranga said. "We are victims. My brother has only one leg. Your friends are shot up, too. They will live, but you have to talk to the police."

"I can't do that. *They* let this happen. It will happen again," Geraci protested. "The white people want the docks, and they used the Provenzanos to do us up."

"You must, Rocco," Macheca said. "If not, the Matrangas will lose their contract with the city, and view this as a dago war. We can't have that. With the Provenzanos off the docks, and you cooperating with the police, it makes us look good in their eyes. We are really victims, and must stand for our rights. You have no choice. Now get dressed in some good clothes. Let's go to the police station, now?"

"They will kill me," Geraci said, dragging his fingers through his black curly hair.

"Not if they hang first," Matranga said.

"Can I bring my pistol?" Geraci asked.

"No," Matranga responded.

Chapter 31

Central Police Station
Tuesday, May 7, 1890
12:30 P.M.

Like maggots on carrion, reporters of the New Orleans newspapers huddled around the front steps of the Central Police Station, waiting for some news about the arrests of the Provenzano brothers. Every paper dispatched reporters to the police station; some had more than two, and *The Daily Picayune* had four. Each reporter had orders to get the facts and report back to their editors on Camp Street, so the story of the "*Mafia Wars*" could be written. The other newspapers were *The New Orleans Daily Times, The New Orleans Times-Democrat, The New Orleans Daily Democrat, The New Orleans Daily Item, The New Orleans Daily States, The New Orleans Daily Delta, The New Orleans Lantern, The New York Times,* and the evening local paper, *The New Orleans Mascot.*

Each paper had block-carving sketch artists to draw and carve on soft wood the images, which their papers would use to create images and excite the readers' emotions. To date, this was the biggest story to weave through the streets, parlors, shops, and cafes of New Orleans. The competition created coveted and jealous copy. The slightest move by a reporter never went unnoticed by another reporter.

Lawrence Hearn of *The New Orleans Mascot* sat on a bench next to his block-carving artist, Abraham Jurrichi, and his newly-minted messenger, Antonio Terranova. The latter two were graduates of St. Aloysius Academy, and both wore stiffly starched white shirts and black bow ties. Hearn and his young staff said nothing but smiled politely when addressed by their competition. When peppered by questions by other reporters about why his newspaper, the one with the least circulation, would be at the police station, Hearn relented and replied, "We are the last paper to go to press and want to get the story accurate." Hearn's terse response worked. The other reporters walked away.

The monotony of waiting was shattered when an impeccably attired gentleman approached the front steps of the police station, doffed his bowler, and tried to climb the front steps. Reporters from *The Daily Picayune* blocked his passage and demanded to know why he was at the police station. The reporters already knew who he was, but wanted to know his motives.

"For the record, please, will you state your name?" one reporter requested.

"You already know my name. Please excuse me," the man said, as he tried to pry his way through the reporters.

"Please. For the record, sir," one reporter persisted.

"My name is Pasquale Corte, and I am the Italian Consulate for New Orleans, and I am here to see that the men arrested are treated fairly and humanely."

"What about the men they shot?" one reporter yelled.

"I will go to Charity Hospital after I leave here," Corte responded.

"So, you admit the Provenzanos shot the Matrangas last night?" a reporter pried.

"I did not say that, and do not report that. This case is under investigation. I am only here to see that the men are treated fairly. So please excuse me," Corte said, as he pushed his way past the reporters.

Hearn leaned over and whispered to Jurrichi and Terranova, "You just saw how not to get the news. Never insult anyone you want information from. And never lie, even by implication. That man is the official representative of the Italian government in New Orleans. If either of you has a problem, go to him. His office is at Number 23 Poydras Street."

"Is he a lawyer?" Jurrichi asked.

"No," Hearne said. "But he can get you an attorney or solve problems because you are Italian. He's a good man. I know him."

After their encounter with Corte, the reporters resumed their vigil. Some played poker, and some took naps. Every time someone entered or exited the police station, the reporters would snap to attention. Antonio Terranova giggled each time the reporters jumped. After about half an hour, the boredom overtook Terranova, and he began to pace in front of the police station, from Tulane Avenue to Gravier Street. He thought the cobblestone business was more interesting than the newspaper business, but understood waiting for something to happen was just part of the process.

At one point, when he reached the intersection of Basin Street and Tulane Avenue, he noticed a carriage stopping about a hundred feet from the intersection, on Tulane Avenue. The driver of the carriage, partially concealed in the shadow of the carriage's canopy, waved him over.

"*Viendi qui,*" the well-dressed man demanded.

Antonio approached the carriage and recognized the driver.

"*Sei Italiano?*" the man asked.

"*Si. Sicilano,*" Antonio responded.

"*Sapete chi sono?*" The man asked.

"Si. Mr. Charles Matranga," Antonio said.

Okay. You speak English?" Matranga asked.

"Yes."

"Do you know these other men in the carriage?" Matranga asked.

"No. But I have seen you around the French Market. I know who you are."

"Are you a reporter for a newspaper?" Matranga asked.

"No. I am just a runner—a messenger," Antonio responded.

Matranga smiled. "I am about to make you famous, boy. Do you know why we are here?"

"Does it have anything to do with the shooting last night?" Antonio asked.

"It has everything to do with the shooting. The man sitting next to me is Mr. J.P. Macheca, and the man sitting next to him is Mr. Rocco Geraci. We are here to tell the police what happened last night. Mr. Geraci saw everything. Where is your pencil and paper, boy?"

Antonio fumbled into his pockets and pulled out a stub of a pencil and a scrap of paper. As he did, a swarm of reporters descended upon him and the carriage. Every reporter knew who the men were in the carriage and blasted questions at them. The three men stepped down from the carriage and ignored all the questions. As Matranga tethered his horse to a hitching post on Tulane Avenue, he turned to the barking crowd of reporters, waved his arms, and said, "We just gave our story to this young man," pointing to Antonio. "We have nothing more to say."

As Matranga, Macheca, and Geraci walked towards the front door of the police station, the herd of reporters followed them, firing question after question. Lawrence Hearn, realizing what had just happened, grabbed Antonio and pulled him across the street to a small park bench. Abraham followed, but Hearn told him to start carving the images of the three men. Once on the bench, Hearn asked Antonio what the men said. Antonio told him, and Hearn leapt with joy.

"I did good?" Antonio asked.

"You did great for your first day on the job. Now, run back to Camp Street and report what happened to our editor. Tell him everything. Stay there. Don't come back here. Abraham and I will get the rest of the story. Now run. I don't want any reporters following you."

><

1:10 P.M.

The main corridor of the Central Police Station buzzed like a hive of honeybees. Uniform police officers and clerks raced between offices on the first floor and up and down the large mahogany stairway. For a moment, no one noticed who had just walked through the front door. But that was about to change.

Sitting at a small desk near the front door, a bespectacled Corporal Francis McDonnell glanced up and froze. He recognized the three men and knew why they were there. McDonnell respectfully stood and greeted J.P. Macheca, Charles Matranga, and Rocco Geraci.

"We are here to see Chief Hennessey," Macheca said. "Will you tell him we need to speak with him?"

As McDonnell started for the stairway, he was intercepted by Captain John Journee, who told him he would escort the visitors to the Chief's office. No words were exchanged while the men ascended the stairway, but Hennessy, Captain Dexter Gaster, and George Vandervoort stood outside the office when they arrived at Hennessy's office. Seeing their guest, Hennessy and his officers went silent. For a moment, only flinty glances and stares communicated each man's purpose.

Hennessy broke the silence. "Mr. Matranga, I am sorry to hear about your brother, but grateful he will survive his wounds."

"Thank you, Chief," Matranga responded. "You are probably wondering why someone like me is in your police station, but I brought Rocco Geraci, who has told J.P. and me what happened last night. He saw everything."

The dour countenance of the police official changed to excitement. "Mr. Geraci, are you willing to give us a full statement about what you saw?" Hennessy asked.

"Yes, sir," Geraci said.

"Great. Come into my office and make yourself comfortable." Hennessy turned to Vandervoort and said, "Please call the mayor's office, and tell them I am delayed and why. Also, ask them to send over Magistrate Guy Dreux of the city's recorder's court. I want Geraci's statement notarized before we present it to the District Attorney."

><

3:45 P.M.

It didn't take long for Rocco Geraci to relive the events of last night. Even his street-tough brashness crumbled a few times, as he recalled facing several shotgun blasts, feeling the shot whizzing past his head in the night, and hearing his friends scream in pain. He knew how close he came to death, and several times during his statement, he drifted off into his own thoughts. Hennessy and other officers' prodding kept him on course, as Magistrate Dreux, using one of the police department's new typewriters, banged on its keys to complete the formal affidavit of Rocco Geraci. After reading his own words in print, Hennessy handed Geraci an inked pen and asked him to sign it as best as he could.

"By signing this, you know the Provenzanos will do me up, for sure. You know that, don't you?" Geraci asked.

"Mr. Geraci, we are all in danger, from time to time. But it's time we put an end to this war between the Matrangas and Provenzanos," Hennessy said. "You are very brave in coming forward, but I must ask why you didn't tell me last night?"

"I was afraid. I am afraid, now. You asked me if I saw George and Vincent Provenzano. I didn't. You asked if I saw Salvatore Giulio. I didn't. You have them in jail now. What will happen to them?" Geraci asked.

"The law says I must release them. We have no evidence to hold them," Hennessy said.

"They will do me up very soon, if I sign this paper," Geraci said.

"Rocco, you were in the wagon last night, and they aimed their guns at you, too. Either way, you are a hunted man. We all are. If you sign the paper, at least we all have a fighting chance. We can take them out without firing a shot. Don't worry about those three *strunzos*. We'll be watching them, as much as they will be watching us," Macheca said.

Geraci took the pen, signed his name in Italian, and placed an "X" after his signature.

><

5:00 P.M.

The flock of slumbering reporters sprang to their feet when the creaking front doors of the Central Police Station opened. Each reporter focused their attention on three bedraggled and unshaven men. With their notepads ready, the reporters waited for words or utterances from the trio who spent the last fifteen hours in a cramped, hot jail cell, with only a bucket of water and a hole in the floor to sustain their humanity.

As George and Vincent Provenzano, and Salvatore Giulio stood on the top step of the police station, they looked around the crowd of reporters, waiting for them to speak. George Provenzano stepped forward and allowed his voice to roar across the heads of the reporters and beyond Basin Street.

"So, look at us. This is what you came to see. Get a good look. We are three innocent men, and there are six more inside. We didn't shoot the Matrangas. We don't know who did, but we wouldn't be standing here if we did," George Provenzano yelled. "This city hates Italians and Sicilians. We know that. You just want our labor and toil. I am an American citizen, but you won't accept me. My brothers are, too. For years, we and other Italians have fed this city, but you don't care. All you want to report is the bad. All you want to write is there's a '*Dago War.*' This city has always been at war and will be. Why don't you report how many tons of cargo we have loaded on and off ships? Report the good and the bad. But your bosses run this city and view us as mules—animals. We are hard-working men who only want a chance."

One reporter yelled, "If you are innocent and they released you, why are your brothers still in jail?"

"They are innocent, too. But liars have come forward to keep us from working the docks. The Matrangas want it all, but they're stupid. They don't know they are next to fall," George Provenzano said.

"What do you mean by that?" another reporter asked.

"Wait. You will see. Your bosses and their friends want to control the docks and our labor. They will tell you what to write. You are being used. And the Matrangas are being used. The police are being used. Now, the courts will be used. Now, excuse us. We're hungry and we're going home," George Provenzano said, as he descended the front steps of the police station with his brother, and Salvatore Giulio.

Chapter 32

City Hall
Mayor's Office
May 8, 1890
10:00 A.M.

David Hennessy and George Vandervoort left Criminal District Court, which was housed inside the old Saint Patrick Hall at Camp and Lafayette Streets, and scurried across Lafayette Square to City Hall. They had just formally presented the Provenzano case to Orleans Parish District Attorney John Finney and were eager to share the information with Mayor Joseph A. Shakspeare. As they ascended the steep steps of city hall, the doorman directed them to the city council chambers, where the mayor, accompanied by J.D. Houston, Maurice Hart, James Richardson, Senior Editor of *The Daily Picayune*, Charles Chaffe, President of the New Orleans Cotton Exchange, Joseph Herwig of the New Orleans Stock Exchange and several members of the city council were waiting. Hennessy and Vandervoort were warmly greeted by each man, but when Houston hugged Vandervoort, everyone in the room took notice, especially Hennessy.

Shakspeare had coffee and English biscuits served to each man and then looked at his chief and said, "David, please tell us about this dago war. Are you ever going to stop it?"

Hennessy took a sip of his hot coffee and began to read from his notes. "George and I have just left the District Attorney's office, and Mr. Finney told me it is his intent to charge the Provenzanos and others with Capital Ambuscade. By the time we left the courthouse, he had the cases lodged in the two sections of the court. The defendants, Joseph, Peter, Vincent Provenzano, Tony Gianforcarro, Tony Pelligrini, and Gaspare Lombardo, were charged in Judge Robert Marr's court with the shooting of Anthony Matranga and Salvatore Sunzeri. The same defendants were charged in Judge Joshua Baker's court with the shooting of Vincent Caruso."

"Why did Finney charge two cases in two different courts?" the mayor asked.

"I believe Finney is concerned with Marr's advancing age," Hennessy speculated. "I think he wants to increase his chances for a conviction."

"Isn't Finney a civil lawyer?" the mayor asked. "Do you believe he knows what he is doing? Can he handle this case? This is very important to this city. This *Mafia* crap has to stop. I want these men hanged and hanged soon as possible."

"He told me he has asked my attorney, Lionel Adams, who was the District Attorney before him, to help him."

Houston began to laugh and snicker, which drew the attention of everyone in the room. "What's so funny, J.D.?" the mayor asked.

"I'm sorry, Mayor, but our fine police chief apparently doesn't know that Mr. Adams has a partner, whom everyone in this chamber knows well."

"Who?" Shakspeare asked.

"Dominick O'Malley, from Cleveland, Ohio."

The city council chambers echoed with moans of discontent, while Hennessy's fists clenched, and his normally pallid face became florid.

"How do you know this, J.D.?" The mayor asked.

"It's printed on the front page of my newspaper," Richardson responded. "It's a two-dollar advertisement, which I was happy to accept. Since I operate the largest newspaper in the state, I was happy to take their money."

"I just happen to have a copy of your newspaper, Mr. Richardson, with me. And I will be more than happy to read the advertisement," Houston taunted.

"Go ahead, J.D.," the mayor said.

O'MALLEY'S DETECTIVE & PROTECTION POLICE
LIONEL ADAMS, Esq.

"Civil and Criminal matters carefully investigated and reported. Uniformed officers furnished day or night on reasonable terms. Missing witnesses found: absent witnesses located; their general reputation investigated; and all matters connected with legitimate detective business properly attended to."

"How can a reputable attorney of Adams' stature associate himself with a gutter rat like O'Malley?" Shakspeare asked.

"Like it or not, O'Malley gets results—one way or the other," Houston responded. "This means that the chances of the Provenzanos hanging have increased. I am sure O'Malley will do anything to help his boss and friend secure a conviction. And the Matrangas' attorney, A.D. Henriques, a close associate of Adams and O'Malley's, will also assist Finney."

"Did you know this, David?" the mayor asked.

"I knew that the Matrangas hired Henriques. I spoke to Macheca and Henriques as I left the courthouse to come here. They wanted to know what my intent was on the Provenzano case, and I told them we just filed charges with the District Attorney. They seemed pleased, but determined to see justice rendered. I did not know about O'Malley, but it seems all kinds of vermin hang around the courthouse. I suppose it makes them feel important," Hennessy said.

"Our neighbor, *The Mascot*, once called him an 'unmitigated nuisance to New Orleans,' given how many times he has been arrested and set free —mysteriously," Richardson said.

"Didn't you have problems with him in the past, David?" the mayor asked.

"Indeed, I did. He was close friends with Thomas Devereaux, whom I killed on Gravier Street. O'Malley spread rumors that my cousin and I were hunting Devereaux the day I killed him, which was a lie." Maurice Hart laughed. "Devereaux still has many friends in New Orleans. And, as I glance around this chamber, I see many of Devereaux's old friends, including you, Mr. Houston, and Mr. Hart. You, Mr. Houston, and Devereaux wanted my job," Hennessy said. "You probably still want it."

"You killed an innocent man, Hennessy," Houston snarled.

"I was found not guilty. It was self-defense, and you know it, Houston," Hennessy growled.

"And who was your attorney back then?" Houston asked.

"Lionel Adams," Hennessy said proudly.

"And now *his* detective *was* Devereaux's friend? You and O'Malley hate each other. Do you think you can properly investigate this case, *Chief?*" Houston asked. "As I see it, Macheca and Matranga are your friends. Lionel Adams is your friend, but his detective is your enemy. How can you not be biased?"

"Adams can keep O'Malley under his control. As for Macheca, Matranga, and Provenzano, I tried to broker a peace between them. I spent months trying. But hot blood runs deep," Hennessy said. "The

Provenzanos were my friends, too. But it's now up to the juries to decide their fate. Not me. But if anyone in this chamber wants me to stop, step away from the case, to avoid any negative press, I will. The case belongs to the District Attorney now. And that includes Lionel Adams and *your* friend, Houston, Dominick O'Malley."

"What more needs to be done to close this case?" the mayor asked.

"As I sit here, Captain Journee is questioning Bastion Incardona and Antonio Locascio. They were in the wagon, too. And with Geraci cooperating, their memories are returning. Once I have their statements notarized, I will give them to Finney. Two cut-down shotguns were found a block away. They are old muzzle loaders; we believe they belonged to the Provenzano brothers. I must admit, I have not seen those types of guns at the Red Lights Club."

"Stay away from that damn place, David," the mayor howled. "And unless you're arresting those prostitutes in that neighborhood, stay away from Customhouse Street and Burgundy Street. Do you understand?"

"Yes, sir."

"Now go back to your police station and make this case stronger. I want no more blood on my docks," the mayor ordered.

><

As Hennessy and Vandervoort left City Hall, Charles Chaffe and Maurice Hart stopped them halfway down the front steps. "We need to chat with you, Chief, if you have a moment," Chaffe said politely.

"Sure, Mr. Chaffe," Hennessy responded.

"It's approaching the middle of May, and that means those cotton boats will be coming down the river soon. To your knowledge, can the Matrangas handle the amount of cotton and cane?" Chaffe asked.

"I'm not a stevedore, Mr. Chaffe, but there are men hungry for work, and having the Provenzanos in the parish prison will make the docks safer. And after the trials, I hope the docks will operate without the impediment of ancient hatreds."

"Are you sure the Provenzanos will be convicted?" Hart asked. "Won't the *Mafia* continue to control our docks?"

"I have written my counterpart in Rome—the *Carabinieri*—and asked him to send me a list of the known members of the various Mafiosos who have left Italy and come to New Orleans. I have not received a response, but I expect one. Since the Matrangas and the Provenzanos have engaged in lawful enterprises, despite their mutual hatred for each other, it's hard for me to claim they are still part of the city's *Mafia*. I know their past. They have been here for a long time—especially Macheca. When I was a kid, he fought for the Democrats, along with other Italians. As I stand in front of City Hall, I have no evidence that Macheca is part of any *Mafia* organization. He, like you, is a Democrat."

"What about the Matranga group?" Hart probed.

"Again, the Matrangas have long been in New Orleans—like the Provenzanos. I doubt the *Carabinieri* will have anything to say about them. I am more concerned with some people who lie about doing nothing."

"But why are they killing each other so often?" Chaffe asked.

Hennessy rubbed his bushy mustache and said, "I can only guess it's the old-world prejudices, coupled with competition for docks. I have read old newspapers about the Battle of Liberty Place in 1874. I was a kid then, hiding with my mother in the Custom House. I heard the cannon and gunfire echoing around the building. Over thirty people died in three days, and many more were wounded. Some of the survivors sit on Canal Street today, with no legs, selling cigars. None of them are Italian, but were motivated by old prejudices, too."

"Are you defending the Italians? Are you comparing our battle for free elections with the *Mafia's* control of our docks?" Hart asked.

"No one has been tougher on the Italian and Sicilian brigand than me," Hennessy said. "Remember who arrested Esposito in Jackson Square, and caught hell from the Italian Colony and your friend, Devereaux, Mr. Hart. Remember, Thomas Devereaux and Esposito were friends, or have you forgotten that?"

Marcel Hart turned away from the conversation, while Chaffe asked one last question. "Chief, can you guarantee a conviction in the Provenzano case?"

Hennessy began to giggle and tapped down his bowler on his head. "Mr. Chaffe, you know as well as I do, courthouses are like brothels and casinos. Everybody loses, except the house."

Chapter 33

Number 12 St. Philip Street
June 17, 1890
8:00 P.M.

When Camillo Vittrano walked into John Matto's winehouse to play cards in the back room with some friends, he had thirty minutes to live. After spending a hot day on the docks of the New Basin Canal unloading a melon barge, Vittrano, who resided across the street with his widowed mother, decided to relax, drink some wine, and gamble the few pennies he kept in his pocket. The backroom was small with a bar, barrels, some bentwood chairs, and one card table. A naked, single-flame gas lamp hovered over the table, casting enough light to read the cards and the players' eyes. John Matto and his fifteen-year-old son, Frank, sat around the card table while Vittrano shuffled a deck and dealt the first hand to the Mattos, Angelo Farola, Leonardo Soldano, and Joseph Brincolari.

When the room filled with cigar smoke, and the air became humid and thick, Matto opened the alley door, which ran parallel to Chartres Street, allowing fresh air to flow through the building. While the men played cards and spoke Italian to each other, the passing breeze, the wine, the game, and the friendship caused the men to forget about their hard lives and the worrisome events of the past several weeks. Last month's ambush of Charles Matranga's stevedores hung over *Piccolo Palermo* like a lead shroud. No one knew when or where the next shot would be fired, but they understood death was part of life.

Vittrano, a strong, tough Sicilian, was twenty-six years old and possessed a placid countenance until provoked. Given his muscular size, provocation seldom came his way. He knew New Orleans' docks well and had worked for the Matrangas, Oteris, and the Provenzanos. He considered himself independent, and would work wherever he wanted to, and enjoyed the respect of his fellow stevedores. He avoided the ancient Sicilian prejudices, which had crossed the Atlantic with the immigrants. But when his family arrived in New Orleans in 1879, he discovered another form of prejudice, which took his brother's life.

On a cold night in 1880, Salvatore Vittrano was walking home from his street cleaning job. His usual path took him through the French Market, where he would stop and purchase some fruits and vegetables from a chignon-capped Creole lady on Decatur Street. For some unknown reason, two New Orleans police officers, witnesses described, set upon Vittrano and shot him to death. The officers were tried and acquitted of the murder, which only reinforced the Sicilian insularity of the area. Fear bolted through the narrow streets and alleys of the French Quarter and all of New Orleans, which endured for years.

Camillo Vittrano, like all Italians and Sicilians in New Orleans, knew their position and understood the social boundaries established by the city's elites after the Civil War, when Louisiana harvested Southern Europeans to do the work they didn't or wouldn't do. Living in New Orleans, for all immigrants, involved acts of endurance, faith, hope, and vigilance. Death in New Orleans could be sudden, and Camillo Vittrano knew that well. His close acquaintances and friends were exclusively Sicilian, Greek, or Croat.

While each player tossed their pennies into the middle of the table, the elder Matto asked Camillo Vittrano about his friend, Tony Pelligrini, who was an inmate in the Orleans Parish Prison, awaiting trial for participating in the ambush of the Matranga stevedores. Vittrano seemed conflicted, as he considered Pelligrini and Rocco Geraci friends. His street instincts taught him well about situational loyalties, even in *Piccolo Palermo*. And after the killing of his brother, his mother seared a Sicilian proverb into his brain: "*Dove c'e poverta, la lealta e sospetta. Where there is poverty, loyalty is suspect.*" And, Vittrano, living in an ethnic vise like New Orleans, knew there were many varieties of poverty, but the worst poverty was a betrayal of friendship.

To avoid answering Matto's question, Vittrano folded his hands, left the table, and went to a barrel of wine against the back brick wall to refill his glass. After returning to his chair, and while a new hand of cards slipped across the table, a deafening blast from a shotgun flashed through the dim room. Immediately, Vittrano's lifeless body fell forward on the poker table, and thick blood flowed from several wounds to the right side of his head and face. Pieces of his nose and mustache covered the table and cards. His poker mates jumped up and ran to the front of the saloon, as shotgun and cigar smoke swirled and twirled in a *danse macabre* around the naked gas flame, hanging over Vittrano's body.

><

Patrolman Thomas J. Roche had just checked in with the Central Police Station from callbox number 44 on Decatur Street when he heard the concussing single blast of a shotgun coming from somewhere nearby. Merchants and customers in the French Market pointed down Saint Philip Street, then known as *Vendetta Alley*. Roche followed their directions while drawing his revolver. When he saw people running from Matto's Saloon, he rushed in and found Camillo Vittrano's body slumped over the table. He called for someone to go back to the police call box and notify the Third Precinct on Chartres Street. About ten minutes later, a police patrol wagon stopped before the saloon, and several officers entered the business. Captain John Journee arrived and took charge of the investigation a few minutes later.

While Journee and the other officers were searching for witnesses, members of the press arrived, including Antonio Terranova and Abraham Jurrichi, who snuck into the saloon when officers were distracted. Abraham gasped when he saw Vittrano's lifeless body draped across the poker table. Antonio remained stoic, as he had already experienced such a scene in Sicily. A police officer, noticing Abraham and Antonio, tried to shoo them away, but when they identified themselves as employees of *The Mascot,* they were allowed to remain in the now-cramped card room. "Just stand against the wall and say nothing," a uniformed officer growled. They complied, and Abraham began tracing an image of the scene on a block of soft wood.

Patrolman Roche found an elderly French woman sitting in the alley near the saloon's side door. She denied seeing anything in broken English, but pointed down an adjacent alley towards Decatur Street. Roche, like before, followed the directions and found a cut-down muzzle—loading shotgun at the end of the alley. Only one barrel had been fired, but it was enough.

About an hour after the shooting, Doctor Charles LeMonnier, the Orleans Parish Coroner, arrived. He lit his oil lantern and examined Vittrano's wounds and pronounced him dead by a shotgun blast to the right side of the head and face. The police and reporters took notes, and the investigation seemed complete.

"We have enough, Antonio. Let's return to Camp Street and tell the story to the editor. Our newspaper comes out at 10 o'clock. We can beat morning papers with what we have," Abraham whispered.

As Abraham and Antonio scurried out of the saloon, George Provenzano ran in and saw Vittrano's limp body being placed on a stretcher. Abraham and Antonio followed him. Provenzano stared down at the ghastly wounds and yelled, "I want everybody in this room to know who did this. It was Matranga and his *Stuppagghieri*. This boy, Vittrano, was going to testify at my brother's trial that he was with Tony Pelligrini. He was their alibi witness. Now he's dead. There will be no fair trial."

The Daily Picayune and *The Daily Democrat* used their ink to fuel the fires in the imaginations of those who needed a *Mafia* war to control New Orleans.

Chapter 34

Central Police Station
June 18, 1890
11:00 A.M.

Chief David Hennessy began to read Captain John Journee's report of the Vittrano murder from the night before, but was interrupted when George Vandervoort escorted Algernon Badger into his office. It had been several weeks since the old friends had seen each other, and the greeting was warm and welcoming, but both knew the conversation's topic. It was on Hennessy's desk. A curious Vandervoort loitered in the doorway.

"I guess you heard what happened on Saint Philip Street last night," Badger said.

Hennessy took a sip of coffee and pointed to a ten-gauge, sawed-off shotgun, with bailing wire wrapped around its rusted barrels, lying on the end of his desk. "This is the weapon," Hennessy said. "He didn't know what hit him."

"The street is buzzing with rumors that the Matrangas did him up—to keep him from testifying. What are you hearing?" Badger asked.

"The same crap. But we have no witnesses. As you know, shotguns always go off in the Italian Colony," Hennessy joked.

"David, the Provenzano trial starts in a few weeks, and I must warn you not to attend the trial."

"Why?"

"Don't go near the courthouse. There's talk in the cafes, and exchanges that you favor the Provenzanos."

"That's crazy. We tried to broker peace between those families several times. I favor none of them. But, as always, I will follow your advice. Does that apply to George, too? He was at the Red Lantern Club that night, when I thought we had a peace."

"No. George needs to go and take notes. He might be a defense witness because he took notes at the meeting. Do you still have your notes, George?"

"Yes, sir. I have them locked away in the safe. Should I give them to Finney?"

"No. Let him or the defense attorneys ask for them. But the Chief's presence in the courtroom will only be a distraction. His absence will manifest neutrality. Let Finney and Adams prosecute the Provenzanos. As I see it, David, you are too connected to this entire affray to be near Saint Patrick's Hall," Badger warned. "Besides, you saw nothing the night of the ambush. You have no evidence."

"That's right, but what about Dominick O'Malley?" Hennessy seethed.

"Well, that is another reason to stay far from the courthouse. You are too entangled with everyone involved in the case. You killed O'Malley's friend. Your attorney has hired O'Malley as his investigator. You brokered a failed peace between the Matrangas and Provenzanos. Some of your police officers will probably testify at the trial. You helped Geraci get off on the Vincenzo Raffo killing in 1886, at Macheca's insistence. Geraci is going to be a state's witness. Macheca will probably be a state's witness. You will be watched as much as that trial. Your every move will be noted. So, stay away, David," Badgered enjoined. "It's for your own good."

Hennessy slumped back in his chair. "This trial sounds like it will be a spider's web of deceit, which will ensnare everyone involved. Those secret Italian societies will be gunning for me, no matter what I do," Hennessy lamented.

"Secret Italian societies? This city is full of secret societies. The Pickwick Club. The Boston Club. Rex and Comus. The Cotton Exchange. The Stock Exchange. Freemasonry. Have you forgotten the war on Canal Street in 1874? Who started that? Look at my leg. It wasn't the Italians." Badger raised his walking cane in the air. "I can't walk without this damn stick, because a secret society declared war, again, on the United States. There. I said it," Badger yelled. "David, at this moment in time, you are like a hub on a broken wagon wheel. The spokes of anger, envy, and hatred all collect right here, in this office. Do you understand?"

"Yes, General. I understand. Do I need a bodyguard?" Hennessy chuckled.

"Yes. Who do you trust?" Badger asked.

"You."

"No. No. I am too old and infirmed," Badger said.

"What about Captain Billy O'Connor with the Boylan Detective Agency?" Vandervoort interjected. "You trust him, don't you?"

"We've been friends a long time, but he can sometimes be arrogant and tedious," Hennessy said. "I will ask the mayor for funding such a position, until this *Mafia* shit blows over. Are you serious about the bodyguard?"

"Yes. Be careful, David. And remember, O'Connor wants your job, too." Badger said. "And arrogance is the shadow of betrayal."

Hennessy laughed and looked at Vandervoort. "Everybody wants my job. J.D. Houston, Dexter Gaster, John Journee, Billy O'Connor, the Chief of Detectives, and Leonard Malone want this job. Do you want my job, too, George?" Hennessy asked.

"No, sir. I am happy taking just notes and getting coffee," Vandervoort said.

"Do you have any idea who did up Vittrano?" Badger asked.

"No. But all indications, thus far, point to some kind of *vendetta*. My officers tell me Vittrano kept to himself most of the time and had no real enemies. The report says he had four cents in his pocket when he was killed. Not exactly a member of the *Mafia.*" Are the newspapers claiming he was another casualty in the *Mafia* wars?" Hennessy asked.

Badger unfolded his copy of the *Daily Picayune* and pointed to a small article on the last page of the daily broadsheet. "Look, here. Vittrano's last breath made the biggest newspaper in New Orleans," Badger said, tapping the article, which began:

AN ITALIAN ASSASSINATED

Hennessy shook his head in sorrow. "Other than his mother, who will remember this poor guy?"

Hennessy read the story about Vittrano's life. He looked up and said, "Mr. Vandervoort, send a telegraph to the Pinkertons in Chicago. Tell them I want to visit their offices and examine all the records they have on any Italian brigands or *Mafia* members who might be in New Orleans. Get me a train ticket for Chicago for the week of the Provenzano trial. Perhaps the trip will be good for my health."

"Wise decision, David," Badger said.

Hennessy turned towards his secretary and ordered, "Mr. Vandervoort, I want you to compile a list of every police officer who testifies for the state, or the defense in the Provenzano trial. This trial will reveal where the hidden loyalties lurk in this city. I have my suspicions, but when one takes the stand, and places his hand on the Bible, he might commit perjury, but he will honestly reveal his loyalties to a cause or side."

"Yes, sir," Vandervoort replied.

"Has the District Attorney asked you to testify in the Provenzano case?" Badger asked.

"No. In fact, I bumped into Lionel Adams at Saint Patrick's Hall and asked him if he planned on issuing a subpoena for me. He said, 'No'. They don't need my testimony," Hennessy said.

"All the newspapers are inciting the public by calling this the 'First Mafia Trial' in New Orleans," Badger said.

"Bullshit. Most of the defendants and victims were born here or came here as children. There are rumors from many origins, including the newspapers, pointing to Matranga and Provenzano being part of rival *Mafia* gangs. I learned Charles Matranga's father, Salvatore, gave him authority over the *Stuppagghieri* when Charles was about twenty years old. Though it has its roots in Monreale, Sicily, I could never link the Matrangas to any organization in Sicily. It was many years ago that they brought those ancient hatreds with them. Over time, both families became businessmen. This case is about who controls the stevedores and the docks," Hennessy huffed. "It has nothing to do with Sicily."

"But they have been fighting each other since you arrested Esposito in Jackson Square. It seems both sides of this feud were friends with him. And Esposito had a connection in Monreale," Badger asserted.

"Thomas Devereaux was friends with Esposito, too. Have you forgotten that?" Hennessy asked.

"Devereaux was jealous of you and the credit you received for arresting Esposito. I'm not sure he had any deep connections with Esposito. But Devereaux was friends with both Matranga and Provenzano. And the day you killed Devereaux was when you made many enemies throughout this city," Badger said.

Badger took a deep breath, stood up, and said, "Sometimes I wonder why Shakspeare appointed you Superintendent— perhaps, to keep both sides of Canal Street under *his* control? If he did, it was a brilliant political move to control a divided city. You are a shanty Irish Catholic; your father was in the Union army. Arthur Guerin killed him for his apostasy to the South. He had more reasons *not* to appoint you than to appoint you Superintendent."

"He knows I know too much about the Cotton Centennial. My badge is his lock on my lips," Hennessy opined.

Hennessy's remark stunned Badger. "Remember that. You are not exactly Pickwick or Rex material. Once Shakspeare exhausts your usefulness, he will replace you. Remember, New Orleans has never surrendered or given up the cause in the Civil War. Union occupation only put a lid on a roiling cauldron of suppressed status, hatred, and delayed wealth. These people can't exalt each other unless they are standing on the sweaty backs of their servants. New Orleans will always be a city menaced by the ancient human emotion to scorn men of a lesser pedigree."

Hennessy slumped in his chair and stared pensively out of one of his windows onto Basin Street. Vandervoort poured him another cup of coffee. The office was silent for a moment until Hennessy asked, "General, am I being used by the mayor?"

"David, when it comes down to politics, we are all being used, until our usefulness is no longer recognized," Badger lamented.

Chapter 35

Saint Patrick's Hall
Criminal District Court
July 16, 1890
10:30 A.M.

After bidding his boss a safe trip to Chicago from the Illinois-Central railway depot on Rampart Street, George Vandervoort drove the chief's carriage to Saint Patrick's Hall, which housed the Criminal District Court for Orleans Parish. After hitching the horse to a post next to Peter Murphy's boiler shop on Lafayette Street, and tipping a blacksmith to care for the horse, the blue-uniformed Vandervoort tucked his writing pad under his arm, and walked across the cobblestoned street to the once grand meeting hall and ballroom erected by the Irish in 1874, and converted in 1880 to the criminal courts building for New Orleans.

As Vandervoort approached the front of the Beaux-Arts designed building, about fifty men, mostly spectators and newspaper reporters, gathered around the courthouse's front door in various knots of graded humanity, measured by their social status. As the gaggle's attention fell upon Vandervoort's brass-buttoned, blue uniformed, and gold-laureled hat, crowning his pale, mustached face, they parted to allow him to enter the large vestibule of the converted hall. As he approached the large stairway leading to the second-floor courtrooms, a deputy exhorted, "Stick around, Mr. Vandervoort. We might need your gun," and then shoved yesterday's edition of *The Times-Democrat* into his chest. "Read this, George, the deputy whispered. There could be trouble in this courthouse and the Italian Colony."

Vandervoort replied, "I don't carry a gun. I'm just the secretary."

"Read the letter to the editor on the first page," the deputy said. "You might need one."

Vandervoort stopped on the stairway and read the first page of the second-largest newspaper in New Orleans. It was a letter authored by all the Italian citrus and fruit importers in New Orleans and several not of

Italian descent. Most prominent signatories were J.P. Macheca, Michael Macheca, Salvatore Oteri, Charles Patorno, J.B. Camors, Dan Fleming, L.P. Schindler, and B.G. Hopkins.

An editorial from the newspaper introduced the letter. It read:

THE PROVENZANO-MATRANGA CASE.

We have very much pleasure in publishing the letter which here follows. In the first place, such a document, with such names attached to it, holds out a strong prospect that, as the frequent undetected assassinations among the Italian community in New Orleans find no manner of sympathy with a large portion of that community, they will in the course of a few years be stamped out altogether for want of moral support. And in the next place, the contents of the letter are calculated to strengthen the hands of the prosecution, and to stiffen the backbone of the witnesses who will be called to give evidence in the Provenzano-Matranga case, which opens today. This is the letter:

New Orleans, July 14, 1890

To the Editor of the *Times-Democrat*:

For a reason appreciated by the entire community, we have heretofore been reticent with respect to the numerous assassinations charged to our countrymen. But we trust that, with the help of the intelligent and independent press of this city, we may be able to stamp out forever the horrible scenes of cold-blooded murder which are charged against our entire people, under the delusion that we all favor a settlement of troubles through the vendetta.

We desire to place ourselves on record as friends of peace and order, and without meaning to prejudice the case now on trial we trust sincerely that the witnesses will speak, and that those, whoever they may be, who have taken part in this midnight assassination may be tried and, after legal conviction, sternly punished.

Vandervoort examined the editorial and each signatory to the letter. He understood the jeopardy the Machecas, Salvatore Oteri, and Charles Patorno had placed themselves in by signing the stunning missive on the eve of the first *Mafia* trial in New Orleans. Though he agreed with the sentiment expressed therein, Vandervoort disagreed with the letter's timing and why the Machecas, Oteri, and Patorno would make themselves potential targets of future *vendettas*. While the aging police secretary hoped for less violence in the Italian Colony, he feared the letter would provoke more. Also, Vandervoort remembered the heated exchange between J.P. Macheca and Hennessy on Canal Street several weeks earlier, where Macheca warned Hennessy to stay away from the Provenzanos and their trial. This confrontation occurred several days after Badger admonished Hennessy to avoid the trial.

Vexed by bloodied images of the past *vendettas*, Vandervoort stepped down from the stairway and went to the first-floor clerk's office, cranked the wall phone, and requested the operator to connect him to the Central Police Station. He conferred with acting superintendent, Captain Dexter Gaster, about the newspaper's editorial and letter, and both men agreed the publication could have a prejudicial impact on the trial and inflame the Italian Colony. Gaster agreed to telegraph Hennessy and request deployment of more officers around the courthouse, the docks, and the French Quarter. Vandervoort, for a few moments and from memory, recited the number of Italian murders in the French Quarter, and on the Picayune Tier, going back to Guiseppi Matranga's body being fished from the Mississippi River on October 7, 1888. The victim orphaned several children and had no demonstrable involvement with the *Stuppagghieri*, but was Charles' older brother. Gaster listened patiently to Vandervoort's history of Italian murders in New Orleans and informed the police secretary of some more disturbing news.

"George, I am hearing several police officers will testify as alibi witnesses for the Provenzanos, and other officers will testify for the Matrangas. We have a major problem on our hands. Finney has decided to indict the Provenzanos *three times* for each shooting victim. That means there will be *three* different trials. Baker has two, and Judge Marr has one. This won't go away soon. Now, Hennessy's policies and relationships have split this department. So, be careful over there. Keep your notes private, and let me know who testifies for each side," Gaster said. "Only share your notes with me until Hennessy gets back."

"Yes, sir," Vandervoort said. "Let's not say anything more on the telephone. You never know who is listening."

><

Vandervoort left the clerk's office and climbed the stairs to the second floor of Saint Patrick's Hall, where Section "B" of the two-sectioned criminal courts was located. Once inside the courtroom, Vandervoort cast his eyes for an empty seat. The only seats available were in the press section, behind a rail, which separated the counsel tables from the press and spectators. A deputy sheriff, recognizing Vandervoort, beckoned him to the press section, where he found a seat next to Laurence Hearn and Abraham Jurrichi of *The Mascot* newspaper.

District Attorney John Finney and his two assistants, Lionel Adams and A.D. Henriques, sat at the prosecution's table with their investigator and well-known rapscallion, Dominick Clay O'Malley. John McMahon and J.M. Pratt reclined at the defense table. The defendants, Joseph Provenzano, Peter Provenzano, Nicholas Giulio, Tony Pelligrini, Tony Gianforcarro, and Gaspere Lombardo sat in the dock, guarded by armed deputies. Lombardo seemed to exude a sallow hue, and each defendant seemed bedraggled and dissipated after spending the last two months in the dank and dark Orleans Parish Prison. Without looking at the defendants, everyone, including the jurors in the box, could smell them.

Judge Joshua Baker sat high above the courtroom on a bench made of black oak. On each end of the bench were brass electric lamps, which cast an amber glow upon the judge and the clerks sitting below him. Everyone was drawn to the judge talking to a clerk and a deputy sheriff on the side of the bench. Though the conversation was muffled, the judge was clearly frustrated with how the jury selection had proceeded, and the court needed one more juror before the trial could start. Since the assigned jury venire had been exhausted, and there were no new potential jurors to call, Judge Baker ordered the clerk to draw up a list of trial jurors and issue summons, "forthwith."

But another issue loomed over the courtroom. Judge Baker, still agitated by McMahon's earlier allegation that O'Malley was sending furtive signals of approval to potential jurors and the prosecution during *voir dire*, allowed McMahon to question each juror to determine if they had any contact with O'Malley before coming to court. This consumed more time, and Judge Baker was not happy. Despite knowing O'Malley's roguish reputation, the judge allowed McMahon, without direct evidence, to proceed. Despite any proof of jury tampering, McMahon requested that O'Malley be removed from the courtroom. Judge Baker denied the request, and the court called a recess until noon. O'Malley stared at McMahon and smirked.

><

The Recess

During the recess, Hearn and Jurrichi went to the café on the first floor of the Parkview Hotel, next to the courthouse. Abraham carried a small canvas sack with several blocks of soft wood and prepared to carve images of McMahon and O'Malley. As they sat at a table near a window overlooking Camp Street, Lafayette Square, and in the distance, City Hall, Abraham asked Hearn about O'Malley. "Who is this man, O'Malley? Everyone in the courtroom seems to know him. Do you know him?"

Hearn laughed. "Oh, yes. I know him too well. O'Malley has a reputation that goes back years, and the stories about him are not positive in any way. He has been arrested for jury tampering, bribery, assault, battery, threatening people, and every other sort of misdeed you can name, short of murder—and he always gets off.

"He's a member of an organization known as "The Ring," and is very close to the mayor's campaign manager, J.D. Houston. He was also close friends with Thomas Devereaux, whom David Hennessy killed in a shootout on Gravier Street, some years ago. Ironically, Lionel Adams represented Hennessy, and Hennessy was acquitted. This angered O'Malley, making me wonder why Adams would associate with O'Malley."

"Is he a dangerous man?"

"Very. He's more dangerous than the men on trial. He walks a very thin line between good and evil. Before he does anything, he has an escape plan. Stay away from him. When Shakspeare was elected, O'Malley tried to get the police chief's job. Houston couldn't help him. The mayor picked Hennessy, which caused a furor throughout the city, which still exists today. Shakspeare knew he couldn't control O'Malley, but he could control Hennessey.

"Shakspeare uses Hennessy to collect taxes on taverns and casinos, which the mayor's enemies own. And it seems O'Malley is friends with those establishments that must pay extra to stay in business. Hennessy and O'Malley hate each other—for many reasons. That's well known. Our newspaper tried to expose Shakspeare's corruption, but the people are too afraid to cooperate with us. So, in essence, there's another war going on in New Orleans, other than the Matrangas and Provenzanos. It's Hennessy against The Ring, and Shakspeare allows it to continue. Why? I don't know."

"Should I carve O'Malley for tonight's paper?"

"No. Carve McMahon is arguing before the judge. I'll write about McMahon's challenge to O'Malley's presence at the state's counsel table. Your image would only make O'Malley more famous in this impressionable city."

><

Noon

When Judge Baker ascended the bench, he possessed a dour countenance, which matched his black suit, white, high-necked, starched shirt, and black silk tie. His long, black curly beard, which fell below his tie's knot, bathed in the amber glow of the bench's lamps, created the grave aura of final judgment. His dark eyes, hooded under black bushy eyebrows, darted around the courtroom. He asked the clerk, Richard Scriven, if enough jurors were present in the courtroom to conclude *voir dire*. Mr. Scriven acknowledged there were and called one name: Abner A. Parker of 436 Coliseum Street.

After the judge and counsel were satisfied Parker could be a fair juror to both sides, he was sworn as the twelfth juror and took his seat with the other eleven men. Scriven stood before the bench and read, in a loud voice, the indictment filed against the defendants. As he did, Antonio snuck into the reporters' gallery and sat between Vandervoort and Hearn. He wore a black suit jacket, white shirt, and dungarees, speckled with gray stone dust. He had a notepad and a thick black graphite pencil.

"Where have you been, Antonio?" Hearn whispered.

"Delivering cobblestones on Basin Street."

"You still have that job?" Hearn asked.

"Only today. I told Mr. Jahnke I must work for *The Mascot* the rest of the week."

Hearn nodded. A deputy sheriff shushed Hearn and Antonio while Scriven read the indictment. Vandervoort inched from Antonio to avoid getting the gray dust on his blue pants. And Lionel Adams' private investigator, Dominick O'Malley, sitting at the state's counsel table, winked at Vandervoort, who remained professionally stoic.

After Scriven read the indictment, both sides gave their opening statements to the jury. District Attorney John Finney alleged, as the indictment read, the Provenzanos had a long and brutal feud with the

Matrangas, which was aggravated by the Matrangas being awarded a larger portion of the stevedoring business on the docks of New Orleans. He promised the jury they would hear from eyewitnesses who were fired upon about midnight of May 5, 1890, and identify the defendants as their assailants.

Defense counsel John McMahon objected to characterizing the "feud," and Judge Baker sustained the objection. "Please keep your comments to the indictment's contents, Mr. Finney," Judge Baker admonished.

After the state's opening statement, defense counsel McMahon began to cast doubt on the state's preview of the eyewitness testimony. "If you have ever traveled Esplanade Avenue, you know it's a very dark street, from the river to Claiborne Street. And at *that* intersection," McMahon bellowed, "one could hardly see one's own hand in front of one's face. While the city is paving the streets, its electrical streetlights have not improved, which cast no brighter light than an oil lamp. Now, put that lamp among the leaves and boughs high in the oak trees at that intersection. What do you see? Nothing."

When McMahon finished his opening statement, the District Attorney began to call his witnesses. Finney's first few witnesses were L.C. Fallon, R.C. Hopkins, and Daniel Fleming, who testified they had been in the fruit and coffee import business for over ten years, and decided to switch stevedoring firms from the Provenzanos to the Matranga and Locascio firm, because they were receiving better service. The defense did not cross-examine Fallon, Hopkins, or Fleming because there was no doubt that several companies had discharged the Provenzanos in favor of the Matranga and Locascio firm. McMahon's defense would center around the eyewitnesses, their character, their veracity, the ambient elements of that evening, and several surprise alibi witnesses.

A crypt-like hush descended over the courtroom when Lionel Adams rose and announced the state's next witness. Everyone knew who was next to ascend the three steps to the witness stand. The prosecution prepared to bore into the core of their case. Reporters gripped their pens and pencils. Spectators sprang straight in their seats. The minute clerk prepared the Crucifix-covered Bible for the oath. Even the judge seemed more alert.

"The State of Louisiana calls Joseph P. Macheca to the stand," the barrel-chested, bespectacled Lionel Adams announced.

Wearing an elegant, gray-tailored suit from a Rampart Street haberdasher, Macheca pranced through the spectator's gallery towards the witness stand. There, he took the oath to tell the truth. After he took the stand and exchanged feral stares with Joseph Provenzano, who sat in the dock with his arms folded across his chest. The hush in the courtroom morphed into a knot of tension, like a hawser line wrapped tightly around an iron bollard on the docks.

"State your name for the court," Adams demanded.

"Joseph P. Macheca."

"How old are you?"

"I am forty-seven years old."

"What is your occupation?"

"I am a fruit importer—the oldest and largest in New Orleans," Macheca vaunted.

"Look into the dock. Do you know the defendants?" Adams asked.

"I have known them for many years. I have known them since we were boys in the French Quarter."

"As a fruit importer, did you ever use the services of Provenzano's stevedores?"

"Yes. For many years, but as time passed, their services were not good, and they became too expensive. I changed to Matranga and Locascio's Stevedores."

"Did that cause problems between your company and the Provenzanos?" Adams asked.

"Yes, we had several arguments over the contract. But when dealing with fruit and citrus, time is important. They were too slow. I needed to get my products to market faster."

"What firm do you use to unload your ships, now?"

"Matranga."

"Are you a member of a club known as the Red Lights Club or the Red Lantern Club on Customhouse Street?" Adams asked."

"Yes, I am."

"Who owns that club?"

"Joseph Provenzanos and his brothers. I have heard the chief of police owns a piece of it, but I'm not certain," Macheca said.

"Did there come a time when you became aware that the Matrangas and Provenzanos were at war with each other?"

Defense attorney John McMahon objected to the word "war," and Judge Baker sustained the objection.

In rephrasing the question, Adams probed into Macheca's knowledge of any dispute between the Matrangas and Provenzanos.

"It was well known they hated each other, and the dispute goes back to Sicily—*before* they were born," Macheca said. "To me, it's stupid."

"Have you ever heard of the *Stuppagghieri*?" Adams asked.

"Yes. It's an old secret Sicilian society that started hundreds of years ago. Some people in New Orleans still claim to be a part of it," Macheca said.

"Are you part of it?"

"No."

"What about the *Giardinieri*?" Adams asked.

"No. I'm not a part of either one. My business is shipping," Macheca asserted.

"Did you ever belong to any secret societies?"

"I tried to join the Pickwick Club, but they wouldn't let me in," Macheca said with a giggle.

The courtroom erupted in laughter, knowing the impenetrable caste system, which existed in a city defined, rivened, and segregated by economics, ethnicity, familial pedigree, neighborhoods, and race. Even Judge Baker tried to conceal his amusement with the answer.

"To your knowledge, do the Matrangas or the Provenzanos belong to either of these secret societies?"

"I only know rumors. People brag about everything on the docks," Macheca asserted.

"Mr. Macheca, I have to ask this question to resolve any doubt in anybody's mind. Are you a member of any *Mafia* family in New Orleans or elsewhere?" Adams asked.

"Absolutely not. I wouldn't be sitting here testifying as a good citizen if I were. The *Mafia*, as you know, has this thing known as *Omerta*. They can't testify against each other. I am an honest businessman and a loyal Democrat. I fought on the Democrats' side in September of 1874. But now, some people want to forget that."

"Did there come a time when you tried to mediate the dispute between the Matrangas and the Provenzanos?"

"Yes."

"When?"

"I remember it was December first, last year. It was unusually cold that night, and we all decided to meet upstairs at the Red Lantern Club."

"Who was there?" Adams probed.

"Well, all the defendants and members of the Provenzano family. Ike Kuhn, Luke Scalzo, Jack Kohl, Charles and Anthony Matranga, Frank Locascio, and a few others."

"Wasn't David Hennessy there, along with Algernon Badger and Tom Anderson?"

"Yes, they were there, but I was the real mediator. I had the most to lose if I couldn't get my ships unloaded faster."

"But you do remember David Hennessy sitting in at that meeting?"

"Yes, he was there," Macheca conceded.

"Tell the gentlemen of the jury what happened that night."

Macheca shifted a little on the witness stand, cleared his throat, and looked at the jury. "Well, that night, we all wanted to put an end to people getting hurt on the docks and find a way to get some business to the Provenzanos while keeping the other importers profitable, too. Joseph Provenzano denied that his company was not doing a good job, and he got irate when he learned that he was losing most of his stevedoring business, not all, but most."

"How did the meeting end?" Adams asked.

"Not good. George Provenzano threatened me and the Matrangas. In fact, Joseph told George to shut up—that he talks too much. And to be honest, I was scared when I left the meeting."

"You were scared even with David Hennessy being there?" Adams asked.

"Well, George was very angry and threatened everyone who was against the Provenzanos. When it appeared nothing would be accomplished, the meeting broke up. I had a porter escort me home."

On cross-examination, conducted by John McMahon, Macheca admitted he was not at the site of the shooting, but arrived there about the time Hennessy arrived. He admitted he had been at the Red Lights Club earlier that evening, and saw the Provenzanos, but they didn't threaten him."

"In fact, Mr. Macheca, since the December meeting, you had many contacts with members of the Provenzano family, and they did not threaten you, isn't that correct?" McMahon asked.

"That's correct."

"And since the December meeting, you went to the Red Lights Club on Customhouse Street many times, and were never threatened. Correct?"

"That's correct," Macheca conceded.

"Mr. Macheca, look into the dock. Look at each defendant. You testified during direct examination that George Provenzano threatened everybody at the December meeting. Correct?"

"Well, not everybody. He didn't threaten David Hennessy. But he did threaten all the fruit importers, and I felt threatened. He told us he had the law on his side," Macheca testified.

McMahon approached the witness stand and stood next to Macheca. "Look into the dock. Do you see George Provenzano sitting there, as a defendant?"

Macheca slumped in his chair and said, "No. George Provenzano is not a defendant."

"So, the most threatening person at the meeting, and a man you have seen since the meeting many times, has not been charged for this crime. Is that correct?" McMahon asked.

"That's correct," Macheca testified.

Hearn scribbled his notes on his tablet and tore off the page. He folded it, gave it to Antonio, and whispered, "Run this back to our office as fast as you can. But come back. Later today or tonight, Geraci will testify. I want you here. Hurry!"

><

1:45 P.M.

After a brief recess, District Attorney Finney called several other witnesses who testified there were bad feelings around the docks, because the Matrangas could wrestle away most of the stevedoring work from the Provenzanos. In fact, many stevedores left the Provenzanos' employment and went to work for the Matrangas. This apostasy didn't sit well with Joseph Provenzanos, his brothers, or his loyal employees.

Salvatore Oteri, an elderly fruit shipper for three decades in New Orleans, took the stand. He started his business on Fulton Street before the Civil War and the ensuing Union occupation. He testified he knew all of the defendants very well and was saddened to be a witness at their trial.

"This should never have happened," Oteri said, immediately after taking the oath.

Finney focuses Mr. Oteri's attention on a chance meeting between the Provenzanos, Lombardo, and Gianforcarro on Canal Street, about a week after the meeting at the Red Lights Club.

"Mr. Oteri, please tell the jury what happened when you ran into to Provenzano's and some of their stevedores last December," Finney requested.

"Well, for the most part, it was pleasant. I've known them all for a long time. They wanted some business back, but Vincent Provenzano told me what it would cost. Their prices were too high, and I hate to admit it, their work was slow and sloppy. I like them all. But I am a businessman."

"Were you threatened?" Finney asked.

"No. Like I said, I've known those boys for many years. But Lombardo and Gianforcarro told me there would be a row if they didn't get some work."

"Row?" Was that their word?"

"Yes."

"Meaning?"

"Trouble on the docks," Oteri said.

On cross-examination, in a respectful tone, John McMahon asked, "Mr. Oteri, since the December Red Lights meeting and this encounter on Canal Street, have any of the Provenzanos or those in their employ threatened you in any way?"

"No. I have known them too long. Since they were kids playing on docks."

"Was there a row on the docks since that encounter on Canal Street?"

Mr. Oteri hung his head and then lifted it slowly. "Not on the docks, but why are we here?"

Finney treaded carefully. "Do you have any evidence to bring before this court that the defendants shot anyone at Claiborne and Esplanade on May fifth or sixth, last?"

"Oh no, sir. I'm in bed every night for eight o'clock," Oteri testified, shaking his head.

The defense asked no questions, but Judge Baker allowed juror Ringold Bronsseau to ask one question. "Mr. Oteri, did you discharge the Provenzanos for purely business reasons?"

"I had many complaints about the Provenzanos. I like Vincent, personally. But their rates were excessive. I had no choice." Oteri said.

><

2:25 P.M.

District Attorney Finney called Doctor Jefferson Davis Bloom to the stand, who testified as to the wounds suffered by the victims. He identified himself as the Assistant House Surgeon at Charity Hospital and was on duty when the bleeding victims were rolled into his operating theater. He testified about the necessity of amputating Antonio Matranga's left leg above the knee, and the nerve and vascular damage the bullets caused to Vincent Caruso's right leg, thus requiring him to use crutches for the rest of his life. Salvatore Sunzeri's wounds were to his right hip, but he would completely recover.

Neither McMahon nor Pratt offered any cross-examination.

><

3:00 P.M.

Before Lionel Adams could call the state's next witness, the back doors of the courtroom squeaked open, allowing the chattering din from the corridor to waft through the courtroom. Everyone was drawn to the back door, where they saw Chief Deputy Sheriff Alcee LeBlanc assisting a crutch-bearing Vincent Caruso through the door, and slowly to the witness stand. As Caruso struggled to the stand, Adams introduced the next witness to the judge and jury.

Since the gaunt Caruso couldn't climb the three steps of the witness stand, Judge Baker allowed him to sit in a chair in front of the bench, and his damning testimony began.

Lionel Adams began direct examination of Caruso with his familiarity with the defendants. "I know them all. I worked for the Provenzanos for twelve years, before going to work for Matranga and Locascio," Caruso said in a weak, but audible voice. The reporters in the gallery had to lean forward to hear the witness.

"To your knowledge, was there bad blood between the two families?" Adams asked.

"Yes. We had a meeting at the Red Lantern Club to calm things down. The chief of police was there, too. But when everyone started screaming at each other, the meeting broke up. Threats were exchanged. I went home."

"Tell the gentlemen of the jury what happened to you on May fifth of this year."

"My brother, James, Anthony Matranga, Salvatore Sunzeri, Rocco Geraci, Bastian Incardona, Tony Locascio, and I had just finished unloading the *Foxhall*. It was nearly midnight. We all got into a wagon to go home. We dropped my brother off at Dumaine and Decatur. We went down the Esplanade towards Claiborne. When we reached the intersection, I heard someone yell in Italian, 'There they are.' I saw four men dressed in dark clothes with guns. They shot at us. They hit me in my leg. I can't use my leg now. I was screaming. I heard others screaming. People came out of their houses. I begged one to call an ambulance. I remember being taken to Charity Hospital. That's all I remember," Caruso testified.

"Did you see the men who shot you and the other men in the wagon?" Adams asked.

"Yes."

Lionel Adams requested that the judge allow the deputies to escort the defendants to stand in front of the witness. Judge Baker agreed, and each defendant, guarded by armed deputies, stood about three feet away from Vincent Caruso. "Do you see any of the men who shot you that night?" Adams asked.

"Yes." Caruso pointed to Joseph Provenzano, Antonio Pelligrini, Gaspare Lombardo, and Anthony Gianforcarro.

On cross-examination, John McMahon asked, "Mr. Caruso, isn't it a fact that when the police first asked you who shot you, you said you didn't know?"

Caruso paused. "I was in pain when I said that. All I wanted was to get a doctor."

"Was your memory better then, or now?"

"My memory was good then and now," Caruso bristled. "I just wanted the pain to go away."

"Was the pain so bad that it made you lie to the police?" McMahon countered.

"Sir, I know what I saw and testified to the truth."

"But you acknowledge you lied to the police," McMahon pressed.

"Like I said, I was in pain, and I was bleeding," Caruso said.

"Before you were shot, do you remember how dark it was at that intersection?" McMahon asked.

"It was dark," Caruso responded.

"In fact, it was so dark you couldn't identify anyone who shot you, and that's why you told the police you couldn't identify anyone who shot you. Correct?"

"It was dark and I was in pain," Caruso said. "Look at my leg. I can't use it anymore."

"Mr. Caruso, we all know you were shot. No doubt about that. But there is doubt about what you saw in the dark that night."

Lionel Adams objected to McMahon arguing with the witness, and Judge Baker sustained the objection. "Move on, Mr. McMahon," Judge Baker said.

McMahon knew he could only ask the wounded victim a few last questions, without appearing to add to Caruso's injuries. He chose wisely. "Sir, as you sit here today, there is no doubt that on May fifth of this year, it was very dark at the corner of Esplanade and Claiborne."

"It was dark."

"On direct examination, you identified four men who shot you and the others in the wagon. Which one shot you in the dark?"

"It happened very fast. I can't say which man shot me, for sure," Caruso said.

"So, you are testifying it was fast and dark?"

Lionel Adams objected, and Judge Baker admonished McMahon not to argue with the witness.

"No further questions, your Honor," McMahon said.

><

4:00 P.M.

After Chief Deputy LeBlanc escorted a wincing Vincent Caruso out of the courtroom, he returned with Anthony Matranga, who, like Caruso, required crutches to hobble to the witness stand. But unlike Caruso, Matranga had only one leg, which required a couple of minutes to traverse the large courtroom's length and reach the witness chair. Everyone in the courtroom focused on the empty left pant leg, which had been rolled up and stitched to his left pocket. The pitiful pageant of a one-legged man, swinging his body between crutches on his way to the bar of justice, dispelled any doubt that an attack had occurred. The courtroom was reverently quiet, and the only sound heard was Matranga's right boot's soft drag against the floor. After flopping into the witness chair, Matranga was sworn and began his testimony.

"Mr. Matranga, before we get to who shot you and where, allow me to clear something up," Finney began. "Are you the same Anthony Matranga who shot and killed a negro in a barroom at the corner of Basin and Poydras Streets in 1881?"

"Yes, I am."

"Were you arrested and tried for that shooting?"

"Yes, I was. I was found not guilty, because it was self-defense." Matranga looked around the courtroom and said, "I think I was tried in this same courtroom."

"Are you a member of the *Mafia*, or any other Sicilian gang?" Finney asked.

Matranga scoffed and said," Mr. Finney, I was born in Palermo, Italy, in 1854. My mother and father brought me here when I was three years old. Our family came here with nothing but the dirt of the old world on the bottom of our shoes. We worked day and night on the levee, loading and unloading fruit boats. My father, brothers, and I built a business on the levee. We had to work to eat and eat to survive. No one helped us. No one cared about us. Our success was our sweat. My father had no time for secret gangs or this thing you call the *Mafia*. In fact, we were victims of the gangs nearly every month—making threats and demands on our success. Now, look at me. I have one leg. I lost my other leg going home from work. No, my family has nothing to do with any secret societies, unlike some other Italians, and the people who run this city."

Antonio began to weep silently, using his jacket sleeve to wipe his tears from his cheeks. Hearn patted Antonio on his knee, affirming the young man's emotional response to the wounded witness.

District Attorney Finney thanked Matranga and quickly had him recite the facts of the evening of the shooting. The direct examination and testimony followed exactly that of Vincent Caruso. Matranga identified Joseph Provenzano, Antonio Pelligrini, Gaspare Lombardo, and Anthony Gianforcarro as the men who shot into their wagon.

"Wasn't it dark that night?" Finney asked.

"Yes, but the streetlight was bright and the moon was out," Matranga said. "I saw what I saw."

Before he began his cross-examination of Matranga, McMahon huddled with Pratt. Both knew that whatever they asked Matranga, the answer would come from a man whose leg was blown off by a shotgun. Though the jurors requested Matranga speak louder, his rolled-up pants leg spoke loudly enough.

McMahon stood by his counsel table and did not approach the witness. In these situations, the attorney knew reverence was measured in inches. He eased into the cross-examination with a dulcet tone.

"Mr. Matranga, you testified that the streetlight was on. Correct?"

"Yes."

"And the moon was out that night?"

"Yes."

"And there were many oak trees around that intersection. Correct"

"There are a few. Yes."

"And, as you know, the streetlight hangs among the branches and leaves of the trees. Correct?"

"Yes, but I could see just fine."

"And the moon cast many shadows on the ground, which is normal. Correct?"

"There were some shadows," Matranga responded.

"And at the time you were shot, you were sitting inside the wagon. Correct?"

"Yes. Behind Vincent Caruso."

"What came first? Did you see the men first, or were you shot first?" McMahon asked.

"It happened very fast. I don't remember. It all happened at once."

McMahon didn't want to ask any further questions, which would allow Matranga to relive the shooting in front of the jury. He selected his next question very carefully. "Mr. Matranga, if the Provenzanos and their employees are convicted at this trial, that would leave only the Matranga and Locascio Stevedore Company to work the docks downriver of Canal Street. Correct?"

"I guess so," Matranga said.

"No further questions," McMahon said, as he sat down.

"Do any jury members have any questions for Mr. Matranga?" Judge Baker asked.

The ever-alert juror Ringold Bronsseau stood and asked, "After you were shot, you fell over in the wagon?"

"Yes, I did."

"You were in pain?"

"Yes. My leg was on fire."

"Could you intelligently answer any questions about your condition, or who shot you at that time?"

Matranga paused and rubbed his mustache with his left hand. "I was in a lot of pain. I didn't tell anybody anything until after they cut my leg off," Matranga said.

With careful timing, and with the strategic intent to divert the jury's attention away Matranga shuffling away from the witness stand, McMahon stood, and in a loud voice said, "You honor, the defense respectfully requests that the jury be allowed to visit the scene of the shooting, at night, before it retires to deliberate." The courtroom trick worked, as the jury's eyes darted between the judge and McMahon, waiting for Baker to respond.

"I have always been in favor of visiting the scene of a crime, and this case should not be an exception. Therefore, after our evening session, the jury will be taken to Esplanade and Claiborne tonight. But there will be no lanterns glowing, no testimony taken, or statements made," Judge Baker enjoined. "The sheriff will provide the necessary transportation and security for the jury. The court will stand in recess until seven o'clock this evening."

But before Judge Baker left the bench, McMahon, Pratt, and several of the defendants reasserted the claim that Dominick O'Malley was, again, sending hand signals and eye winks to the jury. They made an adamant and raucous demand to remove O'Malley from the courtroom. Despite Lionel Adams' fiery protest, Judge Baker instructed O'Malley not to return to the courtroom to protect the integrity of the trial. O'Malley smiled and left the courtroom.

Chapter 36

City Hall
July 16, 1890
4:30 P.M.

As Judge Baker descended the bench, J.D. Houston, sitting in the last row of the courtroom, scooted out the courtroom doors and left the courthouse. He crossed Camp Street and walked briskly across Lafayette Square, breaking a heavy chaffing sweat around his high-starched collar. After entering the city hall, Houston met John Cord Wickliffe, the editor of the *Daily States* newspaper and an attorney. Wickliffe, a Kentucky native and nephew of Robert Wickliffe, the Governor of Louisiana, until 1861, was a Bourbonist Democrat who affected an orgulous personality, according to *his* writers at *his* newspaper. Wickliffe greeted Houston and directed him into the city council chambers. Once inside, he locked the doors.

The mayor and city council sat regally on the dais, and the chamber was filled with members of the Cotton Exchange, Pickwick Club, Boston Club, and other members of the city's elite secret societies. Seeing this collection of city royalty in one room, at the same time, Houston shrank his self-exaggerated sense of self-importance. Some of the gilded gentlemen turned away from Houston, as he represented a more rakish element of New Orleans society—needed—but not invited within the aureate rings of regal societal circles. In New Orleans, one's pedigree surpassed one's ability or utility.

"Come forward, J.D. Come forward, and give us a report on the trial," Mayor Shakspeare ordered. "We are gathered here today to discuss the outcome of the trials and how this city can move forward, once we take control of the docks. So, tell us what's going on. Are the Provenzanos going to hang?"

Houston stood before the mayor, the city council, and the self-sanctified and began his presentation. "Mr. Mayor, the trial seems to be going well. District Attorney Finney is making a sound case, witness by witness. The judge called a recess until seven o'clock tonight."

"Who is going to testify tonight, J.D.?" the mayor asked.

"It should be interesting. More of the victims and witnesses will testify. Still, I got word from a source that some police officers are going to testify *for* the Provenzanos, and some police officers are going to testify *against* the Provenzanos."

The council chambers erupted into a loud din of dissent. "That's outrageous," the mayor yelled. "Are you telling me that the police department is at war with itself over this case? Hennessy knows the Provenzanos and the Matrangas. Why would he permit this case to divide the police department? Didn't he try to mediate their differences? And now he goes to Chicago at the same time this case goes to trial?"

"It appears so," Houston said.

"What is going on here? It appears Hennessy has allowed his department to investigate the case and then interfere with the prosecution. I don't need part of the police department sympathetic with the *Mafia,* and the other part sympathetic with god-knows-what," Shakspeare said.

"Mr. Mayor, may I address the situation?" Wickliffe asked.

"Please do."

"My legal colleagues and I have been discussing the easiest way for the city to gain control over the commerce on the river. It's quite simple, actually."

"Explain, please," the mayor requested.

"Once the Provenzanos are disposed of, the city should use the occasion and the newspapers to force the Matrangas off the docks. We have that power. I am sure James Richardson of *The Daily Picayune* will concur."

Richardson, who sat in the front row of the council chambers, nodded in approval.

"Mr. Parkerson has written a clear legal memorandum attesting to the city's riparian rights along the Mississippi River. Any and all structures the Italians have built on the city's land belong to the city. That includes all wharves, docking facilities, ramps, gangways, and the cotton press located at the end of Esplanade Street," Wickliffe asserted.

"And what happens if the Matrangas won't leave the docks?" the mayor asked. "Do I have to pay them for their improvements and the cotton press?"

"Under the Napoleonic Code of Louisiana, one could make that argument. But if we persuade them it would be in their best interest to abandon the docks, with the hope of future work under city control, then there would be no unnecessary litigation."

"Persuade? Charles Matranga is a bull-headed man, and he and Macheca have made their fortunes down there—to our detriment. And now, I have elements of the police department whose loyalties favor both sides of the *Mafia*? This is insanity. And you assert it's simple, Mr. Wickliffe?" Shakspeare asked.

"Let the thud of the gallows' trap door, or the blast of a Winchester, persuade them. With the Provenzanos gone, they will realize who controls the law of this city, both in the criminal and civil courts."

"The law? The courts? You trust the legal system in this state, Mr. Wickliffe? I don't trust the state Supreme Court. They have too many judges not from New Orleans on that court. They reverse everything we want to do. And doesn't the Napoleonic Code allow for squatter's rights?" the mayor asked.

"Yes. In Louisiana, we call it Acquisitive Prescription. And yes, the Matrangas and Macheca might have a valid legal claim, since they have been down there since before the Union occupation, without interruption by the city or state. There will be no doubt they will plead good faith and demand compensation or ownership," William Sterling Parkerson, another prominent attorney, asserted.

"Gentlemen, you have successfully confused the hell out of me. After the Provenzanos are disposed of, can the city take back the docks, if the law says I can't?" Shakspeare asked. "Can we hire our own stevedores? What about the Aiken Company, which manages the docks? What are they doing to help us?"

"The Aiken Company appears to be part of the problem. They subleased a portion of the docks and market stalls to the Provenzanos. Once the Provenzanos are disposed of, the city can take steps to scrub the rest of the shit from the cobblestones down there," ice-house owner, Maurice Hart, exclaimed. His statement provoked an approving ovation from the audience.

Wickliffe stood, parted his suit jacket with his stubby hands, revealing his rotund belly, and bellowed, "Mr. Mayor, look around this chamber and realize *what and who* sits before you. What do you see? Your friends? Your business associates? Your fellow club members? Your neighbors? No. You are looking at the *law* of this city, which no supreme court can ever deny.

You are looking at the future of this city. You are looking at the wealth of this city. Mr. Mayor, we are developing a plan to save this city's commerce and attract investors without state interference. Trust us."

"I trust you. I want you to consider forming a special committee to address this problem. The members should be of the finest families New Orleans has to offer. Our financial futures rely on control of the river's commerce. But what about the police department?" Shakspeare asked. "They are either corrupt or lazy. And now it appears they will be at war with each other. The city can't survive with an ineffective police department and dago-controlled docks."

"The police will do what their superintendent tells them to do. And, as we all know, Hennessy is expendable, and knows too much," Wickliffe sneered. "Besides, Mr. Mayor, you and Mr. Houston should know about other storms on the horizon."

"What other storms?" Shakspeare asked.

"Macheca and Matranga control a powerful voting block—creole, dago and negro. We can't let our political power drift downriver—literally. This trial is revealing the political fidelities and loyalties, which might be a good thing to know for your next election. You lost your last election because of the dago vote. You can't just focus on the docks. Remember the polls."

"What else?" Shakspeare asked.

"Bales of cotton are piling up on the docks. This trial is bad for business, regardless of who wins. Either way, we must take control of the cotton commerce of this city," Wickliffe said.

Shakspeare pondered Wickliffe's words and directed his attention towards Houston. "J.D., get your ass back to that courtroom. I want a report on what happens every day. I want to know the names of all witnesses. I want to know whom we can trust. And when Hennessy gets back from Chicago, he will have to make some serious changes in the police department, or else. And we, gentlemen, must initiate plans to take over our docks and the vote."

Chapter 37

Criminal District Court
July 16, 1890
7:20 P.M.

The night session of court began twenty minutes late. No one complained because the sun had set, and a breeze breathed fresh air through the courtroom's large windows. The twenty new electric light bulbs, shielded by white opaque glass, yielded twenty different flickering glows, which were enough light for everyone to see across the courtroom. With all the parties in place, Judge Baker took the bench. "Mr. Finney, call your next witness," Baker ordered.

The District Attorney resumed his case with more witnesses from the night of the ambush. Bastian Incardona testified to what he heard and saw through an Italian interpreter. Incardona could only identify Lombardo as a shooter, and no one else. Like the other state's witnesses, Incardona could not remember what came first—Lombardo aiming a shotgun, or the blast, since Incardona dove under the seat of the wagon. And as with other witnesses, Juror Bronsseau interrogated Incardona as to the location of the wagon and the shooters. Reporters scribbled summaries of the immigrant's testimony.

After Incardona left the stand, Finney called the Locascio brothers, who echoed Incardona's testimony. They, too, could only identify Lombardo as a shooter, and McMahon, on cross-examination, could only develop the stress the witnesses were under when the shooting started, leaving the jury with the impression that one under attack might have a flawed memory.

The state's next witness was Officer Albert Rich, who testified he and Officer William Seelhorst found two shotguns on Claiborne Street about twenty-five yards from Esplanade. While the jury's eyes were riveted on the menacing muzzles of the shotguns, Finney handed Officer Rich a third weapon—an old large-bore horse pistol.

"Where were these weapons found?" Finney asked.

"The shotguns were found along Claiborne Street, and the pistol was found in the gutter, near the shotguns," Officer Rich responded.

Finney showed Officer Rich the two shotguns, one with wire wrapped around its barrel to hold it to its forestock, and the horse pistol. Rich identified the weapons as those found on Claiborne Street. McMahon offered no cross-examination.

Aware of the waning hour, Finney followed that testimony with the lead investigator of the ambush, Captain John Journee. Journee, a slight man with close-set eyes and a brown mustache, which seemed to wrap around his thin face. He corroborated Officer Rich's testimony regarding the guns. Without a question, Journee inexplicably volunteered that the defendants were arrested on the strength of Rocco Geraci's statement, which drew an immediate objection from McMahon. Judge Baker sustained the objection, as Finney punctuated Journee's testimony by dropping the weapons on his counsel table with a loud thud.

McMahon, realizing Geraci was going to be the next witness, before the jury went to the scene of the ambush, stunned the courtroom when he demanded that the judge have Geraci arrested for murder, and that he, McMahon, had a witness ready to swear an affidavit to support the allegation. Struggling to compose himself, Judge Baker denied McMahon's disruptive allegation and told the defense attorney to file a complaint with the District Attorney. Finney demurred and insisted he be allowed to proceed with his case. Judge Baker acceded to Finney's request, whereupon Finney, in an attempt to defuse McMahon's combustible demand, called Joseph Lispari, a fisherman who lived in the Louisiana swamps, to the stand.

"Mr. Lispari, do you know Joseph Provenzano?" Lionel Adams asked.

"Yes. I have known him for many years. He once lived on a boat near mine, a long time ago."

Adams approached Lispari with both shotguns. "Have you ever seen these shotguns before?" Adams asked.

"Yes. The one with the broken stock and wire wrapped around the barrel belongs to Joseph Provenzano. He kept it on his boat. The other shotgun also belonged to Joseph Provenzano, but he kept that one at his grocery store and bar on Customhouse Street."

On cross-examination, McMahon challenged Lispari. "When was the last time you saw these guns in Mr. Provenzano's possession?"

"I saw the one with the wired barrel many years ago, and the other, about two years ago," Lispari conceded.

"Do you know if they were in his possession on May 5th of this year?" McMahon asked.

"No, sir," Lispari said.

><

The last witness of the night stood in the gallery and approached the stand without being called. It was Rocco Geraci. A wave of mumblings and whispers washed over the courtroom as the bailiff administered the oath. Everyone in the court was frissoned with excitement and anticipation. The newspaper reporters scratched their pencils against the tablets, and the image carvers etched their sharp knives into their soft Tupelo Gum blocks. Every eye in the courtroom peered into the calloused soul of the muscular stevedore whose reputation spoke before his testimony.

After the perfunctory identification and introduction of the witness, Finney asked Geraci, "Mr. Geraci, were you in a wagon owned by the Matranga and Locascio Stevedore Company when it was beset by gunfire on the midnight of May 5th of this year?"

"Beset?"

"Were you shot at on May 5th of this year?" Finney asked.

"I was."

"Tell the jury what happened."

Geraci detailed the wagon ride from the docks to the fateful intersection of Claiborne and Esplanade. He identified all the defendants as participants in the ambush. His testimony tracked the statement he gave Captain Journee on May 7th, 1890, which triggered the defendants' arrest.

"Were you shot, Mr. Geraci?"

"No. But I jumped out of the wagon with my pistol and chased some of the shooters. I shot at them, but missed."

"Who did you chase?" Finney asked.

"I chased Joseph Provenzano, Anthony Gianforcarro, Gaspare Lombardo, and Pelligrini down Claiborne. When I got to Kerlerec and Claiborne, I saw Giulio and Peter Provenzano hiding behind a tree. When they saw me, they ran towards the river. I was going to chase them, but Salvatore Sunzeri, who was bleeding, came up to me and asked me to help him. So, I helped him back to the wagon."

"Are you sure about the men you saw that night?" Finney asked.

"Yes, sir. I've known them since we were kids."

On cross-examination, McMahon tried to rip into Geraci's testimony.

"Do you live in that neighborhood, Mr. Geraci?"

"No, sir. That place is too rich for my blood," Geraci said, causing the spectators to express a subtle laugh. "I live on Dorgenois Street in Greek Town. It's a muddy street. We just use Esplanade to go home at night."

"Are you the same Rocco Geraci who killed Vincenzo Raffo in 1886?"

Finney objected, but Judge Baker overruled the objection.

"Yes, I killed him. But the police ruled it self-defense."

"And the detective at that time is now the Superintendent of Police— David Hennessy. Correct?" McMahon asked, building a case of witness bias.

"I believe so."

"And Mr. Raffo was close friends with Joseph Provenzano. Correct?"

"I believe so."

"And you used to work for Joseph Provenzano. Correct"

"I did."

"But you quit over a salary dispute. Correct?"

"Yes."

"And that dispute erupted into a deadly fight between you and Mr. Raffo on Conti and Decatur Streets. Right?"

"Mr. Raffo stuck his nose in my business. He was a shoemaker, not a stevedore. He had no knowledge of the dispute," Geraci said.

"But you killed Raffo over a dispute with Joseph Provenzano, who is on trial for his life, now. Correct?" McMahon persisted.

"It was self-defense."

"In fact, you weren't arrested, until last year—four years after the killing. Correct?"

"Yes."

"And the affidavit supporting your arrest was sworn to by Frank Demar, Joseph Provenzano's brother-in-law. Correct?"

"Yes."

"And J.P. Macheca, a previous witness at this trial, and other Italian Democrats got the charges dropped, and you went free to work for the

Matrangas. Correct?"

"I have worked for the Matrangas for many years—about seven or eight," Geraci said.

McMahon approached the witness and put his hands his hips and asked, "Mr. Geraci, so as I stand here tonight, am I to understand that you once worked for Joseph Provenzano, quit over a salary dispute, killed a shoemaker over that salary dispute, got arrested four years later on the strength of an affidavit filed by Joseph Provenzano's brother-in-law, and then was freed on the strength of J.P. Macheca's interference with the investigation conducted by David Hennessy?"

"It was self-defense," Geraci growled.

McMahon turned his back towards the witness and walked away, but he asked one last question before sitting down. "Mr. Geraci, have you ever resolved that salary dispute with Joseph Provenzano?"

Geraci twitched on the witness stand and said, "I forgot about it."

After leaving the witness stand and approaching the doors of the courtroom, McMahon repeated his demand that Geraci be arrested for murder, which occurred in Sicily, based upon the statement of another witness who was prepared to sign another affidavit. Judge Baker ordered that deputies detain Geraci, but after Finney protested and informed the court that any witness McMahon had against Geraci should swear their affidavit before the city's recording judge, Baker ordered Geraci released. Newspaper reporters demanded to know the witness's name, but McMahon ignored their questions, and Geraci left the courtroom.

Before adjourning the court for the night, Judge Baker ordered Criminal Sheriff Gabriel Villere and his deputies to escort the jurors and him to the Esplanade and Claiborne, where they could inspect the scene of the ambush. "The jurors will spend about fifteen minutes at that intersection and thereafter, I am ordering the Sheriff to take the jury back to the upstairs dormitory, where they will be sequestered for the night. The court is in recess until tomorrow morning at ten o'clock."

Chapter 38

Criminal District Court
July 17, 1890
10:00 A.M.

The plea of alibi is the last resort of the condemned. When no other defense is available, one seeks the redoubt of distance or impossibility to commit the alleged crime. Jurors usually see through this feeble defense, like watching a three-act play through a sheer purple veil. All trial lawyers know the hopeless aleatory odds of such a defense, but when the quiver is empty, the lawyer must wield the bow. But McMahon and Pratt were ready to advance their clients' alibis in a very different way.

Once District Attorney Finney announced that the state would rest its case-in-chief, McMahon started calling a litany of brittle alibi witnesses. Newspaper reporters blithely obliged the proceedings by recording the names of the first few witnesses, but when McMahon, realizing he was losing the jury, stood and announced to Judge Baker he had nine members of the New Orleans Police Department prepared to testify for the defense, the courtroom erupted in a roar of disbelief. Even the jurors sprang alert in their straight-back chairs, waiting to see the uniformed apostates testify against the state. Judge Baker spent a minute gaveling order in his court. When the gallery, including the reporters' section, returned to order, Baker summoned all counsel to the bench.

"Mr. McMahon, is this another Geraci-like trick?" Baker demanded.

"No, your Honor. I have nine members of the police department who are prepared to testify that all the defendants were in other places at the time of the ambush."

"Nine officers in different locations, on one night, seeing one group of men who happened to be on trial for their lives, are willing to testify? Those are better odds than you get in one of the mayor's protected casinos," Lionel Adams scoffed.

Judge Baker turned towards the reporters' gallery and summoned George Vandervoort to his bench. Vandervoort's spindly legs wobbled as he approached the bench. "Mr. Vandervoort, what do you know about nine officers prepared to give alibi evidence before this court?" Baker demanded.

Vandervoort's voice quavered. "Judge, there have been rumors that some department members are going to testify for the Provenzanos, and some are going to testify against the Provenzanos. I sent a telegram to Chief Hennessy about this problem. He's on his way home from Chicago now. When he gets to St. Louis, he will get the telegram."

"Did he know about this before he left for Chicago?" Baker asked.

"No one knew for sure, until after the jury was selected," Vandervoort said.

"How did you learn about this, Mr. Vandervoort?" Baker asked.

"I heard it from Dominick O'Malley—in the corridor yesterday."

"Judge, I didn't know until now, "Lionel Adams intoned.

"Mr. McMahon, do you know the upheaval this will cause in this city if you call these officers?" Baker asked.

"No more than my clients being falsely accused of this ambush. Besides, judge, my clients are entitled to a full defense. After all, a gallows is waiting for them on Orleans Street. You can't deny my clients their defense, regardless of the behavior of disappointed people," McMahon asserted.

Baker sat back in his black leather chair and pondered for a moment. "Mr. McMahon, did you know about these officers before or after we picked the jury?"

"I was alerted to their names *after* we picked the jury. That's why I am telling you now. You might want to alert the jurors, because the officers will be known to some of them," McMahon suggested.

"Mr. Vandervoort, how many officers are on the force today?" Baker asked.

"Including the supernumerary officers and ranks, about two hundred. And when Chief Hennessy dissolved the aids department and merged them with the police department, we added about ten detectives."

Baker ordered McMahon to give him the list of the nine officers who were going to testify for the defense. He studied the list and acknowledged he knew most of them. Then he turned towards the jury. "Gentlemen of the jury, it is customary to read the names of all witnesses who will testify at a trial during *voir dire*, or jury selection. This gives all prospective jurors notice that a friend will testify and that their relationship, rather than the evidence, should not sway their verdict. Counsel for the state and defense did not know the names of nine police officers who were about to testify for the defense. No doubt some of you will know these officers, as I do. You are, therefore, cautioned *not* to let your relationship with these officers determine your verdict. You are to judge this case only on the evidence in its entirety. You took an oath to do that when the trial started, and I will hold you to that oath under penalty of law. Do you understand?"

Each juror nodded in the affirmative.

Satisfied, Judge Baker had the clerk read the following names of the nine police officers who were prepared to testify for the defenses: "Captain William Barrett, Captain John Journee, Sergeant John Cooper, Sergeant William Clifton, Corporal Gabriel Porteous, Corporeal Valley Woodworth, Officer Mike Early, Officer Dan Douglas, and Aid Antonio Pecora."

"Do any of the members of the jury find themselves unable or unwilling to honor their oaths, due to knowing any of these officers?"

No juror responded, and the defense began to call the officers to the stand. The reporters and their messengers scribed furiously, as their artists' knives sliced into their soft wood. Each officer testified that the defendants were either at the Eden Theatre at Canal and Royal Streets or attending a prize fight at the Audubon Club at Canal and Rampart Streets. Captain Journee testified he was at the Central Police Station and didn't see any of the defendants on his way to the ambush. Journee further recounted the night at Charity Hospital when the bleeding victims and their unwounded companions arrived. According to Journee, none of the men in the wagon could identify any of the defendants as their assailants. Recalling the earlier sustained objection to Journee's spontaneous testimony about Geraci's statement made the following day of the ambush, which caused the arrest of the defendants, McMahon threaded the needle of this defense carefully.

"Captain Journee, did you arrest any of the defendants the night of the ambush?" McMahon asked.

"No, sir?"

"Why not?"

"Because none of the victims could identify the people who shot them or shot at them."

McMahon thought about his next question, but abandoned the idea and sat down.

><

After all the officers had testified, McMahon and Pratt, feeling confident about their defense, paraded a line of witnesses who were employed at the Eden Theatre, Royal Street bars, the Audubon Club, or customers of those establishments. But McMahon, like the Greek mythical figure, *Icarious*, flew too confidently towards the beaming sun of his own glory.

His next witness was known only as "The Dummy." A slight, dark-haired man attired in the clothes of a common worker, who was illiterate, and unable to hear, nor speak, but frequented the Eden Theater, Canal Street cafes, and Royal Street bars. No one knew his real name, including him.

Through a series of tedious gesticulations, McMahon got the man to testify that he knew Joseph Provenzano, Nick Giulio, and Tony Gianforcarro. When Judge Baker grew impatient with the testimony, Peter Provenzano volunteered to be the witness's interpreter. Though leery of allowing a defendant to be the interpreter for a deaf and mute witness, Baker's curiosity overrode his judgment and allowed it. After "The Dummy" testified, through Peter Provenzano, that Joseph Provenzano, Nick Giulio, and Tony Gianforcarro left the Eden Theatre no earlier than two in the morning, Juror Ringold Bronsseau openly questioned the veracity of the interpreted testimony through a series of questions. Hearing the juror's questions, Judge Baker immediately excused the witness and instructed the jury to ignore everything the witness gestured or interpreted to have gestured.

McMahon immediately requested a recess, which was granted until seven that evening.

><

The Recess

Every reporter dispatched their messengers to their newspapers' offices on Camp Street, accompanied by notes of the day's testimony. Laurence Hearn sent Antonio and Abraham to *The Mascot's* offices with several pages of notes of the police officers' stunning testimony. J.D. Houston ran across Lafayette Square and galloped up the front steps of City Hall.

"Antonio, tell our editor to print **'Unprecedented Police Testimony'** in bold on the front page of our broadsheet. This will shake this town to its roots when the people realize their police department has allegiances with the Provenzanos and contradict the Matrangas. Abraham, have the editor put some of your images on the front page, too."

"You no believe their testimony?" Antonio asked.

"Hell, no. I've been around New Orleans too long to believe nine police officers would testify on behalf of *any* Italian in this city. Something is going on, and we must find out what it is. Now go. Come back about six, and we will have dinner at the Parkview Hotel. Hurry," Hearn said.

><

7:10 P.M.

As a janitor emptied the brass spittoons into a gray iron bucket, Judge Baker gaveled in the night court session. Again, the courtroom buzzed like a beehive, with the gallery anticipating the defendants taking the stand. J.D. Houston and Dominick O'Malley sat on the back row, three seats apart. George Vandervoort sat between Laurence Hearn and Antonio, but no words were exchanged. Each was prepared to take notes as they watched the defense attorneys whisper some final advice to their clients before turning their attention to the judge.

"Mr. McMahon, call your next witness," Judge Baker said.

As expected, the defense called some of the defendants to the stand, who testified consistently with the testimony of the nine police officers. Lombardo, however, provoked a delay in the proceedings when he refused to put his hand on the Bible, which had a crucifix affixed to the front cover. He yanked the Bible from the clerk's hand and flipped it over, proclaiming in a loud voice, "My God is in heaven and not on a cross in this book." He eschewed the police's alibi for him, and testified he was home with his family, and was in bed at the hour of the ambush. His defiance eclipsed his credibility.

When Joseph Provenzano wasn't among the first witnesses to be called by the defense, the jurors' eyes fell upon the Provenzano patriarch— waiting. Instead, when Pratt called George Provenzano to the stand, District Attorney Finney objected, stating the non-defendant Provenzano was present in court when the alibi witnesses testified. His testimony would be just a parroting of the police. Judge Baker, overruling the objection, said, "What do you expect George Provenzano to say? Even the janitor knows what's coming," which drew polite laughter from the spectators.

But Pratt surprised everyone. He requested the clerk to produce the shotguns, which were already admitted into evidence. "Mr. Provenzano, have you ever seen either of these shotguns in the possession of your brother, Joseph Provenzano?"

"No, sir."

"Have you ever seen either of the weapons in his grocery store or at the Red Lights Club on Customhouse Street?"

"No, sir. If you go to the club right now, you will find the only weapons my family owns." "Joseph doesn't like guns. I told him to get some to protect the store from the *Mano Nero*. He didn't, but I did. Those guns you are holding are trash. They're not ours."

Pratt gave the guns back to the clerk and asked George Provenzano about Joseph Lispari's reputation in the community for truth and honesty. "He's a damn liar, and a thief. He stole from our warehouse in Biloxi, Mississippi, but my brother, Joseph, felt sorry for him and didn't call the police. I heard his testimony. He lied."

When District Attorney Finney attempted to discredit George Provenzano. "Mr. Provenzano, do you have any evidence to support what you are saying. If so, produce it?"

George Provenzano's neck and face went florid in anger, and he roared, "I did, until Camillo Vittrano had his brains blown out on St. Philip Street last month. Someone did him up to keep him from testifying today."

Vittrano's brutal murder remained fresh in everyone's mind because of the newspapers' account of another *Mafia* killing in New Orleans. George Provenzano's unexpected response had a mixed impact on the jurors and spectators. Antonio wrote Laurence Hearn a note and passed it to him. It read: *"Does this mean Mr. Vittrano was killed because of the ambush?"* Hearn looked at Antonio, shrugged his shoulders, but was impressed by his messenger's curiosity. Finney, however, realized any further attack on George Provenzano's credibility might elicit another surprise response, so he pretended to be satisfied with what he had and sat down. McMahon, likewise, pretended to be satisfied with the response, but he knew the blood storm of *vendetta* hung over the courtroom, which could easily bleed his clients' innocence away. His last defense card had to be played.

McMahon stood and called Joseph Provenzano to the stand, which stirred the attention of everyone in the court. By law, no defendant may testify in his own defense. Still, when the prosecution heaps evidence of guilt upon the accused, a defendant's Constitutional silence fails to remove him from the courtroom. If a prosecutor adduces sufficient evidence of guilt, the combined curiosity of the jury must be sated by either strong evidence, staunch alibi witnesses, the defendant's own words, or all three.

A jail-haggard Joseph Provenzano took the stand. Weeks in the Orleans Parish Prison etched despair into his wizened rufous visage, and his black Sicilian eyes, hooded by fatigue and stress, affected the gaze of the dead. His old, soiled black trousers hung around his thinning frame, supported by jail-made leather suspenders. He glanced at the jury and waited for the first question.

Not surprisingly, the laconic Provenzano contrasted with his animated brother, George. His responses were short and devoid of any emotion. He denied hating the Matrangas, despite losing much of his stevedoring business to them. He denied owning the shotguns entered into evidence, and being at the intersection of Claiborne and Esplanade on the night of the ambush. When asked to account for his whereabouts on the night of the shootings, Joseph Provenzano paused and testified he had visited several locations that night and early morning.

"I was at Pelligrini's house about eleven. Then we walked to Canal and Royal, and I bought "The Dummy" a drink at a nearby café. Then I went to the Eden Theater. Afterwards, I had another drink at Schoenhausen's Bar. I never went near Esplanade and Claiborne," Provenzano testified. His deadpan demeanor belied a man facing the gallows.

On cross-examination, Joseph Provenzano remained unmoved by the fierce attack on his character and credibility. He denied shooting anyone in the past, but admitted he once shot at James Caruso a long time ago, but only after Caruso shot at him. When challenged about his presence in the area of Canal and Royal Streets on the night of the ambush, Joseph Provenzano stated, "I saw Sergeant Cooper and Corporal Porteous that night. I know them from the docks, and they know me." That testimony caused every reporter to record Provenzano's words about his relationship with the police, particularly the ones who testified for him and his co-defendants.

Every reporter, especially from *The Daily Picayune* and *Times Democrat*, had spent gallons of ink to focus their readers' attention on the internecine Italian violence in the city, secret stiletto societies, the Black Hand, and foreign *Mafia* influence in America's major cities. Still, now the press had to accept that their focus was too myopic. They had reported that Mayor Joseph A. Shakspeare appointed David C. Hennessy to reform the police department from its cultural corruption, which preceded the Civil War, and the Italian immigration.

><

Judge Baker glanced at the jury and noticed several of the gentlemen, though attentive, were yawning. "Mr. McMahon, how many more witnesses do you have tonight. It's after eight, and I want the jury to get some rest before tomorrow's closing arguments."

"We only have a few character witnesses left, Your Honor."

"You have thirty minutes to elicit their testimony. Mr. Finney, I will give you forty-five minutes for rebuttal."

McMahon's remaining character witnesses' testimony had the resonance of a Gallatin Street piano with lead strings. After the last defense witness, John McMahon announced that the defense rests.

With all court observers expecting the state to rest its case without calling any rebuttal witnesses, District Attorney John Finney lanced the new festering abscess plaguing New Orleans—a divided police department, with split loyalties, and questionable veracity. Although the police department already had a dubious reputation, nine officers testifying as alibi witnesses for the defense agitated the imaginations of the public and the newspaper reporters. While many thought the police department was undergoing a transformation under a new superintendent, it was evident to many that Hennessy's efforts, to date, were inadequate. So when Finney called Captain Christopher Collein to the stand, the credibility of the defense's case began to dissolve, but the questions about the alibi witnesses loomed larger.

"Captain Collein, what part, if any, did you play in the investigation of the Matranga ambush?" Finney asked.

"Chief Hennessy ordered me to arrest the defendants based on Rocco Geraci's statements."

McMahon objected, but his objection was overruled by the court.

On cross-examination, in a futile effort to discredit the witness and vicariously Geraci, McMahon asked, "Captain, did you know that Rocco Geraci was arrested for murder?"

"No, sir."

Lionel Adams shot out of his seat and raced to the courthouse corridor.

In a few moments, Adams reappeared with Geraci in court and said, "It appears to me, Geraci has not been arrested."

The courtroom erupted in laughter, and Judge Baker demanded McMahon retract his words, but the seasoned defense attorney refused. Realizing the McMahon's colossal blunder, which might send his clients to the gallows, Judge Baker allowed the matter to rest with the jury.

District Attorney Finney caused another stir in the courtroom when he called James Caruso to the stand. Though Caruso had jumped off the ill-fated wagon in the French Market before the ambush, Finney had one exhibit to show his last witness.

Finney approached James Caruso with the horse pistol, which had been admitted into evidence by Officer Rich. "Have you ever seen that pistol before, Mr. Caruso?"

"Yes, sir."

"Where?"

"It belongs to George Provenzano. I know because there is a piece broken off the hammer. I worked for the Provenzanos, but when they lost work, I left. The morning after the shooting, I went to the police station. The police had it on a table next to two shotguns. Chief Hennessy showed me the guns."

"Are you certain it belongs to George Provenzano?" Finney asked.

"Yes. I used to work for him at his store, and he gave it to me at night to guard his property," Caruso testified. "Also, he gave it to me to bring to the ships we were unloading. One day, it was wrapped up in some clothes. It was heavy. I unwrapped it and saw that pistol."

McMahon shot out of his chair and objected to the hearsay element of the witness's testimony and its overall relevance. "George Provenzano is not on trial. There has been no foundation laid by the state to connect that pistol to any of the accused on trial," McMahon roared.

Finney responded that it was up to the province of the jury to connect the pistol to the defendants. "This is a conspiracy case. Not all conspirators have to be on trial," Finney retorted. Hearing the state's weak assertion, Judge Baker sustained McMahon's objection. Finney relented, satisfied the pistol was found near the scene of the ambush, and had already been admitted into evidence. Though the thrust and parry of counsel are not considered evidence, the ears of the jury, like a river, flow one way.

When both sides rested their case, Judge Baker called a fifteen-minute recess, saying, "It was my hope we would have closing arguments in the morning, but after the recess and despite the hour, we will have closing arguments tonight, and the jury can deliberate tomorrow. I want a verdict tomorrow."

Laurence Hearn leaned over towards Antonio and whispered, "Run back to the office and tell the editor we won't make our normal deadline. We have to get the closing arguments for our next edition. Tell him midnight—maybe. Now go, but hurry back."

><

8:30 P.M.

For the first time during the trial, the judge took the bench on time. Prosecuting attorneys and defense attorneys scribbled their notes in preparation for their closing arguments. For the prosecution, A.D. Henriques and Lionel Adams would urge the jury to convict the defendants of the midnight ambuscade and make them take their last mortal steps on the gallows of the Orleans Parish Prison. Both prosecuting attorneys were accomplished orators, Adams, by far, the best.

For the defense, John M. Pratt would plead to the jury his clients were not guilty, and none of the defendants were near the intersection of Claiborne and Esplanade Streets on the night of the ambush, and that the charges were a calculated step by the Matrangas to use the law to settle their long-simmering *vendetta.* However, no one in the courtroom knew that across Lafayette Square, in City Hall, the mayor and his secret societies were conspiring with other ideas of justice.

Mr. Henriques argued for an hour and twenty minutes. He struck hard at the wounds the victims had sustained in the dark of night by cowards hiding in the city's shadows, willing to kill for their stevedoring business. He held a shotgun in each hand, waving them like steel spears in the jury's faces. He aimed the large horse pistol over their heads, but even in the subdued light of the courtroom, each juror focused on its yawning bore of death. After arranging the guns on his counsel table, muzzles aimed at the jury, Henriques ripped into the only defense proffered by the defendants— alibi.

"Gentlemen of the jury, think. Use your collective common sense. How can more police officers testify for the defense than testify for the state? How can more police officers defend this brutal act than try to solve it? What are the odds of nine police officers being at different locations with different defendants at the same hour, of the same night, miles away from Claiborne and Esplanade Streets? What are the odds? There is only one just verdict in this case: guilty with capital punishment," Henriques said, before sitting down.

Compared to Henriques' heart-pounding closing argument, J. M. Pratt's thirty—minute speech had the aura of resignation. He reminded the jury of the victims' original reticence to identify their assailants on the night of the attack. He pushed the alibi defense and lauded the nine police officers for coming forward to tell the truth in the face of official scrutiny. "It was police officers of several ranks, at several locations, who saw the defendants that night. Did they all conspire to lie for the same reason?" Pratt asked, not realizing he had just inadvertently bolstered Henriques' argument.

The feisty Lionel Adams wasted no time drilling into what was on everyone's mind in New Orleans. Taking a slight risk of impugning the ethnicity of the state's witnesses, Adams launched. "Gentlemen, you are called upon to determine whether or not a series of crimes odious to the people of this country shall continue. You are called upon to say whether or not the *vendetta* of Sicily or Corsica should be grafted upon American institutions—whether midnight assassinations should continue to do away with a witness who dares to assert the truth before a court of justice."

Adams wasn't finished. He took the last shot at the alibi witnesses, arguing, "The Supreme Justice of Massachusetts said of the alibi defense, 'it's the most fruitful of all sources of perjury.'"

McMahon let a great opportunity for a mistrial slip through his hands, as Adams' argument suggested someone had been killed on the night of the ambush. No one had been killed, but Adams' exaggeration, intentional or not, raised the element of undue prejudice before the jury. However, as a sedulous jurist, Judge Baker allowed McMahon the unusual opportunity to rebut Adams. McMahon, instead of moving for a mistrial, decided to go through the lives and character of his clients stating, "it is inconsistent for men imbued with American ideas, as these are, to return to the methods pursued by their more brutal countrymen, and they would appeal to the police, instead of a *vendetta*."

This final argument reminded the jury that the Provenzanos had abandoned Sicily's *Mafia's* methods and sought and received Hennessy's intervention in their feud with the Matrangas. But McMahon's logic redounded in favor of the Matrangas, too, which was not lost on Judge Baker, who would remember that fact for a future trial. McMahon's closing aroused the spectators to applaud, which drew a sharp rebuke from Judge Baker. And with the conclusions of the argument of counsel, Judge Baker charged the jury and sequestered them for the night, until 10:00 the following morning.

Chapter 39

Criminal District Court
July 18, 1890
9:30 A.M.

Despite the rumbling thunder through the gun-metal gray skies, several hundred people gathered in front of St. Patrick's Hall, waiting for the jury to reach a verdict. The crowd's mood seemed celebratory and carefree, anticipating a guilty verdict. No one expected an acquittal, and several men held signs reading, "Hang the Dagos." Even well-dressed ladies, with ruffled umbrellas at the ready, seemed chatty, confident, and buoyant, while they converted their vigil into a soiree. Some food and sarsaparilla vendors stood behind the sheriff's Black Marias, which had just brought the defendants from the parish prison to the courtroom. Their vigil was much more somber.

Newspaper reporters circulated through the crowd to gather opinions and thoughts on the trial. George Vandervoort parked his carriage at the boilermaker's shop on Lafayette Street, followed by three police patrol wagons filled with about twenty uniformed police officers with telegraphed orders from David C. Hennessy to maintain order, regardless of the trial's outcome. As the moments ticked away, the crowd grew larger and more vocal.

Just before ten, Antonio arrived, but he stopped when he saw the crowd and the men carrying signs. He brushed back his black hair from his forehead, buttoned the top button of his shirt, and his black cloth jacket, hoping his appearance projected an air of a newspaper man. As he crossed Lafayette Street, he wound his way through the tight crowd and towards the courthouse's front door. Two deputies and two police officers guarded the front door, but when one of the deputies recognized Antonio, he admitted him into the courthouse. It was the first time in his life that he felt acceptance.

The courtroom was packed with spectators, lawyers, businessmen, and reporters. Deputies kept order, but when the voices became too loud and contrary to the solemnity of the moment, a clerk would use the judge's gavel to maintain the propriety of the moment. The defendants sat motionless, as their lawyers occupied themselves with other matters. The prosecutors remained stoic, like sentinels of justice.

Antonio found a seat next to Laurence Hearn, who instantly read a troubled visage etched into Antonio's face. "Did you have a hard time getting into the courthouse?" Hearn asked.

"No. The guards recognized me and let me in."

"You seemed troubled. Is this your first verdict?"

"Yes. But I need to ask you a question?"

"What?"

"Does everybody in New Orleans hate Italians?"

"You saw the signs, didn't you?" Hearn asked.

Antonio nodded.

Hearn cast glances around the courtroom to detect curious ears, and inched towards his messenger's sensitive mind. Antonio inclined his head towards Hearn and prepared himself to receive the charred and scarred wisdom of a man skilled in the letters of observance.

"Antonio, like you, I was not born in this country. I was born in Ireland. I traveled to America by sail and steam twenty-odd years ago. When I landed in New York, my first impression was a policeman beating a beggar, which reminded me of how a British policeman put his boot in my father's face on a Dublin Street. Though I traveled many miles, I felt I hadn't moved an inch. The British shadow of prejudice followed me across the Atlantic."

Hearn's words clawed Antonio's Sicilian soul.

Hearn continued. "I traveled across America to the Mississippi River and boarded a cotton boat in a city called Memphis. Bales and bales of burlap cotton weighed the vessel down to its water line. Sometimes I thought it would sink under its own weight. But we made it to New Orleans and met a swarm of sweaty stevedores in the shadows of the steamy cotton presses. It was a hot day, like today, and my little leather bag and I immediately set out for accommodations and work.

"I found a little hovel behind the Custom House and looked for work. But my Irish accent strangled my efforts, until I fell upon newspaper row —Camp Street. I got my first job with *The Times-Democrat* as a messenger, like you are today. I carefully study the language and culture of this city. I learned its deep divides, which carve this city to pieces, much like those cobblestones you lay on weekends. But the grout lines are walls. They separate and bind, at the same time, until their granite tongues lie side-by-side, and form this mosaic of contradictions called New Orleans. Are you understanding any of this?" Hearn asked.

Antonio nodded.

Hearne smiled at his student. "This city is built on a swamp by the greed and inspirations of prejudiced men, using the moil and toil of the negro, and now the Italian. It's one of its more blatant contradictions, much like the demimondes prancing in front of St. Louis Cathedral, on their way to Gallatin Street on Saturday night. Those silken men, with their affected pedigrees, are mostly of English stock, which makes it more intolerable for me to countenance. Still, as an observer of the absurd, I must not cast my eyes away while boring into it. And now I exhort you to do the same. Don't accept it or tolerate it, but write about it. Describe it. Reveal it. Speak about it. Shame it, until their prejudices choke them like the nooses they are trying to tie around those defendants' necks."

Antonio cast a forlorn glance at the defendants. "Do you think I can be a reporter like you one day?" Antonio asked.

"I have seen your notes, and so has the editor. We both agree you have great potential. You just need to master the English language and stop mixing Italian words with your English words," Hearn smiled. "It will come with practice and reading American and English literature. Study words and their usage. It will come. You are very smart."

"A Jesuit priest taught me English by reading Charles Dickens. He was English. Do you like him?"

"Mr. Dickens, like you and me, traveled to America and saw prejudice and wrote about it. He experienced prejudice among his own kind. His books are laden with descriptions of all types of hatred and dreadful acts. Study him well," Hearn enjoined. "Not all English are evil. To think that makes us just as bad as those who hate us. We are better than that, because we observe and avoid their example."

Hearn was about to continue when the clerk announced, "All rise for the judge and jury."

"Get ready with your notepad, Antonio," Hearn whispered.

><

It's customary for court watchers and lawyers to look deep into the eyes of the jury as they enter the courtroom to discern even the slightest indication of the verdict. But the twelve jurors remained sphinxlike, which indicated, to many, a dooming conviction. Prosecuting attorneys Finney and Henriques stood next to their counsel table. Lionel Adams had excused himself from being present because of a family function on the Mississippi coast. Defense attorneys McMahon and Pratt, and their clients, stood straight and looked at the jury. It was just minutes before noon.

"Gentlemen of the jury, I understand you have reached a verdict. Is that correct?" Judge Baker asked.

Not surprisingly, the jury had elected Ringold Bronsseau as their foreman, who said, "We have," as he dug into his inside coat pocket and retrieved the verdict form. Minute clerk Richard Scriven collected the form and handed it to Judge Baker, who studied it for a minute.

"Publish the verdict, Mr. Scriven," Judge Baker said.

And in a clear monotone voice, Mr. Scriven read, "New Orleans, Louisiana, July 18, 1890. All Defendants guilty *without* capital punishment. Signed A.R. Bronsseau, Foreman."

Judge Baker showed no emotion, while his courtroom erupted with mixed emotions. Most spectators wanted the death penalty, but some were satisfied with keeping the hangman idle. Members of the Italian community, along with the family of the defendants, openly wept. Italian Consulate, Pasquale Corte, tried to console the family. At the same time, some of the defendants sat motionless in their chairs, except Lombardo and Gianforcarro, who openly wept and called upon God to correct this injustice. The jury of twelve men looked on impassively.

Under Louisiana law, at that time, the verdict had to be unanimous, so McMahon demanded that the jury be polled. One by one, the jury affirmed the guilty verdict. Judge Baker immediately ordered all of the defendants to be remanded to the parish prison, pending their second and third trials for the ambush, and demanded Sheriff Gabriel Villere and his warden, Lemuel Davis, remove the defendants from his courtroom.

Deputies immediately shackled the defendants together, and the clanking of chains echoed off the plaster walls and high ceiling. While families wailed, the spectators looked on with satisfied visages pasted to their pallid faces. J.D. Houston, Dominick O'Malley, and George Vandervoort raced out of the courtroom, down the stairs, and onto the banquette to watch the mournful parade of six dissipated souls pass the jeering crowd, and into the two Black Marias, for their return to the parish prison. Newspaper reporters gathered around the attorneys and the jurors, who dawdled outside the courthouse.

"We have sufficient grounds for appeal to the Supreme Court," McMahon bellowed.

One seasoned reporter yelled, "How can you appeal? You registered no Bill of Exceptions before the end of the trial."

"When there is a fundamental flaw in the trial, no such Bill is needed," McMahon responded.

"What flaw?"

"You have to wait. It's coming," McMahon teased.

Chapter 40

Illinois-Central Railway Station
Rampart Street
July 20, 1890
9:50 A.M.

George Vandervoort tugged on the reins of his single black horse and stopped the police carriage in front of the Illinois-Central railway station. He was about twenty minutes early for the train arriving from Chicago. Dressed in his blue police uniform, Vandervoort looked at the Sunday edition of the *Daily Picayune* and shook his head in disgust. "They didn't have to write the headline like that," he said aloud to himself.

In the distance, he heard the locomotive's whistle and clanging bell echoing throughout the quiet business corridors of New Orleans, announcing the arrival of the passenger train with his boss aboard. He could see puffs of black smoke drifting over the rooftops of the businesses and residences near Poydras Street. People on their way to church stopped to look at the train's black hissing and steaming engine pulling seven dark green passenger cars towards the station.

After the train's iron wheels screeched to a stop, David C. Hennessy, attired in a blue suit, white shirt, and no tie, stepped off the second passenger car, carrying a brown leather grip. Vandervoort greeted his boss and respectfully offered to take the chief's grip, but Hennessy insisted he carry his own luggage.

"George, I need a full report on the Provenzano trial," Hennessy said.

"Yes, sir. The morning edition of the *Daily Picayune* is on the seat. Turn to page six," Vandervoort said. Hennessy sat down, turned to page six, and began to fume. His pale complexion turned florid, and he clenched his jaw. The headline read:

FOUND GUILTY

The Jury Agrees as to Their Guilt, But Spare Their Lives by a Conditional Sentence

---

The Effect Upon the Convicts— They Break Down, Protest Their Innocence and Cry Like Children.

Hennessy read the article and scrunched the pages together in a fit of anger. "The bastards didn't need to write the headline like that. I know each of these men. They are not children. The newspapers love to humiliate everyone. But cast a cynical word their way, and you pay hell for it."

"I have the list of the officers who testified for them and the state," Vandervoort said.

"Give me the list," Hennessy said.

Vandervoort handed Hennessy a folded piece of paper. The young chief read the list of names. He knew them all, but not their motives. "We have a problem on our hands, George. Besides having a corrupt police department, we have a splintered one. I can't retaliate against any of them. It will look like political retribution. What is the mayor saying?"

"He's angry. Rumors are spreading. Some people are blaming you for the officers siding with the Provenzanos. Some say you are siding with the Matrangas. Some say the *Mafia* controls the police department. Some people want you replaced."

"I didn't take sides. I tried to prevent this very thing from happening. The mayor knows about my effort to bring peace to the docks. I had the Provenzanos arrested. The damn city should have taken over the docks in 1865," Hennessy huffed.

"Doesn't he know I went to Chicago to meet with the Pinkerton brothers to get a list of brigands living in New Orleans? The *Mafia* doesn't control the police department. But the Ring and the Regulators do. But they are his muscles. And that shit must stop, too. I am more determined to reform the police department and remove the political vermin from the ranks," Hennessey said, pounding his fist against his knee.

"I think he does. But nowhere in any of the papers do they mention your absence this past week or the reason. It's like you didn't exist," Vandervoort said.

"Damn! I also sent a cable from Chicago to Rome to get a list of fugitives and *Mafia* members Italian police believe are in New Orleans. We should be getting that in a couple of weeks."

"Did the Pinkertons have any information on the Matrangas or Provenzanos?" Vandervoort probed.

"Nothing more than we already knew. Most of them were either born in America or came here as children. They have only ancestral connections to *Stuppagghieri* or the *Giardinieri.* Both families are workers. It's the layabouts we must worry about. The Pinkertons gave me names of members of the *Camorra, 'Ndrangheta,* and something known as the *Sacra Corona Unita Societa,* they believe are here now. These groups are from Naples and the other parts of Italy—the *Mezzogiorno.*"

"What about Macheca?"

"J.P. Macheca was here before the Civil War. He fought for the Democrats in 1874. Remember, he saved General Badger's life," Hennessy said. "He and Monteleone are the richest Italians in New Orleans. But since Monteleone runs a hotel and doesn't work on the docks, he's not under any suspicion. All this *Mafia* shit is about who controls the docks. So, we need to focus on that. With the Provenzanos on their way to the state prison in Baton Rouge, we need to focus on what Rome sends us, and our internal problems," Hennessy said.

"So, is the *Mafia* an exaggeration?" Vandervoort asked.

"No. Not at all. There are foreign secret societies here, but there have always been secret societies operating in New Orleans, even before Louisiana brought the Sicilians here to chop cotton and cut cane. I remember stories about the Knights of the White Camellia. Some of those bastards are members of the Cotton Exchange and other local secret societies. I think men like to feel important when they put on masks, hide in the shadows, assume fake names, and exclude undesirables from their midst. My mother told me how awful they treated the Irish when they came here before the war. In time, we worked ourselves out of the canals and gutters, but we will never be equal to some people. But look at me. I'm Irish and the police chief," Hennessy chuckled.

"Do you think the Italians will ever be considered equal in New Orleans?" Vandervoort asked.

"Not in my lifetime, George."

Chapter 41

Criminal District Court
July 22, 1890
10:00 A.M.

The eight newspapers in New Orleans, including *The Times-Democrat*, showed more preoccupation with nine police officers testifying on behalf of the Provenzanos than with the guilty verdict. Virulent rumors flowed through the city's streets like Yellow Fever, and the police department was a quarantined ward of the afflicted and infected. Every officer, especially the ones who could read well, gulped down the newsprint, as if it were from a pulpit and not a printing press. Impressionable minds do not mature with age.

In its Sunday edition of July 20, 1890, Theodore D. Wharton, a close friend of Mayor Shakspeare and the editor of *The Times-Democrat*, attacked the police department, the nine police alibi witnesses, and challenged Hennessy with a front-page editorial:

"The verdict has discredited this testimony, and we suggest that the chief of police institute a rigid examination into the matter, for he cannot afford to have on his force men who would attempt to screen assassins by false testimony, and we are satisfied Mr. Hennessy will see the necessity of satisfying the public expectation in this regard."

John Wickliffe, a close confidant of the mayor and editor of the *Daily States*, published a similar editorial screed, demanding an investigation into why nine police officers, including three captains, would risk their careers and credibility to testify for the Provenzanos.

For many in New Orleans and throughout the entire police department, suspicion grew, especially among the ranks of the NOPD. Officers' tempers were brittle, and they feared being suspected of corruption and of being fired. Those who manned the Central Police Station, the First, Third, and Fourth Precincts seem to be affected the most by the pervasive and unbidden notoriety. Every café, restaurant, saloon, and tavern was filled with choking rumors, like thick Cuban cigar smoke.

Superintendent David C. Hennessy sat in his office and suffered from the glaring eye of the newspapers, the public, his department, and city hall. He sat at his desk and looked over the list of officers who testified for and against the state in the first Provenzano trial. The city's broadsheets covered his desk. Some of his own men thought it was convenient for him to be in Chicago when the nine officers testified for his friends, the Provenzanos. Hennessy was not immune from suspicion, as the dark phantoms of his past wafted over his transom. The knives of New Orleans memories were long, sharp, and glistened in the hot sun.

Clearer thinkers, however, knew he could have done nothing to stop the nine from testifying, nor would he do anything to encourage them to testify. *Nine people can't be forced to lie and keep a secret. The guilty verdict against the Provenzanos belies any notion of my influence on the verdict,* Hennessy thought. But he also knew an acquittal would mean hell for him to endure, if he could. His guts twisted as the thoughts of nine police officers conspiring to commit perjury, if they did. And he found biting torment knowing the jury took the word of the Matrangas over his nine officers. He felt the walls of his office closing in on him, like the jaws of a blacksmith's vise.

While he spent most of the fitful morning alone in his office mulling over all possible scenarios, the nine officers who testified and two who had not, were on their way to St. Patrick's Hall. There was no evidence that Hennessy knew what they were about to do, as Hennessy had avoided nearly all contact with his officers and staff since his return to New Orleans.

><

As Judge Baker took the bench, Captains Journee, Barrett, and Collein, accompanied by Sergeants Cooper and Clifton, Corporals Seelhorst, Porteous, Bayard, and Woodworth, and officers Douglas and Early stood at the bar. The legion of blue stunned everyone in the court, especially the judge. They stood at attention with a resolute countenance. The courtroom fell into a Requiem silence. After a few tense moments, Sergeant Cooper requested to address the court. Judge Baker granted the request.

"You Honor, in view of the recent publications in some newspapers, the officers who gave testimony in the Provenzano case, hereby ask this court to lay our character before the Grand Jury to preserve or condemn our credibility. The newspapers of this city have blown a dark cloud of impeachment of our credibility, our honor, and our names, not to mention the entire police department."

Judge Baker sat back in his large, high-back chair and pondered the request for a moment. "I am impressed with the posture members of the police department have taken," Judge Baker began, "and I will grant your requests, and take great pleasure seeing that the Grand Jury investigates this matter thoroughly. If it is determined you perjured yourselves, you have no place in the police department, but before the Bar of Justice. Indeed, I find the course you have taken to be a proper one."

As the court sounded the docket for the day, Judge Baker informed the officers that the Grand Jury would be in session that afternoon, and he would formally bring the matter of their request before them. The officers left the courtroom and were immediately besieged by reporters. Sergeant Cooper reaffirmed his testimony on behalf of the Provenzanos and repeated that he had seen Joseph Provenzano on Canal Street the night of the ambush.

The eleven officers descended the stairway and went to the clerk's office to use the telephone. Captain John Journee called the mayor's office to report the request they had made before the court. The mayor's secretary, Joseph Schaumburg, informed the men that they did the right thing. Journee wasted no time telling the reporter from *The Daily Picayune* the purpose and content of the phone call to City Hall. "The credibility of the New Orleans Police Department has been questioned, and we intend to have that question answered, not by the newspapers, but by the courts." Journee produced a printed card, which reflected their position on their testimony and credibility. Several of the officers told reporters they had no allegiance or friendship with the Provenzanos, and they arrested them when ordered by Hennessy and other ranking officers. Journee quickly reminded the reporters of his testimony during the state's case-in-chief, when he told the jury about Rocco Geraci's statement, which Locascio corroborated. "We all did the right thing and testified truthfully," Journee asserted.

><

12:45 P.M.

During the afternoon court session, Attorney William Lloyd Evans appeared before Judge Baker. He stated the Provenzanos had retained him to file a motion for a new trial, but had not had the time to formally present one in writing. He requested until August 1, 1890, to file one. The verbal request surprised Judge Baker because Evans, a well-known defense attorney in New Orleans, had once, along with Lionel Adams, successfully represented David and Michael Hennessy for the murder of Thomas Devereaux in 1882. Now, Evans and Adams would be on opposing sides. Nevertheless, Judge Baker granted the request.

Wary newspaper reporters suspected a connection between the police officers' request and the verbal motion by Evans for a new trial. Soon, Newspaper Row seethed with anxiety and uncertainty. Telegraph keys rattled like voodoo bones in the wind. Wild conspiratorial theories ricocheted off every building on Camp Street, like errant lead slugs. Every reporter covering the Provenzano case sat hunched over their desks, trying to connect the constellation of players to any nefarious plot. At *The Mascot,* Hearn, Antonio, and Abraham exchanged confused glances. "Just when you think you know New Orleans, the sodden bitch gives you a soft kiss, slaps your face, and kicks you in the ass. By the time you get off the floor, she has moved down the bar to tease another man," Hearn lamented.

While the three huddled over their notes and illustrations, George Osmond, the editor of *The Mascot* approached them and said, "Hearn, take my carriage and your two dagoes, and go to the parish prison. Hurry. Reporters are gathering to interview the Provenzanos this afternoon. I understand big-mouth George Provenzano will be giving a speech, too."

As the three climbed into Osmond's carriage, Antonio asked, "Mr. Hearn, does Mr. Osmond hate Italians, too?"

Hearn laughed. "No, Antonio. Mr. Osmond hates everybody, but he hates the mayor the most. Remember, he hired you and Abraham, knowing you are Italian. During his first administration, Shakspeare had him arrested and sought a court injunction to prevent him from publishing the paper. Governor Nicholls took the case to the state supreme court and had the injunction lifted. That only encouraged Osmond to go after anyone in government, and those who think they are beyond the reach of the law. That's why our newspaper, while hated by many, is read by most, in seclusion, late at night, under the flicker of a solitary candle."

Chapter 42

Central Police Station
July 22, 1890
1:15 P.M.

A tomb-like silence permeated the corridors and offices of the Central Police Station. While officers and clerks seemed to busy themselves with contrived work, to avoid contact with their fellow employees, the central telephone switchboard and callbox systems buzzed a faint pulse into the usually bustling nerve center of the police department. The shock of the Provenzano trial lingered like the stench of a dead horse, not the guilty verdict, but how nine cops tried to prevent the guilty verdict. Roiling emotions simmered below the pleasant pretensions of a normal day. Everyone's raw nerves waited for the next development. They knew it was coming, but when?

It didn't take long.

When both front doors of the police station swung wide open with a Banshee screech, everyone stopped to see who was making such a forceful grand entrance. General Algernon Badger, the United States Customs Collector, and Captain William "Billy" O'Connor of the Boylan Detective Agency marched through the center corridor without greeting anyone. He stomped up the stairs to David Hennessy's office. The stunned personnel exchanged glances and immediately went back to work.

Badger and O'Connor greeted George Vandervoort and walked directly into the chief's office and slammed the door. To assist in the free flow and circulation of the July humid air throughout the station, every transom was opened, which denied any conversational privacy. Vandervoort survived as police secretary for many years by strict obedience combined with his vulpine skills of a career bureaucrat. The secretary sat motionless at his desk and listened.

"What the hell is going on, David?" Badger asked. "This city is on fire with rumors and speculations. How can you let nine police officers testify against the state as alibi witnesses?"

"General, I didn't. If you recall, you told me to get out of town for the trial. I went to Chicago to meet with the Pinkerton brothers to gather information on the Sicilian brigands in New Orleans. I had no idea some of my best men would testify for the defense. And if they were hell-bent on doing that, I couldn't have stopped them, anyway. Nor would I encourage them to do so. This was planned well before I left."

People around city hall believe you made the men commit perjury," O'Connor said.

"That's bullshit, Billy. If I wanted to help the Provenzanos, I would have stayed and testified myself. I ordered their arrest on the strength of Geraci's statement, corroborated by Locascio. I had no choice but to file the charges with the District Attorney. If I hadn't, I am sure Macheca and the Matrangas would have screamed favoritism. I won't have that in this police department," Hennessy said.

"The jury didn't believe those nine officers were making a mockery of the police department," Badger said. "Now, I heard those officers are requesting a Grand Jury investigation into *their* alleged perjury. The newspapers are stirring up shit, again."

"Look at my desk," Hennessy said, pointing to a pile of newspapers. "I have spent the morning reading this tripe. The price of lies is just a few pennies. At least Judas got thirty pieces of silver. The entire police department is now under suspicion, and everyone is demanding an investigation, which I will do."

"No. Let the Grand Jury do their job, David. You don't want to be accused of interfering," Badger warned.

"I understand. I haven't spoken to any of the officers since my return from Chicago. But my mind can't escape several facts and questions, which I must discuss with you," Hennessy said.

"What?" Badger asked.

Hennessy smiled and yelled, "George, I know you can hear me. Come into my office and bring your notes. "Vandervoort sheepishly entered the office and sat next to Badger.

"First, let me ask this question," Hennessy said, as he paced the room. "If the Provenzanos didn't shoot the Matrangas, who did? I know everyone, including the jury, believes the Provenzanos did the shootings. But why did nine police officers take the stand under oath and give alibi evidence? Did all nine commit perjury for the Provenzanos? For me? Do people think I ordered them to lie under oath? Why would they risk their careers and freedom for them or me?"

"It's just a rumor, David. But some of my men are hearing stories about a fight on the docks over the Matrangas denying work to some unaffiliated stevedores, who left town after the shooting. I have no proof of that. It's just a rumor," O'Connor said. "I have no names."

"Rumors strangle the truth. Corruption strangles government. Lies strangle justice," Hennessy said. "I need facts. But if those rumors are on the street, who started them and why? Did the Provenzanos start the rumors? George Provenzano has a big mouth."

"Speaking of George Provenzano, the Fourth Precinct called in and said he was going to give some type of speech in front of the parish prison in about an hour," Vandervoort said.

"George, call the Fourth Precinct, and tell them I want a report on whatever that idiot says," Hennessy demanded.

"Yes, sir," Vandervoort said, leaving the office.

Hennessy began to pace. "What if the Grand Jury determines the nine officers lied? What happens? Do the Provenzanos get a new trial?" Hennessy asked.

"No. Remember, they were *defense* witnesses. The jury didn't believe them and convicted the defendants. There is no new evidence, and McMahon has never filed a Bill of Exceptions during or after the trial. As I see it, Finney would have to prosecute the officers for perjury. They took one hell of a risk asking Baker to have them investigated," Badger said. "Either way, it looks bad for the police department. But you don't need to investigate them. Whatever the Grand Jury determines, you can't contradict your own investigation."

"What if the Grand Jury finds they told the truth?" Hennessy asked.

"The trial jury found them guilty, and that verdict will probably stand," Badger opined. "When the reporters start asking you questions, just tell them the inquiry is in the hands of the Grand Jury. David, you're safe. Those nine cops did you a favor asking for an investigation."

"What if it's a plan to destroy me?" Hennessy asked. "What if Journee and his colleagues tell the Grand Jury I ordered them to lie? Then I will be indicted, too, and Finney will use those officers against me." Hennessy turned, looked out his office window, and said, "I know half this city hates me and the other half doesn't give a damn. Mark this moment in time, gentlemen, the rats are scurrying in the gutter, and soon will emerge from the sewers to take me down. They have been trying for years. What do I do, General?"

"Nothing. Let the investigation continue. If the Grand Jury finds they told the truth, they will probably testify again if Finney pursues the Provenzanos again. If they determined they lied, the next two Provenzano cases will go forward, and the officers will be prosecuted. And if they lie and tell the Grand Jury that you ordered them to lie, what is their proof? Admitted perjurers are going to blame the police chief who ordered the Provenzanos' arrest, and then ordered them to lie? And where were you during the trial? In Chicago, investigating the Provenzanos, Matrangas, and every other Italian brigand in New Orleans. David, your mind is chasing phantoms. Relax," Badger advised.

"*Relax?* Why is Billy here? Why do I need a bodyguard? How can I relax when Finney and Adams used Dominick O'Malley as their investigator? I feel betrayed by Lionel Adams that he would use Devereaux's best friend as his investigator. Adams saved my neck, but he knows O'Malley is a devious, lying bastard. Adams and O'Malley damn well knew I killed Devereaux in self-defense. And the same bastards who ambushed my cousin in Houston are ready to ambush me."

"David, you can't have roses without thorns," Badger said. "Adams is a very shrewd trial lawyer. He uses every tool to win. Adams knows O'Malley has contacts throughout this city, and he used them. Adams was furious when nine officers testified against his case. McMahon outclassed him on this one. Besides, early in the trial, Baker threw O'Malley out of the courtroom. So, relax."

"If Finney prosecutes the Provenzanos again, will you testify for them?" O'Connor asked Hennessy.

"Why would I? If the Grand Jury clears the officers, I don't need to testify. I don't know where the Provenzanos were on the night of the ambush. In fact, all of the victims told me they couldn't identify who shot them that night. But those nine officers are now on the record saying they know who didn't. I'm not getting into a swearing contest with my own officers. All I can offer is character evidence, which is about the same as the Matrangas' character. Remember, we tried to broker a peace between both families."

"Did the Pinkertons tell you anything about the Matrangas, or the Provenzanos?" O'Connor asked.

"Nothing new. If there were anything new, they would have been arrested last Sunday. Now, I am waiting for Rome to send me cables about their fugitives hiding in New Orleans," Hennessy responded.

"Do you think Rome has anything on the Matrangas or the

Provenzanos?" O'Connor asked.

"I doubt it. If there is anything, it would have to be from a long time ago, since they have been in New Orleans for most, if not all, of their lives, especially Macheca. He was born here, and Matranga left Italy when he was a baby. Billy, what I need to do is get with the Italian consulate—Corte. The Pinkertons told me he has a list of fugitives from Naples and Sicily. I want that list," Hennessy said.

"His office is at Number 23 Poydras Street, on the second floor of the Italian Labor Union building. Some immigrants go there right off the ships and look for work. Corte will cooperate with you, but keep his cooperation secret," Badger said. "He wants to help, but he got suspiciously sick after having some oyster soup with J.P. Macheca. But despite that, he still remains friendly with Macheca and Matranga. Everybody is seeing shadows behind them. I will set up a secret meeting for you to meet him. What would be a good place?"

"There are no secrets in New Orleans. Does he ever go to the Customhouse?" Hennessy asked.

"Very often. I will set up a meeting in my office soon," Badger said.

Vandervoort returned to Hennessy's office and said, "Corporal Edward Hevron of the Fourth Precinct will attend George Provenzano's gathering. He will write a report."

"Hevron? Isn't he friends with Journee?" Hennessy asked.

Chapter 43

Orleans Parish Prison
Basin and Treme Streets
July 22, 1890
3:45 P.M.

Depending on the direction of the wind, one could smell the Orleans Parish Prison before one could see it. In the daytime, its three-story whitewashed brick walls cast a ghostly, iridescent hue on the dead end of Basin Street. At night, its darkened iron-grated windows would appear like a row of skulls peering from the cells. Its fifteen-foot front gate, regardless of the time of day, struck fear in any man, for many have entered that impregnable iron portal, and never lived to speak of the horrors which dwelled within. Neighbors would often complain to Sheriff Gabriel Villere about the screams coming from the prison day and night. In the summer, inmates would share time at the windows to breathe fresh air. In the winter, the inmates would block the cold wind with their mattresses and sleep on the damp brick floors.

The prison, built in 1834 in the Faubourg Treme, occupied an entire city square bounded by Basin, Treme, St. Ann, and Marais Streets. Because of its forsaken location, among rows of brothels, shadowy opium dens, and cemeteries, the prison was wreathed by four, chert-covered, rutted paths slathered in layers of decay. The streets were among the last scheduled to be paved with Belgian cobblestones, as the more affluent and well-traveled areas of New Orleans enjoyed civic precedence. Behind the forsaken stone, three-storied cellblocks sat a series of small flagstone courtyards, loggia, and livery. The front gates bisected two cell blocks. White Manchac, the women's section, sat on the north side of the prison, above the Fourth Precinct police station, which was located at the corner of Basin and Marais Streets. A small gap between White Manchac, and the larger male block served as the prison gallows, allowing spectators to witness hangings from the neutral ground on Orleans Street, until 1858, when the domino-masked hangman botched his office by not fixing the nooses tightly around the necks of two killers, allowing them to fall to the ground, breaking their legs. Believing in *Providential Interference*, as one reporter noted, the crowd demanded the release of the condemned. But the blood lust of justice had to be sated, and the men were carried back to the trap, the nooses firmly affixed, and their cervical spines judicially separated.

Many reporters and writers of the time were aghast at the prison's mere presence—on a dead-end street, cheek and jowl with two Catholic cemeteries. But the crumbling bastille served its designed purpose—to be New Orleans' charnel house for its prisoners. Any man or woman who survived its walls could easily be identified on the street. Once released, their bent human form, their dissipated countenance, their creased skin by time's serrated edge, and their malnourished bodies were easily recognized. Usually, the first stop for a newly-liberated inmate was a block away from the prison's front gate—the Orleans Street Market—where vendors would feed the former inmates, as a Corporal Work of Mercy. But New Orleans didn't hold the distinction of having the nation's worst prison. Other cities enjoyed consigning their criminals to subterranean conditions, vermin rejected.

Indeed, Charles Dickens, during a 1842 visit to some American prisons, noted in an essay: *"There is a depth of terrible endurance in it which none but the sufferers themselves can fathom, and which no man has the right to inflict upon his fellow creatures... I hold the slow and daily tampering with the mysteries of the brain to be immeasurably worse than any torture of the body."* New Orleans tolerated, if not enjoyed, its prison as long as it remained downriver and downwind from their gilded vicinages, its gentlemen, their pallid wives, beaus, and debutantes. But after a late Friday night bridge game at the Pickwick Club, a cotton factor's clandestine rendezvous with a young mulatto girl in a Treme cottage dissolved all caste structures of New Orleans, at least for a few forgotten moments.

This day suffered the same monotony as past and future days. Wives and children huddled around the main gate, begging admission to see the newly convicted Provenzanos and their colleagues. George Provenzano grabbed the gate bars and gave them a ferocious shake. "Let me in to visit my brothers. Let the families come in to bring them clothes, food, and clean water. Let the newspaper reporters in to see how you keep men locked up like mad dogs," George Provenzano yelled.

Chief Deputy Alcee LeBlanc, accompanied by Warden Lemuel Davis, approached the gate from within the prison. LeBlanc's eyes scanned the crowd, which had gathered. Women, their heads covered in black shawls, and lugging wicker baskets filled with food and sundries, begged tearfully to see their husbands and brothers. He noticed several newspaper reporters and their woodcarvers taking notes. Behind them, NOPD Corporal Hevron watched from a distance. "Damn Lemuel, what should I do?" Leblanc asked, fearing a breach of the gate, reported by the city's newspapers.

"Let them in. Search them for guns and knives, but let them in," Davis responded.

Deputies unlocked the main gate and, one by one, admitted family members and reporters after being searched for any weapons. Corporeal Hevron, a well-recognized member of the police department, slipped through the gate in uniform and armed. Once inside, LeBlanc led the family members and reporters down a first-floor stone corridor, lit by tallow candles and torches. Prison cells of all sizes, immured by heavy iron bars, lined the corridor. The sepulchral stench of the cell block choked the visitors. Women used their shawls to cover their faces, while the men masked themselves with their handkerchiefs. A large cell loomed at the end of the corridor, where all the Provenzano defendants were being held. They already had visitors—their attorneys.

LeBlanc used a large brass key to open the cell and admit the family members, but he refused to accept George Provenzano and the reporters into the cell. For the moment, George was content with talking with his brothers through the bars, as reporters and Corporal Hevron took notes. A large wooden table sat in the middle of the cell, and the women, after hugging and kissing their loved ones, busied themselves with preparing a suitable dinner for the inmates. LeBlanc and Davis tolerated the homemade wine, and even had a small glass themselves with their Italian meal. In New Orleans' *Piccolo Palermo,* it was called *pizzu,* or a protection offering. Soon, the smell of freshly cooked food eclipsed the reeking vapors from the nearby latrine, and the families sat down to share in their prison repast. In those days, the guards welcomed the Italian food, and the families were more than happy to pay the guards the *pizzu,* for the sake of their loved ones.

As the inmates and their families ate, the discussion turned towards why Dominick O'Malley would side with the prosecution, knowing his reputation for jury tampering and locating witnesses to perjure themselves. George Provenzano, sitting on a keg of tallow outside the bars and munching on his dinner, erupted. "If Camillo Vittrano had not been killed, he would have testified as our witness. He knew the *Stuppagghieri* wanted him to lie, but he wouldn't. So they blew his head off."

"What's the *Stuppagghieri*?" A reporter asked.

"It's the secret stiletto society of New Orleans. Tony Matranga is the chief of it. They wanted Vittrano to lie and convict my brothers. He refused. So, they killed him six weeks ago on St. Philip Street at Matto's wine room."

"Did the nine cops lie?" a reporter asked.

"No. They told the truth," George Provenzano yelled. "I guess O'Malley couldn't get to them."

"Calm down, George. I have some news, which might make everyone feel better," Joseph Provenzano said. The reporters readied their pencils. "Our attorneys tell us we have a good chance at a new trial."

Giulio and Pelligrini reminded Joseph Provenzano that McMahon didn't file a Bill of Exceptions. The attorneys remained quiet.

"I was home with my family the night of the ambush. I went to work in the French Market the next morning. If I had shot anyone, do you think I would have gone to the market to be arrested?" Pelligrini asked.

"The jury thought so," a reporter responded.

Joseph Provenzano stood and approached the bars and spoke to the reporters. "I don't know nothing about no shooting of the Matrangas. What I am hearing is that a bunch of laborers didn't get a fair deal after they unloaded the *Foxhall*. So they followed them to a dark spot on Esplanade and shot them. After they shot them, they left the city. We didn't shoot the Matrangas, but we might have to spend the rest of our lives in prison for it. Everybody wants us off the docks."

"What about the shotgun?" a reporter asked.

"That's not my gun. It's trash. I never saw it before it was brought into the courtroom. Yes, I often carried a revolver for my protection. I have been threatened too many times. I never belonged to no *vendetta* gang or secret society. I have worked the docks for many years. All we wanted was a square deal. But Macheca and Matranga kicked us off the docks. The cops told the truth. I was on Royal Street that night. If I knew who shot the Matranga gang, I would have told the police. If they shot the Matrangas, they would shoot us next. Everyone wants to control the docks in New Orleans. All we wanted to do was work and be paid fairly," Joseph Provenzano said.

"What about your new attorneys?" a reporter asked.

Pratt stepped forward and identified William Lloyd Evans as their appellate attorney. "He will be filing a motion for a new trial soon, which we believe has some merit," Pratt said. "There will be two other attorneys as well. Mr. James C. Walker and Arthur Dunn. All I can say is that the trial was fundamentally flawed, and no Bill of Exceptions is needed for a reversal."

"You expect to win a new trial on a procedural defect, and not an evidentiary one?" a reporter asked.

"Absolutely," Pratt affirmed. "I will not say anymore on the matter. Good day, gentlemen."

As the reporters turned to leave the prison, George Provenzano blurted, "We're not finished. Wait and see what happens next." The reporters ignored the outburst and left the prison.

Chapter 44

Recorder's Court
Carondelet and Lafayette Streets
Saturday
July 26, 1890
1:00 P.M.

Nine days after the guilty verdicts were announced against the Provenzano defendants, George Provenzano's parish prison outburst proved prescient. Telegraph keys and the primitive telephone system jammed with the quaking news. Newspaper reporters dashed between the Central Police Station and the Recorder's Court, a distance of about five city squares, to capture the facts. The police, still reeling from the newspapers' accusatory editorials about the nine officers testifying as alibi witnesses during the Provenzano trial, refused to answer any of the reporters' questions. "Who did you arrest this morning?" yelled one reporter at a cluster of officers standing on the front steps of the police station. The officers ignored the questions, and the reporters raced back to the Recorder's Court, where new arrestees are arraigned, and their cases were dismissed for the lack of evidence or held over for a Grand Jury investigation. Reporters had only unconfirmed rumors, which usually sufficed as news in New Orleans.

Laurence Hearn arrived at the Recorder's Court about thirty minutes before the afternoon session. He had already sent Abraham to search for Antonio, who delivered ballast stones for the city street pavers at Canal and Basin Streets. Both boys arrived, heaving and panting, about ten minutes before the court went into session. Antonio, covered in dust and mud, wiped his clothes with Hearn's large handkerchief. "Will I get you in trouble with Mr. Jahnke?" Hearn asked.

"No, sir. I got permission. He knows I work for the newspaper, too. But what is happening? Why are we here on a Saturday?" Antonio asked.

"Do you see that man with black hair sitting in the corner near the prosecution's table?"

"The one that looks nervous?" Antonio asked

"Yes. His name is Frank Demar? Do you know him?" Hearn asked.

"I heard the name during the Provenzano trial," Abraham said. "Who is he? I forgot."

"He's Vincent Provenzano's brother-in-law, and he has sworn out another affidavit on Rocco Geraci for the murder of Vincent Raffo on St. Philip Street in December of 1886. The clerk gave me a quick glance at the affidavit. Things are getting crazy," Hearn said.

"Wait. The District Attorney wants to prosecute his witness in the Provenzano trial for a murder that happened four years ago?" Abraham asked.

"Exactly," Hearn responded. "If you remember, Geraci was cross-examined by McMahon about that killing. Finney knew about it then and did nothing. He knew about it four years ago and did nothing. Today, he had Geraci arrested and wants to put him in the parish prison with the Provenzanos. I'm beginning to believe everybody in New Orleans is smoking Chinese opium."

"What if the Provenzanos get a new trial? Can Geraci testify, again?" Antonio asked.

"Hell no. That's why this is pure lunacy. Finney has lost his mind," Hearn said.

At that moment, Recorder Guy Dreaux took the bench and gaveled the Recorder's Court into session. The docket clerk sounded the docket, and the two police officers escorted a shackled Rocco Geraci to the defense counsel's table. This surprised everyone in the court, which was packed with police officers, lawyers, reporters, and spectators. The room filled with whispers of disbelief, but Recorder Dreaux, sharing the disbelief, ignored the din.

The shock of the moment didn't end there. When Lionel Adams, one of the former prosecutors in the Provenzano trial, stood and announced he would be representing Geraci, the courtroom erupted. Dreaux banged his gavel repeatedly.

"Order! Order! I want to hear Mr. Adams explain this, as much as anybody," Recorder Dreaux yelled. When courtroom decorum was restored, Dreaux asked, "Mr. Adams, how can you represent Mr. Geraci when you are an Assistant District Attorney?"

Adams stood and bravely announced, "Sir, last week, after closing arguments in the Provenzano matter, I decided to be a prosecutor for one last case—the Provenzano case. After that case, I decided to enter private practice and open a law office at Number 22 Carondelet Street. There is no conflict, as Mr. Geraci has been accused, again, of a crime that occurred some four years before the ambush at Esplanade and Claiborne. These are two separate matters. Now, may I proceed with the representation of Mr. Geraci?"

"Any objections, Mr. Finney?" Recorder Dreaux asked.

"None, Your Honor."

"Proceed, Mr. Finney," Recorder Drew said. "Since this is just a preliminary hearing to determine if there is enough evidence to refer this matter to the Grand Jury, I will ask you to call his first witness."

Finney and Adams nodded to each other professionally, and after Adams requested a sequestration of the state's witnesses, the hearing began.

District Attorney Finney, seeming oblivious to the folly he was embarking on, called Frank Demar to the stand. Demar, wiping his brow, took the stand and the oath. Demar testified that on a dark December night in 1886, he heard shots coming from St. Philip Street, between Chartres and Decatur. He testified he had just completed his work as a bookkeeper at Provenzano and Brothers Fruit Company at Number 256 Decatur Street, when he heard many gunshots as he crossed St. Philip Street. He looked down the street and saw muzzle blasts and immediately slammed his body against a building to avoid being shot. He testified he remembered Rocco Geraci, pistol in hand, running past him, but stopped to warn him to say nothing of what he saw. Demar also testified that Geraci came to his house at Number 170 Marigny Street and renewed the warning.

Lionel Adams wasted no time ripping into Demar's belated testimony. "Isn't it true, you are the brother-in-law of Vincent Provenzano, whose brother was recently convicted of attempted murder, and is currently an inmate at the Orleans Parish prison?"

"Yes, sir, but I am telling the truth."

"Didn't you swear out another affidavit against Mr. Geraci about a year ago, and those charges were declined?" Adams asked.

"Objection, Your Honor," Finney interrupted. "Last year, we didn't have the same evidence as we do now."

"Continue, Mr. Adams. This is just a preliminary hearing," Dreaux said.

"How many more affidavits are you going to swear out against Mr.

Geraci?" Adams asked.

"Objection, Your Honor," Finney said.

"Overruled. Continue, Mr. Adams."

"Didn't Rocco Geraci testify against Joseph and Peter Provenzano about ten days ago, thus securing their convictions?"

"Yes, sir, but no one put me up to filing this affidavit," Demar protested.

"How many shots did you hear on St. Philip Street that night, long ago?" Adams probed.

"Oh, about ten or fifteen," Demar responded.

"Mr. Demar, did the pistol you saw in Mr. Geraci's hand or any pistol in the city of New Orleans hold ten or fifteen bullets at one time?"

"I don't think so," Demar responded.

"Did you know Vincent Raffo?" Adams asked.

"I've seen him around."

"And wasn't Mr. Raffo a good friend of Joseph Provenzano?"

"Yes. They were good friends, I believe."

"Is it your sworn testimony that all of those ten or fifteen shots you heard on St. Philip Street came from Rocco Geraci's pistol?" Adams asked.

"I don't know," Demar conceded.

"No further questions," Adams announced.

The state's next witness was the former Deputy Coroner, Stanhope Jones, who testified he first examined Vincent Raffo on December 30, 1886, and decided his death was caused by Erysipelas, secondary to a gunshot wound to his right leg. Dr. Jones further described the wound as having sloughing skin around a deep puncture wound. On cross-examination, Lionel Adams had Dr. Jones concede that Vincent Raffo died of a bacterial infection that ravaged his body while in Charity Hospital, and had he had decent medical care, Raffo would have survived. But Finney objected and reminded the Recorder that the common law of homicide does not place the burden on treating physicians, but on the person who caused the injury. Recorder Dreaux acknowledged the point and directed the District Attorney to call his next witness.

Bonita Banano took the stand wearing a long black dress and her black hair pulled back into wrapped into a tight bun. She testified she was standing on her upper gallery above St. Philip Street when she heard multiple gunshots coming from both sides of the banquette. She looked down into the darkness and saw Rocco Geraci firing what appeared to be a large gun. She stood on the upper gallery, waiting for her fisherman husband to return home, when the shooting started. She heard a man yell in the darkness, while Geraci ran down St. Philip Street towards Decatur Street.

Lionel Adams had one question for Bonita Banano. "Is it a fact that you are the daughter of Gaspard Lombardo, who was recently convicted of firing into a wagon, which Rocco Geraci was riding, last May?"

"My father is innocent," Bonita Banano said.

Laurence Hearn leaned towards Antonio and Abraham and whispered, "I don't understand why Finney is doing this. He is destroying the Provenzano convictions with this hearing. Why does he want to put his star witness in the same prison as the Provenzanos? This is crazy. I'm totally confused."

Antonio and Abraham just shrugged their shoulders.

Finney's most confounding blunder came next. He called Nick Giulio and Antonio Pelligrini to the stand. Both were recently convicted, like Gaspard Lombardo, of ambushing the wagon Geraci was riding in on May 5, 1890. Both witnesses were in chains and escorted by sheriff's deputies. Lionel Adams, like many court observers, was stunned by Finney's strategy. But it was obvious to all that Finney was trying to imprison Geraci, his premier witness in the most famous case he had ever tried. Their dubious testimony echoed Demar's. Adams' cross-examination focused on their recent convictions for shooting at Geraci and others at Esplanade and Claiborne. No one in the courtroom could understand Finney's motive, except that he was up for re-election in the fall and was beholden to Mayor Joseph A. Shakspeare. In New Orleans, the political hand always guided the quill, which scribed the law and balanced the scales of justice.

After Finney called several other witnesses, who gave conflicting testimony, Finney rested his case, and Lionel Adams announced, "Your Honor, considering the character and quality of the state's case, I have no need to call any witnesses. Accordingly, I request that Mr. Geraci be restored to his freedom or, in the alternative, granted some bail pending your decision."

Again, Finney surprised everyone in the courtroom. "I have no objection to granting Mr. Geraci bail, provided it's someone of means and status in this city."

Lionel Adams called former city alderman Anthony Patorno to the bar, who stated he would act as Geraci's personal surety, pending the outcome of this matter.

"Considering the evidence adduced in this hearing, or the lack thereof, I will take this case under advisement, and make a ruling on Tuesday, July 29, 1890. Accordingly, Mr. Geraci is released on a five-thousand-dollar personal surety executed by Mr. Patorno," Recorder Dreaux ruled.

Outside of the Recorder's Court, newspaper reporters fired questions at Lionel Adams, seeking his assistance to help them make sense of what the District Attorney was doing. "I have no idea what Mr. Finney was doing. My client is innocent of murder. He fired at Mr. Raffo in self-defense as Mr. Raffo ran away. The fatal wound suggests Mr. Geraci wasn't aiming at Mr. Raffo's heart. It was self-defense in 1886, it was self-defense when Mr. Geraci was accused last year, and it is self-defense today."

"Is someone out the get Rocco Geraci?" one reporter asked.

"Go to city hall or the Central Police Station and ask that question," Adams bristled, sticking a cigar in his mouth. "Something inexplicable is going on, gentlemen, and when that happens, you can expect more of the inexplicable to occur. That's for certain. Keep your pencils ready."

Laurence Hearn braved one question. "Mr. Adams, didn't this shooting take place outside of Matto Wine House, the same place where Camillo Vitrano was killed earlier this year?"

"St. Philip Street is a very dangerous place. Next to Gallatin Street, it seems to be the most dangerous place in New Orleans. It's a very dark and foreboding pit of doom. I hope you are not going to suggest, in your printed words, Mr. Geraci killed Vitrano," Adams said. "In New Orleans, it seems the blood of truth is often spilled on the city's cobblestones disguised as printer's ink. Stop writing indictments and stick to the news."

Chapter 45

Criminal District Court
Thursday, July 31, 1890
1:00 P.M.

Normally, unless there was an ongoing trial, Thursday afternoons in Judge Joshua Baker's court were days when the staff completed the many ministerial duties required by the sedulous record-keeping requirements of trial courts mandated by the state supreme court. But not today.

After the lunch hour, every newspaper court reporter, including Laurence Hearn and Antonio Terranova, every criminal lawyer, including William L. Evans and Arthur Dunn, and about thirty police officers, including Superintendent David C. Hennessy, sat in the gallery waiting for the judge to take the bench. A man, whom no one in the court recognized, sat alone in the jury box, clutching several pieces of paper in his hands. He wore an ill-fitting gray suit and a crooked blue bow tie. It was obvious to all, the man did not dress formally every day. Spectators riveted their curious eyes on the man in the jury box, who twitched in his chair, discomfited by the attention.

After Judge Baker took the bench, he gazed upon the lone figure in the jury box and solved the mystery. "Mr. Henry Miller, Foreman of the Grand Jury, do you have a report to make to this court?" Judge Baker asked.

Every reporter's pencil snapped to attention, like fresh army privates. "I do, Your Honor," Miller responded.

"Please, in a clear, loud voice, publish your report to the court," Judge Baker ordered.

"As you required, the Grand Jury has thoroughly investigated the charge of Dereliction of Duty by members of the New Orleans Police Department, regarding testimony given by nine officers of that department, and has determined that the charge is unfounded."

"Have you affixed your signature to that report?" Judge Baker asked.

"I have."

"Please give it to the clerk, and with that, this court is adjourned."

Every police officer, including Hennessy, expressed a sigh of relief as the reporters gathered around every officer, peppering them with questions. None of the officers responded, including Hennessy. William L. Evans smiled and glanced at his partner, Arthur Dunn. "If you think this will make the newspapers, wait until tomorrow. We'll rock this city." Dunn said.

Laurence Hearn looked at his notes and then looked at Antonio's. "Let me see your notes. I want to make sure we got Mr. Miller's exact words. Hearne examined Antonio's writing on his notepad and said, "Antonio, great job. I forgot the word 'nine,' but you caught it. Your English is getting perfect. Thank you. Now take the rest of the day off. I'll make the report to the editor."

"What does this mean, Mr. Hearn?"

"Well, it means the officers didn't lie when they testified at the Provenzano trial. But the jury didn't believe them."

"Will the Provenzanos get a new trial?" Antonio asked.

"Not on this alone. It will take much more. But the judge knows the police didn't commit perjury. So does the city. We have to wait to see what their new attorneys do next. Now take a walk along the river. It's cooler there. I'll see you tomorrow in court. Bring your paper and pencil."

><

Antonio left St. Patrick's Hall and walked down Camp Street and turned towards the river on Poydras Street. He was feeling good about himself because of Hearne's compliments. His steps were light, and the air, though heavy and warm, felt good with every breath. As he walked carefree on the uptown, shady side of the street, he met Antonio Marchesi and his son, Asperi, whom he befriended on the docks of Palermo. He traveled to America on the *SS Neustria.* Having not seen each other in the past few months, they greeted each other happily in Italian, and though the meeting was very pleasant, Antonio felt father and son were burdened. After a few moments, the elder Marchesi bent over and whispered in Italian, "Antonio, go to Number 23 Poydras Street—the Italian Labor Union Hall. The Italian consulate has posted a list of Italian fugitives wanted in Italy, for all to see. Check if your name is on the list."

"Why would he do that?" Antonio asked.

The elder Marchesi said nothing and just walked away with his son.

Antonio crossed the street and walked towards the hall. A group of people, Americans and Italians, gather in front, reading a long list of names. Antonio pushed his way through the crowd and began to allow his eyes to follow the list of names. They were not in alphabetical order, so he had to read each name and what they were wanted for in Italy. With each name, he was pleased to see that Antonio Terranova was not wanted in Italy. But a cold shiver jolted through his body when his eyes fell upon the name of *Antonio Carravella of Bisacquino, Sicily—the charge: Omicidio* —Homicide.

Antonio slowly backed out of the crowd and ran down Poydras Street towards Baronne Street. With every stride, his stomach shivered in fear. Beads of sweat streamed down his face, and his clean white shirt became sodden with a mixture of sweat, street dirt, and dust. He ran faster, capturing the attention of men and women seeking shade from the blazing sun. Antonio felt only fear as he raced down Baronne Street towards the Jesuit church and school.

When he reached the Jesuit school, the doors were chained and locked for the summer. He ran down Common Street, seeking anyone, but especially Father Jacques Fontebuis. Antonio, panic-driven by the image of his real name plastered on a wall, pounded on every door and window of the Jesuit school. No one answered. He ran around the corner to Baronne Street and, with both fists, pounded on the Rectory door. No one answered. He leaned against the red-brick wall and caught the attention of a police officer, walking his beat. His pulse pounded in his ears. His eyes widened with fear. "Are you okay, boy?" the officer asked.

"Yes, sir. I'm looking for a priest."

"Go next door to the church. It's open. There's usually one in the church hearing confessions this afternoon," the officer said.

"Thank you," Antonio said, and ran into the Jesuit church.

Because of its marble floors, thick brick and plaster walls, and high ceiling, the temperature in the church was about ten degrees cooler than outside. Antonio's eyes scanned the side of the church and found a Confessional with Father Fontebuis's name on it. He stealthily snooped around the Confessional to see if anyone was inside, but when an elderly woman peeled the blue velvet curtain back from the penitent's box and left, Antonio jumped behind the curtain and waited for the priest to acknowledge his presence. Father Fontebuis opened a small door and prepared to hear the next penitent's confession, but to his surprise, he was met with the frantic whispers of an old friend.

"Father, I need help. Please help," Antonio implored through the confessional's screen.

"Antonio, is that you?" Father Fontebuis asked.

"Yes, Father. I'm in trouble."

"What kind of trouble, Antonio? What did you do?"

"I went to the Italian Labor Union Hall and saw--,"

"The list?" Father Fontebuis interrupted.

"Yes. How did you know?" Antonio asked.

"Calm down. Listen to me. I have heard about that list from many people. I went there yesterday and looked at it myself. I saw the name of a boy who doesn't exist anymore. Remember that."

"But the police will be looking for me," Antonio responded.

"Meet me in the Sacristy. I want to show you something," Father Fontebuis said.

Antonio left the penitent's box and went behind the main altar, into the church's Sacristy, and waited. After about twenty minutes, Father Fontebuis entered the Sacristy and hugged Antonio. "It's been a long time since I've seen you. You have grown a few inches. You look great, and have nothing to worry about. Sit down. I want to show you something."

Father Fontebuis and Antonio sat beside each other while the priest unfolded a copy of *The Times-Democrat* newspaper from several days ago. "First of all, remember, Antonio Carravella doesn't exist anymore. Do you still have to birth and baptismal certificates we made in Palermo?"

"Yes, Father."

"Did you register your name at the Custom House as an Italian Immigrant?"

Yes. Brother Stanislaus took me there when I started school at St. Aloysius."

"Good. As far as anyone in America knows, your name is Antonio Terranova. The Italian police want a boy who doesn't exist anymore."

"Isn't that a lie, Father?"

"No. It's merely a deception to avoid an unjust perception. You were justified in what you did, and you probably saved your own life. Jesus submitted himself to an unjust judgment to fulfill the ancient scriptures, not you."

"Will the police look for me?" Antonio asked.

"The police will be looking for someone who doesn't exist. Besides, that list has been posted in every city in America. Look at this," Father Fontebuis said, as he showed Antonio a newspaper article on page six of the newspaper. "Read those two paragraphs."

Antonio took the broadsheet into his hands and read an article. After a few moments, Antonio asked, "Father, this happened in a place called Boston. Why show it to me?"

"Because an Italian Boston police officer named John Rosatti arrested two Italian fugitives in that city. Their names were Geachini Coochiari and Giuseppe Donati. Their names are on the list posted on Poydras Street. The Italian government has sent America the names of every fugitive they believe is in the United States, not just New Orleans. So, now will you relax?"

Antonio suspired a relieving breath. "Does this mean I can never go home?"

"Not for a long time, if ever, Antonio. Your home is New Orleans. From now on, I want you to visit me often. Come to Mass here. I know you are working for one of the newspapers. That's good."

"But New Orleans is such an unfriendly place. The people treat Italians like we are dirt. I have only a few friends. I don't know if I like America?" Antonio admitted.

"Do you have a girlfriend?"

Antonio blushed. "I like this girl, but her father forbids us from seeing each other."

"I understand. Antonio, each of us is required to make our way in this world. Many places are unfriendly because man has lost his ability to think. There was a French writer and philosopher, Francois Voltaire, who studied with the Jesuits in France, and lamentably, became a harsh critic of the Catholic church—probably for his own good reasons. He wrote: *'Prejudices are what fools use for reason.'* New Orleans has many fools, and they seem to be breeding more of them every day."

Chapter 46

Criminal District Court
Friday, August 1, 1890
10:15 A.M.

Attorney William L. Evans promised a surprise ten days ago, and he was about to keep that promise. Several newspaper reporters waited for Mr. Evans to approach the bar and make a formal appearance for the Provenzano defendants. As Evans entered the court, all eyes, including Judge Baker's, turned to him. Laurence Hearn and Antonio Terranova grabbed their pencils, hoping not to miss a word spoken by Judge Baker or Evans. Arthur Dunn followed close behind.

"May I be heard, Your Honor?" Evans requested.

"You may."

Evans opened his leather valise and removed a thick, hand-written legal document. "May it please the court," Evans began, "I represent all of the defendants in the matter of *The State of Louisiana versus Joseph Provenzano et al.* I hereby request leave of this Honorable Court to file a motion for a new trial based on five individual grounds, singularly and collectively demonstrating my clients did not receive a fair trial, as a matter prescribed by the constitution and by state statute. May it be filed?" Evans requested.

"The clerk is ordered to file the motion into the record. May I see the motion, please?" Judge Baker requested.

As Judge Baker read the motion, Evans said, "I have several copies of the motion printed by a Linotype company, and we are willing to file them as supplements to the record."

"Please do, Mr. Evans," Judge Baker said.

"While Evans gave the clerk the copies, his partner, Arthur Dunn, passed out copies to several newspaper reporters. The scribes devoured them like hungry beasts, looking for imperfections in the trial. The motion listed five errors in complete detail, from how the jury was improperly and illegally selected, to the litany of insufficient evidence to support the jury's verdict. Besides attacking the court personnel for the clumsy and illegal method of jury selection, the trial jury ignored overwhelming proof of alibi evidence, supported by the Grand Jury's finding that nine police officers told the truth at trial.

Judge Baker slowly read the five reasons proffered for a new trial. He stroked his long black beard, and his complexion paled as he read. His court was under attack. He was under attack. His ability to manage an important trial was under attack. Being accustomed to inane and perfunctory motions filed by defense attorneys, Judge Baker knew he had just been tossed a hive of stinging hornets. He looked at District Attorney John Finney, waiting for a response. Finney cradled his head in his hands and read the motion, avoiding eye contact with anyone.

"Mr. Evans, I have read your motion and will schedule a hearing for Friday, August 8, 1890, at ten in the forenoon. I assume you have evidence and witnesses to support each allegation contained in this motion?" Judge Baker asked.

"We do," Evans responded.

"Mr. Finney, is the state prepared to defend the convictions?" Judge Baker asked.

"We will be ready," Finney responded.

"Very well. Court is in recess," Judge Baker said, as he dashed to his chambers.

Chapter 47

Criminal District Court
Saturday, August 9, 1890
10:00 A.M.

The American court system was designed to replace trial by blood, and assertions, *ipse dixit,* forced on court dockets by bias, innuendo, opinion, or prejudice. The legal jeremiads must be splayed on the white-hot anvil of cross-examination to forge the truth, untouched by the sullied hands of corrupt judges or the roiling emotions of the news media. It's the jury's verdict, annealed in the well of a courtroom, which demands justice. Nothing else. No one else.

The law governs how jury trials are to be conducted fairly and honestly. Judges must respect the separation of the determination of the truth by the collective wisdom of twelve unbiased people. But when there is a patent defect in the trial process, or presentation of the evidence to the jury, and a defective guilty verdict is returned, the trial judge must order a new trial to correct the errors of the lawyers or the bench. It's a radical remedy reserved to preserve the fundamental rights of all citizens. A trial judge can destroy all semblance of justice by simply abusing his discretion and vigilance during a trial, which would demand that an appellate court cure the defect. Trial courts hate to be reversed by appellate courts, no matter how softly the reversal is delivered.

Beginning on the morning of August 8, 1890, the blood of advocates flowed freely from the attorneys defending the jury's guilty verdict in the Provenzano case, and those defending the Provenzano defendants' liberty. Legal arguments, however, replaced the clashing of sharpened steel, but not the emotions wielding the weapons of legal trench warfare. Judge Joshua Baker's bench offered no redoubt for him, for his own judicial abilities were on trial. To arrive at a just result, Judge Baker struggled with his emotions and pride. To sustain the guilty verdict, Judge Baker had to ignore the proposition that defective evidence infected the jury's deliberations. The shadow of appellate reversal stretched across Judge Baker's bench. But to decide the Provenzano defendants were denied a fair trial, he must admit, but conceal, his failures as a judge to ensure a constitutional verdict. The latter option allowed him complete control of the outcome, without appellate intervention, while preserving the pretense of an honest jurist.

For over a day and a half, attorneys for the state and defense sparred with concepts and words few in the courtroom understood, especially the defendants. Both sides proffered legal precedents to support their positions. The jammed, sweltering courtroom pulsed with the tension of a bare-knuckled prizefight. The motion caught the attention of many members of the city's commercial elites, while the work on the city's docks slowed to a crawl. Since the ambush, cotton prices remained flat, as reported by several of the city's daily newspapers, which didn't go unnoticed in Galveston or Mobile.

As the blood of warring stevedoring companies began to flow upriver from the French Quarter, the threat of waning fortunes hardened the gentile hearts of the self-affected dilatants of New Orleans. Though the moil and toil of sweaty stevedores never entered their consciousness, members of the commercial elites were now painfully aware how the stench of a dock war could now cross their marble thresholds, and flop down on their embroidered divans and settees, in their silken uptown parlors. Something had to change, and change hung in the humid air of New Orleans.

For over a day and a half, prosecuting attorneys and defense attorneys argued their cases. Judge Baker entertained legal and factual arguments that were not presented to the jury. Most notably, he allowed affidavits of two newspaper reporters, W.B. Stansbury of the *Times-Democrat* and Henry Robinson of the *Daily Picayune,* to be introduced into the record. Both attested that they had asked the victims the night of the ambush who shot them, or shot at them. All the victims failed to identify their assailants. He allowed the attorneys to argue their reasons there, without restrictions. But just as District Attorney John Finney finished his final argument, Judge Baker wasted no time in rendering his decision, to the surprise of everyone in the courtroom.

"It is not a pleasant task for me," Judge Baker began, "to set aside the verdict of a jury, and I would not do so if I could help it, for it is a practice that is not good to indulge in often. Neither do I like to take upon myself the responsibility. But when I feel it to be my duty, I have no desire to shirk the responsibility or deprive myself of my right.

"I consider the jury in this case to be a thoroughly competent one, and do not desire to reflect upon their understanding, but the question that has been given to me is to decide whether or not the testimony warranted the verdict rendered. It would not justify my interference if it were or if I thought it was the circumstances. I would gladly waive the right and avoid the responsibility of doing so. On the other hand, if the testimony given in the trial, and the evidence the defense has since collected, do not, in my mind, justify the verdict, then I feel it is both my duty and privilege to interfere."

The courtroom began to moan and whisper. Some spectators sat numb in disbelief. They knew what was coming and what it meant. Some spectators, notably J.D. Houston and his retinue, fumed with anger. Dominick O'Malley sat like a stone. As Judge Baker read from his written notes, the newspaper reporters and their messengers strained to copy each word, without omission. Some of the defendants exchanged curious glances, while some just listened, without emotion. The attorneys sat quietly, without passion.

"If the testimony of the policemen is good, the alibi was proven by Giulio and Peter Provenzano, and if they were convicted, despite this excellent testimony, it would seem that one could hardly rely on the testimony of the men who convicted them, and it would further seem the conviction of the other accused can hardly be sustained.

"It was said that these men have resorted to 'The Felon's Defense,' which is undoubtedly true. But it is equally true that an alibi is frequently necessary for an innocent man to establish his innocence, and the fact of having resorted to it is nothing against them," Judge Baker said.

Judge Baker went through his analysis of the evidence and testimony given at trial. He also determined that the jury was improperly selected, in plain violation of state law. He set the time of the shooting to be between midnight and quarter past the hour, given the record of the call for the ambulance set at twenty-five minutes past midnight. These facts and the alibi testimony of the nine police officers weighed heavily on his mind and decision, given their professional disinterest in the case.

But just before rendering his decision, Judge Baker announced his most significant reason for reversing the jury's verdict. "Another circumstance which convinces me that the new evidence claimed by the defense is valid, is the fact that neither Mr. Robinson nor Mr. Stansbury is interested at all in this case. Allowances might be made for the statements made to them by men who were either wounded in the affray or suffering from a most natural nervous excitement, but at the same time, it is most probable that these statements were true, owing to the mental confusion that the suddenness of the attack must have produced.

"After talking the matter over with the reporters and others, the Matranga party prevailed upon prosecuting the convicted men, whom they chose from the thirteen that they had at first merely suspected. However, the most convincing reason why the evidence did not sustain the verdict was the testimony of the policemen, who, according to them, neither Giulio nor Peter Provenzano could have participated in the attack. It is not pleasant to me to waste the necessary time, nor to listen to a repetition of the former trial, with a few additions, but under the circumstances, I think that the verdict should not be sustained, and I am, therefore, compelled to order a new trial. Remand the defendants."

Judge Baker left the bench for the sanctuary of his chambers. Sheriff's deputies escorted the defendants downstairs to the waiting Black Maria for their return trip to the parish prison and to wait for their new trial. Spectators and reporters buzzed around the courthouse, amazed at Judge Baker's decision. Some of the defendants wept with joy and expressed smiles of relief. The nine policemen who rendered alibi testimony puffed with vindication. Reporters pounced on the attorneys, seeking an interpretation of the court's decision. The entire courthouse quaked with roiling passions, as if a funeral and a wedding were being conducted in the same church, at the same time.

"Mr. Hearn, if the Provenzanos didn't shoot the Matrangas, who did?" a confused Antonio Terranova asked.

"I do not know, but this dock war is far from over," Hearn responded. "And I fear the worst is yet to come. The lust for blood is seldom peacefully sated in the arrogant or the offended.

Part IV
The Feint

Chapter 48

The Custom House
August 29, 1890
1:00 P.M.

The wealthy of New Orleans escaped August's suffocating heat and humidity for an expanse in the Mississippi River between Wisconsin and Minnesota called Lake Pipen. The slowdown in the cotton and sugar commerce allowed members of those exchanges to leave the city for more welcoming climes and forget their perceived threats to their power, status, and treasure, by the *Vendetta Wars,* as characterized by the various newspapers. On this day, General Algernon Badger planned on taking a train there and spending a week, after he finished some important business at the Custom House.

The economic and social strata below the wealthy took hourly trains to the Mississippi Gulf Coast and established grand homes in the enclaves of Bay St. Louis, Biloxi, and Pass Christian. Their homes faced the Gulf of Mexico, and they would languish under the moss-draped live oaks, or on their wide verandas, swinging in hammocks made of old fishing nets and sail canvas, while sipping bourbon, chilled by ice sold by mule-drawn street vendors. Even Judge Joshua Baker enjoyed the Mississippi coast, and announced in open court he would be vacationing there for the next three months.

Others with means had to settle for West End or Milneburg, on the south shore of Lake Pontchartrain. Though not as exotic as other venues, they did offer casinos, dives, juke joints, and seafood restaurants, for daily or weekend escapes from the urban core of the burgeoning city. Chief David Hennessy had his officers patrolling on horseback since the Lonergran Tavern shootout in Milneburg on Sunday, July 27, 1890.

The sweat-stained plebeians, mostly composed of the immigrant class and Blacks, remained in the sweltering immurements of the city's alleys, markets, patios, streets, and wharves working, only to find an evening respite on their shadow-draped galleries and stoops, as the sun slowly bowed behind their slated roofs. Work meant survival.

Pasquale Corte didn't rest either, regardless of the temperature. His position as the Italian Consulate, stationed in New Orleans, placed him in a vise between his countrymen and an American society, which proved to be welcoming only on a situational basis. Most of his time, he took complaints from his fellow citizens in his second-floor office at Number 23 Poydras Street. But today, he was summoned to the office of Algernon Badger, on the first floor of the United States Custom House. He welcomed the invitation, and despite the swaddling humidity, he dressed in his finest three-piece dark-blue suit, for he was also meeting with Chief Hennessy to discuss the treatment of Italians at the hands of the newspapers, the police, the sheriff, the courts, and the city's elites. Corte was shrewd. He was in the mood to bargain and had something Hennessy wanted.

General Badger, Chief Hennessy, and George Vandervoort warmly welcomed Corte. Two silver pictures of cool water sat on Badger's desk, as the men frequently resorted to their contents during their visit. Badger lifted every window in his office to capture the paltry breeze flowing from the river down Canal Street.

"Mr. Corte," Badger began, "I hope this meeting is fruitful, and we can hopefully solve this problem."

"What problem?" Corte asked.

"The Italian problem. The dock wars. The *vendettas*, which plague this city," Badger responded.

Corte sprang straight in his chair, and responded through his thick Italian accent, but in fluent English, "Gentlemen, I welcome this opportunity to speak with honored men of this city. The mayor refuses to see me, and when we do talk, he shooes me away like a fly. I understand. But I must take issue with your characterization of the problems of New Orleans. May I speak honestly?"

"Please do," Badger said.

"Like you, I read the newspaper every morning. I study the city's commerce page and the court page. I read every headline. And I keep a journal of every crime committed in New Orleans, which every paper reports. Without fear of contradiction, I can attest that my countrymen have not committed most of the crimes in this city. Most mornings, I read Irish names, German names, French names, English names, and the Colored people's names. Most of the people charged with crimes are not Italian or Sicilian. But when an Italian or Sicilian commits a crime, the papers call it a *Vendetta War*, a *Mafia War*, a war between the *Stuppagghieri* and *Giardinieri*. They call their neighborhood in the French Quarter the *Italian Colony*. This is unfair to the good people who were brought here to work in the dirt of this city and to feed this city. All my people want is to be treated fairly."

"Mr. Corte, you must admit there is a crime problem in the Italian community," Hennessy said. "My men in the Third Precinct are always breaking up fights between Italians."

"Are the Italians the only people who fight in New Orleans? I ride through the streets of this city, and I see Italian men, women and children working, sweating, toiling to live a good life. But when one Italian commits a crime, all are suspected and pronounced guilty by the newspapers."

"We don't control the newspapers," Badger said.

"I know. But you are men of influence. You can report your activities without resorting to nationality or race. It's only fair," Corte said. "My people are here to work and become Americans. Reporting their nationality in negative terms delays full citizenship. Remember, Louisiana brought them here with many unfulfilled promises, and they are still here. The *Padrone* system is still here. Go look out your windows. The laboring people will probably be my countrymen. Your view from your office windows is the view of their world, yoked upon them like teams of oxen. They came here to escape what America now demands."

"Again, Mr. Corte, you must admit your countrymen do commit many violent crimes," Hennessy persisted.

"Chief Hennessy, I read where you and your men investigated two murders at Lonergran's Tavern on Lake Pontchartrain about a month ago. No newspaper reported that two Irishmen killed each other, and two more were arrested by you and your men. You are Irish, are you not?"

"I understand your point, Mr. Corte," Hennessy relented. "But you can help in the effort, if you so desire."

"How?"

"Not long ago, I cabled your police in Rome, seeking the names of Italian fugitives who came to New Orleans. I have not received a response. Can you send them a cable for me, seeking the names of those wanted in Italy, before they commit a crime in New Orleans?"

Corte smiled, and reached into his coat pocket and retrieve several sheets of paper. "Here, Chief Hennessy. This is a list of all fugitives currently wanted and believed to be in America. Rome sent me this list three weeks ago, and I have posted at Number 23 Poydras, for all to see."

"How many are in New Orleans?" Hennessy asked.

"How would Rome know how many are in New Orleans, New York, Philadelphia, Boston, or anywhere else in America? You want me to send another cable and ask for the fugitives in New Orleans only? How will Rome know if they are here? Please tell your newspapers that the good Italian people of this city only want to work and prosper, like other nationalities. We don't want to associate with criminals," Corte said.

"What about Matranga, Provenzano, Macheca, Geraci, and other Italians who have been killed in this city? Are they fugitives from Italy?" Vandervoort asked.

Corte laughed. "Which one is guilty of murder? Gentlemen, as you know, those men have been in this city a long time. Macheca was born here. Matranga came here as a child. The men you have mentioned don't like each other, because of how business is divided on the docks, not because they are wanted in Italy."

"Don't the Matrangas and Provenzanos belong to the *Mafia*?" Vandervoort asked.

"If they do, why haven't you arrested them by now for being in the *Mafia*? You know where they live and work. A judge gave the Provenzanos a new trial, because *your* police testified *for* them. Chief Hennessy, you go to Joseph Provenzano's club down the street. You and General Badger tried to broker a peace between the two stevedore companies, not because they were *Mafia*, but because they were fighting for business. You could have arrested them last December, but you didn't."

"Isn't Rocco Geraci an Italian fugitive?" Vandervoort persisted.

"He's not on the list," Corte responded.

"He was arrested, again, for killing Vincent Raffo, a friend of Joseph Provenzano," Vandervoort said.

"Yes, he was arrested, received bond, and is free today. And this morning, the June, July, and August Grand Jury's term has expired. They did not indict Rocco Geraci," Corte asserted. But, gentlemen, I will send another cable to Rome, asking about men they probably do not know."

><

3:30 P.M.

After concluding business with the Italian Consulate, Hennessy and Vandervoort remained behind in Badger's office. But it was evident that a weary Hennessy's attention was splintered in many directions. While Badger and Vandervoort discussed the immigrant issues, Hennessy's lost gaze flowed out the office windows and onto Canal Street. After realizing Hennessy's adrift countenance behind his unblinking blue-green eyes, Badger snapped the young chief's attention back to the matters at hand. "David, are you with us, or are you mired in the black mud of our surrounding swamps?"

"Sorry, General. My mind feels like it's being pulled in many directions."

"Explain, David," Badger said.

"Well, it seems that everyone is focused on the Italians in this city, when we have other problems, especially those affecting the police department and my men. It's not just the Matrangas and Provenzanos. Corte was correct. Most of the crimes in this city are committed by non-Italians. Look in my jail. Go look in the sheriff's prison. Go look in the courtrooms. Look at the dockets. And while everyone is focusing on the docks, we have another war going on, and it's inside City Hall."

"What do you mean?" Vandervoort asked, who considered himself a keen observer of municipal politics. Hennessy ignored his secretary's question.

"General, why did Shakspeare appoint me to be his superintendent. Many older men fought for the job. But he picked me. Why?"

"To be honest with you, David, he appointed you because he could control you and your ambitions. And you know about things that happened during the Cotton Centennial. Your badge has bought your silence. Also, he lost control of the police department before he was re-elected to his second term. Don't you remember?"

"What do you mean, General?" Vandervoort asked.

"The police department, since the Union army left New Orleans, has been a cesspit of political patronage and corruption. Everyone knows that. You almost fell victim to that corruption when you and your late cousin arrested Esposito in Jackson Square. People loved Thomas Devereaux because he knew how to get along. Frankly, David, you don't know how to get along. You are an irritation to many people, like sand is an irritant to an oyster. But what is produced because of that irritation? A shiny pearl. Many men are jealous of you and your accomplishments. You are a shiny pearl glowing in a cesspit. Sorry for the rough language," Badger said.

"So, did the mayor really want to change the police department, like he claims?" Hennessy asked.

Badger laughed as he tried to light his cigar. "Hell, no. Change was forced upon this city by an old friend of mine. Let me tell you a secret, which stays here."

Vandervoort leaned forward with curious expectations, while Hennessy seemed sullen but attentive.

"After the Battle of Liberty Place in 1874, the police department was just a gaggle of rufous bandits who couldn't work at any other job. Remember, I had your job during that period, but a Republican governor appointed me. My friend, Felix Dreyfous, a Democrat state legislator with a reformer's blood, introduced Act 63 of the 1888 legislative session—at my suggestion. That act denied exclusive control of the police department by the mayor, and created the police commission, which the mayor must now share control of the department."

"That's the problem," Hennessy interrupted. "I am caught in the middle of a political battle between three members of the commission and the mayor. The mayor is taking the commission to court, and I'm being forced to choose sides. I am not a politician."

"I know. I have been following that battle in the newspapers. While people's attention is drawn to the *Vendetta* trial, Shakspeare is at war with the police commission, and it has been reported on the same pages of the same newspapers. It's a great distraction for him. The mayor wants to take control of the department by appointing his own members to the commission, thereby hiring those he wants and preventing the firing of unqualified officers. He needs that patronage to sustain his power. And *you* and the commission stand in his way."

"Me? Why me?"

"You, J.C. Denis, Charles Drolla, and James Demoruelle represent reform of the department. Physical exams, literacy exams, training on how to interact with the public, disciplinary proceedings, a code of conduct, and impartiality—these are all your creations and the new commission. The commission took over the department after the state Supreme Court ruled Act 63 to be constitutional. If you remember, that was on February 19th of last year. When were you appointed chief?"

"March 13, 1889."

"And didn't the police commission have to agree with your appointment?"

"Yes. It was a unanimous vote," Hennessy said.

"You know why it was unanimous? Because every other candidate of the mayor's was either a member of the Ring or the Regulators, and the commission would have no control over them. While you were the safest choice, you were the most unpopular choice. There. Now you know the truth. That's why you feel alone in your job," Badger said, giving Vandervoort a flinty glare.

"Now the mayor is starting a new war. Who is Charles Clarke, by the way?" Hennessy asked.

"Clarke is a weasel. As you know, he's on the city council and is a member of the Pickwick Club with Shakspeare. I read in the papers while the Provenzano trial was going on, and you were in Chicago, Clarke filed charges against Drolla, Denis, and Demoruelle, and sought their dismissals from the commission. And as you know, Judge Ellis, of the Civil District Court, upheld their dismissals. Denis, Drolla, and Demoruelle are appealing to the Supreme Court, but until that court rules, the police department is now under Shakspeare's total control and his hand-picked commissioners. As of right now, David, you are alone and under the mayor's control."

Hennessy slowly nodded his head in agreement. "When I notified him this morning that the Boylan Detective Agency and my detectives arrested James and William Nust, along with William Kelly, for those boxcar thefts on Julia Street, which have plagued this city for months, he couldn't care less. And many of his merchant friends suffered great losses because of the Nusts and Kelly. We recovered thousands of dollars in stolen sundries and will return them to their rightful owners. It's as if we caught an apple thief in the French Market. Perhaps Corte was correct. Not all criminals in New Orleans are Sicilian."

"You still don't understand, David. Shakspeare is a famished politician who is never satisfied. Every hour of every day, he seeks power and status in this swamp-bound city. He plays chess alone at the Pickwick Club, under a portrait of Paul Morphy. He believes it sharpens his political skills, and apparently, it does. He once vaunted that his favorite strategic move was called *The Sicilian Defense,* conceived in the sixteenth century for the black pawn. Isn't that ironic? You are the white pawn, David. Be careful," Badger warned.

Chapter 49

New Orleans, Louisiana
September 1890

September in New Orleans dragged into town like a sweaty beggar with a tin cup seeking cool water to slake his long summer thirst. His clothes were ripped and stained by the struggles of the year, but he knew he had more labors to yoke before the cool breezes of autumn rolled across Lake Pontchartrain.

The city streets hummed with muted commerce as the large drayage wagons remained parked until the fall cotton crop flowed down the Mississippi River. Citrus shipments from South America and Sicily docked near the Picayune Tier, while half crews of stevedores rolled barrels of lemons down bouncy gangways, while stronger men shouldered large bunches of bananas on each shoulder, destined for the city's markets. More Italian immigrants, wide-eyed with anticipation, disembarked the steamships, while furtive shipping clerks whispered to the bedraggled newcomers where to sit, stand, and wait.

Three of the city's large steam-driven cotton presses rested their mighty iron jaws, not because of the lack of cotton bales, but because of a labor dispute between the pressmen and the Cotton Exchange. The dispute lasted for nearly five weeks, with the factors agreeing to pay a few more cents per bale to press for shipment to Liverpool, with the mutual condition that no bale exceeded six hundred pounds. This controversy, together with the stevedore wars, gave the wealthy members of the Cotton Exchange more reasons to take over the docks.

Though commerce and life moved more slowly than in other months, life carried on. To the surprise of some, the joy of others, and the dismay of many on the first day of the month, the Orleans Parish Grand Jury, for the September, October, and November term, heard the case against Rocco Geraci, and decided not to indict him for the murder of Vincent Raffo. Liberated from the old charges, Geraci returned to the docks to supervise the Matranga stevedores. The Provenzano stevedores remained in the Orleans Parish Prison, where Sheriff Villere allowed liberal visitation rights of the defendants' family, as long as they cooked enough food for his guards and trusties.

With the adamant urging of Algernon Badger, supported by police surgeon Doctor Henry Bayon, David C. Hennessy took a nearly three-week vacation with his mother to Hot Springs, Arkansas, and Chicago. Captain John Journee was appointed acting police chief. When he returned, Orleans Parish had a new District Attorney—Charles Luzenberg. During Hennessy's well-deserved absence, and for the remainder of September, two things didn't happen. Hennessy did not receive any cables from Rome regarding Italian fugitives hiding in New Orleans, and no one from the Provenzano defense team or family contacted him seeking his testimony for the subsequent trial, docketed for October 17, 1890.

Antonio continued to read English literature and strove to improve his writing. He followed Father Fontebuis's instructions, visited the Jesuit church often, and studied Latin. He became an altar boy, serving Masses at St. Mary's Italian Church on Chartres Street and with Father Fontebuis at his church on Baronne Street. Abraham took art classes from a Creole lady in Faubourg Treme, and both young men continued to work with Laurence Hearn when called upon. Antonio kept his job with Jahnke, delivering granite stones to various locations in the city on Saturdays. Now the deliveries included heavy six-by-six timbers to be used as railroad ties to support the heavier electric street cars. Antonio thought the heavy labor was worth it, as he needed the money, and it gave him an opportunity to see Isla and her smile every Saturday morning.

Chapter 50

New Orleans
October 10, 1890
Canal Street
11:00 A.M.

For the first two weeks of October, Autumn teased New Orleans with gentle northwest breezes and lower humidity. White lace curtains danced to and fro from open windows, like bold maidens beckoning blushing suitors. Men walked along Canal Street, doffed their bowlers to one another, and women finally found pleasure walking the banquettes in their long dresses and high collars. Everyone's mood seemed buoyed by the changing seasons. But in New Orleans, no matter the weather, finding someone with a tetchy temperament wasn't hard, excited by a chance encounter with a nemesis.

J.P. Macheca's deepest unrequited raison d'être was recognition and status in a city that systematically shunned his pedigree. Even after capturing the Republican arsenal and police station behind the city's Spanish Cabildo in September of 1874, the city's Anglo-Saxon leaders refused to give him credit for the daring raid, and gave full credit to Captain Michael Douglas Kirkpatrick of the city's White League. Macheca and his Italian-composed company were loyal to the Democrats, but lost favor with the city's elites when Macheca's men saved General Algernon Badger from Kirkpatrick's sword. Despite the carnage on Canal Street, one newspaper, *The New Orleans Bulletin*, reported Macheca's strategic capture of men and weapons, but assigned full credit to Kirkpatrick. Incensed, Macheca used his own money and placed a four-paragraph story in that newspaper, assigning credit to himself and his men, verifiable by a reluctant Badger. Such a display of vanity didn't sit well with the Democrats, who never forgave or forgot.

On this pleasant sunny morning, J.P. Macheca sauntered down the uptown side of Canal Street, greeting friends and window shopping at the various stores. In the reflection of one plate-glass window, he saw the image of David C. Hennessy, who was sitting in his parked police carriage, talking to a newspaper reporter. Macheca turned around and approached the conversation. Hennessy acknowledged Macheca's presence with a polite greeting, but Macheca wanted Hennessy to answer one question.

"Chief, are you going to testify at the next Provenzano trial?" Macheca asked.

Hennessy, disturbed by the question, a question asked many times in the past few weeks, answered, "J.P., as you know, I have nothing to offer to help or hurt the Provenzanos or Matrangas. I wasn't there the night of the ambush, and neither were you. Let the courts do their job."

"Stay out of it, Chief, if you know what's good for you," Macheca warned.

"J.P., I don't like your tone, and I will not tolerate being threatened by anyone. I will say this one last time. If I had evidence that the Matrangas, Provenzanos, or you were guilty of anything, you all would be in the parish prison now. Now, good day, sir."

Chapter 51

New Orleans
October 15, 1890
8:00 A.M.

David Hennessy kissed his mother's aging cheek and bid her farewell as he left his gray clapboard residence at Number 275 Girod Street and began his four-block walk to his office. Usually, he would take his carriage, but his assigned horse had a split hoof and had to be reshod. As he descended the front steps of his house, his mother said, "David, look at the sky, and the wind is whipping up. Better take a topcoat and an umbrella. The change of seasons is upon us." Hennessy smiled and dutifully took his mother's advice.

"Don't wait up for me, mother. I have hearings at city hall tonight," Hennessy said, as he waved goodbye to his doting Irish mother. With his black bowler hat, coat, and umbrella, he cut an image of a gentleman strolling down Saville Road in London, instead of Basin Street in New Orleans.

As he walked the four blocks to the Central Police Station, his attention was drawn to the Jewish merchants along Basin Street, hanging oil-cloth coats and slouch hats outside their stores, to accommodate the poorer members of the public. The northwest sky looked like a boxer's contused fist, and the wind blew the street debris and dust in all directions. One could smell the pungent odor of an ozone-laden thunderstorm approaching New Orleans. Even the horses and mules bounced and shook their heads, for all animals knew when a storm was approaching. Since it had not rained in a week, the deep and wide gutters carved along Basin Street were dry, allaying any anxiety that a menacing storm would flood the streets again.

As Hennessy approached the Central Police Station, he was met by Captain Billy O'Connor of the Boylan Detective Agency. O'Connor commanded a private patrol crew to watch the fringes of the city's business boundaries and the dock operations near the New Basin Canal.

His company sometimes augmented the NOPD when the police personnel were depleted through resignations or terminations. Hennessy took an aggressive position when disciplining errant officers while building a modern police department. Most members of the Police Commission supported him, but some were troubled by the firings of some men. This caused him political problems beyond his comprehension.

"What brings you out on this stormy day, Billy?" Hennessy asked.

"You."

"Me? Is anything wrong?"

"You have some police hearings tonight at City Hall, don't you?"

Hennessy swung his umbrella over his shoulder like a rifle. "Yes, I do. I have four officers up for disciplinary action. It's not a pleasant chore, but one I must do, if I am to build this department into a professional police agency," Hennessy said.

"I understand. But be careful. Every officer on the department, especially the ones who were there when you became chief, got their jobs through political appointments. Each council member has a friend in the department. Do you understand what I am saying?" O'Connor probed.

"Yes. I know. I get letters from ward leaders, councilmen, and other political types asking me to go easy on some errant officers. But I must follow my own rules and the law. If I show unequal treatment, there is no fairness in the outcome. And that kills the morale of the good officers," Hennessy said.

"I understand your position. But you must be careful who you terminate from the department. It's hard to find jobs after they are fired from the NOPD."

"Why don't you hire them, Billy?"

"Colonel Boylan would not allow it."

"If they can't qualify to be night watchmen, why should I keep them on the force?"

"Wait a minute, David. That's not fair. Boylan officers are more than night watchmen. We really assist your officers in a time of need. In fact, I have J.C. Roe guarding your house every night. He walks the beat from Girod Street to the basin," O'Connor huffed. "In fact, he caught some thieves breaking into the lumber yard on the basin last week."

"Sorry, Billy, for belittling your officers. They do a great job. I'm sorry. Why don't you come upstairs, and we will go over the charges for tonight's hearing? *You* tell me what the consequences of their breach of duty should be," Hennessy said.

O'Connor accepted Hennessy's apology and invitation, and both men ascended the steps of the Central Police Station, as a bolt of lightning struck near Basin and Tulane, rattling the windows of the station, followed by torrents of blowing rain.

><

City Hall

7:00 P.M.

The city council chamber was packed with spectators, newspaper reporters, lawyers, police officers, and witnesses. The Shakspeare-composed police commission lorded over the room, like princes and dukes of some far-away kingdom. Everyone in New Orleans sought a title or position to keep their bodies and souls together. Joseph A. Hincks, a devoted acolyte of the mayor, served as the board's President *pro tempore*. Tonight's meeting was called to adjudicate the guilt or innocence of several police officers accused of an array of charges, ranging from working while intoxicated to demanding bribes. The city attorney served as the prosecutor, while the commission would serve as judge and jury. Chief David Hennessy sat at the right end of the dais and served as the official complainant of those charged. On this evening, Mayor Shakspeare, who by law was an *ex officio* member and President of the commission, sat on the dais behind the commission. His scowling countenance did not go unnoticed.

After hearing cases involving the intoxication of several officers resulting in the docking of their pay as punishment, the commission turned its attention to a more serious case involving Sergeant Patrick Lynch and Officer Henry Thibodeaux of the Eighth Precinct, in a section of Orleans Parish known as Algiers. As Commissioner Hincks called the case, Sergeant Lynch surprised everyone and said, "I am not guilty, but I have not the time to prepare a defense to the charges against me."

As the day-long thunderstorm lashed at the council chamber's large windows, Commissioner Hincks was prepared to continue the case until the next hearing date. But when Shakspeare rose and said the witnesses had traveled across the Mississippi River in the horrible weather, and were ready to testify, Hincks and the other commissioners decided to hear the witnesses' testimony.

Three Algiers tavern owners testified that Lynch and Thibodeaux entered their businesses on Sunday nights and demanded money for selling alcohol in violation of the Sunday Closing Law. John Michel, Phillip Bannerette, and Phillip Geraci, no relation to Rocco Geraci, all testified they were threatened by both officers and paid them money to remain open. Phillip Geraci crowned his testimony by pointing his finger at Thibodeaux and exclaiming loudly, "every time I see him, he calls me a 'dirty dago.' My place is the cleanest tavern in Algiers."

After a long pause, during which the fierce hammering of rain drummed against the chamber's windows, the commission deliberated. Returning to order, Commissioner Hincks stated, "Given the testimony is unrefuted, the Commission finds Sergeant Lynch and Officer Thibodeaux guilty, and they are hereby terminated from the New Orleans Police Department, forthwith."

As the angry terminated officers dragged themselves out of the council chambers, the mayor looked at Hennessy and accused him of not keeping order in the Eighth Precinct, allowing police officers to testify at mafia trials, not keeping the Italian Colony under control, and demanded that he do a better job. A cowering Hennessy assured the mayor he would. J.D. Houston, leaning against the chamber's wall, just smiled.

><

9:45 P.M.

As David Hennessy and Billy O'Connor descended the slick granite front steps of City Hall, a gust of cool air whistled down St. Charles Avenue and pinged them with stinging drops of the waning thunderstorm. Hennessy looked at the black sky, dappled with splotches of exhausted gray rain clouds rolling southward across the city.

"Looks like the storm is over, Billy," Hennessy said.

"I guess my street is flooded again. It's not cobblestoned, yet," O'Connor replied.

"I never asked you, Billy. But where do you live?"

"Number 55 Spain Street—downriver, of course," O'Connor replied.

Hennessy chuckled. "My street is the same. I expect knee-deep ruts by the time I get home. And the gutters will be overflowing. But I welcome the cool weather. I'm tired of summer."

"Are you going back to your office?"

"Yes. George Vandervoort has a carriage waiting for me. Do you need a ride to your car line?" Hennessy asked.

"I would appreciate you allowing me to accompany you to the station and home," O'Connor said.

Hennessy laughed and opened his coat to reveal his nickel-plated Colt revolver. "I can protect myself, Billy. But if you want to come along, no problem. You can tell the mayor you did your job."

O'Connor offered a blushing smile and jumped in the carriage with Hennessy. Vandervoort slapped the reins against the sodden horse, and the carriage faded from Lafayette Street. As they rode through the dimly lit streets towards the police station, the reflection of the new electric streetlights, augmented by the remaining gas-lit lamps, cast an eerie and gauzy glow on the glistening cobblestoned streets. Hennessy prophetically offered, "Billy, look down Lafayette Street. The glimmering lights and their reflections upon the stones remind me of candles glowing in a darkened church before a funeral. After a storm, everything seems shiny and clean." Hennessy said.

O'Connor didn't respond, but instead asked Hennessy a question. "David, are you going to testify in the new Provenzano trial?"

"Damn, Billy. You sound like a newspaper reporter. No. I have nothing to offer against or for the Provenzanos. I have received several threatening letters demanding that I stay away from the trial. I have nothing to offer. I haven't received any response from Rome about the Matrangas or the Provenzanos. If I had anything against them, we would have arrested them."

"Rumors are going around that Luzenberg will call you as a witness for the state," O'Connor said.

"New Orleans couldn't exist without its rumors, Hennessy said. "The Matrangas and Provenzanos have been in New Orleans for years. Are they *Mafia*? Maybe. But all I know is that both parties in that case have worked to build businesses here. If they are part of some secret society, they are doing a poor job of concealing it. I want the Italian fugitives hiding here. I hope I hear something from Rome soon."

Vandervoort stopped in front of the Central Police Station. Hennessy and O'Connor got down from the carriage, and both men went to Hennessy's office, where the young chief made a report of the police commission hearing and the actions taken. "Do you expect any problems from anyone over Lynch and Thibodeaux's terminations?" O'Connor asked.

"I always get the blame for bad officers. The mayor was angry tonight, for some reason. He blames me for everything that goes wrong with the police department. I want literate and honest officers. That's why I now have an entrance exam and physical qualifications, before I recommend anyone to be hired. That has angered many ward leaders and councilmen," Hennessy said. "If the mayor wants a different department, he needs a new chief."

Hennessy looked at his pocket watch. "Damn, Billy. I need to get home. I'm tired, and it's getting late."

"How about we get something to eat before you go home?" O'Connor asked.

"No. I'll just hurry home along Franklin Street and eat at home," Hennessy said. "The banquettes are brick and high on Franklin Street. It won't be flooded. It's a shame the city has ignored this end of Basin Street."

"Come on, David. Let's go to Virget's and get some oysters and a beer," O'Connor insisted. "They close at midnight."

Hennessy reluctantly agreed, and both men left the police station. They took a circuitous route to the Virgets, as Basin Street and the sidewalks were still flooded. Both men walked across Basin Street and then went down Rampart Street towards Poydras. At Poydras and Rampart Streets, Dominick Virgets Oyster Saloon beamed with lights and laughter. Many of the workers at the Poydras Market stopped there before going home or going to work at the all-night market.

Hennessy's presence subdued the chatter and din of the saloon. Hennessy ordered a plate of fried oyster and a glass of milk. O'Connor ordered oysters and a big glass of beer. For about forty-five minutes, the men discussed politics and the police department, the only things they had in common.

><

11:11 P.M.

Their hunger and thirst sated, Hennessy and O'Connor crossed Poydras Street and walked down Rampart Street, which intersects with Girod Street. "Billy, why don't you catch the streetcar to Spain Street. I will be fine going home," Hennessy said. "You're going in the opposite direction.

"Well, I will just see you to Girod Street," O'Connor replied.

Rampart Street was empty and dimly lit, like most streets in New Orleans at that hour. The rumbling of the iron-rimmed wooden wheels of an Italian merchant's pushcart echoed off the cobblestoned street, like a distant, muted thunder. Hennessy and O'Connor cast solitary shadows as they dodged puddles on Rampart Street. As they approached, a misty streetlight hung high above the intersection of Rampart and Girod. The men stopped under the light near the McDonough Schoolhouse, and O'Connor asked, "David, what are your future plans?"

"My future plans?"

"Yes, what do you want to do after you are chief?" O'Connor probed.

"I don't know. I know I serve at the pleasure of the mayor, and he is not happy with me because of that Eighth Precinct case tonight. Maybe politics, if I can be forgiven for doing my job," Hennessy said.

"Politics, David? It's a very dangerous game in this city," warned O'Connor.

"I know very well."

"Know this, David, the voting hordes never improve beyond the ambitions and aspirations of those who lord over them. It's a simple political equation when examined. No man's life and toil will ever improve to a standard of living equal to or exceeding that of the ruling class in New Orleans. If it happens, the political class will find a way to control it. No one sits higher than the glistening crowns of power. Political power will never tolerate any truths that expose their method and means to sustain power. The Provenzanos and Matrangas don't understand that. You should," O'Connor said, jabbing his finger into Hennessy's cut-away jacket.

"Billy, why are you telling me this now?"

"Be careful in your choices, David. Always remember the jealous blade cuts the deepest," O'Connor said, as he turned and walked down Girod Street towards the river, and away from his carline home.

Hennessy turned, walked down Girod Street towards Basin Street, and disappeared into the mist.

Chapter 52

New Orleans
St. Charles and Perdido Streets
October 15, 1890
Earlier That Evening

As David Hennessy and Billy O'Connor ascended the front steps of City Hall for the police hearings, victims and witnesses of the Matranga ambush case met in the law offices of Lionel Adams and A.D. Henriques at Number 22 Carondelet Street. Adams, who agreed to prosecute the Provenzanos stevedores again in the upcoming new trial ordered by Judge Joshua Baker last summer, met with J.P. Macheca, Charles Matranga, James Caruso, Rocco Geraci, Charles Patorno, Salvatore Sunzeri, and Salvatore Oteri to prepare their testimonies. Dominick O'Malley was also there. Each man recited their previous testimony, without deviation.

About fifteen minutes past the hour, Lionel Adams excused himself to attend a Congressional political function across the river in Algiers. His friend, Adolf Meyer, planned to hold a rally there, weather permitting. As Adams left his office, Matranga told him he and his friends were going to the theater, two squares away at St. Charles and Perdido Streets. Since the stubborn day-long thunderstorm remained, Adams warned his witnesses to cover themselves as they walked to the theater. All agreed to meet later at Fabacher's Restaurant at Royal and Customhouse Streets.

After another half hour of witness preparation, Henriques allowed the men to leave. It continued to rain. Macheca, Matranga, Oteri, and Patorno had umbrellas, while the rest of the witnesses had oilcloth coats, which dragged against the soggy stones along the way. They walked fast, as the minutes were ticked by, and they wanted to be seated in their coveted seats in the theater's parquet section. Geraci spotted Captain John Journee on the corner as they stepped between the puddles on St. Charles Street. Geraci asked Journee for the time. Journee didn't respond.

As the men entered the theater and walked to their seats, they were recognized by many people in New Orleans society. On the balcony, they caught the attention of Pasquale Corte, who gave them a warm smile and greeting. During intermission, they mingled politely with the starchy dilettantes of the city's gilded vicinages. They were tolerated, but never welcomed.

When the final curtain came down at forty-five minutes after ten, Matranga and his friends left the theater and splashed their way to Fabacher's Restaurant for a late dinner and wine. On their way, they encountered Captain Journee again, but kept walking towards the French Quarter. Salvatore Oteri decided to go home, as it was past his usual hour of retiring.

The Matranga party arrived at Fabacher's about fifteen minutes after eleven. The rain had finally slackened off, and a cool northwesterly breeze filled the streets of New Orleans. After ordering German champagne and light fare, Lionel Adams, Meyer, and some attorneys entered the restaurant and joined the Matranga party.

"Mr. Matranga, will I have your support and vote for congress," Meyer asked, knowing Matranga and Macheca controlled many votes in the Italian Colony, Creole Treme and the "Back-of-Town" Negro neighborhoods.

"If Mr. Adams is for you, why not?" Matranga said, followed by a toast to Meyer's candidacy.

It was about thirty minutes past eleven.

Chapter 53

New Orleans
Girod Street
October 15, 1890
11:30 P.M.

The rain had finally yielded to a soft, chilly mist. Girod Street glowed in the lambent flickering of gas streetlamps and nascent electrical lights at the intersections. With the mist, the streetscape would be the vision of a drowsy man suddenly awakened in a dimly lit room. But David Hennessy knew his way home, as he fixed his keen eyes on the faint glow of the electric light hanging at Girod and Basin Streets. He was alone, except for a young boy who ran past him, whistling to announce his presence in the gloom. Not hearing the clopping of hooves in the mist, Hennessy crossed Basin Street. Seeing the oil lamp his mother customarily left in the front window at night, Hennessy paused in front of 275 Girod Street to dig in his pants pocket and retrieve his house key.

As he felt for his long brass key, he heard the shuffling of feet behind him. Even in the shadows, he knew he wasn't alone. As he turned to his left, the night exploded with shotgun blasts and pistol fire from five different directions. Hennessy, a strong, tall Irishman, drew his silver Colt revolver and returned fire at the misty silhouettes, as they scattered—some towards Basin Street and some towards Franklin Street. Hennessy's lean body was on fire, but he chased two of his assailants towards Basin Street, firing at least two shots at them. But his exertion caused his wounds to pump blood, and he collapsed on the front steps of the Gillis Store at 189 Basin Street.

Boylan Patrolman J.C. Roe, walking the beat on Basin Street, hearing the fusillade, and seeing shadowing figures wrapped in oilcloth coats, fired a shot at the fleeing figures, which was returned by one of the assailants. The shot creased Roe's left ear. Hearing the shooting, Billy O'Connor raced down Girod Street towards Basin. There he found Hennessy slumped on the steps of the store. "What happened, David? Who shot you?" O'Connor asked.

Hennessy, bleeding profusely and with a pierced left lung, gasped something only O'Connor heard, but when repeated by O'Connor, it would ignite a series of cascading events, which flowed from the muddy streets of New Orleans, to Washington, D.C., and to Rome, Italy. Not even O'Connor could anticipate what would happen next, for an ominous black cloud of ethnic prejudice descended upon America, and remained for decades to come.

><

Midnight

The mist acted like a fisherman's seine, capturing and holding the smoke of the assailant's guns over Girod and Basin Streets, and thickening the air with a dreary amber-gray hue. The windows of the houses along muddy Girod Street blinked alive with lantern lights. Doors flew open, and curious people began to gather around the wounded police chief. The scent of burnt sulphur stung every nose. Someone called the Central Police station from Call Box number 82 at Girod and Dryades Street. Others, who had telephones, called the police and demanded an ambulance. The word of the Hennessy attack shot through the night like an assassin's bullet.

Police from all nearby beats rushed to Basin and Girod. A Charity Hospital Ambulance, pulled by two black horses, arrived to attend to Hennessy and Patrolman Roe. Both were taken to Charity Hospital, just seven squares away. The police switchboard jammed with calls. The city's telegraph system buzzed in the night air, as key operators received and sent messages about the shooting. A few minutes later, a patron ran into Fabacher's and announced that Hennessy had been shot and was at Charity Hospital. The Matranga party paused, but kept drinking. It seemed no one was surprised, given the enemies the young chief had attracted over his short years on earth. Even Officers Hevron and Torregano, from the neighboring Fourth Precinct, attired in plainclothes and ordered by Captain John Journee to follow Matranga and Macheca that evening, showed no emotion.

Hevron slipped out of Fabacher's and met two other officers at Bourbon and Customhouse Streets. He told them to spread the word to all beat officers in the French Quarter. It wasn't long before every window in the city was aglow with light. People began to gather on street corners to exchange rumors. Police patrol wagons raced back to the Central Police Station to await further orders. Whispers of the dagoes killing Hennessy filled every block, café, and tavern. The city boiled and roiled like a cauldron of anger, waiting for confirmation of what they already believed. It didn't take long.

><

Charity Hospital

12:50AM

The front portico of Charity Hospital was clogged with every newspaper reporter in the city. Lawrence Hearn, and fellow *Mascot* reporter, Frank Waters, sensing the heat of the streets, did not call St. Aloysius to awaken Antonio or Abraham. There was no need to put those boys' lives in jeopardy. Curious citizens on horseback and carriages blocked Tulane Avenue. Captain Journee, accompanied by Billy O'Connor, Mayor Shakspeare, Police Commissioner William Beanham, and J.D. Houston, shoved past the crowd. They went to the operating amphitheater, on the first floor of the three-floor, block-long hospital. Hennessy lay nearly naked on the operating table, revealing various gunshot wounds from his left chest down his left leg. A wheezing, gaping wound under his left nipple concerned everyone. He was conscious, but his breathing was labored. Nurses and nuns, the Sisters of Charity, gathered every light in the room to focus on his wounds.

Dr. Samuel Logan, the chief house surgeon, and Dr. Jefferson Davis Bloom, his assistant, began treating Hennessy with Morphine. The doctors had a robust but respectful discussion about how to treat Hennessy. Dr. Bloom, the younger by thirty years, knew how to operate and install a tube into the Hennessy's chest to reinflate his left lung. After that, he wanted to trace the trajectory of the bullets, operate to stanch any bleeding, and retrieve any balls or bullets. Logan overruled Bloom, as he believed both lungs had been pierced, and ordered the nurses and nuns to dress Hennessy's wounds and keep him calm. Logan didn't believe the pericardial sac had been pierced. As the doctors examined Hennessy, the gallery filled with curious, note-taking reporters.

Outside the amphitheater, Shakspeare asked O'Connor what he knew about the shooting. O'Connor said, in the presence of police officers and reporters, "David whispered to me the 'Dagoes did me up,' or words to that effect."

Enraged, Shakspeare bellowed to Journee and everyone in the corridor, "Scour the whole neighborhood! Arrest every Italian you come across, if necessary, scour it again tomorrow morning, as soon as there is daylight enough. Get all the men you need."

Immediately, Journee and his officers pass the mayor's order along to every officer available. Billy O'Connor offered some of his Boylan officers to assist in the arrests. The hospital corridor exploded in a blood-thirsty frenzy, as the nuns tried to keep the voices down. Laurence Hearn, no friend of Shakspeare, recorded the moment, as did other newspaper reporters. In the wee hours of a chilly New Orleans morning, the streets blazed in hate, like hot coals on an iron grate. On the unchallenged words of O'Connor, Shakspeare's unrestrained animus for Italian immigrants lit a fuse which burned from Charity Hospital to the French Quarter and beyond.

Reckless words unleashed the bile of anyone with a gun, and the quarry was any Italian unlucky to be walking the streets, sitting on his stoop, working on the docks, or tending his stall in the French and Poydras Street Markets. For the next few hours and days, Shakspeare's words, repeated by the obsequious newspapers, call for the bleaching of New Orleans streets of people who were regarded not as white, and not as black, but the "Other People." Italian businesses shuddered with fear. Canal Street lost its neutrality. Awakened members of the Cotton Exchange smiled.

><

1:20 A.M.

On Shakspeare's unconstitutional orders, the gates of hell sprang open, and the armed demons raced through the streets looking and searching for anyone who was Italian or Sicilian. Police officers, assisted by angry citizens, arrested over sixty Italian men and jammed them like cotton bales into small cells at the Central Police Station. Many had open head wounds, contused eyes and broken teeth, as a result of their fierce arrests by police officers, cloaked with unlimited authority.

In the racially mixed neighborhoods, Blacks cowered behind cracked doors and heard the screams of Italian women, as their men were dragged downstairs, through alleys, beaten, and tossed into Black Marias. Many older Blacks shivered in fear as they remembered the trauma when the Knights of the White Camelia, hooded in white flour sacks, marauded through their streets, hunting any Black man they could find.

As the streets filled with rampaging police officers and vigilantes, a more somber atmosphere pervaded the first floor of Charity Hospital. Hennessy's mother, Margaret, accompanied by Hennessy's friend, Tom Anderson, and Father Patrick O'Neil, entered the room where the nuns dressed the chief with clean bandages. Shakspeare and his retinue looked on as the Hennessy greeted his sobbing mother with a bit of disbelief. "What are you doing here, Mother? I will be home soon, on the by and by." Not taking any chances, Father O'Neil anointed the wounded chief. After the anointing, Hennessy requested a glass of milk, but the nurse refused his request, and instead, allowed him some chipped ice under his bushy mustache to quench his dry mouth.

Shakspeare ordered city recorder, David Hollander, to take a formal statement from Hennessy, but the chief could not identify the people who shot him, even after several promptings. At this very hour, the only clue the police could act on was the words of Billy O'Connor.

><

1:30 A.M.

Officers Hevron and Torregano maintained their surveillance of the Matranga party, which had moved from Fabacher's to a brothel at Number 11 Burgundy Street. There was no shortage of people at either location who heard the men celebrating Hennessy's shooting, including Hevron, Torregano, and Officer Patrick Cassidy. The officers were familiar with the house's madam, Fanny Decker, and lurked across the street, under a low-hanging canopy, like alley cats.

><

1:45 A.M.

The gravel and chirted bed of Girod Street led to the dwellings of the working poor, or the Protestant dead, entombed in a cemetery at the end of the forlorn lane. Hemmed by deep gutters and a variety of wooden structures conceived by someone's imagination with a pocket full of square nails, an iron hammer, and the will to cobble together a home, Girod Street possessed a sepulchral aura and gloom. Margaret Hennessy's lamp burned brightly behind her louvered window, but no one was home.

Neighbors, some in their night clothes, gathered along the wooden banquette. Police officers carrying kerosene lamps searched Hennessy's home for evidence. Some officers picked shotgun pellets out of the front clapboards of Hennessy's home. Others mucked the gutters, looking for anything.

Other officers arrived on Girod Street and took statements of what people heard or saw. Many stretched credulity, while others honestly admitted they only heard the gunfire and then looked. Some claimed all the shooters were small in height and wore slouch hats and oilcloth coats, suggesting the assailants were Italian. The conflicting witness statements spread across Girod Street like the buckshot. Two of the Boylan Detective Agency's patrol officers, J. C. Roe and James Cotton, told reporters and officers they were shot. Roe claimed to have been hit by one of Hennessy's assailants, and Cotton claimed to have been shot by Hennessy when he returned fire. Police and reporters became suspicious of the accuracy of their stories because that would have placed both officers in the line of fire between the chief and his attackers. Other than Roe's grazed ear, there was no proof proffered by either officer. Cotton had no wounds.

Frustrated officers and newspaper reporters continued to search for clues and talked to putative witnesses. As in any major case, some witnesses want to feel important, while others cowered under their sheets. The first credible witness to be interviewed was John Daure, a bartender who worked at Carondelet and Girod Streets. He resided at Number 316 Frenchmen Street, which was about three miles downriver from Girod. When he heard the shots, he ran down Girod Street and saw Hennessy exchanging gunfire with the attackers. At that point, Daure said he could identify the shooters because he had dealt with them at the Poydras Market. He told officers and reporters they were Italian.

Following Shakspeare's orders, uniformed and plainclothes officers descended on the neighborhood around and in the Poydras Market. Officers arrested Antonio Marchesi and his fourteen-year-old son, Asperi. Officers suspected the younger Marchesi was the boy who was whistling right before Hennessy was attacked. Moments later, Charles Pietzo, a grocer in the Poydras Market, was arrested because an officer saw him with some shotguns days earlier. The Marcheses and Pietzo were transported to the central jail and crammed into the cell with other Italian arrestees.

Sergeant Joseph McCabe, who was very familiar with the Italians in the public markets, went to Vincent Bagnetto's fruit stall in the Poydras Market, looking for the night watchman, Antonio Bagnetto. He wasn't there. Knowing that Antonio lived at Number 155 Dryades Street, McCabe walked down Rampart Street and turned onto Dryades. There, under a streetlight, he found Antonio Bagnetto. McCabe searched him and found a fully loaded gray-metal revolver, typical of the type many people carried in New Orleans at the time. Bagnetto told McCabe he was late for work and always carried a gun to protect his family's produce. McCabe arrested Bagnetto, who protested and offered to give McCabe the gun, worth about three dollars, to let him go. McCabe refused, and according to McCabe, found another revolver in the gutter, near where they were standing.

><

2:15 A.M.

The mayor and several of his political courtesans visited the Central Police Station. By now, the lobby and corridors buzzed with officers. The mayor asked questions about who had been arrested in the roundup of Italians. He was pleased that the few cells were stuffed with scared dark eyes, while other Italians were chained to pipes and heavy furniture. Shakspeare gave another order to Acting Superintendent John Journee. "Captain, I want you to arrest every member of the *Stuppagghieri* known to this department. If your jail is too crowded, call Sheriff Villere and send them to the parish prison." At that moment, Shakspeare failed to see the madness of his command, beyond its unconstitutionality. With one order, Shakspeare killed the upcoming retrial of the Provenzano ambush case, as all the victims were believed to be members of the *Stuppagghieri.* Nevertheless, the order spread like a virulent virus, and the police followed it with great alacrity.

><

2:25 A.M.

Millard Peeler rented a room at Number 267 Girod Street and saw the entire shooting, so he claimed. After mustering enough courage to talk to the police, Peeler approached a knot of officers and told them what he saw. Because the attack, according to Peeler, commenced from across the Girod Street from Hennessy's house, and under the lean-to canopy of Pietro Monasterio's cobbler shop, investigators immediately went to the shop and confronted the cobbler, who was dressed in a nightshirt. The shop was nothing but a small shack built of old, rough-hewed boards and a slanting roof, which allowed rainwater to fall into the gutter. It had one door, facing Girod Street, and one window next to the door. A narrow alley was next to the shack, which provided the owners, the Petersons, and other tenants access to their quarters behind the shack. There was no door from the shack to the alley.

The police entered the shack and searched it without a warrant. They interviewed Monasterio, who spoke little English, but he was able to tell officers that he was in bed when he heard men in the alley next to his shop right before the shooting. Officers found a ramrod for a muzzle-loading shotgun, some muddy shoes, and eight hundred and fifty dollars in cash in the shack. When the cobbler couldn't explain the discoveries clearly, he was arrested and taken to the Central Police Station.

Monasterio's neighbors, the Beverly family and Emma Thomas, supported his statement, but being Italian was enough probable cause to arrest the cobbler. When Thomas told the police that Monasterio had repaired Margaret Hennessy's shoes and was known to the chief, they ignored the statement and put the cobbler in the back of a patrol wagon.

><

2:30 A.M.

On a moonless night, Girod Street seemed like a ghostly trail, leading to the white walls of the Protestant Cemetery. But on this night, kerosene lamps, carried by the police and citizens, speckled the gloomy shadows, like teeming lightning bugs. Loud voices and the sound of horse hooves echoed off the houses and shanties. John Lannigan, a lumberyard watchman, told police that several men, some wearing slouch hats, derbies, and oilcloth coats, ran past him after the shooting on Girod Street. One of the men slipped in the mud and dropped something near Franklin and Julia Streets, but kept running. Police searched the area and found a sawed-off shotgun with a folding stock in the gutter near where the man slipped. Lannigan offered, he asked the men what happened, and the response was, "Me no know," affecting a thick Italian accent. At that time, Lannigan stated he couldn't identify the man. It was too dark.

Throughout the city, packs of police and citizens set upon every Italian they could find. Once the police received Shakspeare's second order to arrest all known members of the *Stuppagghieri,* all pretense of evidence-based arrest dissolved. More guns were found in the streets and gutters.

Curiously, the police had more guns and Italians in jail than the reported number of assailants. But frenzied prejudice superseded mathematics.

Every Italian or Sicilian was a target. Indeed, a monstrous raid on a tavern at Conti and Bourbon Streets resulted in thirty Italians being arrested. The slightest resistance was met with the brute force of the police. Word of the mass arrests seized the Italian Colony, and every house where Italians resided. Cowering Italian mothers hid their children behind bolted doors. The echoes of the police yelling, kicking, and smashing down doors to search homes caused many Italians and Sicilians to question their decision to come to America.

><

4:00 A.M.

Eager to get the story printed and distributed, *The Daily Picayune* and *The Times-Democrat* hastily *"Flashed"* their first edition of the Hennessy shooting. Because of the police raids throughout the city, there was a lack of Italian newspaper boys to go throughout the city and sell papers. Reporters, pressed into double duty, hawked their papers while trying to get updates on the story.

The *Times-Democrat* reported that Hennessy was at Charity Hospital, and resting comfortably, while the *Daily Picayune* printed:

"Another chapter has been added to the already too bloody record of the vendetta in New Orleans, and David C. Hennessy, her superintendent of police, the victim of the tragedy, lies at the Charity Hospital in momentary expectation of the dread summons which must be answered."

The *Daily Picayune* further reported the opinions of the attending physicians, Logan and Bloom, "…**that the wounds were very dangerous, indeed, but were not necessarily fatal at present."**

And during the early hours of October 16, 1890, Hennessy slipped in and out of consciousness. Nurses and nuns hovered around his bed, attending to his every need and praying.

><

4:10 A.M.

Charles Matranga and his party left Number 11 Burgundy Street and went to their respective homes. Little did they know, they were, at that moment, wanted men. Officers Hevron, Torregano, and Cassidy followed Macheca and the Carusos home in a carriage, unaware of the mayor's order to arrest anyone associated with the *Stuppagghieri*. The Caruso brothers followed J.P. Macheca to his Number 279 Bourbon Street residence. There in a loud, sodden voice, officers claimed they heard Macheca boast, "I only wish they done the son-of-bitch up here." All the men laughed and retired for the night.

Chapter 54

New Orleans
October 16, 1890
Dawn

As the sun rose over the wide bend of the Mississippi River, its golden beams stretched across the horizon of New Orleans. But it's autumnal radiance fell upon a city paralyzed by anger, fear, hatred, prejudice, and a rampaging criminal justice system similar to what one would have experienced during Paris' *Reign of Terror,* nearly a hundred years earlier. The French Market, the Poydras Market, and the Orleans Market were almost empty. The docks were quiet. Canal Street was silent, except for police patrol wagons crossing the vast commercial expanse every ten minutes. Bands of police officers and Boylan Detectives roamed throughout the Italian Colony, searching for any Italian male. Italian women slipped out of their residence when no one was near, just to buy some food for the day.

The Camp Street newspapers printed updated stories nearly every hour. Reporters spied on each other to gain some advantage. At the Central Police Station, officers continued to drag in frightened Italian men and boys. The jail population swelled beyond capacity, and the arrestees' sanitation needs began to challenge everyone's senses. Some Italian men were being released if they could prove they had no affiliation with the *Stuppagghieri.* In addition to the already-imprisoned Provenzanos, most Italians had no affiliation with any organization. They toiled just to feed their families, pay their rent, drink a little wine, and pay their tribute to their *Padrone,* who were also hiding deep in the warrens of the Italian Colony.

The nuns moved David Hennessy to a ward on the hospital's third floor. There, they continued to follow the conservative orders of physicians. As the sun shone through his ward window, his hooded, exanimate eyes refracted the sunlight. His skin paled. His facial features slackened. The nuns attended to his every need and prayed the Rosary. Margaret Hennessy wept as her only son's life ebbed. His best friend, Tom Anderson, patted her heaving shoulders.

><

8:30 A.M.

Lionel Adams looked in his bedroom mirror and tied his royal blue bowtie around his starched collar. As he began to slip on his suit jacket, he heard a thunderous banging at his front door. He armed himself with his silver derringer and answered the door. To his amazement, a panting Dominick O'Malley stood on his stoop and shoved a copy of the *Daily Picayune* into his chest.

"I guess you haven't heard? Read the front page," O'Malley said.

Adams unfolded the newspaper and clipped on his round, wire-frame reading glasses. As his eyes scanned the news about the Hennessy shooting the night before, Adams's hands began to shake. "Come in, Dominick," Adams mumbled, without taking his eyes off the page.

Adams sat on a stuffed chair in his front parlor and studied the various sections of the story. His legal mind clicked into high gear as he analyzed each sentence and paragraph. "The headlines say Hennessy has been assassinated, but the story says he's at Charity Hospital. Which is it?" Adams asked.

"I heard he's in grave danger, Lionel. What are we going to do?"

"Nothing. We'll go to my office and wait until we hear more. Shakspeare has ordered anyone associated with the *Stuppagghieri* arrested. That means there will be no Provenzano trial next week. He's a madman. He's stirring a fire he'll never put out, and the *Picayune* is giving him a hot poker."

Adams continued to read the paper. "Damn! Did you read what Billy O'Connor told the newspaper? Of all the nights O'Connor doesn't follow his friend home, the chief gets shot? And the only witness Shakspeare is relying on is O'Connor? Dagoes shot Hennessy? What Dagoes? Who? Hennessy knows them all. Matranga? Macheca? Geraci? Who? I was with a bunch of them last night at Fabacher's. Is Shakspeare going to arrest me, too?"

"It's in all the newspapers. I stopped at the Saint Charles Hotel for breakfast. All of them have the same story," O'Malley said. "People are saying Hennessy was shot because he was going to testify against the Matrangas."

"Rumors? O'Connor doesn't say that. He just said Hennessy said

'Dagoes.' But what Dagoes? And Shakspeare immediately orders the arrest of the Matrangas and the *Stuppagghieri?* Now the Provenzanos and the Matrangas will be in the same parish prison? This is crazy."

"Was Hennessy going to be a witness at the Provenzano trial?" O'Malley probed.

"Why would Hennessy testify against nine of his officers who testified at the Provenzanos' first trial? If he had any evidence against the Matrangas, would nine officers testify for the Provenzanos? Would they go against their chief? Judge Baker relied heavily on the testimony of those nine officers when he ordered a new trial," Adams said. "If Hennessy had incriminating evidence against the Matrangas, they would have already been arrested. None of this makes sense."

"Could Hennessy have new evidence against the Matrangas?" O'Malley asked.

"What new evidence could he have that could be admissible at the next Provenzano trial? David knows I'm one of the prosecutors, and he would have told me. I was his attorney and friend. There would be no reason to surprise me with any new evidence on the eve of the trial. There's more to this than we know. Let's go to my office and wait," Adams said.

><

9:06 A.M.

Despite the golden beams of the morning sun filling the third-floor ward of Charity Hospital, the death pall eclipsed all signs of life. Doctor Logan examined David Hennessy. No radial pulse. No carotid pulse. No signs of breath. Doctor Logan removed his pocket watch and noted the time. He snapped the cover closed and, with a somber voice, told his attending colleagues and nurses that David C. Hennessy had died. He was thirty-three years old.

Logan's pronouncement ripped through Charity Hospital, and soon New Orleans would be whipped into a frenzied, tornadic fire, which would burn through and scorch any semblance of reason. What the White, Democrat, Anglo-Saxon population labeled a *vendetta* when someone was killed in the Italian Colony, they would now adorn themselves with the mantle of propriety. Instead of concealing their blood-fueled deeds in back alleys, they would use every gilded pretense of the institutions of justice to accomplish the same ends.

Within minutes of Doctor Logan's pronouncement, the telegraph keys and the telephone lines spread the news of Hennessy's death. Some police officers openly wept, while others feared for their own lives, given the tense relationship between the police and the Italian community. Within an hour of Hennessy's death, the police had already arrested Pietro Monasterio, Antonio Marchesi, his son, Asperi, Antonio Bagnetto, Bastian Incardona, Peter Natale, Charles Traina, Charles Pietzo, and Antonio Scaffidi.

All were booked for the murder of David Hennessy, but in reality, they were arrested for being Italian, or being suspected members of the *Stuppagghieri*. If proximity to the Hennessy attack had predicted the arrest of Monasterio, the police ignored that element when they arrested Charles Traina at the Sarpy Plantation in Saint Charles Parish, twenty-five miles from New Orleans, and Peter Natale, who was arrested at the Illinois Central station, having just returned from Chicago. Others were arrested for being Italian, living, or working near the Poydras Market. But every witness who tried to identify the assassins all agree on one thing: after shooting Hennessy, the assassins ran uptown on Basin Street or Franklin Street, and away from the Poydras Market.

At city hall, the municipal telegraph office notified public officials of Hennessy's death. Shakspeare huddled with his closest advisors and confidants behind closed doors. Anger, fear, and shock flowed through all neighborhoods of the city. Police and Boylan detectives searched the city for any Italians but made one exception. Boylan officer Roe remembered Zachary Foster running away from the shooting. Foster was not Italian, but Black. The police arrested and separated Foster from the Italians, and brought him to the parish prison, where he remained under a ten-thousand-dollar bond, and segregated from others. The Italians were not granted a bond.

><

11:00 A.M.

Assistant Orleans Parish Coroner P.E. Archinard was called and finally appeared at Charity Hospital to conduct the official autopsy of David C. Hennessy. Hennessy's body was removed to the surgical amphitheater for the procedure. Police officers, medical students, friends, and newspaper reporters took seats above the operating table to witness the final details of medical science. Dr. Archinard opened Hennessy's thoracic body and determined that a large bullet had entered the body about three inches below the left nipple, penetrating both lungs and the liver. The bullet passed through the left eighth rib, traversed the body, and lodged under the skin about four inches beneath the right nipple. There were other multiple gunshot wounds, and Archinard officially determined the cause of death to be internal hemorrhaging. Bullets struck neither the heart nor the pericardium.

By order of the mayor, Hennessy's body was removed to Johnson and Sons Undertakers, across the street from Charity Hospital, for funeral preparations, which would be larger than Jefferson Davis's ten months earlier. Though many hated Hennessy, Shakspeare schemed to use the funeral to stoke anti-Italian sentiment throughout the city, while enhancing his political image. The mayor, the 1882 Rex, and a member of the Pickwick Club knew how to play with people's emotions to gain attention for himself.

><

1:00 P.M.

Police escorted a group of shackled Italian prisoners to a waiting patrol wagon parked in the rear of the Central Police Station. Swarms of officers surrounded the wagon to protect the suspected assassins from an angry crowd demanding vigilante justice for killing their police chief. Captain John Journee, now acting Superintendent of Police, ordered the wagon driver to proceed to the parish prison at Orleans and Basin Streets. Also, some Italians were released from the rear of the jail, allowing them to escape the angry crowd gathered in front of the station. When the wagon passed the crowd, now burgeoning onto Basin Street, someone began a derisive chant, which would haunt Italian-Americans in New Orleans for decades: *"Who killa da chief?"*

Upon arrival at the foreboding, stygian prison, the newly arrived prisoners were housed in a separate section of the sprawling complex, away from the Provenzano prisoners. Sheriff Gabriel Villere and his Warden, Lemuel Davis, didn't want a war within their prison, so the guards and prison trustees were instructed to keep them separated at all times, especially on the yard. Sadistic guards took the orders as opportunities to earn some "yard" money to keep the warring inmates safe from each other. Behind the whitewashed walls of the Orleans Parish Prison, the guards and trustees controlled the prisoners for a price.

><

4:00 P.M.

As the sun began to descend in the deep southwest, the shadows of the Central Police Station covered its front plaza. By now, about fifty citizens remained near the front steps of the building, along with an equal number of newspaper reporters—some from outside of Louisiana. They waited for any new development in the Hennessy case. Their vigil didn't last long.

While reporters exchanged notes for mutual accuracy, a hush washed over the crowd from Tulane Avenue to Gravier Street. With the hallowed and hollow clopping of two black horses pulling a black, draped hearse with oval windows, led by two police officers on horseback, the crowd went stone-silent, for the remains of David C. Hennessy were passing his police station for the last time, destined for his home on Girod Street. Men removed their bowlers and derbies. Some women made the sign of the cross. Every cigar hit the ground and was crushed under a heel. The reality of the moment chilled and seized the faces of the crowd.

Inside the police station, Captain Journee and Secretary Vandervoort prepared arrest warrants for Joseph P. Macheca, Charles Matranga, Rocco Geraci, Frank Romero, James and John Caruso, Loretto Comitz, and Charles Patorno. Despite the well-known alibis for several men, the warrants charged them, and others already arrested, with the murder of David C. Hennessy.

While Vandervoort pounded the keys of his typewriter, six pallbearers removed Hennessy's dark mahogany casket with silver handles from the hearse and carried it up the front steps of Number 275 Girod Street. Mourners had already draped the entrance with black crepe, and bouquets of flowers covered the small front porch. Inside the front parlor, the undertakers removed the lid of the casket, revealing Hennessy's last pleasant countenance, under a sheet of glass. A large silver candelabra was placed near the glass, which cast a pale sallow light upon his final waxen features. His mother fell against the casket, as her heaving breath fogged the glass. Tom Anderson and General Badger comforted her and led her to a chair at the head of the casket. And the wake began.

Chapter 55

New Orleans
October 17, 1890
7:30 A.M.

Fathers Jacque Fontebuis and John O'Shanahan of the Jesuit Church and School pulled into the empty courtyard of St. Aloysius Academy. Since yesterday morning, everyone in the French Quarter's Italian Colony sealed themselves behind closed doors and gates, because of Shakspeare's orders. Brother Stanislaus and other Brothers of the Sacred Heart cancelled all classes, fearing their students would be arrested on the way to school. Even their borders were admonished not to go beyond the school's wall. Antonio, Abraham, and two other borders, whiled their time away in the school library, tinkering on the school's piano, or sitting outside on the school's benches. Laurence Hearn called the school and reinforced that admonishment. There was no call from Mr. Jahnke.

The Brothers greeted the priest warmly and invited them to have breakfast with them. Antonio and the other borders were happy to see the priest and learn any news from beyond the walls of their school. It was bleak. "I have to report that the situation in this city is dire," Father O'Shanahan began. "While our school remains open, you are wise to keep yours closed until this storm of hate blows over. While very quiet, one can feel the tension on every street. On our ride here, we saw only about twenty people on Canal Street. Anyone with dark hair and eyes is being arrested."

"We will keep this school closed until the city returns to normal. Arresting people on how they look is beyond comprehension," Brother Stanislaus lamented. "But I must ask, Father, what brings you here today?"

"I'll get to the point. This afternoon, Chief Hennessy's Requiem Mass will be held at St. Joseph's church on Tulane Avenue. We offered our church because the chief was once a student of ours, but Father Patrick O'Neill said Hennessy was his parishioner. I'll tell you a little secret. The chief always paid a visit to our church on his way home, but we will let Father O'Neill have his way.

"I need altar boys for the service, and Father Fontebuis suggested Antonio and any other Italian boy you can lend us. We want every Italian boy we can get to stand on that altar this afternoon. It will make a respectful statement if you understand my intent."

"Will they be safe, Father?" Brother Stanislaus asked.

"We will have every Jesuit priest in the procession. No one would dare do anything foolish with our eyes upon everyone. Can you get us about four boys?"

Brother Stanislaus looked at Antonio. "Do you want to go? I think you will be safe, which would be a good experience."

"Yes," Antonio said.

"Good. I want some Italian boys to carry candles in the procession. Just follow our orders, and you will be fine. How about you, Abraham?"

"Sorry, but I am Jewish. I know nothing about your customs."

"Good. We will show both of you what to do. Your presence will be appreciated. Besides, don't both of you work for that crazy newspaper, *The Mascot?*"

Everyone laughed. "Good. You will get the story of this historical funeral right—front row seats. How about it?" Father O'Shanahan asked.

Both boys nodded. "Wear black pants and a white shirt. You will be dressed in a black cassock and white surplice. Polish your shoes. Father Fontebuis will be back later this afternoon to get you," Father O'Shanahan said.

><

8:30 A.M.

At city hall, the mayor and his secretary, Wright Schaumberg, put the final touches on the funeral procession. The cortege, though filled with all the accoutrements of a funeral procession, aimed to project the mayor's political power. All politicians love parades, and Shakspeare would not squander an opportunity to display his power.

The Cortege would be as follows:

1. Detail of Mounted New Orleans Police Officers.
2. The New Orleans Fire Department.

3. Louisiana Athletic Club.

4. Citizens on foot.

5. New Orleans Police on foot.

6. Boylan Detail.

7. The Clergy.

8. The Hearse.

9. Family and close friends.

10. Chiefs of the New Orleans Fire Departments

11. Mississippi Fire Company Number 2.

12. Mayor and city council. (Six Carriages)

13. Other State and city Officials.

14. Prominent citizens in carriages.

With the number of participants, the cortege would be about a mile long and would commence at City Hall at two o'clock, with the Requiem Mass to follow. Interment would be at the Metairie Cemetery.

><

9:45 A.M.

Several police officers, along with Secretary George Vandervoort, returned to the Central Police Station from the Recorder's Court with sly smiles on their faces. They proceeded past spectators and reporters and went directly to Captain Journee's office. There, they gave Journee a sheaf of legal documents, with red ribbons and seals affixed to eight cover documents. Journee thumbed through the documents and smiled. He held the arrest warrants for Charles Matranga, Joseph P. Macheca, Salvatore Sunzeri, John Caruso, James Caruso, Rocco Geraci, Bastian Incardona, and Charles Patorno.

"Let's keep this quiet. Go clean up, and get ready for Hennessy's funeral parade," Journee said, despite knowing several of the wanted men were at the Academy of Music and Fabacher's Restaurant on the night Hennessy was shot. "Tomorrow, we execute these warrants."

><

10:00 A.M.

Thomas Duffy, a man of quiet countenance, stood last in line at 275 Girod Street to pay his last respects to a man he idolized. For most of his life, no one paid any attention to Duffy, for he was only known as the man who distributed newspapers for the *Times Democrat*. But today, he would be remembered.

A police corporal told Duffy to move up the line, as he was closing the Hennessy wake and moving it to City Hall. Duffy just nodded and paid his respects. He left 275 Girod Street with tears in his eyes. The image of a deceased David Hennessy in his mind, and a Lefercheaux .32 Caliber revolver in his coat pocket, he walked to the parish prison.

When Duffy arrived at the prison, he approached the front gates' outer iron bars and began executing a plan that would surprise everyone. It was visiting day at the old prison, and deputies were familiar with Duffy, who often visited a friend. A deputy admitted Duffy to an area known as the bullpen, a space between the locked outer gates and the locked inner gates. When deputies asked if he wanted to see his friend, Duffy responded, "Detectives told me to come here to see if I could identify one of David Hennessy's killers," Duffy responded.

"Which one?" the deputy asked.

Duffy paused and remembered only one name—Scaffidi.

The deputy told Duffy to wait in the bullpen while he went to get Scaffidi, who was in the exercise yard. When the deputies returned to the bullpen with twenty-four-year-old Scaffidi, Duffy took a step back and drew his old revolver, and fired one shot, which struck Scaffidi in the right side of his throat, near, but not through his descending carotid artery. Scaffidi collapsed to the ground as his heart pumped blood from the wound. Deputies rushed to stanch the bleeding while other deputies entered the bullpen, disarmed Duffy, and dragged him to the Fourth Precinct police station at Marias and Orleans Streets.

Deputies called for an ambulance, and the wounded Scaffidi, writhing and screaming in pain, was transported to the hospital. There, while still conscious, the wounded man begged Doctor J.D. Bloom and the nurses to call for Father Patrick O'Neill, who was across the street, preparing St. Joseph's church for the Hennessy funeral. Father O'Neill raced across the street and gave Scaffidi the Last Rites of the Catholic Church. City Recorder Hollander also appeared, hoping to get a dying declaration, implicating other Italians in the assassination of David C. Hennessy.

Instead, Scaffidi protested his innocence, while doctors worked on his gushing wound. Hollander took no statement. Reporters were admitted to the treatment room and peppered the scared and wounded Scaffidi with questions. He continued to protest his innocence. When Hollander and the reporters failed to get Scaffidi's confession, they dispersed, leaving Father O'Neill and Scaffidi's family in the room with police officers. After the doctors declared the wounds not to be fatal, they completed their work and held Scaffidi for two days before his return to the parish prison.

While Thomas Duffy was being booked at the Central Police Station, word of his attack only exacerbated the disquietude of New Orleans. Sheriff Villere locked down the parish prison. Almost every Italian began to hide behind bolted doors. Stevedores and fruit vendors ran home and hid. The city quaked with hate and fear.

In front of reporters, Captain Journee asked Duffy why he shot Scaffidi. The chilling response was reported in all the newspapers. "I hope the dago dies. I don't care if I hang. Chief Hennessy was a friend of mine," Duffy snarled.

><

2:00 P.M.

David C. Hennessy's coffin rested on a black-draped catafalque in the council chambers. Every city official made their presence conspicuous to newspaper reporters, each other, and Margaret Hennessy, who continued to weep for her only son. Hundreds of people filed past Hennessy's open coffin, sealed by a pane of glass. Hushed tones of conversation filled the room, but in the center corridor, open discussions about reprisals in the Italian community controlled the topic of conversation. Some police officers emoted anger and fear. Some remained stoic and waited for instructions from the mayor or Captain Journee. Despite the somber occasion, New Orleans coiled like a rattlesnake, waiting to sink its venomous fangs into Italian flesh.

All conversation stopped when the clergy arrived, accompanied by seven altar boys carrying a large gold crucifix and six candles. Led by Fathers Patrick O'Neill, John O'Shanahan, and several other priests, the clergy began taking turns comforting Margaret Hennessy and reading selected offices and scriptures over Hennessy's coffin. When finished, Father O'Neill invited everyone to attend the Requiem Mass at St. Joseph's church. Father O'Shanahan comforted Mrs. Hennessy while she said goodbye to her only son. The undertakers closed the coffin, and the pallbearers, including several police officers, Tom Anderson, and Billy O'Connor, carried the slain Chief down the front steps of City Hall and placed the coffin inside the hearse.

><

4:00 P.M.

After the solemn Requiem Mass, David Hennessy's cortege somberly plodded through the streets of New Orleans for the three-mile trip to Metairie Cemetery. People gathered along the way to pay their respects by bowing or removing their hats. The clopping of horses' hooves against the stone streets, blended with muffled drums, echoed a rhythmic dirge, while the October-setting sun cast a brassy-golden hue against the black funereal carriages. At the red-brick gates of the cemetery, sextons led the cortege to a red-brick, above-ground burial vault.

Pallbearers carried Hennessy's coffin to the front of the open vault and waited for the priests to gather around. Antonio's legs quivered as he led the procession at the head of the coffin. Antonio's mind erupted into a desiderium of memories he thought long suppressed. Hennessy's requiem plunged him into flashbacks, as he gripped the gold crucifix, for fear of collapsing. His dark eyes darted through the crowd as Father O'Neill began to pray over Hennessy's coffin. His attention caught Laurence Hearn in the crowd, which strengthened his legs and spirits.

After the sprinkling of Holy Water and the prayerful last words, the sextons disturb the solemnity of the moment by pushing Hennessy's coffin deep into the vault. The scratching noise screeched through the cemetery as the crowd walked away. As Lionel Adams climbed into his carriage, Algernon Badger approached him and asked, "Mr. Adams, I hope you don't think it indecorous of me to ask you a question at this moment."

"Not at all, General. I hold you in high esteem," Adams responded.

"Rumors are going around that you might be representing some of David's assassins. I know you were his attorney and friend. It was I who recommended you to him when he was indicted for killing Devereaux. So, is it true?"

"Yes."

"Why, sir?" Badger asked, shifting his glare to Tom Anderson, who sealed Hennessy's tomb with a wooden tablet which read: *David C. Hennessy died October 16, 1891.*

"Sir, there are many reasons for me to offer my services. First, I am prepared to prosecute the Provenzanos again for the ambush of the Matranga stevedores. Charles Matranga, J.P. Macheca, Rocco Geraci, and others were in my office all afternoon Wednesday. I was preparing their trial testimony. Afterwards, I left them to attend a gathering of supporters for General Adolf Meyer in Algiers. I gave them tickets for a performance that evening at the Academy of Music. Afterwards, I met with those same men at Fabacher's Restaurant on Royal Street. I was with them about the time David was shot."

"So, you will be an alibi witness, too?" Badger asked.

"No. There were many others at Fabacher's who will testify. Doesn't it seem odd to you that David would be ambushed in the same manner as the Matranga stevedores? Who shot the Matrangas? Why were so many cops watching the Matrangas and none watching Hennessy?"

"What do you mean?" Badger asked.

"You know what David knew about the *Stuppagghieri.* George Vandervoort knows the same information. If they had any evidence contrary to the Provenzano prosecution, don't you think they would have told me? And do you really believe Macheca, the man who saved *your* life, would have killed *your* best friend?"

"Who do you think killed David, Mr. Adams?"

"Right now, Charles Matranga, J.P. Macheca, Rocco Geraci, the Caruso brothers, and several others are in hiding. They know warrants have been issued for their arrest. There are no secrets in New Orleans. But they are in fear of their lives, particularly after what happened to Scaffidi, inside the secure walls of the parish prison. Despite Sheriff Villere's posting armed guards in and around the prison, there is no guarantee these men will make it to trial alive." Adams shifted his gaze to a cluster of men gathered around the mayor's carriage, which was parked about fifty feet away. They were speaking in hushed tones. Badger looked, too. "Looks like the lights will be on late tonight in City Hall, General," Adams said.

Chapter 56

New Orleans
October 18, 1890
Morning

New Orleans roiled like a churning cauldron of hate, which could only be sated by Sicilian blood. The city jail and parish prison immured over sixty Sicilians on gauzy suspicion. The probable cause for their arrest was their names. The police were successful in getting arrest warrants for Joseph P. Macheca, Charles Matranga, Rocco Geraci, Salvador Sunzeri, Frank Romero, James Caruso, and John Caruso. Fearing for their lives, they all arranged to be escorted to the Central Police Station. Macheca had Police Commissioner Frank Barker personally escort him into the city jail to be processed.

Newspaper reporters jammed the corridors, shouting questions to the accused. And at one moment, reporters captured a heated exchange between George Vandervoort and Macheca. Vandervoort attacked Macheca for saying he was happy Hennessy was killed. Macheca denied saying that and retorted that he had nothing against Hennessy and that he considered him a friend. Vandervoort continued the exchange until Macheca broke down and cried, and Captain Journee stepped in to stop the exchange. Wiping his eyes, Macheca said, "If I killed Chief Hennessy, I would be on one of my steamers, on my way to South America. I would not be here. Ask your officers where I was Wednesday night. At Fabacher's."

After the arrest, the men were taken by a Black Maria to First Recorder Court, where they were formally charged with the murder of Hennessy. Recorder Judge Brigier set no bail and remanded the defendants to the parish prison, where they were sequestered from the giddy Provenzano stevedores, who were more than willing to proclaim the Matrangas and the *Stuppagghieri* guilty to hungry reporters through the iron grates of their prison cells.

><

Noon

Hundreds of men crowded the front steps of City Hall, as the mayor, city council, policemen, police commissioners, lawyers, cotton exchange members, and newspaper reporters stomped up the steps with resolute glares in their eyes. Policemen guarded the doors of the large council chambers, where, twenty-four hours earlier, David C. Hennessy's mortal remains rested in homage.

While the council assembled in their assigned seats, the mayor and a select few cloistered themselves behind the locked doors of his parlor. There, among his most trusted friends and associates, Mayor Joseph A. Shakspeare conspired to transform the Queen City of Commerce into a slaughterhouse, where American justice would hang from meat hooks forged by avarice, hatred, and prejudice, drenching the city's cobblestones with innocent blood.

As the noon hour approached, the mayor, followed by attorneys Edgar Farrar, William Sterling Parkerson, George Denegre, John Wickliffe, James Legendre, and about twenty-five members of the Cotton Exchange, entered the council chambers. Everyone rose, as an edgy silence swept over the room. Acting Police Superintendent John Journee and his secretary, George Vandervoort, sat in the front row. Every newspaper had several reporters and the city's recorders in attendance. Laurence Hearn forbade Antonio and Abraham from attending, for he knew their lives would be in jeopardy.

Before Shakspeare had council clerk, Emile O'Brien, read the mayor's statement, he told all gathered that he, too, had been threatened by Sicilians, but offered no proof of that assertion. The room erupted in anger as O'Brien began to bellow the flames of hate, which were recorded verbatim by the city's newspapers.

"To the City Council: It is with the profoundest grief and indignation that I make to you the official announcement of the death of David C. Hennessy, Superintendent of Police of this city, grief at the loss of a true friend and an efficient officer— indignation that he should have died by the hands of despicable assassins. He was waylaid and riddled with bullets almost at his doorstep on last Wednesday night, and he died on Thursday morning at 9:06 o'clock.

"The circumstances of the cowardly deed, the arrest made and

the evidence collected by the police department, show beyond doubt that he was the victim of Sicilian vengeance, wreaked upon him as the chief representative of law and order in this community because he was seeking, by the power of our American law, to break up the fierce vendettas that have so often stained our streets with blood. Heretofore, these scoundrels have confined their murdering's among themselves.

"None of them have ever been convicted because of the secrecy with which the crimes have been committed, and the impossibility of getting evidence from the people of their own race to convict. Bold, indeed, was the stroke aimed at their first American victim. A shining mark they have selected on which to write with the assassin's hand their contempt for the civilization of the new world.

"We owe it to ourselves and everything we hold sacred in this life to see to it that this blow is the last. We must teach these people a lesson they will not forget for all time.

"What the means are to reach this end, I leave to the wisdom of the council to devise.

"It is clear to me that the wretches who committed this foul deed are the mere hirelings and instruments of others higher and more powerful than they. These instigators are the men we must find at any cost.

"For years, the existence of the stiletto societies among the Sicilians in this city has been asserted.

"Appeal was made to me by a prominent Italian during my former administration to protect him from blackmail and murder, but as he was afraid to give me any names, I could do nothing for him.

"It is believed that these horrid associations are patronized by some of the wealthy and powerful members of their own race in this city, and that they can point out who the leader of these associations are.

"No community can exist with murder societies in its midst. These societies must perish, or the community itself must perish.

"The Sicilian who comes here must become an American citizen, and subject his wrongs to the remedy of the law of the land, or else there must be no place for him on the American

continent. This sentiment we must see realized at any cost—at any hazard.

"The people look to you to take the initiative in this matter. Act! Act promptly without fear for favor."

Jos. A. Shakspeare, Mayor

Laurence Hearn scribbled down the mayor's words, and a chill passed through his body. He compared his notes to those of other reporters and immediately discerned a vile lack of candor in the mayor's words. Notably, the mayor's assertion: *"None of them have ever been convicted because of the secrecy with which the crimes have been committed, and the impossibility of getting evidence from the people of their own race to convict."* Hearn asked another reporter, "Did the mayor forget about the Provenzano trial?" The other reporter demurred.

Thereafter, the city council addressed a motion of the mayor to create a Committee of Fifty, composed of the finest citizens of New Orleans, to investigate the secret societies that operated in the shadows of the city. Clerk Emile O'Brien read a list of names, which reflected members of the Cotton Exchange, the Boston and Pickwick Clubs, and some members of the Rex Carnival Club, with the chairman being attorney Edgar Farrar.

Several city council members discussed the motion thereafter and eventually passed it. The mayor immediately motioned the council to appropriate fifteen thousand dollars to cover the cost of all investigations, and to defray the cost of rent of the Cotton Exchange's fourth floor on Carondelet Street, as an appropriate venue to conduct their business. The motion carried, and the council adjourned the meeting and ordered the Committee of Fifty to meet in the council chambers that night at seven-thirty o'clock.

><

3:30 P.M.

The telegraph room at the Custom House clattered with news New Orleans didn't need at the moment. A steamer named *Elysia* had sailed through the mouth of the Mississippi River with a cargo of seven hundred Italians on board. Immediately, telegraph clerks ran through the Custom House and notified the appropriate immigration and maritime authorities. When notified, General Badger, who was just asked to join the Committee of Fifty, blanched and immediately consulted with other government officials. He developed a plan to stop the ship when it arrived at a small port on the river, twenty miles south of New Orleans, known as Quarantine. The *Elysia* was scheduled to arrive near the Picayune Tier on the following Tuesday, October 21, 1890.

Badger and Custom Commissioner Henry Walmouth devised a plan to board the ship with armed guards and process the immigrants, one by one. Any Italian who was known to be a criminal, had no family in New Orleans, identified as a day laborer with no specific skills, or seemed suspicious was to be sent back to Italy. Badger then called City Hall and spoke to the mayor's secretary, informing him of the news, which was not received well. When reporters learned of *Elysia's* arrival, they had a new story to add to their broadsheets, further quaking New Orleans's streets.

><

7:00 P.M.

Members of the newly formed Committee of Fifty, led by attorney Edgar Farrar, gathered in the city council chambers. Each of them, proud of their social status and new purpose in life, seemed animated and eager to seek justice or revenge for the Hennessy murder. Farrar led a few of the members to the mayor's parlor, where they had a private meeting behind closed doors. About thirty minutes later, Farrar's gaggle of righteous men emerged flushed with enthusiasm to execute the mayor's mandate.

As Farrar exited the mayor's parlor, Italian Consulate, Pasquale Corte, tried to see the mayor to complain about the harsh treatment all Italians were receiving at the hands of guards inside the parish prison. Corte's efforts were rebuffed, and the mayor chose to see Charles Peeler, who claimed to be a witness to the assassination. Peeler and his wife lived opposite Gillis' store on the corner of Girod and Basin. Peeler complained about his safety, since the newspapers had printed his name as a witness to Hennessy's murder. Shakspeare showed great compassion for Peeler and sent him, under guard, to the Central Police Station with instructions to increase the guard in and around Girod Street. Corte made another attempt to see the mayor, but a police officer told him to leave City Hall.

When Farrar entered the city council chambers, he was welcomed with polite applause. He took the dais and scanned the room with his piercing dark eyes. S.P. Walmsley moved that all Committee business be done in secret and behind closed doors. The motion carried, and the Committee of Fifty met for two hours behind locked doors. The next meeting would be conducted on the fourth floor of the Cotton Exchange. At that moment in time, New Orleans, accustomed to masquerading as an American city, guided by the rule of law, and seeking international acclaim, entered a new epoch, where the rule of a few men was about to achieve international shame.

Chapter 57

St. Aloysius Academy
October 19, 1890
Noon

As Laurence Hearn drove his carriage down Chartres Street, his nose stung with the stench of rotting fruit wafting up Madison Street from the river. He turned his horse down the street towards the docks, and the smell hung heavier in the air as he did. At Decatur and Madison Streets, he tethered his horse to an iron pole and walked towards the nearly empty French Market. A few bedraggled people were foraging through barrels and crates of fly-infested lemons and oranges. Near the wharf, a rat sat fearlessly on its haunches, munching on a black banana. Hearn removed his handkerchief from his coat pocket and covered his nose, in a futile attempt to filter the fetid air. He asked one stall keeper, "What happened to all the food? Why is it just sitting here rotting?"

An old Italian lady, with sad rheumy eyes, responded in fractured English, "No men to sell food. No men to unload boats. No men. Hiding."

Hearn backed away from the lady and returned to his carriage. He turned left on Decatur Street and caught the crew of one J.P. Macheca's boats dumping its cargo of citrus into the Mississippi River. "Has the world come to an end?" he cried, as he continued his trip to St. Aloysius. At that end of the Italian Colony, there were no other carriages or people moving about. He felt alone in a strange, familiar place. But he knew many eyes were upon him, peaking from behind louvered doors and drawn curtains.

A large chain secured the gate of the school. After descending his carriage, Hearn yanked on a rope attached to an old brass bell to signal his presence. Brother Stanislaus opened the front door and walked across the school yard to the gate. He recognized Hearn and gave him a warm welcome.

"Sorry, Mr. Hearn, but we can't be too careful with what's going on in the city. I hope you understand."

"Completely, Brother. That's why I am here. I brought the Sunday editions of the *Daily Picayune* and the *Times Democrat* to allow you and my helpers to catch up on the news."

"To warn them?" Brother Stanislaus probed.

"That, too."

"Come in. We have just returned from Mass at St. Mary's. Although they are no longer students, we have advised them to stay on the school premises until the city calms down. Antonio is teaching himself the piano, and Abraham is taking art lessons and carving wood to maintain his skills."

"I hope to have them back to work in a few weeks, when it's safe. By the way, how are you getting food?" Hearn asked.

The colored and Creole people are bringing us food from the Orleans-Treme Market. The Ursuline nuns are helping us, too. A Croatian man from St. Bernard brings us goat meat every other day. We will survive," Brother Stanislaus lamented.

"I guess you know about the French Market?"

"Oh, yes. We can smell it when the wind blows across the river. Please come in. The boys will be excited to see you."

After a cheerful greeting from the other Brothers, Antonio, and Abraham, Hearn placed the broadsheets on the dining room table for everyone to read. "I want you to study what's in each of these papers. Pay particular attention to pages three and six of the *Times Democrat*. It will give you an update on the insanity going on beyond the walls of this school. Take your time. I will answer any questions you might have," Hearn said, taking a cup of coffee from the Brother's housekeeper.

Antonio, Abraham, and Brother Stanislaus read the *Daily Picayune*, while Brothers Angelo, Lucian, and Michael read the *Times Democrat*. Hearn sipped his coffee and studied the facial features of the readers. He caught Brothers Angelo and Stanislaus exchanging concerned glances. He watched as Antonio used his right index finger as a pointer under each word. After about twenty minutes of reading, Brother Stanislaus pushed himself away from the table, frustrated and agitated.

"Mr. Hearn, what is this Committee of Fifty? What do you know about them? What is their purpose?" Brother Stanislaus asked.

"The mayor, after having arrested the men he believes killed Mr. Hennessy, has asked the city council to authorize him, the mayor, to appoint fifty of his closest friends to investigate the Hennessy case, and *every* Sicilian in New Orleans. Actually, there are eighty-three men, but it appears our elite citizens can't count. He has requested the city council to appropriate tax money to pay for an investigation he claims has been concluded. But the real purpose, I believe, is to go after every Italian in this city."

"Just the Italians?" Brother Angelo asked.

"Yes. However, a group of Italian merchants wrote a letter to the mayor telling him that the Sicilians were not Italians and asking him not to group them together. That tells me the mayor isn't just satisfied with the men he has in prison, now. One can only conclude it will get worse for anyone who has Sicilian blood," Hearn warned.

"Who are these people—The Committee of Fifty?" Brother Stanislaus asked.

"To be blunt, Brother, they are nothing but a gilded vigilante group, not unlike the White League, which used to ride through the Negro settlements with rage in their eyes. I wasn't here then, but I heard stories about the terror they inflicted in New Orleans after the Civil War. My boss, who hates Shakspeare and is from here, tells me it feels the same now as it did then. So, keep these boys behind your walls until this storm blows over."

"Can the governor stop these men?" Brother Stanislaus asked.

Hearn laughed. "Look at the list. Most of the men are attorneys, doctors, cotton brokers, and members of their own secret societies. But one name leaps off the page to me." Hearn pointed to the name of General John Glynn, Jr. "Do you know who that is?"

"No," Brother Stanislaus responded.

"He is in charge of the state's militia and works for Governor Francis T. Nicholls. He is also a member of the Pickwick Club, as is the mayor, and some of the other members of the Committee of Fifty. It's my opinion, Nicholls knows what's going on, and will do nothing to stop it."

"It appears those men in the parish prison are doomed," Brother Angelo intoned.

"There's one slim hope," Hearn said. "Look at page six of the *Times-Democrat,* under the heading *An Important Witness.* "

The Brothers hovered over the broadsheet and read the article. "The mayor and the police chief interviewed a witness last night who said the Sicilians didn't kill Mr. Hennessy?" Brother Stanislaus asked.

"Yes," said Hearn. "But the reporter who wrote the article is not identified, and neither is the witness. Now, the mayor knows what he told the city council, and his Committee of Fifty is false. And about thirty men sitting in that dungeon of Basin Street are falsely accused."

"Why keep the witness's identity secret?" Brother Lucien asked.

"To protect him, or to keep him from testifying. At least six men know who the witness is, but I feel he'll never testify, nor his identity disclosed. Now the public knows, but that won't stop Shakspeare's persecutions of the Sicilians. Keep Antonio and Abraham here until I feel it's safe. Protect the other Sicilian boys who come to school here. There is a political firestorm blowing through the city," Hearn warned. "It can only be extinguished with buckets of blood."

"But the newspapers say the men were at Fabacher's Restaurant, and the police know that. Isn't that called an alibi?" Brother Lucian asked.

"When there is sufficient hate to carry a cause, passion surpasses careful reflection, usually resulting in death. That seems to be the history and future of man," Hearn lamented. "Remember, we had a civil war in this country, and I don't think it's over, yet."

Hearn cast his gaze towards Antonio, who was cradling his head in his hands, a forlorn look etched into his young face. "You look worried, Antonio," Hearn said. "Just stay here inside the school walls for a while. Everything will be fine."

Antonio looked up. Tears welled in his eyes. His chest heaved. His lips were parched. "What's wrong, Antonio?" Brother Stanislaus asked.

Antonio took a sip of water and began, "I know the Marchesis. I met them on the dock in Palermo. We came here on the same ship. They are good people. They didn't do this. Asperi is my friend. He only knows me and the people in the Poydras Market. We came here for a new life. Now we are hunted like wolves."

Chapter 58

October 20, 1890
Orleans Parish Prison
9:00 A.M.

Lionel Adams, A.D. Henriques, and Dominick O'Malley approached the foreboding front gates of the Orleans Parish Prison and requested admission to see their clients, J.P. Macheca, Charles Matranga, Rocco Geraci, and any other man who had been charged with the murder of David C. Hennessy. Though the prison was filled with suspects rounded up by the police in the past several days, Adams specifically mentioned the men associated with Macheca and Matranga. Two deputies escorted Adams, Henriques, and O'Malley to the second floor of the north wing of the prison, away from the wing that housed the Provenzanos.

Once there, the accused, labeled as the *Stuppagghieri* by the newspapers, the mayor, and his Committee of Fifty, met with their attorneys, and O'Malley in a large group cell. Though Macheca and Matranga were wearing fine suits when arrested, two nights in the parish prison have rendered their garments disheveled clumps of cloth. Adams assumed the role of lead counsel and directed most of his comments to Macheca and Matranga, though the others listened attentively.

"First, let me ask everybody how you're doing?" Adams asked.

"Not good," said Macheca. The food is rotten. It goes right through you. The water tastes like tin. All of us are sick. And the sheriff will not let our families bring us food or new clothing. We're sleeping on straw mats. He said he was following the mayor's orders."

"We'll check that out today," Adams said. "I heard rumors that guards and trustees have attacked you. Is that true?"

"They are threatening us. Some are getting paid by the Provenzanos. Some guards tell us what's going on in here. We're not safe," Geraci said.

"Don't trust any of the guards or trustees. Tell them nothing. NOTHING! It will go back to the sheriff and the police," Adams enjoined.

"Mr. Adams, are you still going to prosecute the Provenzanos for attacking my family and workers?" Matranga asked.

"As of right now, I am—if there is a trial. You still claim you were victims of that ambush, correct?"

The Matranga stevedores nodded.

"But who will believe us now? We are accused of killing Hennessy?" Matranga asked.

"Charles, I'm not going to bullshit you. That's a real problem. Right now, the entire city wants you standing on the gallows upstairs. But someone shot at your people, and we must know who. Advocating your victimhood might help you with your trial," Adams asserted. "We have two ambushes. Remember that. Same setup. Dark streets. Same hour of night. Same type of weapons. And somehow, the docks are involved. It seems too coincidental to be two completely separate ambushes, which could lead to different control of the docks below Canal Street."

"If the Provenzanos didn't shoot my people, who did?" Matranga asked.

"If the Matrangas didn't shoot Hennessy, who did?" Adams retorted. "Remember, I wouldn't be in this stinking cell if I believed you killed my friend. Something is going on in this city, and I think these ambushes are related."

"What's next?" Macheca asked.

"We must mount a defense—a strong one, and we have one. Remember, I was with you when David was killed. Many people saw you at Fabacher's Restaurant that night. Your alibis are strong. Remember how strong Provenzano's police alibis were? You are in the same position. According to the newspapers, you had cops watching you from the theater to the time you left Fanny Deckerts on Burgundy Street. That was four o'clock in the morning."

"That asshole Vandervoort claims I was overheard celebrating Hennessy's death. I didn't, Mr. Adams. The chief was a friend of mine, too," Macheca said.

"Didn't you have a row with Hennessy on Canal Street, some time ago. A newspaper reporter was present and reported it. Did you threaten Hennessy?" Adams asked.

"We had a bit of an argument because Caruso heard Hennessy was paying for the Provenzanos' easy treatment here. I told him to stay out of the case. I told him that if he had dirt on us, then he should arrest us now. I didn't threaten him," Macheca said.

"The newspapers said you told him, something to the effect, 'If you know what's good for you, stay out of the Provenzano case.' Did you say that?" Adams probed.

"I might have said something like that, but we were friends, and we parted as friends," Macheca asserted.

Adams cast a gimlet eye around the dimly lit cell. The morning light filtered through the iron grates bolted to the windows, creating dark shadows in each corner of the coffin-like chamber. Adams pulled Macheca into the shadows and whispered, "J.P., did you rent Monasterio's shop across from Hennessy's house? Tell me the truth."

"No. I swear. I have never been on Girod Street. I don't know Monasterio. I never met him. We met for the first time in the yard."

"How did you know his name? Adams asked.

"It's in the newspapers. He's in the next cell with a man and his boy, a crazy guy named Emanuele Polizzi, Peter Natali, and a grocer named Charles Pietza. There are a few more. I don't know their names. A guard told me the police claim we hired them to kill Hennessy. We don't know them. I swear."

"The guards gave you newspapers?" Adams asked.

"Yes."

"They are trying to prod information from you. Be careful. They want you to respond to the articles. Don't. Talk to no one but us," Adams warned. "Understand?"

Macheca nodded.

"The landlady, Mrs. Petersen, said a well-dressed man who looked like you rented the shanty for Monasterio in August. Did you do that?"

"Mr. Adams, Monasterio is a cobbler and did work for Antonio Monteleone. Monteleone was a cobbler before he bought the Commercial Hotel. Maybe the well-dressed man was Monteleone. It wasn't me. Please investigate that," Macheca insisted. "It's in the newspapers. By the way, Monteleone and I buy our suits from the same Jew on Rampart Street. Go ask him. Please."

"I will."

Charles Matranga had a copy of the *Times-Democrat* and spread it open on the table in the center of the cell. "Look here, Mr. Adams. This newspaper says the police and the mayor found a secret witness who said he saw three of the shooters and they ain't Sicilian. Who is the secret witness? Why are we in here?"

"I read that, Charles, and I'm upset the newspaper didn't identify the witness. But the newspaper editors are the mayor's friends. This means the police know his name; the mayor knows his name. Recorder Hollander knows, too. I don't, but I will definitely ask," Adams said.

"Mr. Adams, can I ask a question?" Geraci asked.

"Sure, Rocco."

"The newspapers say the police were following us everywhere that night, because they believed we threatened Mr. Hennessy. Well, if he had been threatened, why have ten cops on us and none on him? The only person watching Hennessy was that Boylan detective, O'Connor, whose boss is a member of the Committee of Fifty. Why not have more cops protecting the chief?"

Adams shot glances towards Henriques and O'Malley. "That's a damn good question, Rocco. Thanks. I plan on asking that soon. Now gather around. I don't want to say this too loudly. Our voices echo off these stone walls." Adams began to whisper. "Some of the newspaper reporters work for the Committee of Fifty. Read the papers, but don't comment on the articles. Trust no one."

"Mr. Adams, before you go, can you tell us why they are doing this to us?" Macheca pleaded.

"It's simple, J.P. The foundation of all hatred is jealousy. If someone hates you, it's because they see in you that which will never exist in them. You and your friends built businesses on blood, hard work, sacrifice, and sweat. You've made names for yourselves and have refused to be their wards. Remember this: those who hate you can't compete with you so that they will steal from you. If a lion hunts and kills its dinner, lazy lions will gather around and steal the carcass," Adams lamented. "New Orleans is just a jungle with cobblestone streets."

><

On their way out of prison, Adams, Henriques, and O'Malley stopped by Warden Davis's office and asked why the Macheca and Matranga families were not allowed admission to the prison with food and clothing. Davis tried to avoid the question by explaining the rules in an ambiguous way.

"Bullshit, Davis," Adams yelled. "What's the real reason. The Provenzanos are treated like kings in this shithole. Is it a matter of money?" Adams asked, throwing a ten-dollar bill on Davis's desk. "Feed my clients decent food."

"Sorry, Mr. Adams. I'm just following the mayor's orders."

"The mayor? The sheriff runs this prison, not the mayor," Adams said.

"Sorry, Mr. Adams. You have to deal with the mayor on this."

"No. I'll deal with the courts on this matter," Adams said, snatching his ten-dollar bill back.

Chapter 59

New Orleans
October 21, 1890
9:00 A.M.

Lionel Adams and A.D. Henriques sat in their law offices poring over the city's newspapers, looking for any commonality or differences in the reportage. The stories resembled each other in content and tone. According to the printed stories, the Italians were guilty of killing David C. Hennessy, and a trial would be just a perfunctory step to the gallows. *The Daily Picayune*, *The Times-Democrat*, *The Daily States*, and the *Daily Item* were controlled by members of the Committee of Fifty, and the blood lust oozed from the pages. Each editor used his broadsheet like a white-hot poker, stoking the fires of fear throughout the downstream narrow streets of New Orleans.

Upriver from Canal Street, however, the atmosphere seemed calm but resolute. It was just a matter of time and theater before the city heard Italian necks snap at the parish prison, thus liberating control of the docks from the "Other People." Indeed, Canal Street's dark, genteel side pined for the moment when the hangman's axe would slice the rope of the trapdoor.

A feverish *Times-Democrat* researcher dug through its musty files back to 1855, and counted how many Italians were killed by other Italians, thus alerting the pearly, powdered uptowners of the violent predisposition of the rufescent-skinned immigrants. But the *Times-Democrat,* in vainglorious double-bold print, listed the names of thirty-five Italians slain by other Italians. Adams laughed and counted the victims.

"A.D., this newspaper claims the Italians are guilty of killing David Hennessy, because other Italians killed thirty-five Italians in thirty-five years. One per year. They must be bad shots," Adams quipped.

"I guess that's why they use shotguns," Henriques joked.

Both attorneys laughed, but were interrupted by Dominick O'Malley's stormy entrance into the office, his face contorted in anger.

"What's wrong, Dominick?" Adams asked.

"I just returned from the prison, and the guards refused me admittance to see our clients. Again, they blamed the mayor. They wouldn't even let the Italian consulate in. The guards said only clergy are being allowed to see the Macheca and Matranga group. Is that legal?"

"No. Every defendant is entitled to counsel," Adams said.

"The guard at the bullpen told me no lawyers or family members can be admitted until they are formally indicted," O'Malley said. "That could be another month. By then, they could die of starvation."

"We will petition the court immediately for access to our clients. By the way, this sealed envelope was slipped under the door before we arrived today. It's addressed to you," Adams said, handing the envelope to O'Malley.

O'Malley opened the envelope, removed a tri-folded letter, and read it quietly. After reading the letter, O'Malley exploded in anger and tossed the letter on Adams' desk.

"Read this shit," O'Malley yelled. "It's from Shakspeare's Committee of Fifty."

Adams adjusted his round steel-frame spectacles and read the letter out loud.

"To D.C. O'Malley:

The Committee of Fifty demands that you drop all connection instantly with the Italian vendetta case, either personally or through your employees. They further demand that you keep away from the parish prison, the Criminal Court, and the recorders' courts while these cases are on trial or under investigation: that you cease all communications with members of the Italian colony; that you cease in person or through your employees to follow or communicate with witnesses in the matter of the assassination of D.C. Hennessy.

The committee does not deny the accused the right to employ a proper agency. Still, they do not intend to allow a man of your known criminal record and unscrupulous methods to be an instrument for harm to the public at their hands. By order of the committee,

Edgar H. Farrar, Chairman."

"What should I do, Lionel?" O'Malley asked.

"We are going to compose an appropriate response and give it to the *Times-Democrat* to publish tomorrow or the next day. They seem to be working for Farrar and his mob. Let them print it. Do you know how to use the new typewriter?"

"With two fingers."

"Never mind. I will write it," Adams said.

"Sir---Your extraordinary communication of this date has just been received. In response, I can but say that I propose to conduct the business of my office without instructions from you or the committee you claim to represent. Being unable to discover whence you derive any authority to "demand" that I should obey your behests with respect to the character of my employment, I shall continue to reserve to myself the right to think and act without regard to your wishes. Later, I shall have occasion to "demand" at your hands the evidence upon which you have ventured to write of my "known criminal record and unscrupulous methods.

D.C. O'Malley"

"Read this, Dominick, and let me know if you approve it," Adams said.

"I like it."

"Good. Take Farrar's letter and your response to the *Times-Democrat* on Camp Street. Demand they print both letters. They will. While you are there, ask them who the secret witness is who told the mayor and the police that three of the shooters were not Sicilian. They printed the story. We need to know who it is."

><

11:00 A.M.

They pushed their scuffed and worn bodies against the guard rails of the *SS Elysia,* as their restive eyes stabbed the grayish-brown streetscape of New Orleans. Their mortal possessions hung in sacks slung over their shoulders. Their first impression of the city was black smoke pouring from the slaughterhouse's exhaust towers, across from the dock, near the end of Esplanade Avenue. Below them, a crowd of men, with scowling countenances, waited for them. Some men carried sheaves of official documents. A double row of tables stretched from the gangway to empty mule-drawn wagons. About twenty police officers, truncheons in hand, guarded the gauntlet the new Sicilian immigrants would tread as they left the *Elysia*. Men dressed in black suits, white shirts, black ties, and black bowlers sat at the tables, as nearly one thousand new immigrants disembarked and stepped on American soil for the first time. The immigrants had wishful smiles cut across their faces. The men at the tables just glowered.

The ship's captain handed the chief immigration officer a list of passengers, which classified the immigrants by name, sex, and place of birth. Newspaper reporters crowded in to gaze at the list and copy the number of new arrivals. Of the 1043 Sicilians, 672 were males, 151 were females, and the balance were children. After being processed, the single men were forced to climb into the wagons and transported, under guard, to the Picayune Tier, where steamboats waited for them for their trip to the plantations upriver from New Orleans. They were not allowed to stay in the city by order of the Committee of Fifty.

Married men, single women, and children were corralled in pens to be processed to various charitable agencies in the city, which would find them housing and work. Women from the Italian Colony petitioned immigration officials to allow some families to join them, as they were from their hometowns of Bisacquino, Cefalu, Corleone, and Giordano, Sicily. Officials didn't object.

From his third-floor bedroom window overlooking Barracks Street, Antonio watched the immigrants as they flowed through the streets of the lower French Quarter with their sponsors. He smiled, but a chill bolted through him when he recognized an old face from Bisacquino, Vincenzo Trambatore, his father's undertaker. Though he wanted to yell to Trambatore, his delight turned to fright, for fear of being recognized. Antonio remembered his name on the list of fugitives posted outside the Italian Consulate on Poydras Street. He now had another reason to hide within the walls of St. Aloysius.

><

Central Police Station

3:00 P.M.

With a gaggle of reporters, a group of men composed of the police commission, city administration, the acting superintendent of police, his secretary, and several members of the Committee of Fifty stormed into the Central Police Station and climbed the stairs to Hennessy's former office. Their mission was to clear Hennessy's office and inventory his possessions, but every man knew the real reason for such a display of power. The group's apparent leader seemed to be George Denegre, an attorney and a member of the Committee. The obsequious newspaper reporters tried to dance out of the way, but soon they became part of the search team. Wright Schaumberg, the mayor's secretary, told everyone to look for documents that could relate to the assassination.

"Look for any documents from Rome, which support the men in the parish prison are members of secret stiletto societies, the *Mafia, Stuppagghieri, Giardinieri*, or fugitives from Italy. Read every paper you find, then box it and seal it. All personal possessions will be delivered to his mother tonight," Schaumberg ordered.

For over three hours, the men read every sheet of paper. Physical memorabilia from Hennessy's years in law enforcement was packed in boxes and given to his mother. Hennessy's safe, which only contained cartridge boxes and old arrest warrants, was opened. No documents from Rome or any other foreign country could be located.

"Mr. Vandervoort, did you ever see any official documents from Rome, indicating the fugitive status of anyone in New Orleans?" Denegre asked.

"No sir," Vandervoort responded. "We would have locked them in the safe or taken them to the District Attorney."

"Where are the threatening letters sent to Mr. Hennessy?" Denegre asked.

"Sir, I only heard about them. I never saw one," Vandervoort admitted.

After a few more moments, the men carried the boxes downstairs to be placed in storage or sent to Hennessy's mother. Captain Billy O'Connor, of the Boylan Detective Agency, and one of the last people Hennessy allegedly spoke to, tried to lift a portrait of the chief from a hook on the wall, but was stopped by Mr. Vandervoort.

"Mr. O'Connor, don't do that. Mrs. Hennessy asked Captain Journee if he would allow her son's picture to remain on the wall in his office. We had no objection," Vandervoort said. O'Connor nodded and released the portrait. As the search team left unsatisfied, Vandervoort twisted off the electric light hanging over the chief's empty desk and left the office in mournful gloom.

><

District Attorney's Office

3:30 P.M.

After filing writs in the clerk's office seeking a court order to see their clients in the parish prison, Lionel Adams and H.D. Henriques visited the office of District Attorney Charles Luzenberg at the southeast corner of St. Patrick's Hall. They found Luzenberg lounging with some of his assistants as they entered the office. Adams and Henriques just stared into the office for a few moments.

"Come in, gentlemen. Please sit down," Luzenberg said.

"No thanks, Charles. We are here to see about tomorrow's Provenzano trial, and to ask you a few questions about the Matranga group," Adams said.

A somber air filled the room. Luzenberg sat up in his chair. "I guess you know there will be no Provenzano trial tomorrow," Luzenberg said.

"No. We didn't know. You never called us. What's going on?" Adams asked.

"Come to court tomorrow morning, and find out," Luzenberg responded. "But I would say, given this city's current state of affairs, it would be improvident to put the Matrangas and Provenzanos shackled together in the same courtroom. I'm sure you would agree the state would not get an impartial jury," Luzenberg said, giggling. "They would probably want to hang the defendants and the victims together."

"So, no trial tomorrow?" Adams asked.

"Be serious, Lionel. Everyone is focused on the Hennessy case. I heard you and A.D. have been retained by Macheca and Matranga. Is that true?"

"Yes."

"Who is paying your fee?" Luzenberg asked.

"That's confidential."

"You know you're going to lose, don't you?"

"No, I won't. Who is the secret witness mentioned in the *Times-Democrat*?" Adams probed.

"What secret witness?" Luzenberg asked.

"The one who told the mayor and Journee, among others, that he saw three of the assassins and they weren't Sicilian. Who is the witness? I want to know his name," Adams demanded.

"I don't know what you are talking about, Lionel."

"Bullshit, Charles. It was printed in the papers. I know you can read. I have the right to know who that witness is, and I want to know now."

"Sorry, I don't know what you are talking about."

Adams leaned across Luzenberg's desk. Their faces were inches apart. They could feel each other's breath. "You son-of-a-bitch, we have known each other for years, and you are going to send innocent men to the gallows? Are you taking orders from the Committee of Fifty, too?" Adams yelled.

Luzenberg backed away from his desk and just stared at his old friend. "I resent you saying that, Lionel. I assure you that Matranga and his *Mafia* will get a fair trial. What happens after that is up to the jury, Judge Baker, or Judge Marr. Now get out of my office," Luzenberg said.

"I just filed writs to see my clients in prison. Do you have any objection to me representing my clients?"

"It's not my prison. It belongs to Villere. Now go. I will see you in Judge Marr's court tomorrow morning," Luzenberg said.

As Adams backed away from Luzenberg's desk, the District Attorney stated, "By the way, tell Dominick O'Malley he can't work for me or you anymore."

"Go to hell," Adams said, as he and Henriques left Luzenberg's office.

><

United States Custom House
4:00 P.M.

An exhausted, street-torn Pasquale Corte stopped his weary horse in front of the Custom House and stepped down from his carriage. He had gone the entire day without food and shared a bucket of water, kept under his carriage seat, with his horse. But he had one last stop on his mission to ensure his countrymen's fair and honest treatment in the parish prison. He paused and looked at the gray, foreboding government building because he knew what he was about to do would stir another tempest in the streets of New Orleans. But after running between the mayor's office, the governor's office, the Central Police Station, St. Patrick's Hall, and the parish prison pleading for his people's health and safety, he had no options left.

Corte entered the front hall of the temple-like structure and went directly to the official telegraph office of the United States government. The telegrapher knew the consulate, but was shocked by his unkempt appearance. "Can I help you, sir?"

"Yes. You know who I am. I want to send a telegraph immediately," Corte said.

"Is it official business between your government and ours, Mr. Corte?"

"Yes. It must go out now," Corte insisted.

"Do you have a prepared statement, sir?" the telegrapher asked.

"No. May I dictate it to you? It's very official and confidential."

"Sure," said the telegrapher, as he took a lined tablet and his graphite pencil in hand. "Go ahead, Mr. Corte. To whom do I address it?"

"Address it to Ambassador Baron Francesco Fava, Italian Embassy in Washington, D.C., and copy the United States Secretary of State, James G. Blain."

The telegrapher looked up at Corte. "Are you sure you want to copy Mr. Blain?"

"I know I am breaking diplomatic protocol copying the Secretary of State, but what is about to happen in New Orleans will create a crisis between my country and yours. Is that official enough?" Corte asked.

"Go ahead, sir," the telegrapher said. And for the next fifteen minutes, Corte slowly dictated an alarming telegram notifying the Italian and United States governments that unnaturalized Italian citizens where being falsely accused, beaten, maltreated, and imprisoned under harsh conditions of the murder of the city's police chief. Corte dictated that the city and state governments are part of the acts in flagrant violation of treaties existing between the two countries.

"Have you tried talking to Sheriff Villere?" the telegrapher asked, knowing what the telegraph would cause if sent.

"Several times. Today, his deputies denied *me* access to my countrymen. Their families can't bring them food or clothes. Other families are telling me that the men are beaten in the yard on a daily basis. Their property has been stolen. And now, I learned today, the sheriff will not let their lawyers visit them. This isn't America!" Corte cried. "Send the telegraph now. Please."

"As you wish, sir," the telegrapher said.

Chapter 60

Criminal District Court
October 22, 1890
9:00 A.M.

A crowd of men and a few curious women gathered in front of St. Patrick's Hall to await the arrival of the first Black Maria from the parish prison. Bets were being taken on which group of Italians would arrive first from parish prison—the Matrangas or the Provenzanos, for today Judge Robert Marr has set the second trial of Provenzanos' alleged ambush on the Matranga stevedores. Since the Grand Jury indicted the case in two tranches, the first for the attack on Vincent Caruso, lodged in Section "B", Judge Baker's court, today's case was for the shooting of Antonio Matranga and Salvatore Sunzeri, lodged in Section "A", Judge Marr's court. Paradoxically, both the defendants and the victims were in the same parish prison, charged with different crimes, but with common ethnic hatred, weak direct evidence, plausible alibi witnesses, and driven by a maniacal *soi desant* elite mob determined to control the docks, if not the entire city.

The rowdy crowd became excited when a Black Maria stopped in front of the courthouse. People were yelling insults, demanding that the Italians be hanged on the nearest lamp post. Lionel Adams, A.D. Henriques, and Dominick O'Malley, veterans of all types of public blood lust, were shocked as they stood on the front steps of St. Patrick's Hall. Newspaper reporters scribbled the emotion of the moment, trying to use every adjective to capture the heat and fever of the street. It churned Adams' guts to watch ordinary citizens descend to the depths of hell. Some men, dressed in business attire, banged on the back doors of the wagon, screaming the vilest epithets towards those locked behind the double doors.

Shotgun-armed deputies used the butts of their weapons to push the crowd back. As one deputy used a large brass key to unlock the heart-shaped lock, the other deputies endured insults for controlling the crowd. When the deputy unlocked the wagon doors and flung them open, the rapacious crowd fell into a numb silence. The wagon was empty.

Dominick O'Malley and A.D. Henriques stepped into the crowd and peered inside the wagon. The deputies looked at the crowd and laughed. After a few moments, the guards slammed the wagon doors shut and told everyone to go home or to work. The mumbling crowd dispersed as the Black Maria rattled down Camp Street on its way back to the parish prison.

"What the hell was that all about, Lionel?" O'Malley asked.

"It appears the Committee of Fifty now controls the parish prison. Let's go to court and see if they control the D.A., and the judge," Adams responded.

As Adams, Henriques, and O'Malley entered Judge Robert Marr's court, they took their seats at the state's table, but no pleasantries were exchanged between Luzenberg and them. Defense attorneys, E.L. Evans, J.C. Walker, and Arthur Dunn, sat at the defense table reading the morning newspapers. The prisoner's dock was empty, and the gallery had a few people, mostly reporters. The aging and frail Judge Marr entered the court and climbed the bench. Once seated, he called the case, and only Luzenberg registered his appearance for the state, while Evans registered his appearance, along with other counsel, for their absent clients, the Provenzanos.

Evans and Luzenberg entered a joint motion to continue the case until sometime in the future. At first, Judge Marr bristled at the motion, claiming too much time had gone by between the offense and this date. While he scolded both sides for wasting his time, he paused, looked around the court, and said, "I have, however, received a letter from Mr. Edgar Farrar, who represents a group of outstanding citizens of this city. He has registered his concern about going forward with this trial at this time. Therefore, to complete the record, I shall read Mr. Farrar's letter and put it into the record.

"New Orleans, October 22, 1890

Hon. Robert H. Marr, Judge, Criminal District Court:

Dear Sir, I am instructed by the Committee of Fifty to request that, if any application is made today for the continuance of the Provenzano trial, you grant it, and that you will instruct the sheriff not to bring the accused into court or through the streets. There are grave reasons for this request that are unnecessary to detail. Your obedient servant,

Edgar H. Farrar, Chairman."

Without any further discussion, Judge Marr continued the Provenzano trial indefinitely.

"Now you know who runs this city," Adams muttered.

><

Lionel Adams' Office
22 Carondelet Street
Noon

Lionel Adams and A.D. Henriques reviewed the law regarding *Mandamus,* a legal procedure where attorneys file writs against a public official to do their job, according to law. Adams and Henriques, after witnessing Judge Marr's obsequious bow to the Committee of Fifty, had no illusions that Marr would order Sheriff Villere to open the gates of his prison so they could visit their clients. They were preparing to appeal Marr's anticipated order.

Across the office, Dominick O'Malley read the newspapers, well aware that newspaper reporters were acting as investigators for the Committee of Fifty. But while reading the *Times-Democrat,* his attention was drawn to another unknown reporter's story regarding his interview with Antonio Monasterio, which occurred in the parish prison.

"Son-of-a-bitch," O'Malley exclaimed. "You won't believe what a reporter just gave us."

"What did you find?" Adams asked.

"A reporter for the *Times-Democrat* interviewed the cobbler who lived across the street from Hennessy."

"Monasterio?" Adams asked.

"Yes. He gave the reporter his whole life story. He arrived in New Orleans on January seventh of this year and moved into a house on Chartres Street between St. Phillip and Dumaine. By the way, Monasterio's arm was in a sling because a cop clubbed him."

"What else?" Adams asked.

"He arrived on a ship named the *Plata,* and got cobbler work from Monteleone's shoe shop at Royal and Customhouse Streets. He told the reporter that Monteleone gave him tools and leather so that he could work from his house. The reporter writes he verified what Monasterio said, but hasn't interviewed Monteleone yet."

"Really?" Adams asked.

"Yeah. The reporter verified the name of the ship and Monasterio's date of arrival. Then he broke into the cobbler shop on Girod Street, and found a workbench, cobbler tools, twenty square feet of sole leather, and five feet of upper shoe leather. Macheca's theory of Monteleone paying to rent the shanty might be true," O'Malley opined.

"In all reports I have read, the police said there was no evidence Monasterio did any cobbler work in the shanty, despite neighbors saying he fixed Mrs. Hennessy's shoes. Now this?" Adams asked. "I know the police lie, but this exonerates Monasterio, the others, and that secret witness. If the cobbler is telling the truth, so is Macheca. It was probably Monteleone who rented Peterson's shanty."

"What do we do next?" Henriques asked.

"We have to wait for an indictment before we start demanding evidence from Luzenberg. But the bastard knows what we know. Adams said that he reads the same papers as the Committee of Fifty," Adams said. "Dominick, did you ask the *Times-Democrat* for the identity of the secret witness?"

"Yes. When I dropped off Farrar's letter and my response, I demanded to know, and they refused to tell me. They said they would print the letters soon."

"Dominick, we need to get someone to watch that shanty. I don't want anything to disappear mysteriously," Adams said.

><

Parish Prison

5:00 P.M.

The rattling of the brass keys echoed through the stone corridors of the north wing of the parish prison. Two guards, accompanied by Warden Davis, opened the cell door where Asperi Marchesi, his father, and other Italians huddled around an old table, slurping drizzly soup and chewing half-cooked meat of an unknown origin. The presence of the prison officials startled the inmates because they had no more personal possessions to surrender for food or blankets. The cell had two large tallow candles for illumination, which cast a lambent glow upon the faces of the jailers. "Get your stuff, kid. The police said they have no evidence on you.

We are releasing you, but get home before it gets too dark," Davis said.

"I'm free?" Asperi asked.

"Yes. The police are releasing you, but your father stays."

"If the police have no evidence on my son, that means they have no evidence on me," Antonio Marchesi pleaded.

"Shut up. Only the boy can leave. Let's go, kid," Davis ordered.

As the guards pushed Asperi through the bull pen, Asperi turned and asked, "Where do I go? I have no family, but my father?"

"Your record says you live at Number 312 Lafayette Street. I suggest you get your dago ass home before it gets too dark," Davis answered. "Now get!"

Asperi walked down Basin Street, passed the cemeteries and brothels. Women of all hues, shades, and sizes beckoned him to come closer to their stoops. Asperi knew he had just escaped one hell; he wasn't going into another, especially one next to a cemetery. He crossed Canal Street, and a beat cop gave him a piercing stare, but said nothing. The teenager thought about running home, but didn't want to draw attention to himself, given his grimy appearance.

When he arrived at Poydras and Basin, he decided to forage for food from one of the stands at the Poydras Market. He knew many of the merchants, as he and his father worked as delivery men for several. When some of the Italian grocers saw Asperi, they approached him as if he were a ghost. They were cautious, but determined to help the kid, who looked like he had been dragged down a chimney. Several Italian women gathered around him and washed his face as they fed him roasted chicken and beans. Some brought him ill-fitting, but clean clothes. Anna Anguzza gave him several bags of food and clothes and told him to go home. "Stay there for a few days, but come back to continue his delivery route," Anguzza said. Asperi hugged and kissed her, as tears rolled down his cheeks.

Asperi, arms laden with sacks of food and stores, walked down Poydras Street to his small apartment on Lafayette Street, but was stopped by two black males. One he recognized as Joseph Williams. The other, he only knew from the market. Williams competed with others to be a deliveryman for the Italian merchants.

"How you got out?" Williams asked.

"They had no evidence on me," Asperi said.

"You did all that whistling, didn't you?" Williams asked.

"I only whistled when I come up on people on a dark street."

"You were the lookout, weren't you?"

"I'm no lookout for anyone," Asperi said.

"You think you going to get your old job back?" Williams asked

"I hope so," Asperi said, as he continued to walk home.

About midnight, the police kicked down the front door of Number 312 Lafayette Street and dragged Asperi out of his bed. They told him to get dressed and arrested him again. They took the frightened boy to the Central Police Station, where he met Captain Dexter Gaster and a few other detectives. Across the room, Asperi saw Joseph Williams talking to reporters from the *Daily Picayune* and the *Times Democrat.*

"You know that colored boy sitting across the room?" Gaster asked.

"I know him from the Poydras Market."

"Did you talk to him earlier this evening at the market?" Gaster asked.

"Yes."

"Did you tell him you whistled as a lookout for the killers of Chief Hennessy?"

"No."

"Didn't you tell him they let you go from the prison because you are going to testify against your father and others?" Gaster asked.

"No. You released me because you have no evidence."

"Now we do. You told Joseph Williams you whistled that night as a lookout, and you are willing to testify against your father and the other men," Gaster growled.

"That's not true. He wants my delivery job," Asperi said, pointing to Williams.

Gaster instructed his detectives to book Asperi Marchesi based on new evidence and book Joseph Williams as a material witness. When Williams realized he was going to jail, he began to protest, but Gaster ignored him.

At the prison, Marchesi was reunited with his father, and Williams was locked in an isolation cell for his own protection.

Chapter 61

October 24, 1890
10:30 A.M.
Number 22 Carondelet Street

Lionel Adams, A.D. Henriques, and Dominick O'Malley sat around the large partner's desk in the middle of Adams' law office, studying the morning papers. It proved to be the only way they could prepare a defense for Macheca, Matranga, and their associates. Since they were banned from the parish prison, and the courts had not ruled on their *Writ of Mandamus*, they had to resort to the broadsheets for news of what was happening with the Hennessy investigation. They knew the papers were decidedly anti-Italian, with the exception of *The Mascot*, so examining each story provided them leads to pursue, as the reporters wasted no ink convicting the Italians before trial.

"Looks like the state's case got a little weaker," Adams said.

"Why?" Henriques asked.

"The police let little Marchesi out of jail because of insufficient evidence. Then, on the word of a colored street peddler, Joseph Williams, they re-arrest him, because the kid told Williams he was turning state's evidence? That makes no sense. Can't wait until Luzenberg puts Williams on the stand," Adams said. "If the kid was cooperating with the police before they released him, why re-arrest him on information they already knew?"

"Hey, look at this," O'Malley interjected. The *Times-Democrat* printed Farrar's letter to me and my response. This is great. I will never back down from those silk-stocking assholes."

"That should piss them off," Henriques said. "Read on. They are calling for a mob meeting next Monday night in Lafayette Square. Farrar claims it's to update the public on what they are doing. Isn't that why we have newspapers?"

"The Committee of Fifty?" Adams asked.

"Yep. It's on page three of the *Times-Democrat*. I think they are beginning to panic because their case is weak. First, a reporter finds cobbler tools and leather in the shanty, they release the kid, only to re-arrest him on flimsy evidence, the alibis are irrefutable and supported by the police, and they have a secret witness who said three of the shooters were not of the 'Sicilian Element,'" Henriques said.

"The *Daily Picayune* reports gangs of police and civilians are still conducting midnight raids throughout the city, looking for the assassins. If they had enough evidence to lock up our clients, why are they still searching?" Adams asked.

"When I was in law school, I read about the French Revolution and a guy named Robespierre who conducted midnight raids throughout Paris, with his *Comité de Salut Public,* not unlike Shakspeare's Committee of Fifty," Henriques said.

"What happened to him?" O'Malley asked.

"There was a revolt inside a revolt, and Robespierre and his committee lost their heads on the guillotine," Henriques responded. "An unfortunate, unexpected turn of events."

"Do you know where we can buy a used guillotine?" O'Malley joked.

><

Noon

Cotton Exchange Building

The gilded *Penetralium* of the Committee of Fifty sat on the fourth floor of the Cotton Exchange Building, just yards away from Lionel Adams' law office. A gaggle of reporters gathered outside the Exchange, as rumors hummed through the crowd about members of the Committee resigning. The articles in the morning paper fanned the rumor's flames, because of the published letters of Edgar Farrar and Dominick O'Malley, plus the upcoming meeting set for the following Monday night in front of City Hall. Many businessmen expressed concern about Farrar and how much power the mayor had ceded to him. With the accused locked away and the raids continuing, the even-tempered members of the population thought calling for a mass meeting on the next Monday exceeded the authority of the Committee.

Even an editor of the *Times-Democrat*, Robert Warren, expressed concerns about the Committee of Fifty acting like a super Grand Jury, conducting secret investigations, and interviews on the fourth floor of the Exchange. The newspaper openly expressed curiosity about why the Hennessy investigation was not conducted from the Central Police Station. Warren openly challenged Shakspeare and Farrar to cease acting like a city agency and allow the police and District Attorney to do their jobs. In his editorial, Warren admonished the Committee of Fifty not to suspect every Italian in New Orleans of the murder of Hennessy, and to recognize that there were good and bad from every country living in the city.

Despite Warren's editorial, the Committee of Fifty continued their operations and prepared for the mass meeting scheduled for Monday, October 27, 1890. Newspaper reporters listed the members' names as they entered the Cotton Exchange, including Maurice Hart, George Denegre, Joseph Hassinger, S.P. Walmsley, J.D. Houston, Edgar Farrar, and others. The reporters were stunned when a carriage bearing the mayor and his secretary, Wright Schaumberg, stopped in front of the building. As the mayor and his secretary brushed past reporters, they ignored the fusillade of questions, but the mayor was heard muttering, "I'm here to stop that meeting."

No member tendered their resignation from the Committee.

Chapter 62

St. Aloysius Academy
October 25, 1890
10:00 A.M.

Laurence Hearne rang the front gatebell of St. Aloysius. His arms laden with the city's newspapers, Hearn was delivering the Brothers, Antonio, and Abraham, the city's news, while they were continuing their monastic vigil behind the red-brick walls of the school. Brother Stanislaus greeted the reporter and allowed him into the school's dining room, where the other Brothers, Antonio, and Abraham had gathered. Hearn distributed several copies of the local newspapers, which were ravaged by the hungry eyes of people immured inside a school because of fear.

"How are things going in here?" Hearn asked. "Are you getting enough food?"

"Oh yes. The Italian ladies in the neighborhood bring us food every day. You can smell them coming down Chartres Street. They are so kind," Brother Stanislaus praised. "How are things going in the city?"

"Well, as the papers say, things are very uncertain out there. I understand the raids are still going on, despite the mayor praising his police department's quick action in apprehending the assassins. In my opinion, it's all a farce."

"The city sent out an education inspector and asked how many boys we had enrolled. I lied. I told him fifty, but we have less than that. The Italian ladies and the Ursuline nuns escort the Italian boys to school. Sometimes, several police officers stand across the street and watch the boys enter the yard. The boys are scared, and their concentration on their lessons has slacked off. They hear what's going on throughout the French Quarter. With the pleasant weather, we keep the windows open. But the boys stiffen with fear whenever they hear the clop of horses' hooves or wagon wheels against the cobblestones. They are afraid of the police and the men who work for the Committee."

I understand, Brother," Hearn said. "The Italian school at Rampart and

Bienville Street had to close down, because the kids are afraid to walk to school."

"When will it be safe for the kids to play in the street and walk home again?" Brother Stanislaus asked.

Hearn picked up a copy of the *Times Democrat*, and showed the Brother the story about the *SS Elysia*, and what happened to over seven hundred single Italian males. "Without any protest, they just herded them up like cattle, and shipped them upriver to cut cane and cotton."

"Isn't that illegal?"

"It violates the *Anti-Padrone Act*, but it seems no one wants to enforce it," Hearn said. "We must protect Antonio and Abraham from being snatched up and sent to a plantation. They are single and finished school," Hearn said.

"When I lied to the city inspector, I included them in my enrollment. I will keep them here until it's safe. Father Fontebuis brings them books that are beyond our highest grade level. So, it's true they are continuing their education," Brother Stanislaus said.

Antonio looked up from his broadsheet and remembered seeing the Sicilian undertaker, Trambatore, walking beneath his window. His guts spun with fear, knowing not too far beyond his protective walls lived one man who knew his real name and why he was in New Orleans. He knew even an unexpected friendly reunion would be his doom. From that moment on, his mind searched for ways to conceal himself, once it was safe to step beyond the walls.

"Brother, there's another problem brewing like hot coffee," Hearn continued. "The Committee of Fifty is planning a Monday night mass meeting in Lafayette Square. The other side of Canal Street is boiling in rage. Some want the meeting to go forward, and some, even the editor of the *Daily*, printed an editorial condemning the meeting. Read this," Hearn said, pointing to the editorial.

"We feel it our duty here to warn the Committee, to warn the city authorities, to warn the people that it will be a most difficult and delicate matter to handle the thousands of men who will assemble in Lafayette Square to hear the report of the Committee of Fifty upon the progress that has been made in discovering the murderers of Mr. Hennessy, and to consider the state of affairs that the Committee will, at least, be expected to reveal. The

Committee means well, but it is treading on dangerous ground to summon a mob, for that is what will be found assembled upon the summons that is published in this morning's paper. The Hennessy murder has stirred this city to its foundations. No theme could call together so vast a concourse of people of all classes as this proclamation by the Committee. Let the authorities take warning."

"Oh my God," exclaimed Brother Stanislaus. "This is much more serious than I have ever imagined. For a newspaper that is friendly with the mayor to be sending such a warning is frightening. This mob could turn on the entire Italian population, more than the police and the Committee are doing every night."

"It's worse, Brother. They could rush the prison. I don't think the police would stop them. And the sheriff has family members on the Committee, so his deputies will probably surrender the jail," Hearn warned.

"Where is the proclamation the Committee published in today's paper?"

"Hearn, flip the broadsheet over to page six. Here is the pertinent part," Hearn said, pointing to the threatening verse.

"We believe this committee speaks the unanimous sentiment of the good people of New Orleans when it declared that the vendettas must cease and the assassinations must stop. To these things, we intend to put an end, peacefully and lawfully if we can, violently and summarily if we must. Upon your willingness to give information depends which of these courses we shall pursue. We pledge the manhood of this community to protect and defend all those who come forward to assist and give information.

By Order of the Committee of Fifty:

Edgar H. Farrar, Chairman."

"My God, what's going on out there? Another war?" Brother Stanislaus asked.

"It's only my opinion, but it appears all civil authority has been given to this Committee by the mayor and city council. They are conducting their affairs from the Cotton Exchange Building with funds from the city.

They control the newspapers, to some extent, and they have the street muscle to enforce their will," Hearn asserted.

"Street muscle?"

"Again, it's only my opinion, but I walk the streets of this city at night. They know I'm a reporter, so they leave me alone. I see what they are doing and why?"

"They? Who? Why?" Brother Lucian asked.

"The Committee has employed the political muscle of the democrats. There are two groups: one is The Ring and the other is The Regulators. Both groups hold allegiance to the mayor and his closest friends, J.D. Houston, William Sterling Parkerson, and the Committee. These are shrewd political operators who hate the Italians, and didn't like Hennessy much either," Hearn said.

"What else can you tell us?" Brother Stanislaus asked.

"I heard from the colored and creole community that J.P. Macheca and Frank Romero were organizing them, and the Italian Colony into a voting bloc. They want to offer a candidate for mayor and the city council. This, along with the Italian control of nearly half the docks of the city, has lit the fuse on a powder keg. And it won't stop until there is blood weeping on the streets of this city," Hearn lamented. "Like most things in human history, it's a venomous cauldron of money, politics, and power."

"What can we do?" Brother Stanislaus asked.

"Stay here and conduct your classes as normal. Let's see what develops Monday night. I will be in Lafayette Square. After the meeting, I will run back to my office on Camp Street and call you on the telephone. But we must be careful what we say on that device. All calls go through the switching station on Baronne Street, and Captain Journee has officers listening to all phone calls."

Chapter 63

October 27, 1890
City Hall
11:00 A.M.

The corridor to the mayor's office overflowed with reporters from every newspaper in the South, while the city's telegraph operators were flooded with inquiries from nearly every newspaper in the North, most notably from the *New York Times, Chicago Tribune,* and the *Philadelphia Inquirer*—all cities with large Italian populations. Suddenly, Joseph A. Shakspeare's nine-day-old proclamation of war against New Orleans' Italian Colony was no longer confined to the grand crescent of the Mississippi River. The news of the brutal investigation into David C. Hennessy's murder had reached the eyes of millions, including President Benjamin Harrison, Secretary of State James G. Blaine, and Baron Francesco Fava, Italy's Ambassador to the United States. It was clear Pasquale Corte's telegraph had ripped down the veils of the parochial corruption, for which New Orleans was renowned, since the years preceding the Civil War. To the Republicans in Washington, D.C., New Orleans had reverted to the antebellum days, where a man's skin color or national origin determined his station in and for life.

The mayor's secretary, Wright Schaumberg, dodged reporters' entreaties until two from *The Daily Picayune* jammed into a corner, shoved a telegraphed dispatch from New York into his face, and demanded a response.

"Read this. What the hell is going on with the mayor's Committee of Fifty?" one reporter demanded. "Read this."

Schaumberg pinched his spectacles on his nose and read the dispatch. It read:

"The Italian ligation at Washington, upon receiving official reports from the Italian Consulate of New Orleans, in a friendly, yet firm letter, called attention to the State Department to the Proclamation

of the mayor of New Orleans, which they claim is an unjust accusation and gives much provocation to Italians in this country. Mr. Blain, it is said, has telegraphed the Governor of Louisiana regarding this matter."

"So, what do you want to know?" Schaumberg asked.

"Has the mayor spoken to Governor Nicholls, yet?" a reporter asked.

"I don't know, but if he has, and if I know of the content of the conversation, I wouldn't tell you."

"Has the mayor met with the governor yet?"

"I will say they plan on meeting today, before tonight's meeting in Lafayette Square. That's all I have to say on the matter. Excuse me," Schaumberg said, slipping past the reporters.

About thirty minutes later, reporters spied the mayor and his retinue slip out the Lafayette Street door, mount carriages, and speed off.

><

Noon

Royal and Ursuline Streets

Despite moving the Louisiana state capitol from New Orleans to Baton Rouge in 1879, Governor Francis Tillou Nicholls maintained a private-walled residence, ironically, deep in the Italian Colony. Having heard the Secretary of State had sent the governor a telegram regarding a formal complaint about the mayor's statements and the brutal treatment of Italians in and out of the parish prison, Mayor Joseph A. Shakspeare, accompanied by the governor's local state militia commander and a member of the Committee of Fifty, General John Glynn, and others called upon the governor.

The governor's French Quarter residence, guarded by members of the militia, sat behind ten-foot walls and was invisible to pedestrian or wagon traffic. When the mayor entered Nicholls' receiving parlor, the governor remained seated in his leather chair, as he had lost his left arm and foot for the Confederacy during the war. Such wounds and his military record bestowed upon Nicholls a reverent status. A faint coal fire burned in the grate of his marble fireplace to chase the October chill from the room. The pleasantries were brief and perfunctory. Nicholls wasted no time expressing his concern about how the city was handling the Hennessy case.

"Joseph, it's not every day I get a telegram from the Secretary of State, complaining about you. Mr. Blain's inquiry seems to be accompanied by a threat to intervene if New Orleans cannot handle the Italian question within the law. How are you going to handle this meeting tonight? Will this mob your Committee has summoned become a concourse of marauders?" Nicholls asked.

"No, Governor. Your General, John Glynn, who is part of the Committee and a member of my Pickwick Club, is assisting in providing security for the meeting," Shakspeare said.

Nicholls looked at Glynn. "General, do not let anyone cross Canal Street. There are reporters from the North waiting for some type of insurrection. We don't need the Union, I mean, the United States Army living among us, again," Nicholls ordered.

"Joseph, that little Italian Consulate has been a pain in my ass. Every day, he rings my bell and demands to see me, complaining about how his countrymen are being treated. I have ignored him, which probably provoked him to telegraph his ambassador. I'm sure he will be in Lafayette Square tonight. Do you have enough police officers to secure the square?"

"Yes, Governor. We will have the entire square covered," the mayor assured.

"Is there any way you can stop this meeting? Nicholls asked.

"The Committee has already erected a stage on the square with electric lights strung around it. I will be there, too," Shakspeare said.

"If anything goes wrong, you will get the blame. You do understand that?" Nicholls asked.

"Nothing will go wrong. When we leave here, we will go to the Cotton Exchange and meet with the committee. I want to make sure their agenda does not include a march on the prison, or anywhere else."

"That's what I am afraid of. The reporters want that. Keep it brief and to the point. And disperse them in all directions. Don't let them congregate on the corners or start walking towards Canal Street. Put men on horseback and guide them uptown. Put your sheriff on alert until midnight. General Glynn, arrest any group determined to march on the prison or through the French Quarter. I want this meeting to be conducted peacefully. Understand?" Nicholls demanded.

Everyone nodded.

"Let me be honest with everyone," Nicholls began to whisper. "I want those bastards to hang as much as you do, but it must be done legally, or Washington will be down our throats. We don't need another 1874 on Canal Street. We have our sovereignty restored, and can't do anything that will jeopardize our states' independence." Nicholls said.

As the men stood to leave, Nicholls said, "Joseph, I appreciate you sending some of those Italians from the *Elysia* to my plantation in Thibodeaux. We needed them."

"What about Blaine?" Shakspeare asked.

"I'll send him a response after the meeting," Nicholls said coyly.

><

Cotton Exchange Building
1:30 P.M.

A crowd gathered at the corner of Carondelet and Gravier, waiting for the members of the Committee of Fifty to arrive for their meeting. Pasquale Corte and a number of Italian businessmen shouldered their way into the throng. Father Anthony Manoiritta, from St. Anthony's Parish on Rampart Street, stood in the crowd, wearing his black *biretta* and his Bible wrapped in his folded arms. When the mayor arrived, he pushed through the crowd and was followed by Algernon Badger, Walter Denegre, General John Glynn, and other members of the Committee. With Farrar's consent, the Italians were admitted, along with their priest, which stunned the reporters in the crowd.

After taking the stairs to the fourth floor, the mayor was greeted by other members of the Committee. He admonished them to conduct tonight's meeting with order and decorum. He said his police department would be deployed in the crowd and would not tolerate any form of rioting.

Pasquale Corte stood and asked, "May I ask what the purpose of such a large meeting is at a time when feelings against Italians are so raw?"

"The purpose of the meeting, sir, is to inform our citizens of the progress we are making in the Hennessy investigation," Farrar responded.

"Can you not just tell the newspapers of that progress? Besides, you claim to have the assassins in prison, but raids in the Italian Colony continue. Why?" Corte asked.

"We must rid this city of all the Italian secret societies, which perpetrate their *vendetta* murders. We will ask the crowd to report any members of those societies they know," Farrar responded.

"Respectfully, Mr. Farrar, there will be no Italians at the meeting, besides a few men from the Italian business community and me. We know of no secret societies, and your petition to divulge names will only lead to more raids and suspicion."

"I'm sorry, Mr. Corte, but that's my answer," Farrar said.

Farrar turned his attention to the newspaper reporters in the room. "If there be a class of people wanting to sow fear and hate in New Orleans, it's this city's newspapers. Please report the news, and not use provocative language in your stories."

This statement didn't sit well with the reporters, who caused each paper to demand a representative on the stage that night. Farrar agreed.

><

Lafayette Square

8:00 P.M.

They poured from every street surrounding Lafayette Square. Bored men with little on their minds, but hate and shedding blood. Killing excited their primal lust and nature. It gave them purpose. They drew fidelity and identity from their fellow twisted souls, marching shoulder-to-shoulder to receive the Committee's benediction through a shattered stained-glass of glazed self-importance—men of status and wealth.

An illuminated stage stood on the south end of Lafayette Square, ringed with lights and kerosene torches, like a stationary Mardi Gras float. Soon, the city's royalty would ascend the steps and begin to toss morsels and trinkets of diseased anger, which would portend irreversible events to come. Like a flock of hungry raptors, the crowd gathered, waiting for the words of carrion to nourish their empty souls.

Lawrence Hearn leaned against an oak tree near the stage. Through lambent light, he could see the veins and cords bulge in the necks of the raging fools. A few feet away, Lionel Adams, A.D. Henriques, and Dominick O'Malley stood waiting for the flame to light the fuse. Uniformed police, truncheons in hand, waded through the crowd, looking for any type of weapon or pockets of boisterous or drunken men. It didn't take long for a legion of civic leaders to ascend the steps and greet their public. The crowd's cheers fed their insatiable egos, as a sinister symbiosis wafted over the crowd, and under the boughs of the oak trees. Hearn removed his notebook from his pocket and wrote one word: "frightening." This would be the one word he would build his writing around for his next article, if not his life.

Like a specter of the old Confederacy, the mayor, council, civic leaders, and members of the Committee of Fifty stood upon the stage, gazing out over the bowler hats of their faithful. Through the footlights of the stage, one could see clouds of cigar smoke hovering over the crowd. To add a faint air of militancy and propriety to the gathering, the Master of Ceremonies, Colonel Benjamin Eschelman, took the podium. Eschelman was the former commander of New Orleans' Washington Artillery, which was subsumed under the command of General James Longstreet during the Civil War. He stood behind Robert E. Lee when he surrendered to Ulysses S. Grant at Appomattox Courthouse. His presence lent gravity to the situation because he was apotheosized as a war hero, despite defeat.

Eschelman exploited his powers of rhetoric and reminded the gathering of the Committee's purpose. His oratory called down the wisdom of God to descend upon all citizens who seek justice and law. He reminded the crowd that a disease had beset the city, and it was up to the public to rid it from their midst with the full import of the law, established by man. His brief speech ignited the crowd, as they jumped and cheered. Dominick O'Malley began to snicker at the cheap thespian display, and wondered loudly, "How can so many people be so fooled at one time?"

"Shush," warned Adams. "Someone might hear you. Besides, the Committee still wants your ass hanging from a tree, after what Judge Alfred Roman told them about your past."

"I understand. But Roman couldn't prove anything against me then or now, despite my record. Am I still on the case?"

"Yes. They don't control us," Adams said.

"By the way, is this the same Committee of Fifty who warned Judge Marr not to have the second Provenzano trial, because they feared a mob in the streets?"

"Yep. But they didn't control the city then. Now they do, thanks to the mayor," Adams said. "They have the judges and the District Attorney under their boots, too."

As he yielded the podium, Eschelman began a vainglorious introduction to the next speaker—Edgar Farrar. He reminded the crowd to lean heavily upon his words and give him the support he needed.

As the crowd cheered, Farrar waved his arms to be heard. He measured his words with caution and certitude. *The Daily Picayune* printed:

"Your fellow citizens who were appointed by the Mayor under a resolution of the City Council to investigate the existence of murder societies in this city and to devise means to stamp them out and deem it necessary to call this meeting to lay before you their views of the situation, and to test whether they are supported to obtain from you, the people, the authority and mandate, additional to that conferred by their original appointment. We were appointed at a grave condition of affairs. Your beloved Chief of Police was waylaid at the threshold of his own home and assassinated.

"Every fact, apparent and since discovered, shows that the assassination was a result of a widespread conspiracy, and that at least a half dozen men were personally engaged in the killing. We owe to our duty as American citizens to try the law first and to try it thoroughly. We beseech you to be patient and law-abiding.

"The progress of the law is slow and expensive. The thorough investigation of the work we have in hand will take a very long time. It may become necessary to offer large rewards. It may become necessary to bring witnesses from abroad. We have been promised the fullest cooperation from the representatives of the Italian government, and the leading Italian citizens and societies among us, and discover whether they exist or not, and if they do exist, we must then destroy them at any hazard."

Farrar made his final and important appeal. He wanted the good citizens of New Orleans to donate thirty thousand dollars to help their investigation, and see it to a successful conclusion. Completing his appeal, Farrar requested the gathering to give the Committee of Fifty all the authority it needs to complete their investigation.

The crowd cheered.

"Well, I see what's really going on here," Adams said, under the yelps of the raucous crowd. "This city is now under the control of the Committee, and wants the people to support them. Once these damn fools give them money, they can't deny them the power. The money will also subsidize their losses on the docks, while New Orleans bleeds."

"What about the secret witness who saw three of the assassins, and they weren't Sicilian?" Henriques asked. "Who is he, and who are the three shooters?"

"That would kill the Committee's appeal for money. Besides, that witness and the three shooters are probably somewhere in this crowd, and the Committee knows them."

The last speaker was Charles Buck, an attorney and member of the Committee, and a member of the Cotton Exchange. After repeating Farrar's points, he made an ominous statement, which shook Adams.

"Let not our patience be exhausted, until all lawful measures fail."

The crowd cheered louder. Then Buck, also a member of William Sterling Parkerson's Regulators, drilled in with the Committee's true motive for the gathering.

"The people are the makers of the law, and the people are also its executors. In that sense, we appeal to you, and in the spirit of the law, we ask for your help to enforce it."

The crowd, feeling part of a cause larger than their collective selves, erupted in a prolonged cheer, as men waved their bowlers and derbies in the night sky.

"What did Buck mean by that last comment?" O'Malley yelled into Adams' ear.

"Stitch it together. They know our clients didn't kill Hennessy. The state's case is weak. Their witnesses are weak. Our alibis are strong. They're hiding the secret witness. They know who the three shooters are. Several days ago, the Committee placed an appeal in all the newspapers asking the Italian Colony to spy on one another, and come forward with names of Italian fugitives—for a reward. I fear our clients are doomed, and the Italian Colony might devour itself, out of fear or reward."

As the crowd grew more animated, First District Police Commissioner and friend of David Hennessy, W. H. Beanham, seized the ignescent moment. He stood before the stage and waved his arms for silence. His red hair and wide waxed mustache, illuminated by the stage's footlights, cast a rufescent halo around his round head. And once the cheers subsided, he spoke and demanded that the crowd join in a resolution giving the

Committee all the means and power it needed to stamp out the murderous societies in New Orleans. When he asked for a voice vote, the crowd gave fiery assent.

After the speakers finished their appeal, the less-than-an-hour gathering peacefully dispersed, while the Committee of Fifty swelled with their new power. And as promised, Hearne raced back to his office, and called St. Aloysius Academy, and said one word to Brother Stanislaus: "Frightening."

Chapter 64

Executive Mansion
Washington, D.C.
November 18, 1890
9:00 A.M.

On the second floor, on the elliptic side of the Executive Mansion on Pennsylvania Avenue, the twenty-third President of the United States, Benjamin Harrison, thumbed through a stack of letters and telegrams his secretary placed on his large mahogany desk. Harrison, a Union Colonel during the Civil War, fought alongside General William T. Sherman in Atlanta and knew well the Southern condition before, during, and after the war. As an Indiana Republican, he studied, during the battles in the South, the means, methods, and motives of why the Democrats riven his country to preserve their culture, ethos, and values. He understood the death of his nation's youth, fighting a war that he knew would never end, despite handshakes and treaties. He didn't hold his beloved North guiltless, for a battle between families cuts deep scars, which never heal. His life experiences gave him unique insight into the dark souls of man, no matter what color they wore.

As he sat behind his desk, the morning light flowed across his shoulders, casting a grayish hue upon the communications between New Orleans and Washington, D.C., and between Washington, D.C., and Rome. Images of cultural clashes flashed through his mind as he read about how Italian immigrants were allegedly being treated in the South's largest city. During his administration, new states were being admitted into the Union, and a new nation began to emerge, but prejudices festered, threatening the bloom of a new nation.

From the West, he heard of the inhumane conditions of Chinese immigrants. His mind drifted back to the Irish riots in New York during the war. However, New Orleans posed a completely different threat because of its international implications, specifically regarding America's warm relations with Italy. If what he was reading was true, Harrison had a major conflict on America's horizon, which would impact all of its major east coast cities and their labor force. A growing America needed an assimilated and welcomed workforce, devoid of reprised antebellum prejudices. But America would not be the world's dumping ground for its criminal class or fugitives, for that would defeat the purpose of lawful immigration.

Harrison looked at the old grandfather's clock standing sentinel against the wall, as it chimed nine times. Punctually, Secretary of State James Blaine was escorted into the President's office. Both men, from a distance, could be taken as brothers, except that Blaine was taller. Both men had gray hair and closely trimmed gray beards. After the warm greetings and coffee being served by the President's staff, their blue eyes locked. They knew they had a problem.

"James, what is going on in New Orleans?" Harrison asked.

Blaine opened his valise and removed several documents and broadsheets. "Mr. President, on October 15th last, the Superintendent of Police in New Orleans was assassinated. According to newspapers, the city's mayor immediately blamed their Italian or Sicilian community for the murder. The mayor formed a citizens' committee to root out all Italian criminals and bring them to justice. This committee seems to be at the heart of the issue, because it appears it is composed of the city's leading citizens, and claims their commercial interests are now under the control of something known as the *Mafia.*"

"*Mafia*?" the President asked.

"I had my staff research it, and it seems the *Mafia* is loosely known as an organization of Italian and Sicilian criminals, which have entered into America through all of our major ports, including Boston and New York. But in New Orleans, the city claims this *Mafia* has taken over the docks along the Mississippi River, and controls the city's commerce."

"If that is true, this *Mafia* needs to go and go now," Harrison said.

"Well, that's where the dispute rests. The Italian Consulate in New Orleans, the Honorable Pasquale Corte, has sent me and the Italian Ambassador, Baron Francesco Fava, telegrams regarding this case and how the Italians are being treated in New Orleans. He also claims the Italians are innocent. Upon realizing the depth of the problem, I sent Louisiana's governor an official inquiry," Blaine said.

"Who's the governor down there?" Harrison asked.

"His name is Francis T. Nicholls."

"Oh, I remember that name from the war. He was a Confederate General who was wounded several times and lived. Tough Bastard," Harrison said. "What did you tell him?"

Blaine handed the President his telegram of October 21, 1890.

"Department of State

Washington, October 21, 1890

His Excellency, the Governor of Louisiana.

The Italian minister earnestly represents that, according to advice from the Italian consul in New Orleans, the mayor of that city has caused the arrests of innocent persons and issued proclamations tending to excite the whole Italian colony. The minister is confident that the great body of Italians in New Orleans repudiate with horror the act of a few criminals, and have no other desire than to see the law take its course and punish the murderers of the chief of police.

JAMES G. BLAIN"

"Who's the mayor? What proclamation? What did he say? Are the Italians innocent?" Harrison asked.

"According to Ambassador Fava, the police, on the orders of the mayor, have imprisoned many Italians and Sicilians in a jail unfit for habitation. Something akin to Andersonville in Georgia, during the war."

Harrison, remembering touring that prison with General Sherman, became noticeably angry. "I still have nightmares of seeing that place," Harrison said. "New Orleans has a prison like that?"

"I hear it's full of vermin and fifth. It's a huge stone fortress, with a yard surrounded by high walls controlled, in part, by other inmates."

"Who's the damn mayor, and what did he say?" Harrison asked.

Blain handed the President a copy of the New Orleans *Daily Picayune* dated October 19, 1890. Blain followed the President's eyes as he read Shakspeare's proclamation.

"I cannot believe what I just read. This is an abject declaration of war upon the Italian people of New Orleans. No wonder the Ambassador is upset. Who's on this Committee? From where do they get their power? Nicholls is tolerating this?" Harrison asked.

"It's known as the Committee of Fifty and is composed of wealthy businessmen, attorneys, and some doctors. One of Nicholls' generals is a member of this Committee. Many have an interest in the cotton industry, which competes for stevedores with the foreign comestible industries, namely, bananas, oranges, lemons, and other citrus products. It appears the Italians control the stevedores, which creates friction with the cotton barons in Louisiana. This Committee, all Democrats, claim there are secret Italian societies in New Orleans, while Committee members have their own secret societies," Blain responded.

"Are you telling me a police chief was killed over bananas and cotton?" Harrison asked.

"Sir, I think it's much deeper. I have asked the Attorney General to join us soon. He has more details on the matter. But, I am concerned about our relations with Italy, as their Ambassador has cabled Rome to apprise them of the situation."

"Did Nicholls ever respond to your communication?"

"Tersely, Blain said, as he handed the President Nicholls' response.

"New Orleans, La, October 28, 1890

Hon. J.G. Blaine

Washington:

I do not appreciate any trouble; there was, for a time, some excitement resulting from the killing of the chief of police and the manner of his taking off, but there is no occasion, and has been no occasion, for any executive action or unusual action in the premises.

FRANCIS T. NICHOLLS

Governor"

"Did you respond to Nicholls' ridiculous explanation?" Harrison asked.

"No, sir. I had my assistant, Alvey Adee, send Baron Fava Nicholls' response."

"Has Fava responded?"

"Yes. This morning, before I came here, he sent me a letter telling me his Consulate in New Orleans sent him a letter explaining, in detail, how the Italians are being treated. To support his claim, Corte appended a copy of a letter he sent to the Orleans Parish Grand Jury, requesting a formal state investigation. Fava is also formally requesting our assistance in the matter," Blain said, handing the President Fava's of today and Corte's letter of November thirteenth, last.

The President took several minutes to read the communications. Fava's letter was only three paragraphs long, but Corte's eleven-paragraph-long letter included the names of six Italian citizens imprisoned, but not yet formally charged, who bear the bruises and scars of beatings at the hands of inmates, deputy sheriffs, and police officers. Some claim to have money and property stolen from them, and Pietro Monasterio was denied medical attention. Corte also quoted the mayor's denial of maltreatment of the Italians in the prison.

"This is an outrage, and Corte's invocation of our treaty between Italy and America is well asserted. The essence of diplomacy is reciprocity. We can't put our citizens at risk while they're in foreign countries. I am particularly disturbed by Corte's assertion to the Grand Jury, '*You are, no doubt, aware that the eyes of the world are cast on this trial, so much as to have provoked the formation of an extra-judicial body having in view only the Italian element.*'" Harrison exclaimed. "What is this '*extra-judicial body*' Corte writes about?"

"The mayor's Committee of Fifty, I mentioned earlier," Blaine explained.

"Apparently, some people in Louisiana have learned nothing from Reconstruction. James, send Corté's letter to Nicholls. Before we take any action, the governor must be fully apprised of the allegations," Harrison said.

"Yes, sir."

As the President read Corte's letter again, Attorney General William H.H. Miller entered the President's office. Miller, a tall, distinguished man, and attired in a black cut-away suit, was warmly greeted by the President and the Secretary of State.

"Thank you, William, for joining us on short notice, but it seems we have a problem brewing in New Orleans," Harrison said.

"It appears to be serious, Mr. President," Miller said.

"Tell me what you know," Harrison said.

"Our U.S. Attorney in New Orleans is William Grant. He has mailed me the newspapers from New Orleans since the day of the Hennessy assassination. I have exchanged telegrams with him, and to put it bluntly, the situation in New Orleans seems dire."

"How dire?" Harrison asked.

"It's a very complicated matter, which has all the indicia of deep social strife brewing in that city. As you remember, sir, there was a great battle in the streets of New Orleans over the gubernatorial election of 1874. Again, it was Democrats versus Republicans. Many people were killed, and many were wounded. The scars of that battle compounded the scars of Union occupation during the war. To many in New Orleans, the war will never be over," Miller lamented.

"How do the Italians fit into this?" Harrison asked.

"About the time the war in 1874 was being fought, the planter class started bringing in laborers from Southern Europe, specifically Italy, Sicily, Croatia, and Greece. None of these immigrants knew about the Civil War or its reasons. They landed on the cities docks, and put to work on Louisiana' plantations as a labor force to replace the Negroes, who left Louisiana and moved North. Essentially, the immigrants were now the new slaves, but were paid meager wages. If you remember, sir, Congress passed the *Anti-Padrone Act of 1874*, which forbade involuntary servitude, specifically against the Italian immigrants," Miller explained.

"I remember that law being passed," Harrison said. "I thought it to be redundant at the time, since we had the Thirteenth Amendment. I guess I was wrong."

"Sir, I must report that the law has not been enforced, and the *Padrone* system is alive and well in New Orleans, according to Grant," Miller said. "Moreover, the Italians have not been indicted yet, and Grant tells me a preliminary hearing is scheduled in a few days. To make matters worse, the state Supreme Court seems deaf to the fundamental rights of the imprisoned Italians."

"Why?" Harrison asked.

"As I said, it's complicated. Grant tells me the Italians are not welcome in New Orleans and are not allowed to assimilate fully. As such, they have formed very insular colonies or groups in the city to create their own commerce within the city's well-established commerce, to the consternation of the business and professional class of the city. And the Italians seem to have cleave together with the Creole and Negro, and have formed a voting bloc, to the consternation of the city's political class. To make things worse, some immigrants have slipped by American and Italian authorities, who are fugitives from Italy. Grant claims the city's mayor and his friends are using that fact to rid the city of Italians. They have blamed Hennessy's death on a group of wealthy Sicilians who control part of the docks, and some members of the laboring class."

"Does Grant feel the Italians or Sicilians killed Hennessy? Are they part of this *Mafia*?" Harrison asked.

"He stands doubtful. Indeed, there is no proof that any of the accused are part of any *Mafia* organization, and the Italian citizens in prison don't know any of the other Italians. One of the newspapers he sent me, the *Times-Democrat,* had an article last month claiming there is a secret witness who reported to the police he saw three of the shooters, and none were of the '*Sicilian Element.'* Grant doesn't know the identity of the witness, but the *Times Democrat* contradicts another newspaper, the *Daily Picayune*, which has concluded all the Italians are guilty," Miller said.

"*The Daily Picayune* seems to be exacerbating the situation. They have lodged several editorials, condemning the Italian and Sicilian communities," Blaine intoned.

"Explain, James," Harrison said.

"*The Daily Picayune*, conscious of its standing in the newspaper world, responded to an editorial from the *New York Times* of October 28th, last. The *Times* editorial exhorted the fair treatment of all New Orleans and New York immigrants, as they have introduced to our nation many fruit and citrus products, heretofore, not known to New Yorkers. The *Times* also extols the virtues of the hard-working street vendors, who bring much-needed food to their population, and praises the Italian work ethic. *The Daily-Picayune*, in an oblique way, agrees with the *Times,* but its last two sentences reveal where it stands on the Italian issue," Blaine asserted.

"What did the *Picayune* write?" Harrison asked. "Do you have a copy of their editorial?"

"Yes, sir. I do. It's dated the twelfth of this month. I shall read it. '*Let us prove to them that our institutions are free and liberal to all men of good will, but that our laws are just and severe to evildoers. In the treatment of the Hennessy case, every exertion should be made to teach this lesson. The most momentous consequences depend on it.* '"

"Faint praise wrapped in a veiled threat," Harrison quipped. "We all know how dangerous newspapers are. In the words of the French philosopher, Voltaire, '*Those who can make you believe in absurdities, can make you commit atrocities.* 'William, instruct Grant to keep us informed," Harrison said. "I don't trust New Orleans or that Committee."

Chapter 65

Lionel Adams' Office
November 22, 1890
8:00 A.M.

The Louisiana Supreme Court issued split rulings in the matter of the Matranga defendants, jailed for killing Hennessy. Both rulings were a result of the bulldog tenacity of Lionel Adams' approach to practicing law. Earlier in the week, after District Judge Robert Marr denied Adams' *Writs of Mandamus* to compel an Orleans Parish Recorder judge to conduct a preliminary hearing in the absence of formal charges, and to compel the Sheriff Gabriel Villere to allow Dominick O'Malley, and *Times Democrat* reporter, Franklin Michinard, access to his clients to prepare for the hearing, Supreme Court Justice Edward Bermudez authored opinions compelling a preliminary hearing, but denying Adams' investigator, and the newspaper reporter access to his clients. The accused had been in prison for over a month, and Adams had only met his clients once. The *Daily Picayune* printed editorials exhorting the District Attorney to move the Grand Jury to act, and act swiftly.

The Committee of Fifty, leavened by the city councils' public offering of a fifteen-thousand-dollar reward for any information regarding who killed Hennessy, continued its investigation from the fourth floor of the Cotton Exchange building, across the street from Adam's office. As Adams sat alone in his office, he made of list of possible witnesses the state would call to support its claim against the Matranga defendants. In his mind, he prepared his cross-examination of the witnesses, with hopes of discovering the weaknesses in the prosecution's case. The city's legal community knew Adams' stellar reputation as a cross-examiner, and the rare Saturday night hearing was anticipated by many.

As Adams sat at his desk writing notes, Dominick O'Malley entered the office with a curious visage etched across his face. "I went to your house, and your wife told me you were here. Why?" O'Malley asked.

Adams looked up at O'Malley with a stunned expression. "Are you serious? Tonight's hearing is our first break in the case. We'll discover what Luzenberg has been hiding for the last month."

"You haven't heard?"

"Heard what?"

"You haven't read this morning's paper?" O'Malley asked.

"No. What happened?"

"Late last night, the Grand Jury indicted seventeen of our clients—some for murder and some for accessory. Two indictments were lodged again, in two different sections of the court. Both are capital offenses. Since there is now an indictment, the preliminary hearing will be cancelled," O'Malley said.

"Who was indicted?" Adams asked.

O'Malley opened the morning broadsheet and read the names. "For shooting Hennessy, the Grand Jury indicted Peter Natali, Antonio Scaffidi, Antonio Bagnetto, Manuel Polizzi, Antonio Marchesi, the cobbler, Pietro Monasterio, Bastian Incardona, Salvador, Sunzeri, and Loretto Comitz."

"Who are those men? I never heard of them, other than the cobbler. What about Matranga?" Adams asked

"The Grand Jury indicted our clients for Accessory before the Fact. They are. Charles Matranga, Joseph P. Macheca. James and John Caruso, Rocco Geraci, Charles Patorno, Frank Romero, and the kid, Asperi Marchesi," O'Malley said.

"Most of our clients were with me at Fabacher's that night. So were several police officers," Adams said. "If alibi cops are good for the Provenzanos, it should be good for our clients. Matranga and Macheca don't know anyone in the first group. How can you be an accessory to people you don't even know?" Adams asked.

"I guess Eliza Jane Nicholson's editorial achieved its objective," O'Malley said. "What editorial?" Adams asked.

O'Malley spread a copy of the *Daily Picayune* across Adams' desk. "Read that," O'Malley said, pointing to the editorial headline, which read:

"GO AHEAD WITH THE HENNESSY CASE"

Adams read the four-paragraph editorial, pushing the Grand Jury to act while obliquely referring to their inertia, as disturbing not only New Orleans, but the entire nation, since the Hennessy case had captured national attention.

"How do you know that red-hair bitch wrote this?" Adams asked.

"She owns the *Picayune*. She either wrote it or her editor, James Richardson, did. He's a member of the Committee of Fifty, and several days ago, she wrote another editorial extoling the virtues of the Committee, which has a member on the Grand Jury."

"Who?"

"Charles Ballejo—the guy who thinks he is a descendant of the Spanish king."

"Everybody in New Orleans thinks they're royalty. But the truth be known, they are nothing more gilded geldings prancing around the French Opera House on Bourbon Street every Mardi Gras, nuzzling each other's asses for business reciprocations," Adams steamed.

O'Malley laughed. "They accuse our clients of being the *Mafia,* or part of secret stiletto societies, when they are no better. They control the biggest newspaper, the courts, the police, city hall, the District Attorney, the Sheriff, and the Committee of Fifty. They won't be happy until they break every Italian neck in the parish prison."

"When a society thirsts for blood more than justice, it ceases being a collective civilization and becomes a horde of barbarians, their *polite* society, notwithstanding," Adams snarled.

"Remember, it was Eliza Jane who started the society column in the *Picayune*, as her way of having the uptown wives control their husbands. She hides behind her lace and poetry to control this city. She knows there's power in ink," O'Malley said.

"To get the discovery we need, we must devise a way to get the *Times Democrat* and the *Daily Picayune* to gut each other," Adams said. "Luzenberg is hiding evidence, and Baker and Marr won't make him reveal the secret witness Michinard heard about. Our clients are innocent, Dominick. Hennessy was a friend and client. I wouldn't be working my ass off, if I thought they were guilty."

"Nicholson has already attacked the *Evening States*. Read this," O'Malley said, as he turned the page of the *Daily Picayune*.

"The Evening States of yesterday, in an attack upon the Hennessy case, charged the Picayune with having assisted to arouse much prejudice against the Citizens Committee, to the extent of depriving it of its ability to perform effectively the service for which it was organized."

"She's calling it the "Citizens Committee?" Adams scoffed.

"Read on."

"The membership of the Committee embraces some of our best citizens, men who justly command general confidence and respect, and as there were among them solid and cool-headed men of business, and professional men of distinction and prominence, some of whom were trained in the law…"

Adams swiped the paper from his desk with a fierce wave of his left arm. "I can't read any more of that bullshit. That Committee is nothing more than a gang of cotton barons who control Shakspeare's Ring and Parkinson's Regulators. Watch how cool-headed they are if we win this case," Adams said. "And the *Picayune* is tying the hangman's nooses."

Adams sat back in his chair and stared at his notes, which he had been working on since dawn. He felt betrayed and defeated by a system he loved. His mind searched for some path to justice for his clients, but he felt overwhelmed, not by the law, but by an insular society masquerading as justice. Dread washed over thoughts as he thought about the outcome of the case and the deaths of innocent men, impaled on the sword of prejudice.

As he collected his notes, his office door flung open. "Come on, Lionel," A.D. Henriques yelled. "Let's go to the courthouse. Judge Marr is having a morning session with the Grand Jury. We can sit in and listen."

"On Saturday morning?" Adams asked.

"I just left there. They're in recess. He must hurry to get there before they adjourn for the day," Henriques responded.

"What good can we do now?" Adams asked.

"There are four men in prison who weren't indicted. That means we can still have a preliminary hearing tonight for them, and get some discovery," Henriques explained.

Adams, Henriques, and O'Malley sprinted to St. Patrick's Hall and arrived in Judge Marr's court as the Grand Jury returned from its deliberation room. Adams approached the bar and requested to be heard.

"Go ahead, Mr. Adams," Judge Marr said.

"I stand before the bar of justice, cognizant of the Grand Jury's actions last night. I am painfully aware that seventeen of our clients have been indicted for two capital offenses. This court has one of those cases and jurisdiction over the Grand Jury. But with the return of the seventeen True Bills, there remain four men who have not been indicted. They are John Matranga, Charles Pietzo, Charles Traina, and Louis Taormina. Along with the other seventeen, they have been languishing in the dank and dark hellhole of the parish prison. I, therefore, respectfully request this court to either release these four men or cause a preliminary hearing to be conducted in Recorder Bringer's court, as originally scheduled," Adams pleaded.

Judge Marr asked District Attorney Luzenberg if he had any objections, but before he could address the issue, William Roy, the Grand Jury foreman, stood and asked to be heard. Marr agreed.

"Judge, as foreman of this Grand Jury, I must report to you that the work of this Grand Jury is not complete, and we ask that we be allowed to continue our work until noon."

Judge Marr, recognizing the Grand Jury's independence, assented to the request but admonished Roy to return before noon, as he would allow all counsel to remain in the courtroom for the balance of the morning.

><

11:45 A.M.

A loud knocking on the jury deliberation room door announced that the Grand Jury was ready to address the court. Adams, Henriques, O'Malley, and Luzenberg waited for Judge Marr to take the bench. Some newspaper reporters mingled together, waiting to see if there were any more indictments. After a few minutes, the elderly judge climbed the bench and instructed the clerk to admit the Grand Jury.

William Roy led the Grand Jury to the jury box. He was carrying a stack of papers, which aroused everyone's curiosity. Everyone, except the judge, remained standing, which allowed Pasquale Corte to sneak in without notice.

"Mr. Foreman, does the Grand Jury have any more business before this court? Judge Marr asked.

"We do, Your Honor," Roy responded.

"What say you?" the judge asked.

"The Grand Jury for the Parish of Orleans has two True Bills of

Indictment to return," Roy announced.

"Give them to the clerk," the judge said. Marr paged through the documents and instructed the clerk to enter them into the record. To the shock of everyone in the courtroom, the Grand Jury returned indictments for the shooting of David C. Hennessy against Charles Traina and Charles Pietzo. Lionel Adams sank into his seat and began to blame himself for making the earlier motion. He felt he forced the Grand Jury's hand, thus depriving him, again, of a preliminary hearing.

There were nineteen men indicted for killing Hennessy, while a weak witness only saw five shooters, and one unknown witness said he saw three, who weren't of the "Sicilian Element." Several of the accused had strong alibis. Some of the men didn't know each other, and lived and worked in various parts of the city. They were just Italian.

Then the clerk read the second indictment. It charged the prison yard captain, Skip Mealey, with various crimes, including battery and theft, against the men the Grand Jury just indicted for murder, thus giving Corte a pyrrhic victory. Since Mealey was recently released from prison, a capias was issued for his arrest, and Judge Marr ordered John Matranga and Louis Taormina released from prison. There would be no preliminary hearing that night.

Chapter 66

Orleans Parish Prison
November 28, 1890
3:00 P.M.

Lionel Adams smelled the stench of the prison from blocks away. The admixture of body rot, mildew, decaying food, and animal waste assaulted his olfactory senses, like a punch in the nose. His carriage guests, Dominick O'Malley, A.D. Henriques, *Times Democrat* reporter, Frank Michinard, and a new addition to the legal team, Arthur Gastinel, filtered the fetid air with either their sleeves or handkerchiefs. After hitching his horse to an iron hitching post, Adams and his guest approached the front gates of the prison, where they were met by the warden, Lemuel Davis. It was a surprise for all, as Davis was rarely seen at the prison this late in the afternoon. But he was following orders, which caused some concern among Adams and his entourage.

At the front gate, a cluster of weeping Black women gathered around the Sheriff's Black Maria, as five Black men, chained and shackled together, boarded the wagon. Overcome with legal curiosity, Adams approached Davis and asked, "What's going on here? There is no court this late on Fridays. We've just left the courthouse. All sessions are adjourned, and the Recorders don't meet until tomorrow morning. Where are you taking these Negroes?" Adams probed.

"Ain't none of your business, Mr. Adams. Now, go visit your clients," Davis responded.

"I demand to know where these men are going, and why their women are crying," Adams said.

"Ain't none of your concern, Mr. Adams. Now, your clients have been indicted, go visit them. Mind your own business," Davis huffed.

"It's too late for the prison train to Baton Rouge. I demand to know where these men are going," Adams persisted, as the Back women began to stand behind Adams.

Davis reached into his coat pocket and retrieved a letter written by the mayor. "Here, dammit. Read this. It's an order from the mayor himself," Davis said, handing the letter to Adams.

Adams read the three-sentence order signed by Joseph A. Shakspeare. It ordered the sheriff to release five Negro males to the custody of Mr. Edward Scarnnell of the *Cote Blanche* sugar cane plantation in Lafourche Parish, Louisiana.

"Mr. Davis, the mayor has no authority to do this. This is involuntary servitude of the highest degree and is patently illegal. Only a judge can release prisoners from prison," Adams said.

Edward Scarnnell approached Adams and introduced himself. "Sir, it won't be involuntary servitude, as I plan to pay each man over a dollar a day to cut my cane for harvest. I asked the mayor for a favor, conditioned on my paying the men."

"It's still illegal. Only a judge can release men from the parish prison, not the mayor," Adams retorted.

"Take it up with the mayor, Mr. Adams," Davis said. These men are headed to the train depot and then to Thibodeaux. Now, sir, please go see your clients in the prison."

Adams simmered with anger and approached the black women. "You ladies, hear me out. Make sure the money given to these men does not go behind those walls when they return. It will surely be stolen if it does. Tell your men to provide you with the money they earn when they return. You can buy them things they can't get inside the prison. The women nodded their shawled heads and spoke to their men through the bars of the Black Maria.

Lemuel Davis approached Adams and asked, "Mr. Adams, why did you say that to those Negresses? I run an honest prison. Ask Sheriff Villere."

Adams laughed. "You apparently haven't read the newspapers, or heard what the Grand Jury has found inside your prison. It's a veritable shitpit of beatings, filth and corruption."

Davis looked over Adams' shoulder and saw Michinard standing next to O'Malley. Is that Frank Michinard who works for the *Times Democrat*?" Davis asked.

"Yes," Adams responded.

"He can't go in the prison. Only lawyers and investigators are allowed in. No reporters are allowed in the prison. Sheriff Villere's orders."

"So, the mayor can release people, but the sheriff can keep people out?" Adams asked, chuckling.

"Yep. So, if I were you, I would go visit your clients. The sun is going down, and they eat at five. You have to be out by that time," Davis said.

Adams didn't want to pick another fight with a man who held the keys to the prison. He instructed Michinard to take his carriage and return at half past four. "Go find a place to write what just happened," Adams whispered to Michinard.

><

Inside the prison, Adams met his clients and introduced Arthur Gastinel. To his surprise, he found each man clothed well, nourished, but pale, despite the recent *Times Democrat* reports of the foreboding sepulchral conditions of the prison. Adams turned his attention to Macheca. "Excuse me, J.P., but I expected to see men with rags hanging from their bones. Have you read the reports of the conditions in this place?"

"We know about it. We hear the beatings and the yelling every day and night. But if you pay the right people, at the right time, you can escape the beatings, the rocking, and the ragging. Matranga and I are paying off the Villere and Davis for good food, beds, blankets, newspapers, and washed clothes every week. We pay them about fifty bucks a week to live like humans. That reminds me. Go see my wife. Italians from all across America are sending her money to pay for our defense. She comes once a week with the money for Villere and Davis. She also gives the captain of the yard five bucks and a bottle of wine, just to leave us alone. We don't have to rock and rag."

"What's that?" Adams asked.

"It's scraping the flagstones in the courtyards with rocks, then they sprinkle water on the stones. The poor inmates take rags and dry the stones. If they don't do it quickly enough, they get beaten with whips. You can hear the scraping of the rocks and the whish of the whips every day. Some of these men haven't been to trial yet."

Adams shook his head in disgust, but his attention was drawn by the stabbing stares of his clients towards O'Malley. Adams' instincts were correct. O'Malley's presence made some of the clients uncomfortable. To focus their attention, he had the men gather around him. To many, it was the first time they met him, but they knew O'Malley. Adams told them they had been indicted by the Grand Jury in relation to the murder of Hennessy. He read the names of the men indicted for actually shooting.

"For the shooting of Hennessy, the Grand Jury indicted Peter Natali, Antonio Scaffidi, Antonio Bagnetto, Manuel Polizzi, Antonio and Asperi Marchesi, Charles Traina, Bastian Incardona, and Peter Monasterio."

The large cell erupted in denials and weeping. Natali and Traina protested and claimed they weren't in the city when Hennessy was shot. Manuel Polizzi began to wail and had to be physically restrained by the other inmates. "Everybody, calm down," Adams ordered. "These walls have ears. Keep your thoughts to yourself, and never share any information with anyone but me. Now gather closer, I have something to say."

The inmates gathered closer as Adams began to whisper. "Listen to me. This case is very weak. The state knows it, and we know it. Some of you were with me the night Hennessy was shot. We have witnesses who will support that. There's a secret witness who saw three of the shooters. They weren't Sicilian. More guns were dredged from the ditches than there were shooters. The District Attorney, whom I have known for many years, is lying to me, and I know it. This means that the Committee is controlling him.

"The so-called eyewitnesses are very weak and are not sure what they saw that night. Yesterday, the *Picayune* reported that the city council passed an ordinance forcing the electric company to fix their dynamos and keep a steady current flowing throughout the city. The residents of Girod Street have complained they have had no lights for three months. Where was Hennessy shot?" Adams asked.

"Girod Street," Macheca responded.

"And it appears those of you who are accused of the shooting didn't know those who were indicted for accessory. Mr. Monasterio, did you know Mr. Macheca or Mr. Matranga before being arrested?" Adams asked.

The old cobbler shook his head. "I did work for Mr. Monteleone. Where are my tools?" Monasterio muttered through his thick whiskers.

"What about Billy O'Connor?" Matranga asked. "He claimed he heard Hennessy said it was us—the dagoes."

"O'Connor works for Thomas Boylan, who is a member of the Committee. He will say or do what he is told. He will never survive my cross-examination," Adams said.

"Who was indicted for accessory?" Macheca asked.

"You, Charles Matranga, James and John Caruso, Frank Romero, Rocco Geraci, Charles Pietzo, Salvador Sunzeri, and Loretto Comitz."

Again, the cell erupted, and Adams waved his arms for quiet. "Five of you were with me at Fabacher's that night. So were three or four cops. If the cops can be a valid alibi for the Provenzanos, they can be a valid alibi for you, too," Adams said.

"What comes next?" Matranga asked.

"Tomorrow morning, there will be a secret session of both sections of the criminal court where you'll be arraigned. Each of you will plead not guilty. And I have a little surprise for Mr. Luzenberg," Adams snickered.

"May I say something?" Geraci asked.

"Sure, Rocco," Adams said.

"All due respect, Mr. Adams, but we don't trust O'Malley. I will say it right to his face. He has too many friends who hate Italians. He also hated Hennessy, and the yard talk in the prison is that O'Malley was one of the shooters."

The cell erupted, as every dark eye pierced O'Malley's soul. Adams waved his arms again and demanded silence.

"I heard talk about O'Malley being a shooter. But I want each of you to remember this: I wouldn't represent any of you if I thought you killed my friend and client, David Hennessy. As for O'Malley, I wouldn't let him near this case if I believed he was a shooter. He is hated by the same Committee that wants to see all of you hang. In fact, they would love to see him hanged with you. Now, one of Hennessy's arch enemies was a guy named Thomas Devereaux. Hennessy was accused of killing him in 1881. I represented him, and Hennessy was found not guilty. Devereaux hated O'Malley, too. Isn't that correct, Dominick?"

From the shadows, O'Malley nodded.

"I trust O'Malley. In fact, he gave me information, which I intend to share with the court tomorrow to get the indictments dismissed. He has worked hard to gather information to exonerate each of you. He found the *Times Democrat* reporter who found your tools, Mr. Monasterio. I hope y'all understand that.

"It was O'Malley who discovered everyone who has been indicted for shooting Hennessy lives around the Poydras Market, and everyone who has been indicted for accessory, lives in or near the Italian Colony. And only a few of you know each other. I learned long ago that conspirators don't conspire with strangers," Adams said.

Adams removed several sheets of paper from his leather valise and started asking each man questions about their whereabouts on the night of

October 15, 1890. He probed their relationships with each other and any contact with Hennessy. "Be patient with me," Adams said. "I need to reconstruct your lives, before the state tries to destroy them."

><

St. Aloysius Academy

5:15 P.M.

The indictments seemed to have a palliative effect throughout the city, especially in the Italian Colony. Italian men began to walk the streets again, and some returned to their old jobs on the docks. Italian children played on the cobblestone streets without fear, but under the watchful eyes of parents and grandparents, perched on stoops or iron-laced galleries. Every time a beat cop walked down the street, the children would hide. Fruit vendors pushed their wooden, wobbly carts through the narrow streets of the French Quarter, hoping to make even a modest sale, to sustain their lives.

Laurence Hearn rang the bell at St. Aloysius, and Brother Angelo admitted him with a great hug. "We have missed you, Mr. Hearn. The boys will be excited to see you."

"I'm glad to be here. It appears things are returning to normal," Hearn said.

"Are they?" Brother Angelo asked.

"I think so. I see more foot and wagon traffic in the markets. People are moving about, but with caution. How are Antonio and Abraham doing?"

"We've allowed them to climb on the roof, to watch the ships and steamers in the river—to break the monotony of living behind these walls. Both boys are still studying and improving their reading and writing skills. Abraham is becoming an excellent artist," Brother Angelo boasted.

"Great. Are they ready to go back to work?" Hearn asked.

"Is it safe?"

"I think so. We want them to come to court with us tomorrow. The nineteen indicted men are being arraigned in a secret session."

Brother Angelo and Hearn entered the dining hall and met Antonio and Abraham. Dinner was about to be served, and Hearn was invited to stay. "Tomorrow morning, I will pick you up and go to St. Patrick's Hall. The nineteen men accused of killing the police chief are being arraigned. So bring your pads and etching tools. My boss has agreed to pay you each five dollars for your efforts," Hearn said.

Antonio and Abraham were shocked with joy. Brother Stanislaus, hearing the offer, expressed his joy and curiosity. "Thank you, Mr. Hearn, but why so much for one day's work?"

"My boss knows these boys are good workers, and have been locked away from this city. He and others will join us in court tomorrow, as a show of defiance to anyone who wants to wants to express their prejudice against them."

"Others?" Brother Stanislaus asked.

"Yes. Last week, I met a reporter from the *New York Times*. Many eyes are now upon this silty loam of a city populated by *faux* royalty, demanding vengeance for a crime they committed," Hearn asserted.

"Do you boys understand what's going on?" Brother Stanislaus asked.

Antonio and Abraham nodded.

Chapter 67

Criminal District Court
November 29, 1890
10:30 A.M.

Horses' hooves echoed off the brick and stone facades of the buildings lining Camp Street. The lonesome clopping announced the arrival of the Black Maria from the parish prison to St. Patrick's Hall. Nine Italian men sat behind the iron bars of the prison wagon, their dark eyes darting from side to side. Police officers and sheriff's deputies, armed with shotguns and Winchesters, swarmed the rear door of the wagon as the shackled cargo stepped down and entered the courthouse. Other than heavily armed officers, attorneys, and newspaper reporters were the only witnesses to this pathos. Every eye studied the countenance of the prisoners—their clothes, their gait, and their sallow complexions.

One reporter yelled, "Why only nine? I thought nineteen were indicted."

"The other wagon broke an axle. We have to go back and get the other ten," a deputy responded.

Antonio and Abraham stood motionless next to Laurence Hears. Antonio stared at the irons wrapped around the men's wrists and the heavy chains linking each man to the other as they climbed the steps of justice. His thoughts flashed back to his family's vineyard, the shotgun blast, the dead men's blood gushing into the Sicilian soil, his escape to America, and Vincenzo Trambatore walking down Barracks Street, a few weeks ago. He felt the iron against his wrists and wondered if he would take the same walk one day.

Once inside Judge Robert Marr's large courtroom, the reporters took their seats next to the well-guarded dock. The prisoners sat motionless and waited for the others to arrive. Everyone spoke in hushed tones, recognizing the solemnity of the commencement of New Orleans' largest capital trial. Hearn quietly introduced Antonio and Abraham to the New York Times, the Chicago Tribune, and Harper's Weekly reporters. Each reporter recognized their ethnicity and wanted to talk to them, but the deputies hushed the chatter.

When the back doors of the courtroom sprang open, clanging, clinking, and the shuffling of worn leather soles filled the air. Deputies escorted ten bedraggled souls to the dock. Some gazed at the high ceilings of the courtroom, while others just stared into infinity. Across the courtroom, Lionel Adams argued with Charles Luzenberg. Two deputies stood next to the men, but did not interfere with the tense moment. At a quarter to eleven, Judge Marr climbed his high bench and gaveled the court into session.

"In the case of the *State of Louisiana versus Peter Natali, et al, Docket Numbers 14220 and 14221*, are the parties ready for arraignment?" Judge Marr announced.

Lionel Adams approached the bar. "Your Honor, Lionel Adams for all the defense. I hereby file a formal motion to quash the Indictments for several reasons. First, in his haste to indict my clients and avoid a preliminary hearing, the District Attorney allowed Mr. John T. Michel, a court stenographer known to the court, to remain inside the Grand Jury room while the Grand Jury deliberated *before* returning the True Bills against my clients. Furthermore, one of the grand jurors, Charles Ballejo, also known to this court, and a member of the mayor's Committee of Fifty, is also a member of the Grand Jury. And as the court is well aware, this Committee's sole purpose is to see my clients convicted and hanged."

"Mr. Luzenberg, were you aware of the allegations by the defense?" Judge Marr asked.

"I was first made aware of them just moments ago. I haven't had a chance to investigate them." Luzenberg responded.

As Judge Marr began to ask his next question, Ferdinand Armant stood and said, "Your Honor, I represent Charles Patorno, and we do not join in Mr. Adams' motion."

Adams responded, "I was hired to represent all of the defendants, and I have never spoken to Mr. Armant about his participation in the defense."

"The representation of Mr. Patorno is up to him. I will pause the proceedings and allow you to settle this matter with him," Judge Marr said, as he pushed his chair away from the bench.

Adams and Armant spoke to the shackled Patorno while he sat in the dock. It was clear, Patorno wanted Armant to represent him, and the attorneys informed the court of his decision.

"Well, that leaves me with a dilemma," Judge Marr said. "If Mr.

Patorno is not a party to the Motion to Quash, do I arraign him alone?"

Assistant District Attorney, John Finney, rose and stated, "I see no problem continuing Mr. Patorno's arraignment, until after the Court decides the motion. After all, the decision will have an impact on his case, too."

"Do all the parties agree?" Judge Marr asked.

All parties agreed, and it was settled that the motion would be heard the following Saturday.

As Judge Marr left the bench, the deputies escorted the defendants from the box. Asperi Marchesi and Antonio Terranova locked eyes. Young Marchesi's slight build, locked in chains and shackles, cast an incongruous aura throughout the courtroom. Antonio's eyes, welling with tears, clasped his hands and aimed them towards young Marchesi, as if to say, *"I'm praying for you."*

Chapter 68

New Orleans
December 1-28, 1890

Pasquale Corte packed his last crate of documents to complete the move of the Italian consulate from Number 23 Poydras Street to Number 191 Customhouse Street. Since the indictments of the nineteen Italians, he and his small staff had been taunted by the ethnic slurs of non-Italians, which made conducting consulate business untenable. As a parting shot to the American Section of New Orleans, Corte stopped at the Custom House and fired off another detailed telegram to the Italian Ambassador and the United States Secretary of State. He spared no detail in describing how the court system and the parish prison had treated his fellow countrymen. He entreated his government and host nation to intervene for the safety of all Italian citizens residing in New Orleans, describing the situation as "dire."

><

Washington, D.C.
December 2, 1890

Upon receipt of Corte's telegram, Ambassador Fava sent a hand-delivered message to Secretary Blaine, requesting an audience with the President. In the message, Cortes included Mayor Shakspeare's warning, stating:

> **"The Sicilian who comes here must become an American citizen and subject his wrongs to the remedy of the law of the land, or else there must be no place for him on the American continent."**

Baron Fava, incensed by the New Orleans telegram, which included the notice of the mayor's appointment of a vigilance committee to eradicate the *Mafia*, and reports of the *New York Times*, which quoted Shakspeare's and his Committee's ominous words:

"It would proceed to extreme and harsh measures, and by summary means without process of law, means which might strike the innocent as well as the guilty."

Blaine immediately messaged President Harrison. Afterwards, a staff member entered his large office and handed him a telegram from Governor Francis T. Nicholls, sent from Baton Rouge, Louisiana. Before reading it, Blaine took a deep breath and prepared himself for more disturbing news. He opened the envelope and began to read the lengthy missive from Nicholls.

To Blaine's surprise, Nicholls admitted the brutal treatment of Italian prisoners in the Orleans Parish Prison, but hastened to add that such treatment was not limited to one ethnic group. It was pervasive, and the two prison "captains of the yard" had been indicted. He, moreover, asserted the offending position had been eliminated, and three deputies had been hired to replace inmates as part of prison security.

Satisfied with Nicholls' response, Blaine became alarmed that the reports from Corte and Fava were true, and any further reports from New Orleans would be treated with great care. The Secretary then instructed his assistant, William Wharton, to ascertain the nationalities of each of the nineteen men under indictment, as he expected international implications from what could happen in New Orleans.

><

New Orleans

December 3, 1890

"Have you lost your mind?" Dominick O'Malley asked Lionel Adams as he stormed through their office door.

"What do you mean?" Adams responded.

O'Malley tossed the morning editions of the *Daily Picayune* and *Times-Democrat* on Adams' desk. "Read page three of each newspaper. Are you crazy?"

"Sit your Irish ass down, and let me explain," Adams said. "It's not a problem."

"No? You hired Thomas Jenkins Semmes to be lead counsel in the

Hennessy case? Why didn't you tell me? Why do I have to learn this shit in the newspapers?" O'Malley asked.

"Because it wasn't my decision. It was Macheca's."

"Macheca's? What? Why would Macheca hire the president of the Boston Club to be his attorney? This is insane," O'Malley yelled.

"Lower your voice. And listen to me. Trust me." Adams implored.

"But why would Macheca hire this guy?"

"I'll explain, if you give me a chance," Adams said, while beckoning O'Malley to sit down.

"Dominick, this goes back to the *Battle of Liberty Place*—in 1874," Adams began. "If you remember, Macheca fought for the Democrats against the Republicans, because they were afraid they would have a Negro governor in Louisiana. Macheca wanted to curry favor with the Democrats' Ring and their various political machines. Semmes was one of their lawyers and knew Macheca.

"Macheca, to the dismay of many, captured an arsenal of weapons behind the Cabildo, and a ship in the river laden with guns, but the Democrats wouldn't give him full credit for his bravery. He also saved the life of Algernon Badger, the chief of the Republican Metropolitan Police. That didn't sit well with many.

"Semmes is a brilliant lawyer. He graduated from Harvard College, he was a Confederate Senator, the state's Attorney General, and a close friend of Jefferson Davis. Though he is a Catholic, he was invited to join the Boston Club because of his service to the Confederacy."

"But his law partner is James Legendre, a member of the Committee of Fifty," O'Malley said.

"I know. And we talked about that late into last night. He assured me he would be loyal to the case, after I explained to him, the Italians didn't kill Hennessy. And to my surprise, he agreed," Adams said.

"Lionel, he knows the bastards who killed Hennessy, and he is friends with every member of that Committee. Do you really trust him?"

"Yes. Again, it was Macheca's idea to hire him. Semmes will now be hated for taking this case, and knows it. Like us, many people are reading the morning papers in disbelief. At great social risk, he has decided to defend Macheca. I'm sure he will spend the next few days defending his position to all his friends," Adams explained.

"I still don't understand this. Semmes is part of the elite scum that runs this city and killed Hennessy. Now, he wants to defend Macheca, and risk exposing those who did the killing?" O'Malley asked. "Did he accuse me of killing Hennessy?"

"No. He assured me he is a man of the law, and not of any committee. Without any prodding, he told me *our* defenses to the case. He knows what we know and is willing to use his efforts to clear the Italians," Adams said.

"But he will reveal the truth, probably getting himself killed or socially banished. Why would a man of his stature take such a risk? It doesn't make sense, I think he's a spy."

"Dominick, our job is to defend the Italians from false charges, not to prove who killed Hennessy. Our case is very strong, and Semmes has provided evidence we didn't have."

"What evidence?" O'Malley asked.

"One of Luzenberg's main witnesses is Mallard Peeler, who lives upstairs at Girod and Basin. He identified several of the defendants as the shooters, including Salvatore Sunzeri, who was with Macheca, Matranga, Geraci, and me at Fabacher's the night of the shooting. Peeler misidentified Sunzeri because he was drunk, and that can be supported by his neighbor, Mary Wheeler, who warned W.J. Lippert to ignore anything Peeler says."

"Who's Lippert?" O'Malley asked.

"He's a *Times-Democrat* reporter. Semmes knows him. Go find Lippert and get a statement from him. Take Frank Michinard with you. Then find Wheeler. I think Lippert might be the reporter who found Monasterio's cobbler's tools in the shanty, which Journee is concealing. Semmes also gave me a new idea, which I will explain later."

"So, you trust Semmes?" O'Malley probed.

"Yes. Semmes also knows Badger, who is also on the mayor's Committee. They have talked, and Badger encouraged him to take the case. Badger knows I would not have taken the case if I thought the Italians killed David."

O'Malley sat silent in his chair, pondering Adams's words. "Is Semmes going to handle the Motion to Quash the indictments?" O'Malley asked.

"No. Henriques and I will handle that Saturday morning. Semmes hasn't been paid yet, which reminds me, I have to go to Macheca's home on Bourbon Street to get some money. Semmes' fee is very high, and Macheca and Matranga are having money wired from Italians from all over the county."

"Did you read who is on the new Grand Jury?" O'Malley asked.

"Who?"

"Look on page three of the *Picayune*. We have two new members of the Committee of Fifty on the new Grand Jury—Robert Miller Walmsley, father of Sylvester Pierce Walmsley, and Simon Hernsheim," O'Malley said. "If you win the motion, they'll just indict again. And don't forget. The Walmsleys are wealthy cotton barons and want to remove the Italians from the docks."

Adams sighed. "I need to talk to Semmes."

"You still trust Semmes?" O'Malley asked. "Also, he's related to the Walmsleys by marriage. He's Robert Miller Walmsley's father-in-law. This whole damn city is politically and socially incestuous."

"Dominick, Semmes told me about some dark secrets of the cotton barons, which date back to the 1884 Cotton Centennial. Who was the director of security for that event?" Adams asked.

"David Hennessy."

"Why did Shakspeare appoint Hennessy Superintendent in 1888?"

"To stuff cotton in his mouth," O'Malley said.

"There are no secrets in New Orleans," Adams said.

><

New Orleans

December 6, 1890

Lionel Adams, H.D. Henriques, and Arthur Gastinel sat at the defense counsel's table, while Charles Luzenberg, W.L. Evans, and J.C. Walker sat at the prosecution's table, waiting for both judges of the Criminal District Court of Orleans Parish to ascend the bench. Newspaper reporters, police officers, and court personnel sat in the gallery. Since it was a pre-trial motion, the defendants remained in the parish prison.

At about ten o'clock, Judges Robert Marr and Joshua Baker ascended the steps to the bench in a rare tandem appearance. Since the indictments had been bifurcated between the two sections of the court, and Adams' motion impacted the validity of both, both judges decided to hear the arguments simultaneously.

After the case was called, Adams began to argue. It took most of the day, and the defense and prosecution clashed about John T. Michel's presence in the Grand Jury room, during the witnesses' testimony, and jury deliberation. Adams established that Michel was not an authorized shorthand reporter and should never have been in the Grand Jury room. While Luzenberg conceded the fact, he cited old English case law regarding the recordation of testimony, which was deemed customary.

W.L. Evans, in rebuttal, stood next to a stack of law books, known as Annuals, which reported other states' jurisprudence on the matter, and picked through case after case citing the propriety of an unauthorized person being present during a Grand Jury proceeding. Louisiana had no reported decision. Evans crowned his argument with the revelation that the court had not authorized the subpoenas issued by the Grand Jury. Both judges glanced at each other, but said nothing, while Luzenberg argued that an error was merely harmless.

In closing, Adams fired his last shot. "Had the state not been in such a hurry to indict our clients and avoid a preliminary hearing, they would have adhered to the law and conducted the Grand Jury appropriately. I respectfully submit and predict, as this case goes forward, the state will be guilty of further derelictions of their duty."

Judge Marr closed the proceedings by taking the matter under advisement, but promised a quick ruling.

><

New Orleans

December 10, 1890

As Lionel Adams and A.D. Henriques entered the front door of Number 22 Carondelet Street, reporters from the *Daily Picayune* and the *Times Democrat* confronted them. "What do you think of Judge Baker's ruling?" one reporter asked.

"What ruling?" Adams asked.

"Here. Read this," one reporter said, as he shoved his paper towards Adams.

Adams' eyes fell upon the headline: **"QUASHED."** A small smile cracked across his thin lips as he handed the paper to Henriques.

"Are you happy, Mr. Adams?" a reporter asked.

"Only as long as it takes to get to my office. I'm sure the new Grand Jury will indict these innocent men again. But hopefully, I'll get a preliminary hearing to discover whatever evidence Luzenberg is hiding against nineteen men of different backgrounds, neighborhoods, who were scattered throughout New Orleans the night Hennessy was shot, not unlike the night the Matranga stevedores were shot," Adams said, planting doubt in the reporters' minds.

><

New Orleans

December 13, 1890

3:30 P.M.

Lionel Adams's sage instincts were seldom wrong. As he sat in Judge Marr's courtroom, late on a Friday afternoon, he knew what was coming. Only the previous Tuesday did Judge Joshua Baker quash the indictments against his clients. Still, Adams knew the new Grand Jury, led by Boston and Pickwick Club member, and a member of the Committee of Fifty, Robert Miller Walmsley, wouldn't waste time on re-indicting the Italians.

After Judge Marr ascended his high bench, he asked Walmsley what business the Grand Jury had before his court. Walmsley, attired in his customary high starched collar, black bow tie, and dark blue suit, stood and approached the clerk with a stack of official papers. The clerk handed the papers to Marr and announced the new indictments against the nineteen Italians, accusing some with the murder of David C. Hennessy and the others with accessory thereto. Adams chuckled and wondered why it kept Walmsley three days.

><

December 16, 1890

10:20 A.M.

Legions of police officers and sheriff's deputies surrounded the two Black Marias as they parked in front of St. Patrick's Hall. Nineteen gloomed and wrinkled Italians stepped down from the wagons and into the courthouse to be arraigned, again, for a crime the law presumed them innocent, but the people presumed them guilty. Reporters, including Laurence Hearn and his helpers, Antonio and Abraham, looked at the forlorn men as they shuffled up the steps and into the building where the mirage of justice resided.

The nineteen defendants, chains clanging and rattling, were ushered into the dock by guards. Lionel Adams approached his clients, greeted them warmly, and returned to his seat. Thomas J. Semmes did not appear for this arraignment, and reporters duly noted his absence.

As the judge called the case for arraignment, Adams stood and requested to be recognized. "For what reason do you interrupt this court, Mr. Adams?" Judge Marr asked.

Adams shocked the courtroom.

"I hereby file a Motion to Quash this new indictment on several grounds, the most notorious of which is that two members of the December Grand Jury also serve as members of the mayor's Committee of Fifty, and the first indictment has tainted this indictment, and the Committee of Fifty has accepted money from the city council to investigate the death of David C. Hennessy. The prejudice to my clients is as thick as molasses," Adams bellowed.

Judge Marr sat motionless for a few moments, as Adams' words seared through his mind. He knew Adams never engaged in legal frivolities, which impelled him to accept the motion with caution and concern. Adams passed a written motion to the clerk, who passed it to the judge. Marr slid his metal-frame spectacles to the end of his nose and read the allegations. After a few moments, the pale judge said, "I hereby set this motion for hearing for Saturday, December 20, 1890. This arraignment is postponed until the merits of this motion have been heard."

><

December 17, 1890

10:45 A.M.

The clear-thinking people of New Orleans read their newspapers with the clarity of the opacity of the brown Mississippi River. Even the rheumy blue eyes of Judge Robert Marr couldn't follow the *dramatis personae* who stood before him when the clerk called the case of the *State of Louisiana versus Joseph Provenzano et al.* Marr recognized the lawyer's faces, but on this morning, they stood on opposite sides of the courtroom from yesterday's appearances, in the case of the *State of Louisiana versus Peter Natale, et al.* Some local newspaper reporters understood the switching roles of the attorneys, but the out-of-state reporters remained numb with confusion.

When Lionel Adams announced he would be assisting the state in the prosecution of the Provenzanos, along with A.D. Henriques and John C. Finney, Judge Marr grimaced with confusion. "Let me get this straight, Mr. Adams," Marr began. "Yesterday, you were a defense attorney, but today, you are a prosecutor?"

"Yes, your Honor," Adams responded.

"Is there a conflict here, Mr. Finney?" Judge Marr asked.

"No, your Honor. Mr. Adams helped prosecute the first case against the Provenzanos in Judge Baker's court, which, as you know, has been bound over for a new trial."

"And this trial has the same defendants, but a different victim?" Judge Marr asked.

"Yes, your Honor," Finney responded.

"I remember that case. The defendants had strong alibi witnesses, namely the police," Judge Marr giggled.

"That's correct," Finney said.

"So yesterday, Mr. Adams represented the Matrangas who allegedly shot Chief Hennessy in October, but were allegedly shot by the Provenzanos this past May. And today, Mr. Adams wants to prosecute the Provenzanos for shooting his clients? Do I have that correct?" Judge Marr asked.

"That's correct, your Honor," Adams responded.

Marr looked confused. "Okay, this trial will be held on January 12, 1891, when I hope the state and the defense remember who they are," Judge Marr said wryly.

><

December 20, 1890

10:00 A.M.

The corner of Camp and Lafayette Streets was jammed with newspaper reporters, lawyers, and the curious idle. Cigar smoke swirled over the black bowlers and derbies of men of various social rank. The lower-ranked men wore slouch hats or scarves wrapped around their heads to parry the cold north wind blowing off Lake Pontchartrain. Even the morning chill couldn't keep the denizens of justice away from St. Patrick's Hall.

As Lionel Adams and A. D. Henriques pushed their way through the throng, a reporter shouted, "Mr. Adams, what do you think of the Duffy verdict and sentence?"

"What verdict and sentence?" Adams responded.

"Late last night, the jury found Duffy guilty with mercy for shooting one of your clients—Scaffidi. Judge Baker gave him only two years. Any response?"

Adams turned around and entered the courthouse. Once inside, took his seat at the defense counsel table, along with Henriques. After removing their coats, they sat down and reviewed their papers. Since this morning's hearing was Adams' second motion to dismiss the indictments, his clients remained immured the parish prison, as their appearances were unnecessary. While studying his motions and other papers, Adams felt the presence of Charles Luzenberg standing against him, looking down.

"My friend, have you lost your mind?" Luzenberg asked.

"Why?"

"You have issued subpoenas for some members of the Committee of Fifty and their papers. Look at this courtroom. It looks like a meeting of the Boston and Pickwick clubs. You're making enemies."

"I have clients to represent," Adams said.

"Don't give me that *uberrima fides* bullshit, Lionel. You can't just subpoena anyone in New Orleans. These are men of social rank."

"They're not subject to the laws, as you and I are?" Adams asked.

"Yes. But this motion has no merit. Why drag these men into court for a worthless hearing? You just want to embarrass them in front of the newspapers? They won't forget this."

"Are they immune from the law? These men belong to the mayor's Committee. They were given money to investigate Hennessy's death. After my clients' arrest, they continued to get money to continue the investigation. I want to know who gave what and why, while my clients were rotting in that hellhole on Orleans Street," Adams snarled.

"You're making a fool of yourself. You know New Orleans as much as I do. There are some things you just don't do, and you have sullied these men by dragging them into St. Patrick's Hall. These are men of status and power, not the rabble of society, who populate this place every day," Luzenberg said.

"Like us?" Adams asked.

Luzenberg stormed off as both Judge Baker and Judge Marr took the bench.

After clashing over the wording and intent of the motion, Judge Baker allowed Adams to examine R.M. Walmsley and Simon Hernsheim. Hernsheim acknowledged his membership in the Committee of Fifty and explained his roles. He admitted to being the Committee's finance director but didn't have any records to turn over other than receipts for general expenses. Both men admitted that the Committee remained active, even after the arrest of the nineteen Italians. R.M. Walmsley admitted being related to S.P. Walmsley.

Walmsley admitted he agreed with the work of the Committee to rid New Orleans of all criminal elements, but he was not a member. Both Hernsheim and Walmsley admitted there were eighty-three members of the Committee, not fifty, and most of them were attached, in some way, to the cotton industry. After a couple of hours of captious debate, Judge Baker denied Adams' motion and set the formal arraignment for the nineteen Italians for the next day in Recorder's Court.

><

December 21, 1890
10:50 A.M.

Two Black Marias stopped in front of the Recorder's Courts on Carondelet Street, and the nineteen shackled Italians stepped down, followed by a phalanx of police officers and sheriff's deputies into the small courtroom. Since it was a Sunday morning, only reporters, including Laurence Hearn, Antonio, and Abraham, sat in the gallery. After the perfunctory not guilty pleas were entered for each defendant, the hearing concluded.

Outside the recorder's court, Peter Natali asked, "Mr. Adams, do you know what my name means in Italian?"

"No, Peter. What?"

"Christmas."

><

December 28, 1890
The Executive Mansion
Washington, D.C.
11:00 A.M.

President Benjamin Harrison and Secretary of State James Blaine sat around the glowing fireplace discussing the major issues they anticipated for the new year. Since the United States continued to push westward, new government agencies had to be created to handle problems in what was known as "Indian Country," and the protection of people moving to the newly admitted states. The telegraph reports described horrible incidents in the American wilderness, mostly attacks upon the new settlers in the region. Harrison decided to send the army to protect Americans as they pushed westward, but he hadn't forgotten New Orleans.

"What's Grant saying about the situation with the Italians in New Orleans?" the President asked.

"Nineteen men have been indicted for killing the police chief. Their trial is set for sometime in February. Grant doesn't believe they will get a fair trial, given the anti-Italian sentiments rooted in that city," Blaine responded.

"It seems New Orleans' Italians are being treated the same way our settlers are being treated in the western states and territories. Should I send the army to New Orleans, too?"

"No, sir. We must let Louisiana handle this case. Let's see how unfair the trial is, before we act. If it appears the Italians didn't get a fair trial and were convicted, then we might want to intervene if Italy makes a formal request. Although New Orleans is as wild a place as any town in the West, Louisiana has been a state since 1812, with full sovereignty recognized by the Tenth Amendment," Blaine said.

"How many of the defendants are Italian citizens?"

"Grant identified nine men who have not been naturalized as Americans," Blaine responded.

"That means Italy has a valid interest in the outcome of that trial. Instruct Grant to keep us posted. We can't have an international crisis at a time when we are growing our nation. We need to maintain our credibility here and abroad. I don't need New Orleans' insular passions coloring the image of the United States. That city has always been an enigmatic pain in the ass."

Part V
The Anvil

Chapter 69

Number 22 Corondelet Street
January 9, 1891
9:30 A.M.

Dominick O'Malley, A.D. Henriques, and Lionel Adams sat in Adams' office, thumbing through their notes from the first Provenzano trial. With the second trial beginning on the following Monday, the *ad hoc* prosecution team, minus John Finney, prepared to convict the Provenzano stevedores of ambushing the Matranga stevedores on the dark night of May 5, 1890. Because of the weight of the alibi evidence and the doubtful, discordant chimes of the victims' testimony, Judge Joshua Baker granted the alleged shooters a new trial, but this time featuring a different victim, Salvador Sunzeri, and a different judge, Robert Marr. As O'Malley examined the list of the state's and defense witnesses from the last trial, a sense of futility overtook him.

"Lionel, why are we prosecuting these guys again? Shouldn't we be concentrating on the Matrangas? It's all going to be the same witnesses saying the same shit," O'Malley groused.

"If we win, we gather some sympathy for the Matranga stevedores," Adams responded.

"But if we lose?" O'Malley probed.

"Then our alibi case becomes stronger in the Matranga case. We have cops ready to testify in both cases. Usually, an alibi defense is the weakest defense to be proffered by a defendant. But if a jury believes the cops in this case, there's a good chance they'll believe them in the Matranga case."

Before O'Malley could respond, there was a sharp rap on the office door. "Are you expecting anyone, Lionel?" Henriques asked.

"No. Dominick, go see who that is," Adams said.

"O'Malley stepped into the anteroom of the law offices and opened the frosted-glass door. His eyes glowered with roiling hate. Thomas Jenkins Semmes filled the door frame with his large countenance.

"May I come in?" Semmes asked.

"Sure. Lionel is in the next room," O'Malley said.

Semmes entered Adams' office and offered his respects to all present. Adams offered him a seat and hot coffee from a pot he kept on the radiator.

"I guess you're wondering why I'm here," Semmes said.

"Spying?" O'Malley asked.

"Let him speak, Dominick," Adams shot back. "You are welcome here, Mr. Semmes."

"Why don't you trust me, Mr. O'Malley?" Semmes asked.

"Let me see. It's not every day the President of the Boston Club comes calling. It's not every day the law partner of a member of the Committee of Fifty comes calling. It's not every day one of the attorneys for the Cotton Exchange comes calling—that's for starters," O'Malley responded.

"I understand your suspicion, Mr. O'Malley, but I am here to share my thoughts on matters you might find important."

"Go ahead, Mr. Semmes. We'll listen," Adams said, shooting a muzzling stare at O'Malley.

Semmes removed his overcoat and folded it on the back of his chair. He removed his bowler, revealing his gleaming bald head. He sat down and sipped his coffee. His bushy eyebrows furled with delight at the strong black brew.

"I see you preparing for the second Provenzano trial. I hope *our* clients testify truthfully this time," Semmes said. "But if they don't, it won't matter one bit."

"What do you mean?" Adams asked.

"Lionel, whatever the outcome of the case, we win."

"Excuse me," Adams said.

"If the Matrangas tell the truth, the Provenzanos will be acquitted. If they continue to lie, the Provenzanos will be acquitted. Either way, the Provenzanos win, and so do the Matrangas," Semmes asserted.

"Please explain," Henriques said.

"I want you to look at the larger picture here, not just who is telling the truth, or who is lying," Semmes began. "I want you to scrutinize both ambushes—the Matranga's and Hennessy's. Do you see any similarities?"

For a moment, the room fell silent. Adams' keen mind began to spin in multiple dimensions, like a seasoned trial lawyer. "Tell me more," Adams implored.

"As I see it, the Matrangas were attacked by men who would benefit from the shooting, and that wasn't the Provenzanos who, if the police are telling the truth, were imbibing at various taverns a couple of miles away from the fateful intersection. David Hennessy was attacked by men who would benefit from his assassination, and that wasn't the Matrangas, who were with you, Mr. Adams, at Fabacher's Restaurant, a couple of miles away."

"What about the others—Monasterio, the Marchesis, Polizzi, Traina, Natali, and Comitz?" Adams asked.

"The state has no proof any of those men were ever linked to the Matranga's stevedore operations, or Macheca's fruit import business. The only commonality is their Sicilian origins. That's it," Semmes said.

"Mr. Semmes, when I was a law student, I read your treatise on Louisiana's Civil Code. I admired your intellectual capacity, but this is criminal law, the foul renderings of human nature," Adams intoned. "You're accustomed to polite parlor discussions of the abstractions and theories of the law. The courtroom is the crucible where it's decided if men live or die."

Semmes smiled. "I understand your misunderstandings of my position, Mr. Adams. But remember, I was a Confederate Senator, and close friend and advisor to Jefferson Davis in Richmond. There's no tougher crucible than war. I know a man's neck can be snapped on the faith of prevarications. I've seen it. I'm not a pallid debutante at her first ball. My eyes have witnessed the flames of injustice. That's why I decided to take on the Matrangas' defense."

"Not to mention the hefty fee," O'Malley uttered.

Semmes ignored O'Malley and continued. "When I was a law student at Harvard, we studied a case where a popular lawyer took on the defense of eight armed British soldiers charged with shooting five unarmed citizens. In doing so, he hazarded his practice and suffered the opprobrium of his colleagues. But he forged on because he believed the law was the only path to justice. That man was John Adams, and he defended the soldiers in the case known as the *Boston Massacre*." His clients were acquitted, and Adams became our second President."

Semmes paused and reached into his suit pocket, and removed a folded piece of paper. "I, too, have lost friends and colleagues when the newspapers printed that I was lead counsel on the Matranga defense team. Members of the Boston Club have shunned me, and my law partner, James Legendre, is a member of the mayor's Committee. I've been called an apostate from the tribe of Iscariot. I'm neither. Like John Adams, I'm only a lawyer who seeks justice. If I may, I want to read you something from John Adams' diary, written in 1770."

"Please do, Mr. Semmes," Lionel Adams said.

"John Adams quoted an *Italian* legal philosopher, Cesare, Marchese di Baccaria, who, like me, opposes capital punishment. He wrote:

"If, by supporting the rights of mankind, and of invincible truth, I shall contribute to save from the agonies of death one unfortunate victim of tyranny, or ignorance, equally fatal, his blessings and years of transport will be sufficient consolation to me for the contempt of mankind."

"What does that mean?" O'Malley asked.

"It means there is an abundance of tyranny and ignorance in New Orleans, and it seeks the demise of the Italian race. Yes, Matranga and Macheca are paying me well—all of us, for that matter. But what kind of advocates of truth would we be if these men are executed for a crime they didn't commit? I learned many things as a Confederate Senator, and advisor to Jefferson Davis, but I learned more when Abraham Lincoln pardoned me," Semmes said.

"So, you are convinced they're innocent? O'Malley asked.

"Yes, I do. A man in my position hears things other men don't. Most of it is very troubling."

"Like what?" Henriques asked.

"Well, almost every newspaper in the city already has the Italians convicted and swinging from the gibbet. The witness who saw three of the assassins, none of whom were Italian or Sicilian, will never be identified or testify. The Committee of Fifty knows who killed Hennessy. They couldn't let him live for a number of reasons. He knew too much about the city's cotton barons, and their secrets, dating back to the Cotton Centennial of 1884, and continuing to his last night. And, lamentably, David had political ambitions and sought the counsel of Frank Romero's Italian political group. This has disturbed the Cotton Exchange."

"What about David's troubles in the Italian Colony?" O'Malley asked.

"He tried to make peace between the Matrangas and Provenzanos. You must examine closely who Hennessy was a threat to and why. Banana boats and stevedores? Really?" Semmes asked.

"The Cotton Exchange lost money when the Matrangas unloaded Macheca's boats, instead of the cotton boats," O'Malley said.

"They're still losing money, but they will make it up. Remember, New Orleans exports over twenty-five percent of the United States' cotton to Europe. Only Galveston and Mobile come close to ours."

"Doesn't the Cotton Exchange want to control the docks?" Henriques asked.

"Yes. And they are preparing to do that now. After the Provenzanos get out of jail, they are moving across the river. They won't pose any threat to New Orleans," Semmes said.

"How do you know they are going to get out of jail?" Lionel Adams asked.

"Because you are going to lose the case. You need to lose the case, and you will lose the case. It's the only way the Matrangas can win," Semmes insisted.

"Mr. Semmes, I have never lost a case deliberately. It's not who I am," Lionel Adams said.

"You don't have to. The evidence isn't there to convict the Provenzanos, and you know it. Judge Marr knows it, and the soon-to-be-appointed new police chief knows it," Semmes asserted. Your hot anvil of cross-examination will not prevail."

"What new police chief?" O'Malley asked.

"A fellow Ohioan, Dominick. Dexter Gaster. He is no threat to anyone in New Orleans—an obsequious little man."

"Did the Ring kill David?" Lionel Adams asked.

"Excellent question. David knew too much about too many people in power in this city, and they controlled the Ring. The Matrangas are innocent, and Luzenberg knows it."

"How does Luzenberg know it?" Henriques asked.

Semmes stood and placed his cup on the table, sleeved his overcoat, and popped his bowler on his head. "When I leave here, gentlemen, I'm going to the parish prison to meet *our* clients. I am going to exhort them not to speak with anyone except the men in this room. I have it on good authority, and there are no secrets in New Orleans, the Pinkerton brothers have introduced one of their agents into the prison to pose as a counterfeiter. The United States Secret Service is assisting in this charade.

He is trying to gain the confidence of our clients and extract any incriminating information from them. The state's case is falling apart, and the Committee blames you, Mr. O'Malley, for coercing their witnesses to change their testimony."

"Bullshit," O'Malley roared.

"If that's true, why hasn't Luzenberg arrested Dominick?" Lionel Adams asked.

"I'm not saying it's true. I'm just saying it has been said," Semmes responded.

"Are you telling us the United States government and the Pinkertons are trying to gather evidence by beguiling our clients?" Henriques asked.

"Do you have a copy of the *Daily Picayune* from January sixth, last? Get a copy. Turn to page two. You will find an article where the Secret Service arrested a counterfeiter by the name of Antonio Ruggiero in Amite, Louisiana. His real name is Francis P. Diamio. He works for the Pinkertons, and as of right now, he is in the same cell with Emanuel Polizzi," Semmes said.

"Polizzi belongs in an asylum," O'Malley said.

"That's true. But I am told he's the only one talking to Diamio," Semmes said.

"Counterfeiting is a federal charge. Does William Grant know about this?" Lionel Adams asked.

"Yes. Before I came here, I checked the docket sheet at the federal court. Ruggiero appeared before the United States Commissioner yesterday and was given a five-hundred-dollar appearance bond. I'm sure someone will put the bond up soon, and we'll never see Ruggiero again. Grant knows. Have you ever wondered why he has never prosecuted anyone for violating the Anti-Padrone Act? His friends profit from the sinew and toil of the Sicilians. Remember, I was the United States Attorney here under President Buchanan. I know how Grant got his job. As of now, Ruggiero can only repeat the utterings of a crazy man. That's why I must go to the prison, before he wheedles his way into our other clients," Semmes said.

"Do you want me to come with you?" O'Malley asked.

"No. Members of the Ring, especially J.D. Houston, the Committee of Fifty, and the newspapers are watching you. Stay close to Mr. Adams, and stay away from dark streets," Semmes warned.

Chapter 70

Criminal District Court
January 23, 1891
5:30 P.M.

Lionel Adams sat at the state's counsel table, pondering what had happened during the past week. The second Provenzano trial bore no surprises, other than more alibi witnesses. Adams, during his cross-examination of each defense witness, heard the words of Thomas J. Semmes echoing in his ears. He knew his usual approach to challenging the witnesses' words on the white-hot anvil of cross-examination was tepid, at best. Adams knew he could have done better, but his thoughts wrapped around the Matranga trial, just three weeks away. His usual confident countenance waned as A.D. Henriques whispered in his ear, "Finney and the defense team struck a deal. No closing arguments. Just submit the matter to the jury."

"Really?" Adams said.

"What do you think?"

"Let's get out of here," Adams said. "Let Finney take the verdict. I need a drink."

Adams and Henriques gathered their notes, slinked out of the courtroom, and went to a small tavern on Girod Street frequented by attorneys. Both lawyers sipped rye whiskey and hardly discussed the case. It was a ritual for lawyers in New Orleans to imbibe after a trial, like shaking the dust off, after a long carriage ride. But this time, they needed to feel the sting of the liquor descend deep into their souls, for they knew men's lives were on the block of justice, if not in this case, the one starting in a few weeks. In honor of Hennessy's last meal, they ordered pan-fried oysters, but no milk. Adams stared into the bar's mirror as the gas lamps reflected his image. "I could have done better," he mumbled into his glass.

"We did our best, under the circumstances. The jury looked alert and understood the case," Henriques said. "If the Provenzanos didn't shoot at the Matrangas, who did?"

"Semmes knows," Adams responded. "A man like him knows how to warn people without warning them. By the way, where's O'Malley?"

"I sent him home at dusk and told him to stay there," Henriques said.

"Good. I fear they're going to kill him. In many ways, that Irishman is a lot like David, in his ability to make enemies," Adams lamented.

As Adams ordered another round of rye, a newsboy entered the tavern, and yelled, "Provenzanos were just found not guilty."

Adams slugged back his drink as his eyes focused on a quote from the French philosopher Voltaire hanging on the wall over the bar. It read, *"It's dangerous to be right in matters where established men are wrong."*

"That didn't take long. I guess Semmes was right," Adams said.

"He was. The *Times-Democrat* reported this morning that Dexter Gaster is the new police chief."

With sodden courage, Adams grabbed the newsboy by the shoulders, stood him atop the bar and yelled, "Listen to me, everyone." The tavern fell silent. "Despite all the newspapers, the Committee of Fifty, the mayor, the Cotton Exchange, and your gilded secret carnival clubs, a unanimous jury just announced there's no *Mafia* war in this city. It's a contrivance of the prejudiced imaginations of those who seek profit, status, and wealth on the sweaty backs of the Sicilians they brought here to serve their venality. The whip hand is the appendage of the coward."

Adams put the newsboy back on the floor and left the tavern. He waddled to the intersection of Girod and Rampart and waited for the streetcar. As he did, he gazed down Girod Street towards Hennessy's residence. It was dark, and the streetlights offered only a pale halo against the dark sky. He remembered the newspaper reports reciting the inciting words of Boylan Detective, Billy O'Connor, on October 15, 1890. *Dagoes.* Adams remembered it was at this intersection that O'Connor bid Hennessy their final goodnight. Adams remembered O'Connor telling police that after they parted, he walked river-bound on Girod Street, as Hennessy walked home in the opposite direction. Adams, frissoned by an epiphanic flash thought, *O'Connor, where were you going? You live at Number 55 Spain Street—over four miles away—downriver.* And as the streetcar approached, Adams, still feeling the grip of the rye, yelled into the night, "O'Connor, you son-of-bitch, why didn't you catch this streetcar home?"

Chapter 71

Carnival Week

February 1st to 10th, 1891

New Orleans

February 1st

After Sunday Mass, Maria Bertucci served a fine traditional Italian dinner for the Brothers, Father Fontebuis, Laurence Hearn, Antonio Terranova, and Abraham Jurrichi. Although Jewish, Abraham welcomed being included in the Catholic traditions of his home country, especially the indulgences of Brother Angelo's private collection of Chianti wines. As usual, Hearne brought an armful of the city's newspapers, and a discussion of current events ensued, annotated by Father Fontebuis's contribution of the Jesuits, from the other side of Canal Street. And since the neighbors of St. Aloysius Academy could smell Miss Bertucci's cooking, and knew she always cooked more than any group of hungry men could consume in one sitting, tattered children armed with empty baskets gathered at the school's front gate, waiting for portions of the ample leftovers. No one who lived near St. Aloysius went hungry, especially on Sundays.

"The Sunday papers are filled with the excitement of the coming carnival season," Hearn announced. "It appears Eliza Jane Nicholson is using her *Daily Picayune* as the heraldry for the city's faux royalty and their tableaus."

Father Fontebuis leaned forward on the table and lowered his voice. "I have a little secret I want to share with everybody. Can you keep it to yourselves until it's public?"

Everyone in the dining room nodded.

"Archbishop Jenssen visited the Jesuit school last week, and told Father O'Shanahan he planned to issue a Pastoral letter soon attacking portions of the carnival. He knows it will stir up the anti-Catholic emotions in the city."

"What is he going to say?" asked Brother Stanislaus.

"He's aware Freemasonry has invaded the lives of some of the Catholic faithful—those who have climbed the social ladder of the city. He's said the Church is against it for theological reasons, and he will attack it, as well as the many secret societies that form the foundations of the social structure of New Orleans."

"Like the Boston and Pickwick Clubs?" Hearn asked.

"Yes. And there are several more. We have some Protestant students at our school, whose fathers belong to these secret clubs. The Archbishop wanted to warn us that we could lose our enrollment because of the letter. How many Protestants do you have at St. Aloysius?" Father Fontebuis asked.

"None. We have one Jewish student—Abraham—but our entire enrollment is Catholic, and most of them are French or Italian," Brother Stanislaus responded.

"The Archbishop is also attacking the practice of people marrying their first cousins, which seems to be common in New Orleans," Father Fontebuis said.

Hearn erupted in laughter, which drew curious stares. "Why do you laugh, Mr. Hearn?" Father Fontebuis asked.

"Father, that's how they enforce and maintain their family and business structures. Pay attention to the newspapers this week. *The Daily Picayune* and *The Times-Democrat* will publish the names of every family associated with the three main carnival clubs—Rex, Comus, and Proteus. These are the men of the clubs, and most importantly, the Cotton Exchange. They control everything in New Orleans. Your Archbishop knows this. Father O'Shanahan knows it. Everyone knows it, but tolerates it. These people beg to have their names in the society columns. It gives them status. Read the papers. The names never change. That's why Jenssen is upset about these families marrying into each other," Hearn said.

"There are some medical concerns, too," Father Fontebuis said.

"Does the Archbishop know that intermarriage builds and sustains this city's social order and rank, by excluding others unworthy of admission?" Hearn asked.

"The Archbishop used the word 'clannish.'" Father Fontebuis said.

"Excellent choice of words," Hearn said. "Incidentally, on page three of today's edition, the Times-Democrat identified this year's Rex. His name is James S. Richardson; he is the largest cotton planter in the world and sometimes writes for *The Daily Picayune*. He is also a member of the

Committee of Fifty. The gates to this city's kingdom are sealed with affinity and consanguinity, never to be severed by the word of a Catholic cleric."

><

February 3rd

The city's newspapers reported the identity of the petite jurors selected for February. Sixty-six men were selected for Judge Marr's court, and seventy-one for Judge Baker's. Dominick O'Malley sat at his desk and searched each name for any affiliation with the Committee of Fifty, the city's secret societies, or the Cotton Exchange. To his amazement, about twenty names from each section had familial and fraternal connections, which portended a lengthy jury selection in the Hennessy murder case, set for February sixteenth. In O'Malley's mind, he knew behind the sequined masks of the carnival royalty, the eyes of rapacious injustice peered upon the common man, whose worth was measured only by his use, while the laws were designed to enforce the social structure of New Orleans, casting the illusion of equal justice for all.

O'Malley knew the upcoming trial would chart the course of commercial and societal New Orleans for decades to come, and the silly parades, pageantry, and tableaus would announce to everyone who really controls the city. Like hungry beggars, the common population could only watch from afar, and hope for the morsels and trinkets thrown by white-gloved hands. Among the many names listed by the broadsheets, only one shocked him—Thomas Jenkins Semmes, president of the Boston Club.

><

February 7th

After Sunday dinner, Laurence Hearn spread *The Daily Picayune* and the *Times Democrat* across the brothers' dining room table at St. Aloysius. Since he had lived in New Orleans longer than any of the Brothers, Antonio, or Abraham, he assumed the role of instructor of the de rigueur and secret rituals of New Orleans' carnival. First, he used the society columns of the *Picayune*, authored by Eliza Jane Nicholson, to identify the members of the carnival societies. Every name and their position had a purpose and rank. Hearn identified many of the names, families, and their businesses. Hearn explained that the regal names enjoyed recognition and status through the planting, harvesting, and exporting of cotton. Several of the families were known to have cotton plantations, which Hearn annotated by reminding them that Rex of 1891 was regarded as the largest cotton planter in the world.

As Hearn's lecture continued, he emphasized the allure of New Orleans' carnival, which only superseded the draw of the 1884 Cotton Centennial, venued in Audubon Park, about eight miles upriver from Canal Street. "Many of this country's wealthiest men attended that uptown fair and have returned to New Orleans every year to maintain their business relationships," Hearn said with a wink.

"What kind of relationships?" Brother Angelo asked.

"All kinds, Brother. As you well know, the etymology of the word carnival derives from the words '*free from flesh,*'" Hearn said. "But over the years, it's only symbolic, as the Rite of Penance, during Lent, is a tenant of the Catholics, not the Protestants."

"I heard there are some demonic overtones associated with carnival. Is that true?" Brother Stanislaus asked.

Hearn pointed to an article in the *Picayune stating* that Comus will "*Illustrates Demonology*" through its Tableaux. "It's supposed to be mystical satire. But I'll go see for myself."

"Can we go, Brother?" Antonio asked.

"No. You are safer on this side of Canal Street."

"And these are the people who hold the fate of nineteen men confined to the parish prison?" Brother Angelo asked.

"Congratulations, Brother. You understand the pretense of justice in New Orleans," Hearn lamented. "While nineteen innocent Italians sit in the shadows of iron bars, the other side of Canal Street will be celebrating itself, while festooned in the puerile world of mystical fantasies."

"Do you think those men are innocent?" Brother Stanislaus asked.

"Yes, I do," Hearn replied. "I have studied the facts of Hennessy's case, and have concluded that the ones who benefited the most from his death are not in jail. They are parading through the streets of this city, as we speak. The trial will be a farce unless Lionel Adams attacks the state's witnesses and pounds them like a hot mule shoe on an anvil.

"Luzenberg is concealing exculpatory evidence. Why? Because he's been ordered to do so. The jury acquitted the Provenzanos, who are now free, because police officers offered alibi testimony. Some of those same police officers are alibi witnesses for the Matrangas. If a Mafia war existed between the Matrangas and the Provenzanos, why didn't the mayor assemble a Committee of Fifty last May? Hennessy would have loved to have the help, and it could have saved his life. No, some people wanted a *Mafia* war and saw profit in it. The mayor did nothing, because he knew how to rid the docks of the Italians, and get rid of Hennessy, too," Hearn asserted. "Remember, the Provenzanos were in jail until just last week. They have moved across the river—out of New Orleans."

"It sounds like you lay the blame at the Mayor's feet? Why would the mayor want to kill his own police chief?" Brother Stanislaus asked.

"Hennessy knew too much about the mayor and his friends, dating back to the Cotton Centennial. He was trying to broker peace between the Matrangas and the Provenzanos. But Hennessy got caught up in the storm of a family rivalry, exaggerated by the broadsheets. Newspapers are dangerous things. They can convict an innocent man before he is arrested, and the mayor knows how to use the newspapers, except *The Mascot,* which he loathes."

"Wasn't Hennessy killed because he was going to testify he had evidence from Italy that would hurt the Matrangas?" Brother Angelo asked.

Hearn laughed. "There is no evidence from Italy. Even George Vandervoort told the *Picayune* and *The Times Democrat* that. And if the police department had such evidence, Vandervoort could have introduced it at the second Provenzano trial to attack the Matrangas. Every newspaper has asked for it. No one has produced it. I bet it never comes out in the Hennessy trial. Why? Because it doesn't exist."

><

February 10th

Mayor Hugh John Grant of New York City proudly pranced among his New Orleans hosts as he took his seat in the bleachers attached to the façade of the Crescent City Billiard building at the corner of Canal Street and St. Charles Avenue. The building also housed the Boston Club. Grant's amazement showed through his wide blue-green eyes as he looked over the throngs of bands, citizens, and visitors. Mayor Joseph A. Shakspeare sat to his left, and Albert Baldwin sat to his right. Other members of the Boston and Pickwick Clubs, who were not part of the Tableaux and Rex Parade, huddled near their esteemed guests. With the mayor of New York sitting on Canal Street, Shakspeare felt he had fulfilled one of his dreams to make New Orleans a world-class city. In his sodden mind, the long shadow, which reached down Basin Street, would soon be gone. All secrets would be buried. All reputations preserved. All past indiscretions would be forgotten, and a new city of commerce would emerge on the wide crescent of the Mississippi River.

Mayor Grant's gaze settled on a monument erected in Canal Street's middle. It was a bronze statue of a man, facing the river. "Who is the man on the pedestal?" Grant asked.

"That's Henry Clay," Shakspeare responded. He had family ties to New Orleans. We use the monument and plaza as a meeting spot for anything important in New Orleans, like Carnival."

Grant nodded and continued to enjoy the spectacle.

As Shakspeare vaunted the many assets of New Orleans to anyone who would listen, J.D. Houston tapped him on the shoulder and placed a folded copy of the morning edition of *The Times-Democrat* in his lap. Houston pointed to two columns on page eight of the paper. One column covered the Masonic ceremony where Dexter Gaster was awarded a new superintendent's badge by the Excelsior Lodge, accompanied by a citation read by George Vandervoort. In the next column, the newspaper published the Pastoral Letter of Archbishop Francis Janssens condemning Freemasonry, and, among other things, the open practice of New Orleanians marrying their first cousins. Shakspeare's blood roiled, and he shoved the paper back into Houston's hands. "That damn Archbishop should take care of his side of Canal Street, and we will take care of ours," the mayor huffed. "Get me a horse."

Shakspeare excused himself, went downstairs, and met Houston, who held a black spirited horse by the bridle. After the mayor climbed into the saddle, he kicked the horse in the ribs, causing it to buck, slamming the mayor onto the granite cobblestoned street. A doctor and carriage were called, and the mayor was squired home, with severe bruises to his left side. The Ash Wednesday editions of the newspapers reported that the mayor remained in his Carondelet Street home for the balance of the festivities. There was no mention of alcohol being involved in the mishap, or whether it was the second time the mayor had fallen from his horse during Carnival.

Chapter 72

Criminal District Court
February 16, 1891
Morning

As the sun broke over the Mississippi River, golden shards of sunlight dissolved the night's damp shadows. New Orleans awoke to the barking of newspaper boys, hawking their morning broadsheets on every street corner. Though the solemn season of Lent had begun to shroud the penitents of the city, pale, faithless faces gathered in every café, poring over the papers' coverage of the trial of nineteen Italians, accused of killing David C. Hennessy. In a few hours, the grinding and hissing machinery of New Orleans justice would steam awake, like the giant cotton presses on the docks. The laborious process of taking raw facts and ginning them into one neat bale of justice would take about a month. But the magistrates of New Orleans' justice seemed patient with the process, which they believed would end on the city's gallows.

If black coffee didn't stiffen the spine, the list of the state's and defense witnesses would. The state, represented by Charles Luzenberg, J.C. Walker, W.L. Evans, and Arthur Dunn, filed a list of ninety-one witnesses, while the defense, represented by Lionel Adams, Thomas J. Semmes, A.D. Henriques, Charles Butler, and Arthur Gastinel, listed two hundred and fifteen witnesses. Defendant Charles Patorno, represented by Ferdinand Armand, listed thirteen witnesses, for a total of three hundred and nineteen witnesses.

Some of the witnesses resided near Hennessy's home. Some were police officers, some were patrons of Fabacher's Restaurant, and Luzenberg had the audacity to list Fanny Deckert, the Burgundy Street madam, as a state witness. Some reviewed the lists and concluded the trial would be a repeat of the Provenzano trial, while others knew the Committee would insist on a different outcome.

At the Moring Call Café on Decatur Street, Lionel Adams had breakfast while reading the *Picayune*. While the veteran trial lawyer examined the witness lists, one name leapt from the page—William O'Connor. Adams had spent the last few days writing notes and concession points he planned on using to attack O'Connor. He had a map prepared of the corner of Girod and Rampart, and how far it was from O'Connor's home on Spain Street. The map included the streetcar line, which, if taken, would have dropped O'Connor off a half block from his residence. Hennessy's friend had no reason to walk riverbound on Girod to an area of raw concupiscence, known as the *Swamp,* second only to Gallatin Street for its *"Buckets of Blood"* juke joints. Adams knew his plan to use O'Connor to pry open the real plan to kill Hennessy, by linking O'Connor's boss, Thomas Boylan, a member of the Committee of Fifty, was dangerous. As a true advocate, he had to do it.

><

As Adams's cab pulled next to the courthouse on Lafayette Street, he saw a massive throng of well-dressed men, gray-dungaree tradesmen, and curious onlookers chocking the entire breadth of Camp Street. Newspaper boys sang little jingles to attract attention to their wares. Newspaper reporters from New Orleans and across the nation took notes. Laurence Hearn, Antonio, and Abraham were among them, each dressed in black suits, white shirts, and black ties. Legions of mounted police officers and sheriff's deputies patrolled the crowd. Some blood-thirsty entrepreneurs sold hangman's nooses as morbid novelties.

Adams walked to the courthouse, where deputies pushed the crowd aside to make a path for him. Once inside the courthouse, a deputy escorted Adams to the courtroom, where he found the defense team already in place. After Adams greeted the other attorneys, he took his seat and perused his notes. A large pendulum wall clock ticked the minutes away. In an hour, jury selection would begin.

As Adams pored over his notes, he felt a tap on his shoulder. It was Algernon S. Badger. While the men knew each other, they hadn't spoken in months. Adams stood and greeted Hennessy's mentor.

"May I have a private word with you, Mr. Adams?"

Adams nodded, and both men retreated to a quiet corner of the large courtroom. "Mr. Adams, please excuse my intrusion at this important hour, but I must ask you a question. "Do you really believe your clients are innocent?" Badger asked.

"General, I'm convinced they are. I, like you, had a fondness for David. He was my client. I wouldn't take this defense for any amount of money if I felt otherwise. Now, let me ask you a question. Why would you allow yourself to be a member of the mayor's Committee of Fifty? You have nothing in common with those men besides your Masonic connections. By the way, congratulations on being elected Grand Commander of the Knights Templars of Louisiana. I read it in the newspapers," Adams said.

Badger blanched. "Thank you, sir. I lent my name to the effort to seek justice in this matter. Shakspeare needed my *gravitas,* I supposed, and I believed these men were guilty."

"General, how can nineteen men, who have no connection to each other, other than being Italian, conspired to kill David, for no reason? Macheca and Matranga are businessmen—some of these men of just common laborers. One is a cobbler. One is a tinsmith. Others are just fruit peddlers. It's just a hodgepodge of men with long foreign names, unfit for New Orleans' society. That's it," Adams insisted.

"What about the new one-hundred-dollar bill found in the cobbler's clothes? What about the war between the Matrangas and Provenzanos? What about Macheca's threats?" Badger asked.

"I will not reveal my case, but I will only say that Mr. Monasterio had more contact with Antonio Monteleone than Macheca or Matranga. Remember, Monteleone started as a cobbler, too, and Monasterio did piece work for him. And when the Provenzanos were found not guilty of ambushing the Matrangas, that ended the state's theory of a *Mafia* war. This entire case is in a contrivance of the mayor, his friends in the Cotton Exchange, the city's secret clubs, societies, and newspapers. Maybe David was killed because someone wanted his job. Maybe he was killed because he knew too much about the gentlemen of this city and their *lodge* meetings during the Cotton Centennial. Maybe he was killed because he was Catholic," Adams bristled. "And if David wanted to help the Provenzanos, remember he tried to bring peace to both sides."

"Are you suggesting Freemasonry had a hand in killing David? That's repugnant to everything we stand for," Badger responded.

"David was Catholic. He wouldn't bow before any *Worshipful* master. The Archbishop has even recognized these dark fraternities when he published his pastoral letter in *The Times-Democrat* on Carnival morning. David had more enemies on this side of Canal Street than in the Italian Colony."

"Wasn't he killed because he had incriminating information from Rome about Matranga, and some other Italians, and was going to reveal it at the Provenzano trial?" Badger probed.

"Nonsense. If the police department had such information, I would have known about it. Remember, I was one of the prosecutors in the second Provenzano trial. No one from the police department proffered such evidence, and they won't at this trial. It doesn't exist. Sorry, General, but you have aligned yourself with a band of killers hiding behind their fancy names and fake titles to gain control over the commerce of the river and to bury David's secrets," Adams asserted.

"Be careful, Mr. Adams. There are many powerful people watching this trial, and they demand justice for David's death," Badger warned. "After this case, you still have to practice law in this city."

Adams became agitated, but composed. "And what about Mr. Semmes? Must he worry about practicing law, too? The mayor doesn't care about David. His funeral was a political circus—a political feint. The Committee-controlled cops rummaged through David's office the night he was buried. They found nothing," Adams asserted.

"Mr. Adams, remember you are an officer of the law," Badger warned.

Adams inched closer to Badger's face. "When the day comes when American lawyers realize the law is an instrument of control, and not a pathway to justice, or peace, they will rise up, and demand the demons of tyranny be denied all power. When that day arrives, the monarchial oligarchies will be crushed under the boot of freedom and liberty. But until that day, we are all slaves of the magistrates who lord over us from altars *you* kneel before—not me. Now, excuse me. I have a jury to pick."

><

The crowd gathered around the two Black Marias, like vultures on a fence post. The police and deputies had to push the yapping crowd back to create a passage from the prison vans to the courthouse. As the nineteen shackled defendants walked through the crowd, jeers and taunts filled the air. "Who killa da chief?" several men sneered. Deputies hurried the Italians through the teeming throng to Chief Deputy Alcee LeBlanc's office, where they were to wait to be called into court. Newspaper scribes hurriedly described the men. The *Daily Picayune* printed:

"Charles Matranga...His face is full of shrewdness and intelligence. He wears a heavy mustache which, like his hair, is of Latin blackness. He was attired in dark clothes, including a red-striped cravat containing a conspicuous scarf pin of clustered diamonds..."

"Joseph P. Macheca...looked equally prosperous, but not so distinctively Italian in features...The nose is aquiline, the brow sharp and the chin strong... He wore a black suit, tailor-made and of rich material, with quite a display of jewelry."

The other defendants were neatly dressed and groomed, but the newspapers focused on Matranga and Macheca.

In the large courtroom, some potential jurors sat in the gallery. After the defendants were shepherded inside the courthouse, the reporters raced curious spectators to the second-floor courtroom. Charles Luzenberg, accompanied by Assistant D.A. John Finney and attorneys J.C. Walker, Arthur Dunn, and W.L. Evans sat at the state's table. According to Luzenberg, the latter three were being paid by the Committee of Fifty. Thomas J. Semmes, Lionel Adams, A.D. Henriques, Arthur Gastinel, and Charles Butler sat around a law book-ladened defense table. Charles Patorno's lawyer, Ferdinand Armand, sat to the extreme left of the bar.

About half past ten, Judge Baker took the bench. He wore a new black suit, and his long black beard seemed to have been trimmed. After the clerk called the case, Luzenberg stood and stunned everyone in the courtroom.

"May it please the Court, the state of Louisiana wishes to sever the case against the defendants, and proceed to prosecute defendants Matranga, Macheca, Monasterio, Antonio Marchesi, Asperi Marchesi, Incardona, Polizzi, Bagnetto, and Scaffidi, at this time."

"Does the defense have any objection?" Judge Barker asked.

"No, your honor. It's the state's right to sever," Adams responded. "But, I would ask the court to call the roll of the jurors and witnesses, to determine if they are present to proceed. Judging from what I see in the gallery, there are more newspaper reporters than jurors or witnesses present."

Judge Baker agreed. And after calling the roll of potential jurors and identifying witnesses for the state and defense, it appeared many failed to show, as summoned. Baker then issued an order to the clerk to issue new summons for the next day, and for the sheriff to serve them. He also ordered the sheriff to remand the nineteen defendants to the parish prison and return the next day with the nine defendants Luzenberg identified. The court adjourned at about noon.

Chapter 73

Criminal District Court

February 17th to 27th , 1891

10:00 A.M.

On the first day of jury selection, Antonio Terranova, Abraham Jurrichi, and Laurence Hearn sat in the courtroom gallery reserved for newspaper reporters, as the nine defendants entered the courtroom under heavy guard. Asperi Marchesi shambled behind his adult co-defendants, like a bedraggled puppy. He shot a glance and smiled at Antonio, which was readily returned. And while the guards concentrated on the other defendants, Antonio palmed several pieces of Italian candy to Asperi, as a sign of hope. All the defendants were attired well, but months in the parish prison caused their clothes to hang on their bones, like laundry in the wind. Even Matranga's and Macheca's fine suits needed tailoring.

Judge Baker instructed the state and defense regarding the number of peremptory challenges they had to excuse a juror for no cause, other than their intuition. Since there were nine defendants and twelve jurors, Baker allowed the defense two challenges per defendant. Given months of adverse publicity and the city's open hostility towards Italians, the task of picking an impartial jury seemed impossible. But Adams's fearless heart pounded with anticipation.

Of the seventy-one regular jurors called, only one could be seated, which portended a captious, prolonged battle for a fair and impartial jury. Jewish jeweler, Jacob Seligman, braved every question and survived being cut by either side or the judge. As he sat, alone, in the jury box, the judge ordered the clerk to issue three hundred summonses for male trial jurors, randomly selected from the city's directory. Baker intuited it would be difficult to find a fair jury, but he was determined to do so. The court adjourned until the next morning.

><

Day two of jury selection confirmed Judge Baker's intuition. Both parties fought like hyenas over the flesh of each potential juror, seeking the slightest weakness or fault in each man called. Each side riveted each potential juror with questions regarding their nationality, their prejudices, their intelligence, their feelings about capital punishment, their fixed opinions regarding guilt or innocence, and their prejudices about Italians. When one juror expressed a potential bias, the other side would try to rehabilitate the venireman. If Baker detected an impasse, he would cut them for cause.

By the close of the first full day of jury selection, four more jurors were sworn in. Still, the heat of the examinations presaged a ravaging fight, for one side wanting to hang nine Italians, including a young boy, while the other was ordained to protect them from the gallows. Each side maintained tally sheets, numbering the names and challenges used, and calculated how many they had left. And by the end of the week, February twenty-first, eight jurors had been sworn. Judge Baker's tally sheet reflected two hundred and thirty-two veniremen cut for cause, twenty-nine by the state, forty-three by the defense, and forty-four by mutual consent.

An exhausted Judge Baker ordered the clerk to issue one thousand summonses for more trial jurors. Every reporter noted that most of the cuts were for a man's opposition to capital punishment or prejudice against Italians. Since the indictment never mentioned the *Mafia*, Judge Baker cautioned both sides not to mention the word during jury selection.

><

At the close of the ninth day of trial, the jury selection had distilled only ten qualified jurors. Over seven hundred trial jurors were examined by the state and the defense. The tediousness of the process began to wear on the attorneys and the judge. Tempers flared from counsel tables and from the bench. During one examination, a juror said he had read all the newspapers regarding Hennessy's murder and had a fixed opinion of guilt on all the defendants. Angry, fatigued, and frustrated Adams whipped out the October 19, 1890 edition of *The Times-Democrat* and showed it to the potential juror.

"Do you remember reading this newspaper?" Adams probed.

"I read a lot of papers," the juror responded.

"Do you remember this one?" Adams asked.

"Can I read it?"

"Take your time," Adams said.

The potential juror read the pertinent section and rested the paper on his lap."

Adams moved in. "Does that article indicate that a witness saw three of the shooters, and none were of the 'Sicilian Element?'" Adams asked.

Luzenberg objected, but Judge Barker overruled the objection.

"Answer the question," Judge Baker said.

"I remember it, but I still think they did it," the juror persisted.

Baker cut the juror for cause.

><

Charles Boessen, who lived at Number 402 Customhouse Street and worked as a clerk in a small grocery store, was crowned the twelfth and final juror near midnight on February 27th. Judge Baker immediately swore the jury in and instructed the sheriff and his deputies to escort the jury to the hostelry built into the attic of St. Patrick's Hall. That would be their home until they returned a verdict. The sheriff's staff prepared the jurors' meals and sent their laundry to a Chinese vendor on Magazine Street. Doctors remained on call, if necessary.

Judge Baker's complexion paled with fatigue, but he ordered the state to be ready to start their case the next morning at ten-thirty. The newspaper etching artist remained in the courtroom, putting finishing touches on their blocks. Afterwards, given the late hour, Laurence Hearn escorted Antonio and Abraham back to St. Aloysius Academy, admonishing them to get a good night's rest, for they were about to witness how New Orleans justice decides if men live or die.

Chapter 74

Criminal District Court
February 28, 1891
9:30 A.M.

Since it was a brisk Saturday morning, and the first day of taking testimony in the Hennessy murder case, the crowd seemed larger and more animated than on the first day of jury selection. Hundreds of men and women gathered at the intersection of Lafayette and Camp Streets, waiting to catch a glimpse of the nine Italians, whose lives rested in the hands of twelve men they had never met, except through the pages of the city's newspapers. Despite their testimony to the attorneys during jury selection, no one believed each juror's professed ignorance of the Hennessy case. The city swelled with everyone's interpretation of what happened last October, and who did it and why. Every debate seemed annotated by what someone read in the newspapers, which only fomented grist for the rumor mill.

When the Black Marias backed against the curbstones and unloaded the defendants, a phalanx of police officers formed a blue corridor from the wagon to the courthouse's front door. Once inside, the Italians were ushered to the courtroom and seated behind their lawyers. Afterwards, a crowd raced up the stairs of the courthouse, where the stench of stale cigar smoke hung in the air, accompanied by filth, unbecoming of a temple of justice. *The Times-Democrat* called the corridor a "colossal spittoon."

It didn't take long for every seat to be taken by eager blood-lusting spectators. Newspaper reporters from around the country sat next to local reporters, including two anxious boys from St. Aloysius Academy. Joining Lawrence Hearn was the *Mascot's* ribald columnist, Frank Waters, who, like Hearn, knew the Italians were innocent. Both men had keen observation skills and knew the societal sewers of New Orleans. Waters often used his column to harpoon the mayor and his retinue of gilded effete men of self-affected title and status.

At ten o'clock, Judge Baker ascended the bench. His stern

countenance, framed by two tall brass lamps, only enhanced the severity and solemnity of his altar of justice. After the clerk called the docket and the attorneys recorded their appearances for their respective parties, Judge Baker ordered the jury to enter the courtroom. To avoid any mischief between the jury and spectators, Judge Baker ordered Detective John Kerwin to sit between the jury and the gallery to prevent any furtive signals in the jury box's direction. A deputy sat behind Dominick O'Malley.

After the jury was seated, Judge Baker began to read the witness list for the state. If they were present, they were escorted to Judge Marr's courtroom to wait to testify. When Judge Baker read Billy O'Connor's name, a slight smile sliced across Lionel Adams's face, widening when the judge read Boylan Officer J.C. Roe's name. *The Picayune* touted both men as eyewitnesses to the Hennessy shooting, and would seal the defendants' fates.

After reading the state's witness list, Judge Baker read the defendants' witness list and told them to leave the courthouse and return the following Friday. After reading the long lists of witnesses, the judge took a ten-minute recess to allow the attorneys some final moments to prepare their opening statements. During the recess, O'Malley told Adams, "Villere just released Ruggiero from the parish prison. He's gone."

Adams smiled.

><

At one o'clock, Judge Baker took the bench and allowed both sides to give their opening statements. Charles Luzenberg's statement, though fiery, seemed abbreviated and over-promising. He vowed he would provide a litany of eyewitnesses to the assassination. Still, he said nothing about the *Times-Democrat* reporter who overheard an eyewitness telling the mayor and police he saw three of the assassins *"who were not of the Sicilian element."* Lionel Adams seized the moment and attacked the state's assertions, assuring the jury to pay close attention to the quality, not quantity, of the state's evidence. Before sitting down, Adams paced in front of the jury, staring each man in the eye. His steps echoed across the courtroom. At first, he said nothing, but after a few tense moments, Adams said, "Each of you swore you would leave your prejudices outside. I ask you to value these innocent men's lives and honor that oath."

The state's first witness was Dr. P.E. Archinard, the Assistant Coroner for Orleans Parish. Dr. Archinard testified, in gruesome detail, about the wounds Hennessy suffered. Using his own body for illustrative purposes, Dr. Archinard testified that Hennessy sustained three fatal shotgun blasts to his body, with the shot and balls entering his left side, and traversing his stomach, lungs, and liver. Hennessy had shotgun wounds from his left cheek, descending his left side, and down to his left leg. The assistant coroner displayed the fatal balls of lead removed from Hennessy's body to enhance his testimony dramatically. He opined the blasts came from Hennessy's left side, traversed his abdomen with a slight right incline. One ball was removed behind Hennessy's eighth right rib, which supported his opinion. Luzenberg had the clerk distribute the evidence to the jury for their personal inspection.

The cross-examination by Semmes was brief and to the point, achieving a concession from Dr. Archinard that he could not determine from the wounds' trajectory the exact location of Hennessy, or the assassins, at the moment the fatal shots were fired. This concession proved to be important when the putative eyewitnesses would testify in the coming days.

The state's second witness was George Vandervoort, Hennessy's secretary. Adams coiled like a rattlesnake, waiting for Vandervoort's testimony about any incriminating information about his clients emanating from Rome. He intuited the jury knew about the press's wild statements about the alleged motive behind the Hennessy death, and was ready to strike and expose the police department's incompetence to act before the assassination, if the information existed. But to everyone's surprise, Luzenberg had Vandervoort identify Hennessy's blood-stained clothes he was wearing when shot. The garment's stains, now a reddish-brown hue, cast a putrid smell throughout the jury box. The jury foreman, Jacob Seligman, refused to touch the garments. Since Luzenberg never questioned Vandervoort about Italian warrants for his clients, there was no cross-examination, which only heightened Adams's suspicion about who actually killed Hennessy.

The state's next five witnesses seemed confident, but confused. All identified Monasterio, Scaffidi, the elder Marchesi, and Polizzi as being at different locations near or at the corner of Basin and Girod, about the time of the shooting. Adams' anvil of cross-examination glowed so white hot that the judge warned him several times to calm down. Adams once retorted, "I'm just getting warmed up."

Several of the witnesses testified they made in-prison identifications, but when Adams demanded in-court identifications, each witness misidentified the defendants, which betrayed their testimony on direct examination. Laurence Hearn became so angry that he broke two pencil points. Even the vaunted testimony of a young black man, Zachary Foster, proved inconclusive when it met the pounding maul of Lionel Adams' cross-examination. He initially told police he saw who shot Hennessy while running uptown on Basin Street after the first shots erupted. But Foster conceded he couldn't positively identify any of the defendants. But with every witness's testimony, especially Foster's, there was one crucial inconsistency—the brightness of the electric lamp at Basin and Girod, which proved to be an asset for the defense. By the end of the first day's testimony, the only thing the jury knew was what clothes Hennessy wore the night he was shot.

Chapter 75

Criminal District Court
March 2, 1891

Monday morning started quietly, but it didn't take long for the trial to erupt into a day-long torrent of misinformation, innuendo, lies, rumors, speculations, confusion, and ignorance, fomented by Eliza Jane Nicholson's *Daily Picayune* and T.D. Wharton's *Times-Democrat*. As spectators and reporters watched each defendant enter the dock, they noticed all of the accused had stoic visages, but one. Emmanuel Polizzi caught everyone's attention with his tentative steps, darting black eyes, and mumbling lips. As the deputies told the defendant to sit, Polizzi refused. Two deputies pushed his shoulders down until he was seated. But Polizzi continued to mumble in Italian, as the other defendants ignored him.

When Judge Baker took the bench, Polizzi shot up and started to yell at the judge in Italian. Immediately, everyone in the courtroom leaned forward to hear Polizzi's rants. "What is he saying?" Hearn asked Antonio.

"He's saying 'he doesn't want to die, and he wants to speak to the judge in private.'" Antonio whispered to Hearn.

Judge Baker asked Adams and Semmes what their client was saying, but neither attorney could interpret. Adams asked Matranga what Polizzi was saying. "He doesn't want to die and wants his own lawyer— something like that. He's been acting strange since that guy Ruggiero was in our cell," Matranga said.

Judge Baker ordered someone to interpret for Polizzi and called a recess. He demanded that all counsel, Polizzi, and a qualified interpreter go into Baker's private chambers to discuss the matter. Immediately, reporters began to spread rumors that Polizzi was confessing to killing Hennessy, and he wanted immunity to testify against his fellow defendants. Messengers were sent back to newspapers' offices, while J.D. Houston ran across Lafayette Square to tell the mayor. Soon, a crowd amassed outside the courthouse. Members of the Committee of Fifty left their offices and scampered to Judge Baker's courtroom. Louisiana's

Attorney General and one of its state senators were escorted past the throng of spectators to a special seat in the Grand Jury box. Several members of the Provenzano family, who heard bits of Polizzi's comments, interpreted them for the crowd, which only fueled speculation about Polizzi confessing to the crime and implicating his co-defendants.

After nearly half an hour in Baker's chambers, all parties emerged. Reporters shot questions to the attorneys, while an angry judge gaveled order in his court. After the courtroom simmered down, Semmes stood and announced that Emmanuel Polizzi, for the record, has fired his counsel and now seeks his own attorney to proceed with the case. This announcement caused more confusion and speculation among the reporters and spectators. Baker banged his gavel on the bench and demanded silence.

"I have spoken to Mr. Polizzi, and he wishes to have another lawyer represent him. I also understand the District Attorney offers no plea deal with Mr. Polizzi, or a grant of immunity of any kind. Therefore, the court will remain in recess until it can find Mr. Polizzi competent counsel to represent him. Baker returned to his chambers and waited while rumors flared like swamp fire.

Arthur Gastinel, a defense lawyer, told reporters Polizzi's statement was incredible, and Luzenberg would not grant Polizzi immunity to testify. "But I will say this, gentlemen," Gastinel began, "Polizzi stated the men who financed the assassination of David Hennessy are not on trial, and he was home in bed on Julia Street at the time Hennessy was shot. Given everything I have heard since last October, and the adventures and rampages entertained by this city, while Polizzi has been locked up, one must pause and think about why he said what he said, and how he said it."

><

About two o'clock, Judge Baker took the bench and announced that an attorney had been assigned to represent Polizzi. A young criminal attorney, Charles Theard, stood before the judge and reluctantly accepted the appointment. Theard requested enough time to consult with his client and have an independent interpreter appointed to assist in the defense. Baker appointed Frank Marfese to be the interpreter and told Theard to be ready by seven o'clock that evening to resume the trial, as he did not want to waste a day on the Polizzi matter. The judge ordered the sheriff to return the defendants to the prison, but to segregate Polizzi from the other defendants in the prison, and to and from the courthouse.

While the court stood in recess, the newspapers, particularly *The Picayune,* inked bulletins with reckless speculation of what Polizzi told the judge in chambers. Not surprisingly, the published speculation provoked serious consternation among members of the Committee of Fifty and the Cotton Exchange. Rumors flowed through the city like yellow fever. *The Picayune's* newsroom became the incubator of a virulent species of hate and prejudice when it published:

"It is believed that Polizzi protested innocence of any actual participation in the assassination of Chief Hennessy, and claimed he was at home next to No. 5's engine house on Julia Street. He had been in the councils of those who planned and did the shooting; however, he is said to have mentioned the names of several on trial as the men who fired at the chief, as well as two or three others, not heretofore mentioned in the case, but who also took part in the murder

"The poor wretches who fired the shots were merely tools. The instigators were of a higher class and wealthier, and paid well for the removal of the brave police leader, who was determined to oppose them."

The Picayune offered no clarification of their statement or the basis of the published statement. When Laurence Hearn read the bulletin, he tried to ask *Picayune* reporters the source of the information, but they ignored him.

><

As the five-hour recess began, Hearn overheard Adams instructing O'Malley to measure the distance from the intersection of Girod and Carondelet to the corner of Girod and Basin. Adams knew the state's vaunted eye-witness, John Daure, would be called to the stand soon, and Adams wanted to be ready for the cross-examination. Hearn, hearing this, instructed Antonio and Abraham to follow O'Malley and take their own measurements. Hearn, familiar with the neighborhood and Adams's style of cross-examination, wanted his story to have a level of authenticity other newspapers blithely entertained. Daure, a loquacious barkeeper employed at a tavern located at that intersection, had told other reporters he witnessed the assassination. But Hearn, like Adams, intuited that the weather and lighting conditions of that night would strain an owl's eyes to see over three blocks down Girod Street. But both men needed to know the distance. Hearn didn't realize that Adams had a secret witness who would destroy Daure's testimony.

><

As dusk fell upon New Orleans, Judge Baker's courtroom became a murky theater of anticipation. Deputies tried to brighten the new electric lights in the courtroom, but the nascent technology proved elusive. The judge ordered the deputies to resort to oil lamps to illuminate the large courtroom. Still, the oily smoke and fumes permeated the courtroom, requiring the deputies to open the tall windows along Lafayette Street. The oil lamps veiled the capital defendants' ruddy faces from the spectators' gallery in a requiem glow.

The rumors about the night's session brought more spectators to the courthouse. A class of Tulane law students and Louisiana's Attorney General, Walter Rogers, and Senator E.D. White were allowed admission. *The Picayune* had excited public anticipation, which caused many members of the Committee of Fifty, including Edgar Farrar, to slink into the shadows of the courtroom. Many focused their attention on Polizzi, and every twitch of his semi-silhouetted body, while others waited for the next witness to be called.

The state called Mary Wheeler to the stand. *The Picayune* called her a *"bright mulatress,"* who lived in a double, two-story house at the uptown corner of Basin and Girod Streets. Her direct examination, though probative of Scaffidi's guilt, unraveled once Lionel Adams ripped into her perception of the night. On a few occasions, she conflicted herself, to the point she doubted what she saw through the drizzly elements. She was certain Scaffidi wore a rubber or oilcloth coat, but, on cross-examination, doubted its color. She knew she heard dozens of gunshots, causing thick gun smoke to float around the low-hanging streetlight. With several concessions from Wheeler, Adams asked one last question.

"After hearing the gunshots and running to your gallery, did you hear Chief Hennessy call 'Billy, I'm shot?'"

"No, sir," she responded.

After Adams sat down, O'Malley whispered in his ear, "Corondelet and Girod is over three squares away from Basin and Girod—nearly three hundred yards."

Adams nodded.

The state called a series of witnesses who provided conflicting testimony, both on direct and cross-examination. One witness, James T. Poole, conceded that he spoke to police officers during the recess, but refused to disclose the subject matter of the discussion. Adams wasted no time carving the conflicted testimonies from each witness, with the skill of a sculptor's chisel.

With an hour to go before the end of the night session, Luzenberg called what he believed would be his star witness, John Daure. Adams coiled in his chair like a rattlesnake, waiting for cross-examination. In his mind, only two people were in the courtroom—he and Daure. Adams seized every word Daure spoke, and watched the witness's facial expressions and body movement through the flickering light of the oil lamps.

On direct examination, Daure testified he tended bar at a tavern located at Girod and Corondelet Streets. As he was closing the bar for the night and began to walk to his streetcar stop at Rampart and Girod, he remembered seeing Hennessy and another man part company at that intersection, a distance of over two blocks. Shortly afterwards, he saw flashes and heard gunshots coming further down Girod Street, towards the cemetery.

"What did you do after you heard the shots?" Luzenberg asked.

"I began to run towards the shooting," Daure testified.

"What did you see when you got to Basin and Girod?" Luzenberg asked.

"I saw four or five men start in a fast walk from the shed. One of them was Scaffidi, whom I had known for two years. I also saw Antonio Marchesi and Antonio Bagnetto," Daure said, without prompting for Luzenberg. "They all had guns."

Normally, the shrewd Adams would object to the form of the open-ended question and the flowing narrative answer, but he was allowing Daure to spin his own web of deceit.

"What else did you see?" Luzenberg asked.

"Scaffidi fired the last shot. The electric light was burning brightly. I saw others in the vicinity of the shooting. One of them was a boy running on the upper side of Girod Street, between Franklin and Basin. He was running towards the graveyard. I knew it was Asperi Marchesi from the Poydras Street market."

"Are you sure these are the men you saw?" Luzenberg asked.

"Yes, sir."

Luzenberg tendered the witness to an eager Lionel Adams, who snapped on Daure's testimony like a bear trap.

"Where do you live?" Adams asked.

"Number 316 Frenchman Street."

"And you were heading down Girod Street, after closing the tavern to catch the streetcar home?"

"Yes, sir."

"And that's the same streetcar—the Rampart line—which I take home, isn't it?"

"I believe it is. You live on North Rampart Street."

"Exactly. And that car stop is located at Girod and Rampart—the same intersection where you saw Hennessys depart from an unknown man that night?"

"Yes, sir."

"And where were you when you heard the first shots?" Adams asked.

"I was standing in front of the Shakspeare family foundry—on Girod Street."

"And that is over two city squares away from Girod and Rampart, correct?"

"Yes, sir."

"And once you hear the shots, you began to run towards the shooting?"

"Yes, sir."

"And that was at Basin and Girod—over three city squares away, correct?"

"Yes."

"It was dark and drizzly, wasn't it?" Adams asked.

"Yes, I could see. And I heard the shots."

"Mr. Daure, please stand up and clap your hands to approximate the number of shots and duration of those shots, you said you heard," Adams demanded.

After a short pause, Daure asked, "Mr. Luzenberg, do you think it proper for me to do it?"

"If the court says so, do it," Luzenberg said.

"I see no reason why you should not do so," Judge Baker said.

"I have explained it as best as I could," a defiant Daure said.

Adams bored in and demanded Daure clap his hands, consistent with the number and duration of the shots.

"Can you do it?" Judge Baker asked.

"No."

"Why not?" Adams asked.

Daure dropped his head and said, "I don't remember."

In the next volley of questions, Adams demonstrated that the fusillade of shots fired at Hennessy took no more than twenty-five seconds, which was incompatible with Daure's ability to arrive at Girod and Basin to see Scaffidi's face under the streetlight, or any other defendant identified by him. Antonio turned to Hearn and whispered, "Mr. Daure is wrong. The distance is over three hundred yards." Hearn smiled and patted Antonio on his knee and nodded.

Adams wasn't finished with the Daure. "In the time you ran down Girod Street, did you encounter anyone else on the street?"

"No."

As Adams sat down, one juror raised his hand to ask a question, which the judge allowed. "Mr. Daure, how fast can you run a hundred yards?"

"I don't know. But I'm a pretty fast runner."

The gallery snickered as Judge Baker adjourned court to the following morning.

As Adams and the other defense attorneys left the gloomy courthouse for the evening, he cast his eyes across Lafayette Square. He saw the electric lights burning brightly in the city hall's council chambers. "I guess the Committee of Fifty is having a late-night meeting," Adams mused.

Chapter 76

St. Patrick's Hall
March 3, 1891
8:00 A.M.

When Charles Luzenberg arrived at the courthouse on Tuesday morning, a group of men were waiting for him by the back gate, which led to the rear door of the sheriff's office. Luzenberg recognized each scowl as he bid them good morning. Nearly all the men were attired in dark suits, crisp white shirts, and black ties, as if they were attending a funeral. All were members of the Committee of Fifty and demanded to talk to the District Attorney. Most of the men were attorneys, some were members of the Cotton Exchange, and their spokesman, J.D. Houston, expressed their displeasure in how Luzenberg was conducting the case.

Once inside the courthouse, Luzenberg led the men to his private office, where Houston presented their cause. "We decided to meet you and express our concern about last night's testimony," Houston began. "We were at City Hall last night when we received reports that your star eye-witness crumbled like a pillar of salt under cross-examination. Is that true?" Houston asked.

"Lionel Adams got John Daure to make some concessions, which damaged his credibility, but not the case," Luzenberg said.

"Did you prepare his testimony?" John Wickliffe, an attorney and a member of the mayor's committee, asked.

"Extensively. But he was no match for Adams."

"There are rumors going around that people are measuring how long it took Daure to run down Girod Street. It seems no one believes Daure. Do you have witnesses to support Daure's testimony?" Wickliffe asked.

"I have witnesses who can also identify Scaffidi, the Marchesis, Monasterio, Bagnetto, and Polizzi being on Girod Street the night of the shooting."

"Forget the shoemaker. He lives on Girod Street," Wickliffe scolded.

"We understand that there have been discrepancies in the identification made at the prison and made in court. Can you clean that up?"

"I have a series of witnesses who will make the identifications today," Luzenberg said.

"What about Macheca and Matranga? We heard their names have not been mentioned at all during the case. Can you make the conspiracy case?" Wickliffe asked.

"Yes. I have a series of witnesses who will testify they knew of the bad blood between the defendants and Hennessy, and celebrated the chief's death that night," Luzenberg promised.

"Charles, can you tie the men you mentioned to Macheca and Matranga?" William S. Parkerson asked. "So far, the Italians, who have been identified, all live around the Poydras Market—on this side of Canal Street. Can you link them to the other Italians from the other side of Canal Street?"

Luzenberg studied his witness list and became nervous. "I have witnesses who will testify that Matranga and Macheca celebrated Hennessy's murder."

"Who are they?" Houston demanded.

"Two cops and Fanny Decker."

The office erupted in laughter. "Your conspiracy case is based on a Burgundy Street whore and two cops, who will testify they saw some of your defendants at Fabacher's Restaurant, at the time of the shooting? Where is the connection to that rag-tag bunch of fruit vendors and a shoemaker?" Parkerson asked. "Don't you understand people are beginning to laugh at you, Charles?"

Luzenberg's temper flared. "This is the case that the police and your Committee gave me to prosecute. I didn't investigate it. You did. I didn't spend money on witnesses. You did. I didn't put a *Pinkerton* spy in the parish prison to strengthen an already weak case. You did. I didn't get the *Picayune* to run an editorial demanding I hurry up and indict the dagoes. You did. The case I'm prosecuting is not mine, but yours. And whose idea was it to put Semmes on the defense team?"

The room fell silent. Wickliffe patted Luzenberg on his back and reassured him. "Charles, we can't lose this case. We all will be embarrassed, and people will start asking inconvenient questions. Already, some newspapers are asking who shot the Matrangas at Esplanade and Claiborne, after the Provenzanos were acquitted. The people will be asked who shot Hennessy, if these dagoes are acquitted? We can't be embarrassed again."

Luzenberg, his chest still heaving with emotion, said, "I'm doing my best with what I have been given. I urged the defendants to focus the jury on as few defendants as possible. The remaining defendants have a lesser connection to Matranga and Macheca."

"Not Geraci, Romero, or Sunzeri," Houston said. "Why didn't you try them with Macheca and Matranga? They're working to build a voting bloc in the Italian Colony, and the Negro neighborhoods. Maybe there should be twelve on trial."

"I severed the cases to give them a balance on the theory of conspiracy. I omitted Sunzeri because the Provenzanos, or somebody, shot him up. I didn't know about Romero. The Committee demanded I indict him. And Geraci was with Macheca and Matranga at Fabacher's. I didn't want to put too much attention on their alibis," Luzenberg explained.

Wickliffe sat down next to Luzenberg and asked, "Charles, do we have any witnesses who can testify that the nine men you have on trial have ever been in the same room anywhere, at any time, for any reason?"

"No."

"What about the two Negro boys from the Poydras Market—Amos Scott and Joseph Williams?" Wickliffe asked.

"They will only be able to testify that Asperi Marchesi told them he gained his release from the prison by claiming he was going to testify against his father, and that he was a lookout for the shooters. When Hennessy walked in front of the shanty, he was to signal the shooters by whistling."

"What's wrong with that testimony?" Houston asked.

"I have no one in the prison who took Asperi's confession and let him out. So far, all the witnesses have testified that Hennessy was shot just after crossing Basin Street, not in front of the Monasterio's shanty. That the chief was near the glow of the streetlight. Adams's cross-examination ripped apart Daure's testimony. The only credible witnesses I have left are Billy O'Connor and J.C. Roe. But Daure said he didn't see anyone on Girod Street while he was running towards the shooting. I need O'Connor to testify that he saw Daure running on Girod Street, to rehabilitate Daure's testimony."

"O'Connor and Roe are not going to testify," Thomas Boylan, a member of the Committee of Fifty, said.

"What? What do you mean? I need O'Connor. After all, it was he who took Hennessy's dying declaration and started this investigation against the Italians. He must testify. I insist," Luzenberg exclaimed.

"Sorry, Charles, neither will testify," Boylan said. "Besides, O'Connor can't link the defendants together, other than knowing Macheca and Matranga didn't like Hennessy. I know who Adams' alibi witnesses are, and they are men of great stature."

"Who are they?" Luzenberg asked.

"Adolph Meyer, Charles Butler, Theodore Wilkinson, and Lionel Adams. They were at Fabacher's with Matranga, Macheca, Sunzeri, Geraci, and Romero," Boylan said.

"You do realize if O'Connor doesn't testify, you will be gutting my case like a catfish," Luzenberg warned.

"We're sorry, Charles," Boylan said.

"Well, gentlemen, thank you. Be prepared for the worst, and please use the back door when you leave," Luzenberg said, slumping in his chair.

Chapter 77

St. Patrick's Hall
March 5, 1891
9:30 A.M.

Sensing Luzenberg would soon rest his case with his strongest witnesses, spectators, including some of the city's finest ladies, and their genteel escorts, took their seats to watch the final act of the state's opera of justice. The stoic pallid faces, projecting an affected air of sophisticated countenance, only contributed to the clash of classes, pitched between the bar and gallery. Two of the morning papers excited interest in the case, but their divergent accounts triggered mixed emotions among the business and professional elites. A society's intellectual capacity has always been commensurate with its ability to ignore the press, but on this day, New Orleans suffered addled thoughts about a case thought to have been concluded, except for the contrived formalities.

Early yesterday morning, about 2 o'clock, a group of curious men, dubious about John Daure's testimony, enlisted the help of a local athlete, Louis Knuckles, to replicate Daure's run down Girod Street. The event would be timed by horsemen with stopwatches. Sleepy neighbors sprang open their shutters to watch Knuckles sprint from the Shakspeare Foundry on Girod Street to the point where Daure testified he saw Scaffidi fire the last shot at Hennessy. When the signal was given, Knuckles launched and ran towards the block between Rampart and Basin. Spectators speculated the distance was just under three hundred yards.

With all his might, Knuckles covered the uneven streetscape in one minute and sixteen seconds, thus causing more doubt in Daure's testimony, as most witnesses had testified the shooting lasted no more than thirty seconds. The *Times-Democrat* printed the event on page seven of their morning paper, which caused two of their curious reporters to repeat Knuckles' run that afternoon. W.B. Stansbury, a reporter who had been covering Hennessy's assassination from the first day, ran the same distance in one minute and thirty seconds. A fellow reporter managed the stopwatch. The two enterprising reporters discovered that the world record for running the four-hundred-and-forty-yard dash was forty-eight seconds. Today's edition of the *Times-Democrat* printed those results, causing more doubt about Daure's testimony. Lionel Adams read the report and smiled.

Realizing the doubt caused by Knuckles' run, and the conflicting testimony of the state's witnesses extant, Eliza Jane Nicholson printed an editorial on page four of her *Daily Picayune*. It read, in part:

"The testimony developed by the state against some of the persons now on trial charged with the murder of Chief of Police Hennessy appears extremely strong, direct, and incriminating. Unless the position of the State can be overthrown with a decisiveness the means for which are now by no means apparent, it would seem that justice is about to lay its heavy hand upon some, at least, of the participants in this great crime.

"Some, we say, for if the parties to whom the testimony now strongly points should be found guilty, it is plain from every reasonable view of the case that only some of the criminals will have been seized upon. Who are the others? If three or four poor devils did the killing, they were merely tools—it may be said, blind, ignorant tools. They had no personal interest in the death of Chief Hennessy. They were almost strangers in the city. They are almost, if not entirely, strangers to this country. Ignorant, obscure, poor, not even perhaps, speaking the language of the country in which they found themselves, they had no reason, not the slightest, to desire the death of such a high official. If they had any instrumentality in the crime, they were simply agents, hired for money, or more likely driven to it by some more profound and authoritative influence. All this necessitates a conspiracy. Who, then, were the chiefs of it, the arch conspirators?"

Adams and Luzenberg enjoyed reading Nicholson's editorial for different reasons. Adams, by now, knew his clients were innocent and knew more sinister forces dwelt in the opulent shadows of New Orleans' society. He knew the Provenzanos didn't ambush the Matranga stevedores, but whoever did designed Hennessy's ambush. Luzenberg, conversely, thought Nicholson's editorial gave him the basis to point his accusatory finger at Macheca and Matranga, as the architects of Hennessy's death, and his next few witnesses would support his theory.

><

As Judge Baker took the bench, Antonio slipped Asperi Marchesi some more candy. A deputy saw the gesture but ignored it. With the jury settled in their seats, Luzenberg called his next witnesses. The first witness, Amos Scott, testified that Asperi Marchesi told him he followed his father's and Macheca's instructions to whistle when Hennessy approached his house on Girod Street. Adams wasted no time discrediting the convicted felon's testimony by suggesting that the police had prepared his testimony and that he had only seen young Marchesi at the Poydras Market on several occasions. Through tactful leading questions, Adams established that the possibility of an immigrant Italian boy confiding such sensitive information to someone he hardly knew stretched credulity. Luzenberg followed this folly with the same testimony of Joseph Williams, which began to riven the state's case with doubt.

Luzenberg, to stanch the hemorrhage of the state's credibility, called two New Orleans police officers to the stand, followed by Burgundy Street Madam, Fanny Deckert. He knew he had to shift the jury's attention to Macheca, Matranga, and their known associates. Thus far, all the witnesses testified about Italians who lived near the Poydras Market, or activities uptown from Canal Street, but hardly a breath about those who lived, or worked in the Italian Colony of the French Quarter. The strategic pivot appeared to everyone as a ploy to loop in Macheca, Matranga, and others into a *Stuppagghieri* conspiracy to kill Hennessy, but it had unintended consequences.

Sergeant Joseph McCabe, attired in a dark blue police uniform, and gold braid to signify his rank, took the stand, and testified he saw Matranga, Macheca, Geraci, John and James Caruso, Salvatore Sunzeri, and Charles Patorno enter Fabacher's Restaurant, located at Royal and Customhouse Streets, at about ten o'clock on the night Hennessy was shot. He and other officers, Corporal Edward Hevron and Patrolman Peter Torregano, were inside when the news of Hennessy's attack was announced. According to McCabe, the Matranga group cheered.

On cross-examination, Lionel Adams got McCabe to concede he saw Adams, General Adolf Meyers, and several well-known attorneys in the restaurant at the same time, and the news of Hennessy's attack received mixed emotions from the patrons.

Luzenberg replicated McCabe's testimony with Officer Frank McEntee, and Adams's cross-examination elicited the same concession. By the time both officers left the stand, the jury had heard no evidence of a conspiracy by the Matranga group to kill Hennessy. But Luzenberg, knowing men confess to prostitutes more than they do their priest, called Fanny Deckert to testify. The fine-coifed ladies of New Orleans sat stiff in their chairs, as if to cast the appearance of rectitude and righteousness to all present, compared to the raspy-voiced, perfumed Madam of Burgundy Street.

Deckert testified she knew some of the defendants because of their patronage at her brothel. She also acknowledged Macheca's glee while discussing the Hennessy shooting by repeating Macheca's words, "we are all Hennessy's enemies." She concluded her testimony by saying the Matranga party left her brothel about four o'clock in the morning.

On cross-examination, Adams asked Deckert one simple question. "What did Macheca, Matranga, or anyone in their party do or say, which would leave you with the impression they had anything to do with the shooting of Chief Hennessy, and then establish an alibi at your brothel?"

"Nothing," Deckert responded.

Luzenberg, thinking he would seal the Macheca's fate, called two more police officers, Edward Hevron and Robert Pollock. Both officers followed Macheca and Caruso to the intersection of Hospital and Bourbon Streets. Pollock testified they were about half a block away when he heard Macheca say, "I'm only sorry they didn't do that son-of-a-bitch up right here."

On cross-examination, Adams challenged Pollock's ability to hear the conversation between Macheca and Caruso, from a half-block away, while hiding in the shadows. Given the early hour, Pollock conceded the men were talking in low tones. Adams then asked Pollock his understanding of Macheca's use of the word *"they."* Pollock admitted he didn't know who Macheca was talking about. Unwittingly, Luzenberg, through this testimony, again, put Macheca and others further away from Girod and Basin Streets, which the defense exploited.

Between four and five o'clock in the afternoon, Luzenberg put several more witnesses on the stand, who testified that Macheca expressed hostility towards Hennessy in the past. But each witness conceded Hennessy had many enemies in New Orleans. At about five o'clock, there was a pause in the state's case. Judge Baker stated, "Mr. Luzenberg, call your next witness." Luzenberg paused and consulted with his co-counsel. After a few moments, Luzenberg announced the state would rest its case.

The announcement shocked everyone in the courtroom. Reporters sent messengers running down Camp Street to their offices. Hearn scribbled some notes and sent Antonio back to *The Mascot* office with instructions to have his notes printed. Hearn calculated Luzenberg had called only fifty-one witnesses, and had rested his case without calling Captain Billy O'Connor or Boylan patrol officer, J.C. Roe, despite promising the jury during his opening statement, they would testify and establish who shot Hennessy, through the chief's dying words. J.D. Houston and Marcel Hart raced across Lafayette Square to City Hall.

As Luzenberg's words settled in the minds of everyone in the courtroom, the gallery began to hum to a disorderly level. Judge Baker banged his gavel on the bench, and order was restored. Lionel Adams stood and asked Judge Baker, "I'm confused. Will the state put Officer Roe and Captain O'Connor on the stand, as promised? They were mentioned in Daure's testimony. We need to cross-examine them."

"I have no control over the state's case," Judge Baker said.

"Judge, can you ask Mr. Luzenberg for me?" Adams asked, adhering to courtroom decorum.

Before the judge could ask, Luzenberg repeated that the state rested, and he would not call any more witnesses. Adams and Semmes exchanged glances and smiled.

Judge Baker adjourned the court to the next morning and instructed the sheriff to feed the defendants and the jury. The spectators rushed from the courtroom, stunned by Luzenberg's announcement. The garrulous Dominick O'Malley caught George Vandervoort in the dingy corridor and bet him none of the defendants would be found guilty. Vandervoort wisely refused the bet and walked away.

Chapter 78

Despite the Committee of Fifty's investigation, thousands of dollars spent on witnesses, a rabid police department prowling the city like salivating wolves, a Pinkerton spy infiltrating the parish prison, the Provenzanos' acquittal, Eliza Jane Nicholson's *Daily-Picayune* editorials positing notions of a *Mafia*-infested city, fifty-one conflicting state witnesses of dubious veracity, and suppressing exculpatory evidence, Charles Luzenberg sat in his courthouse office realizing he failed to prove any grand *Mafia* conspiracy lurking the drizzly shadows of Girod Street on October, 15, 1890. Indeed, the gap between any probative evidence of an Italian conspiracy and the evidence adduced rivaled the expanse of the giant crescent carved by the Mississippi River a mile away.

However, to support the case, as best as she could, Eliza Jane Nicholson published a three-hundred-word editorial on page one of the *Daily Picayune*, which attempted to summarize the evidence against each defendant. While waiting for Judge Baker, Lawrence Hearn, sitting in the reporters' gallery with Antonio and Abraham, erupted in laughter, drawing the curious attention of those seated around him.

"Why you laughing?" Antonio whispered.

Hearn gave the broadsheet to Antonio and Abraham. "Read this," he said.

The boys sat quietly, carefully reading each word. Sometimes, they had to re-read the same sentence to understand the editorial, but the last paragraph summarized Nicholson's thoughts.

"...The sudden close of the case for the state was unexpected. A strong showing of direct testimony against the men who committed the crime had been made. Public expectations had been aroused to the pitch of thinking testimony as strong would be adduced against the head men, and that strong conspiracy would be proved. In this, there was disappointment."

"What does this mean?" Antonio asked.

"It means all the city's powerful elites have failed to establish that the *Mafia* killed Hennessy. Remember, if the Provenzanos didn't shoot the Matrangas, who did? And if the Matrangas didn't shoot Hennessy, who did? Why didn't Luzenberg call any members of the Provenzanos to testify about the *Stuppagghieri's* control of the docks, if it's true? All the prosecution has is a bunch of sleepy-eyed witnesses whose testimony conflicts with each other about a bunch of Italians who live and work around the Poydras Market, with *no* links to other Italians eating at Fabacher's Restaurant on October 15, 1890. I believe there's a common interest, which motivated both ambushes, and that motivation killed Hennessy," Hearn asserted. "But we can't write that. It's too dangerous to tell the truth in New Orleans."

"What do you mean?" Abraham asked.

"New Orleans is a big city, but a complex little town. Everybody knows something about everybody. That was Hennessy's downfall. He knew too much about too many people, and the mayor put him in a position that only grew that information. He ran the security for the 1884 Cotton Centennial, and probably knew where the Centennial's embezzled money went, where the genteel men went at night, he executed the *"Shakspeare Plan,"* closing down brothels and casinos of the mayor's enemies, he killed Thomas Devereaux and got off, and he associated with the Provenzanos and the Matranga stevedores. Hennessy had a brittle relationship with Macheca, but he never arrested anyone from the Italian Colony for being an Italian fugitive, except Guiseppi Esposito, which, by the way, made him enemies on both sides of Canal Street. Every day, Hennessy sat buck naked on a straight razor."

"Who killed Hennessy?" Antonio asked.

"This city killed him. If Luzenberg and all his silky uptown friends had more evidence on these nine men, we would have heard it by now, and they wouldn't need the *Daily Picayune* to create guilt, where there is none. Boys, pay close attention to what happens next. Like the editorial admitted, perhaps unintentionally, where is the evidence against Macheca, Matranga, or Incardona? We hardly heard their names during the state's case." Hearn asserted.

"Why don't we write an editorial for *The Mascot*?" Antonio asked.

"Mr. Osmond, who is no friend of the mayor, won't let us, until after the verdict," Hearn said. "And even then, our language must be careful.

Osmond already had a shootout with J.D. Houston back in 1885—in our offices on Camp Street."

><

On the fourth Friday of Lent, 1891, near ten o'clock, spectators flowed into the courtroom, anticipating the first defense witness to be called. Little did they know that behind the courtroom, in the sheriff's offices, Manuel Polizzi's erratic temper began to quake, and he began to mumble in an incoherent Italian dialect. Father Joaquin Manoritta comforted him in Italian. His eight co-defendants sat in the guarded dock, waiting for the judge and Polizzi.

As the deputies and Father Manoritta escorted Polizzi to his own seat, away from his co-defendants, he yelled something, bolted for the open courtroom windows, and attempted to jump to the cobblestoned street, two stories below. Every spectator gasped, while some of the coifed ladies bunched against the far wall of the courtroom. Polizzi threw one leg out the window, screaming in broken English and indecipherable Italian. He fought each deputy with flailing fists, punching and kicking to free himself from their grip. His clothes ripped as the deputies tugged on his body. Blood, snot, and sputum sprayed the air. But after several fiery minutes, the deputies subdued him.

When Judge Baker began to ascend the bench, he saw the deputies and Polizzi wrestling on the floor, near the open window. Women held handkerchiefs to their faces, their eyes widened in awe. Men jockeyed for a better position to watch the deputies fight Polizzi with brutal, but necessary force. Judge Baker banged his gavel and ordered the deputies to take the bloodied Polizzi back to their offices while he consulted with physicians and Polizzi's attorney, Charles Theard. Jacob Seligman and his fellow jurors remained in the jury room, debating the reason for the delay.

Theard and Dr. Yves Le Monnier visited Polizzi in the sheriff's offices, but found him totally incoherent and scared. An Italian official, who condemned Hennessy's assassination, Giovanni Rocchi, offered his services as an interpreter to determine what had triggered Polizzi. After visiting Polizzi, Dr. Le Monnier, Rocchi, and Theard reported their findings to the judge. After a lengthy bench conference, Judge Baker allowed Theard to withdraw as counsel and ordered Dr. LeMonnier and another physician to examine Polizzi at the parish prison to determine if he was sane. Baker adjourned the court until the next morning.

Outside, the streets rippled with rumors about Polizzi confessing to being one of the assassins, which only vaunted *The Daily Picayune's* editorial's sting. Antonio and Abraham stood near the courthouse doors, filled with fear, as they watched the fiery force of Louisiana law toss a battered Polizzi in the back of a Black Maria. Antonio's stomach knotted with anger and fear, as his mind flashed images of Vincenzo Trambatore and Sicily.

Chapter 79

Criminal District Court
March 7, 1891

Thousands of ghoulish gawkers gathered on Saturday morning at the intersection of Camp and Lafayette Streets, waiting for the Black Marias to arrive from the parish prison. Escorted by a police patrol wagon, the Marias stopped in front of the courthouse, and deputies and police officers unloaded eight defendants from one, and Manuel Polizzi from the other. Polizzi wore a tattered and stained blue shirt. Darkened and drawn, his face hadn't seen a razor in several days. At first, Polizzi cooperated, but the crowd's ethnic taunts caused him to stiffen, requiring deputies to carry him into the courthouse. The other defendants walked to the courtroom.

Father Manoritta and Giovanni Rocchi accompanied Polizzi everywhere he went, while in the custody of several deputies. About ten o'clock, Judge Baker took the bench and queried Dr. LeMonnier about Polizzi's mental condition. Dr. LeMonnier, swollen with pity, admitted Polizzi was sane, but suffering tremendous fear and loss of all society or purpose in life. Judge Baker, concerned with Polizzi's ability to assist counsel in his defense, demurred on Polizzi's emotions and sought the sterile legal standard to allow Polizzi to proceed as a defendant. Dr. LeMonnier agreed Polizzi could proceed, whereupon Judge Baker appointed John Q. Flynn to represent the volatile defendant.

Father Manoritta and Rocchi escorted Polizzi into the courtroom, but two deputies sat next to him to prevent disruptions. Satisfied with the court's decorum, Judge Baker allowed spectators to enter. Nearly every lady held their hem up, preventing it from dragging along the filthy floor. Deputies opened the large windows but stood guard near each one.

In an odd procedural move, Judge Baker, aware Adams had a witness waiting to attack John Daure's previous testimony, ordered the state to produce their premier eyewitness, and subject him to cross-examination by the defense. Luzenberg reluctantly honored the court's order.

"Mr. Luzenberg," Judge Baker began, "I want the record to be clear as to what, if anything, Mr. Daure saw last on the night of October 15."

Luzenberg called Daure, knowing a stellar defense witness, Captain Achilles Kalinski, of the Fire Night Patrol of Underwriters, loomed on the horizon. Daure took the stand and repeated his original testimony about running down Girod Street when the shooting started. Luzenberg avoided any testimony about Daure's speed, but allowed Daure to shave his original testimony about what he saw and when he saw it. The jury seemed unimpressed with Daure's revisions to his testimony and waited for him to be tendered to Adams.

"Mr. Daure, you live at Number 316 Frenchman Street, correct?" Adams asked.

"Yes."

"Which is about four miles away from where you work?"

"Yes."

"And it is your testimony you ran down Girod Street towards the muzzle flashes, once the shooting started, correct?"

"Yes."

"You were excited and curious, correct?"

"You can say that."

"And after the shooting stopped, you ran back to Corondelet and Girod Street, where you met Captain Achilles Kalinski, correct?" Adams probed.

"He and others were standing on the corner," Daure said.

"And Captain Kalinski asked you who was doing the shooting, correct?"

"Yes."

"And you said, 'someone just done up Chief Hennessy' or words to that effect, correct?"

"Yes."

"And when Captain Kalinski asked you who shot Hennessy, you said, 'I don't know' or words to that effect, correct?"

"Yes."

"In fact, you told Captain Kalinski, as you got closer to the shooting, you ran back to Girod and Carondelet Streets, correct?"

"Yes."

"So, is it correct to say you made the positive identifications of three or four of the defendants, at different locations, after you turned around, and ran back to Carondelet Street and met Captain Kalinski?" Adams asked.

"I saw what I saw," Daure responded.

"So, let's see if we understand what you saw when you saw it. You heard gunfire, and saw muzzle flashes four blocks away, ran towards the fire, got close to see who got shot and by whom, got scared, and ran back to Carondelet Street, and told Captain Kalinski you didn't know who shot the chief, correct?"

"I was scared to say anything at the time. I know these people, and what they can do," Daure persisted.

"And you remained scared for several weeks, before you told the police what you saw or didn't see?" Adams asked.

Luzenberg objected, whereupon Adams announced he had no further questions for Daure.

Judge Baker ignored the objection and announced a brief recess before the commencement of the defense's case.

><

As soon as the last juror sat down, Lionel Adams sprang to his feet and called Captain Achilles Kalinski to the stand. After being duly sworn, Kalinski surprised no one and testified that Daure didn't know who shot Chief Hennessy. With that testimony and the gaping hole in the state's case, Adams, Henriques, and Semmes began to shred the state's case. Reporters, even the ones friendly to the state, began to have doubts. The mood in the courtroom shifted in favor of the defendants—even Polizzi. Seasoned attorneys, watching from the gallery, wondered who shot Hennessy, if not the men on trial. As Adams began to call the defense witnesses, several attorneys, who were members of the Committee of Fifty, along with Marcel Hart and J.D. Houston, left the courtroom and jogged across Lafayette Square to City Hall. As they did, they observed Dominick O'Malley being arrested for carrying a concealed weapon.

For the remainder of the day, the defense called all the alibi witnesses who stitched together the exact footsteps of the Matranga defendants, which excluded Polizzi, the Marchesis, Monasterio, and Scaffidi. He called the employees of the Academy of Music Theater, who sold Matranga the tickets before the show. Boldly, Semmes called Captain John Journee, who admitted he saw the Matrangas before and after the show. He also testified he was standing by the Masonic Temple building and saw Matranga, Macheca, Geraci, Incardona, and the Carusos walk down St. Charles Avenue, cross Canal Street, and enter Fabacher's Restaurant.

Adams called the Italian Consulate, Pasquale Corte, who testified he saw the men at the theater the night of the Hennessy assassination. But Adams wasn't finished. He then called congressional candidate, General Adolph Meyer to the stand, who testified that the Matranga party was dining about the time Chief Hennessy was shot. General Meyer, a man of impeccable reputation, vouched for the Matranga party, which caused reporters to send their messengers running back to their offices. But before the day's testimony had concluded, Adams had one last witness—himself. Adams' testimonial statement seemed like a prelude to his closing argument, as he stared each juror in the eye, and alibied each defendant. Luzenberg offered no cross-examination, and the court was adjourned until Monday morning.

As Adams left the courthouse and took a gulp of fresh, cool night air, a deputy informed him that Dominick O'Malley was waiting for representation in the dock at the Recorder's Court. Adams and Semmes laughed and crossed Lafayette Square to liberate their raffish investigator again. As they walked down Lafayette Street, they peered up at the windows of the mayor's office, which were aglow on a Saturday night. "You think the mayor is working late tonight?" Semmes asked.

"No. He's scheming," Adams responded.

Chapter 80

St. Aloysius Academy
Sunday, March 8, 1891
9:00 A.M.

After attending Sunday Mass at St. Mary's church on Chartres Street, Brothers Stanislaus and Angelo, accompanied by Antonio and Abraham, walked back to St. Aloysius, a few blocks away. Despite being Jewish, Abraham enjoyed attending Mass, despite not understanding the purposes or reasons for the many rituals. As they strolled down Chartres Street, they noticed some Italians draping their iron-laced balconies with the Italian flag to commemorate the forty-seventh birthday of King Umberto I, which would be the following Saturday, March 14, 1891. While being loyal to their adopted country, America, many Italians still honored their king, especially for unifying the country, including Sicily. Some non-Italians bristled at the nationalistic display, but were reminded how the Irish celebrated St. Patrick's Day, despite being under the control of the British crown. And many French residents of the Quarter openly celebrate Bastille Day, with flying France's tricolors. Most residents understood that allegiance to America didn't mean surrendering one's past, but there were those who snarled at such displays on the other side of Canal Street.

When they arrived at the school's front gate, they were surprised to find Johan Jahnke and John Falcone waiting for them, seated in an expensive black carriage. After a warm reunion, Brother Stanislaus invited Jahnke and Falcone for breakfast and the sharing of the day's news.

While Mrs. Bertucci served breakfast, the dominant conversation topic was the nine Italians' ongoing trial. Antonio and Abraham spoke openly about their belief in the men's innocence, which didn't surprise Jahnke, given the recent developments mentioned in the newspapers. But Jahnke and Falcone had an ulterior motive for their Sunday surprise meeting.

"Antonio, when do you expect the trial to be over?" Jahnke asked.

"Maybe this week, sir."

Jahnke looked at the boy's hands. "This newspaper business has made your hands look soft. Are you ready to come back to work for me?"

Stunned by the comment, Antonio said, "I like newspaper work, sir. But it's sad to see these men on trial for something they didn't do. I thought America was better than Italy."

"How much does *The Mascot* pay you to sit in court every day?" Jahnke asked.

"Two dollars."

"If you come back to work for me, I will pay you five dollars a day, starting Saturday. I have a special contract with the city to lay stone in the Treme section of the city—around the Treme Market and the parish prison. The city is going to install electric street cars in that neighborhood, and we need to fortify the stone and iron tracks with new railroad ties. I get a bonus if I finish the job by the end of the month. You want the job?"

"Five dollars a day?" Brother Stanislaus asked. "That's an enormous amount of money."

"The bonus and the chance at future jobs will make it worth it. But it's hard work," Jahnke warned. "Will you meet Mr. Falcone at the Treme Market on Saturday morning?"

Antonio, stunned by the offer, sat silently thinking about the prospect. "If the trial is over by Saturday, I will go to work for you. But only after the trial. I want to finish my job at the paper."

"Great. Meet Mr. Falcone at the market at seven o'clock. You will be paid at six o'clock that evening," Jahnke promised. "Abraham, do you want to work, too?"

"No, sir. I want to complete my art lessons and study the violin," Abraham said.

"Sir, whatever happened to Vito Vittori. He graduated from St. Aloysius, like me, and went to work for you. Will he be there Saturday, too?" Antonio asked.

Jahnke hung his head. "Vito has had a rough time. The night the chief was killed, the police and others caught him walking down Julia Street and beat him severely. He escaped their clutches, ran through the night to my brickyard, and hid for several days without food or water. When Ilsa and Mr. Falcone found him trying to break into my office, looking for food and water, we took him in, bandaged him, and fed him. He shakes every time he sees a policeman. He reads the newspapers every morning and has been following the trial. But he won't leave my business. He's scared to walk too far from my yard, and doesn't talk much. His nerves have been stripped, like bark from a tree. So, he does my bookkeeping. He doesn't talk much, and won't leave the yard."

Antonio rubbed the jagged scar on his nose. "How's Ilsa?" Antonio braved.

"She is fine. She's learning the business, "Jahnke said, as he folded his hands on the table. He looked at the Brothers and then at Antonio. "This entire Hennessy affair has taught many people in New Orleans a lesson in prejudice and tolerance. Some feelings are granite-hard and will never change, while others are changing, but slowly. It's like the War never happened. No war can erase deep, inbred emotions. Those changes must come from within, not from the muzzle of a gun or laws on paper. I don't know what the future holds for this city. I can only pray for justice. I will have Ilsa deliver lunch on Saturday. She will be happy to know you will be there."

Antonio smiled for the first time in months.

Chapter 81

Criminal District Court
March 13, 1891
10:10 A.M.

After a month-long trial, Louisiana's largest capital case in history was coming to an end. In the closing days of the trial, the state tried to tar the defendants with viscid layers of guilt, while the defense attempted to dissolve the prosecution's case in a vat of solvent, based on reasonable doubt, predicated by common sense and truth. In the last few days, both sides fought to convince the jury of the truth of their respective case. Unbeknownst to the defense, the Committee of Fifty was doing some back-alley close-knife work, while the courtroom lights burned into the night.

In Judge Marr's court, a secret Grand Jury prepared indictments against Thomas McCrystol and John Cooney, both known to be associates of Dominick O'Malley. The jury tampering charges were built on a house of cards on a foundation of matchsticks, driven by fear, as the Committee of Fifty prepared for any not guilty verdicts. Before resting, Semmes informed the court that the defense had two more alibi witnesses, one of whom was Polizzi's common-law wife. Neither Semmes nor Adams knew she had been visited by police officers, offering her money not to testify. She refused the offer and testified, along with Polizzi's doctor, Hugh Kelly, who testified he treated Polizzi for a sprained wrist three days before Hennessy was shot. He applied an ointment of Vaseline, belladonna, and opium to deaden the pain, which rebutted the arresting officers' opinion that Polizzi had slipped on Franklin and Girod Streets after shooting Hennessy.

Scaffidi also proffered a strong alibi witness, Carsa Patinia, who served as Mrs. Scaffidi's midwife. She testified that Antonio Scaffidi was home on the night of October 15, 1890, when she assisted in the birth of his son. But the spectators gasped when she testified that the baby died in Mr. Scaffidi's arms, and they disposed of the tiny body in the privy. Her testimony vividly described the privations Italian immigrants suffered, as they fought every day for survival in a strange land.

After the state's last rebuttal witnesses on Tuesday evening, Judge Baker allowed the jury to board carriages and go to the intersection of Girod and Basin. It was dark, and the streetlight burned brightly. However, when an electric light company superintendent informed the judge that the light hanging over the intersection had been replaced with a new light since October 15, 1890, Judge Baker, duty-bound, informed the jury.

><

As spectators crammed into the courtroom on Wednesday morning, attorneys conducted bench conferences with Judge Baker over the length of the closing argument. Judge Baker had two surprises for Luzenberg. "Since the name Bastian Incardona was never mentioned in this trial, other than being at Fabacher's Restaurant on the night Hennessy was killed, I encourage you to dismiss the charges against him," Judge Baker advised. Luzenberg paused, nodded, and returned to his seat, as did a surprised defense team.

"The court has considered the evidence thus far adduced by the parties, and has determined each side should have six hours for closing arguments. After all, this is a capital case, and I want to be fair. Mr. Luzenberg, do you have any motions to make before we commence arguments?" Judge Baker asked.

"Yes, your honor. Considering the paucity of evidence adduced against Bastion Incardona, the state dismisses all charges against him."

The courtroom was concussed in echoes of mixed emotions. Judge Baker banged his gavel while some members of the Committee of Fifty slipped out the courtroom door. Judge Baker made another announcement, which quaked the courthouse to its foundation. "I grant the state's motion, and I also find there has been insufficient evidence adduced against Charles Matranga." Turning towards the jury, Judge Baker stated, "It is my duty to instruct you to return verdicts of not guilty against defendants Incardona and Matranga." The judge then called for a fifteen-minute recess.

Chapter 82

City Hall
March 11, 1891
11:30 A.M.

An ashen Joseph A. Shakspeare sat behind his desk, as John G. Wickliffe, William S. Parkerson, Frank B. Hayne, James D. Houston, Edgar Farrar, S.P. Walmsley, Albert Baldwin, and other members of the Committee of Fifty informed him that all charges against Charles Matranga and Bastion Incardona had been dismissed. The cacophony of their bewildered voices echoed throughout City Hall as other members of the Committee arrived to register their disbelief.

"Let's go to the council chambers where we'll have some privacy," Shakspeare said.

Once inside the council chambers, the mayor ordered two police officers to lock the doors. Once secured, the Committee paced around the chambers like lost children, seeking some understanding of what had occurred across the square.

"Mr. Mayor, we spent thousands of dollars on this case, and Baker dismisses the charges against one of the leaders of our dago problem," Wickliffe exclaimed.

"Everyone, calm down," Shakspeare said. "We must have a plan in place if the jury returns any not guilty verdicts. I don't understand this. This morning's *Picayune* reported that two men have been indicted for jury tampering. Both seem to be friends of Dominick O'Malley. Is this true?"

"It seems both men were hanging around the back of the courthouse near the door to the jury's quarters," Wickliffe said. "Of course, they deny any tampering, but both men are friends of O'Malley and Matranga."

"Alright. Let's build our case on jury tampering if the jury does something stupid. Remember my public statement on the day of Hennessy's funeral? I meant it then, as I do now. *We* will rid this city of this race of people by any means necessary. This is *our* city. *We* are the power of this city. *We* are growing this metropolis into an international venue of commerce. *We* are the law. *We* are justice. If the jury acquits them, *we* will act, for there is no one to stop us. Anyone disagree with me? Do any of the lawyers in this chamber disagree with me?" the mayor asked, his face flushed with anger.

There was no response.

"Gentlemen, this is *your* home where you create *your* wealth and raise *your* families. We will not let *anyone* enter our city and diminish our status. There is no one to stop us from what we must do," Shakspeare said.

"What do you propose, Mr. Mayor?" Houston asked.

"J.D., get the Ring ready, like you would for an election day. Mr. Parkerson, can you lend J.D. some of your Regulators?"

"Yes."

"We need men we can trust to keep secrets. If the dagoes can keep secrets, so can we. Some of you belong to certain lodges and societies that demand secrecy. I know who you are. I belong to a few, also. We control two newspapers and the telegraph system. We control the new telephone switching station. We control the railroads in and out of this city. We control some of the shipping companies, except for the market controlled by Macheca and his half-brothers. That which we don't control must be silenced by *our* law," the mayor seethed.

"What about the state militia? Will they interfere with anything we do?" Houston asked.

"No. Remember, the governor's New Orleans commandant, General John Glynn, is a member of this Committee. I will send for him. I'm sure the governor will not be happy with what has just happened," Shakspeare said.

"What about the judges, the sheriff, the District Attorney, the police?" Albert Baldwin asked.

"What about them? We control them. If they want to retain their positions, they will honor what we must do," Shakspeare said. "Mr. Baldwin, do you have an inventory of new weapons?"

"I have crates of new Winchesters and shotguns. I have crates of new pistols, too. I have them hidden in my warehouse uptown on the river. It's our private arsenal."

The mayor smiled. "Good. We need it now. Tonight, I want you to move about twenty rifles and ten shotguns to Hayne's house at Bienville and Exchange Place. Any problems, Frank?"

"Not at all," Hayne responded.

"Once there, I want you to secure them, until we see what this damn jury does."

"Are we going to raid the Italian Colony again?" Houston asked.

"No. We can't do that again. We will focus on the beneficiaries of the tampered jury. If the dagoes are found not guilty, we will say it's because the jury was bribed. That's our message to the public. The *Picayune* will help us."

"Why do you think Judge Baker directed the jury to find Matranga not guilty?" Wickliffe asked.

"Because Thomas J. Semmes, that apostate, represented him. It was Matranga who attracted the money to pay the lawyers," Shakspeare responded.

"Doesn't Baker's jury instruction to find Matranga not guilty belie any notion of jury tampering?" Houston asked.

The council chambers fell silent for several moments as the Committee and the mayor pondered Houston's question. "If we take any action adverse to the jury's verdicts, we must be careful how we handle Matranga. Semmes still has many powerful friends in the city," Wickliffe intoned.

"I understand. Do you, J.D.?" the mayor asked.

Houston nodded.

Shakspeare checked his pocket watch. "It's a little after noon, and the closing arguments are being made. Let's hope the jury does the right thing. Wickliffe and Parkerson meet me here tonight at eight o'clock. Polish your oratory skills. J.D., get your people ready. Remember, only people *we* can trust to keep secrets," Shakspeare demanded. "When the courts of law fail, the people become the law."

Chapter 83

Criminal District Court
March 12, 1891
10:30 A.M.

For the two days, members of the Committee of Fifty's paid prosecution team and the defense argued for the lives of six men and one boy. Bastian Incardona and Charles Matranga, though acquitted in Judge Baker's court, remained in the dock because they faced charges of "Lying in Wait" in Judge Marr's court. Charles Luzenberg strategically charged and split the cases to increase the odds that the defendants' last shadow would cast on the prison gallows.

For two days, lawyers became, as Luzenberg acclaimed, "priests in the temple of justice." The prosecutors demanded the death penalty for the remaining defendants' attack on civilized society, by gunning down the highest representative of law and order, David C. Hennessy. They stressed if Hennessy couldn't walk the streets of New Orleans safely, no one could. But Lionel Adams wasted no time ripping the state's case to rags.

"I ask the gentlemen of the jury to consider the following when you deliberate. I knew David Hennessy. Do you think I would represent his killers? Do you believe a bartender can run fast enough down Girod Street to make positive identifications in the dim, gloomy night? Do you think Kalinski was lying when he said Daure didn't know who shot David Hennessy? Why did Daure wait so long to tell the police what he saw or claimed to have seen? Examine what the state didn't prove. Whose guns were found? Where were the defendants at the time of the shooting? Not on Girod Street. The state failed to establish any personal or professional relationship between each of the defendants. In fact, the state offered no proof of any relationship or conspiracy between these men. Remember, Judge Baker will instruct you to find Matranga and Incardona not guilty, because of the lack of proof of their guilt. I would offer that there is more reasonable doubt in this case than any I have ever tried.

"What was the motive to kill David Hennessy? If there was a war going on between the Matrangas and the Provenzanos, as the newspapers have stated, these defendants had more motive to kill the Provenzanos than David Hennessy. Remember this: David Hennessy ordered the arrest of the Provenzanos on May 5, 1890. So, gentlemen of the jury, it comes down to one question. Who killed Chief Hennessy? If you don't know, that's reasonable doubt, and you must find the defendants not guilty."

But the prosecution hammered on two points, one of which the defense didn't aggressively challenge, and that was the animus between Hennessy and Macheca. But the defense agreed that Macheca and Hennessy were at odds with each other, but not to the extent that Macheca would assemble *nineteen* men to kill him, of which two have been acquitted. The second point the state seized upon was the *Mafia* influence in matters of the city, and its willingness to kill David C. Hennessy. Judge Baker, hearing enough about the *Mafia*, stopped prosecutor W.L. Evans in mid-sentence and warned him that the state had not introduced any evidence of the existence of the Mafia or the defendants' membership therein.

Reporters for the *Daily Picayune* and the *Times-Democrat* were surprised by Baker's interruption of the closing argument, but understood the reason. The state failed to introduce any evidence that the Mafia or *Stuppagghieri* had killed Hennessy, despite months of newspaper articles suggesting the contrary. And the state offered no evidence that Hennessy had incriminating evidence from Italy regarding any of the defendants, thus destroying any rumor or theory that supported that motive, as reported by the newspapers.

But the defense drove a spike deep into the heart of the state's case, and an ailing Thomas J. Semmes wielded the hammer, as he appealed to the jury's common sense.

"The state promised you they would call two witnesses to prove their case. J.C. Roe and Billy O'Connor. Where are they? In the absence of Officer Roe, who stood guard at Hennessy's house, and spoke to Hennessy after he was shot, and Captain O'Connor, who was the last man to leave Hennessy, and probably the first to reach him after the murder, could not but add to the doubt in your minds. The absence of those witnesses under these circumstances, when they might have established a certainty as to the men, was a matter for question. The only hypothesis is that, if they had appeared, they would have given evidence which would have cleared the accused."

After Luzenberg made a flailing thrust to justify the differences in perceptions of eyewitnesses, the judge charged the jury as to what law to follow in their deliberations. Judge Baker rapped his gavel and adjourned court until the following morning. As the jury filed into the deliberation room, Judge Baker exhorted them to get some rest that night and take their time, for the lives of several men and a boy rest with their judgment.

As the spectators left the courthouse and gathered on Camp Street, torrents of rain failed to scatter them. Thunder rolled across the contused sky, like wooden casks rolling on a cypress floor, but the crowd huddled to predict the verdicts. Despite the sheets of rain, the police pushed the crowd from the street, allowing a drayage wagon, laden with two heavy crates from Baldwin's warehouse, to splash past the gossiping gaggle.

Chapter 84

Criminal District Court
March 13, 1891
Morning

The Camp Street newspapers worked through the night, chronicling the last day of the much-vaunted Hennessy murder trial. Each paper had hand-etched images of the lawyers pitted in battle for the necks of eight men and one boy. Each provided the malleable minds of New Orleans with their interpretation of the case. But the *Daily Picayune* went further. Eliza Jane Nicholson took one last stab at the Italians when she printed a story about the trial, which started on page one and continued through page three. The last two paragraphs of the story attempted to capture the deserved pathos of the moment, while provoking febrile anticipation of guilty verdicts.

"It was a dark, rainy, threatening night, the crowd around looked grim in the gloom, and the ominous weather was not calculated to cheer the heavy hearts of the men charged with having dealt out death to David C. Hennessy.

"Of course, there are no means of learning the deliberations of the twelve men charged with deciding the fate of the accused. But rumor is always busy, and the rumor late last night was the jury had agreed upon a verdict against most of the accused now before the bar."

When Antonio, Abraham, and Hearn arrived at the courthouse, they found the streets adjacent to the old hall clogged with people and carriages, reflecting every strata of society. Across from the courthouse, in the square, they noticed the families of the accused huddled around Pasquale Corte, who was taking notes. Emmanuel Polizzi's common-law wife screamed allegations of police misconduct to Corte, but in Italian, to avoid any further retribution.

As Antonio crossed Lafayette Street, Johan Jahnke and John Falcone beckoned him to approach Jahnke's carriage. Antonio complied and was greeted warmly by both men.

"You look like a great young gentleman, dressed in that black suit, Antonio," Jahnke said.

"Thank you, sir."

"I know you have been very busy working for *The Mascot* and covering this trial, but it might be over today. Tomorrow is Saturday, and I have mounting pressure to finish the paving job around the parish prison, behind Congo Square. I need you, and anyone else who can help. I am willing to pay you five dollars for a day's work. Will you work for me tomorrow if this trial is finished today?" Jahnke asked.

"Yes."

"That's right," Falcone said. "That's more money you make with the newspaper. We need to lay large stones and new streetcar ties. We need about ten boys to complete the job. Is your friend willing to come?" Falcone asked, pointing to Abraham. Antonio called Abraham over to the carriage, and Falcone repeated the offer. Abraham changed his mind and agreed to work for Jahnke. Hearn overheard the conversation, and was disturbed at the venue of the boys' offer—next to a courthouse where a jury would soon determine if men would live or die.

"Great. I will pick you up at St. Aloysius at seven o'clock tomorrow morning. Wear old clothes. I will have some leather gloves for both of you," Falcone said.

"Thank you, boys," Jahnke said. "In the future, I will have more work and pay you well." Then Jahnke bent down and whispered in Antonio's ear. "Believe it or not, I hope they find these men not guilty. They didn't kill Hennessy."

Antonio smiled and nodded. He was tempted to ask about Ilsa, but silenced his heart and lips.

><

The edgy crowd gathered around the courthouse's front door throughout the morning, pacing and waiting. Rumors tore through the crowd like a virulent fever. Many expressed their impatience with the jury's lengthy deliberations. To many, their prejudice overruled their logic, which caused them to ignore the weaknesses in the state's case. They demanded instant justice despite the nearly month-long trial.

A little after noon, a member of the crowd noticed two police patrol wagons coming down Lafayette Street from Magazine Street. Captain Journee sat atop the first wagon, which stopped at the courthouse's side entrance. The crowd watched as police officers and sheriff's deputies rushed the defendants through a side door and into the courthouse. The crowd, including newspaper men, swarmed the front doors, elbowing men and women alike. In the excitement, no deference was given to one's gender or status.

Once inside the courtroom, the spectators rushed for seats. The newspaper reporters, some from New York and Chicago, pressed into the seats. Soon, the defendants filed into the courtroom, expressing no outward emotion. The court clerks move around their desks, pretending to be busy. About twenty minutes later, Judge Baker cracked open his chamber doors and stood behind his bench. He instructed a deputy to let the jury into the courtroom. As the twelve men entered the jury box, each wore a white boutonniere, perplexing veteran court watchers and the judge. What signal was the jury sending? Was it a signal, or just some inscrutable expression of completing their job?

"I understand the jury has a question," Judge Baker said. "Will the foreman step forward?"

Jacob Seligman stepped forward and announced that the jury could not return a verdict on some of the defendants, but could return a verdict on others. Judge Baker instructed the jury to return to the jury room to await further instructions. As the court clerks huddled around the judge, more spectators poured into the courtroom, including members of the Committee of Fifty. After about ten minutes, the judge ordered the jury to return to the courtroom and render their verdicts.

After the jury was seated, Judge Baker asked Seligman to give his clerk, Richard Screven, the verdict form. Screven then passed the form up to the judge and slowly unfolded the papers. Judge Baker sat back in his large black leather chair and studied the verdicts as the spectators focused on the judge's eyes and wavy brow. After a few minutes, the judge asked Seligman, "Mr. Foreman, are you telling this court you cannot return a verdict as to Polizzi, Monasterio, and Scaffidi?"

"Yes, that is correct."

In a visibly stunned state, Judge Baker handed the verdict form to Richard Screven and ordered him to publish the verdict.

"New Orleans, March 13, 1891," Screven began. He read each name of the remaining defendants, with the pace of a tolling bell. "Bastian Incardona, Charles Matranga, Antonio Bagnetto, Asperi Marchesi, Antonio Marchesi, Joseph P. Macheca. Not Guilty."

Antonio and Abraham hug each other, their eyes welling with tears. Most of the reporters uttered words of disbelief. Family members wept. Spectators growled in disbelief. As the verdicts flowed from the courthouse, the crowd on Camp Street erupted in anger. Judge Baker ordered the defendants to be returned to the parish prison, partially for their own safety, and the remaining dubious charge of Lying in Wait, pending in Judge Marr's court.

Reporters besieged each jury member, hurling insults and questions at each of them. Since they had agreed not to discuss their deliberations, most of the jurors honored that oath. But Jacob Seligman spoke out, thinking he must defend his brethren's verdict. "We were told we would hear testimony from O'Connor and Roe. We didn't. Why? That planted reasonable doubt. We didn't believe Daure's testimony. That was more reasonable doubt. The state's case was weak, and we believed most of the alibi witnesses."

One reporter braved an insult to the jury. "Were any members of the jury bribed?"

"Bribed? How could we be bribed? The judge found Incardona and Matranga not guilty. We followed his instructions. The mistrial votes were equally divided among the jurors. We followed the judge's instructions about reasonable doubt, and we had reasonable doubt," Seligman asserted.

As members of the jury were escorted from the courthouse, the crowd hurled insults, which were ignored. Police officers escorted some for several blocks for their safety. Inside the courtroom, attorneys for both sides lingered to answer questions from reporters.

Lionel Adams took this opportunity to approach his old colleague, Charles Luzenberg. While they shook hands, Adams asked. "Charles, are you ever going to tell me who the man was who saw three of the shooters who were not Sicilian?"

"What do you mean?" Luzenberg responded.

Adams reached inside his suit pocket and pulled the *Times-Democrat* newspaper article from October 18, 1890, where a reporter heard a man tell the police and the mayor he saw three of the assassins, and none were Sicilian. Luzenberg refused to answer the question.

><

Later in the afternoon, the crowd began to dwindle. Antonio, Abraham, and Hearn left the courthouse and walked down Camp Street towards their office. Hearn spotted a group of well-dressed men standing under a Magnolia tree in Lafayette Square. Most of them were members of the Committee of Fifty. Hearn stopped and watched the men from across the street. Though he couldn't hear them, it was clear it wasn't a social gathering. Their normal pallid complexions were florid with anger.

"You boys go back to your school, and don't go anywhere tonight," Hearn warned.

"Why?" Antonio asked.

Before Hearn could answer, half the group peeled off and walked towards City Hall. The other half walked towards Canal Street.

"I'll take your notes and carvings back to the office. Stay inside tonight," Hearn said.

"What about our work tomorrow on the streets?" Antonio asked.

"I think you will be safe in the daylight," Hearn said.

As they walked on the riverside of Camp Street, their eyes followed the men walking on the opposite side. When they arrived at the intersection of Camp and Commercial Place, they met another group of men and entered the offices of William S. Parkerson.

"Boys, I have a bad feeling. I want you to run back to school and stay there. The mayor's Committee is planning something."

"How do you know?" Abraham asked.

"Those men are usually home on Friday evenings sipping bourbon and smoking a cigar before dinner. But they are now meeting at a lawyer's office? And are members of the other newspapers following them? Go. Run. I'm going to stay here and see what happens. I will contact you later. Stay inside tonight."

Antonio and Abraham jogged back to St. Aloysius. The mien of the Italian Colony seemed more cheerful than it had been for months. Some Italians were celebrating the verdicts and King Umberto's birthday the next day by draping Italian flags over the ornate ironwork on the galleries above Chartres Street. Other than Antonio and Abraham, no one knew there was a toxic cauldron of hate roiling across Canal Street.

><

Lawrence Hearn leaned against a wall on Camp Street, watching a pack of reporters waiting outside Parkerson's office. After about an hour, a large group of men, some attired in expensive suits and bowlers, and others in dungarees, walked down Camp Street towards Canal. Hearn and other reporters followed them. As the men crossed Canal Street, Hearn's fears churned his guts. Most of these men lived uptown. *"What are they doing in the French Quarter on Friday night?"* Hearn thought. The reporters followed the men to the intersection of Bienville and Exchange Place, where Franklin B. Hayne lived. J.D. Houston and other members of the Committee of Fifty, Houston's Ring, and Parkerson's Regulators jammed into Hayne's residence for several hours. Reporters waited outside, knowing the verdicts rendered earlier were not the end of the case, but a burning torch lighting a fuse. Their anticipation filled the air like black acrid smoke from a funeral pyre.

Hearn paced the intersection and exchanged some thoughts with the other reporters. As he waited for anything to happen, he noticed the large drayage wagon parked in an alley near Hayne's residence. A large green canvas tarp covered its cargo, but the wagon's owner's name was visible, painted in large black letters. Even in the gloom of night—**A. BALDWIN HARDWARE**—pierced Hearn's eyes.

The Haynes' front door opened about nine o'clock, and the men filed out. Some walked down Exchange Place towards Canal Street. Some lingered behind and took positions near the drayage wagon. J.D. Houston, accompanied by his men, approached the reporters for the *Daily Picayune* and the *Times-Democrat,* and handed them each a piece of paper.

"Go tell your editors to print this message in tonight's paper, so everyone can read it first thing in the morning," Houston demanded.

Hearn moved towards the reporters, as they looked at the message under a streetlamp. It read:

MASS MEETING!

"All good citizens are invited to attend a mass meeting on SATURDAY, March 14, at 10 o'clock a.m. at the Clay Statue to take steps to remedy the failures of justice in the HENNESSEY CASE. Come prepared for action."

Sixty-one names appeared below the message, including A. Baldwin, John Wickliffe, W.S. Parkerson, Septime Villere, Omar Villere, Edgar Farrar, Frank B. Hayne, James D. Houston, S. P. Walmsley, Walter Denegre, George Denegre, T.D. Wharton, other members of the Cotton Exchange, secret carnival clubs, Freemasonry, and the Democrat scions of men determined to perpetuate the social structure of the old South in New Orleans. And as Hearn read the ominous missive under the flickering gas lamp, a chill coursed through his body, for he knew a new weapon had been forged, not of iron, lead, or steel, but of ink and paper.

Part VI
Pro Bono Publico

Chapter 85

March 14, 1891
Morning

As the morning sun crested the horizon beyond the Mississippi River, its brilliant beam shot down Canal Street, sparking life into the peaceful commercial center of New Orleans. Already, newsboys were strategically planting stacks of the morning papers at all the city's main street intersections, waiting for customers to pay two cents for the foreboding news of the day. At the center of the intersection of St. Charles Avenue and Canal Street, in an area known as the *Neutral Ground,* a twenty-five-foot bronze statue of Henry Clay stood, facing the river. The statue rested on a large granite pedestal atop a base three steps above the street level. A four-foot wrought-iron fence circled the base, which had a small gate installed to allow speakers to stand before a crowd and bellow speeches.

Many people used Clay Statue as a meeting point in the city, as the street cars from uptown and downtown would converge at that point, and allow their passengers to commerce on the broad avenue, without fear of being attacked for their ethnicity. The grand monument of the "Great Compromiser" reminded everyone that Canal Street carved New Orleans into two cities, and the social order ordained during the antebellum times still applied. What the city's political and wealthy elites had planned for this day would reflect behavior from the shattered mirror of history, which occurred deep in the lawless fields and woods of plantations, not in an ersatz sophisticated metropolis.

About a dozen men sat on the steps at the base of the Clay Statue, reading the various editions of the morning papers, waiting for the cafes to open. These were working class and tradesmen, waiting for the call of work, of any kind. Most had a casual acquaintance with the current events, because foraging for work consumed their daily lives. Whatever occurred on either side of Canal Street held no value to them unless it meant work, and work meant survival. But as these day laborers, some barely literate, spread their broadsheets in the morning sun, they read the ominous notice of a "Mass Meeting" printed on page three of the *Times-Democrat* and page four of the *Daily Picayune*. Realizing where they were sitting, the men scattered towards the docks or disappeared into the depths of the French Quarter.

><

As Pasquale Corte walked down Canal Street near Rampart Street, he bought a copy of the *Daily Picayune* and read the notice regarding the meeting at ten o'clock. He raced to city hall and breathlessly ascended its front steps. A guard stopped him at the front door. "I demand to see the mayor," Corte screamed.

"Sir, this is Saturday morning. The mayor is usually at the Pickwick Club, having breakfast," the guard responded.

Corte scampered down the steps and ran to the Pickwick Club and demanded to see the mayor. Two doormen denied him admission because Corte was not a member. "I need to see the mayor at once," Corte demanded.

"Sorry, sir. We cannot let you in," a doorman said.

"Can you take him a message? He must stop this meeting at ten o'clock," Corte entreated.

"What meeting?"

"The meeting printed in the newspaper—a block away from here," Corte pointed.

"Sorry, sir, we know nothing about a meeting today," the doorman said.

Frustrated, the Italian Consulate walked onto Canal Street's neutral ground. From a block away, he could see a crowd beginning to muster at the base of the Clay Statue. He saw an Italian tinsmith riding his horse towards the statue, and warned him to go home, but to lend him his horse. The tinsmith obliged, and Corte galloped towards a bawdy section of New Orleans, known as West End, on Lake Pontchartrain, where Governor Francis T. Nicholls was known to frequent on the weekends. West End had casinos and hotels, which curried to gentlemen, not wanting to be noticed after dark. But Corte's business included knowing the habits of public officials in New Orleans.

When he arrived at West End, he noticed a detail of Louisiana militiamen standing guard outside a weather-beaten clapboard hotel and casino, near the mouth of the New Basin Canal. Corte breezed past the guards and entered the lobby, where he found the governor having breakfast with several gentlemen. "With all due respect, Your Excellency, but I must talk to you," Corte said.

"What is it, Mr. Corte?" Nicholls asked.

"Are you aware of a mass meeting downtown at the Clay Statue. I fear some violence against my countrymen who were acquitted yesterday. It's in the newspapers," Corte said.

"I heard rumors about some meeting, but I will not get involved in a local affair. Let the city police handle the matter," the governor responded.

"But your General Glynn is part of the mayor's Committee of Fifty," Corte protested. "You must stop this now," Corte pleaded.

"Sorry, Mr. Corte. This is purely a local problem. The state will not intervene. Now, please let me finish my breakfast."

Corte left West End and galloped back to Canal Street, remaining a few blocks from the Clay Statue. But now, the crowd had grown, and both sides of Canal Street were blocked with carriages and wagons. It was only eight o'clock.

><

At the parish prison, the inmates were finishing breakfast. The recently acquitted Italians sat at a long table under a loggia near the kitchen. Removed from the shadow of the gallows, their mood seemed relaxed. Once-exiled Emmanuel Polizzi sat at the end of the table, his dark eyes darting from side to side. Even the guards relaxed near the table. But J.P. Macheca had some unfinished business to conduct with Pietro Monasterio. He approached the old cobbler respectfully, but a fire burned in his heart.

"Mr. Monasterio, did you hear what I told the reporters in the courtroom yesterday afternoon?" Macheca asked.

Monasterio nodded, but didn't say a word.

"Why didn't you tell the police I didn't rent your shanty on Girod Street, as the witnesses stated? Who rented your shanty? Please tell me," Macheca implored.

"I cannot say. I only got a mistrial, and can be tried again. You were acquitted."

"Who told you that?" Macheca asked.

"Polizzi's lawyer—Mr. Flynn. He said we are not to talk to anyone about the case."

"But you know I didn't rent your shanty, and you could stop them from prosecuting me, but you didn't. Who rented the shanty?" Macheca demanded.

"J.P., let it go. We have been found not guilty and will be released Monday morning. Leave the cobbler alone," Matranga intervened. "We will be back to work soon."

"I want to know who rented the shanty," Macheca persisted. "I've been put through hell, and lost my reputation because of some bullshit shanty I never saw?"

"It doesn't matter anymore," Matranga said. "Let's focus on our work."

Macheca relaxed, and then he noticed the loggia and yard had fewer guards than usual. "Where are all the guards? Usually, we can't shit without someone watching us," he asked.

"We were found not guilty, and will be out of here Monday morning when Judge Marr takes the bench," Matranga said. "Relax."

The inmates didn't know Sheriff Villere had stationed dozens of armed deputies outside the gray-white walls of the old jail, as a pretense of security.

><

Workmen began ripping up old cobblestone outside the parish prison and laying new railroad ties to accommodate the heavier electric street cars. The crews, most Italian and Black laborers, drove iron spikes into the grout lines and lifted the heavy stones, one by one. Wagons, laden with six-by-six creosote-coated ties and granite stones, lined up at the Orleans and Treme Streets intersection. The echoes of the sledgehammers slamming iron spikes bounced off the gray-white walls of the most foreboding structure in New Orleans. On the banquettes, in front, and on the side of the parish prison, deputies walked with shotguns cradled in their arms. Their presence only added to the mournful ambience leaching from the iron-grated windows of the prison. Sometimes, a forlorn face of an abandoned soul peeked through the grates and waved to the workman. Common decency demanded an acknowledging wave from the workman.

A Jahnke foreman assigned Antonio and Abraham to unload the ties from the wagon and carry them to where the workman had cleared the street for their installation. Although smaller than Antonio, Abraham struggled with each tie but wouldn't quit. Fortunately, each boy wore leather gloves and a leather farrier's apron to protect their hands and clothes. After stacking the ties, Antonio paused and searched each window of the prison, hoping to spot Asperi Marchesi. Sometimes the foreman would complain and admonish Antonio to hurry, because their goal was to reach Hospital Street by dusk.

As the work continued, Lawrence Hearn parked his carriage on Basin Street and approached the workman, looking for Antonio and Abraham. His eyes searched each crew and found the boys near a stack of ties on Treme Street.

"Listen to me. You boys must get back to school at once." Hearn warned.

"Why?" Antonio asked.

"There's a mob gathering at the Clay Statue on Canal Street, and I think they might be coming here," Hearn said.

"Why would they come here?" Antonio asked.

"To lynch the men who were found not guilty yesterday."

"What does lynch mean?" Abraham asked.

"They will break into the prison and kill the Italians. You're Italian. It looks like most of the men working here are Italian. If this mob comes here, everyone is in danger. You must go now."

"But they were found not guilty, right? How can they kill them? Isn't that against the law?" Antonio asked.

"*They* are the law in New Orleans," Hearn said.

The foreman, Jack Lenningham, approached Hearn and demanded that he leave the work site. Hearn refused and expressed his concern about the mob coming to the prison. "Let them come. We have work to do. Mr. Jahnke is paying everyone five dollars to work today. We have to get to Hospital Street by dusk," Lenningham said.

"Most of your crew are Italians. If that mob comes here, they might be in trouble, too," Hearn said.

"If that damn mob comes here, they will be after the dagoes in the prison, not the ones working on the street. I'll just tell the crews to stand aside and let the mob do their job," Lenningham said. "Now, get your ass off my work site, or I'll get one of those deputies to run you out of here."

Hearn looked at Antonio and Abraham. "If that mob shows up, run and hide," Hearn said, before returning to his carriage.

Chapter 86

Clay Statue
Canal Street
Mid-morning.

Like a gnomon of an ancient Greek sundial, the Henry Clay statue cast a mid-morning shadow across the dark side of Canal Street, between the buildings which housed the Boston and Pickwick Clubs. As the ten o'clock hour neared, the crowd had swelled to over five thousand people, some on foot, some on horseback, some in carriages, and some in elegant coaches. Some men were dressed in their best clothes, crowned with bowlers and derbies. Pistols bulged in their waistbands, while others slung their rifles and shotguns over their shoulders, like hunters preparing to stalk their prey. Women sat in the rear seats of carriages, boldly displaying their bonnets, resplendent in bows, flowers and ribbons. The mood embraced an ecumenical sensation, but was devoid of any stained glass.

A block and a half away, at Franklin Hayne's Exchange Place home, J.D. Houston began to distribute Winchesters and shotguns to a select group of men, all dressed in black suits, white shirts, and black ties. After a final briefing, five wagons carrying about fifty men rolled down Exchange Place to Canal Street, where they waited for further instructions. Although the wagons were about a hundred feet away from the statue, they could hear the exhortations filling the air from three of New Orleans' finest attorneys.

At ten o'clock, three ministers of the law, William Sterling Parkerson, Walter Denegre, and John Wickliffe, stepped through the small wrought-iron gate and ascended the steps to the plinth of the monument. Parkerson spoke first.

"People of New Orleans. Once before, I stood before you for public duty. I now appear before you again, actuated by no desire for fame or prominence. Affairs have reached such a crisis that men living in an organized and civilized community, finding their laws fruitless and ineffective, are forced to protect themselves. When the courts fail, the people must act. What protection or assurance of protection is there left when the very head of our police department, our Chief of Police, is assassinated in our very midst by the *Mafia* society, and his assassins are again loose on the community? Will every man here follow me, and see the murder of Hennessy avenged?"

The crowd roared with approval. Parkerson then asked, "Are there men enough here to set aside the verdict of the infamous jury, every one of whom is a perjurer and a scoundrel?"

The frissoned crowd roared louder, and some demanded they march on the parish prison. Parkerson fueled his angry flames with the promise to hunt down Dominick O'Malley, whom he blamed with jury tampering. He closed his remarks with an incendiary question. "Men and citizens of New Orleans, will you follow me? I will be your leader."

Parkerson's words had the effect of stomping on a mound of fire ants. Some of the crowd began to walk down Canal Street towards Basin, while Walter Denegre and John Wickliffe gave speeches admonishing the crowd to follow Parkerson. As the crowd approached the intersection of Exchange Place and Canal Street, the wagons carrying the assigned executioners began to roll towards the prison, followed by a crowd of over six thousand blood-lusting, rabid people.

Chapter 87

Orleans Parish Prison
Basin and Orleans Streets.
10:40 A.M.

Antonio and Abraham continued to heave the large railroad ties onto a pyramid-shaped pile on the Treme Street side of the parish prison. Their leather gloves and aprons protected them from shards and splinters from the rough-hewed, blackened timbers. The Jahnke crew pounded their iron pikes and pried the cobblestones apart, carving new rail beds for the new street cars. Both Italian and Black men worked well in teams and were inching towards Hospital Street, with hopes of going home with money in their pockets at dusk. But the harmonious labor ceased when the crews heard the rumbling of iron-ringed carriage and wagon wheels rolling on the granite stones, accompanied by the din of thousands of people marching up Basin Street, and across Congo Square.

Jack Lenningham, remembering Hearn's earlier warning, scattered his workmen. The Italian workers ran in all directions, while some of the Black workers remained around the prison, since they were close to home. Antonio and Abraham ran across Treme Street, but Abraham tripped on a broken stone and sprained his right ankle. He cried in pain as he attempted to put his weight on his right leg. Antonio hoisted Abraham onto his back and carried him into the clump of hedges that lined Congo Square. They hid from the wrathful crowd, with a clear view of the Treme Street side of the prison.

The crowd jammed Orleans Street, from Rampart to the Treme Market, then snaked around to Treme Street. The prison was surrounded on two sides. Deputies tried to disperse the crowd, but ran away when their efforts proved futile. A police wagon from the Fourth Precinct drew the ire of the crowd and was pummeled by pieces of broken street stones and mud. They retreated to their station at Marais and Orleans. The rabid, labile mob was the law.

A dauntless Pasquale Corte sat on his borrowed horse in Congo

Square, near Orleans and Basin Street. He reached into his coat pocket, retrieved his notebook, and began to record the swarm of hate engulfing the prison's front gates. From his saddle, Corte witnessed Parkerson, Houston, and other members of the Committee of Fifty arguing with Warden Lemuel Davis through the tall iron bars of the prison's gates. Parkerson demanded the keys to the gates, but Davis refused. A heated exchange between the men continued until someone in the crowd yelled that a wooden gate and door were on the Treme Street side of the prison.

Parkerson, Houston, and their henchmen ran to the side of the prison. There, a group of men grabbed one of the railroad ties from the stack. and used it as a battering ram to splinter the wooden gate and door. A group of both Black and White men held the railroad tie and slammed it several times against the door. Each time, the noise of the ram echoed throughout the prison. Davis gave the order to release the nineteen Italian prisoners accused of killing Hennessy, and let them hide anywhere they could inside the prison.

"Give us some guns and let us defend ourselves," J.P. Macheca demanded.

"No. Go hide," Davis responded, as the ram continued to boom throughout the stone corridors of the prison.

One deputy advised the Italians to hide in the women's section on the third tier. Rocco Geraci, Frank Romero, Pietro Monasterio, James Caruso, Loretto Comitz, and Charles Traina ran up the stairs, entered the women's section, and hid. J.P. Macheca, Antonio Scaffidi, and Antonio Marchesi ran to the other side of the third tier, known as the Condemned Unit, and hid on the barred gallery outside the cells. Asperi Marchesi followed his father's advice and hid in Davis's doghouse and kennel.

Emmanuel Polizzi, seemingly dazed by the commotion, remained squatting on his cell floor. Antonio Bagnetto also remained in his cell, behind the locked door. Charles Matranga hid in an empty cell under several mattresses. The rest of the nineteen found similar redoubts in garbage heaps and latrines. Fear quaked the prison.

Parkerson, abandoning the idea of breaching front gates, decided to assemble his men near the Treme Street door, as the men continued to ram. He told Houston to station several men near the door, and not to allow anyone in, except those they selected last night. "Do you have a list of the men we want?" Parkerson asked.

"Yes," Houston said, as he pulled a piece of paper from his coat pocket.

Then, Parkerson whispered, "J.D., don't kill Matranga."

"What? Why?"

"Just do as I say," Parkerson said.

><

Antonio crawled on his belly to the edge of the hedges and parted the branches just enough to see a group of armed men file through the shattered door. They held their Winchesters and shotguns against their chest, as their legion of death began their mission. At one point, he saw two uniform police officers join their ranks. The crowd cheered as the men breached the door, but were angry they were denied admittance. To Antonio, the wild mob could only be satiated by the blood of the nineteen Italians, which caused him to shake and remember Sicily.

Inside the prison, the men who sought shelter in the women's section were betrayed by a Black female inmate. "Dey ran up dem steps to hide," she blabbered.

Twelve armed men ran up the steps, while the Italians found a stairway leading down to the first-floor courtyard. Finding no way to escape the prison walls, the six men huddled together and begged for their lives. From ten feet away, their executioners opened fire on the men. They cranked their Winchesters and blasted their shotguns repeatedly into the pile of men. Standing beyond the walls, newspaper men from New Orleans and New York heard over a hundred shots. Corte heard the volley. Antonio heard the volley. The crowd's blood boiled with each fusillade, which concussed the morning air. They wanted to be part of the slaughter of the Italians and demanded entry, but several of Parkerson's men, mainly from the Ring and Regulators, blocked their passage.

As the killers stood over the six dead men, they marveled at the wounds they had caused. Each body was riddled with bullets and shot, from head to toe. Rivulets of blood streamed down the flagstones of the courtyard.

Meanwhile, another squad of executioners found Macheca, the elder Marchesi, and Scaffidi on the gallery near the Condemned Unit. Macheca had armed himself with an Indian Club, used for exercise, but it offered no protection from rifles and shotguns. As Macheca turned away, a single rifle shot dropped him, and the killers opened fire on Scaffidi and Marchesi. One of the killers took the Indian Club and beat Macheca's head until it was almost unrecognizable. Those shots rang out over the walls, and the crowd, already frenzied, pushed against Parkerson's guards, demanding participation. The final volleys echoed over the prison walls when Bagnetto and Polizzi were shot in their cells.

Although Bagnetto and Polizzi were mortally wounded, they were still alive. Parkerson and Houston, realizing the mob outside the prison was growing impatient with just standing around, had members of the executioners grab Bagnetto and Polizzi, and serve their dying bodies to the fanatical crowd. The crowd broke into two groups, one carrying Bagnetto to a tree on the corner of Orleans and Treme, and one carrying Polizzi to a lamp post along Treme Street. The sacrificial ritual continued.

Antonio watched in horror as the mob hung Bagnetto from a tree and began shooting his dying body. When the limb broke, a neighborhood boy climbed the tree and slung the rope over a robust branch, and the crowd yanked the rope, lifting Bagnetto high in the air. Again, armed members of the mob unloaded their weapons into his twisting body, while others cheered on the morbid display.

Near Antonio's hiding place, another mob hung Polizzi on a lamp post. Still possessing some strength, Polizzi managed to grab the crossbar on the lamp post and pull himself up, avoiding the tightening noose around his neck. Someone climbed up the post, tied Polizzi's hands, and his body dropped, strangling him slowly. Armed members of the mob fired their weapons into the helpless Polizzi, as his body twitched with every piercing round. The crowd roared.

Parkerson stood on the stack of railroad ties and declared that justice had been served. Members of the mob hoisted Parkerson on their shoulders, like a victorious king. As the crowd carried their leader back to the Clay Statue, they left their Lenten oblation to the gods of bigotry and ignorance hanging in the morning sun and lying lifeless on the prison floors.

Chapter 88

Orleans Parish Prison
March 14, 1891
11:30 A.M.

The eyes of the soul never blink, and Antonio's young soul witnessed what he thought were the limits of the evil of man. In his seventeen years, he has killed, nearly been killed, and watched men kill other men, for no reason but hate. Life, to him, had no purpose but to suffer in various ways until numbed by death. The meaningless journey through life promised no hope of a better life. America, to him, meant he must hide behind bushes to survive. He closed his eyes, buried his face in the dirt beneath the branches of his redoubt, and wept.

Lying on his back, facing Rampart Street, Abraham asked, "Antonio, is it over?"

Antonio lifted his head and cast a gaze towards Treme Street. Looking past the dangling bodies of Bagnetto and Scaffidi, he saw the crowd leaving. "Yes. They're leaving."

"Can we leave, yet? My ankle is hurting me."

"No. Stay still. Stay here."

"Where are you going?" Abraham asked.

"I have to check on Asperi."

"Are you crazy. They'll kill you."

"It looks like it's over, and everyone is leaving. I must go see Asperi," Antonio said.

"I'm getting hungry. We've got to get out of here," Abraham said.

"I'll go to the Orleans Street market and get some fruit. Stay here. Stay quiet," Antonio said.

"Be careful. Hurry back. I need a doctor for my ankle."

"I will," Antonio said, as he mustered enough strength to crawl from under the bushes and walk across Treme Street. As he did, he noticed a carriage filled with women stopped near the body of Scaffidi, and gawked at the mangled man hanging by his neck. One eye bulged open, and his tongue hung from the corner of his mouth. Blood streamed from his bullet wounds and down his clothes. The gruesome image had no impact on the women, as two of them dipped their dainty handkerchiefs is the puddle of blood beneath Scaffidi's feet.

Antonio entered the Treme Street door of the prison. The smell of rifle and shotgun smoke filled the air inside the walls. The guards offered no resistance to his presence, as they watched the neighborhood people empty the pockets of the dead. He stepped towards a pile of dead men, looking for Asperi. Numbness filled his soul as he turned away and walked alone through the hellish corridors of the prison.

As he approached the warden's office, guards carried three dead men down the stairs from an upper tier. He looked away. When he reached the warden's office, he took a furtive peek inside and saw a doctor trying to sedate Asperi, who was crying for his father. Antonio, feeling grief and relief knowing his friend was alive, scurried out the prison's front gates and walked towards the market.

><

About noon. Antonio left the market with a small sack of fruit and returned to Abraham by running down St. Ann Street, behind the prison. Because he was still wearing his leather gloves and apron, the police and deputies paid him no attention. When he returned to the hedges, Antonio gave Abraham an apple and a banana.

"Where did you get the money to buy this?" Abraham asked.

"I have money. I save my money. *Mangia,*" Antonio said in Italian.

As the boys ate, two deputies carrying a ladder cut Scaffidi down. It was the first time Abraham saw the results of the mob's assault on the prison. He felt sick. The deputies put Scaffidi on a canvas stretcher and carried him inside the prison. In the distance, other deputies cut Polizzi down and brought him into the prison.

"How long are we going to stay here?" Abraham asked.

"After we eat, I'll carry you back to St. Aloysius. But I must be sure Asperi is fine, before we leave."

After eating, Antonio re-entered the prison through the broken side door. By now, eleven dead men were lying side-by-side under the prison's loggia. He recognized some of the dead as men who were on trial for the Hennessy murder, but five of the dead were part of the nineteen indicted, who were never tried. A group of men hovered over the bodies, removing the blood-soaked clothes, while counting the wounds and taking notes. Antonio recognized one of the men as the Orleans Parish assistant coroner, who testified for the state at the Hennessy trial. Their cold stoicism struck Antonio as they dealt with the irrelevant dead.

Antonio's senses saturated his mind with images of his father's death and what he did in Sicily. He remembered nearly being shot by bandits in the Sicilian mountains while escaping his homeland for a better life. He wondered how he survived the perilous Atlantic crossing. Every hopeful emotion drained from his body as he resigned himself to an early death. As he turned away from the carnage, funeral home wagons were entering the prison yard, followed by priests and nuns. Family members demanded access to their dead, but were denied, until they were released to the undertakers. The pleas and wails of the families stabbed Antonio's ears, as he hung his head and walked towards the prison's front gates. But a yell stopped his steps.

"Antonio Carravella. Is that you?" a man yelled.

Antonio ignored the call. Chills ran through his body. *"Who is calling me?"*

Antonio, it's me. Vincenzo Trambatore—from Bisacquino. You remember. I buried your friend and father," the man said in a Sicilian dialect.

Antonio slowly turned around and saw the Sicilian undertaker sitting on a Thomas E. Lynch's undertaker wagon. "I got my old job back here in New Orleans," a jovial Trambatore said, jumping down from the wagon.

Trambatore hugged Antonio. Antonio returned the gesture and whispered, "Speak English. This is the last place you want to speak Italian or Sicilian."

"I learn English at the Italian work hall. I got my job there. But my accent is still thick, so they say. It's good to see a familiar face. You fine?"

"I'm fine."

"Why you dressed like that? So dirty. Why?" Trambatore asked. "What happened to your nose?"

"I have a job paving streets. I fell down," Antonio said. "I was working here when this *revolta* happened. I'm glad to see you, but I must leave here."

Trambatore grabbed Antonio by the arm and walked him away from the prison gates. They stopped on the neutral ground on Orleans Street, and the undertaker whispered, "Antonio, you are wanted in Sicily for what happened in your father's vineyard. Things are bad in Sicily, so I ran, too. There is a *ricompensa* on your head. I see your name posted on the wall of the work hall on Poydras Street. Did you know that?"

"No," Antonio lied.

"You must hide. Not all Italians or Sicilians are loyal. If you get arrested, they will put you in this prison. They send you back to Sicily. Three hundred dollars will make people whisper in the wrong ears."

"Thank you. I must go now," Antonio said.

"Where you stay?" Trambatore asked.

Antonio hesitated. "I live in a small shack on Girod Street," Antonio uttered impulsively, and ran towards Congo Square.

When he returned to Abraham, he said, "We gotta go. Quick. I'll carry you on my back."

"What's wrong. You see a ghost?" Abraham joked.

"We must leave here. It's too dangerous to stay." Antonio put Abraham on his back, jogged across Rampart Street, and entered the empty streets of the Italian Colony. Every door and window was closed. The familiar neighborhood assumed the aura of a foreign cemetery. When the boys reached St. Ann and Dauphine Streets, Antonio found an old Italian street vendor pushing an empty fruit cart. He gave the man two dollars and put Abraham on the rickety cart. Antonio pushed the cart back to St. Aloysius. The old man followed without saying a word, his creased face and sagging eyes hiding in the shadow of his brimmed hat.

Chapter 89

St. Aloysius Academy
March 14, 1891
12:30 P.M.

From the moment William Sterling Parkerson stepped down from the Clay Statue to the last shot fired at the parish prison, New Orleans became a city which relapsed to its anti-bellum culture, with murderous secret societies, driven by the passions of hate, status, and title, while masquerading as a city ready for the Twentieth Century. Louisiana's deep cultural roots clawed deep into the alluvial soil and refused to abandon its old ways while preserving its bloodlines and wealth by destroying any perceived threat to its insular existence. The Committee of Fifty successfully cast a pall over the Italian Colony, reinforcing a social cast system now ordained by the city's lynch law.

When Antonio pushed the cart down Chartres Street, the rumbling of its wooden wheels echoed against the red-brick shuttered homes and businesses. Occasionally, he caught the suspicious eye peering through green louvered doors. A palpable fear hugged the Italian Colony like a cold winter fog. The news of the prison lynchings spread through the city like yellow fever, immuring Italians in their locked homes, with memories of the night raids of the previous October.

As Antonio approached St. Aloysius, he noticed several carriages and horses hitched to an iron post on the banquette. As he pulled Abraham from the cart, he heard the school's front gate creak open. He looked up and saw Brothers Stanislaus and Angelo, Father Fontebuis, and Laurence Hearn pouring out of the gate.

"Are you okay?" Brother Stanislaus asked. "What happened to Abraham?"

"We're fine. He hurt his ankle when we ran from the prison. So we hid until it was all over," Antonio said.

"Did you see what happened?" Hearn asked.

"I saw it. I heard it. I smelled it." Antonio fell into Father Fontebuis's arms and began to weep. Brother Angelo picked Abraham up and carried him into the dining room of the brothers' residence. Brother Stanislaus paid the old Italian fruit vendor five dollars and warned him to go straight home.

Once inside the dining room, Mrs. Bertucci looked at Abraham's swollen, contused ankle. She borrowed Father Fontebuis's carriage and took Abraham to the fish market to wrap his injury in ice and rags. While they were gone, Antonio told everyone in the dining room what he saw. While Hearn took notes, his complexion paled. Antonio spoke slowly without interruption for nearly thirty minutes, reliving his experiences. He paused and stared at the floor when he got to the part about seeing Trambatore. He said nothing for a few moments.

"What's wrong?" Father Fontebuis asked. "Are you okay?"

Antonio looked at Hearn, because he was the only one in the room who didn't know his past life in Sicily. "Father, do you remember Vincenzo Trambatore from Bisacquino?"

"Yes. The village undertaker?"

"He's here. He works for an undertaker in New Orleans. He was at the prison picking up the dead. He recognized me," Antonio said.

The priest and the Brothers immediately understood Antonio's reticence.

"Do you want to talk anymore?" Father Fontebuis asked.

Antonio shot a glance at Hearn and asked, "Father, can I talk to you alone?"

Antonio and the priest left the dining room and went to an empty classroom. He told the priest that Trambatore knows he's wanted in Sicily, and there was a reward for his arrest. "Do you trust this man to keep silent?" the priest asked.

"You and the Brothers are the only ones I trust you with this knowledge. Mr. Trambatore told me to be careful. Even Italians will inform on each other. I saw that between the Matrangas and Provenzanos. They would do anything for money."

"Does Trambatore know where you live?" the priest asked.

Antonio laughed. "I told him I live in a shack on Girod Street. That's all I heard about for the last month—a shack on Girod Street. So, it's the first thing I thought. I didn't want him to know I lived here. But I did tell him I worked for the company paving the streets."

"That's enough information to help the police find you. We must move you."

"Where? And what do I tell Mr. Hearn?" Antonio asked.

"We'll tell him you are afraid of being a witness to what the mob did, and they will come after you. Did he see Abraham, too?"

"No. Just me."

"We have to move you. Sooner or later, the police will come here."

"Where?

"After dark, I will take you to the Jesuit school. We'll hide you there. I don't think Father O'Shanahan will have any objections. Now, clean up and pack your things. I will tell the Brothers and Mr. Hearn."

"What about Abraham?"

"We'll tell him the same thing. Listen to me, Antonio. You know better than most that life is full of goodbyes."

Chapter 90

The Cotton Exchange
March 14, 1891
1:30 P.M.

After Parkerson stood on the steps of the Clay Statue and admonished the excited crowd to go home, being proud of accomplishing justice for New Orleans, he boarded a carriage with J.D. Houston and William Wickliffe and rode to the Cotton Exchange. Robert Chaffe, the Exchange's president, had called a meeting of the Committee of Fifty and members of the various commercial exchanges in the city. Newspaper men from New Orleans and around the country followed Parkerson into the building.

Inside, the princes of commerce and politics entered a self-congratulatory caul, puffing on cigars and patting each other on the back. The crowd cheered when Parkerson arrived and ascended a dais with Chaffe. The room glowed with a virtuous fury, while eleven slaughtered Italians were being hauled to various funeral homes in the city. A group of lawyers huddled in the corner, preparing for any attack on their self-righteous exercise of tortured due process. Deep from the breasts of these men, a benediction of criminal immunity poured forth, blessing every shot fired at the parish prison. As the bourbon flowed and numbed their senses, howls of enduring justice filled the room.

"Let's go hang the jury," shouted one florid derby-crowned man.

"Where's Dominick O'Malley?" shouted another.

"Let's take all the dagoes for a ride tonight," a lawyer yelled.

Sensing his audience was feeding off its own roiling flesh, Chaffe waved his arms and demanded order. They settled down to listen to his remarks, which were printed and circulated in the next day's *New York Tribune,* which, along with a detailed account of the lynchings, ignited an international crisis.

ELEVEN ITALIANS LYNCHED.

WORK OF A NEW ORLEANS MOB.
A PUBLIC MEETING HARANGUED WITH TERRIBLE RESULTS.

***

"A meeting of the Cotton Exchange was called to order 1:30 o'clock by President Chaffe who state that he had been called upon by at-large committee of members with the request that he convene the institution in general meeting for the purpose of adopting a suitable resolution indorsing the action of the people of New Orleans in the deplorable affair of the morning. Mr. Chaffe said that inasmuch as all were familiar with the occurrences, it was not necessary to dilate upon them. They knew the facts and the necessity of the situation. He then caused the following preamble and resolution to be read by the secretary:

"Whereas, the deplorable administration of criminal justice in this city, And the frightful extent to which the bribery of juries has been carried, rendered it necessary for the citizens of New Orleans to vindicate outraged justice: be it Resolved, That while we deplore at all times the resort to violence, we consider the action taken by the citizens this morning to be proper and justifiable."

Moments later, members of the New Orleans Stock Exchange expelled jury foreman Jacob Seligman and denied his access to all forms of commercial society. Some members thought social expulsion to be an insufficient sanction and wanted to smell and spill more blood.

Chapter 91

The Custom House Telegraph Office
March 14, 1891
4:00 P.M.

Italian Consulate Pasquale Corte spent two hours handwriting what he entitled a "Memorandum," in his own bridle-veil cursive, to memorialize the salient facts of the Hennessy case and subsequent lynchings. He intended to telegraph its contents to the Italian Ambassador in Washington, D.C., Baron Francesco Fava. But given its length and details, he decided to telegraph Fava with a terse emergent description of the state of affairs in New Orleans.

As he left his office, people on the streets accosted him and hurled invectives at him. The city he thought he knew had become a hostile bed of hot coals, and after seeing what he saw a few hours earlier, his fright was justified.

The telegrapher recognized him as he entered the Custom House on Canal Street and knew what he wanted. He cleared the wires for Corte's message to the Italian embassy in Washington. Corte dictated the following telegram:

"New Orleans, March 14, 1891

Minister of Italy, Washington:

Mob led by members of the committee of fifty took possession of jail; killed eleven prisoners; three Italians, others nationalized. I hold many responsible. Fear further murders. I am also in great danger. Reports follow.

CORTE"

After dictating the urgent telegram, Corte left the custom house and met Algernon Badger on the front steps. Corte's chest heaved in anger and fear as he glowered into the eyes of a man who had lent his name to the

Committee. For a moment, they said nothing, but Badger broke the fiery silence.

"I regret what happened today," Badger said.

"Regret, Mr. Badger? Your friends have butchered eleven innocent men, and you only have regrets?" Corte asked.

"I took no part in that assault on the prison."

"Yes, you did. I saw your name in the paper this morning. You allowed the mayor to use your name without you knowing?" Corte asked.

"I knew he wanted to use my name, but I never authorized it. And that's the truth," Badger said. "I was friends with David Hennessy and Lionel Adams. I would have never agreed to this type of action."

"You will have to explain yourself one day. You work for the American government, and your name endorsed the mob's actions. These men were innocent. They were killed only because they were Italian. And some of the men were Italian citizens. I have just reported this to my government. Why did they do this?" Corte asked.

"Some believe the jury was bribed," Badger said.

"That's impossible. The judge instructed the jury to find Matranga and Incardona not guilty. Was the judge bribed, too? And the jury was split on Monasterio, Polizzi, and Scaffidi. How could the jury have been bribed? Thank God, they didn't kill Matranga and Incardona," Corte said.

"Matranga is alive?" Badger asked.

"Yes. They didn't kill the leader of the New Orleans *Mafia*. So, why did they kill eleven innocent laborers and let Matranga live? It makes no sense. There's a reason, and I will discover it—for my country," Corte said.

"What about Macheca and Romero?" Badger asked.

"They're dead—shot to pieces," Corte said.

Badger stood silent on the steps and stared into the sun setting over Canal Street. A cool breeze swept his face as he pondered Corte's statements. "Mr. Corte, I promise to cooperate with any investigation. But believe me, I did not approve of these lawless acts. I would be honored if you allow me to buy your supper."

"Supper? I have no appetite. I must go into the Italian Colony and visit the families tonight, even if it means my own death."

And as Corte stepped down from the Custom House, he saw a mule pulling an old streetcar with a large advertisement plastered on its side. It announced Giuseppe Verdi's Italian opera, *Trovatore,* to be performed that night at the French Opera House at Bourbon and Toulouse Streets, roughly six blocks from the parish prison. Some members of the Committee of Fifty were patrons of the arts.

Chapter 92

Secretary of State's Office
Washington, D.C.
March 14, 1891
6:00 P.M.

By late afternoon of March 14, 1891, nearly every major newspaper in America had received news of the Italian lynchings in New Orleans. Many of the newspapers reported the mass slaughter of the eleven innocent men as a positive development in American justice. Cities with large concentrations of Italians began to experience a breakdown in the civil order. In Pittsburgh, there was a riot at the city hall. The insouciant manner in which American society accepted the mass lynchings only inflamed Italian-American citizens and immigrants. But the anger didn't remain within America's shores, as the news swept to Europe by cablegrams.

Consulate Corte's telegram cut through Washington, D.C. like a straight razor, sparing no pretense of diplomatic comity. Italian ambassador, Baron Francesco Fava, caught Secretary of State James Blaine leaving his office on a cold Saturday afternoon, and demanded an audience. Having already been alerted to the events in New Orleans, Blaine obliged Fava's request, and the men adjourned to the Secretary's office. A career diplomat, Fava conducted himself in all the formalities owing to such a crisis. There were no pleasantries exchanged, only a demand that the United States take action against the members of those responsible for the mass lynchings. Blaine listened to Fava's demands and the conveyed fears of Corte, but said the United States could not get involved in local affairs. Fava pressed Blaine and reminded him that at least three of the victims were Italian citizens, and the mutual aid treaty of the United States gave Blaine jurisdiction to act. Blaine, again, refused to commit any action on the part of the American government until he spoke to President Harrison.

Fava, detecting Blaine's diffident posture, stood, bowed, and left the

Secretary's office. Blaine then began to review the telegrams and cables about the lynchings. His staff notified him that the Premier of Italy, Marchese Antonio di Starabba Rudini, had been sent a cablegram by Fava. Blaine, already beset by personal and political problems, knew America faced a serious domestic and diplomatic challenge because of the lynchings.

Late that night, as the news of the massacre spread across the world, President Harrison sent a message to Blaine's residence, in which he decried the lynchings, and instructed Blaine to contact Governor Francis T. Nicholls, to protest the slaughter, and demand protection for all Italians living in Louisiana, in accordance with the existing treaty between the United States and Italy, dated February 26, 1871. Blaine spent the night crafting a telegram he knew would ignite, not only old parochial prejudices made dormant by time, but now laced with international consequences. He chose each word carefully.

Chapter 93

New Orleans
March 15, 1891

Lenten Sunday mornings should be filled with peace and penance. As the church bells toll the hours, penitents should seek the redoubt and refuge of the many churches, identifying the diverse faiths of New Orleans. Preachers and Priests prepare for their services, while the congregations, dressed in their finest attire, huddle together in solemn prayer—but not this Sunday. On this somber morning, a gun-metal gray pall hung over the city, whose most notable landmark was a Catholic cathedral.

In most cities, the newspapers defined the mood of the people, and they worked hard to do so. From their inked pages, they derive revenue and power to control the thoughts of the thoughtless, the feelings of the numb, and the actions of the indolent. It's a power relished by many, for it enjoys the immunity of the First Amendment—an immunity which blesses distorted perceptions of the truth. Those who control the ink control the power, for the contrarian voices are only dissenting echoes, after the newspapers are printed and read. Like a fired, red-hot bullet, it can't be stuffed down the barrel of the gun after the trigger is pulled. Even stray bullets kill.

No one knew this more than Eliza Jane Nicholson and Thomas D. Wharton, who controlled the *Daily Picayune* and the *Times-Democrat,* respectively. Nicholson's editor, James Richardson, was the 1891 Rex, carnival king, and a member of the Committee of Fifty. Wharton was also a member of the Committee of Fifty. They published accounts of the lynchings very differently, but with the palpable intent to influence public opinion of the Lenten massacre. Both took their newspapers down divergent paths of perverted analysis, but arrived at the same conclusion: the lynchings were justified.

Nicholson buried the mass killings on page four of the *Daily Picayune* under the four dissembling headlines. The first read:

WHEN THE MINISTERS OF THE LAW FAIL.

In the following seven paragraphs, the *Daily Picayune* published a detailed exegesis justifying a society administering justice when the instrumentalities they deigned to do so failed their mission.

"Yesterday, the people of this city rose in wrath and indignation at the corruption and perversion of the machinery to which was delegated the administration of justice. They did not overwhelm and sweep away the officials, but brushing them aside, they took in their own hands the sword of justice…"

Anyone reading this section of the paper concluded the actions of the Committee of Fifty had the complete approval of commercial and political leaders of the city, despite the twisted logic employed by the paper to support their thesis.

The following headline and content had a veiled warning to anyone who would find the mob's behavior abhorrent. The headline read:

"ADMINISTERING POPULAR JUSTICE"

The *Daily Picayune* posited the theory of the popularity of the mob's restraint by describing how worse it could have been if this occurred in any other city, thereby exacting only a popular and limited justice.

"Yesterday, the work done was a marvel of moderation, when we consider the terrible nature of the forces at work. In any other city on the continent, it would have been impossible to restrain the vast concourse of people assembled at the call of the mass meeting yesterday."

In a veiled warning, the newspaper described what could have happened in other less sophisticated cities. The specter of riots, burning of homes, and indiscriminate race war was avoided by the execution of moderate murderers within the walls of the parish prison. The clear import of Nicholson's message to her readers was to be proud of how city leaders employed deadly, but tempered justice. She didn't stop there when her next headline evoked a lethal parochialism.

"OUTSIDE OPINION NOT TO BE FEARED."

The *Daily Picayune*, sensing some form of dissent from beyond the swamps of New Orleans, struck an insular tone to protect the city's burgeoning commerce among other cities of the world. At this point, on page four, all pretense of reporting facts vanished. The paper marched as the vanguard of the Cotton Exchange and all ancillary industries that served the port, and was led by members of the Committee of Fifty. The paper attempted a pre-empted attack when it printed:

"The almost complete stoppage of business which yesterday's tragedy occasioned, gave rise in some quarters to fears that the affair might result injuriously to the business interests of the city by creating false impressions in the North and West as to the law-abiding character of our people. The question was asked, might it not divert investments of outside capital to other fields?"

This section of the article boldly attacked other cities, which had exercised their right to the lynch law to settle their domestic disputes, and those cities in the North and West had no ground to complain about New Orleans, for they had done the same when their institutions of justice had failed.

It is the final flurry of attacks, the newspaper attacked the people responsible for the assault on the prison. At no time did Nicholson, or any of her editors, identify any member of the Committee of Fifty by name, or the men who shot and hanged the eleven Italians. Using its power of print, the paper wanted to divert responsibility away from the city's elites.

"JUROR SELIGMAN AND THE STATE'S ATTORNEY"

There's no doubt Eliza Jane Nicholson wanted to shift all the burden from her society friends to Juror Jacob Seligman, a Jewish jeweler who operated a store on Gravier Street. Reports and rumors claim Charles Luzenberg knew about Seligman's potential biases, which were not specified, when he allowed him to sit as the jury foreman. The paper devoted several paragraphs to attacking Seligman and blamed the not guilty verdicts on his leadership in the deliberation room. Then the article pivoted to Sheriff Villere and the guards at the prison for allowing the mob to defeat the prison's security. *The Daily Picayune* ended its tirade against Seligman by writing:

"Seligman was a juror for the defense. The State was informed of the evidence that declared that fact. In spite of this, Seligman was retained by the State. The State is responsible for keeping him in a place where he was able to paralyze the entire power of the court to convict notorious criminals."

With these assaults on Seligman, the jeweler's life was put in jeopardy. He fled New Orleans and remained absent for several years. Again, the newspaper never printed the names of the killers, but through clever draftsmanship, successfully converted responsibility for the lynchings to everyone, except those with their fingers on the triggers and hands on the ropes.

><

The *Times-Democrat* took an equally insidious, but under a different veil of deception, in their publication. While Nicholson took a more editorial tenor in the *Picayune's* publication, Wharton openly celebrated the lynchings with several full-page etchings of the victims, and the crowd gathered around the prison, under the headline:

"AVENGED"

The *Times-Democrat* left nothing for anyone to interpret from the headline or the story that followed. The image of the crowd around the prison, complete with the image of Bagnetto and Polizzi hanging from a tree and a lamp post, sent the message to New Orleans. Wharton asserted that what occurred at the prison was justified under the law, which is the will of the people, despite a jury's verdict. Wharton's reporters devoted six pages to various aspects of the lynchings, from the meeting at the Clay statue to the actions and celebrations of the Cotton Exchange when Parkerson arrived and delivered the macabre news.

The *Times-Democrat* took a more thorough reportage on the entire matter, leaving the larger *Daily Picayune* to splash the city with its blood-drenched editorials. Wharton displayed pictures of Parkerson, Hennessy, and several of the dead Italians. He reported on the insouciant ignorance of the mayor and governor on the matter, as if mass lynchings are a daily occurrence. He printed telegraphs from around the country supporting the great citizens of New Orleans. The only dissenting telegraph was from William Pinkerton, who equated the lynchings with the murder of his friend, David Hennessy.

><

Antonio left his apartment above the Jesuits' livery stable and entered the refectory of the rectory for breakfast. Fathers Fontebuis and O'Shanahan sat at the end of the large table. The morning editions of the *Daily Picayune* and the *Times-Democrat* were spread across the table. Both priests poured over the content of each broadsheet until they saw Antonio standing near them, attired in a black suit, white shirt, and black tie.

"Good morning, Antonio. Please sit down and have some breakfast. Eleven o'clock Mass is an hour, but we will dispense with the normal fasting requirements," Father O'Shanahan said.

Antonio nodded, sat at the long table, and stared at the open newspapers. His eyes caught the illustration of the crowd outside the prison, published in the *Times-Democrat*. The priests noticed his fixed gaze. "Is this accurate?" Father Fontebuis asked, pointing to the illustration.

"Yes. I was hiding in the bushes and saw it all. They hung two men, then shot their bodies with bullets and laughed. Blood splattered with every shot. The people just laughed," Antonio said. "I thought this was America. It's worse than Sicily."

"Eat your breakfast, Antonio," Father O'Shanahan said. "After you eat, I want you to wear a full cassock every day and everywhere you go. You must assume the role of a seminarian."

"Again?"

"Yes. I'm sorry. After nine o'clock Mass, I heard discussions of what's going on in New Orleans. It's not good. That Committee of Fifty and their henchmen are looking for Mr. O'Malley and Mr. Seligman. They also got a list of Italian fugitives from the police, and are searching everywhere in New Orleans for them. I fear they will use a man's fugitive status to feed their bloodlust. What happened yesterday is far from over, I fear. Do you understand what I am saying?" Father O'Shanahan asked.

"Yes."

"You will be safe here. The boys will view you as one of us. You are bigger than most of them so that they won't ask questions. Keep the stable clean, and work in the library when you can. Wear the cassock. Try not to have conversations with the boys. You still have a pronounced accent. I don't want to draw any suspicion to our school."

"How long must I stay here?" Antonio asked.

"Soon, we will be building a church and college upriver from the city on St. Charles Street. The police hardly go there, and we will move you there once a place is built for you to stay. Probably a year from now," Father O'Shanahan said."

"Then what?" Antonio asked.

"You will enroll as a student at the college. In about a year, these harrowing moments might subside. Until then, you must hide. The history of our church is filled with people who flee tyranny. So, embrace your time here. You will grow. This I promise," Father O'Shanahan said.

"Antonio, I will be serving the eleven o'clock Mass," Father Fontebuis said. "Put on a cassock, and stay in the Sacristy during Mass. There will be too many curious eyes in the congregation, and I will use my sermon to attack what happened yesterday. I'm sure it will upset some people, but it must be said. So, hide in the Sacristy."

"Like during my father's funeral in Sicily?" Antonio asked.

"Yes, like in Sicily."

Chapter 94

New Orleans, Rome, Washington, D.C.
March 15th through April 27th, 1891

March 15, 1891
New Orleans

Father Fontebuis's sermon seared through the newspaper-conditioned minds of his congregation. He spared no words condemning the lynchings of the eleven Italians, and anyone who accepted it as justified. Even in his thick French accent, he splashed tarring guilt on anyone who took joy in the massacre. While scorching the Jesuit church from his pulpit with analogies of Biblical injustices, another fusillade of words fired up the telegraph lines between New Orleans and Washington, D.C., and the Transatlantic cable between Washington, D.C., and Rome. While the Committee of Fifty basked in their local newfound glory, the diplomatic relations between the United States and Italy began to fray. With an army exceeding two million men and a navy boasting eleven heavy battleships, Italy eclipsed the military power of the United States tenfold, which wasn't ignored.

><

March 15, 1891
Washington, D.C.

On the quiet Sunday morning, Secretary of State Blaine went to the telegraph office of Madison Place, took a resolute breath, and sent the governor of Louisiana a tense telegraph. Blaine spent most of the night crafting his words, fearing inflaming the crisis, but determined to avoid a larger one.

"Washington, D.C., March 15, 1891
It has been represented to the President by the Minister of Italy

accredited to this Government that among the victims of the deplorable massacre which took place in the city of New Orleans yesterday were three or more subjects of the King of Italy. Our treaty with that friendly Government which under the Constitution is supreme law of the land guaranties to the Italian subjects domiciled in the United States 'the most constant protection and security for their persons and property,' making them amenable on the same basis as our own citizens to the laws of the United States and of the several States, in their due and orderly administration.

"The President deeply regrets that the citizens of New Orleans should have disparaged the purity and adequacy of their own judicial tribunals as to transfer the passionate judgment of a mob a question that should have be adjudged dispassionately and by settled rules of law.

"It is the hope of the President that you will cooperate with him in maintaining the obligations of the Unites States towards the Italian subjects who may be within the perils of the present excitement, that further bloodshed and violence may be prevented, and that all offenders against the law may be promptly brought to justice.

Very Respectfully,

JAMES G. BLAINE."

Blain, to assuage the Italian minister, Baron Fava, sent a copy of the Nichols telegram to him, with the intent to demonstrate the United States' resolve to seek justice in this matter. He closed his telegram to Fava, thusly:

Washington, D.C, March 15, 1891

"Trusting that you will see in the telegram the desire and intention of the President to do justice to the Government of Italy,

I am,

JAMES G. BLAINE."

That afternoon, the United States Ambassador in Rome, A.G. Porter, sent an urgent Transatlantic cable to Blaine exhorting him and President Harrison to take whatever steps necessary to protect all Italians in the United States. Blaine immediately responded to Porter, copying the Nicholl's telegram he sent earlier to New Orleans. At that moment, Blaine knew there was a roiling cauldron of emotions spilling into a Roman fire ignited by the political, prejudicial, and venal natures of Mayor Shakspeare's Committee of Fifty.

><

No. 16 South Rampart Street

New Orleans

Late Sunday night, Italian Consulate Pasquale Corte sat in his residence, and using a new Densmore typewriter, wrote an eleven-paragraph letter to Baron Fava, describing the lynchings of the day before. He used his notes, which he had scribed, as he witnessed the rabid citizens of New Orleans defeat the locks and walls of the parish prison and slaughter eleven Italians. Using only his index fingers and under a bare electric light, Corte punched out the emotional letter to Fava, describing details of the massacre. He had to hurry to get this letter to the Southern Railway mail train by midnight for the fifty-eight-hour trip to Washington, D.C. His first paragraph set the tone of the letter:

> *"Mr. MINISTER: I have not time to describe the horrors of the slaughter which the populace, under the leadership of the principal members of the vigilance committee, has committed against the unarmed prisoners, some of whom had been acquitted and some of whom had not yet been tried."*

Corte blamed the lynchings on the confluence of a blood-thirsty mayor, his elite friends he selected for his Committee of Fifty, and the *de facto* immunity fomented by the city's newspapers. Corte described his activities of the day before, including pleading with the Sheriff, the state's Attorney General, and the state's Governor to stop the mob's attack on the parish prison. No public official would intervene unless the mayor ordered it. But no one knew where the mayor was hiding. Later, Corte discovered the mayor was secreted behind the secured doors of the Pickwick Club, a block away, and with a clear view of the mob gathering around the Clay Statue.

Corte emphasized the dangerous conditions prevailing in New Orleans for all Italians. He described attacks on the relatives of the victims, who sought sanctuary at his offices. A small gang arrived late Saturday night at

Corte's residence, banged on his door, and pulled his doorbell for hours. Corte informed Fava he was carrying a pistol for his own protection, as the police were useless, and the governor would not deploy his militia to protect the Italian Colony. Corte closed by enclosing a copy of a letter he was sending to the governor seeking protection of all Italians in the state.

The letter to Governor Nicholls spared no pleasantries.

"Dear Sir: The killing yesterday of the defenseless Italian prisoners, a part of whom were acquitted and a part not yet tried, has affected the civilized world. His Excellency, the Marquis di Rudini, minister of foreign affairs, whilst he informed that he has made steps to the U.S. Government to provide energetic and immediate precautions, orders me to apply officially to Your Excellency to be assured that similar acts are not to be renewed."

Corte formally demanded that Nicholls dispatch a protection detail in the Italian Colony and near the Italian consulate. He also demanded that all remaining Italians in the parish prison be released unharmed. After sealing the diplomatic envelope, Corte shoved his pistol into his waistband and took a taxi to the train station near the customs house. Ironically, it was the same depot where J.P. Macheca had saved Algeron Badger's life in 1874.

><

March 16, 1891

Washington, D.C.

Secretary of State James Blaine received a terse telegraphed response from Governor Nicholls. It read:

New Orleans, March 16, 1891

Hon. James G. Blaine

Secretary of State, Washington, D.C.

Your telegram was received late last night. I will answer it hereafter by mail. Everything is now quiet here, and there is nothing to lead me to anticipate further trouble. The recent action was directed against particular individuals; their race or nationality was not a factor in the disturbance."

Nicholls's insouciant manner and his election to correspond by mail infuriated Blaine. He now knew everything Fava had said was true, and Nicholls' characterization of the mass lynching as a "disturbance" was a lie. Blaine, an experienced diplomat, felt fear in his heart. He knew that if the New Orleans Italian community was cowering, newspapers from other major cities would report upheavals in their Italian communities, which wouldn't go unnoticed in Rome.

Not long after receiving Nicholls' telegram, Blaine received a cable from the American ambassador in Rome, A.G. Porter. Porter reported that Rome demanded that the United States take immediate action to protect all Italians in America. Porter reported he had assured the Marquis di Rudini that the President and the American people were taking *"energetic measures for the protection of Italians."*

><

March 17, 1891

New Orleans

Not surprisingly, *The Daily Picayune* and *The Times-Democrat* foolishly insinuated their editorial opinions into the delicate balance of international diplomacy. Having deep passions for the old South and its stubborn traditions, both broadsheets attacked the United States government's handling of the international crisis while ignoring their relationships with various members of the blood-stained Committee of Fifty. Shifting the attention from the massacre, the *Times-Democrat* attacked the defense attorneys and claimed the attorney fees were paid by *"The Mafia."* The newspaper offered no evidence to support their position, but the reporting further inflamed relations between the United States and Italy by purposely ignoring who was responsible for murdering three innocent Italian citizens.

The Daily Picayune embarked on a parallel scheme to divert the world's attention from the lynchings. It reported that the jury had been bribed and that Lionel Adams' investigator, Dominick O'Malley, had distributed money to various members of the jury, especially its foreman, Jacob Seligman, who was in hiding. Judge Joshua Baker was not attacked for taking bribes, despite instructing the jury to find Incardona and Matranga not guilty. Though several of the lynched Italians were now buried in a potter's field, the newspapers used their publications to slam the sexton's shovel against the bloodied tilled soil of the victims' graves, depriving them and their families of the truth.

Another newspaper, *The New Orleans States*, claimed it had interviewed an anonymous member of the jury, who was offered three thousand dollars to vote a certain way. The paper's editor, George Dupre, and a member of the Committee of Fifty, refused to identify the juror or the person offering the bribe. Just as they did before the trial and the lynchings, the city's newspaper deigned itself as the sacred courier of the truth, while enjoying its role as the courtesan of the Committee of Fifty.

While the New Orleans broadsheets continued to pump their effluent of lies, District Attorney Charles Luzenberg snuck into St. Patrick's Hall, and dismissed the remaining charges against Charles Matranga, Bastian Incardona, Asperi Marchesi, Peter Natali, Charles Pietza, Charles Patorno, Salvatore Sunzeri, and John Caruso. He then called the parish prison and told the sheriff to release the eight men into the night, thus gutting his own case.

><

March 18, 1891

New Orleans

Within four days of the mass lynchings in New Orleans, the civilized world knew what happened through the spreading prairie fire ignited by the cities' newspapers. Most of the newspapers throughout the United States sided with the anarchic mob's version of justice, dispensed by rope and shot. One newspaper, *The Chattanooga Daily Times*, echoed the accounts described in the *Daily Picayune* and *The Times Democrat*. In fact, the Chattanooga newspapers ran a four-day account of the lynchings and the aftermath, cleverly mimicking the accounts of the New Orleans papers. But there was one thing Chattanooga had, which New Orleans didn't: a statement from the brother of the Rex of 1891, and a member of the Committee of Fifty.

John P. Richardson, brother of James S. Richardson, told *The Chattanooga Daily Times, "The lynchings in New Orleans Saturday is just the thing that should have occurred. It looks bad on its face to those away from there, but the people who are acquainted with the status of affairs can do nothing but commend the action taken."*

Like his brother James, John P. Richardson was a wealthy landowner in Louisiana and Tennessee, and used his lofty position to curse the Italian race, claiming the lynchings to *"be a blessing for New Orleans."*

But other American cities, particularly ones with large Italian populations, demanded that the members of the lynch mob be brought to justice. European newspapers decried the lynchings and demanded justice, which only made the diplomatic channels between Rome and Washington more fragile.

In New Orleans, harassment of Italians persisted throughout the city. Italian Consulate Corte demanded police protection for his residence and the consulate, four blocks away. Police Superintendent Dexter Gaster agreed to provide protection, with the assurance that Corte would disclose the identity of Italian fugitives in New Orleans. Corte provided a list of all known Italian fugitives in America, but couldn't guarantee who among them were in New Orleans. Gaster seemed satisfied, as he exploited the list to support the prevailing sentiment that New Orleans was a sanctuary for Italian criminals, and that a diligent search for the fugitives would continue.

The morning edition of *The Daily Picayune* published police secretary George Vandervoort's theory of who killed David C. Hennessy. His statement, though annotated with flimsy facts, supported Hennessy's assassination to be the work of the *"Mafia."* Vandervoort opined that Hennessy's arrest of Giuseppe Esposito in Jackson Square in 1881 spawned the *vendetta* against Hennessy. Vandervoort did not explain the nine-year gap between Esposito's arrest and Hennessy's assassination.

In an effort to be fair, the newspaper published two jurors' statements regarding allegations that they were bribed. Soloman Mayer and William Yockum both stated that the evidence against the defendants was weak and contested. Mayer repeated the fact that Judge Baker instructed them to find Matranga and Incardona not guilty, which the jury did. Mayer denied that anyone on the jury was bribed.

Yockum also denied being bribed and followed Judge Baker's instructions. He added, *"I only had a nickel in my pocket, so I had to walk home."*

><

Newspaper Row

March 18, 1891

The first three blocks of Camp Street housed the gray-facade publishing houses for the city's seven newspapers. From the night of the verdict, it resembled a disturbed anthill, with reporters and messengers running in and out of the houses. The large papers, *The Daily Picayune,* and *The Times-Democrat* maintained internal telegraph offices to send and receive messages from other papers in the country. Their publishers were well aware of the country's sentiment regarding the mass lynching.

The newspapers printed nothing about the District Attorney dismissing the remaining charges on the surviving Italians, despite the fact that reporters were in St. Patrick's Hall the day before, covering Judge Marr's new charges to the Orleans Parish Grand Jury to investigate the lynchings. Some grand jurors were also members of the Committee of Fifty. To perpetuate the illusion of due process in New Orleans, Judge Marr's charge was reported in *The Daily Picayune* on March 18, 1891, on page one:

"Gentlemen of the Grand Jury—since your last adjournment, New Orleans has been the scene of a deplorable tragedy which terminated in the death of eleven persons, prisoners in the custody of the law, charged with complicity in the assassination of David C. Hennessy.

"I say deplorable tragedy because, without reference to the causes, all good citizens must and do regret the taking of human life without warrant of the law.

"The details and incidents of this alleged homicide and its causes and antecedents are matters of public notoriety; they are discussed in the columns of the daily press, and they largely occupy the public mind at home and abroad."

Judge Marr chose his words very carefully. He knew who he was charging and who was taking notes. He directed the foreman, William Chaffe, to report the results once their investigation was completed.

><

Washington, D.C.

March 21, 1891

It wasn't a surprise. The telegraphs and transatlantic cables ping the news of the lynchings at a blistering pace. Rome, now in possession of the three names of the Italian citizens slaughtered during Lent in New Orleans, forced the Italian government to make two demands. The Marquis di Rudini cabled Baron Fava and demanded that the United States hold the responsible parties responsible for the death of their citizens, and that reparations be paid. Rudini's cable closed with ominous words:

"A simple declaration, though cordial and friendly, is not sufficient: we want positive facts.
RUDINI"

Fava and Blaine exchanged telegrams across Washington, D.C. Fava told Blaine he would seek confirmation and names of the three slain Italians and formally informed the United States:

"The Marquis di Rudini does not speak, of course, of those people who are American citizens. But he insists that the murderers of the three Italian subjects be brought to justice. And I trust your high cooperation in this.
FAVA"

Secretary of State Blain left his office and raced to the Executive Mansion. Knowing the lethal strength of the Italian navy far exceeded that of the United States, and knowing a city-ordained lynch mob had killed three Italian citizens, any official demur by Washington could be interpreted as acceptance of the murders by the United States. He knew the only way to assuage the Italian government was to punish the Committee.

Harrison, a careful lawyer, demanded that the United States Attorney in New Orleans, William Grant, seize the District Attorney's files and conduct a federal investigation into Hennessy's death. This would, hopefully, demonstrate the United States government's sincere interest in determining the truth.

Later that day, Governor Francis T. Nicholls sent a telegram to Blaine, wherein he acknowledged that several of the victims were Italian subjects. He also assured Blaine that local tempers have cooled, and a judge has empaneled a Grand Jury to investigate the matter. Nicholls closed by stating:

"I am satisfied that most of the persons killed were American citizens, but it is possible that two or three were Italian subjects.
Francis T. Nicholls"

Blaine shared Nicholls' telegram with President Harrison. It didn't sit well with him. Indeed, it was a formal acceptance by a state that they had killed two or three innocent Italian citizens, and every newspaper condemning the action correctly reported the lawless act. To Harrison, the citizenship of the victims did not, in any way, establish justification, but established a basis for condemnation.

><

March 24, 1891

Washington, D.C.

Marquis Rudini pulled the threads of diplomacy tighter. He sent Fava a cable notifying him that Italian patience, regarding the murder of three Italian citizens, began to fray. He repeated his frustrations with the United States' lack of immediate attention. He closed the cable by writing"

> *"…if concrete provisions were not at once taken, I should find myself in the painful necessity of showing openly our dissatisfaction by recalling the minister of His Majesty from a country where he is unable to obtain justice.*
> *RUDINI"*

Fava wasted no time in communicating Italy's formal position on the matter and demanded responses by nightfall. None came. Instead, early the following morning, Fava sent Blaine this telegram, which could split Italy's and the United States' relations asunder.

><

March 25, 1891

Washington, D.C.

"My Dear Mr. Blaine: In compliance with your request, I have the honor to enclose herewith a copy of the report just received from H.M. consul at New Orleans, relating to the persons murdered in that city who are undoubtedly Italian subjects, and nine other whom Mr. Corte

*does not think can be considered as American citizens according to the
Constitution of the United States.*
FAVA"

Blaine, upon receipt of Fava's telegram, immediately notified
President Harrison that Italy was revising the number of its citizens killed
in New Orleans from three to nine. Corte had provided Fava with an
amended list. Only J.P. Macheca and Frank Romero were American
citizens.

While diplomatic communications went silent, *The Daily Picayune*
blared its editorial horn and attacked Blaine, while not siding with Italy. It
perpetuated its Southern arrogance when it wrote:

**"It has been for years so common for representative Republican
sectional politicians to charge that the Southern people have been
murdering Americans, that we felt no surprise when Mr. Blaine
charged the inhabitants of the city with having murdered
Italians… But when in his character as Chief Minister of the State,
for Foreign Affairs, treating with a foreign power which does not
recognize sectional distinctions in use by Republican politicians, he
drags in these local distinctions, and complicates his case."**

In their haste to protect their Democrat power, *The Daily Picayune*
chose a path of sectional politics to attack the United States government,
not realizing Italy's jaundiced eye towards anything flowing from New
Orleans, and confirming Italy's belief the city was ruled by a lawless mob,
not unlike the *"Mafia,"* for which they blamed for all their economic and
political woes.

><

March 26, 1891
Washington, D.C.
Blaine's undiplomatic silence to Fava's entreaties didn't sit well with the
Italian government. The revision of the number of victims worsened the
nations' relationships. Italy made further demands for the murderers to be
brought to justice and for reparations to be paid to the victims' families.

Fava made another attempt to elicit a response from Blaine. Frustrated, he wrote:

"Not having received up to today, 26th (6 p.m.), the answer you promised me, I am now compelled to request you to let me know how I must interpret your silence...
FAVA."

Blaine agreed to meet with Fava at the latter's convenience. During the meeting at the State Department, Blaine and his associates tried to explain America's system of Federalism to the Italian minister. While Italy became a unified monarchy after its War of Unification, the American Constitution created a system of sovereign states with their own power to prosecute crimes. Absent a specific criminal statute, the United States had no power to prosecute members of the lynch mob, but the government was willing to study the issue of reparations.

Fava reminded Blaine that New Orleans' finest citizens murdered nine Italian citizens, and Italy demanded justice, pursuant to the treaty between the two nations. Having heard reports from Porter about Americans being arrested in Italy, Blaine promised he would instruct the federal attorney in New Orleans to explore all options available to the federal government. Unsatisfied, Fava stood, excused himself, and returned to his embassy.

Blaine, expecting Fava to notify Rome of *his* interpretation of American law, cabled Porter and instructed him to explain the powers and limitations of American law personally. Blaine wanted to avoid any misinterpretation by Fava, accidental or intentional.

><

March 31, 1891
Washington, D.C.

The spongy words of diplomacy often beget granite consequences. And on March 31, 1891, Marquis Rudini, fatigued by America's perceived diffidence in exacting justice in the case of nine murdered Italian citizens, formally recalled Baron Fava from Washington, D.C. to Rome. In diplomatic venues, such an act is a prelude to war or some other punitive act. Secretary Blaine, aware of Italy's formal action of severing diplomatic relations, notified President Harrison. Both men knew Italy's capacity for a naval blockade of the Mississippi River, which would cripple America's maritime commerce significantly, and cripple the coveted positions of the men who participated in the lynchings. Pasquale Corte knew New Orleans.

Italy's recall of Fava spread through Washington, D.C. like a virulent plague. Transatlantic cables rippled across the ocean to all European countries. The nation's newspapers snared the news, and the telegraph keys punched the news across the country. *The New York Times* boldly declared Fava's recall as a declaration of war. In a matter of hours, the United States knew it was on the precipice of war with a powerful European country because the United States failed to care for foreign citizens near the cotton wharves of New Orleans. Soon, every newspaper published the bellicose news, which provoked various degrees of patriotic reactions. Not surprisingly, *The Daily Picayune* proffered their own thoughts on the matter, which didn't salve the situation. The Italian newspaper, *L'Opinione,* attacked American newspapers for their aggressive and war-seeking stances, while ignoring the original international question of the safety of foreign citizens in the United States.

At the Jesuit School in New Orleans, Father O'Shanahan collected every American and foreign newspaper. From past experiences, the Jesuits knew that their Order protected itself by possessing a clear understanding of geo-political events, which could bang on their rectory doors in the middle of the night. They had to be prepared for any eventuality, especially since the Jesuit's superior had an office in the Vatican, and Protestants controlled New Orleans with a demonstrated penchant for mob rule.

><

April 2, 1891

New Orleans

The rabid *Times-Democrat* wasted no time reporting Fava's withdrawal and the views of American politicians regarding the portent of Italy's actions. The broadsheet devoted eight columns over two pages to the controversy. The clear import of the publication was, like the anti-Italian sentiment before the lynchings, to inflame the temperament of the city's citizens. On page one, it emblazoned its headline:

"TROUBLE WITH ITALY."

The newspaper attacked everyone, except the Committee of Fifty, for the lynchings. It blamed the Italian government for hastily removing Fava, and exciting rumors of war. It blamed the Republican administration for exploiting sectionalism, casting unnecessary opprobrium on Southern culture. It obliquely blamed city officials for not protecting the victims while in the custody of the sheriff. It blamed the jury for not rendering a just verdict. Then on page one, to give the lynchings an aura of legitimacy, the paper published a conversation between the former disgraced Republican governor of Louisiana, Henry C. Warmoth, and Republican Iowa Senator, William B. Allison, both of whom witnessed the Clay Monument speeches, on March 14, 1891, from Morreau's Café on Canal Street.

"You see, Senator," said Warmoth, "that New Orleans is a peaceable, orderly, and law-abiding city. Our Committee of Fifty is now on its way to the prison to execute ten or twelve murderous criminals. When it is finished there, it may execute ten or fifteen more...The ladies are out shopping as usual, and we are enjoying our lunch in quietude. Yes, New Orleans is a peaceable, orderly, law-abiding city."

Readers, no matter where they were, knew New Orleans possessed an unrepentant attitude towards murdering Italians, and embraced *posse comitatus* in the body of the Committee of Fifty, as the regnant sovereign of the city.

The Daily Picayune reported copies of the diplomatic correspondence between American and Italian officials. Their reporting, again, omitted culpability for the lynchings, while accusing the Italian government of hasty actions by recalling Fava. The paper described Italy's ignorance of American law, especially the concept of *"Federalism,"* which prevents the United States government from prosecuting anyone associated with the lynchings, absent a federal statute. There was none, leaving the matter in the hands of Charles Luzenberg, the District Attorney for Orleans Parish, and his state Grand Jury. The broadsheet reported William Grant, the U.S. Attorney in New Orleans, was investigating the matter, which didn't sit well with the Committee of Fifty or the mayor.

><

For most of April 1891, with the suppression of the Italian community in New Orleans, the city's broadsheets allowed the lynchings to slip from their pages. While there were some slight references to the ongoing diplomatic communications between Washington and Rome, much of the daily reporting seemed normal, as if the city's cobblestones were never stained with blood. The newspapers knew their power in shaping public attitudes, and used their ink, like a Renaissance master's palette.

Under the shroud of apathetic minds, the New Orleans city council enacted Ordinance 5256, which transferred control of the docks of New Orleans, from Toledano Street, southbound to Piety Street, and provided for the creation of the Louisiana Construction and Improvement Corporation. The benign-sounding name caught no one's deep attention at the time. But further investigation revealed a clever transfer of ownership and control of the Port of New Orleans to a corporation led by members of the Committee of Fifty, most notably J.T. Houston, Marcel Hart, E.T. Leche, and members of the Cotton Exchange.

Houston was appointed its President, and immediately took control of over three miles of wharves on the east bank of the Mississippi River. Mayor Shakspeare wasted no time in having Houston commandeer the port's infrastructure, including all buildings along the river, including those built by J.P. Macheca. There was no resistance. Further, the new control over the docks meant the control over all stevedoring operations, which gave Houston control over the sweat and toil of Italian and Black labor.

But throughout the Italian Colony, it was clear why Hennessy was killed, and why nineteen Italians were charged with his murder, and eleven lynched. No newspaper made the connection between the May and October 1890 ambushes on the city streets, or the conflicting testimonies in both the Provenzano and Matranga trials, or the lack of direct evidence of culpability in either, while proffered alibi testimony was admitted in both. *The Times-Democrat* failed to expose the weaknesses in the state's case, while knowing one of their own reporters possessed information that would have exonerated the Italians charged with killing David C. Hennessy.

But in the city's marketplaces, where nine Sicilian dialects were spoken, along with Itablian dialects, the hushed whispers of the immigrant understood that American newspapers controlled political power, and political power controlled justice. The immigrant knew the best way to survive was through self-reliance and avoidance of any form of government until their suffrage would be honestly recognized or they repatriated themselves to Italy.

><

April 27, 1891
Department of Justice Communication
New Orleans to Washington, D.C.

During the entire month of April 1891, the United States and Italy continued to communicate through diplomatic transatlantic cables. The fear of war only appeared in various newspapers across America, but no formal threat from Italy ever materialized. American military experts knew Italy's naval power could present a maritime problem, given its formidable size. However, A.G. Porter reported that there were internal political factions inside the Italian government, which could prevent any kinetic action by Italy. So, in good faith, the countries continued to communicate.

On April 27, 1891, William Grant formally reported to Attorney General Miller the results of his investigation. The six-page document, which the prosecutor exercised great circumspection regarding the guilt of any member of the lynch mob, instead, focused on those lynched, and a brief biography of each. Grant concluded that nine of the victims were Italian citizens, while Macheca and Romero were American citizens. Grant found no connection between the deceased and any *Mafia* organization or their attempt to bribe any jurors. Only Polizzi and Geraci had previous records of violating the law, but not in New Orleans. Grant added he found no evidence of any *Mafia* society in New Orleans, despite common attribution to criminal offenses committed by Italians over the past twenty-five years.

Grant revealed his opinion as to the guilt or innocence of the men lynched, while noting some victims had never stood trial. He wrote:

> *"I have not attempted to examine into the guilt or innocence of the persons accused of the murder of Hennessy. The evidence in the case against them submitted to the jury is voluminous, covering some eight hundred pages of typewriting. Both as a whole and in detail, it is exceedingly unsatisfactory, and is not, to my mind, conclusive one way or the other."*

Grant's opinion weighed heavily on officials in Washington, though no one expressed surprise, given his residency. While Grant never ascribed guilt to any of the victims of the lynch mob, he never ascribed guilt to any member of the lynch mob, which was interpreted as a bow to the obduracy of haunting Southern values.

Chapter 95

New Orleans
May 6, 1891

After school had commenced, Antonio snuck into the rectory for breakfast. Father O'Shanahan had *The Daily Picayune* and *The Times Democrat* spread across the dining room table, searching both broadsheets for any discrepancy in the shattering news. The priest's complexion, ordinarily an Irish pallor, seemed waxen, as his green eyes traced the print. Antonio's presence startled the old priest.

"Sit down, son. You need to know this," the priest said.

"More trouble, Father?"

"I'm afraid so. But it was expected," O'Shanahan said, passing his hand through his white hair. "Both newspapers have printed the Grand Jury report regarding what happened at the parish prison. Not surprisingly, Eliza Jane Nicholls and T.D. Wharton are celebrating."

"What did they say?" Antonio asked.

Father O'Shanahan went through the broadsheet, column by column, and explained the report. First, he addressed *The Daily Picayune's* characterization of the Grand Jury's report through their headlines:

"THE MAFIA A FACT. A LARGE NUMBER OF ITALIAN FUGITIVES IN NEW ORLEANS."
"LYNCHING FOUND TO BE A POPULAR MOVEMENT."

The priest explained the Grand Jury found the existence of a secret *Mafia* society, but didn't name any of the members, including the men killed in the prison. The report, nearly five thousand words, tortured logic, and concealed the honest purpose of conducting a Grand Jury investigation, namely, determining the culpability of those who killed the eleven men. Instead, the Grand Jury placed the blame on the trial jury for being bribed, the collusion of the jury commissioner, and the sheriff.

"This conclusion will shake this city," Father O'Shanahan said. "The report is long on words, but short on proof. It shifts the blame from the lynch mob to the omissions of others and the participation of Matranga and Romero. Those men didn't die by mysterious means. Like the other nine, they were slaughtered, like ensnared animals. Do you know what the word contrivance means, Antonio?"

"Not really, Father."

"It means this report is filled with diversions, lies, and trickery, designed to protect the guilty. I want to read you the last paragraph of the report. Listen to this: '*It is a noteworthy fact in connection with the uprising that no injury whatever was done to either persons or property beyond the one act which seemed to have been the object of the assemblage at the Parish Prison. We have referred to the large number of citizens participating in this demonstration, estimated by judges at from 6,000 to 8,000, regarded as a spontaneous uprising of the people.*'"

Father O'Shanahan pounded his fist on the table. "Pardon me, son, but it was not a '*spontaneous uprising*'." The newspapers printed a notice of a meeting at the Clay statue the morning of the lynchings. I have those papers. It was well planned and organized."

Father O'Shanahan continued to read the report. "Listen to this tripe: '*The magnitude of this affair makes it a difficult task to fix the guilt upon any number of the participants—in fact, the act seemed to involve the entire people of the parish and city of New Orleans, so profuse is their sympathy and extended their correction with the affair.*' I can't believe what I just read to you. I have the list of the men published *that* morning in *these* newspapers. In fact, three of the Grand Jury members were members of the mob." The priest's complexion went florid, from his forehead down to his Roman collar.

He sipped his coffee and continued. "This is the best part, Antonio. '*In view of these considerations, the thorough examination of the subject has failed to disclose the necessary facts to justify this Grand Jury in presenting indictments.*' No one got indicted. No killers. No *Mafia* members. No one for taking a bribe. It's like it never happened."

"What about the Italian fugitives in New Orleans? Are they still searching?" Antonio asked.

The priest paused and hung his head. "Sorry, Antonio, but I heard the police have been to St. Aloysius and the Jahnke yard. Someone has alerted the police about you for the reward. But you are safe here. After supper tonight, I want you and Father Fontebuis in my office. I have a plan."

><

Noon

Pasquale Corte sat at his desk, resting his beleaguered head in his trembling hands. His elbows rested on a copy of *The Daily Picayune,* as his tears plopped on the ink of despair. He read the paper's report of the Grand Jury findings, knowing a city had gone mad and killed eleven of his countrymen with impunity. He was convinced Hennessy's murder wasn't a result of an Italian secret society, but an American one, which now has complete control over the entire commerce of New Orleans. Being a man of letters and words, Corte knew any attempt to challenge the report would just be scattered like the dust of the dead, gone, buried, and forgotten. Even his own government relented, and sought only reparations for families. Corte's dreams of America lay shattered and splintered on his floor, as he accepted the New World was occupied by old human, immutable instincts. America would never be free of prejudices, no matter how many laws are written, because the powerful of any community decide what laws are to be enforced, and what laws would be symbolic. And any concept of justice for the plebian would be aleatory, at best.

As his last act as the Italian Consulate in New Orleans, Corte penned another note to be sent to Rudini and Lionel Adams. He had one last point to make before preparing for his recall to Italy. He wrote:

"Among those who participated in the killing, besides prominent politicians, there were, as I said, several employees of the city & policemen, namely Dennis Corcoran, who, besides taking an active part in the killings, pointed out the different Italians to be killed. This & other circumstances of the affair were of public notoriety.

"Notwithstanding these facts, the Grand Jury did not indict anyone & wants to make it appear the entire population of New Orleans participated in the act or approved it... But it appears from the official report of the police that Sergeant Hevron was wounded in the prison & from the report of General Glynn of the State Militia, also a member of the Committee of 50, that the militia was not called out... I can prove that the head members of the same were in the mob, when the mayor was not to be found & governor replied to me he could not do anything without a request of his Honor. When Mr. Sheppert, another reporter of the Times-Democrat & other persons worthy of belief assured me

that some members of the Grand Jury were in the mob..."

Corte sipped a glass of warm whiskey, wiped his eyes, and continued his heart-scalding rambling thoughts.

"Notwithstanding the fulfilling of my duty, I fear nothing & no one it is natural that if it is true what the Grand Jury affirms, that two American citizens managed the temple of justice at their pleasure corrupting the jury & officers of the court, or as I believe, a Second power exist besides the constituted authorities to which only I am accredited, I am compelled before recognizing this government in effect to consult my government."

Consumed by drink and grief, he allowed his pen to drift down the page in despair.

><

7:30 P.M.

In the somber chamber of Father O'Shanahan's office, a mahogany grandfather's clock ticked the moments of time. The old Jesuit, yoked between the pressures of the sacred and the secular, pondered the future of his Order in New Orleans. Even with all his ecclesiastical training, he wrestled with a city's failures and mores running wild on the cobblestone streets, just beyond his windows. His studies taught him that the tribulations of man will exist as long as man pursues power over his fellow man, instead of living consistently with Holy Scripture.

The Bible's Testaments recorded and foresaw such times, and the zeitgeist of New Orleans validated everything he learned as a young seminarian. He studied the birth of man, the oppression of man, the death of man, and his unquenchable desire to live as a free man, regardless of rank or station, imprinted at birth. From the old streets of Jerusalem to the streets of New Orleans, Father O'Shanahan knew his clock ticked away the hours, but man remained indifferent to his mortality.

A soft knock on his door snapped him from his thoughts to the dangerous task at hand. Antonio and Father Fontebuis entered the office, illuminated by a single lamp on Father O'Shanahan's desk. The light carved deep creases and shadows in the old priest's face, giving his guests the appearance of a familiar apparition.

"Come in and please sit down," Father O'Shanahan said.

Antonio and Father Fontebuis sat on a davenport, their eyes fixed on every expression of Father O'Shanahan's aging face.

"I have always been taught to do the right thing," Father O'Shanahan began, "but there are times when God's law supersedes the facades of man's laws. As head of this Order, I know almost everyone by sight or by voice, if you know what I mean."

Antonio and Father Fontebuis said nothing.

"I know this city and its sins. There are many and varied. It's a city that has tasted power, money, status, and blood and enjoys all their pleasures on one plate. It's a very dangerous place for those who won't accede to its societal demands. Its intuitions have become rotten and spoiled like fruit left on its docks—only the rats rejoice. Churches and synagogues are tolerated filigree to those whose true god is money and status.

"I know you are wondering why I called you here at this late hour. For the past few weeks, I have seen this city deny itself an honorable place among the legions of prosperous cities because of the arrogance of its leaders and journalists. New Orleans' status quo is its destiny. It has always been a bare-knuckle, bawdy slice of land, devoted to lubricity, instead of the liturgy. Therefore, I have come to the conclusion that both of you must leave the city at once."

"Both of us?" Father Fontebuis asked. "Why?"

"Yes, both of you must leave. Antonio is an Italian fugitive who will not get justice in this country or in his own. If he is arrested in New Orleans, the police will imprison him in that dungeon at the end of Basin Street. I'm sure they will beat him and feed him maggots. If he survives the trip back to Sicily, the corrupt powers there will kill him. I can't take that chance."

"And me?" Father Fontebuis asked.

"I have been informed that your sermons, while true to Scripture, have incited some wealthy elements of this city. You have attacked the heart of their beliefs, which they leave outside the church every Sunday, like an old mule, only to mount the beast, and go home and resume their carnality. Unlike the wealthy Catholics, their Protestant counterparts make no pretense of the deception. Father, you have drawn too much attention to the Church and the Order. For your safety, and the safety of this Order, I must send you away with Antonio."

"But where, Father?" Antonio asked. I have no home."

"Before you came to New Orleans, Father Fontebuis, didn't your superior in Italy promise you that if you came to New Orleans and completed your mission here, he would allow you to return to France?" Father O'Shanahan asked.

"Yes."

"Your mission here is complete, and I want you to leave and take Antonio with you. It's not safe for you or him. I will never tell you what to preach. That's a priest's sacred mission. Besides, everything you have said from the pulpit is true."

"Am I in danger?" Father Fontebuis asked.

"You could be. Some powerful people are very angry, and we need the city government's approval to build our college uptown." Father O'Shanahan opened his desk drawer and removed a large brown envelope. "I've booked a passage on a cotton steamer, leaving New Orleans for Le Havre, France. It has six cabins. I have booked two—one-way. There's a Jesuit seminary near there. I have cabled them and informed them of your arrival."

"Father, why didn't you tell me this before, or give me a voice in your deliberations?" Father Fontebuis asked.

"Fair question, and you deserve an honest answer. While you are a great preacher and teacher, our flock has deep-rooted prejudices and is prepared to isolate our church and school. There are other Catholic churches in New Orleans that they can attend. As you know, Jesuits have a long history of expulsion from various lands. It happened here once. I will not allow it to happen again. Don't you want to go back to France?"

"Honestly, I never wanted to come here, but the promise of returning to my own country motivated me to come. Despite its moral and physical decay, the city grows on you, like a beard of moss. But if that's your order, I will go. Perhaps the sea air will scrape this city from my mind."

"The trip will be a tonic for both of you," Father O'Shanahan said. "Antonio, you have been through too much for a young man. I know the circumstances that made you escape Sicily. You were justified, but as you see in New Orleans, it's not the law people follow, but their passions, and passion is always stronger than logic. Your new home will be in France under the French name we gave you in Palermo—Antoine Caravelle. You speak French?"

"A little," Antonio whimpered.

"You will have over thirty days to polish your French with Father Fontebuis. I have prepared all necessary documents for your travel, and have all documents demonstrating Antonio's French citizenship." Father O'Shanahan pushed a folded document with red ribbons tied around it toward Antonio. "These are your ordination papers. You will travel as a French priest to France. I know it's a deception, but one which favors God and the perpetuation of life. Do you understand, Pere Antoine?"

Antonio looked up and giggled. "I'm now a priest?"

"Just until you get to Le Harve. Once you land there, you will be on your own. The Order will help get you settled. Keep the French name. It will be documented in the Cathedral in Le Havre. I know you have a darker complexion than most in Normandy, but they are a fair breed of people, and won't question you, as long as you speak French or English. It, too, is a port city. Never speak Italian or Sicilian. Understand?"

Antonio nodded.

"When do we leave?" Father Fontebuis asked.

"Tomorrow at six in the evening. The ship's name is the *Nordica*. It will be laden with tons of Louisiana cotton. What an irony. You're escaping evil wrought from the very crop, which has made New Orleans an evil place. Do me a favor. Sit on a bale and laugh all the way to France," Father O'Shanahan said with a smile.

"Can I ask a question, Father?" Father Fontebuis said.

"Sure."

"This seems so planned. When did you make this decision?"

"Honestly, the day Antonio moved in here. I knew there would be more trouble."

"How will we get from here to the dock without the police arresting Antonio?"

Father O'Shanahan laughed. "We have it well planned. The Archbishop and I will escort both of you to the dock, near Esplanade Street, in the Archbishop's fancy coach. No one will stop us or question us. Now, go pack."

Chapter 96

New Orleans
May 7, 1891
Dusk

The afternoon sun reflected off the black-lacquer coach built for royalty. Its brass fittings and decorative finishes refracted the sunlight upon the red-brick walls of the Jesuits' livery yard, like shafts of eternal light. A tuxedoed black man gingerly stepped down from his black leather seat, above the coach, and placed his smooth brown hand on a winged-shaped handle affixed to the coach's side, and cranked open the scarlet-red upholstered door. The black man extended his hand and grasped Archbishop Jenssen's hand, assisting the prelate's exit from the coach. Two black horses stood reverently still, locked in their brass harnesses.

From his second-floor room about the livery, Antonio watched the Archbishop and several Jesuit priests greet each other, with a firm grasp on their upper arms. After the prelate and priests entered the rectory, Antonio continued to pack his brown leather satchel. From a secret pocket within the wall of the satchel, Antonio removed a black leather pouch containing three hundred American dollars. A mild fortune for a boy of eighteen years, but earned in betrayal, blood, death, dust, and treachery from his many encounters with people. He dropped his pants to his knees, and using two small leather straps cut from the liveries' old tack, he tied the pouch to the inside of his right thigh. As he hitched up his pants, he heard three knocks on his door. It was Father Fontebuis, and he was carrying the clerical garments Antonio needed to wear during his escape from New Orleans.

"Put these on," Father Fontebuis said, as he held the long cassock open for Antonio to slide over his clothes. After buttoning the cassock, Father Fontebuis wrapped a white Roman collar around the boy's neck and plopped a *biretta* on his head.

"There. You look like a Jesuit. Come on. It's getting late. Let's go meet the Archbishop, and get something to eat, before we go," Father Fontebuis said.

Antonio took one last glance around his borrowed room and followed the priest to the rectory. In the rectory, he met the Archbishop, resplendent in garments of his office, who blessed both wayfarers and wished them a safe trip to France. No one mentioned the reason for their departure.

While eating a hearty meal of roasted beef and potatoes, the silent atmosphere at the dinner table reminded Antonio of Lawrence Hearn's stories about condemned prisoners' last meals. But Antonio found solace in knowing he was escaping death.

After dinner and the farewells, Antonio climbed into the Archbishop's coach and sat motionless for the ride to the dock. Occasionally, he would peek out a window and watch New Orleans slip by. As the wheels of the coach bounced on the cobblestoned streets, Antonio listened to the horses' iron shoes beat a sorrowful dirge against the stones. Inside the coach, nary a word was spoken, leaving Antonio with the full measure of his thoughts.

At various intersections, uniform police officers would stop traffic and allow the Archbishop's coach to pass. One officer even bowed. Antonio's eyes searched every face on Canal Street, looking for anyone familiar, but everyone seemed estranged from him and themselves. Already, he felt detached from his being, or former self, drifting through a strange, familiar city, with clashing thoughts of the vineyard and the parish prison. The setting reflected off blank faces, going from nowhere to nothing.

Antonio's turbid thoughts pulsed through his body when the Archbishop's coach turned off Canal Street and into the Italian Colony. The worn buildings, their forsaken empty windows and galleries facing the docks and wharves seemed abandoned by a people who only wanted an opportunity to live in peace. Antonio identified with the gray-tombstone facades of the French Quarter buildings. He continued to stare into the cracked mirror of his short life, punctuated by blood.

On the dockside of the coach, Antonio watched a few stevedores lugging handcarts of cargo from steamboats and ocean steamers. Their leathered skin glistened in the waning light. The coach stopped in front of Jackson Square, and two police officers stuck their heads through the windows. They immediately recognized the Archbishop and bowed. When they arrived at the Esplanade dock, a security checkpoint had been erected from old boards and barrels. A customs officer and a police officer demanded the papers of anyone who planned to board the *Nordica*.

"The captain said there were only two passengers and twenty tons of cotton for the voyage," the customs officer said. "Who are the passengers?"

The Archbishop stepped forward and handed the officer two packets of paper, tied with royal blue ribbons, and sealed with red wax. The customs officer shook his head. "There's no need to open them, Your Excellency." Jenssen returned the favor by blessing both officers.

The *Nordica's* holds were closed, and the ship's officers waited for their two priests at the foot of the gangway. Few words were spoken, but Antonio's nerves quaked in his muscular body. He tried to control his weakened legs as he walked towards the ship. Father O'Shanahan and Fontebuis approached the ship's captain, and they exchanged greetings in French. Antonio smiled because his memory allowed him to understand what they were saying. The conversation lasted several minutes, which allowed Antonio to rest his satchel on the ground.

As he waited, his right foot kicked a piece of cobblestone near the dock. He picked up the fist-sized piece of granite and slipped it into his cassock pocket. It was a piece of New Orleans and his past. After hugging the Archbishop and Father O'Shanahan, Antonio and Father Fontebuis walked up the rickety gangway to their spacious cabins compared to their cabin on the *Neustria,* a couple of years earlier.

"Come on, Antonio. Let's go on the fantail as the ship pulls away. We can watch New Orleans shrink from our memory," Father Fontebuis joked.

As they went on deck, Antonio found a hunk of cotton floating above the planks. *"Another souvenir,"* he thought. They leaned on the rails of the fantail and watched two steam-powered tugs pull the ship into the swirling currents of the old river. At first, the tugs pulled the *Nordica* upstream, allowing its steam engine enough time to develop self-sustaining power. As the ship pulled away from the dock, the setting sun used its palette to splash the firmament with a cinnabar-scarlet hue, laced with streaks of gilded-edged gray clouds. The silhouetted peaked roofs of the Italian Colony submitted to the shadows of the St. Louis Cathedral's jetting spires. Antonio watched as the evening lights flicker in the empty windows, lending life to crippled streetscape.

"They look like a cluster of old tombs and votive candles," Antonio remarked.

"They are. We are leaving the living dead to care for themselves. This city has wrought pain and death upon many people. But as long as the powerful are unsullied by the lives of the unwashed, they will remain content in allowing death to roam free on its narrow streets. You have seen many horrible things in your eighteen years, Antonio. You are much older and wiser than the people we're leaving. Thank God for this chance to shake the dust of this city from your soul. Look forward to a long life, serving others, unlike what you have experienced so far. You have been given a second or third chance to start a new life. Be grateful for that, son."

Antonio dug into his pocket and retrieved the piece of broken cobblestone. He wrapped it in the swath of raw cotton he found on the deck. He took one last look at New Orleans, rubbed the jagged scar on his nose, and heaved the cotton-wrapped stone into the swirling wake of the ship's engine, allowing it to sink into the murky waters of his orphaned memories.

THE END

ACKNOWLEDGMENT
& RESEARCH BIBLIOGRAPHY

While *Cobblestones* is a book of Historical Fiction, the author spent over six years researching and re-investigating the subject matter to insure the reader is satisfied with the accuracy of the horrible events depicted herein. While most of story is real, the real events are wrapped around the *bildungsroman* of the main fictitious character, Antonio, who traveled from Sicily to New Orleans during adverse conditions wrought by the post-Civil War conditions in the American South, and the post-War of Unification in Italy in the late Nineteenth Century.

Many of the characters are real, and their identities have been culled from numerous documents and sources, hereinafter identified for the sake of accuracy and proper attribution. The author hopes the reader is transported back to a time when Italian immigrants were mere commodities, used and consumed for another's accretion of social status and wealth of gilded Americans.   The title, *Cobblestones*, was selected to assist the reader in understanding the human tragedies painted on the metaphoric canvas of the times, which represent the streets of Sicily and New Orleans.

To accomplish the literary objective of *Cobblestones*, the author, using his life and work-life experiences conducted a modern "cold-case" homicide investigation into the Nineteenth Century assassination of New Orleans Police Superintendent, David C. Hennessy, and the ensuing furor, paroxysms, and overt prejudices manifested by the businessmen, mercantile class, newspaper publishers, professionals, and the politicians of Post-Reconstruction New Orleans. While Louisiana took aggressive steps to attract Southern Europeans to work the city's and fields of the state, the welcome was conditioned on the silent servitude of the deracinated immigrant. Any attempt to sneak across the formidable social boundaries established before the Civil War, was greeted with a kinetic reminder of the ruling class.

While many of the sources are in the public domain, the author believes the work of others, both deceased and living, should be gratefully acknowledged, also, to bring belated justice, albeit in literary form to the victims of the Lenten Massacre of 1891. Accordingly, here are some of the sources reviewed by the author which assisted him in his writing of *Cobblestones:*

1. The Italian-American Resource Center of the Jefferson Parish Library, Metairie, Louisiana.

2. The newspaper achieves, accessible through the Jefferson Parish Library, Metairie, Louisiana, for the newspapers of the Nineteenth Century.
    a. *The Daily Picayune.* New Orleans, Louisiana.
    b. *The Times Democrat.* New Orleans, Louisiana.
    c. *The Daily Democrat.* New Orleans, Louisiana.
    d. *The Daily Item,* New Orleans, Louisiana.
    e. *The New Orleans Mascot.* New Orleans, Louisiana.
    f. *The New Orleans Delta.* New Orleans, Louisiana.
    g. *Harper's Weekly Magazine.* New York, New York.
    h. *The New York Times.* New York, New York.

3.Books, Documents and Publications:
    a. *Vendetta.* Novel by Richard Gambino.© 1977.
    b. *Empire of Sin.* Novel by Gary Krist. ©2014.
    c. *Deep Water.* Novel by Thomas Hunt and Martha Macheca Sheldon. ©2007.
    c. *Crescent City Lynchings.* Novel by Tom Smith. © 2007.
    e *The Hennessy Case.* PhD. Dissertation by Barbara Brotein. ©1975.
    f. *Report of the Bureau of Immigration to the Louisiana General Assembly, January 1869.* Louisiana State Archives.

g. *The Killing of Prisoners: New Orleans: March 14, 1891.* Department of State. United States of America. Government Printing Office. Washington, D.C. 1891.

h. *Handwritten memorandum of Pasquale Corte, 1891.* Eleven pages.

i. Transatlantic Cables between the United States Government and the Kingdom of Italy. 1891.

j. On-line records of Carnival Krews of Rex. 1880 to 1900.

k. On-line records of the Boston and Pickwick Clubs of New Orleans, Louisiana. Nineteenth Century.

l. Obituary and burial research of the members of the Committee of Fifty.

m. Transatlantic cables between Pasqual Corte and Baron Fava. March 1891.

n. *Il Regno: The Murders of Sicilians in New Orleans:* © *March 14, 2011. (*Author unknown).

o. *Lynchings and Criminal Justice in South Louisiana 1878-1930;* © Michael Pheifer 1999. Louisiana Historical Association.

p. The Kemper Williams Resource Center of the Historic New Orleans Collection, New Orleans, Louisiana.

q. The Jefferson Parish Library System, Metairie, Louisiana.

r. The Orleans Parish Library System, New Orleans, Louisiana.

s. The investigation of miscellaneous on-line documents and monographs at various research facilities and university libraries.

The author would be remiss if he didn't acknowledge the work of Attorney Michael Santo of New York, who lead the effort to obtain a formal Proclamation from the city of New Orleans, apologizing for its participation the slaughter of the eleven innocent Italians on March 14, 1891.

*****

I would like to acknowledge and thank the hard, tedious work of Dee Marley and her team at Historium Press in processing a long, raw manuscript into a literary quality product, worthy of their imprint, and the readers' valuable investment of their resources and time in understanding a tragic episode in American history.

ACTUAL HISTORIC PHOTOS

DAVID C. HENNESSY

THE COTTON EXCHANGE BUILDING

THE ITALIAN COLONY

CITY HALL

THE PICKWICK CLUB

THE BOSTON CLUB

THE PICAYNE PIER – NEW ORLEANS

DAVID C. HENNESSY'S HOME ON GIROD STREET

ST. PATRICK'S HALL (CRIMINAL COURTS)

CLAY MONUMENT

NEW ORLEANS DOCKS

ORLEANS PARISH PRISON – MARCH 14, 1891

LIONEL ADAMS, ESQ.

THE HONORABLE THOMAS J. SEMMES,
President of the Jesuit Alumni Association, New Orleans, La.

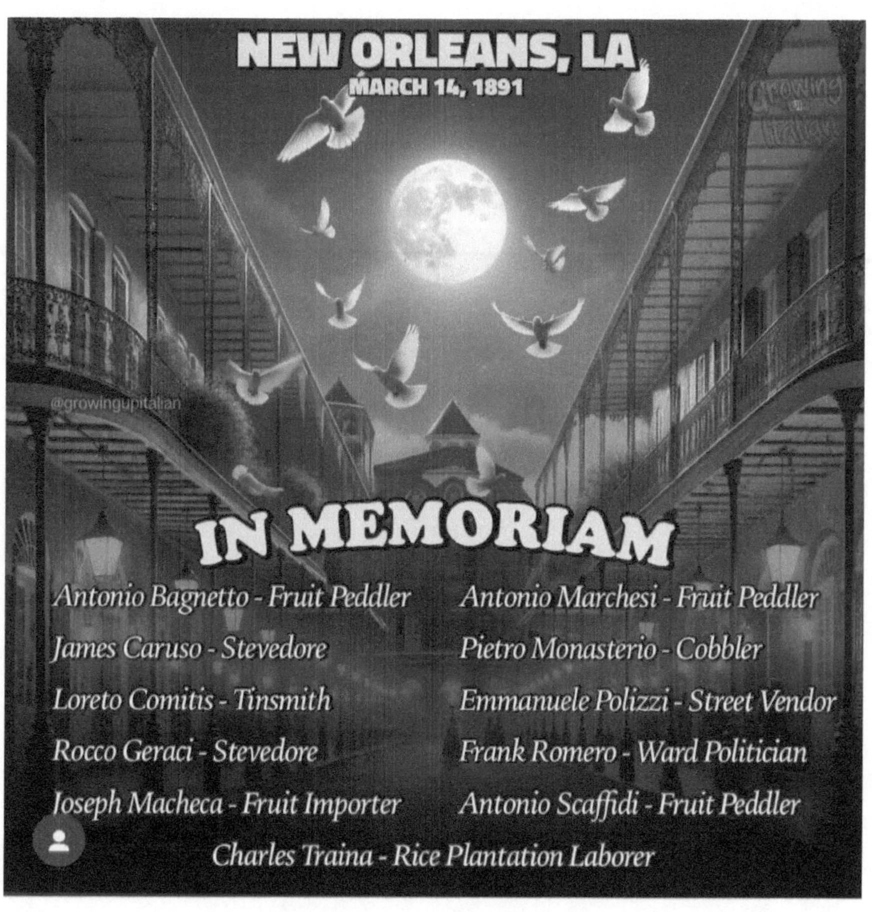
NEW ORLEANS, LA
MARCH 14, 1891
IN MEMORIAM
Antonio Bagnetto - Fruit Peddler
Antonio Marchesi - Fruit Peddler
James Caruso - Stevedore
Pietro Monasterio - Cobbler
Loreto Comitis - Tinsmith
Emmanuele Polizzi - Street Vendor
Rocco Geraci - Stevedore
Frank Romero - Ward Politician
Joseph Macheca - Fruit Importer
Antonio Scaffidi - Fruit Peddler
Charles Traina - Rice Plantation Laborer

ABOUT THE AUTHOR

Sal Perricone, a graduate of Loyola University of New Orleans with a BA (1975) and JD (1979), has dedicated his career to law enforcement, legal practice, and public service. Beginning as a sergeant with the Jefferson Parish Sheriff's Department, he progressed to detective with the New Orleans Police Department before practicing law privately in New Orleans. In 1985, he joined the Federal Bureau of Investigation as a Supervisory Special Agent, specializing in financial crime investigations and organized crime.

In 1991, Sal Perricone transitioned to the U.S. Attorney's Office for the Eastern District of Louisiana, where he served as Chief of the Organized Crime Strike Force and Senior Litigation Counsel until retiring in 2012. Over his illustrious career, he prosecuted significant cases involving La Cosa Nostra, public corruption, and white-collar crime. He earned numerous accolades, including multiple Director's Awards and the Attorney General's Award for his role in establishing the Katrina Fraud Task Force.

An adjunct professor at Tulane University and the University of New Orleans, Sal Perricone has trained law enforcement professionals across the nation. Post-retirement, he has authored two novels with positive Catholic themes, *Blue Steel Crucifix* and *The Shadows of Nazareth*. A Brother Martin alumnus, he continues to inspire with his dedication to justice and ethics.

Visit the author's website at www.historiumpress.com/sal-perricone

www.historiumpress.com